'[A] wonderfully inventive novel set in eighteenth-century England. As the heroine and narrator Red seeks the truth about her origins and possible connection to the wealthy De Lacy family, the reader's expectations are constantly confounded with one twist in her tale after another'
The Times and *The Sunday Times*, 'Best Historical Fiction of 2023'

'A big, complex mystery: rich in memorable, scheming characters and vivid historical detail, full of daring twists ... I didn't want it to end'
S. J. Parris, author of the Giordano Bruno series

'A corkscrew plot, full of ingenious twists and turns, a charismatic heroine, a rogue's gallery of aristocratic rascals in Georgian England and a dangerous family feud ... a hugely engaging, entertaining read'
Daily Mail

'What a magnificent novel ... Meticulously researched and beautifully written, this is one of the most intriguing books I have ever read'
Liz Nugent, author of *Strange Sally Diamond*

'Exquisitely, meticulously plotted and you'll want to curl up and absorb it all in as few readings as possible'
Belfast Telegraph

'Filled with period colour, clever twists and turns, and the best set of characters this side of Dickens ... *The Square of Sevens* shows a novelist approaching the peak of her powers'
Daily Express

'A clever story ... its characters flit between London's slums and palatial estates where misdirection and conspiracies abound'
The Washington Post

'What a magnificent rollercoaster ride of a book ... Laura Shepherd-Robinson writes with such a fluid, easy style, with a knack for putting in just the right amount of detail to perfectly paint the world she is describing ... I am in awe'

James Oswald, author of the Inspector McLean series

'This is a book to relish, not rush through. Rich in historical detail, it's immersive, authoritative and Dickensian in scope. Fundamentally though, it's a damn good story, brilliantly told. I loved it'

Harriet Tyce, author of *Blood Orange*

'This is a fabulously evocative novel, with a heroine who proves the most wonderful company, and a finely spun mystery which keeps you turning the pages. *The Square of Sevens* invites you into a magical world which you won't want to leave'

Elodie Harper, author of The Wolf Den trilogy

'It's impossible to overstate the brilliance Laura Shepherd-Robinson demonstrates in her work ... *The Square of Sevens* is an exquisite feat in storytelling: intelligent, dark, surprising, moving, and always entertaining'

Charlotte Philby, author of *Edith and Kim*

'Suspenseful and intricately planned, *The Square of Sevens* is a work where every page seems to hold the promise of a new thrilling secret. More than a mystery, it is a book that radiates a deep love of storytelling and the magic of a well-told tale'

Katherine J. Chen, author of *Joan*

THE
SQUARE
OF
SEVENS

Laura Shepherd-Robinson worked in politics for nearly twenty years before re-entering normal life to complete an MA in Creative Writing. Her debut novel, *Blood & Sugar*, was a Waterstones Thriller of the Month and won the Historical Writers' Association Debut Crown and the Specsavers/CrimeFest Best Debut Novel prize. Her second novel, *Daughters of Night*, was shortlisted for the Theakston's Crime Book of the Year, the Goldsboro Glass Bell Award, and the HWA Gold Crown. *The Square of Sevens* is her third novel and became an instant *Sunday Times* bestseller on publication. She lives in London with her husband Adrian.

Also by Laura Shepherd-Robinson

Blood & Sugar
Daughters of Night

LAURA
Shepherd-Robinson

*

THE

SQUARE

OF

SEVENS

PAN BOOKS

First published 2023 by Mantle

This paperback edition first published 2024 by Pan Books
an imprint of Pan Macmillan
The Smithson, 6 Briset Street, London EC1M 5NR
EU representative: Macmillan Publishers Ireland Ltd, 1st Floor,
The Liffey Trust Centre, 117–126 Sheriff Street Upper,
Dublin 1, D01 YC43
Associated companies throughout the world
www.panmacmillan.com

ISBN 978-1-5290-5370-8

1 3 5 7 9 8 6 4 2

A CIP catalogue record for this book is available from the British Library.

Map artwork by Hemesh Alles
Card illustrations by Paul Heneker

Typeset in Adobe Caslon by Jouve (UK), Milton Keynes
Printed and bound by CPI Group (UK) Ltd, Croydon, CR0 4YY

Visit **www.panmacmillan.com** to read more about all our books
and to buy them. You will also find features, author interviews and
news of any author events, and you can sign up for e-newsletters
so that you're always first to hear about our new releases.

To Holly Shepherd-Robinson

*This new forth-setting of an old mystery
is cordially offered*

Author's Note

A complete guide to the method of fortune telling, as well as a full list of the meanings of the cards, can be found in *The Square of Sevens: An Authoritative System of Cartomancy* by Robert Antrobus (John Gowne, 1740). The first edition is extremely rare, but the second edition, edited by E. Irenaeus Stevenson (Harper and Brothers, 1897), will meet the needs of any fledgling cartomancer.

'The truth may be stretched thin, but it never breaks, and it always surfaces above lies, as oil floats on water.'

Miguel de Cervantes, *Don Quixote*

BOOK ONE

Concerning a fortune told
of Mr Robert Antrobus

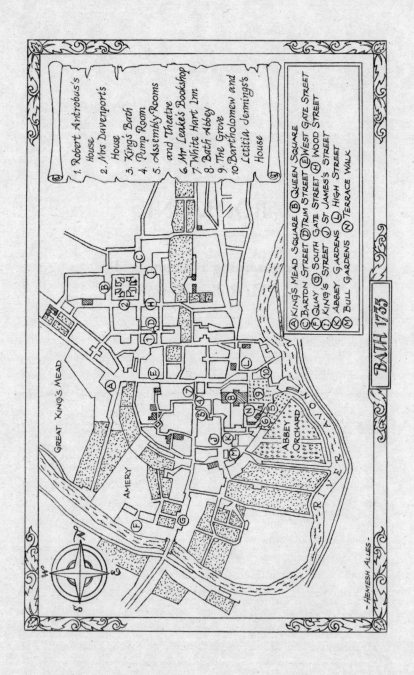

BATH 1735

1. Robert Antrobus's House
2. Mrs Davenport's House
3. King's Bath
4. Pump Room
5. Assembly Rooms and Theatre
6. Mr Leake's Bookshop
7. White Hart Inn
8. Bath Abbey
9. The Grove
10. Bartholomew and Letitia Jennings's House

(A) KING'S MEAD SQUARE (B) QUEEN SQUARE
(C) BARTON STREET (D) TRIM STREET (E) WEST GATE STREET
(F) QUAY (G) SOUTH GATE STREET (H) WOOD STREET
(J) KING'S STREET (J) ST JAMES'S STREET
(K) ABBEY GARDENS (L) HIGH STREET
(M) BULL GARDENS (N) TERRACE WALK

GREAT KING'S MEAD

AMERY

ABBEY ORCHARD

RIVER AVON

- HEMESH ALLES.

CHAPTER ONE

Eight of spades, influenced by a heart:
an illness to another, dear to one.

PEOPLE LIKE TO say they seek the truth. Sometimes they even mean it. The truth is they crave the warm embrace of a lie. Tell them they're going to be rich or fall in love, and they walk away whistling. Give them the hard, unvarnished truth, and you're looking at trouble. Now I am told to do just that. Tell the truth and nothing but. Well, my story begins with a story, it begins with a lie.

November, 1730. I never knew precisely where. A few hours' walk south of Tintagel. A neap tide and a quarter moon. A rain that fell in fat, cold droplets like quicksilver. It ran off the inn sign in a torrent, washing away a crust of soot and salt, revealing a queen's head and bright beads of scarlet blood. I edged closer to the door and the light and the warmth, straining to hear over the patrons' laughter. Father was weaving one of his tales: a sick man and a motherless child (that part true), a robbery on the road and a dead dog (that part lie).

'I don't care if you're St Christopher himself,' came the innkeeper's retort. 'I said no gypsies.'

'I am not a gypsy, sir,' Father said. 'I am a cunning-man, a—' I heard a crash, a splintering of china.

Father emerged from the door, grim-faced. 'I tried, Red. It'll have to be that barn we passed a mile back.'

I whispered a curse to Joan the Wad, licked my thumb, and pressed it against the wall of the inn. A departing couple had followed Father out, and the woman frowned. 'She's not yet ten years old. She should be in bed.'

The trouble with being a child, was people expected you to act like a child. To cry over a late night, or a missed meal. A year on the road is worth two in a town, Father liked to say, which, by my reckoning, made me fourteen rather than seven. Yet I smiled up at her, wide-eyed, clutching Joan the Wad like a toy, and her expression softened.

'Try the Seven Stars,' she said, in a kindlier tone. 'It's about a quarter-mile out of town.'

The man by the woman's side had edged into the shadows, lowering his head to hide his face beneath his cloth hat. Father had taught me about fishing towns. How the women took up with other men while their husbands were away at sea. I often saw it in their eyes when I told their fortunes. The men suspicious, often seeking the name of a rival, the women tormented over worthless choices. Then they had the brass to tell you when you should and shouldn't be in bed.

'The Seven Stars?' Father murmured. 'Aye, we would be thereabouts.'

'Do you know it?' I asked.

He merely grunted, tipping his wide-brimmed hat to the woman, and we battled on through the rain. Like most Cornish ports, the town was a maze of ancient, narrow streets. My numb feet slipped upon the cobbles, my hair plastered to my icy cheeks. To my frustration, Father kept stopping to rest. Some weeks ago, we'd passed through a village where the mood had turned ugly. A farmer had accused us of souring his milk, and his friends had ducked Father in a millpond to see if he would float. Ever since, his chest had troubled him, the hollow rattle of his breathing keeping us both awake at night.

On the outskirts of town, we turned onto a steep road that climbed a windswept headland, the waves crashing against the rocks far below. The inn looked as if it had stood there on the clifftop for a thousand years or more. An arch with a lantern above it led to the stable yard, which was surrounded by timber buildings, some tiled, some thatched. A strong smell of fried fish greeted us as we staggered into the taproom. The drinkers stared.

Father cut a tall, striking figure in his long indigo coat embroidered with hieroglyphs and hexafoils. On his back, he carried a knapsack, tied to it a cumbersome arrangement of bedroll, market wallet, and leather portmanteau. The rain was dripping from his hat and he pushed it back on his head. I found the change in him disturbing. All the fat had gone out of his face. He asked the innkeeper if there was a room for the night.

'Gypsies, is it?' The man had mean eyes, ink-stained fingers and a hard, thin mouth.

'I am a pellar, sir,' Father said. 'A Cornish cunning-man.'

The innkeeper shrugged, as if he didn't understand the difference. 'Two shilling a night,' he said. 'Supper, three shilling for two. If ye wants to be selling fortunes or like what-not in my taproom, then I'll take half.'

We were being fleeced and royally so, but we were used to that. Give us greed over hate, over fear, even over charity. There was much less chance of things going wrong.

The landlord's eye fell upon Joan the Wad. 'What's that witchcraft?'

People often had that reaction to Joan's twisted wicker limbs and braids of woven horsehair. Afraid their comments would hurt her feelings, I'd had Father make her a patchwork dress much like my own. One day, I'd make her a crown out of a nugget of purest gold, and then all our journeys would receive her nod of good fortune.

'She's just a doll, a child's plaything,' Father said, and I pressed my fingers over her ears so she couldn't hear.

Father gave me a nod, and while he signed the register, I counted out the coins from the purse at my belt. The innkeeper studied the pile of shillings I laid on his counter, selected one and bit it. I smiled at him sweetly. These were no butchered bobs, filed farthings and the like. Father had carved the mould from chalk and mixed the metal in his crucible. Possessing smaller and steadier hands, I had stamped the coins myself, and polished them up with aqua fortis and cream of tartar. The innkeeper grunted, sweeping the coins into the pocket of his apron.

The rooms we were given overlooked the dung heap in the stable yard and smelled as one would expect. Yet the place was warm and dry, and when I ran my hand over the mattress of the large oaken bed, only one or two lice scuttled out. Father sank into an old leather chair in the parlour and asked the innkeeper, Mr Chenoweth, for a bottle of brandy. 'And food for my daughter. A pie, something like that.'

'Father, please eat.' Joan the Wad had told me to make sure that he did.

He waved me away. 'Brandy will revive me.'

'Another two shilling for the brandy,' Mr Chenoweth said. 'If you read my cards tomorrow, you can have it for half.'

'My daughter will do so gladly.'

He gave me a contemptuous glance. 'She's just a child.'

'Seven years old, and more gifted than any cartomancer you will ever meet.'

The innkeeper stared at Father intently. 'Do I know you, sir?'

Father gave him a long look. 'I don't believe so.'

He frowned. 'My mistake.'

After he'd gone, I scowled at the door. 'If I read his cards tomorrow, he'll learn some hard truths.'

Father smiled. 'I don't doubt it. But soften it, will you, my love? We need his goodwill. Remember what happened with that farmer.'

Guilt made me fierce in my defence. 'I can't help what's in the cards.'

'I know,' he said gently. 'But sometimes you scare people. We don't want to end up in any more millponds, now do we?'

Father was in a strange mood that night. Several times he went to the window to look out at the stable yard, and he seemed unusually distant in his talk. In bed, I whispered about it to Joan the Wad, but she didn't know why. When I awoke the next morning, the brandy bottle was empty.

Father's chest seemed worse. Nor was the weather any better, and when I asked him if we could stay another night, to my surprise, he agreed without argument. Two nights turned into three, then four. On our fifth night, we made the acquaintance of a doctor named Kilderbee, who was staying at the inn on his way to St Ives. He declared an interest in natural remedies, and Father offered to show him his herbal grimoire the following morning.

When the doctor came to our rooms, I was sent outside as the weather was brighter. I ran across the grass to the edge of the cliff, my hair blown wild by the wind. Worming forward on my belly, clutching Joan the Wad very tight, I discovered that we could look right down the face of the cliff to the rocks below. My head swam and my stomach lurched, even as danger held a strange allure. When I could stand it no longer, I gathered a pile of stones and stood back from the edge, hurling them out to sea. The sun gave the tips of the waves a shine like the inside of a seashell, the little fishing boats like the toys of Bolster the Giant.

When I returned to our room, Father was sitting in his chair, lost in thought. I put my hand on his arm, he ran his fingers through my tangled red curls, and told me to put on my cap and mind my books. Our small library travelled with us on the road: an almanac; Father's grimoire and magical books; and a few battered novels. My favourite was *Don Quixote*, the adventures of a mad Spaniard who had become a knight errant at the age of fifty. Father often read it to me aloud, and I knew all Quixote's quests by heart. I turned the pages slowly, whispering the stories to Joan the Wad, but rewriting them to give them better endings. I imagined Father as Quixote, me as his vengeful squire, finding the constables who'd beaten him and making them beg for their lives, enjoying the humiliation of the men who'd ducked him in the millpond.

That night at supper, a gentleman, a new arrival, was seated at the next table, and several times I caught him staring at Father and I. The dining room was hung with paintings of ships, and as the walls and floor were all askew, and the roar of the sea faintly heard, it was easy to imagine yourself aboard one. Mr Chenoweth's pot-boy cleared our plates, and in the lull, the man leaned over and introduced himself. 'Robert Antrobus, a visitor to these parts from the city of Bath.'

Father shook his hand. 'George the Tenth of Kernow, glad to know you, sir.'

This delighted Mr Antrobus. 'I had no idea I was in the presence of royalty. You are, I think, a gypsy king?'

When he smiled, two little red circles formed high on his lightly lined cheeks. Throw into his lap a parcel of knitting, and with his snow-white wig and tortoiseshell spectacles, he would have resembled a benevolent grandmother. Not that I had much knowledge of grandmothers, benevolent or otherwise, but I knew such women existed, for I had told their fortunes.

'I am no gypsy,' Father said, 'though I hold the Romani people in naught but the highest regard. Neither am I a king, but merely the tenth man named George in a long line of cunning-men. My forefathers have walked this land since the days of the Saxon invaders.'

'Which makes you a king indeed.' Mr Antrobus raised his glass and they drank.

'My daughter, Red,' Father said.

'Red,' Mr Antrobus repeated, beaming at me. 'An unusual name, but I rather like it.'

He made no jokes about my hair, and I liked him better for it. All told, he looked a very good catch indeed. Soft, plump hands; his coat a fine brown woollen broadcloth with silver-gilt embroidery; his watch chain indisputably gold.

I inclined my head. 'I am very happy to make your acquaintance, sir.'

'What pretty manners,' he exclaimed. 'Your daughter does you credit, Mr George.'

'Indeed she does. Her mother was a lady, and I have endeavoured to teach her a lady's comportment and speech.'

'Then her mother . . . ?'

'Taken from us before her time. Red has never known a mother's care.'

'I regret to hear it.' He peered sympathetically at me. 'But I don't believe you have made all the introductions.'

I smiled, liking him more. 'This is Joan the Wad, sir. The Queen of the Piskies. Show her respect and she'll light your journey, but if you are unkind to her, she'll call down the mist and lead you astray.'

'Then I *am* in the presence of royalty!' He sketched a little bow in her direction. 'I'd never dream of showing anything but respect to Her Majesty.'

'Do you have children of your own, sir?' Father said.

'Alas, no. I am a bachelor. Rather more by accident than design.' He took a sip of wine and changed the subject. 'I have never had the good fortune to meet a cunning-man before, though I have studied the ancient traditions that survive in the furthest reaches of this realm. That is my avocation, an antiquarian. I have published several volumes on our island's history to some small acclaim.' He smiled modestly, glowing a little pink. 'Lately I have been studying the language of the Romani, hence my rather clumsy introduction.'

'Is it your studies that bring you here to Cornwall?' Father asked.

'A rather more sombre matter. I was called to the bedside of an ailing cousin, who regrettably died of his illness two weeks ago. I would have returned to Bath by now, had I not learned that the dear man left me a small bequest: a farm and some other landholdings. My intention is to sell them, but I have been forced to wait while some rather tiresome legal entanglements are resolved. In the meantime, I felt a little sea air would do me good.' He patted his chest.

Father eyed him appraisingly. 'Perhaps you desire a charm or amulet to bring you fortune in your affairs? Or a horoscope to consult the fates? I see from your expression that you are sceptical, sir.'

Mr Antrobus chuckled. 'I confess I struggle to believe that if I buried an egg and a packet of pins under an oak tree on full moon, it would ease the passage of probate.'

'For a matter of money, I too would advise against using an egg,' Father said. 'Yet you should not dismiss our arts too lightly. There is a reason they have endured. They hold more power than your science, and have more adherents than your reason.'

'Hence my interest. Anything that holds the common people in thrall is worthy of closer study, however implausible.'

It was my task, at such moments, to sit modestly and hold my tongue. People felt soothed by the presence of a child, their fears and suspicions allayed.

'My daughter understands the powers of which I speak,' Father said. 'She is herself already adept at the art of cartomancy. We use an ancient method that has been passed down in my family from pellar to pellar for generations. That's what people here call the cunning-folk.'

Mr Antrobus nodded. 'Etymology, I believe, tells us that "pellar" derives from the word "expellers". Is that another of your talents? Driving out witches and evil spirits?'

'True witches are rare in the modern age,' Father said. 'More often than not, the finger of suspicion is pointed at women who have committed no crime greater than growing old without a husband. For that reason, when I am asked to undertake such work, I tend to decline.'

'I would be interested in hearing more about your work, sir. If you were able to spare the time?'

I waited for Father to name a price, but to my surprise, he only regarded Mr Antrobus thoughtfully. 'We will talk, and Red will tell your fortune.'

These words were barely spoken, when the door to the cliffside burst open, and a blast of freezing, salty air extinguished the candles. A figure strode into the dining room, his hair wild and demonic in the moonlight. Something glinted in his hand, as he moved towards us.

Father rose from his chair, his staff levitating to his hand. Mr Antrobus uttered a little cry, pushing himself back into his chair. I scraped back my own chair, snatching up a knife from the table. Father had instructed me to flee if ever his enemies caught up with us, but I would not leave him to face them all alone. His staff scythed through the air, sweeping the figure's legs out from under him. I darted in, pressing my knife against his throat.

Somebody screamed. A glare of light filled the room. Mr Chenoweth appeared, holding up a lantern. 'Shut that damn door,' he said.

The inn's scrawny pot-boy was on the floor. He flinched from my knife. In his hand, he held a small hand rake, which he let drop.

'Thatcher left it in the stable yard,' he stammered.

Rising, my face colouring, I dropped the knife onto the table, and then guided Father's taut body back to his chair. I had never fully understood his fear – nor the identity of the mysterious enemies who inspired it – but it was always brimming in his watchful gaze, spilling over in moments like this.

Mr Antrobus was making fulsome apologies, smoothing things over with Mr Chenoweth.

I bent to pick up Joan the Wad. 'Father, it draws late. We should go to bed.'

'Your daughter speaks sense, sir,' Mr Antrobus said, turning. 'That lad gave us all a fright. Let us continue our discussion tomorrow over supper.'

Still with those haunted eyes, Father allowed me to walk him back to our rooms. I lit candles, and he collapsed into his chair.

'Who did you think he was?' I asked. 'The pot-boy?'

He beckoned me forward with a candle to light his pipe. The tobacco crackled softly, as he drew deeply, then exhaled. 'What did you make of him? Mr Antrobus?'

I frowned, wanting an answer to my question. 'He seemed kind. Though something troubles him behind his smiles.'

'I feel as if I know him. As if I have met him before.'

'Like the innkeeper did with you?' I was still curious about that conversation. Every time I'd tried to bring it up, he'd avoided my questions. Yet I was convinced Father had stayed at this inn before.

'No,' he said. 'Not like that.'

I sighed. 'Where would you have met Mr Antrobus? In London?' I knew my father had spent time in that city prior to my birth.

He pointed with his pipe to the cards on the table, and it took me a moment to work out what he meant.

'You think he's my king of diamonds?'

Every time he'd told my fortune, that card appeared, influenced by a heart. It figured a kind and sensitive man, easily moved in his mood.

'How can you be sure? We barely know him.'

He answered me roughly. 'Because I have to be.'

The bleakness of his expression made my throat close up. I remembered the grave face of Dr Kilderbee when I'd seen him in the taproom earlier. Father's long silences ever since their talk. The way he'd started looking at me when he thought I was unaware.

That was the moment when I realized my father was dying.

CHAPTER TWO

Ace of hearts, influenced by a club:
a talent or gift to be made much of.

T HE ROOM WAS silent save for the whisper of the cards.
Outside a storm raged – a match for the one building inside
of me – but there in our small parlour, filled with the scent of a
birchwood fire, all eyes were fixed on the pack of cards I shuffled
seven times.

'Do you have a query for the cards?' I asked. 'A matter of money?
Or the heart? It helps to know the generality, if not the particular.' I
always began this way, and I rarely stumbled over the longer words
any more.

Mr Antrobus thought for a moment, and some private emotion
seemed to mist his lively black eyes. 'A matter of the heart,' he said.
'Yes, why not?'

The candle flames flickered, as a particularly violent gust of wind
rocked the inn, followed by a-slithering and a-shattering of dislodged
roof tiles. I held out the shuffled pack. 'You must take three wish-
cards. Keep them in your care, but do not look at them, or you will
be cursed.'

Mr Antrobus chuckled, slipping the three cards into the pocket
of his forest-green waistcoat. I laid the square using the remaining
forty-nine cards, starting with a diagonal line of seven cards, followed by flanking lines of six cards each, then five, then four, and so
on. 'The Square of Sevens,' I said, as I placed the final corner card,

and we took a moment to admire the seven rows of seven cards laid out on the table. 'The Square contains great power, an arrangement of cards unique to you. Out of it will arise your parallelogram, the cards of fortune.'

'Fascinating.' Mr Antrobus removed his spectacles, polished them on his cravat, and replaced them to study the arrangement again. 'Of course, seven is a fortuitous number to many peoples and religions. Seven sins and seven virtues. The seven blessings of the Israelites. The seven planets. The seven sacraments. The seven demons of the Magdalen.'

As he chattered on, my thoughts drifted on a tide of despair. If only I hadn't upset the farmer with my fortune. If only I'd made Father see a doctor weeks ago. I'd told Joan the Wad my new secret last night. She'd said I had to listen to Father. That a little girl couldn't light her own way. I'd said she was wrong, and she'd called me names, so I'd shut her away.

A sharp creak from Father's leather armchair tugged me back to the present. He was cast entirely in shadow, save for the glow of his pipe. I could almost hear his silent admonition: *This is no ordinary fortune, Red. Remember what we discussed.*

Except I didn't want to remember. I didn't want to be nice to this gentleman, when my heart was constricted like a fist, when the awfulness of everything churned inside me. And yet Father had spelled it out to me. Choice was a luxury I couldn't afford. *This is your story, Red. You must tell it well.*

You want me to lie to him about his cards? I'd asked.

Of course not. He'd sounded shocked. *But you heard him express regret. It will be there in his cards. Figure it large.*

'I begin the Reduction,' I said, taking the card in the top right corner, a club, and laying it upon another club to its immediate left. 'The cards of like suit in each row are gathered together into piles, save the leftmost card, which is the master-card, and always stands alone.' My hands moved swiftly, despoiling the Square, Mr Antrobus watching with great interest.

'Now we come to the Sacrifice,' I said, when it was done. 'This is a further reduction of the Square, achieved by discarding the right-most suits in each row, so that only the master-card and the first two suits remain. Only the uppermost card in each pile has significance to us now, leaving us with a parallelogram of twenty-one cards, composed of seven rows of three cards each.'

'A lot of labour, that business with the shuffling and the Square,' Mr Antrobus said. 'Could one not simply deal twenty-one cards from the off?'

'The Square is the father of the Parallelogram,' Father said, 'what Jacobus of Utrecht called the soul. From the soul is distilled the essence of the fortune.'

'I see,' Mr Antrobus said, with a little smile that suggested he did not.

'Hearts are the suit of the affections and passions,' I said, 'whereas diamonds signify matters material. In clubs lies judgement, the intellect and will, whilst spades are the suit of doubtful prognostics, figuring matters of misfortune and loss.'

I gazed down at his parallelogram, dismayed. All those spades and inauspicious clubs.

'Now I know why you named your daughter "Red",' Mr Antrobus addressed my father, seemingly unconcerned by his adverse fate. 'It is the colour of good fortune, is it not?'

Father inclined his head. 'My daughter would bring any man good fortune.'

'Each card in the Parallelogram is influenced by the card directly to its left,' I said. 'Only the master-cards are without influence, each possessing a singular meaning. Sometimes the cards figure a querist's past, sometimes his present, sometimes his future. Sometimes they concern events of which the querist is unaware, but which have a marked influence upon him.'

My patter concluded, I pointed to the first card in his fortune: the eight of spades, influenced by a heart. 'An illness to another, dear to one,' I said.

Mr Antrobus gave another of his knowing smiles. 'That would be my late cousin, I presume. The man I told you about last night.'

I looked him in the eye, ignoring his scepticism. 'The first card in the Parallelogram holds the greatest significance of all. Often it figures a great change. The heart is an influencing card of good fortune, casting a light upon the darkness of the spade. In this moment of loss, perhaps something new will be found.'

Father gave a soft grunt of approval, and I pointed to the second card. 'A talent or gift to be made much of.' Then the third: 'A sad or serious duty or care.' Frowning, I pointed to the first card again. 'Their meanings may relate to the change figured by the illness. The talent and the duty, that is. Often proximity signifies a connection.'

'And this one?' Mr Antrobus said, pointing to the next row. 'The lady?'

'The queen of spades, influenced by a club,' I said. 'She figures a female enemy, intellectual and audacious.'

'Good gracious,' he said. 'How devilish she sounds. I know nobody like that, I am happy to say.'

'Perhaps she lies in your future,' I said.

Father's chair creaked again, and I knew he wanted me to move on. The dark queen was not helpful to our cause. So I worked my way through the rest of Mr Antrobus's fortune, speaking of love, regret and decision wherever I could. It was no easy task. His cards figured loss, unhappiness, hurt and underhand dealings. Yet I did my utmost, seeking to plant a seed within his mind, as Father had instructed, that in fruition might guide him to the right decision. When I came to the final card, the words caught in my throat.

'Four of spades as master-card. Affecting some near concern to the querist. It shall end less well than was hoped.'

I stared at the cards, trying to find words that might soften the bleakness of his fortune. But Mr Antrobus only burst out laughing. 'How solemn you look, young Red. Pray, do not worry on my account. It likely refers to a barrel of biscuits or a bottle of wine gone to blight.' He fished the wish-cards from his pocket. 'What of these?'

One diamond, one heart, one spade. 'The red cards dominate, which means you can make a wish for yourself.' I waited until he gave me a nod. 'The cards are high, which means your wish will be fulfilled.'

Mr Antrobus smiled a little wistfully. 'I cannot think how.' He cast his gaze down to the table a final time. 'Remarkable, especially in one so young. I can well imagine the effect such a performance would have upon the credulous. If the cards can be said to hold true power, I suppose that is it.'

In other circumstances, I might have tried to explain. How, just as the querist influences the cards, so the cards influence the querist, but not at all in the way that he imagined. Faced with their fortune, people open up like books, and if you understand the language of souls, then you can read them. Mr Antrobus might call it sensibility. The common folk call it magic. Whichever word one chooses is another sign, there to be read.

Mr Antrobus, for instance, was plainly a man in love. His cards had figured both secrets and temptation. When I had spoken of their meanings, I saw guilt and fear in his eyes. Another man's wife, was my best guess, a forbidden desire.

Father reached for his pouch, and it jingled as he shook it into his palm. 'Here, sir.' With a snap of his fingers, one of his charms soared through the air, ringing a high, pure note as it span. Mr Antrobus caught it rather clumsily in one of his pudgy palms. He held the little golden heart up to the candlelight.

'To bring you luck,' Father said. 'Will you join me in a glass of wine?'

Mr Antrobus peered at him doubtfully. 'You would not rather sleep?'

'It will help me to do so.'

'Then I shall step out to the taproom and procure us a bottle of Lisbon.'

Once the door had closed behind him, I rose and went to Father's side. 'I'm sorry.'

'Don't be,' Father said, taking my hand. 'You did very well.'

'But he doesn't believe.' A waver of panic had entered my voice. 'You heard him.'

'Many people say such things,' he said. 'They lie to themselves as well as to you. The truth will find him.'

Father sent me to bed, but I listened to his conversation with Mr Antrobus through a crack in the door. My head pulsed, heavy and hot against the wood, the tempest of emotion somehow sharpening my concentration. I'd taken Joan the Wad out of the drawer, so that she could listen too. Men often told one another things they didn't like to say to piskies and children.

'Here, sir,' Father said, raising his voice over the howl of the wind. 'I have something to show you.'

Reaching into his shirt, he took out his red leather document tube, which he carried on a string around his neck. He unbuttoned the lid and took out the most precious object that we owned.

'This document explains the method of cartomancy you just witnessed,' he said, placing the scroll in Mr Antrobus's hands. 'It is a secret of ancient power, known only to my daughter and myself.'

Mr Antrobus leaned forward into the candlelight, examining the fragile pages eagerly. 'Fascinating,' he said, after a few minutes of careful study. 'The use of language.' His voice was softer than Father's, and I struggled to hear him over the rattle of rain. 'And yet it cannot be so very ancient. Two hundred years at most – the pack of cards did not exist in like form before then.'

'I said the power was ancient, sir, not the secret. People have used different methods over time to harness that power. Witness the oak-seers, and the men who built the stone circles.'

'A rare document of antique provenance? A lost secret of magical power? Why, my publisher, John Gowne, would give his eye teeth to get his hands on this.'

'Ordinarily, I would never part with it.' Father drew on his pipe and exhaled slowly. 'Yet the truth is, sir, my time draws near. Doctor Kilderbee tells me it is a canker. A matter of weeks, he says, perhaps much less.'

I pressed my fist against my mouth to stop myself crying out, hardly aware of my teeth cutting into my skin.

'Oh, Mr George,' Mr Antrobus said, tearing his eyes away from the parchment. 'I'm so dreadfully sorry.'

Father made a dampening gesture with his hands. 'My concern is not for myself, but for my daughter. When I pass into the next realm, she will be left all alone in this world. I fear for her future.'

'You have no family or friends who could take her?'

'My family are dead, and my marriage caused an estrangement between myself and my friends. Even if I could find them in time, they would not help me.'

'Then her mother's family . . . ?'

'They don't even know of her existence.' His voice rose. 'They *must* not know.'

'Whyever not?'

'I have enemies, sir. Men I have hidden from for many years. I changed my name, kept on the move, because if they knew my daughter lived, they'd want her dead.'

A chill crept over me, as I struggled to make sense of his words. If Father had changed his name, then what was his real name? Were his enemies my mother's family? Or someone else? And why would they want me dead? I was just a child. I asked Joan the Wad, and she whispered that it was just a fakement to bend Mr Antrobus to Father's will.

I could tell that Mr Antrobus shared her scepticism. 'Sir, lower your voice. You might wake the girl. She would be frightened to hear such words.'

'Fear may be the only thing that saves her. Unless compassion extends a hand.' Father skewered him with his gaze. 'I offer this document to you, sir. It is all I have to trade. In return, I ask that you undertake the care of something more precious still.'

Mr Antrobus stared at him, aghast. 'You mean your daughter?'

'I wish her to be raised as a lady, like her mother. Did you not speak of your childless state with much regret?'

A life of comfort, Father had said. Yet where lay comfort without him? Certainly not with this stranger, for all that he had a good heart. Yet no one seemed to care about what I wanted.

'I sympathize with your predicament,' Mr Antrobus said. 'Truly I do. But you must see that I cannot take on the charge of a little girl I barely know. I have no wife . . . people would talk . . . I would scarcely know what to do with her. Surely another solution can be found?'

'A workhouse?' Father said roughly. 'An orphanage? A life on the street?'

'Perhaps your friends will change their minds, once they have met her? She has a face to melt even the hardest heart.'

Father's gaze was unrelenting. 'The evidence suggests not.'

'Come now, sir. It is hardly the same.'

'It was there in your cards,' Father persisted. 'The change, her gift, your duty of care. She will enrich your life, if only you will let her.'

Mr Antrobus sighed. 'You are desperate, sir, and little wonder. But I am not the answer to your prayers. You must see that.'

When Father came into the bedroom a little later, he had that weary, ravaged look on his face again.

'What do we do now?' I asked.

'There is still time,' Father said. 'Your king of diamonds. We will find him.'

'What if there is no king of diamonds?'

Father turned away, his voice thickening. 'Go back to sleep.'

CHAPTER THREE

Three of clubs as master-card:
a sad or serious duty or care.

I AWOKE TO find Father shivering next to me, soaked in sweat. When he tried to get up, he fell back against the sheets. I ran to fetch Dr Kilderbee, who came at once.

Word of his condition quickly spread throughout the inn. Mr Antrobus, his conscience pricking him, insisted that we swap rooms, in order that Father might be made more comfortable. The pot-boy and Mr Chenoweth carried him on a mattress between them, and laid him in a four-poster bed with velvet curtains. All of this seemed to happen in a place outside myself. I clutched Joan the Wad, staring at the commotion all around me.

For three days and nights, I sat with him, trying to feed him soup he wouldn't drink, as he drifted in and out of fever dreams.

'I'm sorry about the farmer,' I said, during one of his lucid periods. 'I didn't mean for this to happen.'

'Look at me, Red.' Father spoke fiercely. 'This is not your fault.'

Yet I knew that it was. Unable to look at him any more, I left the room to empty his chamber pot. When I returned, he cried out: 'Are you there, my love?'

I parted the bed's curtains. 'Always.'

He looked wildly around. 'Where is she? What have you done with her?'

'Who, Father?' I said. 'It's me, Red.'

He gasped. 'My dearest girl. This room. I thought for a moment that you were her. Your lovely hair.'

My voice faltered. 'Do you mean my mother?'

He hardly ever talked about her, and had answered few of my questions. I knew little more than the scant facts he'd told Mr Antrobus. She'd been a lady, her family had disapproved of their match, and they'd eloped together. He'd never spoken of her death, but I presumed it had been in childbirth.

His face darkened. 'Don't let her see me. Not now when I am weak.' He thrashed feebly, until I put my arms around him.

'It's all right. I'm here. I'll never leave you.'

Only nothing was right. I knew no enchantment to counter this, and Joan the Wad had no suggestions. I lay there, holding him, until he slept again. Somehow, sleep eventually claimed me too.

I awoke feeling very cold. Through the crack in the curtains, I could see that it was light outside. Father was still in my arms. His hand was icy to the touch. I sat bolt upright to look at him. His lips were stiff and pale. I placed a finger upon his mouth, and no breath stirred.

'Father?' My voice rose, cracking. 'Father?'

In the dying echo of that word, I felt such pain as I had never felt before. I could not conceive of a life without him. He was my world and I was his. I lay back down beside him, resuming our embrace. If I refused to let him go, then it hadn't happened. I told myself that I would wake to find it all a dream.

I sat in Father's chair in our old rooms, my eyes hot as coals – as if they might set fire to my thoughts, if there were any left inside my skull to burn. A shadow fell across me, and I looked up into the sorrowful face of Mr Antrobus. 'Dearest Red,' he said. 'I'm afraid it is time.'

We followed the undertaker's cart down the hill into town. An odd trio of mourners: Mr Antrobus in his fine broadcloth, Joan the Wad and I in our patchwork dresses. My eyes never moved from the coffin. Was it possible to hate a thing with so much venom? The world seemed different, unmoored from reality, as if it might take flight and carry me away with it.

The church was ancient: a wooden tower and a stunted stone nave. Mr Antrobus had explained to me that the vicar had refused to say the proper words, because Father was a cunning-man. So he was buried silently, on the cold north side of the churchyard, with the suicides and the murderers and the still-born infants. Amidst my tears, I thought of Sancho's words to Don Quixote: *There is a remedy for all things but death.*

Mr Antrobus was at the counter, settling his account with Mr Chenoweth. Outside, the ostlers and the pot-boy were loading his carriage with trunks and boxes.

'What will happen to the girl?' I heard him say.

'Orphanage is coming for her at noon.'

'They are good people?'

'Good as any.' Mr Chenoweth smiled at the coins in his hand. 'Right Christian of you, sir. I hope you'll return.'

Mr Antrobus crossed the room to speak to me. 'In our short acquaintance, your father made a great impression upon me. As you did yourself. Whatever the future holds, I know you will endure.'

I looked for any sign that the seed I had planted during his fortune had taken root. His conscience loomed large in that room: in his liquid eyes, his tremulous mouth, taking form between his twisting hands like a genie. Yet he only reached for his purse, and pressed a handful of coins into my palm. Then he took Father's charm from his pocket – the little golden heart – and folded the fingers of my other hand around it. 'Your father said it would bring me luck. But I think you are more in need of it than I.' He bowed to Joan the Wad, who was sitting in my lap. 'Your Majesty. Farewell, young Red.'

He walked out into the stable yard, I heard a carriage door slam, and the shout of his coachman to the horses. Opening my hand, I counted seven golden guineas.

Within seconds, Mr Chenoweth was looming over me. He grabbed my wrist, forced my hand open, and took the coins.

'Owing on your bill,' he said.

I knew it couldn't be true. Those coins would have kept Father and I on the road for many weeks. But in that moment, I hardly cared.

Mr Chenoweth returned to his counter, where he sat scribbling in a leather-bound ledger, occasionally glancing up at the clock. Just before noon, a clatter in the stable yard heralded the arrival of a carriage. Mr Chenoweth went outside, and returned accompanied by a plump lady of middling years in a box-pleated gown of russet silk, and a young man in a long black coat and a frizzled wig of coarse hair, probably goat.

'Stand up,' Mr Chenoweth said to me. 'Let Mrs Sandbach look at you.'

The lady had rosy cheeks and cupid's bow lips, that might have suggested a benevolent character, had it not been for the coldness of her gaze. She wore a string of fat amber beads around her neck, and in one, I glimpsed the shadow of an entombed insect.

Dumbly, I rose from my chair. I felt pounded by grief, all my sharp edges ground away.

'She's called Red,' Mr Chenoweth said. 'Father was a gypsy.'

'Heathen, I suppose. Where are her things?'

Mr Chenoweth pointed to Father's knapsack and portmanteau. The young man opened the knapsack and tipped its contents onto a table. Mrs Sandbach stirred the pile of clothes. 'Little better than rags.'

The man moved on to the portmanteau, unbuckling with his busy fingers. He took out our books, a bundle of papers tied with red string, and the red leather document tube containing *The Square of Sevens*.

'Good Lord, what is that?' Mrs Sandbach snatched Joan the Wad from my lap, holding her up as if she was a dead mouse. In two strides, she'd crossed to the fireplace, and tossed her into the flames. I screamed and tried to run to her, but the man in the goat-wig caught my arm and boxed my ear.

Twisting in his grasp, I watched in anguish as the flames crackled and surged.

'Turn out your pockets,' Mrs Sandbach said. 'Give everything you have to Edward.'

'Murderer,' I cried, and Edward boxed my ear again. Choking back sobs, I handed over my pack of playing cards, a threepenny bit, and the golden heart charm.

'Put it on the carriage,' Mrs Sandbach said to Mr Chenoweth, gesturing to the portmanteau. 'I know a man who'll take the books. You may dispose of these clothes as you see fit.'

Edward marched me out to the stable yard, all my griefs mingled as one. Mr Chenoweth followed us out with the portmanteau, and I was bundled into the carriage, Mrs Sandbach on one side, Edward on the other. Panic seized me and I reached for the door, but Edward roughly returned me to my seat. Mrs Sandbach rapped on the roof with her parasol and the carriage moved off. Edward tossed Father's golden heart into the air and caught it in the same hand.

We had barely reached the shadow of the stable yard arch, when the vehicle halted suddenly, jolting us together. I heard a commotion outside and, moments later, the carriage door was flung open. Startled, we stared into the flushed face of Mr Antrobus.

'What is the meaning of this?' Mrs Sandbach said.

'My name is Antrobus,' he said. 'I wish to speak to this girl.'

His peremptory tone, coupled with his gentlemanly dress, shocked her into outraged silence.

'Before he died,' Mr Antrobus said, 'your father asked me to undertake the charge of your guardianship. Believing myself unworthy of that great trust, I declined. Yet in one short hour upon the road, I fell to wondering . . . My studies provide me with much contentment, and yet sometimes I find myself asking whether life shouldn't contain something more. A house too large, too quiet, and all the rest. It was in that spirit that I discovered I could not stop thinking about our time together here.' He drew a breath, twisting his hat in his hands. 'I do not seek to replace your Father – I would scarcely know how – but

I do possess a great willingness to learn. In short, I offer you a home, Red, if you think it will serve.'

Having experienced a few short minutes of Mrs Sandbach's tender care, I was already halfway out of that carriage. Mr Antrobus held out his arms to lift me down, but I turned back to snatch Father's golden heart from Edward's hand. Then I surrendered to Mr Antrobus's awkward embrace.

'Unload her things,' he ordered, spurring the ostlers into action. 'That portmanteau. Everything. Now.'

CHAPTER FOUR

Queen of spades, influenced by a club:
a female enemy, intellectual and audacious.

S O TO LONDON. To Hanover Square, specifically, on a crisp April morning in the year 1740 – nearly ten years after the little girl known only as Red went to live in Bath as the ward of Mr Robert Antrobus.

Lazarus Darke walks along the street. A lean man, neither tall nor short, his head is thrust forward, eyes darting, always watching – giving him a look of vibrancy and caution all at once. He wears no wig, his own hair black and long – one bobbing forelock escaping the tie – and though he is approaching forty, not a hint of grey. A high forehead, angled black brows, and a polite smile for the ladies, who turn to admire his shapely calves from behind. In dress, he favours sober colours of fashionable cut: an olive-green coat trimmed with a narrow strip of gold braid; a matching waistcoat and knee breeches; silk stockings with embroidered clocks; a three-cornered hat, the brim upturned; a froth of lace at the throat, secured with a black cravat. On his left hip, he wears a silver-hilted small-sword, a convenient station for him to sometimes rest a cocked hand. The keen of eye might observe that his shoe buckles too are silver – rather than gold to match the braid – and conclude that Mr Lazarus Darke is a gentleman who takes great pride in his appearance, without quite having the means to carry the whole thing off.

He pauses outside the door to number twenty-nine, to brush a piece of lint from his coat. If appearance matters to Lazarus Darke, today it matters more.

The house, as most will know, has been owned by the Lords Seabrooke since its construction nearly twenty years earlier. Lazarus has called here only once before, in circumstances that do not bear thinking about, but which have some small connection to the business that brings him here today.

The footman who answers his knock, the sort to notice silver buckles rather than gold, frowns when Lazarus asks to see the Dowager Countess of Seabrooke. 'Do you have an appointment, sir?'

'I do not. But she'll see me.' And if she won't, he utters silently, I have words to change her mind.

He is shown into an anteroom, the first footman watching over him, while a second is dispatched with Lazarus's card to consult his mistress. The room is dominated by eight Ionic pillars of green scagliola, each surmounted by a bronze god or goddess. Golden shadows dance across the walls and across Lazarus himself, so that he feels like Zeus visiting Danaë in a shower of gilded rain. Here and there amidst the splendour, he picks out signs of wear: a crack in the scagliola floor; a flaking of the gilt plasterwork. The late Lord Seabrooke's debts were the talk of the town. The family hasn't been in affluent fortune since the South Sea Bubble burst.

The second footman returns. 'If you will follow me, sir.'

She hadn't needed convincing. His heart skips a little faster. They progress through a grand hall, the footman throws open a pair of double doors, and in he walks.

The salon is vast. More gilt plasterwork, a painted ceiling, marble and mirrors. More signs of wear.

None on the lady who rises from the sofa to greet him. The countess is still in half-mourning, her black satin trimmed with white lace, a black lace headdress drawn up over her white wig. Her widow's weeds, meant to diminish her, only enhance her porcelain skin and narrow blue eyes. She is not yet thirty-five years of age, and he supposes she will have her share of suitors should she wish to marry again.

On the table in front of her is an arrangement of playing cards. She believes they have the power to predict the future. In another woman, such foolish notions might imply fear or desperation, but Lady Seabrooke does not lend herself easily to such emotions. He searches her face for a trace of their past, but sees only the cold, hard present.

'How long has it been?' she asks. 'I hardly remember.'

Lazarus wonders at the lie, about her reasons for making it. Sixteen years, five months, eleven days is the answer – and still he can smell the dying trace of her perfume, still feel the constriction of his embattled heart.

He bows to her and to the red-headed youth puzzling over a chess problem at a nearby table. Her son, Leopold, he presumes, the fourth Earl of Seabrooke.

'I was sorry to hear of the death of your husband, My Lady. Fate can be cruel indeed.'

The third earl had dropped dead over an oyster supper at the age of forty-two. An apoplexy, the newspapers said. *We never know the hour.*

'He was murdered,' his widow says. 'By worry and work and regret. By my enemies. If they hoped I would surrender now that he is dead, then they are wrong.'

Lazarus has read that too. The boy regards him with his mother's eyes. 'Who is this man, Mama? What does he want?'

She arches an eyebrow. 'A good question, Leopold.'

'I bring news of a certain document, My Lady. One that purports to contain an ancient secret of cartomancy. It was stolen sixteen years ago, believed destroyed.'

Her eyes widen. Her right hand grips her left wrist. 'Speak its name, sir.'

'*The Square of Sevens*,' Lazarus says. 'There was said to be only one copy in existence.'

She breathes deeply, then shakes her head. 'My husband employed agents. His father before him. They made enquiries. I would know if it had survived.'

'I believe it did.'

He can feel her torment, a reflection of his own. Their desires have different roots, but are entwined. The boy watches them, his chess problem forgotten amidst the curious tension that has filled the room. His mother's gaze hardens. 'Do you mean to bubble me, sir?'

Lazarus bites back his instinctive response: 'How can you ask me that?' He is afraid of the answers she might give, and where they might lead.

'If I am to act, then I should do so quickly,' he says. 'Before the other party comes to hear of it.'

'How is this even possible?' she murmurs. 'Who has it?'

'I don't know,' Lazarus says. 'But I mean to find out.'

The tip of her tongue moistens her lower lip. He watches, entranced.

'And what does Lazarus Darke desire in return?'

There is so much he wants to say, but he could search for years and not find the right words. 'We are neither one of us as rich as we might be.'

A flicker of private emotion fleetingly lights her cool gaze. 'Very well, Mr Darke,' she says. 'Let us talk terms.'

Chapter Five

Five of clubs, influenced by a diamond:
a strong temptation.

I WILL NEVER forget my first sight of the city of Bath. Five hundred houses of yellow stone nestled in a misty valley, an ancient black abbey arising from their centre. The townhouses were taller than any I had ever seen, and between them I glimpsed gardens and terraced walks, empty in the rain-washed pewter half-light. Despite the weather, the streets jostled with crested carriages and sedan chairs. I spied bewigged women within, their faces in profile, gemstones glittering, like the queens in a pack of cards. The city breathed both wealth and possibility. I gazed down at my father's golden heart in my damp palm. It glowed in the light of the shop windows like a piskie's lantern.

Mr Antrobus had explained to me on the journey that if I was to be raised as a lady, then I must never speak a word to anyone about my former life. It would damage my reputation, he said, not to mention my marriage prospects in the future.

'I know how to play a part,' I reassured him. Despite everything, I could still do that. 'In the villages, I wore an amulet and a headscarf. Sometimes I said a spell, though the cards need no incantation. You have to do what people expect, Father said.'

He nodded a little uncertainly. 'Then let us make sure never to disappoint them.'

Mr Antrobus lived in a large three-storey house on a quiet road of honeyed stone named Trim Street. He kept four servants: a house-keeper, Mrs Fremantle; Mathias, a manservant, who doubled as his valet; Mrs Grainger, his cook; and a yellow-haired maidservant, whose name was Letitia, but was known to all as Lettuce. I was intro-duced to them in a bewildering blur of faces as Rachel, the former ward of Mr Antrobus's late Cornish cousin on his mother's side. My new guardian announced that my surname too was henceforth to be Antrobus.

Life in that house took some getting used to. I was given a bed-room of my own, in which I slept beneath a quilted counterpane. No meals were ever missed, and they were served at a mahogany table laid with porcelain and silver. Nobody seemed to resent my presence, or called me a vagabond, and Mrs Fremantle went out of her way to offer me comfort. If you'd asked me before to imagine a housekeeper, I would have described an old, shrewish creature dressed all in black, whereas Mrs Fremantle was younger than my father. She would sit on my bed at night and talk to me, her yellow petticoats neatly arranged, black ringlets gathered at her temples, her green eyes creased with tenderness or amusement. Sometimes in those early days, I would awake screaming from a nightmare, to find her sitting there, strok-ing my hair as I wept. I had never known the proximity of a woman before, and I was suspicious of her motives at first. In my experience, people rarely did something for nothing.

'Rachel has been showing us her talent with the cards,' Mrs Fre-mantle said, one night at supper, a few weeks after my arrival. 'She has foretold true love for Lettuce and peace of mind for Mrs Grainger. You know how she worries about her son. Your kitchen is as content a place as it has ever been, sir.'

Initially, Mr Antrobus had said I could not tell fortunes any more, but Mrs Fremantle, the only other person privy to the secret of my former life, soon talked him round. She said lots of young ladies told fortunes and most people considered it harmless fun.

'Mathias is worried that Rachel might open a door to a demon,' Mr Antrobus said now.

Mrs Fremantle smiled. 'He's always saying he'd like another pair of hands around the place. His demon could bring in the coal and take the parcels to the post.'

Mr Antrobus laughed. 'I told him he was as credulous as Lettuce.'

My head was turning from one to the other, still trying to make sense of this strange new household. 'I don't think I can summon a demon. I could try to, if you wish?'

'Of course you can't,' Mr Antrobus said. 'There's no such thing.'

'Mathias says that there are demons in the bible.'

'Indeed there are,' Mrs Fremantle said. 'Witches too.'

Mr Antrobus sighed. 'Not you as well, madam?'

'You scoff,' she said, 'but only the other day, Rachel's cards told me I would be lucky. And this morning, I found a half-guinea in the street.'

'Which proves what? That coincidences happen?'

'You'd want proof if I told you the sky was blue.'

'In point of fact, madam, Sir Isaac Newton—'

'Don't,' she said, laughing. 'If you're about to tell me that Isaac Newton said the sky was green, I declare I shall pack my bags and leave this house this very night.'

Mr Antrobus smiled at my look of alarm. 'Well, that will never do.'

Each member of the household undertook some aspect of my education. The formal part of this endeavour fell naturally to Mr Antrobus. Our lessons in arithmetic and the classics, logic and rhetoric, took place variously in the library or the study or the print room – the house possessing any number of rooms with little evident purpose except to store books. To the delight of Mr Antrobus, I never had to pretend to take pleasure in my studies. It felt like a part of my life that had been missing up until now. I read voraciously and uncensored, learning much about the world beyond Trim Street. Mr Antrobus, preferring his understanding rooted in theory rather than practice, rarely ventured out into that world himself. Aside from our walks to church on Sundays, and his visits to Mr Leake's bookshop in Terrace Walk, his only forays into Bath society were the occasional dinner with gentlemen who shared his scholarly interests.

For all matters beyond our front door, I applied to Mrs Fremantle, who accompanied me on our walks to the Grove and to the High Street. She had spent her youth working as a lady's maid in one of the grand mansions of London, before her marriage to her late husband, a Bristol milliner. She was therefore well-suited to the task of educating me for polite society. Buttoned into boned bodices, my waist cinched with a sash, a bibbed apron worn over my petticoats, a frilled cap on my newly tamed curls, I felt like the wooden doll of the old queen, Anne, which sat stiffly on the dresser in my bedroom. (I never asked Anne for advice, as it would have felt disrespectful to Joan the Wad. From then on, I kept my secrets close.)

I would not like to claim that my new role always came easily. My grief crashed upon me in waves, choking me, pushing me under. I'm ashamed to say that Mrs Fremantle often received the brunt of my rage. There were tears, slammed doors, many times I said words that I later regretted. In those moments, I longed to be outside. Not on my stiff walks with Mrs Fremantle, but free to run about, as I had that day on the clifftop. Once, when I was nine years old, I slipped out of the house when Mrs Fremantle was arguing with the apothecary's boy about his master's prices, and ran all the way to the abbey. I strolled the Grove and the Terrace Walk, wishing I had money for the cake-houses, hiding whenever I recognized a face from church.

When I returned to the house, Mrs Fremantle gave a little cry and fell upon me, crushing me to her breast. Mr Antrobus had tears of relief in his eyes. I had my excuses prepared, but the words caught in my throat, choked by an uncharacteristic attack of conscience. If once I had been my guardian's duty, it seemed plain I was now his delight. Mrs Fremantle's motives too were no longer so much of a mystery. During the course of our readings of the cards, I had sensed a shadow in her past, I guessed a dead child. Some roles we choose to play, others are chosen for us. Sometimes those roles become indistinct from our true selves.

Dismayed by my disobedience that day at the abbey, Mathias, our manservant, took it upon himself to offer me moral instruction. A thin, dark, solemn man, who sang overly loud in church, he was alarmed by Mr Antrobus's liberality in thought and feared for my salvation. Not that I minded, for I have always been fascinated by what people do and don't believe. Understand their fears and uncertainties, their limits and possibilities, and you understand their soul. I would sit and listen to Mathias's sermons, as he stropped Mr Antrobus's razor or brushed his waistcoat, learning about the prophets, the apostles, and Satan's realms.

Conversely, our cook, Mrs Grainger, tried to inspire me to insurrection. The object of her ire was the King's First Minister, Mr Walpole, whom she called 'The Skreenmaster General', because he'd protected his rich friends in the aftermath of the South Sea Bubble. I would cheer as she railed against government corruption, slamming down a piece of dough, or pounding a sugarloaf to a fine powder. I knew Mathias suspected Mrs Grainger, whose grandfather had fought the roundheads at Marston Moor, of papist sympathies – even going so far as to suggest that she was a supporter of the Stuart prince over the water. Mr Antrobus had laughed when this was put to him. 'As long as she's not hiding the Pretender in my coal cellar, she can pray to Osiris himself, if that is her fancy.'

Finally, Lettuce tried to teach me about men. They were an object of fascination to her, even the dullest examples of the species. Mr Leake's boy, who delivered Mr Antrobus's books, the man who drove the vintner's dray, the young deacon at church. Mrs Grainger said the men of Bath prayed for Lettuce's wedding day, because only then would they be safe from her depredations.

'You'll understand when you're older,' Lettuce told me. 'You'll have your pick of the gentlemen then. Mr Antrobus told Mrs Fremantle that he means to make you his heir. Half his fortune will go to you, and half to his cousin, Henry, who is at sea.'

I liked the idea of Mr Antrobus's death even less than I liked the thought of sharing his wealth with a husband. When that dreadful day came, I decided, I would be like Don Quixote's Marcella, who rejected her suitors and her inheritance to live as a shepherdess. Only, unlike Marcella, I wouldn't renounce my wealth, because to me that seemed a very odd thing to do.

Despite my contentment in that house, I could never entirely forget my life before Bath. Certain questions gnawed at me. What was my father's real name? Who was my mother? Did her family really not know of my existence? Would they want to know?

My mind kept straying to the portmanteau, which, ever since my arrival, had been stored under Mrs Fremantle's bed. There had been a bundle of papers inside it, and I wondered if they might hold some answers. One night after supper, when I was about twelve years old, I asked if I might look in it.

'Is there something in particular you need?' Mrs Fremantle said.

'I wish to know more about my parents.'

She and Mr Antrobus exchanged a glance.

'Well now,' Mr Antrobus said. 'That is understandable, of course. And yet it took you a long time to settle to your life here. I am not sure it would be wise for you to be reminded of the past.'

'That is why I ask now,' I said. 'Because I feel ready.'

'The thing is . . .' Mr Antrobus polished his spectacles upon his cravat. 'Sometimes . . . That is to say . . .' He gazed helplessly at Mrs Fremantle.

'When you're older,' she said firmly.

'How much older?'

'Patience is a virtue, Rachel. Remember that.'

As was so often the case, Mrs Fremantle's word upon the matter was final. Over my years in that house, I had observed much. How Mr Antrobus kept no secrets from her. How he deferred to her judgement on countless matters. How he sometimes bought her little gifts. How she made him laugh. How she did not sleep downstairs with the other servants, but had the room between Mr Antrobus's and mine. How her bed was not always slept in.

It was on just such a night, hearing the creak of my guardian's bedroom door, that I took up the candle in the hall, and went to her room. Sliding the portmanteau out from under the bed, I ran my hand over the cracked black leather.

The sight of our old things brought a lump to my throat. The books from our travelling library; Father's briar pipe; the red leather document tube. The tube was now empty, *The Square of Sevens* on display downstairs in Mr Antrobus's cabinet of curiosities. He had toyed with the idea of sending it to his publisher, Mr Gowne, but Mrs Fremantle had talked him out of it. A woman who abhorred a mirror's breakage, and disliked a Friday's errand, she was afraid that revealing the secrets of the cunning-folk might bring us bad luck. Mr Antrobus had scoffed at the suggestion, but he was ever unwilling to distress her.

Eventually, I found what I was looking for. Untying the ribbon that bound the little bundle of papers, I spread them out on the floor. I don't know what I had hoped to discover – letters between my parents, perhaps – but there was no correspondence at all, and nothing that seemed likely to give me the answers I sought.

Most of the scraps of paper appeared to be mementoes of London entertainments. There were tickets to plays and operas, and the menagerie at the Tower of London, as well as handbills advertising astonishing spectacles: a museum of waxworks, the exhibition of a mermaid, and another of an Essex giantess, seven feet tall. I came across a few poems, written in an elegant hand; a folded engraving to commemorate the Duke of Marlborough's funeral procession; and a receipt for half a dozen silk ribbons, on the back of which was penned the scores from a *partie* of piquet. Above each column of numbers was an initial: *J* and *L*. *J* had won the game by 132 points. Between the initials someone had inked a tiny black heart. Gazing at the little horde spread out on the floorboards, I wondered why Father had kept them – we had always travelled so lightly on the road. I concluded that they must have held sentimental worth to him.

Returning to the portmanteau, I took out an unfamiliar pack of cards tied together by a gold locket on a black ribbon. Opening the locket, I found myself gazing at an oval miniature of a young woman, her red hair curled in a low, old-fashioned style. Nestled in the other half of the gold casing was a tiny coiled plait of red and black hair woven together.

Mother! I knew it was her. The black ribbon suggested a token of mourning. Her nose was longer than my own, her forehead distinctly higher. Yet her lower lip was considerably fuller than the upper, just like mine.

As I stroked the little plait with my fingertip, a door creaked open in the hall. I thrust the pack of cards and the locket into the pocket of my nightshift. Piling everything back into the portmanteau, I slid it under the bed, just as Mrs Fremantle appeared in the doorway.

'Goodness,' she exclaimed. 'You gave me quite a fright. Whatever are you doing down there on the floor? Here, give me that candle – you'll set fire to the place.'

'I was looking for you,' I said. 'I couldn't sleep.'

She frowned, and I followed her gaze. The end of the portmanteau was sticking out from under the bed. I hated seeing the disappointment in her eyes. She sat down heavily on the bed, and pointed to the spot next to her. 'You disobeyed Mr Antrobus. And you lied to me.'

'I only wanted to find out more about my parents.'

'I won't hear excuses, Rachel. Lying is a sin.'

Stung by the unfairness, my voice rose. 'I lie every day because you tell me to. Even my name is a lie.'

'That's different,' she said. 'Some lies are necessary to protect yourself or the people you love. Others are not, and that sort of lie is very wrong.'

Seeing that further argument would not serve me, I allowed her to lead me back to bed. Yet I also saw the flaws in her reasoning. Weren't all forms of lie a protection of the self? Was it so very bad to lie in search of the truth? Surely judgement was in the eye of the beholder – unless one counted God. And for all Mathias's sermons, I never did.

Chapter Six

Nine of diamonds as master-card:
a valuable possession.

I GUARDED MY new-found treasures with a dragon's cupidity. Every night, before I went to sleep, I would kiss the miniature of my mother. I spent many hours thinking about those mysterious initials *J* and *L* and the heart inked between them. Father had said that he'd changed his name. Was one initial his, and the other my mother's?

Sometimes, when I was alone, I'd play patience with the pack of cards, feeling a connection to my parents as I touched their greasy surface. The cards were highly unusual in design. First, they looked expensive, with a printed image on the reverse in two colours: six golden stars, each with seven points, forming a circle around a large red heart. Second, and most intriguingly, all of the queens in the pack had red hair. Finally, a little scroll with a motto in Latin was printed upon the ace of hearts: *Fortuna Favente*.

Much to the dismay of Mr Antrobus – who spoke Latin, Greek, Hebrew, French and German, as well as any number of more obscure tongues – languages were a great struggle for me, the words and their meanings never lodging in my head for long. But with the aid of a Latin vocabulary, I translated the motto: *With fortune's guidance*. Auspicious words, ones that fanned the flames of my obsession with my parents' story. My mother rich, my father poor, their love undeniable, her family and his friends arrayed against them. I imagined them stealing away together: a dramatic ride on galloping horses, or a silent voyage by moonlight down a river.

More answers might lie in the portmanteau, for I had barely examined half the contents. A week or so after my first visit to Mrs Fremantle's room, when once again I heard the creak of my guardian's bedroom door, my desire found a path through the cracks in my conscience. Kneeling to look under Mrs Fremantle's bed, I gave a start of dismay. The portmanteau was now secured by a little brass padlock.

I searched everywhere for the key, but failed to find it. Refusing to be discouraged, I returned several nights' later with a hairpin. I knelt there on the floor for two hours, attempting to pick the lock, trying to remember from my days on the road with Father how it was done. But the pin was awkward to manoeuvre compared to the lockpicks we'd used in the old days. Eventually, after achieving nothing more than numb fingers and a stabbed thumb, I conceded defeat.

Over the years that followed, I dwelled often upon my parents and my past, embroidering the few facts in my possession, weaving fantasy where I had none. Every birthday I asked if I might look in the portmanteau, but older never seemed to be old enough.

In the winter of 1738, shortly after my fifteenth birthday, Mr Antrobus's cousin on his father's side, Henry, returned from his travels abroad. My guardian introduced us in his study.

'Dearest Rachel,' Henry said, holding out his hands for me to clasp. 'She is even lovelier than you described, cousin.'

I smiled uneasily. On my walks, I had lately become aware of a new interest on the part of the young gentlemen we passed. I understood it and yet at the same time, I did not. I knew about desire, of course, from my days on the road telling fortunes with Father. I'd seen it on men like madness, on women like grief. I had witnessed it first-hand in our house, its attendant emotions of guilt and resentment. But observing isn't knowing, not in its true sense.

Henry Antrobus was not young, being over thirty years of age, and both his gaze and his words were perfectly proper. His head was rather oddly shaped, almost triangular, and his wig was resultingly wide, with two rows of tight sausage curls, further emphasizing the narrowness of his chin. Similarly, his grey eyes were spaced far apart, and his mouth was very small. His clothes were of fashionable cut, and he took particular pride in his walking cane, which was topped with an ivory parrot's head with rubies for eyes.

Birds, it transpired, were Henry's passion. On that first day, he showed us a box of strange and exotic eggs of different colours. 'I mean to write a book,' he said. '*The Birds of the Eastern Oceans, Together with their Eggs*. An artist I know will paint the plates.' He selected the largest egg in his box, a vivid dark green in colour. 'I thought this one would look very fine in your cabinet, sir. I am told it is the egg of a flightless bird from New Holland.'

My guardian's cabinet of curiosities was his joy, occupying a whole section of wall that might otherwise have been devoted to books. The polished interior was divided into many differently sized compartments, in which Mr Antrobus had arranged his collection according to Quiccheberg's formula of *Artificialia*, *Naturalia*, *Mirabilia*, *Ethnographica*, and *Scientifica*. I had spent many hours gazing at the treasures within: polished jaspers and agates; the teeth of ferocious beasts; a blackened human skull; coiled snakestones; ancient parchments like *The Square of Sevens*; a small scarlet frog; and a Turkish dagger with a blade shaped like a wave. Many of my guardian's most prized pieces dated from Roman times: coins, pots, seals and small statues that had been found in the fields around Bath. Mr Antrobus placed the egg in the cabinet alongside his other *Naturalia*, and we all exclaimed at how pretty it looked.

'You must soon be thinking of introducing Rachel into Bath society,' Henry said, when we were taking tea.

Suddenly more interested, I set down my bowl. Though I had lived many happy years in that house, I was beginning to chafe at its constraints. The idea of entering Bath society had a second appeal to me too. Ever since my discovery of the tickets and handbills in the portmanteau, I had retained a fascination with London: the city where I was convinced my parents had met and fallen in love. Many visitors from the capital came to Bath in the summer months, and I entertained the possibility that in society I might meet people who had known my mother.

Mr Antrobus raised his eyebrows. 'Rachel is not so ill-behaved as that. Should she really be punished in such a fashion?'

'You jest, sir, but you would not wish your ward to grow up a bumpkin, I am sure.'

Mr Antrobus grew more serious. 'She's rather young for all that.'

'Oh, there are many girls of fifteen out upon the town. And Rachel seems very mature for her years.'

'I should like to see the baths, and visit the Assembly Rooms,' I said.

'That is because you have never been,' Mr Antrobus said. 'Once you do, you will thank me, for sparing you that torment for so long.'

Henry gave me a smile of complicity, suggesting he well understood that it was Mr Antrobus's own displeasure of society that underpinned his reluctance. Mrs Fremantle had been afraid that Henry might be upset to learn that Mr Antrobus had decided to leave me half his fortune. Yet I could discern no sign of resentment on his beaming face. I smiled back, thinking he might prove a useful ally.

I now bring my scrying glass to bear upon a call Henry paid to our house some months later in the late spring of 1739. His visit caught me home alone except for Mathias and Mrs Grainger. I received him in the drawing room, where he apologized for calling unannounced. 'I could not wait, for I have hit upon the most magnificent scheme.'

By then, we were all used to Henry's enthusiasms. Often, he'd stop by with a plan for a proposed excursion involving a hamper and a pony-and-trap, or a public lecture with learned speakers that would be perfect for the Assembly Rooms, or a proposal for the book he planned to write next, or the one after that. These plans invariably came to nothing, but I was not averse to hearing a grand idea. Too few people dreamed large enough, I'd always thought. Besides, we had few enough other visitors to Trim Street, and later, once he'd exhausted himself, I could always question him about London.

'You must tell me all about it,' I said.

'Oh, indeed, for it concerns you, and I guarantee it will delight. But first, I would like you to tell my fortune.'

Henry and I settled ourselves at the tea table, and Mathias poured him a glass of Madeira. I placed Father's little golden heart next to me, for I liked to have it close when I told fortunes.

'Thank you,' Henry said. 'You may leave us now.'

Mathias frowned. 'But Miss Antrobus—'

'We are all but related,' he said, waving a hand. 'I assure you that Mr Antrobus would not object. My secrets are for Miss Antrobus and the cards and no one else.'

Still frowning, Mathias withdrew. I turned to Henry, intrigued. 'Your secrets?'

He sighed rather dramatically. 'My query concerns a matter of the heart.'

Henry had often lamented in my hearing that he had not the means to marry, but he anticipated that this would change when his egg book made his fortune. Sometimes he talked to me about all the things he'd buy when he was rich. I knew little about publishing, but when Mr Antrobus and Mrs Fremantle had discussed the subject, she had made sceptical noises and he'd said nothing to contradict her.

After I'd shuffled the cards, Henry drew his wish-cards, and I laid the Square. While I was busy despoiling it, he rose to refill his glass, and poured one for me. I was not supposed to drink wine except on Sundays, and we exchanged one of our smiles of complicity.

Studying his parallelogram, I saw that his cards were highly auspicious: an array of hearts and diamonds. 'Your first card is the ten of hearts influenced by a diamond. It figures a marriage with money in it.'

Henry smiled.

'Your second card is the queen of diamonds, influenced by a high heart. She figures a woman of great affection.'

'I never doubted it,' Henry said, with much feeling.

'Your destiny and hers are much bound together,' I said. 'There are no kings or knaves in this fortune, no male rival to discern, but many hearts, much intensity of emotion.'

'Indeed there is,' Henry breathed.

I wondered if he had intentions towards his landlady, Mrs Davenport. She was older than Henry, but Lettuce had said she was very handsome. The thought of love made my mind drift, as it so often did, to my parents. Their romance must have caused a great outrage at the time – a cunning-man and a lady, an elopement, a child – but though I had been up to the attic where Mr Antrobus stored his old newspapers, I had found nothing, not even a hint, about the scandal. I wondered if my mother's family had hushed it all up – Mrs Grainger had told me that the rich often used their money to protect themselves. Distracted by this idea, I rattled my way through Henry's fortune.

'The ace of diamonds, influenced by like suit,' I said, pointing to the penultimate card. 'An affair of purchase, bargain or sale, much to advantage. Perhaps it refers to your book?'

'One can only hope so,' he said. 'Did I tell you that this is my best coat?' He spread his arms wide so that I could admire his pink-spotted velvet with silver spangles, then poked his little finger through one fraying cuff. 'Such a tiny hole to ruin such a pretty thing.'

As I murmured my commiserations and read the final card, Henry cupped a hand to his ear. A key rattled in the front door, Henry swiftly drained my glass, and gave me a wink.

'Cousin,' he said, rising, as Mr Antrobus entered the room, 'you will forgive the intrusion, I am sure. My business absolutely could not wait. I have struck upon the perfect solution to your problem.'

'My problem?' Mr Antrobus said, looking fondly from Henry to me.

'Rachel and her introduction into Bath society. You take no pleasure in the town – no, sir, don't deny it – for it matters not. This morning at breakfast, I was discussing Rachel's situation with my landlady, Mrs Davenport, and she has made a most delightful offer. If you were willing, she would like to give Rachel a Bath season. She is entirely respectable, and sits on several of the committees. Mr Nash himself often solicits her opinion. Now, what do you say?'

'Well, I don't know,' Mr Antrobus said. 'Rachel?'

I smiled happily. 'I should like it very much.'

'Then that's settled,' Henry declared, before Mr Antrobus could change his mind. 'I'll arrange a dinner for the four of us very soon.' Taking his wish-cards from his pocket, he passed them to me. 'In all my excitement, I almost forgot the most important thing of all: my matter of the heart.'

His wish-cards were all red. 'You may make a wish for yourself.'

'Oh, I've made it already. You can guess what it is, I am sure.'

I smiled sympathetically. 'The cards are low, which means your wish will not be fulfilled.'

He glared down at them. 'Are these fates set in stone? Can they be altered?'

'Of course,' I said. 'This fortune is a reflection of the man you are now. Change your character and your fate might look very different. But true change is as rare as the eggs in your book.'

'Then I shall hope to be the exception,' Henry said, 'for I don't like to be thwarted.' Turning, he addressed my guardian. 'Sir, might I beg a confidential word?'

That night Mr Antrobus and Mrs Fremantle had one of their rare quarrels, something about money and a person who took advantage. Ordinarily, I would have made it my business to get to the bottom of it all, but I was caught up in a larger concern of my own.

Sometime after Henry had left, I'd realized that I did not have my golden heart charm. I searched everywhere, all over the house, but I could not find it. After several days hunting, in which the charm did not materialize, I even had Mathias lift the floorboards in the drawing room. All to no avail. I cried many tears of self-reproach. To me, it felt like an ill omen.

CHAPTER SEVEN

King of hearts, influenced by a diamond:
a man of wealth.

EVERY YEAR, WHEN Parliament rose in May or June, Bath was transformed. The cream of London society trundled west in their private carriages or aboard the 'Flying Machine', taking lodgings at the White Hart and the Three Tuns, or at private houses in the fashionable new streets around Queen Square. Ostensibly they came to take the waters, but a greater allure were the dances, assemblies and levées that filled the Bath season. To me, it was our visitors who held the allure. At last, in that summer of 1739, I was to witness my mother's world.

My guide to this menagerie – a favourite phrase of my guardian's – was Henry Antrobus's landlady, Mrs Araminta Davenport. Not yet fifty years of age, the childless widow of a quarrier in Bath stone, she seemed less to mourn her lonely situation, than to rejoice in it. Tiny in stature, her hair a vibrant, natural yellow, she talked very fast, her words clattering together like the peas in a child's rattle.

'You must look upon Bath as an opportunity,' she told me. 'Nowhere else in the kingdom save London could one mix in such exalted circles. But unlike London, no one shall cut you here, not even a duke, for Mr Nash has decreed it – and he would banish a duke for breaching his rules against snobbery just as surely as he would you or I.'

This gentleman, Beau Nash, dubbed the 'King of Bath', could

often be seen at the balls and assemblies we attended. Elegant in dress, sharp in wit, rather more amusing than kind, he was the arbiter of everything – from fashion to manners to music – even going so far as to draw up a set of laws that all must obey. To my eye, he was a magician. Who was Beau Nash, after all? A nobody. A glazier's son. Yet by acting and dressing the part, by always being in the right place at the right time, by pronouncing his judgements with the utmost confidence, he had convinced these fine people, so far above him in rank and station, that he strode among them like a demi-god.

So as not to fall foul of Mr Nash's standards, Mr Antrobus had bought me many new gowns: brocade and silk creations with hooped skirts and fine embroidery. At Mrs Davenport's suggestion, he had also engaged a dancing master, though I fear that I was far from his finest pupil. She also said I should dye my hair – red being a most unfashionable colour – but I opted to heavily powder it instead. I did not enjoy the balls, finding the dancing a breathless torment. I tried politely declining, but to my private fury, Henry informed me that a lady wasn't allowed to refuse a gentleman. Curious about his heart's desire, I observed his interactions with Mrs Davenport, but though he was perfectly charming, I witnessed him pay her no special favour, nor to any other lady of our acquaintance. It made me wonder if the woman he loved lived in Oxford or London, cities he visited on occasion.

Of far more interest than either the dances or Henry's private affairs were my morning promenades with Mrs Davenport. We would stroll along the Terrace Walk, or around Queen Square, stopping to shop for silk ribbons or paste-glass stones. Sometimes we would take a basin of vermicelli in Mr Moss's pastry shop, where Mrs Davenport would introduce me to her friends. To their great delight, I would often tell fortunes, and then we would talk about who had lately arrived from London. As a young unmarried woman, I could hardly raise the topic of my parents' elopement. Yet I kept my ears open, hoping to hear some snippet of the scandal, before learning that another of Mr Nash's wretched rules was that ladies and gentlemen must never indulge in malevolent gossip.

On days when the weather was fine, we went to the baths. One such August morning, as Mrs Davenport and I were approaching the King's Bath, a particularly lavish town coach drew up outside. It was lacquered in chocolate-brown and cerulean-blue and pulled by six glossy horses. The liveried coachman heaved upon the reins, and two of the most magnificent footmen I'd ever seen jumped down from the back. I stared at the armorial crest painted upon the door: a dragon and a unicorn flanking a shield, on which was painted a ring of golden stars and a large red heart. Above the crest was a scroll bearing the motto: *Fortuna Favente*. The same design as the pack of cards that I'd found in the portmanteau!

One of the footmen flung open the carriage door, and a gentleman of about thirty-five stepped out. Broad-shouldered but narrow-hipped, he wore an exquisite black silk coat embroidered with butterflies in coloured thread, and black slippers with diamond buckles that twinkled like evening stars. Pink and freckled in complexion, his chin was square and his eyes deep-set. His hair was the colour of burnished copper, tied back with a white silk ribbon. A white beaver hat, of the style favoured by Mr Nash, was tucked under his arm.

'Well,' Mrs Davenport said, her eyes following him into the bath-house. 'I didn't know the De Lacys were in town.'

'Who is he?' I asked.

'Only one of the richest men in England. Without his wife, I see. Lady Frances is the daughter of the Earl of Macclesfield. For all the De Lacy money, she married beneath her. Kept her own title, as one would, I suppose. Doesn't want anyone forgetting her rank, least of all her husband.'

I wanted to ask more, but we were drawn into the bustle of the bathhouse. We showed our tickets to the attendant and climbed the stairs, emerging onto the terraces that overlooked the bath below. We passed the next half-hour promenading, stopping to converse with Mrs Davenport's friends, watching the bathers traversing the waters in their yellow canvas suits. I looked for Mr De Lacy in the pool and on the terraces, but I did not see him.

We rarely ventured into the waters ourselves, the purpose of a visit to the baths less to bathe, than to be seen. Soon we retired to the Pump Room, where we joined a table presided over by the Countess of Arundel. Though Mr Nash had deemed snobbery the greatest sin, it was universally acknowledged that an acquaintance made at the spa should not extend in London. Despite the amiable party we made that day, Mrs Davenport had told me that if we encountered the countess walking in St James's Park, she would cut us dead!

I had spotted Mr De Lacy the moment I walked into the Pump Room, standing at the centre of a knot of gentlemen, sipping a glass of the sulphurous Bath water. I watched him holding court, barely listening to the conversation at our table, which ranged from the ravages of the Ottomans in Austria, to everyone's hopes that the roads would be much safer now that the highwayman, Dick Turpin, had been hanged. Only when the countess asked if I would tell her fortune, was I forced to tear my eyes away from Mr De Lacy. I had brought a pack of cards with me in anticipation of such requests, and everyone watched as I laid the Square and made the Reduction. When I was about halfway through the reading, Mr De Lacy happened to pass by our table. He stopped and stared.

'The Square of Sevens,' he said. 'Good Lord. I haven't seen it done in years.'

My heart beating, I looked up. The crest on the carriage had made me wonder if he was related to my mother. Now I wondered if he'd once known my father.

'Julius,' the countess said. 'I didn't know you were in Bath.'

He kissed her hand, still staring at the cards. 'Just for the one night. I'm on my way to Devonshire.'

'Lady Frances isn't with you?'

'She's already there. I was delayed in town on business.' He gestured to a vacant chair. 'You don't mind? I'd like to see this.'

A ripple of excitement ran through our party. As the appropriate introductions were made, Mr De Lacy studied me curiously.

'Where did you learn the Square of Sevens, Miss Antrobus?'

The well-practised lies tumbled easily from my lips. 'My late guardian, Mr Williams, had a servant who taught it to me.'

'Was this in London? Or in Bath?'

'Neither, sir. In Cornwall.'

'Yes, that would make sense,' he said. 'I was told there was a Cornish connection.' He peered at me, and I flushed under his scrutiny. 'Your father was a gentleman?'

'Yes, sir, a landowner. I was born in the county of Staffordshire.'

'And your mother?'

Our party would normally have considered such questions impertinent. Yet coming as they did from one of the richest men in England, everyone simply looked at me expectantly.

'She was the daughter of a Warwickshire solicitor. She died in childbirth – and my father of the smallpox not long after. That's when I was sent away to Cornwall. When my guardian died, his cousin, Mr Antrobus, brought me to Bath.'

'So you have been passed around from pillar to post? You poor girl. Yet your misfortune is our gain.' Mr De Lacy gestured to the cards. 'It's all coming back to me now. The Square. The Parallelogram. Pray continue.'

I pressed on with the reading, Mr De Lacy listening to my interpretations as intently as the countess. When I turned over her wish-cards, the ladies let out a sigh.

'It was merely an idle query.' The countess stared down at the cards. 'It makes no odds.'

'Not to worry, My Lady,' Miss Fiennes said. 'Think how you always win at whist. You were born lucky.'

'My father used to say that luck was a matter of preparation meeting opportunity,' Mr De Lacy said. 'It's Seneca, I believe. Words my father lived by – and he had his share of luck, good and bad.'

Miss Fiennes, a celebrated beauty, smiled, her cheeks dimpling. 'You should go next, sir.'

He gave her a flash of his square white teeth, before turning to me. 'If you have no objection, Miss Antrobus?'

Inclining my head, a pale imitation of Miss Fiennes's elegance, I shuffled the pack seven times. 'Now you must take three cards.'

'And not look at them, or I will be cursed. I remember. My query concerns a matter of money.'

I noticed several of the ladies exchange knowing looks. Mr De Lacy placed his large freckled hands upon the table, his eyes bright and keen. I wished to give him a beneficial fortune, in the hope that it might inspire a closer acquaintance, and was pleased to see his parallelogram was awash with hearts and diamonds.

I pointed to the first card. 'The queen of hearts, influenced by a diamond. She figures a gifted woman, esteemed in society.'

Mr De Lacy bestowed his broad smile upon me. 'I can already tell that you are that, Miss Antrobus.'

He was a man who liked to admire and be admired – his authority and charm lending weight to one another. Yet I sensed that his charm was entirely dependent upon his own pleasure, and that one might see an entirely different Julius De Lacy were he ever displeased. The fortune I gave him made it easy for him to be delightful. When I turned over his red wish-cards, the ladies applauded.

'The cards are very high,' I said, 'meaning your wish will be granted.'

Reaching into his coat, Mr De Lacy withdrew a small jewelled case. 'Well, Miss Antrobus, you have certainly brightened a dull morning.' Taking a card from the case, he placed it in my hand. 'Should your guardian ever bring you to London, I hope you will call upon me there. I know my mother would very much like to see the Square of Sevens again.' Rising, he bowed. 'Countess. Ladies.'

He walked back to join his friends, and I studied his card.

Julius De Lacy Esq.

DE LACY HOUSE, PICCADILLY
LONDON

The countess sniffed. 'We won't see him again until November.'

'Such a conquest,' Mrs Davenport declared. 'To be invited to his house. It is one of the grandest in London. And the De Lacys are very select. This is quite unprecedented.'

'It doesn't take a fortune teller to guess what his wish concerned,'

Mrs Harper said. 'The newspapers say the Seabrooke suit is coming to a head at last.'

'The Lords Seabrooke and their De Lacy cousins have been battling it out in court for years,' Mrs Davenport explained. 'Mr De Lacy hopes this latest case will soon be settled in his favour.'

The countess sniffed. 'That family have always been a superstitious lot. It's how the De Lacys made their money in the first place. Old Nicholas, Mr De Lacy's father, was the second son of the first Earl of Seabrooke. His inheritance was a fraction of his elder brother's, but he married well, and invested his money, as we all did, in the South Sea Company. In those days, everyone was convinced that the price of stock would rise forever – but Nicholas met a gypsy fortune teller who told him when to sell up. He got out just before the bubble burst, unlike his brother. Now the family fortunes are reversed. The Seabrooke side have their title, but little else.'

I had stiffened at her words. People had often mistaken Father for a gypsy.

'There was another story about that gypsy, as I recall,' said Mrs Endellion, the wife of Mrs Harper's brother, a government minister.

The countess eyed her beadily. 'Hardly one suitable for the ears of Miss Fiennes and Miss Antrobus.'

'Hush,' Mrs Harper addressed her sister-in-law. 'Mr Nash is just over there and you know how he feels about gossip. When you are banished from Bath, don't expect us to follow you to Tonbridge.'

Chastened, Mrs Endellion retreated behind her fan, and the conversation moved on to other things. Later, of course, when we were alone, I tried to revisit the subject of the gypsy, but mindful of the countess's censure, she would not be drawn.

Yet the various connections – the crest on the carriage, the colour of Julius De Lacy's hair, his familiarity with the Square of Sevens, the gypsy fortune teller – had convinced me that his family were connected to the mysteries of my past. I resolved to find out everything that I could about the De Lacys.

CHAPTER EIGHT

Eight of diamonds, influenced by a spade:
a plan that in success is troublesome to another.

LAZARUS DARKE LIKES to think of himself as a servant of the truth. He aspires to honesty in all his dealings, even if it is to his detriment, which has proven the case with rather alarming regularity. Yet the lies he has just told Lady Seabrooke do not trouble him unduly, as they serve, to his mind, a greater form of truth: the man he knows himself to be – who would never normally welcome another man's death, or call upon a lady with dishonest motives.

In the interests of truth, he examines those motives now. There is an element of personal revenge to it, undoubtedly. Her enemies are also his, and the thought of Julius De Lacy in the poorhouse is not an unpleasant one. But mostly, it comes back to the lady herself and the demands of his conscience. Any other feelings he might have upon the matter are surely irrelevant. Only a fool would entertain hope for the future, alongside his remorse for the past. Yet even as Lazarus tells himself this, he thinks of Lady Seabrooke's own lie, and that flicker of emotion he thought he'd seen in her eyes.

It had been in the service of truth, that Lazarus's father, a playwright, had accused his leading actor of an adulterous liaison with his wife. In the resulting duel, fought with swords on Hoxton Fields, his father was run through, and died from his injuries. His mother promptly married her lover, whereupon Lazarus, then fifteen years of age, swore to have nothing more to do with her. The generosity of an uncle sent him to Oxford, after which he worked for some years as a private secretary to the De Lacy family, which suited his talents for diligence and discretion. That employment had come to an abrupt end in a courtroom sixteen years earlier. Knowing that his evidence would be detrimental to his employer's interest, Lazarus had nevertheless opted to tell the truth.

Dismissed without reference, finding himself unemployable as a secretary, he had sailed for Bombay, where he had worked for over a decade, clerking for the East India Company. On his return to England two years ago, he had looked up some of his old India connections, who had lately set themselves up in the insurance trade. As if his stars had aligned, they offered him a well-remunerated role investigating the verisimilitude of claims made against their company. It was in this present guise as a servant of the truth that Lazarus had learned of the survival of *The Square of Sevens*, a document he, like everyone else, had believed destroyed.

It had happened quite by chance, the night before his visit to Lady Seabrooke in that April of 1740. The unlikely scene is a cockfight, the creaking timber galleries of the Holborn pit packed with men drinking and shouting, screaming encouragement to the birds slashing and skidding in the bloody slick of the pit below.

Lazarus is meeting his man in James Barclay's bank, a scrawny clerk with drooping eyes, a barrel chest, and a beak of a nose – an appearance not unlike that of the fighting cocks below. 'No overdue loans,' he says, in a nasally Welsh drawl. 'No mortgage. No history of trouble. The bank thinks him a valued customer.'

The man whose financial affairs they are discussing – John Gowne, a wealthy publisher – has lately made a claim upon Lazarus's employer, Pardew and Clare, after a burglary at his fine house in Warwick Court. There is nothing overtly suspicious about the claim, but the amount is significant, and one likes to be certain. Lazarus has already established that Gowne is not a gambler, nor a whoremonger, nor is he overly fond of drink. He owes nothing to the moneylenders, and has no dealings with the pornographers, nor the political pamphleteers.

'Any debts at all?' he asks.

'Just the one. Two hundred pounds. Short terms, to fulfil a large order. Gowne is publishing a new book that he says will make him a fortune.'

'Good luck to him.' It makes up Lazarus's mind. 'Less so for my masters, but there we are.'

As Lazarus fishes for his purse, his informant grins. 'Your masters should read Gowne's book – but then you'd be out of a job.'

'Why's that?' Lazarus is distracted, looking down at the pit. A black cockerel is bleeding badly, slashed by a smaller white bird. The crowd roars, and the white bird's spurs flash as he comes at the cockerel again. The resulting spray of blood almost reaches the spectators in the gallery.

'This book tells you how to predict the future. It's called *The Square of Sevens*. The author has some ancient document that spells it all out. What with the new laws against witchcraft, Gowne says it will fly off the shelves, magicked into gold to fill his pockets.'

Lazarus turns, uncertain that he has heard him correctly. He presses the man to repeat himself, resisting the urge to shake the words out of him. When he speaks, Lazarus listens intently, trying not to betray his astonishment.

After his informant has departed – a little puzzled by the intensity of his questions – Lazarus remains standing, oblivious to the din, his mind drawn down the passage of years. He remembers John Jory laying the Square, the entranced faces of the De Lacy sisters. Most of all, as he stares down at the carnage in the pit, he remembers Lady Seabrooke.

◆

Now, his visit to Lady Seabrooke as fresh in his memory as a summer peach, he pauses on the threshold of the Mask bookshop, Paternoster Row. The shadow of Paul's recalls a more distant memory: Lazarus clutching his father's hand, gazing up in awe amidst the crowds, as the son of the late Mr Wren places the final stone atop the cathedral's lantern. He misses his father more than he can ever put into words.

The street is known for the book trade. Every other shop deals in antique volumes or the newest novels or alphabets or hymnals. The Mask sells novels, plays, travel guides, jest books and poetry. Witchcraft is a popular subject, judging by the grimoires, spell books and occult pamphlets on display. A few customers peruse the shelves, watched over by a young shop clerk behind a counter. Lazarus asks for his master. The lad sighs beneath his breath and nods to a corner of the shop. 'In there.'

Rounding the bookshelves, Lazarus discovers a red curtain. It leads to a small office overlooking a yard and a print-shop beyond. A gentleman sits at a desk scribbling, pigeonholes lining the wall above him. Lazarus eyes the protruding documents hungrily.

Gowne looks up. 'Can I help you, sir?'

He is perhaps thirty, with dark, almost Italianate looks. In Gowne's intense gaze, his tapping foot, the calluses on his writing hand, Lazarus recognizes the same enterprising spirit that resides in many of his former East India acquaintance, men who are now considerably richer than Lazarus Darke.

'I'd like to talk to you about *The Square of Sevens*,' Lazarus says.

The publisher frowns. 'How did you hear about that?'

'Does it matter?'

'It does to me.' Gowne swivels in his seat to skewer Lazarus with his gaze. 'Other than myself and the author, only a handful of people know about this project. If one of them has been talking, then I'd like to know who.'

'It's the author I'm interested in,' Lazarus says. 'Do you happen to know how the document came into his possession?'

Gowne rises. 'Who sent you here? Lappett? Or Pierrepont? You may tell them that they're too late. The contract is signed.'

'I don't work for your competitors, sir, though I do represent an interested party.'

As if by magic, a golden guinea has appeared in his hand. Gowne eyes it contemptuously. 'If you wish to find out more about this book, then you may do so at the same time as everybody else – by buying a copy on the day of publication.'

Lazarus can hardly go to Lady Seabrooke with a book that she might buy herself in a shop. Yet he can see Gowne will not be moved. Tipping his hat, he takes his leave.

Two hours later, he is back. This time he loiters outside, until such a time as the shop is busy, the clerk distracted by customers. He slips inside unseen, and takes up a position between the shelves where he is obscured from the view of both the clerk and anyone coming through the curtain. A boy enters the shop. His name is Cato, the son of Lazarus's landlord. He grabs two volumes from a shelf, makes a very rude gesture at the clerk, and then dashes through the door onto the street.

The clerk cries out: 'Thief, sir, thief!' He runs after Cato, still shouting. Peering around a bookshelf, Lazarus watches as John Gowne hurries out to take the clerk's position behind the counter. He casts a gimlet eye over his customers, but he doesn't spot Lazarus slipping through the curtain into his office.

Cato will run just fast enough to give the clerk hope that he might catch him. Most men last at least five minutes before giving up. Lazarus works quickly, glancing over the documents on Gowne's desk, then turning to the pigeonholes. Each compartment seems to relate to a different book published by Gowne, and it doesn't take him long to locate the one he seeks. He leafs through a bundle of papers relating to *The Square of Sevens*: orders from bookshops, dockets relating to ink and paper, and a thick bundle of correspondence between Gowne and the author. Lazarus commits the name and address to memory: *Mr Robert Antrobus, Trim Street, Bath*.

CHAPTER NINE

Ace of spades as master-card: a special misfortune, unhappiness,
or hurt to one's life, perhaps not discernible at once.

T HE DE LACY family swiftly became my new obsession. I spent
many hours up in the attic in that autumn of 1739, wedged
between a moth-eaten crocodile, a broken astrolabe, and the tusk of a
narwhale, curiosities banished here by Mrs Fremantle. Mr Antrobus,
who hated to throw anything away, stored a great many tea chests up
here too, full of magazines and newspapers dating back many years. I
pored over them all, seeking mention of the De Lacys.

My rewards for these labours were few, yet I carefully clipped each
article I found, and pasted it into my album. In the legal pages of the
newspapers, I discovered several references to *Seabrooke v De Lacy*,
the legal battles that the ladies at the Pump Room had mentioned. It
seemed the late Earl of Seabrooke had pursued a great many different
suits against Julius De Lacy: in the Prerogative Court, in Chancery, in
Doctor's Commons, before the High Court of Delegates, and before
the King's Bench. All appeared to have ended in failure. I found the
legal terms confusing: bills, testators, replications, rejoinders – and Mr
Antrobus's books on the law proved just as impenetrable. All I could
ascertain was that these cases had been grinding through the courts
since at least 1724, and concerned the estate of Julius's late father,
Nicholas De Lacy.

In a copy of the *Daily Courant* dated 17 November 1723 – only a few weeks after my own birth – I found a short obituary of that gentleman.

The Hon. Nicholas De Lacy
(1681–1723)

At Leighfindell, Devonshire, aged 42, The Honourable Nicholas De Lacy of that place, and of De Lacy House, London. The second son of the first Earl of Seabrooke by his second wife, Anne, daughter of Lord Hearnshawe. He inherited, through his maternal great-aunt, Lady Elizabeth (Lilibeth) Woodbead, the manor of Castle Clifton. Later, he purchased the estate of Leighfindell from the Radclyffes of Devonshire, as well as considerable property and other titles from his brother, the second earl.

He attended New College, Oxford, where he proceeded MA in 1698, and through adroit speculation acquired a considerable fortune. He married Mirabel Tremaine, eldest daughter of Admiral of the Fleet Sir Richard Tremaine KB, and by that lady he had issue five children. By royal sign-manual, dated 20 September 1721, he adopted the arms of Seabrooke differenced by a heart and a motto: **Fortuna Favente.** *The irony of the latter, given the tragedies befallen this family, of untimely death and filial estrangement, we shall not dwell on here. It is enough to say that he will be mourned by his disconsolate widow and wide acquaintance.*

Taking out the locket, studying the miniature, I wondered if my mother could be one of Nicholas's five children, perhaps the 'untimely death' mentioned in the obituary? If so, that would make Julius my uncle!

Finally, in another edition of the *Daily Courant* from April 1721, I found an article entitled 'A Scale of Beauty', which ranked twelve fashionable women according to their countenance, figure, elegance, grace and wit. Most were women of title, but halfway down the list a name leapt out at me.

Jemima De Lacy is the eldest daughter of The Honourable Nicholas De Lacy. Entranced as we are by this flame-haired Circe, we fear the bachelors of London will truly run amok as swine when she is soon joined in society by Patience, her younger sister.

J and *L*, I thought. Was that my mother's name? Jemima De Lacy?

In early November, electricity came to Bath. For one night only, Mr Alexander Ravencroft, master of the art of electrical fire, was to perform at the Assembly Rooms, his visit marking the end of our dwindling season. I wanted desperately to go. Not only to see the spectacle, but also because I hoped that Julius De Lacy, like so many other gentlemen returning to London for the parliamentary session, would stage a stop in Bath to coincide with this event. Mrs Davenport was out of town visiting relatives that week, and Henry was in Oxford for a dinner, which meant that I had to convince Mr Antrobus to take me. Predictably, he refused.

'The man's a charlatan. Electricity should be studied for its properties, not performed as a conjuror's trick.'

'Can't one do both?'

'Not if you expect me to sit and applaud.'

'I could take her,' Mrs Fremantle said, surprising us both. 'Well, why not? I should like to see what all the fuss is about.'

It was unlike her to express an interest in the entertainments of the town. Yet I believed I understood her motive. I had been so busy with Mrs Davenport over the summer, we had hardly spent any time together at all. Resolving to do better by her, I begged Mr Antrobus to let us go. Between the pair of us, his resistance was soon worn down.

Tickets were duly purchased and the crackle of excitement that had consumed the city entered our home. Mrs Fremantle curled her hair, and wore her hooped petticoat and quilted pink gown. I left my hair unpowdered, in the low, old-fashioned style of the lady in the miniature.

The Assembly Rooms were a short walk from our house, and it was agreed that Mathias would accompany us there, and then return at ten o'clock to escort us home. We had barely left the house, when the heavens opened. We jostled together beneath Mrs Fremantle's umbrella, which Mr Antrobus had ordered for her from Italy. The Terrace Walk was bustling with sedan chairs disgorging their passengers into the Assembly Rooms. Two of the chairmen, a constant source of trouble in Bath, had barricaded a gentleman inside their chair and opened the roof – presumably a dispute over his fare. The poor passenger was getting drenched, hammering on the window, all the chairmen laughing mightily at his plight. Hurrying past them, we made our way inside, and down the stairs to the theatre in the basement. Threading our way through the crowd, we found our seats. I scanned the tiered rows of benches as they filled up, my disappointment mounting. Julius De Lacy wasn't here.

Once everyone was seated, a boy came onto the stage, and asked for the candles to be extinguished. The room was plunged into darkness, only to be lit up once more by a great crackle of blue sparks, accompanied by a powerful stench of sulphur. Mr Ravencroft strode onto the stage and Mrs Fremantle squeezed my hand.

'Ladies and gentlemen,' he addressed us, in a Scottish accent, 'I bring to your city Electricity, the youngest daughter of the sciences. Tonight, you will see her fire harnessed and you will admire her beauty, enchanting as the Aurora Borealis herself.'

In the half-light of a burning brazier, the boy carried a curious contraption onto the stage: a large wheel encased in a wooden frame, a glass tube attached to it by a cord. The boy handed the tube to his master, and then worked the wheel with a handle, spinning it faster and faster. A ripple of amazement ran through the audience, as the glass tube began to glow. Ravencroft held it high above his head, and his long brown hair flew up to meet it, prompting a flurry of incredulous applause.

Further tricks followed. We gasped and clapped as Ravencroft made paper puppets dance and a bell ring, all through the power of electricity alone. Finally, the boy was secured under the arms and legs by long silken ropes and hoisted into the air, as if he was flying. Ravencroft applied the glowing tube to him, and the boy was able to turn the pages of a book with one finger, despite being suspended several feet above it.

'Tonight,' Ravencroft said, when the applause had died down, 'I shall perform a new experiment. It is named "The Chaste Diana" and I require a volunteer. A young woman, one unmarried.'

Several bold young women cried out, but Ravencroft's eye fell upon me. 'Cast by Titian himself. Miss, will you be my Diana?'

'Don't be afraid,' Mrs Fremantle said. She'd always had a daring side. 'I'm sure he'll let no harm come to you.'

As I walked up onto the stage, I felt only exhilaration. Electricity seemed to me something marvellous. It spoke of danger and transformation and possibility. Yet I knew that the crowd – like Mrs Fremantle – would expect nerves, and so I stepped hesitantly onto the stage, blinking in the light and all the rest. Mr Ravencroft guided me to a chair mounted on what looked to be a large block of resin. The boy turned the handle of his machine again and the glass tube glowed. 'It won't hurt you,' Ravencroft whispered, as he swept the air around me, never quite touching me with the pulsing light.

'Here sits Diana,' he addressed the audience, 'goddess of the glade. Is there an Actaeon among you, one brave enough to court our virgin queen?'

The hands of many men shot up, amidst ribald shouts. Ravencroft pointed, and a young gentleman rose from his seat. I watched him walk onstage, taking in his fair hair, his long legs and self-deprecating smile.

'I invite you, sir, to kiss the goddess, Diana. Go ahead, sir, on the lips. If you dare.'

Now my palms grew moist. My fingers tensed upon the chair. I glanced at Ravencroft, who gave me a reassuring smile. The theatre quietened, a drawn-out breath of anticipation.

The young gentleman gave me a crooked grin of mutual embarrassment. Unsure what else to do, I raised my eyebrows. His face blurred, then sharpened, as he lowered it to mine. I could smell his civet scent. His skin was damp where it met his cravat. The hairs of his eyebrows against his skin were like threads of spun gold.

Then there was a great flash, a popping noise, and a smell of sulphur rising. My Actaeon drew back sharply, clutching his lips.

'And lo,' Ravencroft declared, 'Diana remains inviolate.'

A thunder of applause echoed throughout the theatre. Ravencroft drew me from the chair by the hand, and the three of us took a bow. Filled with a tingling excitement that I put down to my brush with electricity, I rejoined Mrs Fremantle, who was full of praise for my boldness. 'You will be the talk of Bath,' she said. 'I am afraid to even touch you. So will the gentlemen, after that display – which will afford Mr Antrobus much peace of mind.'

We applauded Mr Ravencroft as he gave his final bows, and the curtain came down. As it was still a few minutes to ten, conscious of the raucous antics of the chairmen, Mrs Fremantle suggested I wait in the lobby, while she went to see if Mathias had arrived. People filed past me, and I received many plaudits for my bravery. Somebody clutched my arm and I turned. I found myself facing an elderly gentleman, his hair white and wispy, his hands and scalp covered in liver spots. His eyes were bright, but rather wild, his mouth slack and toothless.

'Remind me of your name, my dear,' he said. 'I never could tell you De Lacy girls apart.'

I stared at him. He seemed not quite right in his wits. Yet he had somehow recognized me as a De Lacy! 'My name is Rachel, sir.'

He stared at me, bewildered, his nails digging into my arm. 'Who is your father, girl?'

Emboldened by his confusion, I answered him forthrightly. 'He was a Cornish cartomancer. Do you remember him, sir? He won Nicholas De Lacy a great fortune.'

'John Jory,' he said, slowly. 'Clever fellow.'

John Jory? Was that my father's real name? Jory was the Cornish form of George.

J for John Jory. But then who was L? The De Lacy daughters were named Jemima and Patience.

'My father eloped with my mother,' I said. 'Do you recall it, sir?'

He frowned, his white eyebrows drawing together. 'They told me you were dead.'

'Whoever told you that was mistaken, sir.' I smiled reassuringly. 'Do you remember my mother?'

'Of course I remember her,' he said, rather crossly. 'Pretty girl.'

'Can you tell me her name?'

He scowled. 'You don't know the name of your own mother?'

'I never knew her, sir.' My voice faltered a little. 'I know nothing about her.'

He blinked, his watery eyes focusing unsteadily upon my face. 'Such a monstrous thing. You poor girl.' Reaching out a trembling hand, he stroked the side of my face with his long yellow nails.

'My mother's name, sir?' I prompted, resisting the urge to pull away.

Before he could reply, a thickset, well-groomed gentleman in a red-and-black-striped coat and a flowing, white Adonis wig barrelled up to us. 'There you are, Father. What are you doing? Unhand this poor lady at once.'

'Poor lady?' the old man echoed. 'She is a De Lacy. Rich as Croesus.'

The second man spoke through a sigh. 'She's just some red-haired girl from Bath. Now come, sir. Remember where you are.' He tugged rather hard at the hand of the old man, who only tightened his grip upon my arm.

As the pair of them grappled like this, the three of us locked in an awkward dance, a younger man hurried up to us. With a start, I realized it was my Actaeon. Evidently, he knew the pair, for he tried to prize the old man's fingers loose. Our dance now a *pas de quatre*, I stole a second glance at him: his torso trim in his charcoal-and-topaz coat; his soft brown gaze, his gentle hands, his ragged smile.

The old man's grip came loose at last, and the second man drew him aside, speaking to him rather sharply. The smile of my Actaeon broadened in recognition. 'You!' he exclaimed, touching his lips ruefully. 'For one moment there, I feared I might burst into flames.

Please accept our apologies, miss. Old Mr Radclyffe's wits sometimes wander, and girls with red hair always seem to set him off.'

I'd been puzzling how it was that this old man had taken me for a De Lacy, when Julius clearly hadn't discerned any great resemblance.

'I understand,' I said. 'There was no harm done. I'm quite all right.'

At that moment, Mrs Fremantle bustled up to us. Apparently alarmed by the old man's expression, she pulled me away. 'Mathias is waiting. Come, quickly now.'

As she steered me through the crowd, I turned back to see the gentlemen watching us. My Actaeon lifted his hand in farewell.

I wanted to ask him who he was. I wanted to ask the old gentleman, Mr Radclyffe, more about the De Lacys. Above all, I wanted to know my mother's name.

The old man shouted after me. 'I know you!' he cried. 'You're supposed to be dead.'

CHAPTER TEN

Three of hearts, influenced by a club: a visit.

THREE WEEKS LATER, Lettuce gave in her notice. She was to marry Mr Leake's boy, now very much a man, promoted chief clerk overseeing his master's business. No one could have been more delighted than Mr Antrobus to learn that all his deliveries of books had at last attained a practical application. We held a supper that night to celebrate – all the servants sitting at table, the meal cooked and served by Mrs Fremantle and myself. Looking at their faces, all aglow in the candlelight, I was filled with a fierce protective love. I went to bed that night a little warm from wine, and drifted off into a fitful sleep.

Sometime in the early hours, I awoke with a start. The house seemed to quiver with the dying trace of a loud noise. Listening hard, I discerned the faint, rattling scrape of someone opening a window downstairs. Mr Antrobus sometimes worked late into the night and I presumed that he desired some fresh air.

For a few minutes, I tried and failed to get back to sleep. Eventually, feeling unusually thirsty, I decided to fetch a bowl of milk from the kitchen. I walked softly downstairs, my eyes adjusting slowly to the light. At the foot of the stairs, I made out the pail of hot ash and lye that Mathias prepared last thing at night, so that Lettuce could scrub the tiles in the morning. Making my way around it, I paused in the hall by the door to Mr Antrobus's study. Seeing a crack of light, I decided to ask him if he wanted anything from the kitchen.

As I opened the door, someone grabbed my arm and hauled me inside. A hand was clamped over my mouth, one arm wrenched tightly behind my back. I struggled fiercely, but my assailant held me easily.

Fighting to breathe against the rough, dirty hand over my mouth, I tried desperately to take in what was happening. There were two men in the room: the one holding me, and a big man with a black beard, who was rifling through Mr Antrobus's desk drawers. A bulls-eye lantern on the desk cast a low light on the mess of papers the man had thrown to the floor. My heart raced in rising panic. *What would they do to me?*

'Now what?' the man holding me whispered fiercely.

'Just hold on to her,' Black-Beard said. 'Keep her quiet while I look.'

Their accent was one I heard often in Bath, on the lips of the footmen, coachmen and maids who filled the city in the summer season. London villains.

I watched helplessly as Black-Beard continued his search, fears chasing one another through my mind. Eventually, he stood back from the desk, grunting his frustration. 'It isn't here.'

'Try that fancy cupboard,' the man holding me said.

Black-Beard crossed to Mr Antrobus's cabinet of curiosities and opened the doors. He grabbed a fistful of garnets and thrust them into his pocket. Then he peered at a couple of the ancient maps and parchments, before tossing them to the floor. Seeing *The Square of Sevens* crushed beneath his boots, my head filled with a pulsing rage.

It took me back to the Seven Stars inn, that day when Edward from the orphanage had rifled through our things. Back further still, to the day when the constables had beaten Father. Their leader had gripped him from behind, as this man was gripping me now. Father had driven his head up and back, breaking the man's nose. We'd tried to run, but the other constables had caught us. Their blows had rained down on Father, one of them holding me, kicking and screaming. They would have killed him, if a local landowner hadn't intervened.

The man behind me wasn't tall. I could feel his hot breath against my ear. 'She might know where it is,' he said.

Black-Beard turned. 'If you scream, missy, it'll go the worse for you.' He nodded to his friend, who removed his hand from my mouth. 'Where is it?'

'Where is what?' I managed to say.

Black-Beard had a veined complexion and close-cropped black hair. 'Your strongbox. Where the master keeps his valuables.'

'There is no strongbox,' I said, truthfully.

He smiled nastily. 'You wouldn't be lying to me now, would you, darling?'

Sensing that things might take a turn for the worse, I judged that it was now or never. I let my weight sag at the knees, then brought my foot down hard on my assailant's foot, using the momentum to propel myself up and back towards his face. Only I had misjudged the man's height, and the back of my skull only caught him on the chin in a glancing blow. It still took him by surprise. He cried out and his grip loosened. Shoving him away, I ran into the hall, shouting for Mr Antrobus and Mathias.

My foot caught on the rug and I sprawled forward onto my face. I heard voices above and below, footsteps coming. Turning, I saw Black-Beard bearing down on me. Scrambling to my feet, I ran a few more paces, almost colliding with Mrs Fremantle at the bottom of the stairs. Taking one look at the burly shadow coming towards us, she pushed me behind her, snatched up the pail of hot ash and lye, and hurled the contents into Black-Beard's face. He howled, clutching his eyes.

His friend, the one who'd been holding me, had followed us into the hall. I caught a flash of a green coat, a white face pitted like a cheese, and dark-rimmed eyes. 'Come on,' he cried, making for the front door.

While he struggled with the bolts, Black-Beard turned on Mrs Fremantle. 'Bloody bitch,' he cried, hurling her to the floor. Her head struck the tiles with a sharp crack.

I screamed. Green-Coat seized Black-Beard's arm, pulling him away. 'Christ's sake, let's go.'

They ran out onto the street. I heard rapid footsteps on the kitchen stairs, and Mathias burst into the hall, clutching an ancient blunderbuss.

I knelt by Mrs Fremantle's side. Her eyes were closed, and when I shook her, she wouldn't respond. 'Mathias,' I cried, my voice rising in fear. 'Fetch the doctor.'

Chapter Eleven

Four of clubs, influenced by a spade:
the cost will not be valued for its worth.

I F TIME WITH those we love is measured by the hourglass, then God's greatest cruelty is not to let us see the size of that vessel. Know how much time you have, and you could ration each grain of sand. Fill every moment with kindness, say all the words left unsaid. One can ask the cards, but their meaning is often obscure. Sometimes they figure a death, but it could be months or years from now. Or it could be tomorrow.

'I fear the assault upon your housekeeper has caused an apoplexy,' the doctor informed Mr Antrobus later that morning. Mrs Fremantle being a mere servant in his eyes, he made little attempt to soften the blow. 'I have bled her eighteen ounces in an attempt to rebalance the humours. If you wish, I could return this evening to undertake a scarification. But her situation is grave, and you may wish to spare yourself the expense?'

Afraid my guardian might strike the doctor, I laid a hand upon his arm. 'Anything, sir,' I said. 'Anything that might save her.'

The doctor returned that night to cup her, but there was no improvement in her condition. At five o'clock the next morning, her breathing grew noticeably shallow. Not an hour later, she died.

♣

I can hardly bring myself to write of those desolate weeks that followed her death. The thieves had not been caught, though the magistrate had scoured the county. When he'd learned that they'd had London accents, he'd nodded gravely. 'They probably heard some story in a tavern from a footman or a groom about a diamond necklace or a hoard of gold under a bed. I imagine they got the wrong house.' He shook his head. 'Import London money and manners, and you import their villains too.'

Mrs Fremantle's funeral was a quiet affair. A stormy sky, a wind like a knife. Mathias praying, Lettuce weeping on the arm of her fiancé, Mrs Grainger and I consoling Mr Antrobus. His white face and red eyes impressed the vicar as a true model of the benevolent master, and yet if he'd known the source of that grief, he'd have denounced it as a sin.

My own grief is as raw now as it was then. The truth is, Mrs Fremantle was a mother to me, the only one I ever knew. My greatest regret is that I did not realize it until it was too late. As salt meets ink, and these words bleed into the page, I remember the pair of us taking the ferry-boat back from the Spring Gardens, the dying sun hitting the water, shadows consuming the golden pools one by one.

About ten days after the funeral, I went up to Mrs Fremantle's bedroom to sort through her things. I boxed up her clothes, her romance novels, and her porcelain figurines for Mathias to take to the charity office. These sad tasks accomplished, I sat on her bed, her brass chatelaine belt in my hands.

To be too practical is madness, says Cervantes. Better that than the wandering madness of grief. Like Heracles, we labour, and the monster we vanquish is named loss. Sit idle again, and like the heads of the Hydra, grief snakes back.

Upon the chain of the chatelaine belt hung a needle case, a notebook, a vinaigrette, a purse, and the household keys. Opening the purse, I listlessly counted a handful of silver. Then I opened the needle case, and the sight stirred me from my languor. Nestled amongst the rows of needles was a tiny brass key.

When you're older, Mrs Fremantle had said. Well, I am older now, I thought. I feel as if I have aged a hundred years.

Lifting the portmanteau onto the bed, I slid the key into the padlock. Inside were all our old things: our books, the document tube, the bundle of papers, father's pipe. Some things it took me a moment to remember, others I didn't recall at all. In the corner of a threadbare shawl of bright red silk, I found a tiny embroidered design: six yellow stars surrounding a red heart outlined in black thread. Supposing it must have belonged to my mother, I pressed it to my cheek.

My memories of our days on the road were fading, scattered fragments of a childhood that seemed so distant now. Fingering the scraps of velvet and lace in our old mending box, I recalled a barn in winter, Father sewing Joan the Wad's patchwork dress, telling me stories about witches: how they rode on ragwort stems, how if I wanted to become a witch, I should go to a logan stone at midnight and touch it nine times. With reverence, I placed each item upon the bed: Father's pens, ink and paper, his tobacco pouch, his razor and brush. Each held a story, but not the one I wanted told.

Untying the drawstring of his herb bag, I shook out ancient sprigs of lovage, agrimony and belladonna. They crumbled to dust between my fingers, leaving the faintest trace of their scent in the air. In the bottom of the bag something crackled, and I discovered a folded sheet of paper, which I recognized at once as an astrological chart.

Father had never taught me astrology, believing the Square of Sevens to be a far superior method of divination. Struggling to remember his charts, I identified the symbols for the planets and the star signs. In one corner of the paper, Father had scribbled a set of coordinates: *Lat. 51° 32 m.*

I was unlikely to find any books on astrology in Mr Antrobus's library – and nor would I find an astrologer to consult in Bath. The Witchcraft Act, passed a few years earlier, had abolished the execution of witches on the grounds that claims to possess magical powers were not diabolical, but fraudulent. Consequently, it had been made

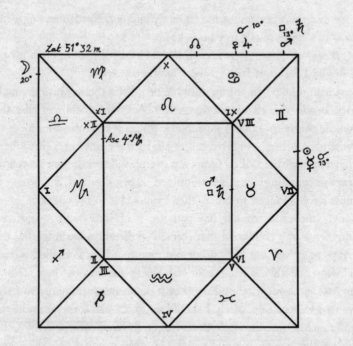

illegal to tell fortunes and cast horoscopes for money. As I refolded the paper, I noticed that someone had inked a little heart across the fold, just like the one on the piquet score. Might my father have drawn this chart for my mother?

Rolling it up, I tucked it neatly inside the document tube to study later. I sorted through the rest of the portmanteau, but found little else to give me answers. My head slumped in frustration. To have waited so long and for so little!

My eye fell on the bundle of papers, and I decided to go through them again, to see if I had missed anything significant the first time around. I made three piles on the bed: theatre and opera tickets; handbills; and other mementoes.

When I came to one of the handbills, I paused. It advertised a show that had been held at a tavern named the Crown and Magpie, Smithfield, in May 1722. There were several acts: a performance of puppetry, an exhibition of an Indian chief, and a conjuror.

THE FAMOUS WIZARD OF THE WEST JOHN JORY JAGO

Performs his most surprising tricks by dexterity of hand,
with his cards, Indian birds, mice and money,
known to no other in the kingdom.

NB Fortunes told and horoscopes drawn by prior arrangement.

Reading my father's real name, I felt a great surge of emotion. He had been skilled at legerdemain, often making his golden charms appear and disappear, plucking them from the sky, from a woman's sleeve, or a cat's ear.

But who was my mother? And what was her connection to the De Lacys? I was no nearer an answer to either question.

Only a few days later, an opportunity fell into my lap. Mr Antrobus and I were sitting in his study after dinner. Every now and then, I would glance at him over my book. Since Mrs Fremantle's death, it had been hard to get a word out of him.

'It's the guilt as well as the grief,' Lettuce had said to me after the funeral. She could sometimes take you by surprise like that. 'He thinks he didn't do right by her. But he did, in a manner of speaking. What else could he do? Marry her and Bath society would have laughed at him.'

'He didn't care about that,' I said. 'He cared that they would have laughed at her.'

The thought of Mrs Davenport and her friends dissecting Mrs Fremantle for their own amusement made me want to tear out their feathers and crush their jewels beneath my feet.

'Goodness,' Mr Antrobus said, breaking the silence, 'are you girl or gargoyle? Isn't that what she used to say?'

I offered him a fractured smile.

'I have been thinking . . .' he went on. Immediately I laid my book aside. 'I thought I might see if John Gowne wishes to publish *The Square of Sevens*. I am in need of a project to rouse me from this malaise. Mrs Fremantle had her superstitions about it, but they surely cannot distress her now.'

I had shared her misgivings about the wisdom of publication, and I also liked being the only person in the world who knew the Square of Sevens. Yet I wanted more than anything to see Mr Antrobus smile again, and so I told myself that the method was nothing without an understanding of the language of souls. Another, less honourable motive also spurred me on. 'Will it necessitate you going to London?'

'Undoubtedly,' Mr Antrobus said. 'I'd need to visit Mr Gowne.'

'Then I think it a fine idea. May I come too? I should hate to be parted from you at this time.'

'I don't see why not. I should be glad of your company.'

London, home to the De Lacys. And to the Crown and Magpie tavern, haunt of John Jory Jago.

Chapter Twelve

Seven of spades as master-card:
a tempting proposal that must be declined.

LAZARUS DARKE IS aboard the Bath 'Flying Machine'. Were he travelling on his own account, he would be perched up top on the carriage roof, but with Lady Seabrooke's coin in his pocket, he sits inside, wedged snugly between a country parson and a widow from Stroud, who keeps falling asleep on his shoulder. To his masters at the insurance company, he has pleaded a leave of absence on personal grounds. His work for them is exemplary, and yet they agreed without any great display of understanding. Lazarus barely notices the lurch of the carriage, as it bounces over holes and humps, with such vigour the widow remarks that they might indeed take flight – into a ditch. But Lazarus is on a different journey altogether, the years flitting past like the villages of Kensington, Hounslow and Slough.

He is in the mansion on Piccadilly, sitting in the study of his then employer, Nicholas De Lacy. Lazarus is only a few days in post, still feeling his way around. His new master is about forty. He has a scholar's slender build, a lawyer's clear, grey gaze, and a musician's delicate hands. Wigs he derides as an effeminate conceit – and all the gentlemen of the house, Lazarus has learned, wear their own hair long in homage to his neat brown locks. To date, he has had only courtesy from Mr De Lacy's lips, and yet he senses that the mind behind that high-domed forehead is so coolly dispassionate, so logical, so reasoned, that he could command an execution without breaking sweat.

Not that he can imagine Mr De Lacy sweating. Lazarus admires his immaculate tailoring almost as much as he admires his speed with a calculation, or his analysis of the ministry's intentions towards the joint stock companies. All of which makes the rumours about the fortune teller and the faith that Mr De Lacy places in him, so deuced odd.

His master is meeting with his elder brother, Lord Seabrooke, together with the latter's son and heir, Peter, Viscount Lisle (that same gentleman who, eighteen years later, will die of an apoplexy over an oyster supper, and be much mourned by all, excepting Lazarus Darke). The meeting is ill-tempered; the South Sea Bubble has lately burst, and property is exchanging hands on adverse terms for the senior party. When Lord Seabrooke bangs the table, Lazarus is sent out upon the pretext of fetching documents.

He opens the door and steps into the hall, nearly colliding with a young woman. The De Lacy daughters have friends visiting that day, sometimes Lazarus has caught a peal of laughter, or the bark of a lapdog followed by applause. He presumes she is one of the daughters, or one of the friends. Her eyes are blue and startled; her wig powdered a pale blue with orris root. Her teeth are small and white, like little seed pearls. Besides her beauty, he is aware of a shimmer of midnight-blue silk, sapphires winking at her throat, and a scent of ambergris that fills the air between them. Also her proximity – she was surely listening at the door? Move a little closer and he might feel her breath upon his cheek.

He is then nineteen years old, and aside from the odd tumble with a barmaid or a lady of the night, innocent of the ways of women. He judges that she is not a day over sixteen, and waits for her to act accordingly: to blush at getting caught, or to step away in shyness at his presence. She only scrutinizes him frankly. 'So you're the new secretary,' she says. 'The reports are true, for once.'

He swallows. 'What reports are they?'

She raises a finger, which he watches as it draws closer to his breast. It comes to a rest. Taps twice. 'You have a button loose. Better get that fixed.'

Her laughter rises at the shock on his face – bold as any barmaid, more unobtainable than even the most expensive lady of the night. She turns with a glide of her hip, and he calls after her, agitated. 'My name's Lazarus Darke. What's yours?'

But she has passed through another door, her laughter trailing. Lazarus wants to follow, as a knight might follow the notes of a harp to find a maiden lying in a bower. And yet he has read enough Malory to know that such temptations tend to end badly for said knights.

A blast from the coachman's horn rouses him from the memory. As he gazes at the Wiltshire countryside rolling by, he wonders how it is that his nineteen-year-old self had so much more restraint than he does now.

♠

Incredible though it seems, only thirty-eight hours after departing Ludgate Hill, the carriage disgorges its yawning passengers into the yard of the White Hart Inn on Stall Street, Bath. Lazarus takes a room with a half-tester bed, dinner and a hot bath thrown in. Before leaving London, he had spent a few days making inquiries about Robert Antrobus amongst scholars of his acquaintance. Thus he is prepared, when he reaches Trim Street, to find that Antrobus's house is both substantial and in fine repair, not one of the sixteen windows bricked up to avoid tax. The door is answered by a dark-haired man-servant, and Lazarus apologizes for calling unannounced. He drops the name of John Gowne into his rather vague explanation.

He is shown into the study of Robert Antrobus, who looks exactly as one would imagine a provincial gentleman scholar to look. He appears tired, his eyes bloodshot, but there is no discernible drinker's tremble in the pudgy hand he shakes. Lazarus's keen eye notices a jet pin in his cravat and wonders for whom he is in mourning.

'I am told you might be able to help me with a matter of close personal study,' Lazarus begins.

'I am always willing to help a fellow scholar. What is your subject, sir?'

'A method of cartomancy named the Square of Sevens.'

Antrobus raises his eyebrows. 'I am surprised that Gowne mentioned it. He impressed upon me the need for absolute secrecy in this endeavour. He's afraid one of his competitors might steal a march on us.'

'I wondered if I might examine the original document?'

Antrobus frowns. 'I sent it to Gowne. He didn't tell you?'

Lazarus waves a hand. 'A presumption on my part. Might I enquire from where you originally obtained it?'

'It was a gift,' Antrobus says, equally vaguely.

'Can I ask who gave it to you? I am especially interested in the document's provenance.'

'You sound like Gowne,' Antrobus says. 'Wants me to claim it's a gypsy secret. Would give it *authenticity*, he says. It's got nothing to do with gypsies, I told him, but does he care?'

Lazarus restrains his impatience. 'If not a gypsy, then who?'

Antrobus doesn't seem to want to answer the question. 'What precisely is the nature of your scholarship, sir?'

Lazarus is at his most comfortable when the truth will serve him best. 'I am looking into this matter on behalf of a client, the rightful owner of a document also named *The Square of Sevens*. That parchment was stolen many years ago. Hence my interest in the provenance of your document.'

'Stolen!' Antrobus exclaims. 'I hope you don't mean to suggest that I—'

Lazarus raises a hand. 'I have no interest in causing trouble for you, sir. I do not even wish to deprive you of *The Square of Sevens*. It isn't the principal object of my interest at all.'

'Now you're talking in riddles,' Antrobus says crossly. 'You've spoken of little but *The Square of Sevens* since you arrived.'

Lazarus feels as if the conversation is slipping away from him. He speaks calmly in an attempt to draw it back.

'When *The Square of Sevens* was stolen, a second document – of a legal nature – was taken alongside it. It is this latter document that I am trying to locate. For a long time it was believed that both documents had been destroyed, but if *The Square of Sevens* has survived, then so might the other. My client is willing to pay a great deal of money for information leading to its recovery. They are also content to overlook the circumstances in which you acquired your document.'

'Overlook? Circumstances?' Antrobus's lip trembles. 'How dare you suggest that I would be in possession of stolen property! That I would lie to conceal it!'

'Sir, I did not mean—'

'Tell your client that I know nothing about his precious document. Now leave my house, sir, before I call for the constables.'

His indignation appears genuine. Seeing that he will make little headway here, Lazarus murmurs an apology and withdraws. As he opens the door to the hall, he glimpses the back of a young woman, a flash of red hair as she turns into another room. It is an echo down the years, a picture within a picture. He blinks and the moment is dispelled.

Lazarus is not giving up yet. In the course of his London inquiries, he has learned that there is a second scholar named Antrobus living in Bath, a cousin to the first. Only a few minutes after leaving Trim Street, he turns into Queen Square. Four grand terraces of new town-houses surround a large garden with an obelisk at its centre. When he knocks at Henry Antrobus's door, he is told by his landlady that the gentleman is not at home, but is invited inside to await his return. Mrs Davenport is tiny and very handsome, with vibrant yellow hair. She mentions four times that she is a widow, and Lazarus, who has learned a great deal about women since his first encounter with Lady Seabrooke, soon has her perfectly charmed. They take tea together, and he senses that he could take greater liberties than tea if that was his wish.

When her lodger returns, his landlady reluctantly leaves them. Henry is an odd-looking man of about thirty. His wig is yellowed in patches, and there is a loose button on his worn silk coat. *Better get that fixed.* These grand lodgings must be costing him a pretty penny. In the words of Lazarus Darke's mother, Henry looks like a man who would dine on cold cuts and water at six, that he might invite an earl to his box in the theatre at half past eight.

They go upstairs to Henry's parlour, which is full of polished wooden cabinets displaying birds' eggs. Lazarus explains his business frankly. 'I regret to say that your cousin rather took offence at my questions. Let me assure you that I meant no trouble to him, nor to anyone else. Quite the contrary. My client is willing to pay a large sum of money for information that might lead to the recovery of her property.'

'I wish I could be of help,' Henry says. 'My cousin showed me *The Square of Sevens* once, but I don't believe he ever said how he came by it.'

'Is it several pages in length? Written in an old-fashioned hand on parchment? With diagrams of the cards?'

'That sounds very much like the document I saw.'

'Might you be willing to speak to him on my behalf? Help him to see reason? I only wish to ask him a few questions. He did not let me get so far as to speak of an amount. We could do so now?'

Henry laughs. 'Oh, my cousin has no interest in money. He's not a worldly fellow at all. He can be stubborn too, especially when out of sorts. He was the victim of a burglary recently, you see.'

Lazarus frowns. 'A burglary?'

'Yes, my cousin's housekeeper was attacked and killed. I'm afraid he's taken it all rather badly. That being so, I suspect there is not an amount you could offer that would induce him to change his mind.'

Lazarus hesitates a moment, his mind working its way through various possibilities. 'And you, sir? Do you share your cousin's lack of interest in money?'

There follows a long pause, during which Henry turns the loose button on his coat, round and round, until – *snap* – off it comes. He regards it thoughtfully, before meeting Lazarus's gaze.

'No, sir, I would not say that I do.'

CHAPTER THIRTEEN

*Queen of diamonds, influenced by a club: a woman of
some audacity, restless and self-depending.*

N O AMOUNT OF books or maps or conversations with Henry
could have prepared me for the materiality of London. Mr
Antrobus had speculated on the journey from Bath that over five
hundred thousand people now inhabited the capital. It was easy to
believe, watching the crowds from the comfort of our hired coach.
Scores of hackney carriages and town coaches clogged the wide
thoroughfares, sedan chairs weaving in and out of narrow alleyways
to escape the traffic. On the foot-pavements, barrowmen, servants
and porters with towering baskets barged through the dawdlers and
the shoppers. Stalls sold Brazil nuts and China oranges and every
delicacy one could imagine, the cries of their sellers interweaving like
chaotic evensong. And the smell! Henry had warned me, but still I
found myself reaching for my handkerchief. Excrement, ammonia,
yeast, fish, sweat – the sum somehow worse than its putrid parts.

As the carriage came to a halt on Paternoster Row, Mr Antrobus visibly brightened. He had been in a pensive mood ever since
the mysterious, well-dressed stranger had called at Trim Street. My
guardian had not mentioned the visit to me, but I had overheard
part of their conversation. The man had claimed that *The Square of
Sevens* was stolen property – and he'd mentioned a second document
of a legal nature, also stolen. I didn't understand it. Father had been
given *The Square of Sevens* by his own father. It had been in his family

for generations. The only other papers in the portmanteau were the mementoes of London and the star-chart – neither of which could possibly be described as a legal document. I told myself that it must be a mistake.

Mr Antrobus's publisher, John Gowne, had secured us lodgings next door to his bookshop: a comfortable second-floor apartment above a stationer's shop, with two bedrooms, a dining room, and a small parlour. Once we had unpacked, Gowne showed us the printing-house behind his shop. Three presses clanked away, each worked by a team of six guildsmen, and we were forced to raise our voices over the din.

'I present to you, sir, *The Square of Sevens*.' Gowne handed my guardian a slim volume bound in green calfskin tooled with gold lettering. Mr Antrobus turned the pages eagerly, as Gowne chattered on about the type-setting, the quality of the paper, and the vermillion ink used in the illustrations of the playing cards.

'Everyone frustrated by the witchcraft laws will be queuing up to buy this book,' he said. 'An ancient secret that will enable people to tell the fortunes of their family and friends in the privacy of their homes. I already have orders from bookshops from Perth to Penzance.' He drew our attention to a large number of identical volumes stacked on wooden pallets. 'Tomorrow I have arranged for us to meet with representatives from publishing houses in Sweden, the Dutch Republic, and Savoy. Your book will be famous, sir.'

We dined that night with Gowne's family at his house in Warwick Court. 'I have taken the liberty of organizing a small banquet on Thursday,' he said. 'The guests are to be seven persons of note in London society to whom we will introduce *The Square of Sevens*. My idea is that each of those seven will then hold a second banquet with six of their friends, making a square of sevens. The newspapers, I am certain, will adore the conceit. Word is already spreading, sir, despite my best efforts to keep our endeavour under wraps. The Dowager Countess of Seabrooke herself has approached me and asked to be one of our seven champions.'

Seabrooke. The other party in the lawsuits against the De Lacys.

'Lady Seabrooke has an interest in cartomancy?' I asked.

'I would say more than an interest – a very great passion. She has been a frequent customer of my shop of late, always on the look-out for rare books about clairvoyance or prognostication. I have heard it said that she is trying to divine a strategy for her latest legal suit. Win or lose, she will be a fine patroness to have.'

Mr Antrobus's face glowed – not from the wine and the candle-light, but from the ambition of Gowne's plans. His smile filled my heart, and yet I also felt uneasy – about the impending fame of *The Square of Sevens* and the attention it might attract – and about my own plans for my time in London.

◆

The following morning at breakfast, I told Mr Antrobus that while he was in his meetings, I intended to visit St Paul's.

'You cannot wander the streets of London unescorted,' he said.

'Mrs Davenport told me that it is not unusual for a lady to walk unescorted in the mornings,' I said. 'As long as it is in a respectable place, such as a park. And there can be nowhere more respectable than a cathedral.'

Without Mrs Fremantle to put iron into his resolve, I easily talked him round. Promising to return to our lodgings in time for us to take dinner together, I stepped out onto the street with exhilaration. London – at last!

Instead of cutting south towards the cathedral, I headed north onto Newgate Street. Mrs Davenport had warned me that any lady consulting a map on the streets of the capital would make herself the target of beggars and thieves. To that end, she had lent me a most ingenious fan. Patterned ordinarily on one side, the other was printed with a map of London, enabling a lady to study it for directions discreetly. Guided by my fan, I made my way past the for-bidding black walls of the Newgate Prison, onto Giltspur Street. I was halfway down the street when I heard an extraordinary noise: a lowing, bleating, grunting and squealing, as if a giant had plucked up a farmyard and dropped it into the middle of this busy city. It was matched by a thick stench of manure that grew steadily stronger, so that I was hardly surprised when finally I emerged into the vast open site named Smithfield to see a vast number of animals in pens, their owners buying, selling and bartering all at great volume. The ordure was ankle-deep, apart from where narrow paths had been scraped through the filth. I held my handkerchief over my mouth to avoid inhaling the flies that swarmed in the rising steam.

Dozens of taverns ringed the market, farmers and drovers drinking outside. I walked all the way around the site, which must have covered a dozen acres, but I found no tavern named the Crown and Magpie. Eventually, I asked a passing butcher, carrying a great mass of bloody entrails in his apron. 'Take the passage next to the Blue Boar,' he said, barely checking his stride. 'You'll find it there.'

I remembered passing the Blue Boar, and so I retraced my steps, until I found the narrow, dripping alley. I walked down it, emerging into a large yard, filled with yet more animal pens and drinking men. From the black and white smear upon a sign that hung outside one of the buildings, I took it to be the Crown and Magpie. Ignoring the drinkers' stares, I walked into a low-ceilinged taproom with cracked plaster walls and straw on the floor. Cheap tallow candles filled the room with an odorous smoke, and I made out more men drinking, some in pairs, some sitting alone. The tapwoman behind the bar was deep in conversation with a pair of customers. They all turned as I approached, and looked at me in surprise.

'Can I help you, miss?' the tapwoman said. Her accent held a trace of Cornish. 'Do you need a room?'

'I'd like to talk to you about a man named John Jory Jago. He performed conjuring here once many years ago.'

The woman's plump breasts were spilling out of her loosely laced stays, making an odd contrast with her austere black ale-wife hat. She rested her thick arms upon the bar. 'John Jory Jago? Now there's a name I haven't heard in a long time.'

'You knew him?'

'Met him the first summer he came to London. 1712 it must have been. John Jory was with the Cornish Players then. They've always lodged here during the charter fair. What's he to you?'

'I think I knew him once.'

She gave me an odd look. 'He's been dead years, love. Before your time.'

'Could you describe him for me? His looks, his manners?'

She nodded to her barrels. 'Buy a pot and I will.'

I handed her a coin, and she filled a leather cup from the tap. Not wishing to offend, I sipped the lumpy, yeasty brew as we talked. Her customers, a pair of gnarled old men with a mangy dog at their feet, leaned forward to listen.

'Best person to describe John Jory would have been John Jory himself,' she said. 'Always with his face in the looking-glass, though I'll admit there was much to admire. Thick black hair and brows, fine grey eyes. Six foot tall and lean as a dog in Lent. He wore an old indigo coat embroidered with magical what-nots, and a broad-brimmed hat with a feather. Always reading that book of his: *Donkey Zotee.*'

I swallowed rather painfully. 'That's him.'

'Girls used to queue for hours to have him tell their fortune. They liked John Jory, and he liked them – until he didn't, anyway.'

'Didn't what?'

'Like the girls any more.' She smiled wryly. 'Sometimes he was invited to give a private reading in the fancy houses up west, telling fortunes and drawing up horoscopes for the gentry. One time he got lucky, gave a good fortune to a gentleman, and made him rich. After that, the gentleman came to rely on John Jory for advice about everything. He was always off to Piccadilly, or to some big house down in Devon. That's where he met his grand lady, and they fell in love.'

Hearing about my parents' romance first-hand like this, I felt as if I'd imbibed the purest drop of sweet emotion. Julius De Lacy had been on his way to Devon when I'd seen him in Bath. Surely the tap-woman was describing his father, Nicholas?

'Can you recall her name?' I asked eagerly. 'John Jory's lady?'

The tapwoman frowned. 'It was a funny name. Give me a moment. It might come back.'

'Was it Jemima? Or Patience?'

She shook her head. 'Ted, can you remember the name of John Jory's lady? The one he ran off with?'

Ted had a dirty yellow beard, the sort that made a good home for mice. 'Luna,' he declared. 'Like the moon, he used to say.'

J for John Jory. L for Luna. But who was she? Luna didn't sound like a diminutive form of either Jemima or Patience. Another De Lacy daughter? One who hadn't been mentioned in the article I'd found? Or was she some other connexion of the family?

'Can you remember anything else about her?' I asked.

Ted shrugged. 'Only that her family was dirty rich.'

Disappointed, I pressed on. 'When did you last see John Jory?'

The tapwoman thought for a moment. 'It must have been the winter of '22. He'd good as left the Players by then – and that caused some bad blood, I can tell you. But when he was in London, he'd still stop in here for a pot for old times' sake. That last day we saw him, he said he was going back to Devon, so we didn't think nothing of it when we didn't see him for a time. Then in the late spring of '23, some men came here to talk to us, looking for John Jory and the lady. That's when we found out that they'd run off together. Threatened my Pasco, God rest his soul, though he didn't know where they had gone. Nobody did. Then sometime the following winter, I heard that John Jory was dead.'

'There was a song about it,' Ted said, turning to his friend. 'Do you remember it, Pete?'

Pete grinned, baring the greying stumps of his teeth:

> *'John Jory Jago, as I've heard many say,*
> *John Jory Jago, met a girl who would say nay.*
> *But he'd caught her eye,*
> *They'd laugh, she'd sigh,*
> *A kiss and a flirt,*
> *She raised her skirt –*
> *And he had her where she lay.'*

Ted joined in as the song came back to him, the pair of them slapping the bar in unsteady time.

> *'John Jory Jago, as I've heard many say,*
> *John Jory Jago, met a girl who would say yea.*
> *Her stays grew tight,*
> *They took flight in the night.*
> *Ten men gave chase –*
> *One drew the Ace,*
> *Came upon them as they lay –'*

They broke off, grinning at one another.

'What happened then?' I asked, a little breathless. Their bawdy lyrics suggested that my mother had been with child when they'd eloped – presumably, given that I was born in the October of 1723, that child was me. Were those men who'd come after them the enemies Father had always feared?

'Can't remember,' Ted said, scratching his beard.

'Do you know how John Jory was said to have died?'

I surveyed their blank faces. Apparently not.

'Who told you he was dead?'

'One of his friends,' the tapwoman said. 'Morgan Trevithick, I think.'

'Who's he?'

'The automaton man. Captain of the Cornish players. John Jory was his partner.'

'Do you know where I can find him?'

'He'll be on the road now,' she said. 'Be back in London come August for the charter fairs.'

Maybe I could convince Mr Antrobus to bring me to London again in the summer. I asked a few more questions, but they could tell me little else. Eventually, the landlady leaned in close, lowering her voice. 'You want a horoscope? I've got a girl upstairs. A shilling for a half-hour consultation.'

I hesitated, tempted by her offer. The astrological chart was in my pocket, and I was eager to learn more about it – but what this woman was proposing was now a crime. True, the offence was on the part of the seller, rather than the buyer, but I could well imagine Mr Antrobus's reaction were I to be escorted home by angry constables. I'd never be let out of his sight again. And yet there had been a time when I had faced the dangers of the law every day . . .

Meeting the landlady's eye, I nodded, handing over the coins. She pointed to a door next to the bar. 'Up the stairs, second room on the right. Knock twice. Take a candle.'

Following the tapwoman's instructions, I climbed a flight of dark, narrow stairs to the landing above, and knocked at the second door. 'Enter,' a woman said.

The room was small, with a sloping roof, the walls hung with black velvet and mirrors. Through the tallow-smoke, I made out a girl, a little older than myself, seated at a table. 'Welcome,' she said. 'Please, take a seat.'

On the table in front of her were two large leather-bound volumes, several round brass plates inscribed with astrological symbols, an amulet on a chain strung around a thick candle, and several parchments covered in spidery hieroglyphics.

Smiling inwardly at the theatrics, I studied the girl, who was arresting in appearance. Olive-skinned, with a narrow nose and an oval face, her eyes were a startling blue with thick black lashes. Dressed chastely in a high-necked white chemise and a blue woollen bodice with matching sleeves, her hair was a rich amber in colour, falling to her shoulders in soft waves.

'Do you seek insight into your past or your future?' she asked.

'My past,' I said. 'That is to say, I don't want a reading. I'd like to ask you about this chart.' I extracted it from the document tube, and handed it to her.

'Whose chart is it?' she asked. 'Your husband's?'

'No, I'm not sure. I'd like to find out.'

'It is unusual, to seek insight into a stranger.'

'I believe it might have belonged to my mother. I never knew her.'

She studied the chart. 'What is it you'd like to know?'

'Can it tell you the date of birth of the person for whom it was drawn?'

'That depends. Do you know if it is a horoscope or a natal chart?'

'What's the difference?'

'A horoscope is a query in the present. Were you to ask me a question now, I would draw a chart for this current time and place. I would then interpret the placements of the stars and planets to give you an answer.'

Like the queries my sitters asked of the cards. 'I understand.'

'Whereas a natal chart is drawn for the time and place of a person's birth. The placements of the stars and planets reveal truths about the querist's character and their life. If this is a natal chart, then these coordinates would give the place of birth, and I can work backwards from there to find the time and date. But if it is a horoscope, then the chart would tell us only when and where it was drawn.'

'These coordinates are for London, are they not?' I had been able to divine that much, at least, from Mr Antrobus's books.

She nodded. 'The astrologer, William Lilly, called it the city of Gemini. In this chart, the sun is in Gemini too. Would you like me to consult an ephemeris to try to determine the date? It will take a little time.'

'Please do.'

For the better part of my allotted half an hour, I sat there, watching her, as she pored over one of her leather-bound books. The pages were printed with tiny columns of numbers and tables and astrological signs. She ran her finger lightly down them, and sometimes she paused to make a note upon her parchment, or to refer again to my chart. Sitting there in her presence, when I should have been fearing the heavy tread of constables upon the stair, I felt oddly becalmed by her serene manner, and the silent movement of her lips.

Finally, she sat up, rubbing the back of her neck, and pointed to the open page. 'The stars and planets align exactly. This chart was either drawn here in London at three o'clock in the morning, on the fourteenth day of June 1705, or for somebody born in London upon that date. The time suggests to me that this is a natal chart.'

To me too – not least because Father would have been only fifteen years old in 1705, and the tapwoman had just told me that he'd first come to London in 1712. If I was right, and this chart had been drawn for my mother, then she would have been just eighteen years old when I was born.

'It is an interesting chart,' the astrologer said. 'The conjunctions, the voids, the Dragon's Head. The sun in Gemini. The moon in the twelfth house, Pisces. The moon speaks of motherhood, whereas Pisces is the ruler of lost things. There is a shadow here, it speaks of sorrow. I could tell you more, if you wish, for another shilling?'

I hesitated, sceptical that the stars could tell me much about a woman who had been dead for sixteen years. I believed, as Father had, that the placements of the planets at the time of one's birth could have an influence upon one's character, just as the moon influences the tides. Yet I also believed that people were ultimately the masters of their destiny. My cards divined the truth by reading the querist in the present, not at the fixed moment of their birth, with all life's challenges to come. Nor did I have the time, not if I was to visit De Lacy House, and get back to Paternoster Row without incurring the disappointment of Mr Antrobus.

'Perhaps another time.'

She smiled, as if sensing my scepticism. Rising from the table, I held out my hand for the chart. To my surprise, she took my hand in hers, her skin soft and dry like rag paper.

'There are dualities in this chart,' she said. 'Light and dark, love and hate, truth and lie. In Gemini, we see the twins, but the gap between them figures large. In Scorpio rising, something is lost, something is missing.' Releasing my hand, she passed me the chart. 'Come back tomorrow if you change your mind.'

CHAPTER FOURTEEN

Ten of clubs, influenced by like suit:
one of troublesome conflict of conduct or advices.

I F SMITHFIELD AND the Magpie tavern was my father's London,
then the elegant houses and shops that I passed as I headed west
were indisputably my mother's world. I recognized many of the names
from the bundle of tickets and mementoes that I'd found in the portmanteau: Drury Lane, Covent Garden, the Haymarket Theatre.

On Piccadilly, this feeling of proximity to my mother was only
enhanced. The south side of the street was a parade of fashionable
shops: perfumiers, peruke-makers, sellers of snuff and toys and parasols. On the north side, grand mansions loomed behind high walls,
many times larger than even the finest townhouses in Bath. I identified the De Lacy residence by the coat of arms on the gates: six
seven-pointed stars surrounding a large red heart.

The house was set back from the street by a large gated courtyard.
Vast and white, with Venetian windows, a wide flight of steps led up
to the bronze front doors. A curved colonnade on either side joined
the main residence to two secondary villas that flanked the courtyard,
an Italianate fountain at their centre. Two Herculean footmen in
red-and-yellow livery stood either side of the gate, arms folded, eyes
directly ahead, to discourage all but the boldest of visitors.

'My name is Rachel Antrobus,' I told the nearest footman. 'Mr De
Lacy invited me to call upon him and his mother.'

His gaze swept over me, and I could almost hear my transgressions being tallied: no appointment, no carriage, no chaperone, not even a servant. In Bath, I would sometimes call upon Mrs Davenport unannounced and unaccompanied, but we were well acquainted. I already had my excuses prepared – I'd say that Mr Antrobus was ill and the maid could not be spared – but I knew it would be considered most irregular, if not a little scandalous. Yet under the circumstances, I did not see that I had very much choice, and I was hoping that the De Lacys' desire to see the Square of Sevens again might prompt them to overlook the usual formalities.

Alas, I was to be disappointed. 'Neither Mr De Lacy nor his mother is at home,' the footman said.

I had come prepared for this eventuality. Fishing in my pocket, I withdrew a letter I had written earlier that morning. 'Then please pass on my regards and this note. My address in London is enclosed. I shall be in town another week, before my guardian and I return to the West Country.'

As I said this, someone gave a shout behind the gates, and they began to open. A young gentleman strolled out, and I was astonished to recognize my long-legged Actaeon from the electricity show. He was followed by two footmen carrying a trestle table, and a third labouring under the weight of a large hamper. The footmen on the gate bowed to him. 'Good morning, sir.'

The quartet waited for a carriage to pass, then crossed the road, heading through another gate into the park opposite. Did this mean the young gentleman was a De Lacy? It rather looked that way. The footman noticed me looking, and grinned insolently. Giving him an imperious nod, I went after them.

The park was laid to lawn, with a few copses of trees and ornamental plantings. To the west lay open countryside – at last I had reached the edge of this vast city! To the south was a large mansion built of yellow stone, which my fan informed me belonged to the Duke of Buckingham. Ladies and gentlemen strolled the gravel paths, walking lapdogs, laughing and flirting, the sun passing in and out of hen-scratch clouds.

The footmen had set the table down on the grass. They exchanged a few words with their master and then walked past me, back towards the house. The third footman placed his basket upon the table, and stood a little way off, under a tree. The young gentleman opened the basket, and took out a red-and-yellow-striped ball. It was about two feet in diameter, and appeared to be made of coloured paper, glued over some sort of frame.

I watched him surreptitiously, as I made a slow perambulation of the paths. He removed more objects from his basket and fiddled with his ball. I glimpsed a piece of wood, what looked like a small clay dish, and a canvas bag. He seemed to be attaching the piece of wood to the hollow base of the ball, by means of wire. Once he had accomplished this task, he lit a taper with a tinderbox, which he used to ignite a small fire in the clay dish. Holding his ball in one hand, with the other he carefully slotted the flaming dish into a hole in the piece of wood. Then he held the ball aloft, and cast it into the air. Caught by a gust of wind, it sailed across the lawn, before gliding to the ground not far from my feet. It fell on its side, the dish spilling burning splints and paper onto the grass. I stamped them out before they could set fire to the ball.

The gentleman had set out across the grass in pursuit of his contraption. I picked it up and handed it back to him.

'Thank you, miss.' He looked a little crestfallen. 'Lest you think me perfectly mad, this endeavour is in the interests of scientific discovery. The ball is supposed to fly into the air, but I must be doing something wrong.' He bowed, rather awkwardly, given his burden. 'Archibald Montfort. I would say at your service, but plainly it is the other way around.' He frowned. 'But you look familiar. Have we met?'

'Yes, at the electricity show in Bath, though we were never formally introduced. My name is Rachel Antrobus.'

'Of course, Diana!' He looked a little alarmed by the memory.

While we'd been talking, I'd been making a study of Mr Montfort at closer quarters. Mrs Davenport, who never liked a man to be over-embroidered, would have approved of his plain buff woollen coat – though his riding boots might have prompted a dry enquiry after the health of his hounds. She would have been horrified by his hair, which was his own, curled neatly with pomade, secured by a ribbon to resemble a tie-periwig. He'd powdered it only lightly, his natural lustrous gold shining through. Julius De Lacy had not worn a wig either, I recalled, an affectation that Mrs Davenport had laid at the door of arrogance and wealth. Otherwise, the two gentlemen bore little similarity to one another, and nor did Mr Montfort resemble the miniature of my mother.

Feeling as if I should say something, I pointed to the ball in his hands. 'Perhaps it is too heavy?' I suggested. 'I believe Gusmão conceived his idea after seeing a soap bubble rise above a candle's flame. Doesn't that suggest that weight might be a factor?'

He stared at me. 'You know of Gusmão?'

Which is more astonishing, a lady in possession of a mind, or a ball that flies? To look at Montfort's face, you might have thought the former.

'My guardian corresponded with Gusmão in his youth,' I said. 'We studied his experiments last year. Did you know that he designed a flying craft that could carry a man?'

'The *passarola*,' Montfort said. 'Some reports say he built it and raised himself into the air, just before he fell foul of the Inquisition.' He considered. 'Perhaps, if I remove the wood, I could refashion the wire to hold the dish. That would make it lighter.'

We walked back to his table together, where Montfort uncoupled the wires. 'May I ask what brings you to London, Miss Antrobus?'

'My guardian is here on business. He was feeling a little unwell this morning, and so I thought I'd take the opportunity to pay a call at De Lacy House.'

'My uncle's house,' he said, in some surprise.

'Good heavens,' I exclaimed. 'Now there's a coincidence.'

'I should add that he is my uncle not by blood, but by marriage. My step-father is Mr De Lacy's younger brother.' He looked at me quizzically. 'You are a friend of Miss De Lacy?'

I had read in the newspapers that Julius had a daughter, and I presumed that Mr Montfort must be referring to her. 'I have not yet had that pleasure, but I was introduced to her father at the spa last year. I told his fortune with playing cards, and he invited me to call upon his mother.'

Montfort frowned. 'Then he should have had more sense.'

Seeing me blanch at his words, he softened his tone. 'I'm sorry, I don't mean to be rude. It's just that my family have long had a foolish obsession with fortunes and horoscopes and all manner of matters occult. It has made them a target for mountebanks and frauds.'

I spoke crisply. 'I am not a fraud.'

'Which is – forgive me – what they all say. Including the villain who betrayed Mr De Lacy's father's trust in the most devilish way imaginable. Mrs De Lacy should be protected from such people, not encouraged.'

Sometimes opportunity drops into your lap like a gift. 'Do you speak of the elopement, sir?'

He spoke roughly. 'What elopement?'

Did my family make a habit of them? 'Why, that of Luna and John Jory Jago.'

Their names seemed to anger him greatly, for he glared. 'Is that what the gossips say? How they delight in human misery. Elopement. It makes my blood boil.'

'What else would you call it?'

'Many other words which propriety forbids me from saying aloud. That villain preyed upon a girl half his age while her household was in mourning. Her eldest brother had just died tragically, her father was distracted by grief – and the rogue took full advantage of her lack of protection. He abducted her from her home and forced her into marriage. Nor was she the only one who suffered. Nicholas De Lacy's health never recovered from the shock. To lose another child was simply too much for his heart to bear.'

Then my mother was one of the De Lacy daughters after all! Yet in that moment, my indignation rising, I was focused more upon Montfort's cruel words about my father.

'They were in love,' I cried.

He stared at me. 'I can only presume that you do not know the half of it. Otherwise, you would not stand here defending such a man. I say in all honesty that a greater villain has never lived. My family still lives in the shadow of his crimes. Then these soothsayers and other charlatans tell Mrs De Lacy that she can talk to her dead children. Their deceits reopen old wounds and inflict pain anew, all the while costing her a fortune.'

My fury was mitigated somewhat by the realization that Montfort had plainly been told a pack of lies, and in his naivety believed them. Nor did I wish to jeopardize my invitation to De Lacy House. 'I would never charge Mrs De Lacy nor anyone else money for a reading,' I said, in a conciliatory tone. 'Mr De Lacy merely thought it would entertain.'

'Doubtless my uncle had the best of intentions,' Montfort said. 'But good meanings and good wishes can pave a reckless path. Aha, that's it.'

He had succeeded in securing the dish with wire. Holding his ball in one hand, he opened his bag with the other, and made an awkward attempt at filling the dish with kindling.

'Here, let me hold it,' I said.

He allowed me to take it from him, while he filled the dish. Then he lit the taper and set the kindling ablaze.

'Go ahead,' he told me, a little more kindly. 'Whatever our present disagreement, this experiment is now yours as much as it is mine.'

I waited until the next gust of wind, and then tossed the ball lightly into the air. It dipped slightly, but then rose and kept on rising. Montfort clapped his hands together, and I couldn't refrain from a cry of delight. Shading our gaze, we watched the ball float up and away over Piccadilly. People in the park turned to stare, and one man surreptitiously crossed himself.

'You can see why the Inquisition thought it was witchcraft,' Montfort said.

I could not resist a pointed rejoinder. 'People always use words like that about things they don't understand. Fraud, mountebank, charlatan. Those are others.'

He regarded me with a troubled expression. 'Miss Antrobus, you are undoubtedly a clever woman. Perhaps you are also what you claim to be: a lady of honour. It is with that possibility in mind that I speak candidly. If you have any compassion at all for the suffering of an elderly lady, I beg you to stay away from the De Lacys.'

CHAPTER FIFTEEN

Ace of clubs as master-card: an event of material weight, involving use of judgement, will, shrewdness or decision.

DESPITE MY BEST efforts not to dwell upon Montfort's allegations, they darted in and out of my head like a plague of wasps. To claim that my father had preyed upon my mother . . . That he'd taken advantage of her innocence . . . To insinuate that he was guilty of worse crimes still . . .

How dare the De Lacys spread such foul lies about a good man? And yet, perhaps, like Montfort, they believed those lies to be true. They had loved my mother, just as I had loved my father. It was important to give them the benefit of the doubt.

Dwelling on all the things I had learned that day, I retraced my steps back across London. By the time I reached Paternoster Row, it was well after one o'clock, the time I'd promised Mr Antrobus I'd return. Yet an idea had come to me on my journey, and instead of hurrying back to our apartment, I walked along the street until I came to a bookshop that dealt in second-hand volumes. The shopkeeper, in answer to my query, soon found me a copy of *The Peerage of England*. I had tried to pursue this line of enquiry in Bath, but Mr Antrobus had no interest in the nobility and he didn't have *The Peerage* in his library. In vain, I had tried Mr Leake's bookshop on the Terrace Walk, but all I'd been able to find were new editions of *The Peerage* which had been published long after Nicholas De Lacy's death.

Conversely, the volume I held in my hands had been published in

1712, over ten years before he'd died. Ignoring the mounting indignation of the shopkeeper, I turned the pages until I came to the entry for Thomas De Lacy, the second Earl of Seabrooke. The Honourable Nicholas De Lacy, as his younger half-brother, merited a short entry beneath. Five children were listed; three sons and two daughters – in order of seniority: Virgil, Jemima, Julius, Patience and Septimus.

No daughter named Luna or anything close. Yet as I studied the entries for the De Lacy daughters, my pulse picked up pace.

Jemima Maria Anne Elizabeth Carolina, born Castle Clifton,
Warwickshire, 29 April and baptized there 26 May 1703

Patience Louisa Ursula Natalia Augusta, born Bloomsbury Square,
London, 14 June and baptized there 10 July 1705

I breathed deeply. There it was: 14 June 1705. The same date that the astrologer had given me earlier.

Louisa
Ursula
Natalia
Augusta

I had found my mother.

At the entrance to our lodgings, I almost collided with a gentleman coming out. He apologized and, with shock, I realized that it was the same well-dressed stranger who had called at our house in Trim Street. I stepped aside to let him pass, and his eyes skirted over me. I watched him walk off down the street, and then hurried upstairs to find Mr Antrobus.

I discovered him sitting at the tea table in our parlour, a troubled expression on his face.

'Who was that man? What did he want?'

He looked up sharply. 'Rachel, where have you been? It's after three.'

'I will explain, but first tell me about that man. He called on us once before, in Bath.'

He sighed. 'His name is Lazarus Darke. I don't know quite who or what he is. Except that he's becoming rather a pest.' I listened as he summarized much the same facts as I'd overheard in Bath: *The Square of Sevens*. An alleged theft. A stolen legal document. 'I didn't mention it before, because I'd hoped we'd seen the last of him.'

'Did he tell you the name of his client?'

'Not precisely. He claimed *The Square of Sevens* was stolen from a gentleman named Nicholas De Lacy, a famous financier who died many years ago. I presume Mr Darke is working for his heirs. He said he represented the rightful owner.'

I supposed that was Julius De Lacy. Did that mean he knew that I was his dead sister's daughter? It certainly hadn't seemed that way in Bath. Nor just now with Mr Darke. He had barely looked at me. From what Mr Antrobus had said, all he seemed interested in was this precious document. I wondered, then, if Father had always told me the truth. Might he have stolen *The Square of Sevens* from Nicholas De Lacy?

'I wanted to be rid of him,' Mr Antrobus went on, 'so I told him I'd found *The Square of Sevens* amongst the papers of my late Cornish cousin. I thought that would fit with your story about learning it from one of his servants. Only Mr Darke didn't seem to believe me.'

An alarming possibility occurred to me then. 'Those men who broke into the house – could they have been looking for this legal document too? They seemed very interested in the papers in your desk.'

He frowned. 'How is that even possible? I didn't write to Mr Gowne about *The Square of Sevens* until some weeks after Mrs Fremantle's funeral.'

Reassured by both his logic and his conviction, I endeavoured to think. 'I wonder if we should tell the De Lacys the truth.'

Now I knew for certain that I was related to that family, it seemed a logical – and yet momentous – step. I gave little thought to Father's warnings that if my mother's family knew of my existence, then people would want me dead – that had been a fakement to change the mind of Mr Antrobus. Yet if they hated my father, as Mr Montfort had implied, then they might not take kindly to me at all. On the other hand, how would I ever find out, if I did not act? As for Mr Darke, I would happily tell him everything I knew about *The Square of Sevens*, though I could be of no help at all with his missing document.

'The truth?' Mr Antrobus said. 'About *The Square of Sevens*?'

'About my mother and father.' I gazed at him anxiously. 'My mother was Nicholas De Lacy's daughter, Patience.'

'A De Lacy?' Mr Antrobus exclaimed. 'Rachel, what are you talking about?'

'My father's real name was John Jory Jago. He eloped with my mother before I was born.' Seeing that I needed to explain everything from the beginning, I told him about the portmanteau and how it had led me to Julius De Lacy at the baths.

As I talked, my guardian's expression grew more and more dismayed – and not a little angry. 'You lied to me,' he said. 'Many times.'

'Only because you would have tried to stop me. I had a right to know about my past.'

'I only ever sought to protect you. Mrs Fremantle thought it for the best. My dear, this is a terrible mistake. You must have nothing more to do with any of those people.'

Guilt lit the fuse of my rage. 'You're just jealous. You want me to forget all about my parents. Well, I can't.'

His face crumpled in shock. I had never spoken to him like that before. Immediately, I regretted it, and ran from the room, ashamed. I lay on my bed and refused to come out, even when it was time to go for supper with Mr Gowne.

'I shall say that you are unwell,' Mr Antrobus said eventually, after his efforts to persuade me had failed. 'I shall walk over to Gowne's now, and ask him if we can postpone supper until tomorrow.'

Once he had gone, seeking consolation after our argument, I took the document tube from my pocket, and shook out my mother's natal chart and the locket. Studying the miniature, I was comforted by the thought that my mother now had a name as well as a face. I would ask for nothing from the De Lacys, except to learn about her past. Surely Mr Antrobus could not object to that?

As I mulled the matter over, turning the document tube in my hands, I spotted something I had never noticed before. On the inside of the tube, just below the leather hinge of the lid, three initials had been embroidered in a slightly darker thread: NDL. Nicholas De Lacy. Entranced by this new connection to my family's past, I ran my thumb over the raised ridges of the embroidery. As I did so, I felt a curious crackle. I ran my thumb back and forth and felt it again. There was something under there. Something sewn into the satin lining of the document tube.

Hurrying to the dresser, I hunted through my sewing box until I found an embroidery hook. I drew a lamp close, and carefully unpicked the stitches of the lining. Sliding my fingers into the gap, I pulled out a folded sheet of linen paper.

In the name of God, Amen, I, Nicholas De Lacy of Leighfindell in the county of Devonshire, being weak of body, but of sound mind and memory, praise to God, do make this codicil to my last will and testament, to be accepted and taken as part thereof as fully and effectually to all intents and purposes as if the same had been actually inserted therein and I do by this my codicil revoke my said will so far only as the same is incompatible herewith.

As concerns my temporal goods that God hath endowed me, I give and bequeath them in manner and form following . . .

To my son, Julius De Lacy, the sum of one shilling.

To my son, Septimus De Lacy, the sum of one shilling.

To my daughter, Patience De Lacy, the sum of one shilling.

To my nephew, Peter, Viscount Lisle, heir to the earldom of Seabrooke, the sum of one shilling.

The remainder of my goods moveable and unmoveable, I give and bequeath to my firstborn grandchild, lawfully begotten, the estate to be administered by my trustees until such time as my heir is of age.

In witness whereof I have hereunto set to my hand and seal the 21st day of September 1723.

An elaborate signature, embellished with paraphs and other flourishes, left me in no doubt as to the significance of my find.

The Hon. Nicholas De Lacy Esq.

Two further signatures followed.

Witness: George Montfort of Leighfindell, Devonshire.
Witness: Lazarus Darke of Leighfindell, Devonshire.

Lazarus Darke. There he was again. No mere agent, but a participant in these events. This had to be the document for which he was searching. His interest suggested that it was genuine. I read it through a second time, every nerve tingling.

Was it possible that *I* was the true heir to the De Lacy fortune?

CHAPTER SIXTEEN

Six of spades, influenced by a club:
must be read an unfavourable sign.

THE CODICIL WAS dangerous. That much I knew. Both Julius De Lacy and the Seabrooke side of the family claimed that Nicholas De Lacy's estate was rightfully theirs. If my instincts were correct, and this codicil made me his true heir, then it was a threat to both their interests. Little wonder Lazarus Darke was so keen to get his hands on it. I thought again of Father's conversation with Mr Antrobus all those years ago. His claim that if his enemies knew of my existence, they'd want me dead. I still thought he'd been exaggerating. Families like the De Lacys didn't go around murdering people. And yet the codicil did at least provide a motive for his fears.

We were due to meet Lady Seabrooke at the banquet the day after tomorrow. Did her interest in our book come from a place of malevolent intent? It surely wasn't a coincidence. I recalled Mr Antrobus's queen of spades: a female enemy.

As for the De Lacys, did I even want their money? It didn't seem to have brought them very much happiness. If I destroyed this codicil, or surrendered it to Mr Darke, I would no longer be a threat to anyone. And yet Father had never done so. He had kept it safely hidden for all those years. Had he hoped that one day I would claim my fortune?

It seemed plain to me that I needed to confide in Mr Antrobus. This was too momentous a matter to be left to my judgement alone.

Between my boldness and his caution, we would come to a sensible decision. When Mr Antrobus returned later that night, I duly intercepted him in the hall. 'I'm sorry for everything I said. I didn't mean it.'

He embraced me with tears in his eyes. 'I am sorry too. I should not have grown angry like that. In your shoes, I'd want to know too. But I am not jealous, I am afraid for you.' He sighed. 'I wish Mrs Fremantle was here. She always knew just what to do. Oh, Rachel, I miss her so very much.'

Our tears started flowing then, and in that moment our loss seemed so much more important than the De Lacys and the will and Lazarus Darke. We adjourned to the parlour, where we talked truthfully about Mrs Fremantle for the first time. Mr Antrobus told me that he'd loved her, and I told him I'd always known it. We spoke of guilt and loss and desire and all their old secrets. The codicil can wait, I told myself, not wanting to spoil the significance of that moment. I'll tell him everything over breakfast tomorrow morning.

The man with the green coat and the white, pitted face was in my bedroom. His hand was clamped over my face, smothering me, choking me. I twisted in the bed, trying to get away from him. His hand moved to my throat, squeezing. I struggled to breathe. Behind him, his friend Black-Beard held Joan the Wad over a fire in the grate. Grinning, he cast her into the flames. I tried desperately to break free, I tried desperately to scream – but Green-Coat's hand only tightened around my throat. I awoke with a violent start, my heart racing, sucking air into my lungs in heaving gasps.

The air tasted acrid, full of hot smoke that burned my throat. I leapt from my bed, and opened the door to the hall. A great blast of hot air greeted me, and I stared in horror. Flames were licking the door to the parlour, running along the wallpaper above the door and the stairs. I could hear someone shouting on the street outside.

'Mr Antrobus!' I cried, inhaling a great lungful of smoke. I doubled over, coughing, stumbling along the corridor. My arm across my face,

I groped blindly for the handle of his bedroom door. As I crashed into the room, he sat bolt upright in bed. I pointed wordlessly at the smoke.

'Are you hurt?' he cried, throwing back the covers.

I shook my head and, together, we returned to the hall. To my dismay, in that short time, the fire had taken hold in the stairwell, the timbers blazing fiercely, the hallway filling with an even thicker black smoke.

'The window in the hall!' Mr Antrobus cried. 'It overlooks Gowne's shop. We can get out that way.'

We groped our way along the hall, barely able to see for the noxious smoke. When we reached my bedroom door, I pulled away. I ran to my dresser, opened a drawer, grabbed the document tube, and thrust it into the pocket of my nightshift. Mr Antrobus had followed me, and he dragged me back to the hall.

Our hair crackled in the heat. We edged past the blazing parlour door to the window. Mr Antrobus heaved it open, and cold air flooded in. We inhaled it greedily as, behind us, the flames billowed and surged. Looking down, I saw it was about an eight-foot drop to the roof of Gowne's shop.

'I can lower you onto it,' Mr Antrobus said. 'Quickly now.'

Climbing onto the sill, I awkwardly squeezed through the frame. Gowne's print-shop was also ablaze, all but consumed by the flames. All that paper, oil and ink. All those leather-bound editions of *The Square of Sevens*.

I took hold of Mr Antrobus's hands, and he leaned from the window, lowering me down. 'Ready?'

He let go and I plunged through the air, hitting the slate in an odd crouch, jarring my ankle. 'Hurry, sir,' I cried, looking up.

He smiled down at me, his face darkened with soot. 'I won't fit,' he said. 'Don't worry. I'll find another way out.'

I stared up at him in horror. How had I not realized? I had barely squeezed through the window myself. He'd said nothing, because he'd known I would never have left his side. 'Sir,' I cried, tears pricking my eyes.

'Everything will be all right,' he said. 'I will see you very soon.' Turning, he disappeared into the smoke and the flames.

I needed to fetch help. The shop had a timber gallery on the first floor, with stairs leading down to the street. Awkwardly, I manoeuvred myself to the edge of the roof, clinging to the leaden guttering. Every time I looked down, my head swam from the smoke and my panic. I slid further over the void, and heard something crack. Then the guttering gave way beneath my weight, and I was falling through the air again. I hit a railing, which pitched me backwards onto the gallery in a bruising tumble of limbs. My nose bloodied, my cheek smarting, I hauled myself up, and hurried down the stairs. A crowd had gathered on the street, staring up at the blaze.

'My guardian is inside,' I cried. 'Please help him.'

They turned, a sea of concerned faces. Then someone pointed and a hush fell over the crowd. Mr Antrobus had appeared at the dining-room window, and seemed to be struggling to open it. The curtains were on fire, an inferno blazing behind him.

'It must be twenty feet to the ground,' somebody cried. 'Fetch blankets.'

Still the window wouldn't open. People just stood there staring. Some turned away.

Mr Antrobus disappeared again, and I gave a violent sob. Then the flames dipped, as if disturbed by a violent rush of air, and Mr Antrobus crashed through the window, shattering glass and frame. Sparks showered from his body, as he plunged to the street below.

CHAPTER SEVENTEEN

Nine of clubs, influenced by like suit:
several persons or circumstances oppose, perhaps slyly.

LADY SEABROOKE IS pacing the salon. When she turns, her eyes are bright, her face tight with tension.

'Will he die?'

'I believe so,' Lazarus says. 'He has not regained consciousness after the fall, and his burns have become infected. His cousin has arranged his return to Bath by covered wagon. The doctors say it is only a matter of time.'

'Then he can tell us nothing?'

Lazarus inclines his head.

'Who is your informant, the cousin?'

She has always been like this, her thoughts leaping like quicksilver. 'Henry Antrobus has applied for power of attorney. Should he find the codicil, he'll sell it to us.'

'You are certain?'

'As much as I can be.'

'What if he doesn't find it?'

Lazarus has no answer that will give her the reassurance she craves. She turns, black satin rustling, and places a hand on the fireplace. It is inlaid with mosaic depicting the Seabrooke crest: seven stars of seven points. 'If only we knew how Antrobus had acquired *The Square of Sevens* in the first place,' she says. 'Are you certain he wasn't telling the truth about this Cornish cousin?'

'I've known a lot of liars in my time. Antrobus wasn't a good one. First, he said it was a gift, then a bequest. He's hiding something.' Lazarus pauses a moment. 'There's something else. Last November, there was a burglary at Antrobus's home. His ward disturbed the villains and they fled empty-handed, but his housekeeper was attacked and died of her injuries.'

Lady Seabrooke draws a deep breath. 'You think Julius knows about Antrobus?'

'I'm keeping an open mind. He is not the only one with motive.'

She arches an eyebrow. 'Are you accusing me of murder?'

She's probably capable of it, Lazarus thinks, but he remembers the look of astonishment on her face when he'd told her about *The Square of Sevens*, several months *after* the burglary in Trim Street.

'I was thinking of a third party, someone who hoped to find the codicil and profit by its sale.'

'It would have to be someone close to the family for them to have made the connection.'

Lazarus nods. 'Or it might simply be a tragic coincidence.'

'I don't believe in those.' She thinks for a moment. 'Are you quite certain that this fire was an accident?'

Lazarus has had Pardew and Clare's fire-man look into it. The blaze started in the print-shop. The foreman swears he extinguished the candles. There was no stench of lamp-oil. No sign of a break-in. No other evidence pointing to arson. 'I believe so.'

'I don't.' She smiles thinly. 'Julius will stop at nothing. Don't forget, he has killed before.'

Lazarus likes his speculations to be supported by a scaffold of evidence, especially when accusing a very rich man of murder.

'There is nothing to suggest that the fire was anything other than a chance misfortune. I would also add that my old suspicions were based upon the assumption that *The Square of Sevens* and the codicil had been destroyed. The survival of the former puts that theory into doubt.'

She shakes her head. 'Julius killed that poor maid. I know he did.'

Lazarus sighs. The fate of the maid in question has troubled him for years, a mystery interwoven with the theft of the codicil and *The Square of Sevens*.

Lady Seabrooke has no time for his uncertainty. Her truths are simple ones, constructed upon the bedrock of her beliefs. Yet such truths can easily founder. Life should have taught her that. After all, she had once believed in him.

Chapter Eighteen

*Knave of clubs as master-card: a man selfish in inclination,
or too easily influenced by others of greater art.
Not to be relied on as one would gladly do.*

M R ANTROBUS SOMETIMES stirred when I came into the
room. His eyelids would flicker, and occasionally he'd moan.
But his eyes beneath his raw red lids were rolled back into his skull
and he never spoke. He was heavily sedated with laudanum. Almost
his whole body was wrapped in bandages. The room stank of vinegar
and the troubling sweetness of decay.

The door opened and the Richardsons came in. 'I need to change
his bedding,' Mrs Richardson said briskly. 'Come along, miss. He
wouldn't want you moping about.'

I gave her the coldest look in my lexicon. The Richardsons, husband
and wife, were our new housekeeper and manservant. Downstairs, in
the kitchen, were a new cook and housemaid. Henry's first act upon
taking up residence in Trim Street had been to dismiss Mrs Grainger
and Mathias. I had begged and argued with him to no avail.

'Mrs Grainger's son, I hear, has been in and out of prison for
years,' he'd said. 'It wouldn't surprise me if she was a party to that
burglary.'

'That's ridiculous,' I said. 'It had nothing to do with Mrs Grainger.
Those men forced open the study window.'

'Or it was left open for them. Rachel, I know you speak from the
heart, but you are very innocent of the ways of the world.'

'And Mathias? You cannot think him guilty of involvement? He's a God-fearing man.'

'Too God-fearing,' Henry said. 'Forever neglecting his duties to attend a sermon or a meeting. Always silently judging a man for heaven knows what. Mr Antrobus was too easily imposed upon.'

'Mrs Fremantle used to say that too,' I said. 'That he was too easily persuaded to another person's advantage.'

Perhaps he caught the edge to my tone. 'Yes,' he said, 'well, if anyone knew about that, then it was her.'

I had managed to snatch only a few words of farewell with Mrs Grainger, while her bags were being loaded onto the horse and cart. She'd never been one for embraces. 'Watch out for that one,' she'd said, nodding towards the house. 'Say a prayer for the master for me, won't you now?'

The cart was to take her to Bristol from where she would catch a coach back home to the north. Mathias was destined for Herefordshire, where his sister lived. He embraced me stiffly.

'Remember, the Lord grants us but a portion of his blessing in this life,' he said. 'One day, the higher joys of eternal life will be yours.'

I felt he could have chosen more comforting words, but he meant well.

Now, without friend or ally in this house, I watched as Mr Richardson raised Mr Antrobus from the bed, whilst his wife slid the soiled sheet out from under him. Feeling indescribably lonely, I walked downstairs.

Henry was in the study. He had met with the lawyer earlier that morning, and now he was searching for the codicil. I knew that was what he was doing, because he'd questioned me about it after my return from London.

'Did you ever see Mr Antrobus with any legal documents?' he'd said. 'Think carefully now.'

'Like the house deeds? Or the contracts for his books?'

'More like his will.'

'He keeps it in the middle drawer of his desk.'

'I know that,' Henry said patiently. 'I said *like* his will.'

Our faces were twin masks of inscrutability. I'd hidden the codicil beneath the loose floorboard in my bedroom. I couldn't think about it now, and yet Henry's search demanded that I did. How did he even know about the codicil? Lazarus Darke, I presumed.

'No matter,' he said, when I offered nothing more upon the subject. 'I want to talk to you about that old parchment of my cousin's: *The Square of Sevens*.'

'It burned in the fire,' I said. 'Only a few copies of the book survived.'

'But where did it come from originally? Did he ever say?'

'From my former guardian, Mr Williams.'

'You're sure about that?'

'His servants liked to read it. It's how I learned to lay the Square of Sevens.'

'Do you know how Mr Williams acquired it?'

'No,' I said. 'But I was very young then. I'd scarcely remember.'

Since then Henry had never stopped looking for the codicil, opening every drawer, every cupboard. I didn't know how to stop him. I didn't know how to stop any of this. I rested my head against the newel post at the bottom of the stairs.

'Rachel, is that you? Can you come in here, please?'

Henry was standing by the mahogany cabinet, some folios in his hand. More papers were piled upon the desk. The doors of Mr Antrobus's cabinet of curiosities were open. Henry had replaced some of the lesser treasures with his favourite birds' eggs. More eggs in glass-fronted cases were arranged around the room.

Henry followed my gaze. 'They look very well there, don't you think?' Without waiting for an answer, he invited me to sit. 'I met with Mr Edwards today. The power of attorney has been granted. Only, it seems we have another lamentable business upon our hands. Mr Edwards informs me that Mr Antrobus's estate is heavily encumbered by debt. I'm afraid my cousin has been rather reckless in his spending. He wanted you to have the best of everything, and so we shall not fault him overly much, but once his debts are settled, I regret to say there will be very little money left.'

I stared at him. 'That cannot be true. Mr Antrobus was never reckless about anything in his life. That lawyer must be lying. Mrs Fremantle never trusted him.'

'I've been over the figures myself,' Henry said. 'I'm afraid that it's true. Please don't distress yourself, my dear. I have a little money, enough to secure this house. We shall not starve.'

'Where are the accounts?' I said. 'I'd like to see them.'

He placed a hand upon my arm. 'My dear, you are distressed, and little wonder. I feel rather conflicted in my emotions myself. But you must not doubt his love for you. Your welfare was always uppermost in his mind. In the event of his incapacity or death, your guardianship passes to me, a trust that I am honoured to receive. Indeed, given the parlous state of my cousin's affairs, it makes me wonder if he had a particular design in mind.'

I frowned. 'What design?'

He was looking at me strangely, his eyes rather misty. An odd little smile played on his lips, much like the one he'd worn that day last year when I'd told his fortune. 'My cousin saw and understood much,' he said softly. 'Perhaps more than we even did ourselves.'

His matter of the heart. I stared at him, comprehension dawning. How could I have been so blind? I, who called myself a reader of souls? I pushed back my chair violently, disturbed as much by my own failures, as the realization itself.

'We shall ask Mr Antrobus when he is better,' I managed to say. 'Then we shall be in no doubt as to his plans.'

Henry's eyes brimmed with sympathy. 'Oh, Rachel—' He started to say more, but I fled from the room, unable to hear it.

Chapter Nineteen

*Nine of hearts, influenced by a spade: a wish fulfilled,
but followed by some detrimental event.*

IN THOSE DREADFUL days after London, I thought often of the past. The woman who had given birth to me. The men who had raised me. The men who had wronged me.

To this latter list, I added the lawyer, Mr Edwards. I was convinced he was lying about Mr Antrobus's money. One day, having tried in vain for several weeks to see the accounts, I took myself off to his office and demanded a meeting. But he only sent for Henry, who escorted me home and gave me a lecture about leaving our household affairs to him. I was perplexed by his lack of concern. He wouldn't listen to my attempts to convince him. My frustration festered, until it more closely resembled suspicion. Had Henry and the lawyer conspired to defraud me of my money? Did he plan to coerce me into marriage, the only alternative a life of poverty?

My anger fed upon my distress. I felt powerless to act. I shut myself away with Mr Antrobus, emerging only for meals, or to take long walks across the countryside when it all became too much. One day, when I returned home from one of these walks, a hired coach was pulled up outside the house. Henry was in the hall in his travelling cloak, talking to Mrs Davenport.

'Ah, Rachel, there you are,' he said. 'I have to go to London unexpectedly. I don't like leaving you at such a time, but it is unavoidable. Mrs Davenport has offered to stay here with you while I am away.'

I heard this news with some relief. 'How long will you be gone?'

'The best part of a week. I hope not too much more.'

Later, after I had sat with Mr Antrobus, Mrs Davenport and I played cribbage in the drawing room. She chattered on about inconsequential matters, one of those people who respond to tragedy by banishing it from the room. Every time I opened my mouth to speak, she looked nervous.

'I called on Julius De Lacy while I was in London,' I said. 'He was not at home, but I met his nephew, a gentleman named Archibald Montfort.'

She seized gratefully upon the topic. 'Archie Montfort, now there's a feast for the eyes. I don't suppose he told you that his father was the De Lacys' former steward?'

'I don't think he mentioned it,' I said.

'I imagine not.' She smiled rather unkindly. 'After Archie's father died, his mother married Julius's younger brother, Septimus. A poor match for a De Lacy, though she is a great beauty.'

I recalled that a George Montfort, presumably Archie's father, had been the second witness to the codicil. And Septimus had been mentioned in the codicil too. He had been left the sum of one shilling, just like his brother, Julius; my mother; and their cousin, Peter, the late Earl of Seabrooke.

'I hear the De Lacys remain in London,' Mrs Davenport went on. 'They normally summer at their Devonshire estate. Did Montfort say what is keeping them in town?'

'I'm afraid not,' I said. 'We mainly talked about the elopement of Patience De Lacy.'

Mrs Davenport's eyes snapped up from her cards. 'It is talk like that which will get you into trouble. The De Lacys are a powerful family and very sensitive to malicious gossip. Especially given their legal affairs. Neither Julius De Lacy nor Lady Seabrooke are the sort to forget a grudge. Guard your words carefully, my dear.'

Disappointed by her circumspection, I changed tack. 'I confess I find all this legal business rather baffling.'

'You seem rather fixated upon the De Lacys,' Mrs Davenport said, but her tone lacked censure. She always appreciated an opportunity

to demonstrate her knowledge of current affairs. 'The two are connected, of course: the family schism, and the scandal of which we will
not speak. They say it was the night Nicholas De Lacy discovered his
daughter missing, that he suffered his first apoplexy. His second, a few
months later, was the one that killed him. Under the terms of his will,
his eldest surviving son, Julius, inherited the bulk of his estate, with
smaller bequests for his widow, his daughters, and his younger son.'

'But the Seabrooke side of the family contested it?'

'Certainly they did. To understand it, you have to first understand
the family history.' Mrs Davenport paused to lay down her cards,
count her points, and move her peg. 'Like most disputed wills, it
all comes down to bad blood between fathers and sons. Nicholas's
father, the first Earl of Seabrooke, was a natural son of the second
King Charles. His mother was an actress, born plain Bess Lacy. They
say the first earl never quite got over not being made a duke like the
King's other natural sons. One man's gift is another man's grudge,
that's what I always say.'

She paused, smiling, as if in contemplation of male vanity.
'Nicholas's resentment was rather more understandable. His father
lavished everything upon his heir, Thomas, and had no time at all
for his younger son. The half-brothers were never close, and relations
between them worsened after the Bubble burst, when Thomas, by
then the second Earl of Seabrooke, lost most of his fortune. Conversely, Nicholas, thanks to his gypsy fortune teller, became very
rich. He bought up his brother's estates, and those of many other
ruined investors. Farms, mining concerns, land on the western edge
of London on which he built houses. Sadly for him, his good fortune
did not extend to his children. His eldest boy, Virgil, died young,
without issue, and Julius became his heir, as we have discussed. Yet
both Julius and his brother, Septimus, proved a disappointment.'

'Why was that?'

Mrs Davenport gave me a look: another forbidden topic. 'All we
will allow, is that Nicholas was known for his unforgiving nature. He
disinherited both his sons, and as he desired a male heir, he sought
a rapprochement with his half-brother. He then drew up a codicil to

his will – a document which has become known as the Seabrooke Codicil – leaving the bulk of his estate to his nephew, Peter.'

A codicil that presumably predated the one beneath my floorboard, which was dated only a month before Nicholas De Lacy's death.

'Yet in the autumn of 1723,' Mrs Davenport went on, 'following his first attack of apoplexy, Nicholas burned the Seabrooke Codicil. That part, at least, is uncontested. He died only a short time later, and Julius laid claim to the estate under the terms of the original will. Well, Lord Seabrooke and his son didn't accept it, not for a moment. They contended that Nicholas hadn't been in his right mind when he'd destroyed that codicil. It was even suggested that he had been prevailed upon to do so.'

'By Julius?'

'Or his mother. Or the steward, George Montfort. Or other members of the family, who did not wish to see their cousin enriched. That first suit failed in the Prerogative Court and on appeal before the High Court of Delegates. So Julius inherited the lot.'

'Then why are legal cases still being heard today?'

'Because the Earls of Seabrooke aren't ones for giving up. When Peter inherited his father's lands and title, he brought new suit against Julius – his wife was said to be the driving force behind it. Where there was money – and the Seabrookes borrowed heavily – their lawyers found new avenues for legal redress. There was a suit in Chancery that dragged on for years, and a sensational trial before the King's Bench, where all manner of wrongdoing was alleged. After the death of her husband last year, Lady Seabrooke continued the fight on behalf of her son, Leopold, the fourth earl.'

'Was anything ever said in court about a second codicil?'

Mrs Davenport smiled. 'The Grandchild Codicil. I was just coming to that part. Long ago, during that first suit in the Prerogative Court, Nicholas's secretary testified that he had witnessed the signing of a second codicil, leaving the estate to his eldest grandchild. Given that he had no grandchildren at the time, it would have prompted quite a dash to the altar – but George Montfort testified that he had witnessed his master destroy that codicil too.'

Lazarus Darke must be the secretary in question, I thought. And George Montfort must have lied. Surely the codicil in question was the one in my possession?

During my hours sitting with Mr Antrobus, I had attempted to draw up an ancestral tree of the De Lacy family, and this conversation with Mrs Davenport had filled several gaps in my knowledge. Most of all, she'd cemented my belief that I was the rightful heir to the De Lacy fortune. The codicil had been signed only a month before my birth, and no elder grandchildren had existed at the time. The only part that confused me was why my father would have stolen it. By doing so, he had ensured that his own child was disinherited. It made no sense.

'The whole episode with the second codicil did rather add to the impression that Nicholas had been behaving erratically before his death,' Mrs Davenport went on. 'Julius was said to be furious, and dismissed the secretary from his family's service. Since then, of course, everything has been visited and revisited many times. The Seabrooke Codicil, the Grandchild Codicil, Nicholas's state of mind – all to the benefit of nobody but the lawyers.'

Did that mean Lazarus Darke wasn't working for Julius De Lacy after all? Who, then, was his client? Lady Seabrooke? Were there matters of personal revenge at work here, on top of everything else?

The conversation also raised a moral question in my mind. Even if I wanted to lay claim to the money, even if I found the means to do so, would it be right? If Nicholas De Lacy's mind had been impaired when he had destroyed the Seabrooke Codicil, then any subsequent codicil did not reflect his true intention. Yet he had asserted in the Grandchild Codicil, that whilst weak in body, he was sound in mind.

I wondered whether I could glean any sense of his sanity from his signature. To my memory, it was written in a bold, ostentatious hand. I duly made my excuses to Mrs Davenport, and went upstairs. Fetching a bodkin from my sewing box, I knelt to pull back the rug. Carefully, I prised up the floorboard, and gazed into the void below. A cold, sick dread broke over me.

The codicil was gone.

CHAPTER TWENTY

Ten of spades, influenced by like suit:
a disgrace.

THEY SIT IN the shadows, at a table sticky with spilled wine. In the centre of the room are four larger tables, on each a silver platter. On each platter stand two naked girls, writhing, kissing, and licking. The girls are too young for this sort of work, but Henry Antrobus insisted upon meeting here. Lazarus wonders if that is why he chose it.

Then Henry produces the codicil from his pocket, banishing all Lazarus's concern for the girls and his dislike of the man in front of him. He takes it in his hands and draws it close.

It is nearly seventeen years since he held it last. He recognizes Nicholas De Lacy's flamboyant signature, his own jagged penmanship, and the neat copperplate of the late, self-serving traitor, George Montfort.

'Where did you find it?' he asks.

'In the house,' Henry says, vaguely.

Lazarus frowns. 'I wonder why your cousin didn't admit to having it. It was no benefit to him.'

'I cannot say.' The topic plainly bores Henry. 'Perhaps we might discuss the terms of sale?'

'I'll give you five hundred pounds for it.'

Henry smiles. 'Do you mistake me for a country farmer, come to London atop my turnip wagon?'

'Heaven forbid,' Lazarus says. 'Farming is an honest trade.'

'I know the value of this document to your client, sir. I also know that there are other courses of action that I might take.'

'And then my client would be forced to involve the law.'

Threat and counter-threat. Neither of them mean it. Henry wouldn't be sitting here now if he wasn't intending to agree terms. They haggle for a time and settle upon twelve hundred.

Lazarus would have paid more. *As much as it takes*, is his instruction from the lady. As he counts the notes, he wonders from where she obtained them. A moneylender? A friend? A lover? The thought makes him hesitate, just for a moment.

Henry tucks the money away. He takes a tiny golden heart from his pocket, and presses the charm to his lips, in what Lazarus takes to be an act of celebration.

Their business concluded, Lazarus rises to leave, and a memory weaves its way through his curt farewell.

He is in the drawing room of De Lacy House. Ten large windows overlook Piccadilly and the darkened park beyond. Anyone else would have ordered the curtains drawn by now, but Nicholas De Lacy likes the world to admire his wealth. A hundred candles burn, three vast fireplaces blazing against the winter chill. Lazarus sits next to his employer at a mahogany table, the not-yet dead, not-yet traitor George Montfort on his other side. They are discussing a proposal to establish a proprietary colony in the Americas, between the fertile soil of the Carolinas and the swamp of Spanish Florida. George Montfort is all for it. Lazarus, who fears the land is more swamp than fertile soil, has reservations.

Normally, he could clean his boots with Montfort, but tonight he is distracted by a different rivalry altogether. At the other end of the room, a small crowd is gathered around a second mahogany table. John Jory Jago is telling fortunes for the De Lacy daughters. Two red heads are bent to look at the cards. John Jory's hair is black, thick and wild, neither short nor long. His thin face is a place of hollows in which shadows pool in the candlelight. The flames glint on the golden guineas stacked by his side and on the golden embroidery of his indigo coat. Lazarus asked him the meaning of the hieroglyphs once, but Jago only smiled. He wonders if Jago even knows himself.

Lazarus doesn't like the hold Jago has over his employer, and he is far harder to see off than George Montfort. How can you counter the arguments of a man who laughs at reason? Who deals in stars and omens and fortunes? Mr De Lacy calls him a gypsy, but that is an insult to the Romani. He is a charlatan who once got lucky in the small matter of the South Sea Bubble. Lazarus doesn't like Jago enriching himself at the De Lacys' expense. He doesn't like the confidence of Jago's years and his awareness of his own good looks. Nor does he like the way Jago watches Patience De Lacy, just as he's watching her now. Her voice rises: *Turn over my wish-cards* – no patience there! – hence Luna, her pet-name used by intimates.

The girls are flirting, touching their hair, making warm eyes at Jago. Another rivalry there, though it's only for sport. They'll laugh about him later when he's gone.

I made John Jory blush.

You never did. He doesn't blush.

He gave me one of his stares.

He gives everybody stares.

Not like this.

A pair of lapdogs burst into the room, chasing one another, knocking over a sewing basket, upending a game of backgammon, scattering ivory and jade counters into the air. Nicholas mutters his irritation. Jemima gives chase, followed by Etta, her lady's maid. In the ensuing distraction, Jago takes something from his pocket, holding it between his thumb and index finger. In the moment before he presses it to his lips, the little golden heart catches the light. He hands it to Luna, who smiles and slips it into her pocket. Turning slightly, she catches Lazarus watching her and swiftly looks away.

Not my business, he tells himself. Nobody challenges Jago's place in this house and wins. To console himself, he takes George Montfort's arguments apart, piece by piece.

Now, as Lazarus steps into the chill night air of Covent Garden, the Grandchild Codicil stowed snugly in his pocket, his mind lurches unbidden to Cornwall, to the fishing town named Tretelly. To the room in the inn on the clifftop, to the bloody carnage of the four-poster bed. Luna naked, her eyes glazed, his rising panic.

'Where is he?' he had demanded of the tap-girl who had shown him there. 'Her husband. The fortune teller. Where is he?' She only shrinks from him in speechless terror.

He asks the same question, moments later, of the innkeeper. 'You need to speak to my head ostler,' Chenoweth replies. 'He saw it all.'

CHAPTER TWENTY-ONE

Four of spades as master-card: affecting some near concern to the querist. It shall end less well than was hoped.

I COULD FEEL Death's presence in that room. Sometimes he grinned at me from behind the bars of Mr Antrobus's bed, or from the shadows next to the window, behind the curtain. Sometimes I glimpsed him leaning against a wall, sharpening his scythe. I wanted to snatch it from him and drive it through his skeletal ribs, smash his grinning skull to pieces.

Mr Antrobus never stirred any more. He was still, but I knew he was not at peace. I sat on his bed, consumed by anger, helplessness and guilt, until I heard the clatter of a coach drawing up outside. Rising and going to the window, I watched the guard dismount and open the door. Henry stepped out and greeted Mr Richardson, who had come out to take in the luggage.

It had been six days since I'd discovered the theft of the codicil. I knew immediately who had taken it. I thought of Henry's search. His sudden trip to London. And yet how had he known where to find it?

I'd taken the codicil out of its hiding place to study the night before Henry's departure. Could he have somehow seen me do it? I went from my bedroom into the hall, and knelt to look through the keyhole. It afforded a view of my bed, but not the rug and the floor-board beneath. Returning to my room, I stood on the rug, and looked around. My eyes came to rest upon the wall which divided my room from Mrs Fremantle's old room, where Henry now slept. I walked over to the wall, and ran my hand over the panelling. My finger slid inside a small hole. I stood on tiptoe to put my eye to it, but I could see nothing.

I went next door to Mrs Fremantle's room, and studied the wall from the other side. There was a picture hanging next to the bed, a watercolour of Exeter Castle. I removed it from the wall, and examined the hole behind it. I put my eye to it and looked directly into my bedroom. I could see the rug very clearly. It was where I got undressed at night. I felt sick.

The front door closed, and I heard Henry talking to the servants in the hall. I walked downstairs and followed him into his study.

'Rachel,' he said, with a delighted smile.

I closed the door behind me. 'Where is it?'

He raised his eyebrows at my tone. 'I had rather anticipated an apology.'

'You spied on me,' I said, hardly able to bear thinking about what else he might have seen.

'Only because I suspected that you were lying to me. That document was stolen property. You could have got yourself into a great deal of trouble. As your guardian, I had a responsibility to act.'

'Did you sell it to him? To Lazarus Darke?'

'I merely returned it to a party with a legitimate interest in this matter. Mr Darke was kind enough to offer me a small reward for my trouble.'

'How much?'

'Really, my dear, you sound quite mercenary – and at such a time.'

'*How much?*'

'Two hundred pounds. It will come in useful given everything.'

So many words gathered force in my head, a pulsing maelstrom of fury. But before I could speak, the door opened, and Mrs Richardson hovered there, looking flustered. 'It is the master,' she said. 'I was just standing there, folding a sheet, and he slipped away.'

♠

I scarcely remember all the comings and goings after that. The vicar, the undertaker, neighbours came to pay their respects. I moved through those conversations like a ghost. Mr and Mrs Richardson laid Mr Antrobus out in his best suit. I kissed his cold forehead, trying to stop the tears from falling.

Much later, up in my bedroom, I gazed at my reflection in the looking-glass. My eyes were red, my face white and blotched. I thought of that little girl who'd come here, nearly ten years ago, saved from want and brutality and loneliness. I remembered running through this house, the light reflecting the stone outside, each room bathed in a golden glow.

Those walls were narrowing now. Everyone I'd loved in that house was dead. The codicil had been stolen. My money too.

'My name is Red,' I said to the ghost in the looking-glass. 'I am the daughter of John Jory Jago and Patience De Lacy, whom people called Luna.'

Whether Lazarus Darke was working for Lady Seabrooke or Julius De Lacy, the codicil had surely been destroyed. Yet that at least put an end to the complications. Nobody would want me dead now – if indeed they ever had.

Despite all the troubles of the past, the De Lacys were still my family. If I explained my situation, then they might help me. But how to prove that I was who I said I was?

The codicil was gone. *The Square of Sevens* had burned in the fire. All I had to connect me to the De Lacys was the locket, my mother's shawl, the pack of cards, and my knowledge of the Square of Sevens. Yet I could also be persuasive in the telling. For all these years, I had convinced people with my lies, surely now I could do so with the truth?

Kneeling to reach under the bed, I pulled out the portmanteau, which I had stored there ever since Henry had moved into Mrs Fremantle's room. I packed lightly. Two day-gowns, one wrapping-gown, one nightshift, two petticoats, my mother's shawl. Stockings, two lace caps, gloves, handkerchiefs and ribbons. My jewellery box containing my trinkets and paste-glass stones. A brush, hair-powder, soap. *Don Quixote*, a few packs of playing cards. I had only a little money of my own, not quite thirty shillings, and Henry kept his money locked away in a strongbox like a goblin king. I thought about stealing something of value and selling it, but the thought made me nervous. It might enable Henry to track me down, or prompt him to get the law involved. No, I would earn my own keep, I decided, as I had in the old days. My experience in London had led me to believe that people would pay a lot of money for an illicit fortune.

At a little after midnight, I heard Henry climb the stairs. I lay in bed for another two hours, until I was certain he'd be asleep. Then I dressed and crept downstairs, carrying the portmanteau. I went into Mr Antrobus's study, where I lit a candle. In the desk drawer, I found the key to the cabinet of curiosities. Crossing the room, I fitted it into the lock. I wanted something to remember Mr Antrobus by, a new talisman to replace my golden heart. My eye came to rest upon a snakestone. I traced its tight coils with my finger, remembering our discussions about its origin. Mr Antrobus had scoffed at the notion that the snakes had been turned to stone by St Hilda or St Cuthbert. 'There will be a scientific explanation,' he'd said. 'One day we will know it.'

The snakestone fitted neatly into my palm. I liked the feel of its weight. I was about to close the cabinet, when my eye fell upon the large green egg that Henry had given Mr Antrobus on the day he'd returned from his travels. Taking it from the cabinet, I carried it to the desk. I placed it upon the blotter, and looked at the snakestone in my hand. Then I brought it slowly down upon the egg, crushing the shell to tiny pieces.

There were other eggs in the cabinet. And many more in Henry's wooden cases around the room. One by one I fetched them, placed them upon the blotter, and silently ground each to a fine powder.

When I'd finished, I slipped the snakestone into my pocket. Picking up the portmanteau, I went to the front door and eased back the bolts. The street was dark and still. Somewhere a bird was singing. There was a scent of honeysuckle on the air.

I felt as if I was back on that clifftop, the waves roiling far below – but when life gave you a push, what choice did you have?

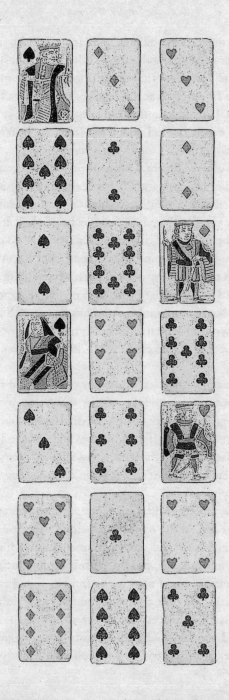

BOOK TWO

**Concerning a fortune
told of Lady Seabrooke**

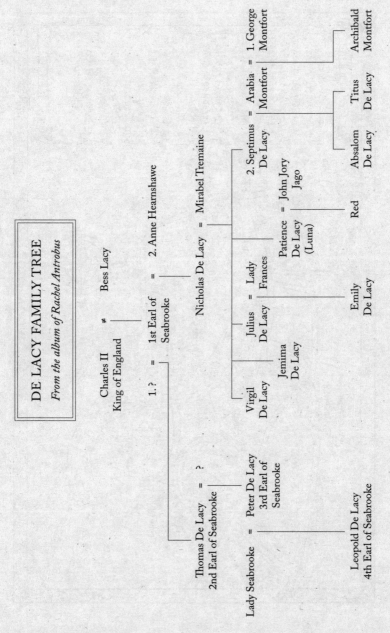

DE LACY FAMILY TREE

From the album of Rachel Antrobus

Charles II
King of England

≠

Bess Lacy

1. ? = 1st Earl of = 2. Anne Hearnshawe
Seabrooke

Nicholas De Lacy = Mirabel Tremaine

Thomas De Lacy = ?
2nd Earl of Seabrooke

Virgil
De Lacy

Jemima
De Lacy

Julius = Lady
De Lacy   Frances

Patience = John Jory
De Lacy   Jago
(Luna)

2. Septimus
De Lacy

Arabia = 1. George
Montfort   Montfort

Lady Seabrooke = Peter De Lacy
3rd Earl of
Seabrooke

Emily
De Lacy

Red

Absalom
De Lacy

Titus
De Lacy

Archibald
Montfort

Leopold De Lacy
4th Earl of Seabrooke

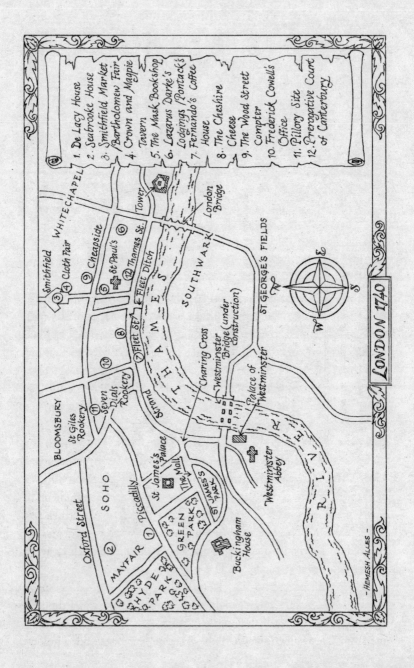

LONDON 1740

1. De Lacy House
2. Seabrooke House
3. Smithfield Market / Bartholomew Fair
4. Crown and Magpie Tavern
5. The Mask Bookshop
6. Lazarus Darke's Lodgings / Pontack's
7. Fernando's Coffee House
8. The Cheshire Cheese
9. The Wood Street Compter
10. Frederick Cowell's Office
11. Pillory Site
12. Prerogative Court of Canterbury

— HEMESH ALLES —

CHAPTER ONE

Three of hearts, influenced by a diamond: it is in part a matter of money – and may be associated with an entertainment.

ONEY. FOR YEARS I had barely thought of it. Now the light-ness of my purse was all too readily apparent.

It cost over a pound to board the Bath Flying Machine, but for half the price a passenger could take a seat upon the roof. I would happily have walked to London, keeping to the quieter roads, as I had walked all those years ago with Father. But if Henry tried to find me, a young red-haired lady journeying alone would make a conspicuous traveller in the country villages. Whereas in London, I could lose myself in those busy, anonymous streets. Which meant getting to the city as swiftly as possible.

In the yard of the White Hart Inn, I reluctantly parted with the fare – nearly half of my meagre fortune – and my portmanteau was loaded into the basket hanging from the back of the coach. One of the ostlers lifted me unceremoniously, and the guard hauled me up to join the other passengers on the roof. As the church bells struck five in the morning, the coachman gave a long blast on his horn, and we lurched out of the yard, the taller passengers forced to duck to avoid the inn sign over the gate.

As Bath receded into the distance, the carriage picked up speed along the turnpike. Clinging tightly to the wooden handle, I thought of that other carriage ride long ago, when Mr Antrobus had taken me from Cornwall to live in Bath. A seven-year-old child, a golden heart clutched in her small damp palm, sullen with grief and loneliness and suspicion. I wanted to hug that little girl, to reassure her that Mr Antrobus was the best man who ever lived. I thought of our last argument and reconciliation. His face in the window of the burning house. I watched the lambs playing in the fields, haymakers at work, the glint of a scythe. I mouthed a prayer for him, words neither one of us had ever truly believed.

'What's with the Friday face?' A voice broke in upon my thoughts, one of a pair of young gentlemen travelling together. 'A smile cures the wounding of a frown, you know.'

His companion, who wore a red cockade with a jet button in his black felt hat, burst out laughing at my expression. 'I do believe you have been turned to stone, Jerry.'

There were eight of us on the roof. Nine, if you counted a boy perched in the basket with the luggage. Ten, if you counted a live turtle strapped to a box – clearly destined for some nobleman's pot – which sometimes turned its head to regard me rather mournfully.

The coach stopped frequently to change or rest the horses. By Marlborough, my stomach was growling, and I ventured into the coaching inn. My fellow passengers crowded around the innkeeper, purchasing cakes and ale, but when I asked the price, I was rendered speechless by the sum. The innkeepers along the Bath Road evidently took full advantage of their monopoly. Returning empty-handed to the yard, I watched the sun dissolve in a haze of rose and gold over the fields, trying to forget the gnaw of hunger and all the perils that might lie ahead of me. Before too long, the coachman blew a few bars of 'Black-Eyed Susan' on his horn, and everyone piled back into the carriage.

Though the day had been warm, once darkness fell it grew bitterly cold up there. I'd brought only a summer cloak, and deeply regretted my lack of foresight. Jerry's friend, the gentleman in the hat, offered me his brandy flask and, despite my misgivings about their company, I took it. The spirit possessed a delightful transgressive burn that helped mitigate my shivering a little. I passed the flask back, and the gentleman brushed my fingers, exclaiming at their chill. Opening his great-coat, he suggested I huddle inside. I replied frostily, and no more nips upon his brandy flask were forthcoming.

I slept only a little, terrified I would lose my grip on the handle and be pitched into the road. Rarely had I been more relieved to see the dawn. The rising sun slowly restored life to my numb limbs, but by eleven o'clock I longed for the cool night air again, the sun fierce in its indifference to those denied the shelter of the carriage below. Sticky, sun-burned, hungry, and exhausted, my spirits nevertheless surged as I glimpsed a yellow streak upon the horizon that slowly took on the form of the great metropolis.

We stopped twice more – at Turnham Green and the village of Kensington – and then we were racing alongside the Hyde Park, startling the deer, the coachman blowing his horn to warn strollers of our approach. Finally, at just after half past five, we clattered into the yard of the Bell Savage on Ludgate Hill. My legs wobbled uncontrollably when the ostler set me down, and I queued for my portmanteau amidst a bewildering press of people: relatives embracing my fellow passengers, waiters carrying trays of punch, men trying to sell us sweetmeats and plaster models of St Paul's.

'You look half-famished,' a woman told me. 'I have a house just around the corner, where I'll give you a hot meal. I don't like to see young girls all on their own in this dangerous city.'

She was respectably dressed, in a cygnet-grey gown and feathered hat, but I caught a glitter of calculation in her eye. There were women like her in the novels Mrs Fremantle had used to read. A hot meal became the offer of a place to stay, then a loan of money. The innocent maiden thus ensnared, her debt would be called in, and though Mrs Fremantle's books had only hinted at the disgrace that awaited such a foolish girl, I could hazard a guess. Turning my back on the woman, gripping my portmanteau tightly, I walked out onto Ludgate Hill.

The stink was more intense than on my last visit, the taverns busier. Otherwise, the city looked the same – and yet everything was different. I had no guardian, no fine apartment, only sixteen shillings to my name. Nor did I have very much of a plan, beyond calling upon the De Lacys at the first opportunity. Yet I could hardly present myself at their door in my current condition: travel-soiled, portmanteau in hand, the very portrait of a desperate supplicant only interested in their money. No, I would call upon them respectably, confess my identity at a suitable moment, and when they enquired about my circumstances – as they surely would – I'd tell them everything.

All of which meant that I needed to find accommodation for the night, somewhere I might get some rest and some food and some hot water. I'd met many London acquaintances in Bath, and yet here in the capital, I would be lucky if they raised their hats to me in the park. Nor could I run the risk of word getting back to Henry. Taking fashionable lodgings was out of the question, given my scant funds, but I recalled that on my last visit to London, the landlady of the Crown and Magpie had asked me if I was looking for a room. She had seemed pleasant enough, and she might let me tell fortunes in her upstairs room. I could also enquire there after Morgan Trevithick, my father's old friend, who I'd been told would be back in London in the summer.

The last time I had walked up to Smithfield, I had been greeted by a farmyard cacophony. This time, a great clatter of hammers and a rigorous rasping of saws drowned out everything else in the surrounding streets. When I reached Smithfield, I discovered that all the animal pens had been cleared away, the vast site colonized by dozens of carpenters and other labourers, busily erecting wooden booths, sheds, stalls, tents and other more elaborate constructions, some two or three storeys high. Hundreds of coloured signs dazzled the eye: *The famous WIRE-WALKERS of Russia*; *Mr Punch's Puppetry Show*; *Mr Harris's WAXWORKS: true to LIFE*.

I had, of course, heard of the Bartholomew Fair. Some said it was the largest charter fair in all of Europe. I could believe it from the scene in front of me. All the houses and taverns on the perimeter seemed to have been taken over by the fair, the signs outside advertising plays, drolls and operas. The sign outside the passage that led to the Crown and Magpie announced that *The Distressed Lovers* would be performed there nightly. More hammers and saws echoed in the yard, where a stage was being constructed. A few labourers were resting outside the tavern, drinking ale in the sun. Threading a path between them, I attracted many crude comments about my hair, until my cheeks burned with a righteous indignation. More eyes regarded me in the smoky taproom. The same buxom woman in the ale-wife hat was behind the bar and she greeted me with a half-nod of recognition. 'Back again, darling? What can I do you for this time?'

'Last time I was here you offered me a room.'

'That's right. Three shillings a night.'

'Are the bedclothes made of silk? The chamber pot of gold?'

She laughed. 'You won't find cheaper round here. Not now, during the fair. But a young lady like you surely don't need to quibble over the shillings and pence.'

'Would I be looking for a room here if I did not?'

She grinned. 'Two, then. But don't go telling my other guests.'

'Or I might find out you let it to them for a shilling?'

'There's enough clowns out there in the fair,' she said. 'You want the room or not?'

Reluctantly, I passed her the coins, and she held out her hand for me to shake. 'My name's Kerensa.'

I hesitated for the barest moment. 'Mine is Red.'

She smiled at the name. 'Follow me, Red.'

She showed me upstairs, past the room where I'd visited the astrologer, through another door, down a crooked corridor and up another flight of stairs. I was given to understand that the tiny taproom was deceptive and the Magpie had colonized the upper storeys of the neighbouring buildings. Finally, we halted in a narrow passage, where Kerensa unlocked a door.

The room was so small that a narrow bed and a worm-eaten cupboard nearly filled it entirely, the remaining patch of floor covered by a scrap of threadbare carpet, so dirty I could barely discern the design. The soot-blackened fireplace was barely big enough to toast a slice of bread and Kerensa had informed me on our way upstairs that coals and kindling would cost extra. A cracked chamber pot and a dog-eared psalm pasted to the wall above the bed completed the inventory of my new home.

'There's a washstand down the hall,' Kerensa told me. 'You'll find a candle in the cupboard. Any trouble from the other guests, be sure to let me know.'

Rachel Antrobus might have baulked at laying her elegant head in such insalubrious surroundings, but Red had once slept in barns and ditches and had no such scruples.

'I was wondering if I might tell fortunes here,' I said. 'Cartomancy is my gift, an unusual method.'

'You'll get no customers here. Not now. Fair's full of fortune tellers.'

'How do I get a booth at the fair?'

'They've all been booked for months now.' She scrutinized me frankly. 'I could sell your clothes for you, if you like? Buy you something cheaper? I know a man in the Strand who'll give me a good price.'

Already conscious of the sorry state of my gown, I could hardly go calling upon the De Lacys in anything less. I declined her offer politely, silently praying that all would go well tomorrow. I had barely enough money to last me a week in London.

'When I was here last, you mentioned a Cornishman named Morgan Trevithick. Is he staying here now?'

'Aye, but he's gone to the Norwood to buy lumber. He'll be back tomorrow afternoon.'

Once Kerensa had returned downstairs, I inspected the bed, and discovered a residue of sand between the sheets, suggesting that they had not been washed since the last occupant had slept in them. Yet I spotted no lice, and the linens were not overly stained. Overcome by weariness, I slept for over two hours, waking at a little after nine o'clock. Feeling ravenous, I went downstairs, where I was greeted by delightful wafts of roasting meat. As I studied the prices chalked on the slate, my despondency must have shown, because one of the customers suggested that I could find cheaper food out in the fair.

I wandered the stalls for nearly half an hour, bewildered by the noise and the crowds and the choice. Men sold toys and singing birds, puppy-dogs and gingerbread, ribbons and ratafia wine. Canary organs warred with fiddlers and bagpipers and marching troupes of boys with drums and trumpets. Hawkers outside the larger booths tried to entice me in: 'Come see the tall Dutchwoman, miss.' 'Come see the tiger.' 'Come see the man with no bones.' Despite all this gaiety, being alone in the fair at night made me nervous. The men breathed gin and anticipation, the women gaudy in dress, everyone's laughter a little too shrill. Eventually, I found a booth selling roast quail for sixpence, and I queued to hand over my coin. The birds were impaled on an elaborate mechanism of spits, turned by a dog running on a wheel attached to the ceiling.

Clutching my warm parcel to my breast, I headed back to the Magpie, taking care not to meet any man's eye. To my relief, I reached the passage unaccosted. As I hurried down it, a man entered from the tavern side blocking my path. He didn't retreat to let me through, simply strode towards me. I pressed myself against the dripping wall to let him pass, but to my horror, he swivelled round, grabbing hold of me. Pressing his face to mine, he ran his thick tongue over my lips.

I cried out, pushing him violently, and he stumbled in his drunkenness. My parcel slipped from my grasp, but I didn't stop to retrieve it. I ran full-pelt down the alley, followed by a volley of vicious curses. More men called out to me in the Magpie's taproom, but I barged my way through them, and fled up to my room, where I collapsed on the bed.

The vulnerability of my position, the disgusting liberties of Henry and that man in the alley, the loss of Mr Antrobus and Mrs Fremantle and the home that had been mine – all pressed in upon me and I wept. I could still taste the man's beer and garlic breath – and another flavour too: the bitterness of rage. Anger eventually staunched the flow of my tears. I rose, breathing heavily, and lifted the portmanteau onto the bed. Digging through the contents, I pulled out one of my silk stockings and slid the snakestone inside, tying a knot to secure it tight.

I swung my makeshift weapon, enjoying the feel of its weight in my hand. I imagined cracking Henry's skull like I'd cracked his eggs, the skull of the man in the alley, the skulls of Lazarus Darke and the men who'd assaulted Mrs Fremantle.

The next time a man tried to lay his hands on me, he would be sorry.

CHAPTER TWO

Three of diamonds, influenced by a spade:
a death to another likely enters into it.

I AWOKE TO the rippling notes of a flute. For a moment, I lay
there, my mind fogged with sleep and confusion. The narrowness
of the bed and the lumps in the mattress contributed to the sense of
dislocation – until it all came flooding back in a great onslaught of
exhilaration and dread. London. The De Lacys. Opportunity. Danger.

A drum had begun to beat outside, as if in time with these
thoughts, followed by a great fanfare of trumpets. Kneeling upon the
bed to look out of the window, I saw actors were rehearsing on the
stage out in the yard. Beneath an arch of woven branches, a young
man in a suit of armour was clasping hands with a yellow-haired
girl in a white robe. A few people were standing around in the yard,
watching or talking or drinking, pigeons pecking in the dirt at their
feet.

'Whether our love brings joy or sorrow,' declared the knight. 'Harvest the day, and burn the morrow.'

Taking these words to be a good omen, I dressed and went downstairs, where I paid a penny for a bowl of hot water to be brought
up to my room. Taking my time over my toilette, I washed away the
memory of the Flying Machine and pinned my hair as best I could,
leaving my curls unpowdered in the hope that the family resemblance
between myself and the De Lacys might be more marked. Having
secured my stays, hoops and petticoats, I put on a clean day-gown

from my portmanteau. Studying my reflection in my looking-glass, I pulled a face. Inelegant for a London house call, inelegant even for Bath. But given my current situation, it would have to do.

I hadn't eaten in two days and felt faint with hunger. Deciding that I needed my wits about me, I went downstairs and paid the boy behind the bar sixpence for a dish of hog's pudding and potato cakes. Having made short work of this repast, I walked out into the sunshine.

I had tried not to think about Archie Montfort, but as I walked west across London, his sneers and cruel insinuations on my last visit to De Lacy House came flooding back to me. Would he be there today? I could well imagine how he would respond to my story – with his witchfinder's nose and his suspicion that I was after the De Lacys' money. Especially as the bitter truth now was that I *did* need their money. How I wished that I was calling there in more propitious circumstances.

Upon arrival at the mansion on Piccadilly, I gave my name to one of the footmen on the gate and asked to see his master. He gave me no warmer reception than the last fellow, but this time the gate was unlocked and I was escorted across the courtyard to the front door. Presumably this meant Julius De Lacy was at home.

Walking into that house was like entering a cathedral, one filled with a divine light. The entrance hall ceiling soared three storeys above me, sunlight cascading down from a row of high arched windows near the roof. This ecclesiastical impression was rather dispelled by a first-floor gallery of semi-circular balconies with intricate lattice screens that called to mind a sultan's seraglio from the *Arabian Nights*. Everything was painted, gilded, carved, mosaiced, marbled, or otherwise embellished.

A bewigged butler – dressed so finely he would not have looked out of place at the Bath Pump Room – took my card. Clearly, I couldn't give the De Lacys the address of the Crown and Magpie, Smithfield – not if I wanted them to believe that I was a respectable woman. I had therefore written the address of a coffeehouse on Fleet Street that I had passed on my walk, which had advertised its services for receiving mail in exchange for a small fee. The De Lacys would probably assume correctly that I was staying in an unfashionable part of town and wished to conceal that fact, but they would imagine a small townhouse in the City with only three or four servants, rather than a low tavern full of fairground folk. They would likely pity me, shame at genteel poverty being a perfectly acceptable form of duplicity in polite society.

The butler asked me to wait in an anteroom separated from the main hall by a row of pillars. A painting hung over the fireplace, depicting a pair of young women in diaphanous robes, dancing in a glade, their red hair garlanded with flowers. The De Lacy sisters, I presumed. I was still trying to decide which one was my mother, when I heard voices behind me.

Turning, I saw that a girl had walked into the hall, followed by a footman and an older woman who had the look of a governess. The girl was a little younger than myself – I guessed fourteen or fifteen years of age – small, thin and rather pale. Her blue silk gown had pagoda sleeves and a matching petticoat, a modest fichu of white lace covering her bosom. Her hair was dark, worn in low curls, her hat a small blue lace affair with beading and feathers. Wondering if she was Julius's daughter, my cousin, I felt very conscious of my own shabby dress.

The girl gave me a distracted smile and walked out of the front door, trailed by the others. Almost immediately, I heard new footsteps approaching, and Julius De Lacy walked into the anteroom. Greeting me warmly, he kissed my hand, professing his pleasure. 'I am only sorry that you did not call again in the spring, Miss Antrobus. I did write to the address that you provided.' He was wearing another of his exquisite suits, this one of grey metallic satin embellished with sequins and blue-glass spangles.

I explained that I had been forced to return to Bath unexpectedly after the death of my guardian, and he murmured all the appropriate sympathies.

'I am only pleased that you felt able to call on us today. You are fortunate to find us at home. Normally we retreat to Devonshire at this time of year, but I have been detained in London on business. Upon that note, I regret that I am unable to receive you today. Mr Walpole is here and I can only step out for a moment.'

His dismayed expression intimated that the King's First Minister was a wretched inconvenience keeping him only from the pleasure of my company. Concealing my disappointment, I murmured that I entirely understood.

'But my mother would be delighted to meet you,' Julius went on. 'I told her all about our charming afternoon at the Spa. She is intrigued to see the Square of Sevens again.'

'I should be honoured,' I told him, my spirits rising at the prospect of meeting my grandmother.

I wish here to pause to say a few words about my motives. I have been honest from the first that I wished for assistance with my material circumstances. Yet whilst pressing, it was far from the whole story. All those years in Cornwall and Bath, I had gazed enviously at children with their brothers and sisters, aunts and uncles, grandparents. None of this was to denigrate my father, nor the little family we had made in Trim Street. And yet neither situation had been the normal order of things. I ached for that normality after the upheavals of my youth. I was not so naive that I felt certain that I would find it here with the De Lacys, but I would be lying if I said some small part of me didn't cling to that possibility.

Julius frowned. 'You have no chaperone? No servant?'

He was probably also wondering why I wasn't wearing mourning dress. I told him that I was staying with a family friend, a rather elderly lady, who had sadly fallen ill since my arrival in London. Due to her condition, neither her maid, nor her manservant could be spared to accompany me on my walk.

'It is rather irregular,' Julius said. 'I don't know how things are done in Bath, but in London a young lady does not pay a house call all alone.' He drew a jewelled snuffbox from his waistcoat pocket and took a sniff. 'Then again, I sat for a female portrait painter the other day, a Frenchwoman. She had no servant with her, and nor did

I remark upon it. Because she had come here to provide me with a service. As you do too, in a manner of speaking.'

'That is certainly the case,' I agreed.

He went on in a brighter tone: 'And my mother is a very liberal sort of woman. I am certain she will understand. As I said, she is decidedly eager.'

I had been counting upon this eagerness. The rich, in my experience, devise many rules to keep others out, but those rules can be bent at will or discarded altogether, if the object of that transgression is their own convenience.

His smile fully restored, Julius offered me his arm. 'Mother is in her cabinet. Let me take you up.'

We proceeded along a hall and up a great sweep of a grand staircase, Julius providing a short history of the house, pointing out paintings, sculptures and bronzes of particular note. We walked along the gallery I had seen from below, until Julius knocked at a door, and we entered. The room was tiny and octagonal, the polished wooden interior inlaid with Venetian mirrors and tortoiseshell panels. Despite the brightness of the day outside, lamps and candles had been lit against a thick fug of tobacco smoke.

'A caller for you, Mother. I present to you Miss Antrobus from Bath, the girl I told you about. Miss Antrobus, my mother, Mrs Mirabel De Lacy.'

My grandmother almost filled an entire Ottoman chaise, her face large and white, soft around the jowls, with high cheekbones. Jewelled pins glittered in her piled silver hair, which was striped through with a ghostly streak of red. Her dark eyes, nestled in little pockets of flesh, held a glint of humour, though the lift of her chin was imperious and her mouth careworn. Her silks rustled as she leaned forward to inspect me more closely, her gown a bonfire of plum and gold and garnet.

'The girl who knows the Square of Sevens,' she said. 'I remember.'

I curtseyed, my legs unsteady in the moment.

'Oh, your lovely hair.' Mirabel turned to her son with a look of reproach. 'Julius, you did not tell me that.'

'It's just hair, mother.' He smiled a little tightly, before repeating my explanation for my lack of chaperone.

'These modern girls, so bold.' Mirabel favoured me with a smile. 'You will find no objection in this quarter.'

'Good, then.' Julius nodded to me. 'Now I must go, before Mr Walpole takes offence.'

'*Coach for Mr Walpole.*'

I whipped round. Through the pall of smoke, I made out the golden eyes of a large grey parrot edging along a gilded perch. '*No peace without Spain,*' it squawked, and I stifled a smile. How ridiculous to hear the slogan of those who opposed Mr Walpole in Parliament on the beak of a bird!

'Must you teach it such sedition?' Julius asked mildly. 'Miss Antrobus did not call here to be corrupted.'

Mirabel gave me an amused glance. 'Did you not?'

I chose to answer in the spirit of her expression. 'My guardian's manservant used to say that my fortune telling was the work of the devil, so I fear it may already be too late.'

Mirabel laughed. 'Go, sir, attend to your precious Mr Walpole. Miss Antrobus and I shall be wicked together and have a merrier time by far.'

'That would hardly prove difficult.' Julius raised his eyebrows in my direction. 'We're in shouting distance of the Horseguards should you need them.'

Witnessing these little intimacies filled me with a pleasure it is hard to describe. Mirabel gestured me to a chair upholstered in ochre brocade, and rang a silver bell. A maid duly appeared, bearing a decanter of red liquor and two implausibly delicate glasses.

'Cherry gin,' Mirabel said, when the girl had poured and withdrawn. 'From our orchards at Leighfindell.'

She pronounced it 'Liffingdell'. It had always amused me how the aristocracy liked to lay traps to trip the unwary, so that not just fashion and manners, but the pronunciation of mere words became barriers between themselves and all the rest. Could I ever truly be one of them? I told myself that if I could make the journey from Cornwall to Bath, I could make this one too.

'Where do you stay in London, Miss Antrobus?' Mirabel asked.

The words of my confession stuck in my throat. I had little sense of my grandmother yet, beyond her arch humour, and it was impossible to predict how she might react. The little speech I had rehearsed on my journey here had been intended for Julius De Lacy, not his mother. I had warmed to her immediately, but I decided to take her measure first – to judge whether I should appeal to emotion or duty. Knowing the right words to use with a person, I'd often thought, was a skill in itself.

'At the house of a family friend, Mrs Illingworth,' I said. 'My new guardian has business abroad in Ireland, and she was kind enough to offer me a place to stay.'

It was the first name that popped into my head. Mr Illingworth owned the haberdashery in the Bath High Street. I did not like lying to my grandmother, but in the great scheme of things, I was sure it would be understood.

'Illingworth,' she mused. 'It is not a name I know.' She reached for a mother-of-pearl box on a side table, taking from it a pack of cards. The design on the back was identical to the one that I'd found in my father's portmanteau. 'The Square of Sevens has a special significance to my family,' she said. 'I had believed that the secret was lost for ever.'

I took the cards from her outstretched hand. 'Is there something in particular you wish to ask me about?'

'A matter of family,' she replied, with barely a pause.

What subject could be more apposite than that? And what better way to get to know my grandmother than by reading her cards?

As I laid the Square and despoiled it, Mirabel's beady eyes flitted back and forth. 'The method appears the same,' she remarked. 'I did wonder. Julius was little more than a boy when last he saw it done. I wasn't sure if he could tell true gold from pyrite.'

Her fortune consisted almost entirely of hearts and spades. A fortune of the passions, my father would have said, of the blood and the beating heart and the eye of the storm.

'The five of spades, influenced by a club,' I said. 'It signifies a death.'

Mirabel let out a long sigh. From her reproachful eyes, I was given to understand that it was not a sign of pleasure.

'And I had such high hopes for you,' she murmured.

'Mrs De Lacy?'

She took a wax taper from her box and held it to a candle, then used it to light a long silver-and-ebony pipe. Smoke curled around her face like a materializing djinn.

'Do you know how many diviners and soothsayers have sat where you are sitting now?' she said. 'More than you can count. And every one of them has begun with the death of someone close to me.'

'If a loss figures large in the heart, it figures large in the fortune,' I said. 'Perhaps they all saw the same imprint upon your soul?'

'Which loss would that be? Were you intending to tell me about my husband? Or about my son? Or about my daughter?' She smiled sardonically, her teeth crooked and tobacco-stained. 'I presume you read the newspapers, Miss Antrobus.'

'Sometimes,' I said cautiously.

'Then you know how my husband died?'

'Yes, I do.'

'At least you're honest. Apoplexy runs in my husband's family. The men die young. It was that which sparked my husband's interest in the occult, one I came to share. He wanted to know when he would die.'

'The cards cannot figure that,' I said.

'So he learned. Is it his death you see here?'

'I cannot yet know. Not without more cards.'

She drew on her pipe and exhaled. 'Then do go on.'

Determined not to falter under her withering stare, I indicated the next card. 'Five of clubs, influenced by a heart. A wound or bruise.' I frowned. 'This card suggests that the death might have been violent.'

'Not my husband,' she said. 'He died in his bed.'

'No,' I agreed, 'and yet the master-card is the knave of hearts, which does suggest the death of a man.'

'My son, then.' Mirabel gave a long sigh that turned into a cough. The parrot squawked: '*Bad for you, mother.*'

'Be quiet, Ocho. You're worse than Julius.' Mirabel gestured dismissively at the cards. 'Virgil died in a fall from a horse at the age of nineteen. He hit his head, a blow which killed him instantly.' She skewered me with her gaze. 'Now can you tell me something that you couldn't have read in a newspaper, Miss Antrobus? Or is this all just a waste of my time?'

I had met disbelieving querists many times before, usually men enamoured with the new school of reason. Evidence was their watchword, but show them evidence of my talent at reading their soul, and they would seize upon any explanation their clever minds could conceive, rather than accept the truth in front of their eyes. Mirabel was a different prospect. She had the intense gaze of a true believer, but one who wanted to make certain that I was worthy of that belief.

'Why do you smile?' she asked.

'I met your step-grandson, Mr Montfort, the last time I called at this house. He was unimpressed that I proposed to tell your fortune. He feared that I would take advantage of your grief.'

She chuckled. 'Archie is a good boy. He believes I need protecting – a poor old woman! Old I might be, but I have no truck with charlatans.'

'I am not a charlatan, Mrs De Lacy. These cards are a reflection of your soul and the query inside your heart. If they figure a death, it is there for a reason – whether or not that death has appeared in the newspapers.'

Her face was bland, still unconvinced, but I rather liked her frank manners and cunning eye. When I had finished her fortune, I decided, I would tell her my story and do so plainly. No manipulation of the emotions. No appeals to duty. Only the facts.

'The knave of hearts as master-card figures a close friendship. It points to feeling, rather than judgement. Sometimes the friendship is false.' My eyes moved to the next row. 'The three of spades influenced by a diamond signifies a breach or quarrel.'

'One between the friends?'

'I would think so.'

I could see my answer interested her. She edged forward, hands resting upon her knees.

'The six of diamonds,' I said, 'influenced by a spade. It signifies an error or untruth, one with adverse consequences.'

She licked her lips, sticky and scarlet from the gin. 'Can you say which? An error or a lie?'

I could tell the question meant something to her. 'Not presently. The other cards might tell us more. It likely has a connection to the quarrel, to the false friends. Perhaps also to your son's death.'

She made an impatient gesture: *the next card.*

'The ace of spades,' I said. 'As a master-card, it figures a misfortune or hurt.' The next card was also ominous. 'The king of spades, influenced by a club. It figures a man unsuspected for his real malevolency.'

Her breath seemed to catch in her throat. As I witnessed the effect of my reading upon her, I wondered at the cause – might it have a connection to my parents and their elopement? Before I had time to question her further, the door opened, greatly startling the parrot. 'Forgive me, Miss Antrobus,' Julius De Lacy said, rather curtly. 'An urgent matter has arisen that I must discuss with my mother.'

I gazed up at him with dismay. To have come so far and be forced to leave without having fulfilled my principal objective – why hadn't I blurted out the truth when I'd had the chance? I thought about doing so there and then, but, observing Julius's forbidding expression, my courage failed me.

Rising, I curtseyed to him and his mother, murmuring my thanks for their hospitality. Mirabel was still staring at the cards, and had to be prompted by her son to bid me farewell. A footman was waiting outside, and as he escorted me to the stairs, I heard Julius's voice rise in agitation: '*Three damn months.*' His mother said something I couldn't discern, then Julius's voice came even louder: '*Lady Seabrooke . . .*'

Feeling utterly dejected, I made my way out onto Piccadilly, not knowing when or if I'd ever be welcomed back. But before I had gone a hundred yards, a hand touched my arm, and I turned. It was the maidservant who had brought the gin, looking rather red in the face. She bobbed a curtsey. 'Mrs De Lacy asks if you will please come again this time next week.'

As I walked on down the street, a new buoyancy to my step, I tallied the events of that morning. In my nervousness to speak, I had shown myself a coward more than once. I hadn't the first idea how I was going to survive in London until next week. But when it came to Mirabel De Lacy, I had conquered.

CHAPTER THREE

King of spades as master-card: a particular man,
our enemy, resolute and powerful.

LAZARUS DARKE'S THOUGHTS, at that moment, are also consumed with Lady Seabrooke. He is standing on her doorstep,
her footman gazing at him levelly. 'The Dowager Countess is not at
home.'

Lazarus restrains a grunt of frustration, this being the fourth time
he has called at Hanover Square and received this same response.
'Tell her it's not about the money.' He is still owed half of his
commission for finding the codicil. 'It is imperative that I see her.
Something has happened.'

That something is named Julius De Lacy. The previous evening,
Lazarus had dined at Pontack's, an establishment conveniently sited
next door to his lodgings in Abchurch Lane. Pontack's is popular with
City bankers and stock-jobbers, who come for the fine French food
and the very best clarets.

Lazarus dines alone, on a ragout of stewed snails, and poussins in
elderberry sauce. His booth is lined with striped velvet, portraits of
prominent Romans upon the wall. He debates who makes a more fitting supper companion: Mark Antony, who followed a woman to his
own destruction, or Cicero, who never knew when to stop. Sometimes
he remembers Lady Seabrooke's expression when he placed the codicil in her hands. When Julius Caesar unrolled the gift of a carpet to
find Cleopatra nestled inside, his eyes never shone with such delight.

It gives Lazarus pleasure just thinking about it, though he has barely seen her since. She is always closeted with her lawyers, plotting Julius De Lacy's destruction.

At that moment, to his surprise, the principal object of her hatred walks through the door. Not known for an unobtrusive entrance, Julius is preceded by a yellow-and-scarlet peacock of a footman, another following in his wake. Heads turn. Julius spots Lazarus in his booth. He walks over, and sits down uninvited.

A waiter hurries to pour him wine, but Julius waves him away. 'I know you've had dealings with her. The moneylenders are taking her notes again. What's going on?'

It's the first time they've laid eyes on one another in sixteen years. Their last meeting was not a pleasant one, and it is like Julius not to acknowledge that fact.

'You don't know?' Lazarus says. 'You used to employ better people.'

Julius smiles. He wears his father's intaglio ruby on his little finger. It is carved with a heart in a ring of stars, mined in the valleys and mists of Mandalay. 'I know she's bringing a new suit in the Prerogative Court. What possible grounds does she have?'

'You'll have to ask her.'

'Come, Darke. We worked well together once. What do you say?'

This offer of a bribe to turn traitor sets Lazarus thinking. How much does Julius already know? Which facts is he missing? Lady Seabrooke's lawyers are embarked upon new plans. The codicil safely recovered, she believes nothing can frustrate them. Witnesses are being sought, depositions taken. A spirit of optimism has entered Seabrooke House.

'Tell her to give it up,' Julius says. 'If Lady Seabrooke wants to depart the battlefield with what's left of her dignity and reputation, she must do so now. If you have any care for her at all, then you'll convince her of that. There are certain matters that I have never aired in court, out of deference to my mother, who retains a measure of affection for Lady Seabrooke. But if she forces my hand, then be in no doubt that I will use them.'

He is plainly rattled – to come here like this, issuing threats. 'Speculation and gossip,' Lazarus says. 'The court will never allow it.'

'Oh, I have evidence to prove it. A certain report you wrote for my father in the September of 1723.'

Lazarus's expression betrays nothing of his inner turmoil. Like the codicil, he'd thought that document had been destroyed long ago.

'What did the newspapers call you the last time you testified?' Julius goes on. 'An honourable man in a nest of serpents? A speaker of truths? The servant who refused to lie for his master, even though it cost him his post? Well, that episode cost me too. You cast me in a bad light. I rather like the thought of you doing the same to her.'

Lazarus has a sudden vision of Julius De Lacy sprawled across the floor, his face bloodied, surrounded by his teeth. The footman nearest Lazarus seems to sense it, tensing a little in readiness. Lazarus offers him a disarming smile.

'If we are in the business of traducing reputations,' he says, 'I am surprised to find you so cavalier about your own. Lady Seabrooke's lawyers have long counselled her to avoid any unnecessary escalation in hostilities. But if you plan on scorching the earth, don't expect her to listen.'

'You mean that old story about the maid?' Julius laughs. 'Preposterous. I barely knew her name.'

That much Lazarus doesn't doubt. Julius was ever careless with his women. 'I worked for your father, remember. Sparing the family blushes, cleaning up the mess. Maids always were your weakness, as I recall.'

Julius's expression tightens. 'And Lady Seabrooke was always yours.' He retrieves a snuffbox from his waistcoat pocket and takes a pinch. He has one for every day of the year, each more exquisite and bejewelled than the last. 'Convince her,' he says. 'Or they'll be singing songs about her in every low tavern and gin-shop in the kingdom. The sort of scandal that never dies. That her son will read and know his mother was a whore. She'll blame you. It won't be fair, but there it is.'

CHAPTER FOUR

Two of diamonds, influenced by a club:
an interview of consequence.

ON THE STAGE in the Magpie's yard, men in armour were fighting – swords clashing, spraying a lot of red paint about, to the accompaniment of drum rolls and crashes of cymbals. Atop a rickety tower, a red devil and a small, fat cupid were boxing. The devil delivered the cupid a mighty blow, and he sailed gracefully to the floor on what looked like wires. In the yard, men were carrying lumber back and forth from the alley, a one-armed man with a yellow beard directing them where to put it.

Spotting Kerensa, I asked her where I could find Morgan Trevithick and was told he was up at the fair. 'His booth's on the north side: *Machina Mundi*. Past the waxworks, next to the dancing bears. I told him you was looking for him yesterday.'

The crowds at the fair were thicker today, packed close as a barrel of dates. Men and women called out to me from their stalls: 'Spin the wheel, win a half-guinea!' 'Come see the Whore of Babylon!' 'Come to the Whelp and Bacon music booth!'

I passed three waxwork booths, but could see no *Machina Mundi*, nor anybody advertising dancing bears. Pausing by a Wig Dip, I asked the stallholder if he knew where it was. His customer had his arm buried deep in the barrel of sawdust. He pulled out a scraggy wig that looked as if it had been made from a cow's tail, swore, and threw it to the ground.

'Don't lose heart,' the stallholder told him, pointing to his own handsome peruke. 'There's wigs in there that would have made the Sun King simper.' He turned to me, and I repeated my question. 'Think it's over there,' he said, vaguely, waving an arm.

I might have wandered the fair for hours, had a young woman not thrust a pamphlet under my nose.

MACHINA MUNDI

THE MECHANICAL WIZARD

MORGAN TREVITHICK

DISPLAYS HIS

INGENIOUS AUTOMATA

INCLUDING

THE FAMOUS GOLDEN GOOSE AND THE

PENNILESS PLAGIARIST

Entrance: ONE SHILLING

I called out to the girl and she turned. With a mixture of shock and pity, I saw that her face was cruelly disfigured, the cheekbones sunken, the nose misshapen, a patch worn over one eye. 'Can you show me the way?' I said, indicating the pamphlet.

Beckoning me to follow, she plunged into the crowds. I struggled to keep sight of her up ahead, but, eventually, she stopped and pointed at a booth painted with cogs, wheels and dials. A young African man in a powdered wig and purple velvet coat lounged in the doorway. He nodded to the disfigured girl. 'Right, Meg?'

She pointed at me, and I asked him for Morgan Trevithick. He glanced over his shoulder into the booth. 'Show's started.'

'Can I go in?'

He shrugged. 'Cost you a shilling.'

Reluctantly, I parted with the sum. My finances – or rather the lack of them – were very much on my mind. Later, I planned to wander the fair and see if anyone had a spare place in their booth for a fortune teller.

The audience were seated on benches, the booth only about half full. I crept inside, taking a seat near the back. A man I presumed to be Trevithick stood onstage. He was tall and robust, with shoulder-length black curls, his saffron waistcoat unbuttoned a little way to display a silver shirt-buckle with a large rock-crystal at its centre. The automaton in operation could only be the Golden Goose. Cogs whirred, and the bird pecked spasmodically at a sack of grain. It turned its head as if to observe us, then, twitching, laid a golden egg. Trevithick held it up to much applause.

'*Machina Mundi*,' he said. 'The machine of the world. Only with Newton's discoveries are we beginning to comprehend God's greatest gift to man: the Clockwork Universe. Fully understand the laws of motion and our lives will be transformed. Just as we can now predict the movement of the planets, so we shall soon predict the weather, the winner of the Queen Anne stakes, the perfect wife for every man, the winner in every war.'

With his wild black hair and the messianic glow to his eye, he better resembled a prophet than a wizard. I found myself listening with interest, thinking about the Square of Sevens, how it might fit into this idea of a Clockwork Universe. For all his scepticism, Mr Antrobus had once commented on the method's mathematical neatness, and I had sometimes mused upon the harmony of its arrangement. If everything in the universe worked like a clock, then presumably people did too. Viewed in that light, the Square of Sevens might be seen as a sort of manual, for understanding and predicting the actions of humankind.

'Imagine a world,' Trevithick said, 'in which your clothes are sewn by an automaton tailor, your boots made by a clockwork cobbler, your wig by a peruke-making machine. Imagine your wealth tallied by a machine abacus, your carriage driven by a clockwork coachman, your verses written by an automaton poet.'

With these words, he pulled aside the cloth covering another machine to reveal a lifelike figure of a man seated at a desk, dressed as a gentleman, quill in hand.

'*The Penniless Plagiarist*,' Trevithick said. 'Would anyone care to pay a penny for a verse?'

Several hands shot up. He pointed to a gentleman, who rose and made his way up to the machine. Trevithick pulled a lever and the automaton's hand jerked into the air. At his urging, the gentleman dropped a penny into the figure's palm. A murmur went up from the audience as the automaton pocketed the coin, then dipped his quill into his inkwell and began to write on a paper in front of him. When he had finished, Trevithick urged the gentleman to take the paper and read it aloud.

> '*All the world's a stage,*
> *And all the men and women merely players.*
> *They have their exits and their entrances;*
> *And one man in his time plays many parts.*'

'It's *As You Like It*,' someone cried.

More hands rose, everyone eager for a verse. The automaton wrote six in total, lines from Milton, Dryden, more Shakespeare, and the *Beggar's Opera*. My mind was still racing at the possibilities of these machines and their magic. Might an automaton really be taught to walk, to speak, to think?

'Thus,' Trevithick concluded, 'will we overcome the frailties of flesh and bone, freeing man from drudgery, unleashing his mind to new feats of understanding. The gears grind, the clock ticks, the universe rotates. And so we touch the face of God.'

Everyone applauded, and he bowed several times. Whilst the rest of the audience filed out, I remained seated. Trevithick busied himself with his machines, until he looked up and noticed me.

'Can I help you, miss?'

Rising, I approached him. 'My name is Red. I was hoping to talk to you about John Jory Jago.'

Trevithick had an aquiline nose, weathered skin, and eyes the colour of old French brandy. His long, hard look gave little away. 'What about him?'

'He was my father.'

Trevithick shrugged. 'Might be a whole pack of little John Jorys running about London, for all I know.'

'He died when I was seven years old. There's so much I don't know about his life. I was hoping to ask you some questions about him.'

His eyes narrowed. 'How old are you?'

'Sixteen.'

'Then someone's been telling you a fairy tale, my darling. John Jory died back in '23.'

'I know that was what you were told,' I said. 'But it isn't true. I think he wanted people to believe that he was dead.'

'Tell that to the folk in Tretelly. There's a man there who saw him jump.'

'Tretelly?' I asked. 'Is that in Cornwall?'

'It sound like Yorkshire to you?'

I frowned. 'What do you mean a man saw him jump?'

'He leapt from the cliff above town, a self-murder. I've been up that clifftop for myself. Nobody could have survived that fall.'

The cliff above town. Had Tretelly been the name of the little fishing port where we'd first met Mr Antrobus? The innkeeper had seemed to recognize Father, and I had suspected that he had stayed at the inn before.

'Perhaps he only pretended to jump?' I said. 'Or paid that man to say he saw him do it? Father believed he had dangerous enemies. That would have given him a good motive, don't you think?'

Trevithick studied me a moment. 'What's all this about, hey? Did your mother give you my name? Send you here on the jig?'

'I never knew my mother, but I think perhaps you did? Her name was Patience De Lacy, though my father called her Luna.'

'And I'm the Midnight Washerwoman.' He laughed. 'Look, I

don't know what sort of fakement you're chousing here, but I've been dealing with sharps and jilts and wheedlers all my life. And even if I was the longest-lashed milk-cow in the pasture, I still wouldn't give you any money, because if John Jory Jago had enemies, then I count myself among them. Fine try, though, my darling. I'll give you that.'

'I don't want your money,' I said, seeking words that might convince him. 'My father was John Jory Jago, though he called himself George the Tenth of Kernow. He was alive for seven years after you believed him dead. In our days on the road, he sold horoscopes and charms. He taught me cartomancy, a method called the Square of Sevens. He wore a long indigo coat embroidered with hieroglyphs and hexafoils. He smoked a pipe and carried a blackthorn staff. He could produce golden charms from a milkmaid's ear or a pigeon from a locked box. His favourite book was *Don Quixote*, as it is mine. He was your friend and partner once, whatever happened to set you at odds. All I want is to learn more about his life before I was born.'

He was looking at me strangely, his hands upon his hips. 'What was your name again?'

'Red,' I said.

'You're telling me, Red, that you know the Square of Sevens?'

'Yes, I do.'

He regarded me a moment longer. 'Come with me.'

I followed him outside, into a smaller booth next door, which had a sign over the door:

STEP INSIDE
THE ENCHANTED BOWER
A SECRET TOLD
A SUMMER FLOWER

The walls and ceiling of the booth were hung with green cloths embroidered with leaves and flowers. A table covered in green velvet was flanked by two chairs. Trevithick handed me a pack of cards from his pocket. 'Show me.'

As I shuffled and laid the Square, he watched me as intently as

Mirabel had done earlier. He seemed disinterested in the fortune I told for him, but he listened to my patter with a faint smile.

'Can you start today?' he said, when I had finished.

'I'm sorry?'

'Kerensa told me that you was looking for a pitch at the fair. Isn't that what all this other fiddle faddle is about? Well, I don't give a damn about John Jory, but I do give a damn about my profit. The Square of Sevens is good business. Always was.'

'I wasn't lying about my father.'

'Let's just say I don't care and leave it at that. Well? Can you start today?'

I resented his disbelief, but I needed money to live on until I could call upon the De Lacys again. Working for Morgan Trevithick would also give me the opportunity to earn his trust. Perhaps, given time, he might open up to me about my father. 'On what terms?'

'You'll charge a shilling a fortune – never more, never less. I take half of everything you earn.'

'Half?' I objected.

'This pitch cost me four quid. Your board and lodging comes out of my share. I pay off the constables too. Those are Company terms. You won't find better.'

For all I knew it might be true. 'Very well.'

'All right, then.' He gave me a hard stare. 'But I want no more fudge about John Jory, do you hear? When he walked out on the Cornish Players – that's the name of my troupe – things went very badly for a time. I'm not the only one who was sore at him, and if you go around calling yourself his daughter, there's folk who'd be sore at me for giving you a pitch. You understand?'

I nodded.

'Good – because you cause me any trouble and you're out.'

The booth darkened, as three women walked through the door, carrying baskets of flowers in their arms. They stared at us in surprise, the one in the rear jostling against the others. The booth was barely large enough to squeeze us all in.

'This here's Red,' Trevithick said. 'She's going to be telling fortunes with us for the duration of the fair. This is Tamson. You'll share this booth with her.'

To my surprise, I realized that the girl he was looking at was the same astrologer I'd consulted in the spring about my mother's chart. 'I know you,' she said, brushing a lock of amber hair from her piercing blue eyes. 'The lady who doubts the wisdom of the stars.'

'She'll bunk in with you at the Magpie,' Trevithick said.

One of the other girls shot me a hostile look. She had long yellow hair coiled in a plait and wore a yellow-and-black-striped gown that fitted her like a skin. I recognized her as the actress I had seen on stage that morning. Right now she reminded me of an angry wasp.

'Ladies don't tell fortunes. Not real ones,' she said.

'This one does,' Trevithick said. 'She knows the Square of Sevens.'

The girl shrugged. 'Means nothing to me.'

The third woman was older, with a round, red face and greying black hair. Her pebble eyes narrowed. 'It brought us seven years' bad luck.'

'That's foolish talk,' Trevithick said. 'It made us a lot of money, and there's naught more lucky than that.' He raised his voice: 'Roland.' The young African poked his head into the booth. 'Have another table and two chairs brought up from the Magpie.' He introduced me, and Roland gave me a friendly nod. 'You call Roland if you have any trouble from the customers. Remember what I said and we'll do good business together.'

So began my days telling fortunes at the Bartholomew Fair.

That first evening, I had a slow, yet steady stream of customers. An apprentice who wanted to know if he would be rich; a pretty girl anxious about a proposal (rightly so); her friend who wanted to know if her grandfather had remembered her in his will; two young lads who had just taken the King's shilling, their nervous demeanour saying everything; and an old man who feared his young wife had made him a cuckold.

The baskets of flowers had been hung on hooks around the walls of the booth, giving the impression of stepping into a woodland bower. Red and yellow roses, pinks and carnations, palest primroses and lilies of the valley. After each fortune, I'd give my querist a flower. In between customers, I listened to Tamson interpreting her customers' horoscopes and natal charts. Sometimes I caught her watching me, and I wondered if Trevithick had told her to keep an eye on me. In the lulls between customers, I asked her about the fair and the Cornish Players. She answered all my questions with polite reserve.

'Do we really not need to worry about the constables?' I asked, still a little nervous about the illegality of my new trade.

'They patrol the fair, but Morgan pays them off. It's the magistrate you want to watch out for. You'll know him if you see him: a big, florid man with a brandy nose, always with a pair of greyhounds at his heels. He's a man of God,' her voice was thick with contempt, 'and he hates those who practise magic with a dark passion.' She rose from her chair and peered outside the booth. 'Meg,' I heard her call.

The same disfigured girl who'd given me the pamphlet joined us in the booth. Tamson introduced me. 'Show Red what it is you do when you see the magistrate.'

The girl put her fingers to her lips and let out a distinctive whistle, like a warbling bird. Tamson went to the back of the booth and raised a section of the green cloth. I saw that a hole had been cut into the wood, and on the ground outside sat a basket.

'You hear Meg whistle, you put your cards and anything else incriminating into the basket. Meg will run round and take it away. If the magistrate asks what business we're in, we're selling flowers.'

'He'll believe it?' I asked.

'It doesn't matter what he believes, only what he can prove.'

'What happens if we are caught?'

'A year in prison – and a few sessions in the pillory.' Tamson glanced at Meg, who looked away. 'But it won't happen. Not if we're careful.'

We stayed open long into the night. My hands ached from all the shuffling, my mind fogged with weariness – and yet I felt proud of the money I earned that day. When the church bells struck two, Tamson rose, stretching her back. 'It's just drunks after two. I'm famished. Let's go get dinner.'

As we walked down to the Magpie, Tamson explained that the Cornish Players all ate together, outside in the yard, at around this time. Most members of the troupe were actors in the play, though a few had booths like us out in the fair. Roland was standing guard at the door to the enclosure in the Magpie's yard. He gave us a broad grin as we walked in. About three dozen people were eating at trestle tables and benches, the ground littered with orange peel and walnut shells, presumably dropped by the audience earlier. Kerensa was spooning stew from a cauldron into wooden bowls. A few men and women were dancing to a fiddler's tune, others beating time upon the tables.

We queued for food, and then Tamson led us to a table where the women I'd met earlier were sitting. She introduced me properly, and I learned that the older red-faced woman was named Naomi – she made all the costumes for the play – and the wasp was Gwen. They greeted me coolly.

I ate ravenously, Gwen and Naomi pointedly making little effort to include me in their conversation. Occasionally, Tamson would interrupt to explain something to me, and when Gwen and Naomi got up to dance, she laid a hand on my arm. 'Don't mind them. They take a while to warm to newcomers, but I'm sure they will.'

I resisted the urge to say that they could rot in chains for all I cared.

'Gwen is worried you're an informant for the magistrate,' Tamson went on.

'Why would she think that?'

'You're a lady. It does seem odd that you're telling fortunes at the fair.' She smiled. 'But if I was going to send an informant, I wouldn't choose a lady. It would make everyone suspect that she was an informant.' She ran a crust of bread around her bowl. 'As for Naomi, she thinks you're a Jacobite spy. Don't go looking for reason where there's none. She thinks the world is full of Jacobites. If there were that many in this realm, I told her, then Prince Charlie wouldn't need to invade. But Naomi is Naomi. If she gets a pimple, she thinks it's a papist conspiracy.'

I smiled. 'What did Naomi mean earlier, when she said the Square of Sevens had brought seven years' bad luck?'

'It's what some of the older Players say. Morgan once owned an ancient document that revealed the secrets of the Square of Sevens. It was sold to a rich man and the Players' luck turned. People made the connection.'

'What was his name? This rich man?' I asked, hoping to draw her out upon the topic.

'I don't know,' she said. 'It was before my time.'

Surely it must be Nicholas De Lacy. Had my father subsequently stolen it? And taken the codicil at the same time?

I looked around the Players, studying the faces of the older men and women, wondering if one of them might prove more knowledgeable about these events. Morgan Trevithick was watching me from across the yard, his arm around a woman with silver curls piled tightly like a helmet. Our eyes locked, and he gave me an unsmiling nod.

I judged him a hard, venal man, one who danced to the promise of coin. I sensed he didn't fully trust me – and rightly so. I had little compunction about breaking my word to him. Hadn't he called himself my father's enemy? And he should never have asked me to make a promise that I couldn't keep.

CHAPTER FIVE

Two of clubs, influenced by a spade:
advice seemingly good, but not so.

THE FOLLOWING MORNING, I moved into Tamson's room at the Magpie. I didn't like the idea of her observing my comings and goings, but it would save me money, and I reasoned that it might help my efforts to learn more about my father. Tamson was clearly popular in the Cornish Players, and if I stayed close to her, people might talk to me more freely.

Thankfully, both the room and the bed were larger than those I had vacated. Tamson had also made more of an effort to give the place a homely feel. A pretty oil lamp stood on the press, next to a tulip vase displaying five red flowers. A patchwork counterpane covered the bed, and an embroidered shawl was pinned to the top of the window to serve as a curtain. In front of the window stood a table, a row of books upon on it, as well as an album and a box of watercolours. A few bunches of herbs were hanging from the window frame and the air was filled with their fragrant scent.

While Tamson emptied one of the drawers of the press so that I'd have somewhere to put my clothes, I examined the spines of her books. A few novels, a herbal grimoire, some poetry.

'Do you practise herbalism?' I asked.

'A little. Gwen keeps me busy. She's always complaining about a head-pain or a toothache.'

'What do you paint?'

'Flowers and plants, mostly.'

She didn't suggest that I look in her album, and I didn't ask.

'There.' She'd finished emptying the drawer. 'You don't have much, do you?'

It was as close as she'd come to curiosity about my situation. I put down my portmanteau. 'All that I need.'

After I'd unpacked, we walked up to the booth together, the fair kindling to life around us. I spotted Meg, pamphlets in hand, standing outside a booth where a dog played dominoes. We waved to her and she gave us her lopsided grin.

'Was it the pillory that made her that way?' I asked.

Tamson nodded. 'She used to work in the booth with me. Scrying was her trade. But an unhappy customer 'peached on her to the magistrate and she was arrested. This was last year, before we used the lookout and the basket. On the eve of her first session in the pillory, a local baby died, and a rumour went around the taverns that Meg had laid a curse on it. Two hundred of them turned out, and they came armed with half-bricks. The Players tried to fight them off, but there were too many. The sheriff stepped in eventually, but Meg's poor sweet face was ruined. Her wits are addled too.' Observing the horror on my face, she paused. 'My mother used to say that the worst people were not angry men, but frightened men.'

I thought of the man I had scared all those years ago, the one whose friends had ducked Father in the millpond.

'That's why I was in London in the spring,' Tamson went on. 'The Players usually return to Cornwall for the St Ives Fair and winter there. But the magistrate let Meg out early because of her injuries, and she was too ill to come on the road. So I stayed to look after her.'

'That was good of you.'

She shrugged. 'I don't mind staying in one place for a change. Even London.'

Those first few days at the fair all blur into one. Long hours telling fortunes in the booth with Tamson; hot nights of music and dancing down at the Magpie; a few hours' snatched sleep lying next to Tamson in our bed, both exhausted. Sometimes a party of gentlemen would come into the booth and I'd worry that I'd meet someone who'd recognize me from Bath. But I never did – the only hazard I faced was the occasional customer who was amorous or just plain rude. 'We deserve a medal,' Tamson would sometimes remark, 'for services to patience.'

Through talking to her, I learned that several of the Players had been with the troupe in my father's day: three of the actors in the play; one of the trumpeters; a husband-and-wife team who had a puppetry booth in the fair; Tamson's friend, Naomi; Pierre, the one-armed man, who was a sort of odd-job man for the Players; and Morgan's wife, Rowena, the tall, slim, grey-haired woman I'd seen him sitting with on my first night there. She had a rope-dancing booth in the fair, and had once crossed the Avon Gorge upon a wire, making her something of a heroine to the younger women in the troupe.

Although Morgan seemed pleased with the money I was making him, I was always conscious of his beady eye upon me. I couldn't risk my questions getting back to him, not if I wanted to keep my place in his booth, and so I was cautious about what I said and who I said it to. But I deliberately sought out the older Players, hoping that the subject of my father might arise naturally. I could hardly be blamed for any crumbs they might let drop.

One night, I was sitting with Gwen and Naomi, watching Tamson and Roland dancing to the wild Cornish tunes. Roland was spinning her fast, her skirts rising. Frank, the actor playing Tristan to Gwen's Iseult, bounded up to us.

'Have a dance with me, Gwen?'

He was a strapping, sandy-haired man of about twenty-five. I often saw him out in the yard of a morning, his white shirt clinging with sweat to his muscular torso, repeatedly lifting two heavy bells with the clappers removed. These 'dumb-bells' were not his only vanity. Tamson had told me he wore a night mask for his freckles, and he was fond of powdering his face, even when he wasn't on stage.

'I'd sooner dance with the Prussian dwarf,' Gwen replied.

Frank's face fell. I'd seen them reject him like this before, though they seemed happy enough to dance with the other men in the troupe. It made me wonder if Frank had done something to offend them.

'How's your new admirer?' Naomi asked Gwen rather pointedly, so that Frank would get the hint.

Gwen smiled. 'He brought me flowers after the play. Said he'd come again tomorrow night. Wants me to take a walk with him.'

'Are you going to go?'

'I don't know. My sore throat's come back. And I've got a lump behind my ear. Have a look, will you?'

While she lifted her hair, and Naomi prodded her, Gwen turned to me. 'Do you have a sweetheart, Red?'

'No,' I said shortly, not liking her sly expression.

'What, no fine gentleman who farts guineas?'

I turned back to watch the dancing.

'Have you never kissed a lad?' Naomi asked, a little more kindly.

'No.' I thought of the electricity show. 'I came close once.'

'Was he very handsome?'

I considered the question. 'He was the most beautiful man I ever saw.'

'So what went wrong?'

'He turned out to be a disappointment.'

Naomi laughed. 'They always do.'

When the dance had ended, Tamson and Roland came and sat with us, the firelight making a dance of its own across their glowing faces. I sat there silently, marvelling at how far I had come in only a few short days. When Roland and Gwen got up to dance, Tamson caught me watching her.

'My grandmother was Indian,' she said, rather hotly. 'That's why I look the way I do. I don't mind it one bit, so don't go feeling sorry for me. And don't ask me about Bombay or Calcutta. I've never been there.'

'I wasn't—' But I couldn't explain why I had been looking, not without feeling a fool. How to say: I never had a friend before?

The next morning, when I awoke, the other half of the bed was empty. I dressed and went downstairs, where I found Pierre talking to Frank out in the yard. I asked them if they'd seen Tamson.

'She'll be over by St Bartholomew's,' Frank said. 'There's a garden near the church where she likes to paint on quieter mornings.'

'Want to catch a show?' Pierre asked, in his slow, Cornish drawl. 'I was just off to see the dancing bears.'

Naturally I accepted, and he offered me his good arm. Tamson had told me that he'd lost the other one whilst changing a wagon wheel. A trim, yellow-bearded man who reminded me of Mrs Fremantle's porcelain gnomes, he carried a dark grey kitten named Ash around in his coat pocket. It was in the interests of his pet that we stopped off at a cock shy stall on the way up to see the bears. Pierre paid a penny and was given three stones to hurl at the cockerel. At the Bath fair, they used a live bird, but I was relieved to see that this one was fashioned from forcemeat. Pierre's aim was good, and we walked on, Ash breakfasting greedily on the forcemeat in his pocket.

We paid at the door of the bear booth, and took seats around the perimeter upon bales of straw. A flute and drum began to play, and two walnut-skinned men in Levantine hats drove in a procession of six black bears of varying sizes. The creatures rose upon their haunches and danced in pairs, a passing resemblance to a minuet.

'They train them on hot metal platforms,' Pierre whispered to me. 'The bears lift their paws to escape the heat, while the flute and drum are played. Over time, they come to link the burning of their feet with the music.'

I didn't enjoy the bears nearly so much after that. Pierre had much to say upon the topic. I had met his sort before: affable enough, neither as clever nor as interesting as he believed himself to be, fond of dispensing wisdom to younger women. I made all the appropriate noises of enthrallment, until he was quite puffed up with pride at my captivation. Then I asked him about himself and how he'd met Morgan. For a while, he waxed lyrical about the triumphs of his youth, when he'd been a juggler. Had it not been for his accident, it seemed, he might have been rich and travelled the world. 'That was a bad business,' he concluded. 'It was almost enough to make me believe we was truly cursed.'

'Cursed?' I asked, seizing upon the topic.

'Aye, that's what some folks say. It was your Square of Sevens that started it all. We had a fellow with us back then – Morgan's old partner – who told fortunes using that method. It was an old secret in his family, and he had an ancient parchment that spelled it all out. Well, him and Morgan argued, and Morgan sold that document for a handsome pile of gold. After that, the women said that we was cursed. There's some who're nervous about you using it even now. Rowena, for one.'

'Morgan stole his partner's document?' I asked, trying to make sense of it all.

Pierre shook his head. 'It wasn't theft as such. John Jory had wanted to borrow some money from Morgan. But Morgan didn't trust him no more, so he insisted upon a surety.'

'His old document?'

Pierre nodded. 'It was worth a lot of money and it was also precious to John Jory. So Morgan knew he'd be back for it. But John Jory used the money to run off with some rich man's daughter and didn't return. The father's agent caught up with us that summer in Cambridge, looking for the girl. He said John Jory had taken her by force, and that Morgan could be charged with kidnapping as an accessory. So he told them everything.'

My fists clenched. More De Lacy lies. And yet I reminded myself that they might be as deluded as everyone else. Once they knew the truth, things might be different.

Pierre paused to applaud. The largest bear, his black fur grizzled with grey, had been harnessed to a cart, driven by a pair of chattering monkeys wielding whips. The bear lumbered around the booth, pulling them along.

'The agent had some pet constables with him and they broke up Morgan's machines. He was sore at John Jory, and so he sold that agent the Square of Sevens. Morgan said John Jory almost killed him when he found out.'

I looked up sharply. 'Morgan saw John Jory again? After the elopement?'

Pierre shrugged. 'That's what he told me. Wanted me to watch his back, though as it turned out, we never saw John Jory again. After that nothing went right for us. Lost pitches, burned wagons, arrests, we had it all. Some blamed the Square of Sevens, some said Jack the Lantern and Joan the Wad had it in for us. But for my part, I don't think we was cursed, I just think Morgan needed John Jory, for advice and all the rest. Between the two of them it worked better, that was all.'

Later, in the booth with Tamson, I struggled to make sense of what I'd learned. I refused to believe that my father had taken my mother by force, but I gave other parts of Pierre's story much more credence. If Father had believed that the Square of Sevens was rightfully his, sold unlawfully by Morgan Trevithick, then it would explain why he had decided to steal it back. But when had he done so and how? And why had he taken the codicil at the same time?

'Well?' my customer demanded, breaking into my thoughts. 'Which one will serve me best?'

He was a squinting, sallow-faced clerk, trying to decide between two women. One he'd described as ugly but rich, the other pretty but poor.

'The four of hearts, influenced by a spade,' I said, 'implies that your query is based on error or lacks full insight.'

He frowned. 'What does that mean?'

'I see a marriage with money in it, and a woman of beauty and charm. I believe you might have both with a little ambition.'

'Both?' He thought for a moment. 'There is my employer's daughter. He is a wealthy merchant, and she is very beautiful. But I can't think he'd entertain my suit. He'd be more likely to dismiss me for the mere presumption.'

'I can only tell you that the cards suggest you should aim high.' I pointed again. 'But this card here, the ace of diamonds, influenced by a heart, suggests that success in this marriage is contingent upon the closure of matters open. You must break off your current attachments before pressing your suit.'

'What if her father does not look kindly upon my proposal? I'd be left with nothing.'

'That is a choice only you can make. But Venus, like Fortune, favours the bold.'

He departed extremely satisfied. I was not displeased myself.

'I saw that,' Tamson said.

'What do you mean?'

'Those cards you gave him. They didn't fall naturally that way.'

I shrugged.

You want me to lie to him about his cards? My question to Father all those years ago had planted a seed in my own mind. I knew it wouldn't be hard. As a little girl, Father had taught me his legerdemain: *See the lady. Watch the cards. Watch her disappear.*

The first time I'd tried it, Lettuce had been upset over a man, and I'd decided to figure Mr Leake's boy in her cards, who was by far the kindest and most intelligent of her suitors. So it had come to pass – they had fallen in love – and everybody concerned was better for it. I no longer thought of it as lying. A fate and a fortune were mirrors of one another – and you could always find the truth reflected there.

'It isn't your place to decide his destiny,' Tamson said.

'You never know,' I said, grinning. 'His employer might want him for a son-in-law. Either way, those other women will be spared marriage to such a man.'

She frowned. 'Don't you believe in the cards?'

'I believe people get the cards that they deserve.' It was a flippant answer, but I was annoyed by her judgemental tone.

'It's wrong what you're doing. It's disrespectful. It's dangerous.'

I laughed. 'I don't think he'll be back. And Roland will drop him in the river if he tries anything.'

'I don't mean him,' she said. 'The cards can curse, the cards can kill in defence of their power. Rowena told me.'

I laughed again, a little uneasily this time. 'It's not happened yet.'

'Are you sure?'

I thought back to that day I'd told Lettuce's fortune. Only a week or so later, I'd lost my golden heart charm. Then there was that day at the Pump Room in Bath, when I'd given Julius De Lacy a propitious fortune that had made him smile and invite me to his house. It had only been a few months later that those villains had broken into Trim Street and killed Mrs Fremantle. And there was Mr Antrobus too, I thought in sick dismay. I'd encouraged him to profit from the Square of Sevens, and then he had died.

I told myself the idea was ridiculous – just Player superstition. But the thought buzzed around in my head and refused to be swatted. Was it possible that their deaths had been my fault?

CHAPTER SIX

Nine of spades as master-card:
an unwelcome meeting.

TWO DAYS LATER, I called again at De Lacy House. I went there determined to tell Mirabel De Lacy everything. Tired of all the lies I had woven around myself, I believed this day would mark a new beginning. Yet when the butler showed me into a very beautiful Chinoiserie parlour, I was dismayed to find Mirabel taking tea with Archie Montfort.

'Miss Antrobus,' my grandmother said, rising to clasp my hands. 'I am so pleased you have returned. You are acquainted with Mr Montfort, I believe.'

He bowed his golden head, then fastened his eyes combatively upon mine. 'When I learned that I'd missed your last visit, I was determined to be present for the next.'

The way he looked at me left me in no doubt of his feelings. I had disregarded his entreaty to stay away from his family, and he was highly displeased. Had I been prepared for his presence, then I might have answered him with self-possession. As it was, my cheeks grew warm and I looked away. Anxiety compounded my unease. How could I speak the truth in front of him? I could well imagine the contempt with which he'd greet my claims.

'Julius asked me to apologize for his conduct the last time you were here,' Mirabel said. 'You should know he treated poor Mr Walpole in equally brusque fashion – though in his case, not entirely undeserved.'

We exchanged a smile, the King's First Minister firmly established as the object of our private amusement, though I'd never held any particular opinion of him before. Mirabel invited me to sit at the marquetry tea table, a pack of cards already waiting there for me. Archie remained on the sofa, his long legs elegantly sprawled.

'I regret that we did not have time to finish my fortune on your last visit,' Mirabel said. 'The death, the quarrelled friends. It intrigued me.'

'A fortune may be interrupted, Mrs De Lacy, but the truths it contains hold fast. Keep those cards in your mind as I shuffle. The death, the injury, the friends . . .'

'The error or lie,' she said, 'the misfortune, and the man of malevolent character.'

A slight hiss escaped Archie's lips, something like *pissssht*.

'Archie is an unbeliever,' Mirabel said, giving him a fond glance. 'He is entitled to that view, though you or I might pity him for it.'

He grinned. 'I believe only in what I can see and put to the test with scientific method, Nonny. If Miss Antrobus can tell me the next winner of the Newmarket Town Plate, I shall drink a bumper to her talents with my winnings.'

'My cards look into the human soul, not horse races,' I said. 'Though I met a man recently who believes that one day we will be able to use Newton's laws of motion to predict everything. That the world works as an ingenious clock, a mechanism the finest minds might understand. Sir Isaac was certainly a man who gazed far into the future. He was also greatly interested in the occult, I believe.'

'Newton's method was extremely rigorous,' Archie said, a little stiffly.

I met his gaze with flint of my own. 'So is mine.'

Mirabel laughed. 'There, Archie. You have met your match in Miss Antrobus. Now I said you could only stay if you promised to be quiet.'

Archie spread his arms wide. 'I shall be a veritable Trappist, Nonny. You will hardly know I'm here.'

I was aware of very little other than his presence. As I laid the Square, and a maid appeared with wine, I watched him out of the corner of my eye. His languid posture, his still gaze, his mocking smile. Unbidden, my mind lurched to the electricity show in Bath, those same lips drawing ever closer to mine. I wished I could give him a shock now, to startle him out of his complacency. I also wished that it was not quite so hot in that room.

I thought about figuring my mother's elopement in Mirabel's cards, to get a sense of her feelings upon the subject – and yet I fretted over Tamson's warnings: *The cards can curse, the cards can kill.* It was not that I believed her, precisely, but I harboured enough doubt to let the cards fall naturally, desiring no bad luck to sour this day.

'The king of clubs, influenced by a high heart,' I said. 'An affection for a near relative. The heart in question is the queen, here influenced by a spade, indicating a woman either not of firm health, or not of firm virtue.'

'Yes, of course,' Mirabel murmured, her eyes darting over the cards. 'She would be figured here.'

'Mrs De Lacy?'

But she only waved a hand, indicating that I should continue.

'The six of spades as master-card figures a disappointment.'

She gazed at Archie. 'Can you deny it now?'

'Certainly I can,' he said. 'These meanings are generalities. A disappointment. A female relative. You see in them the things you want to see.'

'But in these combinations . . .'

'I do agree it is a remarkable coincidence.'

Mirabel caught the inference in his tone. 'But how could she know? Nicholas went to great lengths to keep these events out of the newspapers.'

'There is always gossip,' Archie said. 'Bath is not so very far from Devon.'

Given my failure to learn any of the family's secrets in Bath, I might have laughed.

'You are wrong,' Mirabel said. 'She has a true gift.'

His insolent eyes met mine again. 'That Miss Antrobus is gifted, I don't doubt.'

Trying to ignore him as best I could, I addressed Mirabel: 'The more you can tell me about the patterns you see within these cards, the better I can guide you to understanding.'

'Yes,' she said, nodding, her eyes very bright. 'I believe you can.'

The chatty Trappist can say what he likes, I thought. This battle is already won.

Mirabel took a sip of wine. 'The lie figured here,' she said, 'relates to the manner of Virgil's death. A lie I repeated to you the other day. My son did not die in a fall from a horse, though that is the story my husband concocted, and was reported as fact by the newspapers.' She smiled sadly. 'Virgil was a handsome, athletic boy. Rode like a centaur, fenced like a dancer. Ever dutiful to his father. The dogs adored him. If he had a failing, then it was an impractical sense of honour – and a hot-headedness in that cause which led him to ruin.'

'The quarrel between the friends was a matter of honour?' I asked. 'Over a woman?'

'How swiftly you see the truth.' She sighed. 'Virgil's dearest friend was named Little Piers. Everyone called him Little Piers because that was also his father's name, but he was a tall, vigorous youth, just like my Virgil. They must have climbed every tree at Leighfindell together, swum in every pond. The woman who came between them was my eldest daughter, Jemima.' She stroked the queen of hearts with the tip of her little finger. 'She and Virgil were twins. If my husband's family curse is death, the blessing of my own is abundant life. I was a twin, I gave birth to two sets myself, and Septimus too has sired twins. Some twins form a bond in the womb. So it was with Virgil and Jemima. They loved the same dogs, the same food – and the same people.

'Suffice to say, Little Piers dallied with Jemima's affection and then rejected her. She took it very badly. The truth is, Miss Antrobus, she lost her mind. Virgil's distress at his sister's plight was terrible to witness. He blamed Little Piers for his false promises, and on the next occasion that he showed his face at Leighfindell, Virgil called him out. They met on the island on the lake, wreathed by the dawn mist. Virgil was the better shot, but his pistol misfired. The bullet fired by that cowardly poltroon, Little Piers, struck my Virgil just below the heart. A physician was summoned, but there was nothing he could do. Jemima asked for her brother every day, but nobody could bear to tell her the truth. She believed he too had forsaken her, and she died of a broken heart.'

'Nonny,' Archie said softly. 'Stop this. You will only upset yourself.'

'It was nearly twenty years ago,' she said, giving him a steely look. 'I won't rend my garments.'

Still wrestling with grief myself, my heart went out to her. 'There is an error figured here again too. This time as a separate card to the lie. Does that mean anything to you at all?'

'Perhaps the error is mine? Had I not been so wrapped up in my concerns about Jemima, then I might have realized what Virgil intended and prevented the duel.'

The king of spades was also present again, influenced by a club, casting his malevolent gaze over her fortune. I danced over this ill omen, not wanting to upset her further, and was reading the final row of her parallelogram, when a footman opened the door to admit two ladies.

The first, a woman of middling years, sailed into the room, fanning herself ostentatiously. 'We are not too late, are we?' she said, pausing to kiss Mirabel and stroke Archie's hair. 'There was a queue in the millliner's. Do say that we are not. I have not been so excited since Julius took us to the palace.'

I had learned a thing or two about fashion under the tutelage of Mrs Davenport, whose keen eye could price a woman by the yard. This lady's caraco jacket of embroidered black brocade was of the very latest French fashion, as were her pink silk petticoats and golden lace sleeves. Throw in her diamond earrings and an elaborate necklace of pink gemstones nestled in her plump bosom, and I tallied her at over a thousand pounds. Her chestnut curls were pinned high in elaborate coils; her large dark eyes alight, her smile wide.

Following in her wake, less boldly, but no less fashionably, was the same small, dark-haired girl I had seen in the hall on my last visit here. Mirabel made the introductions: 'I present Miss Rachel Antrobus of Bath. This is my granddaughter, Miss Emily De Lacy, the daughter of my son, Julius. And her aunt, Mrs Arabia De Lacy, the wife of my youngest son, Septimus.'

Archie's mother, who had formerly been married to the family steward. I rose to curtsey, more conscious than ever of my shabby gown. The ladies joined us at the tea table, and inwardly, I sighed, my hopes of being left alone with Mirabel entirely diminished.

While I finished Mirabel's fortune, the other ladies watched with great interest. 'Who is next?' Arabia said, her eye fastening upon Emily. 'You, dear? I'm sure you have much to ask?'

At her aunt's teasing tone, a pink bloom rose on the girl's cheeks. 'You go first, Aunt Arabia,' she said. 'I'd like to watch.'

Arabia arched an eyebrow. 'You cannot be coy for ever, child. I hear your father's business with Mr Walpole was concluded most satisfactorily.'

'Who told you that?' Emily asked, a little sullenly. Her eye came to rest on Archie Montfort.

'Not I,' he said, shortly.

I observed this exchange with interest, though little understanding. Arabia re-pinned her hair with a jangle of bracelets. 'My turn, then. I wish to ask you about a matter of friendship. Someone has been spreading unkind stories about me in the salons, and I am determined to find out who it is.'

'Mother, all you and your friends do is spread unkind stories in the salons.'

'Only when they are warranted, at which juncture, they cease to be unkind. Now, I don't want you to hold back, Miss Antrobus. I want your perfect honesty.'

Archie smiled thinly. 'Miss Antrobus will tell you she is scarcely capable of anything less.'

'We all know how you set such great store by honesty,' Emily said quietly.

I wondered at the cause of the evident hostility between them. Archie lowered his eyes, and a hint of something – anger or shame, perhaps – darkened his expression. So, my enemy had a weakness. The knowledge gave me pleasure – and a keen desire to find out what it was.

I shall not bore my reader with the banalities of the many fortunes I told for Arabia that day. She trilled and billed and cooed as if it was all the most delightful game. Eventually, the clock striking three, Mirabel thanked me for coming, and I saw this was my signal to depart. As I rose, she took out a small purse of sky-blue silk and passed it to Arabia. 'A guinea a fortune,' she said. 'Miss Antrobus, you will find that I have also settled our account from last week.'

Arabia frowned. 'I am quite certain that Miss Antrobus . . .'

'Oh, I couldn't possibly . . .' I said, though I confess my heart had soared at the thought of all that money.

Mirabel spoke over us both. 'Remember what we used to say? A fortune unpaid is idly laid and may be unmade.'

'Who told you that?' Archie asked. 'Let me guess. A fortune teller?'

'Oh yes, it was,' Arabia cried. 'John Jory Jago.'

Immediately, she looked stricken, as if she'd spoken without thinking. Archie gazed at Mirabel, concerned.

'The beast,' she said, with great feeling. 'The man who bewitched my Luna. He used his powers to turn her against us, and then stole her away.'

'Nonny,' Archie said gently, with a reproachful look for his mother. 'Try to forget.'

Mirabel waved his concerns away. 'You understand people, Miss Antrobus, better than any of us here. Tell me this . . . Do you think a mother could ever forget the man who murdered her child? Ever forgive those she holds responsible?'

Murder? As I stared at her sincere, impassioned face, a sharp needle of doubt slid into my heart.

'Close your ears, my dear,' Arabia murmured to Emily.

'I am not a child,' she retorted. 'I know all about the elopement.'

Mirabel was still looking at me for an answer. 'Perhaps,' I said, my throat dry, 'if the facts were different to those she believed. Or if something happened to heal the wounds of the past.'

Mirabel smiled faintly. 'The facts are set in stone, I fear, but I shall always live in hope of a brighter future.'

Arabia dropped four guineas into the purse with a sour expression. 'You can buy yourself something nice. Perhaps a new dress.'

'What riches,' Archie remarked. 'Did you foresee such a sum in the cards?'

'It's impossible to tell one's own fortune,' I said, still dwelling upon Mirabel's words.

'I am sure it is.' Archie's eyes dropped to the purse in my hand. 'What would be the point?'

CHAPTER SEVEN

Knave of diamonds, influenced by a club:
a sudden discovery as to a person.

T HAT NEEDLE OF doubt worked at me all the way back across
London. I told myself that my kind, gentle father could not be
a murderer. Mirabel must have been told a pack of lies. Yet why had
Father never told me how my mother had died? Why had he changed
his name and hidden from the world? Was it possible he'd been afraid
of the hangman's noose?

When I reached the fair, I immediately sensed an odd feeling in
the air. There was a look of tension in the eyes of some of the stallholders, and a mood of suppressed revelry to the crowd. Catching
sight of Meg walking purposefully towards the Magpie, I was about
to run after her, when I noticed the basket in her hand. I soon spotted
a man striding between the stalls, who could only be the magistrate
Tamson had told me about. Corpulent, about fifty, with a large be-
veined nose, he carried a silver staff in one hand and the leads of two
sleek greyhounds in the other. He was flanked on either side by a
muscular constable, each armed with a much more practical wooden
staff. I hurried up to the booth to find Tamson.

'Where have you been?' she demanded, when I walked through the
door. Her face was taut with nerves, her hands fluttering.

'With a private client.'

'Morgan won't like it. He stopped by, asking where you were. I said you'd gone to buy a pie, but he put his head in again later and you still weren't here.'

'Tamson,' I said, 'do you remember when you read my mother's chart?'

'Are you even listening?'

'Don't worry about Morgan. I'll deal with him. You said you could tell me more about that chart. Could you do so now?'

'Haven't you seen? The magistrate's out there.'

'He was heading off towards Cock Lane. Besides, it's not illegal to read a chart, just to take money for it. I'll keep watch by the door, and if I see him coming back, you can give it to me.'

'I thought you didn't believe in the stars.'

'I never said that.' I was ready to grasp at anything that might support my conviction that my father was innocent. If the stars held true meaning, then surely an event as momentous as a murder would be figured there?

Sighing faintly, Tamson took the chart from my outstretched hand.

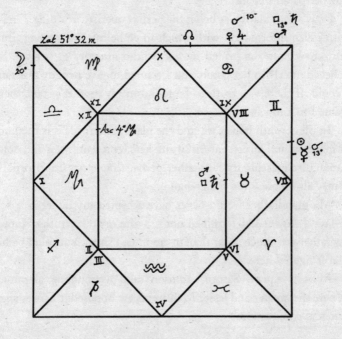

'I remember,' she said, after a few moments' study. 'It is a highly unusual chart, the first six houses void of planets. Scorpio is in the ascendant, the sign of physical passion. I would expect this woman to possess charm and magnetism, perhaps physical beauty.'

'I am told she was very beautiful,' I said.

'I can believe it.'

I smiled at the compliment, hoping this meant my absence earlier was forgiven.

'These houses mostly relate to family and childhood,' she went on. 'As I said, they are all void of planets. There is much mystery here, almost as if a veil has been drawn across it. The third house is ruled by strict Capricorn, figuring an authoritarian influence in childhood. Given that your mother's sun is in youthful Gemini, it is a combination that does not auger well. It may be that her childhood was unhappy.'

'I think it must have been. She eloped with my father and never saw her parents again.'

I was aware that I was being the perfect querist, providing Tamson with much information with which to embellish her reading. But I also knew how she prided herself on the integrity of her art. She believed utterly in her charts and I wanted to give her any assistance I could. If there was truth to be found in my mother's stars, then I wanted to know it.

'In the seventh house, we find the planet Saturn. This is the house of marriage and lovers. Saturn sitting here represents rules and domination, also masculinity. Her father, perhaps, our strict Capricorn. But it may also represent a father-figure.'

'My grandfather would never have accepted my father as a son-in-law.' I frowned, determined not to write my own truths. 'Though my father was much older than my mother. I suppose it could be him that is figured here.'

'Mars is square Saturn,' Tamson said, 'a troubling alignment. Where the greater and lesser Malificents are opposed it figures anger, fear, and combustion.'

Kidnap? Rape? Murder? But again, I caught myself. If I mustn't write my own hopes, nor must I write my own fears.

'In the eighth house, we find the Sun and Mercury conjunct. This is the house of passion and secrets, also the house of death. Here it is ruled by Gemini, the twins, which may point to children. Mercury is the story-teller and messenger of the zodiac. It suggests there is a story yet to be told.'

'A story relating to me, her child? Or a story about her death?'

'Perhaps both.' She tapped her finger upon the chart. 'Mercury in Gemini is an attractive combination, but also fickle. It can sometimes figure infidelity or a secret tryst. If your parents eloped together, then that might explain it. Eighth house themes are often dark, but here the Sun may shine a light.'

'On the truth?'

'If that is what you seek, then I would take it to be a good omen. The ninth is the house of freedom, ruled here by Cancer, the sign of family. There is a discordance, which fits with what you have told me. Venus, Mars and Jupiter are all present here, a turbulent combination. Also the Dragon's Head, signifying destiny. Venus figures love and passion, Jupiter is the planet of material things, whereas Mars figures anger and war. I see conflict everywhere in this house.'

Passion, money, war. Apt words to describe the De Lacys' legal battles with their Seabrooke cousins.

'There are themes emerging in this chart,' Tamson went on. 'Secrets and death on the one hand, freedom and discovery on the other. The remaining houses are void, save for the moon in the twelfth house. The moon is the sign of the mother, and the twelfth house is a place of dreams and lost things. I see sadness here, I see a shadow.'

'The shadow of death?'

'I cannot say. It is a chart that evades certainty. The water element is everywhere. In Scorpio ascendant; in the strength of the ninth house, Cancer; the Moon in the twelfth house, the realm of Pisces. I feel the push and pull of the waves and the rage of the storm.' She gazed at me across the booth with those extraordinary blue eyes. 'You cannot catch water in your hands. It drains through the fingers.

There is something at the heart of this chart that evades and escapes, a mystery, a secret.'

Normally, I might have said that this was all very convenient. A reading like this, sprinkled with caveats, might apply to anyone. No doubt Archie Montfort would say that everyone had parents and secrets, and households without conflict were rare indeed. Most had love affairs, many had secret passions, death figured large over us all. And yet all the things I'd feared the most were figured here too. A dominant father-figure, passion, fear, rage. Was this the true story of my parents' marriage?

◆

I was still dwelling on it later that night in the Magpie's yard. Trade had been slow that day because of the magistrate, and everyone was talking about a poor tasseomancer who had been taken up by the constables. Frank bounded over to our group.

'Dance with me, Gwen. Come on, there's no harm in it.'

'I'll piss on your oysters before I'll dance with you.'

Seeing his face fall, wanting distraction from my morbid thoughts, I smiled up at him. 'I'll dance with you, Frank.'

It was the first time I had danced at the fair. The music was fast, the movement lawless – so different to the regulated steps of the Bath Assembly Rooms. I surrendered to the saw of the fiddle, the beat of the drum, laughing as Frank span me round and round. I glimpsed Tamson talking to Meg; Gwen and Naomi watching me, scowling. In that moment, I forgot everything: my grief, my resentments, even the question of my father's guilt or innocence.

When the music stopped, we applauded, breathless and perspiring. Frank pressed me to dance again, but, not wishing to give him the wrong idea, I declined.

'Where's Tamson?' I asked, as I rejoined our group.

Naomi eyed me coldly. 'Seeing to Meg.'

'What's wrong with Meg?'

Before she could reply, a shadow fell across us, and I looked up into the unhappy face of Morgan Trevithick.

'A word, my darling.'

I followed him out of the enclosure, into the Magpie. A few of the Cornish Players were drinking there, and at a nod from Morgan they vacated their table.

'Where were you today?' Morgan said, as we sat down. 'I expect everyone to be at their booth during fair hours.'

'With a private client.'

'You don't take private clients during the fair. That's stealing from me and my troupe.'

'I was going to give you half.' Reaching into my pocket for Mirabel's purse, I shook out three guineas and placed them on the table.

He eyed the gold greedily. 'You made three yellowboys in one day?'

'I made six. That's your half. Are we agreed that I can see my private clients whenever I want?'

Morgan grunted. 'Sounds fair to me.' He reached for the coins, but I swiftly covered them with my hand.

'There's another part to this bargain. Or I'll take my money, and you can give my pitch to someone else. I want you to tell me about my father.'

Morgan shook his head. 'Not this again.'

'I'm not lying to you,' I said. 'My father was John Jory Jago and my mother was Patience De Lacy.'

'Is that where these yellowboys came from? The De Lacys?'

'What do you care?'

Perhaps seeing the logic of my position, he grunted again. 'Take a walk with me, then, but don't go repeating what I say to anyone else. If Rowena thought for a moment that you really was John Jory's daughter, she'd want you out.' I lifted my hand from the gold, and he swept it into his pocket.

We walked up into the fair, the laughter of drunken revellers mingling with the stallholders' cries: 'Come buy my nuts and damsons and fine Burgamy pears!' 'Best pig and bottle-ale in the fair, sir.' 'Fine velvet caps.' 'Here's the German dwarf who paints!' 'See the elephant of Siam!'

'John Jory Jago and I first met at the St Ives fair,' Morgan said.

'I was in the card business then. Not fortunes, but Find-the-Lady. Some marketmen took exception to my talents, and John Jory took exception to the odds against me. Not that it made much difference. They beat and robbed us both. But John Jory had a yellowboy hidden in his boot, and as we drowned our sorrows that night, we founded the Cornish Players.' He grinned, a flash of gold tooth. 'Now those were good times.'

For the next few minutes, I listened to him talk about my father and the Players' golden days. The plays and operas, the audiences of up to a thousand, the actors and singers who came from France and Italy and Russia to join their troupe. 'We was making a small fortune, and so John Jory encouraged me to follow my dream. I went to Paris to learn to make automata at the workshop of the great Jean-Martin Hippolyte. Sometimes I wonder if things would have turned out differently if I hadn't gone. It was while I was in France, that John Jory took up with the De Lacys. He neglected the Players and we lost some of our best people. When I came back and saw how things stood, I wasn't happy.'

Pausing by a stall, he paid a farthing for an egg-pot of gin, and knocked it back. 'John Jory had made good money from the De Lacys – there was no denying that. He said we could make much more, that we should milk that prize-cow dry. I let him talk me round, dazzled by all that gold. I didn't realize then that John Jory was dazzled by something else.'

'My mother,' I said.

He gave me a look. 'If you say so. When I found out, I told him he was Bedlam-bound. Patience De Lacy was the granddaughter of an earl, for pity's sake. She wasn't about to marry a Cornish fortune teller. But he said she loved him, that he'd seen it in her cards. His moods had always been up and down, but I'd never seen him like this before. One minute low as a winter sun, the next high as the cross of Paul's. All he ever wanted to talk about was his precious Luna – that's what he called her. Then he refused to come on the road with me, saying he wanted to stay with the De Lacys. He said he'd be back once he'd made Luna his wife.'

We were on the fringes of the fair now, near the entrance to Cock Lane. Women in bright silks smiled at Morgan from the entrance of their booths. Each had a sign of a bird over the door, the so-called 'soiled doves' of the fair. 'Ease your comfort for a half-guinea, sir.' 'Come inside, have dinner.'

'What could I do?' Morgan said. 'I couldn't force him to come on the road, and I didn't want to lose him as a partner. I assumed when the girl laughed in his face, he'd crawl back, his tail between his legs. We wintered in Cornwall as usual, and in the spring, we headed back east for the charter fairs. We often camped at Tavistock and while we was there, John Jory paid me a visit. He was staying nearby, at the De Lacys' Devonshire estate, and he must have had someone watching out for us on the road. He said Luna had agreed to elope with him, but he needed two hundred pounds to fund their escape, and he only had half. Wanted to borrow the rest from me. After some wrangling, I lent him the money.'

'In exchange for *The Square of Sevens* as surety. Which you then sold to my grandfather's agent in Cambridge.'

He frowned. 'Who have you been talking to? Pierre, I suppose? Yes, I sold it. There's no shame in it. John Jory lied to me. Made me complicit in a crime.'

'You can't believe he really took her by force?'

Morgan spat on the ground. 'I don't know what I believe. I do know he was obsessed with her. He once told me he'd do anything to be with her.'

'Was she with him when you saw him after the elopement? When he threatened to kill you?'

He scowled. 'Pierre has got a loud mouth. Yes, she was with him. It must have been October month. We was in St Ives for the charter fair and I had a message from him asking to meet me in secret by an old boathouse we both knew. I thought about not going, but in the end I did. It was the first time I'd laid eyes on her. She was heavy with child, pale and sweating. I told John Jory that she should be in bed, but he said that all was well. That she had another two months to go and they intended to go to Ireland for the birth.'

'Did you see any evidence that she was there against her will?'

'She looked scared, was what I thought. But I couldn't tell if she was scared of John Jory, or of her father and what he might do if his agents caught up with them. John Jory said he didn't think they'd rest until he was dead. Which was why they had decided to go abroad. Only John Jory couldn't bear to leave his precious document behind him. He said he'd send the money to me as soon as he had it, which was some damn brass. We argued about it for a time, and in the end, to shut him up, I told him I'd sold it. Well, he called me every name you can imagine and threatened to stick me with his blade. The girl calmed him down, we exchanged some more hard words, and then they left. I never saw either one of them again.'

My mind was working furiously, still wondering when and how Father had stolen *The Square of Sevens* and the codicil from Nicholas De Lacy. Yet what did it matter, now that the codicil had been destroyed? The thought of my lost inheritance left a bitter taste in my mouth, but I forced myself to concentrate on the part that mattered most.

'I need to ask you about Tretelly,' I said. 'I've heard things here in London. The De Lacys say my father was a murderer.'

He nodded grimly. 'They say that in Tretelly too. There was a witness to the crime, the head-ostler at the inn where they was staying. He wouldn't talk to me. Nor the innkeeper. I suspect the De Lacys paid them off. But in a small place like that, word gets around.'

'Then you believe it?' My voice cracked.

He shook his head slowly. 'In the old days, I'd never have said John Jory would have been capable of such a wicked crime. But he was so different by then, mad with passion, angry at the De Lacys – and sometimes, yes, angry at her. I think they must have argued – perhaps she changed her mind and wanted to go home – and the thought of losing her drove him to the darkest place of all.'

Lights span around me. Feeling sick to my stomach, I forced the words out. 'What did he do to my mother? How did he kill her?'

Morgan frowned. 'Don't sport with me, my darling.'

'What sport? Just tell me the truth.'

He looked at me for a long time, his eyes narrowed with suspicion. 'You don't know?'

'I just said so, didn't I?'

Still with that odd expression on his face, he spoke with quiet deliberation: 'Patience De Lacy wasn't murdered, not by John Jory, nor anyone else. One of her father's agents caught up with them in Tretelly, not long after she'd given birth to a baby daughter. John Jory was already dead by then, jumped from the cliff, as I told you. The agent took her back to London, to the house of her uncle, the second Earl of Seabrooke. When the second earl died, she married her cousin, Peter, the third earl. She's been estranged from the rest of her family ever since.'

I stared at him. Lady Seabrooke. My mother was alive.

So many thoughts and emotions assailed me in that moment – and yet none of it made sense. Why hadn't Mrs Davenport told me that Lady Seabrooke was Julius De Lacy's sister? Or had she alluded to it, but in the midst of my misconceptions, I had paid it little heed? The newspapers had talked about Lady Seabrooke and mentioned a family at war, but I had presumed this was a reference to her husband's family. Something else confused me too. Hadn't Morgan just said he believed John Jory might be a murderer?

'If she isn't dead, then who is my father supposed to have killed?'

I was treated to another of his heavy-lidded stares. 'If you are who you say you are, my darling, then that would be you.'

CHAPTER EIGHT

*Ten of clubs, influenced by a spade: an inheritance, or a matter
needing much watchfulness and care when known.*

THE GRAND EATING Room at Hanover Square is forty feet
in length, painted a dismal shade of grey inexplicably named
Celadon Green. Seven marble gods and nymphs, plundered from
Sicily by the second Earl of Seabrooke, occupy niches around the
walls. Celebrated in its day as the pinnacle of gentlemanly taste, the
room stands now as a testament to hubris. There are discoloured
gaps between the exquisite plasterwork where Italian paintings once
hung. The shelves, filled in past times with Lamerie silverware and
Meissen china, now hold cheaper imitations. One of the goddesses
has a broken arm – and yet she's still standing. She reminds Lazarus
of the mistress of the house.

Lady Seabrooke has at last received him, but not alone. Her lawyers
sit around the table, ten of them, headed by the illustrious founding
partners of Molyneux, Godwin and Brooke. The Grandchild Codicil that Lazarus purchased from Henry Antrobus is now the subject
of a new suit that will be heard in the Prerogative Court in the new
term. If that document is found to be genuine, then fourteen-year-old
Leopold De Lacy, the fourth Earl of Seabrooke, stands to inherit an
estate said to value over half a million pounds. A folio of papers is
stacked in front of each man, the document they presently peruse a
copy of Lazarus's old testimony before the Prerogative Court in the

original suit of *Seabrooke v De Lacy* sixteen years earlier. They are all talking about him as if he isn't here.

'Julius De Lacy has been to see me,' he says, tiring of their chatter.

Eleven pairs of eyes swivel to face him. Hers are the ones he meets. 'He knows about my visits here. I believe you have a spy amongst your people.'

'There are spies all around me,' she says. 'There is no one I trust.'

The men bristle at the implication, Lazarus most of all.

'Your brother says if you do not withdraw your suit, he will destroy your reputation. His lawyers will paint you as a woman of low character and loose morals, who has lied about her past for years.'

She waves a dismissive hand. 'What can he say that is not already whispered in drawing rooms? Without evidence, the court will rule it out of hand.'

'He has evidence. A report concerning your elopement with John Jory Jago.'

'You believe it can hurt me?'

'I know it can,' Lazarus says. 'I wrote it.'

Her face twists in distress. 'Leopold,' she says.

Evidence laid before the court can be printed in the newspapers. Words whispered become words spoken aloud. At Eton, for instance, where Leopold currently studies. Boys can be unkind when it comes to the subject of mothers. Lazarus should know.

Aside from that fleeting flicker of emotion during their first meeting at Seabrooke House, this is the first evidence he has witnessed that she cares about anything other than the court case and destroying her brother. Almost immediately, she recomposes her features. She sees love as a weakness, he thinks – a vulnerability to be exploited by her enemies. Even in the old days, she'd been wary of her feelings – unlike her sister, Jemima, the great romantic.

'If this report is so damning, then why hasn't Julius used it before?' asks one of the lawyers, reasonably enough.

'He says out of deference to his mother.'

Lady Seabrooke gives a hollow laugh. 'Julius would slit Mother's throat, if he thought it would give him an advantage over me.'

'I think he's bluffing.' Lazarus has given the matter a lot of thought since Julius took him by surprise at Pontack's. 'The report might be damaging to your reputation, but it's also damaging to his own case. That's the real reason he's never used it before.'

She gazes at him impassively, but he can tell how much she wants to believe him. 'Elaborate,' she commands.

'On the same day your father received my report, he drafted the Grandchild Codicil. When I arrived at Leighfindell a few days later, he had it ready for us to sign. He didn't do so upon a whim, as George Montfort tried to claim in court, but because he'd just learned of the imminent birth of his first grandchild. I could say nothing of this in my first testimony, not without damaging your reputation, but if Julius chooses this path, then I'll tell them everything. About your father's buoyant mood, how the news seemed to dissipate his anger. How he called the child "a new beginning". He was convinced it would be a boy – wrongly, as it turns out.'

She turns away, and he suspects it's so that the lawyers won't see her flinch. 'None of this proves that Montfort lied when he said Father later destroyed that codicil,' she says.

'Maybe not,' Molyneux says. 'But it speaks powerfully to your father's motivation. And when you combine it with our other evidence, notably the large payment made by your brother to Mr Montfort only two days after his testimony, it all starts to paint a compelling picture.'

'Which is why I believe that Julius will think again,' Lazarus says. 'If his lawyers don't talk him out of it, then Septimus will. Even Julius won't risk his entire fortune for an act of revenge.'

Lady Seabrooke thinks for a moment, evidently reassured by this line of reasoning. 'What of the maid?' she asks the lawyers. 'The one who disappeared from Leighfindell around the time of my father's death?'

'We are making inquiries,' Molyneux says. 'Speaking to any servants we can find from your father's day. Mr Brooke believes he may have tracked down Jemmy Woodford.'

'The old pond-man at Leighfindell?' Lazarus says, giving the lawyer his full attention.

'That's right,' Brooke says, smiling rather immodestly. 'I have a man heading for Lancashire to talk to him as we speak. If anyone can give us some definitive answers about the maid, then it will be Woodford.'

'We will hear what Mr Woodford has to say,' Molyneux ventures cautiously. 'And yet we must take care not to muddy the waters.'

Lady Seabrooke arches an eyebrow. 'A rather callous metaphor, given the circumstances.'

'I concur,' Godwin says, addressing Molyneux. 'Even supposing this man Woodford tells us what we anticipate, it proves nothing of substance.'

'We don't need to prove anything,' the lady says. 'We only need to put Mr Woodford before the court. People will draw their own conclusions: that my brother is a liar and a cold-blooded killer.'

'But in so doing, we would raise a great many questions to which we don't presently have the answers,' Molyneux says. 'Not least how the codicil survived, and how it came to be in the possession of this scholar, Robert Antrobus. I counsel restraint, My Lady, when it comes to the subject of the maid. Victory is within your grasp. Mr De Lacy can say nothing to alter that.'

'And how it must enrage him.' She smiles slowly. 'Very well. But we keep Woodford and the maid in reserve. If this becomes a battle of character, then I won't submit without a fight. *Vincit qui patitur* – isn't that right, Mr Molyneux?'

The lawyer inclines his head. 'And we shall, My Lady.'

The point won, Godwin swiftly moves things along. 'Shall we return to Mr Darke's testimony?'

With a rustle, they all bend their heads to their folios.

'Etta,' Lazarus says.

Molyneux raises his head. 'I beg your pardon, Mr Darke?'

'That was her name. The maid. Her name was Etta.'

CHAPTER NINE

Two of spades as master-card:
you must say 'NO', when you would say 'YES'.

MY MOTHER WAS alive. My mother was Lady Seabrooke. Patience De Lacy. Luna. A woman I had believed to be my enemy, in all likelihood responsible for the corruption of Henry and the theft of the codicil.

'Tell me the rest.' My voice rose in impatience.

We had headed back into the fair, Trevithick halting next to the swinging chairs. As if he needed to be surrounded by lights and music, the excitement and joy of strangers, to talk about that terrible night in Tretelly.

'All I know is that the baby came early and John Jory took rooms at the Seven Stars, that's the name of the inn. The birth was difficult, I was told – a physician was called and Patience lost a lot of blood. But she survived and was delivered of a baby girl.' His eyes followed the course of a swinging chair, the shrieks of its occupants like the cries of carrion birds. 'A little later that night, in the midst of a great storm, John Jory took that child from her mother's arms, walked out of the inn to the edge of the cliff, and threw himself and the baby off it.'

'No. The man who saw it must have been mistaken. Or lying.'

'Nobody in Tretelly thinks so. The De Lacys don't think so.'

'Were any bodies ever found? There couldn't have been. So there you are.'

'Bodies wash up along the coast all the time – what's left of them.'

'Then that proves nothing.' I fell silent a moment, thinking. 'So my mother has always believed I died that night?'

Trevithick shook his head. 'If you're thinking about tears and reconciliation, you can forget it. The De Lacys aren't a sentimental breed.'

'But I'm her daughter.'

'Whether that's true or not, she didn't want John Jory and she didn't want his child.'

'You don't know that,' I cried.

'People heard them arguing that night. Why else would he kill his own baby except for revenge?'

'I'm telling you, he didn't.'

'Have it your way, then. Why did he take her child away from her? Deny you a mother?'

'I don't know.'

Hands upon his hips, he looked down at me. 'You've paid three yellowboys to hear this, and so I'll give it to you straight. If this is a fakement, then I doubt you'll ever see a penny from her. And if it's not – if you really are her daughter – then heed my words. The De Lacys are trouble. They'll chew you up and spit you out. I don't need a pack of cards to tell you that.'

♠

I barely slept and rose early, determined to act on everything I'd learned. Kerensa lent me an inkpot and paper, and I sat in her taproom composing a letter to my mother.

I had already decided against putting the truth into written words. Better that my mother should meet me in person, that she might gaze upon my face and see my sincerity when I broke the news. So I wrote that I'd heard of her interest in *The Square of Sevens*, and as a practitioner of that art, I wondered if she'd be interested in a private demonstration. I remembered from my last visit to London and my conversations with Mr Gowne that Lady Seabrooke lived in Hanover Square. I gave my corresponding address as the same coffeehouse on Fleet Street that I'd given to the De Lacys. Having signed and sealed the letter, I walked down there.

I'd visited the coffeehouse a few times since my visit to De Lacy House, to see if I'd had any correspondence from either Julius or Mirabel De Lacy. Fernando's was a respectable establishment of black timber and white plaster, a relic from the days before the Great Fire. Though ladies were generally discouraged from entering such places, Fernando's held periodic auctions of property, and there were usually one or two women sitting at the tables with their gentlemen of business. The coffeehouse's owner and namesake, a rotund Portuguese, greeted me with a nod of recognition. I passed him my letter, and he stowed it with the other mails to go out later that day. He also handed me a letter from his pigeonholes.

The large red wax seal held the imprint of a heart. Prising the paper apart, I broke it in two. Inside the enclosure was a card embossed with the De Lacy crest. My name and that of Mrs Illingworth were written across the top.

'I know a bank where the wild thyme blows,
Where oxslips and the nodding violet grows.'

Mrs Septimus De Lacy
requests the pleasure of your company
at a concert au jardin to celebrate the seventh birthday of

TITUS AND
ABSALOM DE LACY

22 August
at 2 o'clock

At De Lacy House, Piccadilly.
An answer is requested.

Two days ago, the invitation would have thrilled me. Today, even the De Lacys couldn't hold my attention for long.

Would my mother know me the moment she saw me? Would she even need to be convinced? Could I bring about a reconciliation between my mother and my grandmother? These were the questions that chased themselves around in my mind. To Morgan Trevithick's warnings, I gave very little thought at all.

CHAPTER TEN

Nine of clubs, influenced by a heart:
there is a wounding of tenderer feelings or relationship in it.

I WISH TO state quite clearly, in full knowledge of the accusations subsequently levelled against me, that my only thoughts at that moment were about my mother. Lady Seabrooke's suit could not have been further from my mind. Ever since Henry had stolen the codicil to give to Lazarus Darke, I'd presumed it had been destroyed. Had I thought a little more about the wider implications of my latest discovery, then perhaps I might have paused to question this assumption. But for years, my mother had been my driving obsession. How I'd longed to put a name to her lovely face. To discover that she had been alive all this time, that she too had wrongly believed me dead, was an event of such astonishing magnitude, I hardly stopped to think about anything else.

That night, when we were finishing up at the booth, Tamson said she needed to talk to Roland about something. I offered to wait, but she told me to go on ahead. Distracted, I walked through the crowds, imagining my first conversation with my mother. But as I entered the alley that led to the Magpie's yard, I glimpsed two shadowy figures ahead of me, which snapped me out of my reverie. My hand slipped into my pocket where I always carried the snakestone and stocking. Yet as the figures drew closer, I recognized Naomi and Gwen.

'Where are you going?' I asked, in some relief.

'We're looking for someone,' Gwen said.

'You.' Naomi pushed me hard against the wall. 'Shitten fuckstress.'

I stared at them, my blood rising. 'What's all this about?'

'What do you think?' Naomi said. 'Prancing about with Frank like that. Shaking your bubbies, letting him put his hands all over you.'

The unfairness of this accusation almost made me laugh. 'We were just dancing. And what's Frank to you anyway? You don't even like him.'

'Don't listen to her,' Naomi cried. 'Jacobites are always full of lies.'

I sighed wearily. 'I'm not a Jacobite.'

'You're a whore, though.' Gwen struck me hard on the shoulder.

Winding my hand around the stocking in my pocket, reassured by the hard ridges of the snakestone, I met her gaze. 'Do that again, and you'll be sorry.'

'She doesn't know.' We all turned at the familiar voice, and I glimpsed Tamson in the shadows behind me. 'Leave her alone. She doesn't know.'

'Know what?' I said.

'It isn't just Frank,' Gwen said. 'She's been off with Morgan too. Pierre saw them together last night, heading up towards Cock Lane. That how you convinced him to give you a pitch, eh? A hot little fumble in the dark?'

'Girl's common as a barber's chair,' Naomi said. 'One out, the other in.'

I addressed Tamson: 'We were just talking.'

I could see a flicker of doubt in her eyes. She and Rowena were friends, and she admired the older woman deeply. 'Why couldn't you talk down here in the yard?'

I hesitated, unable to think of a convincing lie, and in that pause, Tamson frowned. Gwen turned to say something to her and, seizing my chance, I pushed between my two assailants. Naomi caught hold of my arm, but I shoved her away. As I walked swiftly down the alley, I heard Tamson telling the others not to go after me.

I went upstairs to our room, where I lay in bed, my thoughts a feverish jumble. About an hour later, when Tamson came up, I tried to talk to her. 'I wasn't doing anything with Morgan. Not with Frank either.'

She regarded me solemnly in the half-light. 'I don't want to talk about it now. It's rather late.'

Stung by her refusal to believe me, I rolled over. Tamson undressed and climbed silently into bed. Telling myself that I had more important matters to worry about, I thought of all the things I'd tell my mother, all the lost time. Yet as I listened to Tamson breathe, her warm body lying inches away, I wished that her lack of faith in me didn't hurt so much.

For the second night in a row, I barely slept, rising at a little after six. Fernando's opened its doors at seven, and I was determined to be the first in line. Tamson was still asleep, her eyelashes fluttering against her cheek. I told myself I didn't care what she thought of me. She was just some fairground girl. I was the daughter of a dowager countess. Soon we would be reconciled. Then I'd never need to talk to any of the Cornish Players again.

On Fleet Street, the pamphleteers were out in force, thrusting their papers under my nose. '*JACOBITE CONSPIRACY*', '*Walpole's swine in the trough*', '*Toothache cured without drawing*'. When I presented myself at Fernando's counter, he gave me a long look.

'What is it?' I said.

He reached under his counter, then placed a pamphlet in front of me.

MISSING GIRL:
TEN POUNDS REWARD

MISS RACHEL ANTROBUS,
a young lady, run away from her home in Bath on
the night of August the third, while it is supposed
temporarily deranged in the mind. Presently believed
to be in London, Miss Antrobus is sixteen years old,

**five feet three inches tall, of slim stature,
a pale complexion and red hair.**

**Send information to Mr Henry Antrobus Esq.,
Trim Street, Bath.**

A chill wave of panic prickled my skin. I looked up and met Fernando's curious eyes. 'Two men give these out on street,' he said. 'I not let them come in here.'

'Fernando—'

'It not my business,' he said, turning away towards his pigeonholes.

My throat was dry. 'I'd have thought ten pounds would be anybody's business.'

He shrugged. 'There's good business and bad. I not like their faces. Be careful they not mistake you for this mad girl.'

I had been complacent in assuming that I could lose myself in London. What if the De Lacys happened to chance upon one of these pamphlets? Everyone else knew me only as Red, and yet I stood out at the fair as a lady. I resolved to powder my hair from now on and keep a close watch around me.

My gratitude towards Fernando increased when he laid a letter on his counter, the yellow seal stamped with a seven-pointed star. Breaking the seal eagerly, my spirits soared as I saw it was from my mother. The letter said that she was at home that evening and would be delighted to receive me – or otherwise at my earliest convenience. I pressed the letter to my lips, sick with nerves and excitement.

CHAPTER ELEVEN

Six of hearts, influenced by a spade: an inclination or desire, not wholly honourable, or of brief realization.

In an attempt to restore himself to the good graces of his employers, Lazarus spends the day looking into a man he suspects of staging a burglary in his jewellery shop. At a moneylender's on Oxford Street, he discovers that the man owes five hundred pounds, a small fortune he has almost certainly spent on his pretty mistress.

As he trudges wearily home, he reflects with some irony upon the things a foolish man will do for love. He thinks about the court case to come, the testimony he will give, what his employers will make of his role in this public scandal. Julius De Lacy's lawyers will try to discredit him in the eyes of the judge, naturally. They will say he is disgruntled, seeking revenge on his former master. They might even make allusions to his feelings for Lady Seabrooke. Yet did not the Prerogative Court once commend him for his honesty? His East India paymasters too used to remark upon his integrity, with a faint air of resentment, as if he made the rest of them look bad. Whereas Nicholas De Lacy had praised it, even as he judged it a weakness he didn't quite understand.

The truth is, Nicholas De Lacy didn't know the half of it.

Luna. Even her name is like the taste of something forbidden. Lazarus remembers those days as a slow descent into darkness, into a cavern filled with wondrous treasures and danger lurking under every rock. At first, he tries to ignore her flirtations, just as he ignores those of her sister, Jemima. The girls have more success with John Jory Jago, and all the young, perfumed fools who call at the house with eyes like thieves. They even flirt with George Montfort, who views them with a cold, contemptuous lust.

There is certainly much to admire, and Lazarus doesn't just mean their looks. Their wit, their rarity, the brightness with which they burn, the sense that you never quite knew what they were thinking. Jemima is fond of the sort of novels that the newspapers despise. She listens to her suitors talk about themselves, and her replies make them feel like the conquerors of worlds. Luna is the clever one. She can debate a point of principle for hours, often to enraging effect. Fast with a quip or observation, she strikes a man wherever he is most vulnerable. Men desire Luna – and her father's fortune naturally – but Jemima is the one they fall in love with. All except John Jory Jago and Lazarus Darke.

When Lazarus catches himself watching her, he feels only disgust. Because of her age – she is sixteen, a gap of three years that feels significant. Because of his position of trust in the household. Because he doesn't want to be predictable like the perfumed peacocks, or disrespectful like George Montfort, or troubling like John Jory Jago.

He refuses to take part in her games. He'll fetch a parasol when requested, even if it isn't fit work for a secretary, but he never joins a hand of quadrille, or presents his palm to be read on demand. This wall preserves him – until the day it is breached asunder.

It is nine months since he began working for Nicholas De Lacy. Death has yet to tear the family apart with his cold scissor-claws. There are whispers that Jemima is in love. That her father does not approve. She is at the family's new estate of Leighfindell with her father and brothers, but Mirabel has remained in London with Luna. Lazarus too has been kept in the city on De Lacy business.

The library is the largest room in De Lacy House. Some say it is the third largest room in England. The bookcases are by Hawksmoor, the fireplaces and overmantels carved by Gibbons, and the ceiling painted by Thornhill with scenes of Caesar entering Rome.

The painting is allegorical, Caesar's bulbous blue eyes and sharp nose closely resembling those of King George the First. As Lazarus peruses the shelves, seeking a volume, he hears a sob. He follows it to its source: a little reading nook in one of the two octagonal towers to the rear of the house. Luna is curled up on a window seat, a discarded book by her hand. Her fist is pressed to her forehead, red ringlets shielding her face. She looks up, startled, and he catches a glimpse of her reddened eyes.

'Forgive me.' He turns to go.

'Wait.'

And of course he does, passing her a handkerchief. 'Why are you crying?'

She wipes her eyes, straightens her skirts. 'Father means to send my tutor away and not replace him.'

He doesn't ask why. Nicholas De Lacy doesn't need reasons to torment his children. Family, to his master, is one long competition – for his affection, for his money, for the right to be kicked, then praised, then kicked again. Success is rewarded, failure is punished. A diamond bracelet or a new hunter; a favourite servant dismissed or a pet dog shot.

'Do you know Descartes?' Luna asks, indicating her volume.

'Of course.'

'Will you talk to me about him sometime? Because my Latin . . .' She makes a gesture.

'Can't you ask one of your gentlemen callers?'

'I'm asking you.'

'If I have time.' Meaning not on your life.

She rises, her hand trailing down the spines of the volumes on the shelves. 'Descartes says if a person cannot follow what is true, then he should follow what is probable. Do you believe that?'

'It is a path that will take one closer to the truth.'

She smiles wryly. 'What is truth?'

'For that you'll have to read Francis Bacon. Or the Bible.'

'I already have. Bacon says truth is the daughter of time, not authority. I don't believe that. When powerful men die, their lies still endure.'

The thought offends him, even as he wonders if she might be right. 'Well, I'd better get along.' He holds out his hand for the handkerchief.

'You won't tell my father, will you?' She presses it into his palm, still warm from her hot tears. 'That you found me like this?'

'I won't tell a soul.'

Before he knows what she is doing, she stands on tiptoe to plant a kiss upon his cheek. Her lips are soft, her skin damp, her eyes very bright. He makes no effort to narrow the gap between them, merely surveys the wreckage of his defences.

CHAPTER TWELVE

Queen of spades as master-card:
a female enemy, evil-wishing or evil-working.

ONCE AGAIN, I was standing on that clifftop. One leap and my life might change for ever. The hackney carriage turned into Hanover Square, and I peered from the window, the mansions of Mayfair aglow like ornate lanterns in the dusk. Seeking employment for my slick palms, I smoothed my petticoats. That afternoon, I'd spent nearly all my money on a new gown of striped blue-and-cream silk, determined to appear respectable when I met my mother. It had been hastily altered to fit, and the carriage smelled faintly of vomit, but three guineas didn't buy you made-to-measure and a coach-and-six.

The carriage rolled to a gentle halt outside Seabrooke House. My stomach was a swill, my forehead damp. As I stepped down from the vehicle, the ground seemed to shift beneath my feet. The skies were clear, but I could taste the metallic edge of the storm. Then I was at the door, banging the knocker, dull claps like thunder.

The footman was clearly expecting me. He showed me into an anteroom decorated with green marble pillars, where he asked me to wait. Scuffing a broken patch of marble with the toe of my slipper, I surveyed the faded grandeur around me.

The footman shortly returned and informed me that Lady Seabrooke would receive me in her card room. We walked down a long corridor to a small oval room, where a lady seated at a faro table rose to greet me.

'Miss Rachel Antrobus of Bath,' the footman announced. 'The Right Honourable Dowager Countess of Seabrooke.'

I stared mutely, taking in my mother's pale flawless skin, the feline curves of her small skull, her narrow blue eyes. She was still only thirty-five years of age, but she might have passed for even younger. Her red hair was concealed beneath a tall, white wig, and I searched in vain for other similarities between us. In my youth, when I'd studied the miniature, I'd told myself that portraits were always exaggerated in their perfection. But I saw now that it was the miniature which had failed to do justice to its subject. I struggled to imagine how anyone would believe that I was the daughter of this perfect creature – it made the task before me seem all the more daunting.

'It is an honour, My Lady,' I stammered.

She smiled, not very warmly. 'Do sit down.'

More footmen appeared. One pulled out my chair, another poured wine, another presented me with a pack of cards on a silver tray. 'I have many questions to ask you,' my mother said. 'Principally regarding the document owned by your late guardian that was burned in the fire.' She scrutinized my face. 'If you are surprised by the extent of my knowledge, I will tell you that the Square of Sevens has long been the subject of my close interest and study. But before we discuss it further, I should like you to tell my fortune.'

Feeling like a simpleton, I could only murmur again that it would be an honour.

'I am sure you have heard of my legal battles against my family,' she said. 'You will learn with little astonishment that I wish to consult the cards about that great matter.'

Following her gaze, I saw that the walls of the room were pasted with articles clipped from newspapers. All related to the various suits of *Seabrooke v De Lacy*. Some dated back years, to when the second Earl of Seabrooke was still alive. Others were much more recent, an obsession undiminished even by the deaths of those who'd nourished it.

'Well?' my mother said. 'Am I to grow as old as Noah's wife before we begin?'

All the words I'd so carefully practised had dried on my tongue. Trying desperately to gather my thoughts, I picked up the pack of cards. Tell her fortune, I thought, and I'd have time to compose myself. The moment would arise naturally, and the words would all come back.

The black cards in the parallelogram I laid that day figured enemies and opposition at every turn. Even several of the red cards were ominous in aspect.

'The knave of diamonds, influenced by a club,' I said. 'This card figures a sudden discovery about a person. I see a wounding of feelings here, and also acts of manoeuvre. These cards suggest you have fallen victim to a deception.'

'A spy?' she said sharply. 'I am constantly vigilant against them.'

I hesitated, hearing Father's voice down the years: *figure it large.* 'Not a spy, I don't think. I see change figured here. Trust taking the place of deceit. There is a turbulent past in this fortune, leading to a reconciliation. Perhaps a family member? Someone whose love has been denied you?'

'I don't want reconciliation. I want to win.' She frowned. 'I see the final master is the eight of diamonds, the unlucky red card. The man who first showed me the Square of Sevens told me it was the unluckiest card of all.'

'That is true,' I said, carefully, 'but the misfortune figured there may relate to the original deception, rather than to the revelation of its falsity.'

'What deception?' she said, rather crossly. 'What has this got to do with my suit of law? I must see the wish-cards. Are they high?'

She snatched them up from the table and turned them over. The cards were high indeed, though all of them black. 'Your wish must be for somebody else,' I said, 'but it will be granted.'

My mother let out a long breath. 'My son, Leopold. All I ever wanted was his happiness.' Seemingly content again, she savoured a sip of wine, considering the cards on the table with a mellowed expression. 'You have a true gift, Miss Antrobus. I applaud it. Did you learn this method from your guardian's document?'

'I studied it often, but I also had a worthy tutor in my youth.'

'Indeed? I am curious to learn all about it. Most of all I'd like to know how this document came into your guardian's possession in the first place.'

No more delays, no obfuscations, no more lies. 'It was given to Mr Antrobus by my father, a Cornish cunning-man. He was the tutor to whom I just referred.'

She frowned. 'A cunning-man, you say?'

Even now, I don't know how I forced the words out. My days on the road. My father's death. Mr Antrobus. Bath. Julius De Lacy. The Bartholomew Fair. My quest to find the truth about my mother.

As I spoke, her imperious mask cracked. Emotions chased across her face: confusion, distress, fear. I reminded myself that the day of my birth must have been the worst day of her life. To have her child taken from her arms after labour. To believe her daughter murdered by the man she'd loved. As the truth spilled from my lips, I watched in vain for the softening gaze of motherly tenderness.

'Just two nights ago, I learned the truth,' I concluded hesitantly. 'That my mother had not died in Cornwall, but had returned to London alive. My Lady, my mother – may I call you that?'

Still she stared at me in apparent horror. Then her lips contorted into a vicious snarl. 'Lies,' she said. 'All of it lies. My lawyers warned me that something like this might happen. Of course, you would have known that I bought the codicil.'

'This has nothing to do with the codicil,' I said.

'Don't take me for a fool, girl. That codicil bequeaths a vast fortune to the eldest grandchild of Nicholas De Lacy: my son, Leopold. And now here you are claiming to be my long-lost child.'

'I didn't know,' I cried. 'I'd assumed you'd destroyed it. All I desire is to know you as a mother.'

'How dare you call me that?' Her eyes burned with contempt. 'You may have picked up a few crumbs of gossip about my past in whatever middling salons you frequent, but if you repeat this laughable claim in public, then you will be sorry.'

I hastened to reassure her. 'I understand why you have always sought to keep the truth out of the public realm. Especially as you believed that I was dead. Our reconciliation can be a private affair. There is no need for this to damage your reputation.'

Immediately, I saw that I had said the wrong thing. She rose to her feet, scattering the cards from the table. 'Blackmail, is it now? Well, know this, Miss Antrobus: you cannot be my daughter, because there was no daughter and no elopement. I reject your claim utterly, do you hear?'

'But we both know that isn't true,' I protested. Taking out the locket, I opened it to show her. 'My father treasured this. Later, I did too. I kissed you every night before I went to sleep.'

She took it from me, glanced at it, then tossed it back across the table. 'My sister, Jemima. My father had at least a dozen copies painted after she died. He gave them to everyone who'd known her. Her friends, even her servants. Where did you pick this one up? In a pawnshop?'

'It was in my father's portmanteau. The codicil was there too, together with *The Square of Sevens*, and other things that you'd once owned.'

She gave a hollow laugh. 'It will take more than a family trinket and a head of red hair to scare me. I'll pay you nothing. Do you understand me?'

I rose from the table to face her. To my shame, my voice faltered. 'I don't want money. Please, you are my mother. You have to believe me. I will prove it.'

Her hand cracked across my face and I cried out. But the sting was nothing compared to the pain she inflicted next.

'Let us suppose for one moment that by some miscarriage of justice a court believed your lies – about this elopement, my supposed child, about your risible claim. You would still be entitled to nothing, do you hear? *Lawfully begotten*, those are the words in that codicil, and a forced marriage to a monster has no basis in law.'

'My father was not a monster,' I cried.

She rang a bell for her footman, fixing me with an expression as chill as a blackthorn winter. 'Persist with these lies and I will make you suffer. I will make you wish that you had never been born.'

In that moment, hearing those cruel words from my mother's lips, I already did.

Chapter Thirteen

Knave of hearts, influenced by a club:
a friend of judgement and good at advice.

BLACK-BEARD AND GREEN-COAT visited my dreams again that night. Like wraiths, they fed upon my distress. Green-Coat had hold of me, crushing the air out of me. Black-Beard was slamming Mrs Fremantle's head against the floor again and again. I wanted desperately to shout out, to tell him not to hurt her, but I couldn't breathe. Twisting violently, I pulled away, but Green-Coat wrestled with me, trying to keep me close. I fought, struggling against him, until Tamson's voice broke through my terror. 'Red, it's me. It's just a bad dream.'

She had her arms around me, and I allowed her to lean me back onto the bolster. The sheets were damp with sweat, a shaft of moonlight silvering Tamson's concerned face. She stroked my hair back from my forehead. 'You were crying for your mother.'

I took a breath, and it came out as a wrenching sob. 'Here,' Tamson said, drawing me close again. She pulled up the blanket and stroked my hair, making soothing noises. It had been so long since anyone had laid a comforting hand upon me. I closed my eyes, not wanting to sleep, not wanting to wake.

In the morning, Tamson and I walked up to the booth together. I kept my eyes upon the ground, embarrassed to look at her after my histrionics in the night.

'I want to talk to you,' she said. 'It's about Frank.'

Despite everything else, I hadn't forgotten our quarrel. 'I don't care about Frank. I never did.'

'I know.'

'You didn't before.'

'I wasn't sure then. I am now.'

I lifted my tired gaze to the sky. 'What made you change your mind?'

She shrugged. 'I just thought about it more. It didn't seem like something you would do.'

'That's an apology, is it?'

She smiled. 'I'm sorry. But you can't blame me entirely. You're up to something, Red. I know you are.'

I watched the gulls soar overhead, trying not to think about my mother.

'Going off all the time, the Lord knows where. Rowena says you're giving money to Morgan, a lot of money. And you were doing something with him the other night that you didn't want the rest of us to know about.' She held up a hand. 'I don't mean that. But it was something.'

I hesitated, on the brink of telling her everything. And yet after last night, I hardly knew where to start. My mother's words still cut me to the quick. Little wonder that my father had taken me away from her. If I never laid eyes on that cruel, cold-hearted woman again, I would be content.

Yet the news that the codicil had survived threw up further problems. How could I possibly declare myself to the other De Lacys now? They would surely react like my mother, suspecting I'd come to cheat them out of their money. I wasn't sure that I could bear any more rejection. But what else could I do?

I would never go back to Henry and Bath, but I supposed I could earn my living telling fortunes. I could go on the road like the old days, perhaps with Tamson and the Cornish Players.

Yet amidst these thoughts of an itinerant life, another possibility wormed its way into my mind. If I really was the rightful heir, then why shouldn't I lay claim to my fortune? My grandfather had meant his money to come to me. The very idea made my pulse race with excitement. With all that money, I'd need nobody. Not my mother, not Julius De Lacy, not Henry, nor any other man. Like Don Quixote's Marcella, I'd be the mistress of my own destiny. But rich.

'Don't tell me, then,' Tamson broke in upon my thoughts. 'Just be careful, Red. Whatever it is.'

'Be more worried about Naomi and Gwen,' I said, wanting to change the subject. 'I won't be hit by them again. They'd better watch out.'

'I've already spoken to them. Naomi won't give you any more trouble.'

'And Gwen?'

She gave a crooked smile. 'The thing you have to understand about Gwen is that she's bloody to everyone. You would be too, if you thought every nosebleed was caused by a tumour.'

'If she comes near me again, I'll give her a nosebleed.'

'I don't think she will. She was just worried about Meg.'

'What did I ever do to Meg?'

'She's married to Frank. That's what I wanted to explain.'

'Married?' I turned to look at her. 'Why didn't you tell me before?'

'He doesn't like strangers to know. Not any more.'

I thought of Meg's ruined face and her simple smile. Frank and his dumb-bells, his clumsy flirting.

We had arrived at the booth, and while we removed the dying flowers from their baskets, Tamson told me all about it. 'I don't think I ever saw two people as much in love as Meg and Frank. He loves her still, I don't doubt it. It was only a Player's marriage, nothing bound him to her legally. He could have walked away, but he's still here. It's not easy for him, though. It doesn't feel right to him to treat her like a wife – which makes him angry, so he loses himself in drink. Sometimes he likes to dance with other girls, and sometimes he likes more. Meg doesn't understand much, but she understands that.'

I shook my head, contemplating the bleakness of this tale. 'I'd never have danced with him, if I'd known. I'll not do it again.'

Tamson sighed. 'It's not a solution though, is it? To any of it. I hate him. Not Frank, the magistrate. I'll never understand the evil in people's hearts.'

'You said it before, they're afraid of us,' I said. 'In the old days, the authorities believed our powers came from the devil. They tortured and burned us to death for being witches. Now they don't believe any more, but they punish us anyway. They say it's for tricking folk, but I think it's because people listen to us as much as them.'

She gave me a sidelong glance. 'Some of us do trick folk, though, don't we? Tell me you've stopped all that. I don't ever want to see you wind up in the pillory like Meg.'

'I'm more than a match for that magistrate,' I said, sitting down at my table.

Tamson gazed at me unhappily, but her reply was forestalled by the arrival of our first customer. 'Do you seek your destiny in the stars, sir,' she asked, 'or in the cards? A shilling will buy you a fortune or a natal chart.'

'Here's half a crown,' the gentleman said. 'I want you to disappear for half an hour, so I can talk to your friend.'

Tamson gave me an uncertain look, but I was glaring at the gentleman, my anger rising.

He was wearing a soft blue coat and hat, each embroidered with silver thread, and a silver small-sword upon his left hip. Examining me with his shrewd, dark eyes, he gave a formal bow and introduced himself.

I already knew his name: Lazarus Darke.

CHAPTER FOURTEEN

Six of clubs, influenced by a spade:
a sudden opposition.

THE ANGLO-INDIAN GIRL exchanges a few quiet words with Red, and Lazarus waits while she leaves. Red gives him a hard stare as he sits down.

'I was very sorry to hear of the death of your guardian, Miss Antrobus.'

'My name is Red. How can you say that, when all you ever did was threaten him?' Her face is taut and angry. There is a slight resemblance to the De Lacys, and it isn't just the hair. Not much, but it's there.

'That is not how I recall it.' His tone is gentle. 'A phrase about ravens chiding blackness comes to mind.'

'Who have I threatened?'

'Why, Lady Seabrooke, of course. You surely understand the consequences of your claim?'

'All I have said is that I am her daughter.'

And therein lies the problem. Lady Seabrooke had sent for him late last night. He'd found her pacing the salon, wild-eyed. 'A girl came to see me. She claims to be my dead daughter. She says John Jory never jumped from the cliff, that he raised her alone in Cornwall. This is a threat, Lazarus. A shot across my bows.'

'Did she ask for money?'

'She didn't need to.' Lazarus listens as Lady Seabrooke recounts the story. The girl's claim is extraordinary, an elaborate work of fiction that he struggles to take seriously. Yet Lady Seabrooke believes victory is at last within her grasp, and she is terrified of anything that might upset that balance.

'I saw her in Bath when I first approached Antrobus,' he says. 'She was listening at the door. I suppose she heard the Cornish part of the story in Bath.'

Lady Seabrooke is ahead of him. 'When Antrobus found the codicil, she must have glimpsed an opportunity. She is about the right age and looks the part, more or less. She had one of Jemima's miniatures. Do you remember them?'

Lazarus has one himself somewhere. The original was painted on ivory by Bernard Lens, Nicholas De Lacy's idea of grief to transform his dead daughter into a valuable possession. Much as he'd treated her when she was alive.

'I will take care of it,' Lazarus tells her.

And so he has come here to the Bartholomew Fair, home of liars and tricksters, conjurors and three-card-trick men who seduce the unwary with their games of chance. He is here to show the girl that this is a game she cannot win. Not unless she plays by his rules.

'I am surprised to find you living here like this,' he says. 'Am I to presume that your guardian's death left you in straitened circumstances? Henry surely did not turn you out?'

She lifts her chin. 'I left of my own accord. I wanted to find my mother's family. Was it you who brought her back from Cornwall after the elopement? I heard it was one of my grandfather's agents.'

He can see that she knows too much to be satisfied by an outright denial, but he chooses his words carefully. 'If Lady Seabrooke were ever forced to give an account of that distressing episode in court, she will maintain that whilst lost in the madness of grief, she was kidnapped from her home and forced to submit to a sham of a marriage out of fear for her life. She will prove that the daughter born of that crime died at the hands of John Jory Jago, but even if she had survived, the marriage of her parents was unlawful. She would have no claim at all to the De Lacy fortune.'

'So she told me. Except we both know that it's a lie.'

'Lies are a topic you seem to know a great deal about.' He meets her gaze. 'You don't seem like a cruel woman, Miss Antrobus. Why would you want to put a lady you barely know through such a painful and distressing experience to no good end?'

She studies his face. 'You care about her,' she says, sounding interested.

Before he can refute the allegation, her expression hardens. 'She might lie to the world, but she cannot lie to me. My father was a good man. Not a rapist. Not a murderer. And my mother can't wish me away. I will not let her.'

Lazarus is intrigued by her anger. It makes him wonder what lies behind it. Antrobus's death, he presumes. Perhaps also his dealings with Henry over the codicil.

'Will you tell me your story?' he says. 'Let me ask you some questions?'

'So you can try to prove me a liar?' Her glare might start fires.

'If you're telling me the truth, then I won't succeed.'

'That's right. You won't.' Her gaze falls on her pack of cards. 'Only if I can tell your fortune.'

Whatever will get her talking. 'Very well.'

She smiles, rather slyly, as she shuffles the pack. 'Do you have a question for the cards? A matter of the heart? Or of money?'

'I'm afraid I don't believe in all that nonsense.'

'You don't believe in the cards, you don't believe in me. Is there anything you do believe in, Mr Darke?'

'The truth,' he says, aware that it makes him sound rather pompous.

'Who died and made you pope?' Her smile curves. 'In that case, I shall ask a question on your behalf. Will Mr Darke obtain his heart's desire?'

At her urging, he takes three wish-cards from the pack and places them upon the table. As she starts to lay her arrangement of cards, a memory rises. Two red heads bent over a card table, John Jory Jago's tangled black curls. A golden heart pressed to the rogue's lips, his own heart pierced by a sharp spike of jealousy.

'Let's start with Cornwall,' he says. 'Your childhood, your father. Anything you remember.'

She tells him a tale about life on the road: father and daughter, reading charts and cards, sleeping in hay wains and barns, defrauding simple country-folk. It is rich in detail, light on facts. He reminds himself that Antrobus wrote books about such people – about folk traditions like piskies and Joan the Wad. The girl could easily have researched it.

'I knew hunger,' she says. 'I knew the discomfort of a ditch at night. But I also knew the warmth of a father's love.'

He asks her about her first meeting with Robert Antrobus, and she tells him about her father's death, his golden heart charm, and her move to Bath. She displays emotion in all the right places, wearing it well, but not too well. He wonders if she ever made a living upon the stage.

'When did you decide that Lady Seabrooke was your mother?'

'I didn't *decide* it. I worked it out.' She tells him about the portmanteau and the things she supposedly found inside it, how they led her to the house of Lady Seabrooke.

When he pauses to compose his next question, she points to the first card in his fortune. 'The four of spades, influenced by a club. It figures a loss.'

He gives her a wry smile. 'Lady Seabrooke's loss, I suppose?'

She only points to the next card. 'Three of clubs, influenced by like suit. A choice of two things, both desired much, but one to be dismissed.'

She is watching him, just as John Jory Jago used to do when he told fortunes, looking for any sign of human weakness to exploit. But two can play that game, and Lazarus will play it better.

'Do you really expect me to believe that you didn't know Lady Seabrooke was Patience De Lacy until three days ago? All that time you spent up in the attic reading newspapers?'

'I wasn't interested in the Seabrooke side of the family. Nor the legal suits.'

'Nobody in Bath society ever mentioned it?'

'People don't gossip in Bath. Mr Nash deplores it.'

'People gossip everywhere.'

She frowns. 'I tried to get people to tell me about the De Lacys, but I didn't ask the right questions, I suppose. Don't forget, I believed that my mother was dead.'

'Let's return to your father. Is there anyone who can corroborate your claim that he lived for another seven years after everyone assumed him dead?'

'How could they? I told you he used a different name. Hid from the world.'

'Someone must remember the pair of you on the road? A cunning-man and his red-haired daughter?'

'I would think so.'

'So give me the name of a place. A date when you were there.'

'I was very young. I don't remember.'

'You remember Tretelly well enough.'

'The place, not the name. Morgan Trevithick told me.'

Lazarus remembers Trevithick. He had dealings with him in Cambridge, when he was searching the country for Luna. A canny, covetous fellow, unlikely to be motivated by sentiment.

She rattles off another reading, and then comes to a card she likes. 'Three of spades, influenced by a heart. A failure.' She smiles, as if the failure is surely his.

'Strange,' Lazarus says, 'that your scheme should be figured so starkly in my cards. Can anyone corroborate your first meeting with Mr Antrobus at the inn?'

'He was in Cornwall seeing to the affairs of his late cousin, Mr Williams. There will be a record in the court of probate.'

'I don't doubt that he was in Cornwall. I'm interested in his meeting with John Jory Jago.'

She thinks. 'You could talk to the innkeeper. His name was Chenoweth.'

Lazarus remembers Chenoweth too, a man who could have taught Morgan Trevithick a thing or two about venality and acquisition. For many years, Chenoweth had received a pension from the third Earl of Seabrooke to forget he'd ever met John Jory Jago and his child bride. 'Chenoweth died two years ago,' Lazarus says. Something the girl could have easily discovered by writing to the parish priest or the town physician or some other local worthy. 'How about Mr Antrobus's coachman?'

'He always used a hired carriage. I suppose the driver or the guard might remember.'

'Do you know their names?'

'No, why would I?'

'How about the names of the people who came to take you to the orphanage?'

'Mrs Sandbach,' she says, after a moment's thought. 'Her assistant was called Edward.'

'Was this orphanage local to Tretelly?'

'I don't think so. Mr Chenoweth wrote to them and they took four days to arrive.'

Which means this orphanage could be just about anywhere in Devon, or Cornwall, or even Somerset. It is, shall we say, rather convenient. 'Do you remember the name of the doctor who examined your father at the inn?'

'Kilderbee,' she declares, rather triumphantly. 'I don't remember much about him, except that he was old. I expect he'll remember us, if he's still alive.'

So it goes on. Lazarus asking questions, the girl parrying with her answers. If he ever pauses for thought or breath, she leaps in with her damn fortune, taking great delight in any adverse cards. 'A hindrance.' 'A grievance.' 'A fall.'

Eventually, he sits back. 'There are so many holes in your story, I could sell it to a Switzer for a cheese. I know Mr Antrobus liked to purchase collections of papers from the archives of dead scholars. I think that's how he acquired the document tube and *The Square of Sevens*. When you discovered the codicil concealed inside it, you started asking questions about the De Lacys. Perhaps you planned to sell it to them or to Lady Seabrooke, but Henry found it and sold it first. You were angry, you sought revenge, and you remembered how that old man in Bath had mistaken you for a De Lacy. You'd heard gossip about Lady Seabrooke, rumours of a dead child, and thus your scheme fell into place.'

'That isn't true. I was asking questions about the De Lacys long before I ever found the codicil. Then after Henry stole it, I thought it had been destroyed. I didn't know differently until my mother told me.'

'And now?'

Her eyes flash. 'If I am entitled to that money, then why shouldn't I claim it?'

She cannot seriously hope to succeed. Blackmail must be her motivation. Lazarus is loath to reward her efforts, but a pragmatic approach might save everyone a lot of trouble.

'If it's money you need, then perhaps we might come to an arrangement.' Reaching inside his coat, he produces a banknote to the value of fifty pounds. He lays it in front of her, alongside a document hastily drawn up by Lady Seabrooke's lawyers earlier that morning. The girl eyes it as if it might bite her.

'Lady Seabrooke, upon my counsel, is prepared to offer you this sum, on condition that you sign this paper renouncing your claim that you are her child.'

'You want me to lie?'

'We can call it that if you wish.'

'I won't do it.'

'Think carefully,' he urges. 'Lady Seabrooke's lawyers will question you in court, without the nicety that I have shown today. They will go after your character, your reputation, and they will prove you to be a liar. You might end up in prison for perjury, and don't imagine that is the only danger you face.'

'Are you threatening me, Mr Darke?'

'I merely remind you that you are playing for very high stakes. Do you remember the burglary at your house in Bath? Your housekeeper was killed?'

She frowns. 'Of course I remember. It had nothing to do with any of this.'

'Are you sure?'

'It was only when Mr Antrobus sought to publish *The Square of Sevens* that people learned of our link to the De Lacys. That was after Mrs Fremantle's murder.'

'That was when *I* took an interest, certainly. But someone else might have discovered it sooner. You were telling your fortunes openly, using this long-lost method. You were asking questions about the De Lacys all over town. Someone with knowledge of the facts could have easily surmised a connection between you and the codicil. Your guardian had *The Square of Sevens* on display in his cabinet, after all.'

'You mean Julius De Lacy?' She shakes her head. 'He doesn't know who I am.'

'Someone does. A third party is my best guess. That codicil was worth a lot of money to the right person. Lady Seabrooke was willing to pay a small fortune to get her hands on it. Julius De Lacy would likely have paid much more to see it destroyed.'

The colour has drained from her face. It's the first time he's seen her unsettled, and he presses home his advantage. 'I can be a friend to you,' he says. 'Help you extricate yourself from all this mess.'

'This mess is my life,' she says quietly. 'None of it was of my own making. I'll not lie any more. Especially for her.'

Sometimes people need a little time to change their minds. Lazarus returns the banknote and the document to his pocket, putting his calling card on the table in their place. 'Think on it,' he says. 'You can find me here.'

He rises, and she gazes up at him sullenly. 'Don't you want to see your wish-cards?' She flips them over with her finger. The two of clubs, the two of hearts, and the two of diamonds.

'Your heart's desire,' she says. 'Whatever it is, you won't obtain it. You will fail utterly.'

Lazarus has known that for nearly twenty years. 'That makes two of us,' is his rather peevish response.

CHAPTER FIFTEEN

Three of spades as master-card:
a suddenly changed plan, a discomfiture.

I REFUSE TO repeat all the vile accusations that Lazarus Darke made to me that day at the fair. Suffice to say, he slandered me in every way imaginable: calling me a liar, ascribing venal motives to my actions, trying to trick and trip me at every turn.

After he had gone, I kept hearing my own rejoinder: *If I am entitled to that money, then why shouldn't I claim it?*

Easy words to say. My words had come out in an angry flood. The false calumnies against my father, the threats and cruel taunts of Lady Seabrooke, now Lazarus Darke. I would make them sorry for it all. I would make them pay.

Yet how to go about it, when I had not the first notion of the workings of the Prerogative Court? I knew Darke was right to say I'd need proof of my claims. I would also need money. Mrs Davenport had told me that Lady Seabrooke's lawsuits had cost her nearly all her fortune (I refused to think of her any more as my mother). I didn't know the cost of a good lawyer, but I imagined I would need many hundreds of pounds.

Refusing to be daunted by the scale of the task ahead of me, I recalled how on my last visit to De Lacy House, Mirabel had started to open up to me about the elopement. Stay close to my family, I reasoned, and I might unearth the evidence I sought. Which meant concealing my true identity. The audacity of the idea left me quite breathless, and yet I also felt it could work. Julius De Lacy didn't seem to know that Lady Seabrooke had acquired the codicil from Henry Antrobus, or he'd never have let me through his door. Even Archie Montfort, who thought me a fraud, did not begin to suspect the true nature of my deception. The De Lacys' estrangement from Lady Seabrooke meant they were unlikely to hear about me from that quarter. Nor were they likely to guess who I was. Everyone was convinced that I'd been dead for many years.

I would be lying if I said that the prospect of deceiving the De Lacys and taking their money did not give me a moment or two of moral qualm. But I reminded myself that Julius had almost certainly told lies in court to obtain my money under false pretences. I also reasoned that when I inherited my fortune, I would be in a position to help those members of my family who merited my largesse. Mirabel, certainly. Emily, perhaps. Archie Montfort could beg on the street for all I cared.

Lazarus Darke's warnings also occasioned me some concern. In refusing his offer of a bribe, I had made Lady Seabrooke my enemy. I had already experienced her vindictiveness and Darke's machinations for myself. He might write to Henry and tell him where I was. I cursed myself for telling Lady Seabrooke about the fair.

Yet I dwelled most of all, not on my present situation, but on Darke's suggestion that my enquiry had somehow been responsible for Mrs Fremantle's murder. It had been bad enough to think that my manipulations of the cards might have brought tragedy upon our household. The prospect that I may have played a more direct role still made me sick to my stomach. I could not deny that those villains had seemed to be looking for something, and they'd travelled all the way from London to obtain it. Was it really my fault? Or was Darke simply trying to unsettle me? I sat there fretting over this alarming possibility until Tamson returned.

Three days later, wearing my new blue-and-cream silk, I called again at De Lacy House. Many carriages were drawn up in the courtyard, the gates crowded with urchins and onlookers, eager to catch a glimpse of the De Lacys' guests. They looked rather disappointed in me, and who could blame them?

A footman showed me through the house, out onto a terrace overlooking the garden. More akin to a private park, many acres of lawn surrounded a serpentine lake and areas of cultivated wilderness. On a wide plateau of grass in front of the house, about fifty ladies, gentlemen and their offspring sat in little groups upon sofas or on furs laid out on the grass. An orchestra in a white stone pavilion was play-ing Handel's *Water Music* and children were riding miniature horses along the shores of the lake. I spotted Julius De Lacy by the entrance to a Turkish-style tent, talking to a group of his guests.

I descended the steps to the garden, and my heart sank as Archie Montfort came forward to greet me. 'Miss Antrobus, here you are again.' He smiled to offset the ambiguity of these words. 'Mrs Illing-worth is unable to join us?'

'Regrettably her illness is little better,' I said.

'I hope that you did not travel far all by yourself. Where was it that you said you were staying again?'

'Near Cheapside,' I said, naming an unfashionable part of town. I did not trust Archie Montfort's motives at all in asking me these questions. 'It was very kind of your mother to invite us here today.'

'She was greatly entertained by your fortune telling, and wishes to show you off to all her friends.'

I had rather anticipated that I'd be expected to sing for my supper. 'I should be honoured to read for them,' I said.

Archie smiled. 'Such a pity that this will be the last opportunity we'll have to appreciate your talents for quite some time.'

I gazed at him in concern. 'Oh?'

'Why, yes, we're off to Leighfindell for the rest of the summer.'

His beaming face suggested he took enormous pleasure in impart-ing this news. Struggling to contain my dismay, I spoke with a slight croak: 'Your grandmother is to go too? And your uncle?'

'All of us,' he said. 'We won't be back until the Prerogative Court reconvenes for the new term.'

How on earth would I ever prove my case now? I'd already exhausted Morgan Trevithick as a source of information, and I knew of no one else here in London who could help me. I'd thought about travelling to Cornwall – to try to prove that my father and I could have survived that night on the clifftop. Perhaps I might also find someone who remembered me from the old days. But none of that would do me any good, if I couldn't also prove that my birth was legitimate.

'There are several other rich widows here today,' Archie remarked. 'They might provide suitable appreciation while we're away? I could introduce you, if you wish? Or do you have an eye for such people? I imagine you do.'

Insufferable man. To think I'd ever considered him handsome. Thankfully, I was spared any further discourse on his part by the intervention of his mother.

'Miss Antrobus,' Arabia cried, detaching herself from a group of guests and coming to greet me. 'We have all been waiting for you. My friends are simply longing to have their fortunes told.'

She was wearing a forest-green gown embroidered with oak leaves and acorns, and a golden tiara with ruby flowers and emerald leaves. I'd already noticed that all the footmen and maids appeared to be wearing fairy wings. Recalling the inscription on the invitation, I presumed my hostess was supposed to be Titania.

She led me into the tent, where several tables draped in damask held silver punch bowls and chocolate pots, elaborate arrangements of spun sugar, and platters piled with cherries, strawberries and jewel-like confectionary. About a dozen ladies were sheltering from the sun, all dressed to the height of fashion, fanning themselves. Several amused pairs of eyes studied my gown.

'Our cartomancer has arrived,' Arabia announced, guiding me to a table covered with a fringed cloth. 'Miss Antrobus will divine all your secrets, even ones you didn't know you had.' She lowered her voice confidingly. 'Next time we will have to dress you up to look the part. A veil, embroidered stars, and so on. Sometimes it's better to stand out, than to attempt to fit in.'

Still reeling from the news that the De Lacys were leaving town, for the next few hours, I duly told fortunes. I proved a great success, the ladies crowding around my table, applauding every auspicious card and each wish granted. Matters of the heart and of money, of false friends and wayward sons and unfaithful husbands. Though I accrued a great many golden guineas, nobody seemed in the least bit worried about the illegality of this act. I supposed the rich did not much worry about such small trifles as the law.

As afternoon bled into evening, sunlight filled the tent with a ruby glow. Some of the ladies ventured outside again, and more followed when Arabia announced that the children were about to play hot cockles. Emily De Lacy, who had been watching the fortunes, lingered by my table during this exodus.

'Would you like me to read your cards?' I asked, when we were alone.

She shook her head, smiling faintly. 'Mother wouldn't like it. She said Aunt Arabia would have done better to invite the butcher's boy to cast some entrails.'

'People are entitled not to believe,' I said. 'My guardian never did.'

'I hope he was kinder than Mother and Archie. I'm sorry he was so bloody to you the other day. He can be very superior at times.'

Her fitted yellow overdress had a low, loose bodice, the silk embroidered with all the usual fancy embellishments the De Lacys favoured. It was a garment for a woman in her prime, and it made Emily seem even younger than her years, like a child dressing up in her mother's clothes. I recalled her words on my last visit: *I know all about the elopement.*

'Mr Montfort was only concerned for your grandmother,' I said. 'He fears I might take advantage of her trust, like the cartomancer who seduced and kidnapped your Aunt Patience.'

Clumsily done, perhaps, and yet it elicited the desired result. Emily came to sit in front of me, her dark, feverish eyes intent upon mine. 'Except it isn't true, all the bad things that they say about John Jory Jago. My Aunt Luna – that's what the family call her – was very much in love with her fortune teller. I think that's why she's so angry with us now. Because she lost her one chance of happiness.'

It was comforting to find a fellow believer in my father's innocence, even if I was now sceptical that my mother had ever truly loved him. Yet I have always found pulling a better method than pushing in such circumstances. 'Didn't he murder their child and then jump to his death?'

'I don't believe that either. Why would he kill his own baby, when he loved Luna so very much? I think their deaths must have been a terrible accident.'

'Your grandmother doesn't think so. Nor Mr Montfort.'

'Everybody thinks the worst of John Jory because that's the story that Luna told her uncle, Lord Seabrooke, when she returned to London after the elopement. She sought sanctuary at Seabrooke House because she was too ashamed to return home. But she had every reason to lie, don't you see? Lord Seabrooke would never have helped her if he'd thought she was a Jezebel, so she made out that she was a victim of the piece.'

'What makes you so certain she was lying?'

'My aunt was bold and determined and clever beyond her years. A girl who knew her own mind. Everybody says so, even Nonny. And Aunt Arabia says that John Jory was very handsome and mysterious. There is a grotto at Leighfindell where he and Luna used to meet in secret. The walls are covered in mosaics, and John Jory carved their initials into the eye of King Neptune. I found it when I was just a little girl.'

Hardly evidence that would convince in a court of law. 'That isn't proof that she returned his feelings.'

'Maybe not, but proof exists. There is a report that goes into everything: the elopement, their marriage. I overheard my father arguing about it with my Uncle Septimus. Father was going to use the report in court to cast doubt upon my aunt's character. But Uncle Septimus talked Father out of it.'

It was as if I had turned over my wish-cards to find the ace, king, queen of hearts. 'Have you read this report?'

She shook her head. 'Mother would have me whipped if she knew I was even talking about it.'

'Do you always do what your mother tells you?'

She looked a little affronted. 'Of course not. But Father is very careful with his documents. The report is locked away at Leighfindell with my grandfather's papers.'

I considered this last piece of news rather gloomily. 'Why does your grandmother believe Lady Seabrooke's lies? Hasn't she read this report?'

'I don't know. Perhaps. Father says Nonny only ever believes what she wants to believe.'

I told myself that Emily was surely right about one thing: my father's innocence. And this report seemed to contain the proof of it, as well as much else that I would need – proof of my parents' marriage, of my legitimate birth, perhaps more. But how on earth could I ever lay my hands on it?

'Did you hear about the codicil that my aunt claims to have found?' Emily said. 'It was in all the newspapers yesterday. Mother says we might lose everything, though Father believes the court will rule it a forgery.'

I smiled sympathetically. 'It must be a concerning time for you all.'

'I suspect Father will be proved right. He usually is.' She studied me curiously. 'You don't have any money, do you? Aunt Arabia said to Mother that you use a corresponding address because you're embarrassed about where you live, and if you're not embarrassed by your clothes, then you should be.' She broke off, looking aghast. 'I'm sorry. That was unkind. Sometimes I speak quite without thinking.'

'It's usually better to know the truth,' I said. 'You should always feel as if you can tell me anything.'

She smiled, toying with her fan. 'Did you know that my cousin, Leopold, is just three months older than I am? Otherwise, under this codicil, everything would come to me. Then nobody could tell me what to do. I hope he'll drop dead, like his father did. There, now I've told you my very worst thought.'

The De Lacys certainly spent a lot of time thinking about their inheritances. Emily struck me as rather innocent, eager to impress, perhaps a little lonely. I liked her sweet manners and her open heart. Most of all I liked her candour. I think she might have told me more, had not a tall, striking woman of middling years chosen that moment to enter the tent and approach our table.

'Come away now,' she addressed Emily. 'Mr Radclyffe has arrived, and the archery is about to start.' She made no acknowledgement of my presence, not even a nod.

'This is Miss Rachel Antrobus,' Emily said. 'Nonny's fortune teller. Miss Antrobus, this is my mother: Lady Frances De Lacy.'

I knew instinctively that Lady Frances and I were not destined to be great friends. She examined me with a look that one might offer a puddle of cat sick, or a beggar defecating in the street. I tried not to take it personally, the deep grooves between her eyes and the pull of her downturned mouth suggesting that displeasure was far from an unusual state of being. Her strong, rather masculine countenance was plastered thickly with white lead paint, her hair caked with so much powder, I could scarcely discern its original colour. Diamonds glittered at her breast, on her fingers, at her wrists, their colour a match for her rather jaundiced eyes.

'Forgive me if I do not partake of your services,' she said. 'I find fortune telling neither a rational, nor a Christian pursuit.'

That told me. Emily rose, offering me an apologetic smile of farewell, and followed her mother out of the tent. It took me only a few minutes to come up with a plan.

CHAPTER SIXTEEN

*Four of hearts, influenced by a club:
it is apt to lead to acts of manoeuvre . . .*

FAMILY SECRETS. WHICH brings me to the Radclyffes of Devonshire.

Everybody had gathered on the lawn to watch the archery. I stood at the entrance to the tent, looking around for Mirabel, but I couldn't see her. Little boys weaved in and out of the crowd, brandishing miniature bows. Two dark-haired boys, extremely alike, were presumably Archie's step-brothers, the twins, Titus and Absalom. The first archers stepped up to take their shots, Archie Montfort among them. The thud of arrows hitting their targets sent a flock of doves into the air.

The second party of archers took the places of the first, and Archie walked over to join Julius, his wife and Emily. They were talking to a thickset gentleman wearing a long, white wig, a blue striped coat, and a golden small-sword. He seemed slightly familiar, and I studied him a moment, wondering if I'd made his acquaintance in Bath. Archie bowed to the gentleman, his shirt clinging to his torso after his exertions with the bow.

'Delightful view,' a rich, lilting voice remarked.

Turning, I saw a grinning, dimpling man in a green velvet waistcoat and ruffled lace jabot, a jewelled crown adorning his rust-red curls. Oberon, I presumed, though his diminutive stature and impish countenance owed more to Puck.

'A beautiful prospect of the lake,' I agreed, ignoring the insinuation in his tone and expression.

The gentleman examined me with unabashed interest. 'You must be our fortune teller. Septimus De Lacy, at your service.' He gave a very low bow, twirling one wrist.

'I must say,' he went on, 'it is a delight to finally meet our woman of mystery. A dead guardian in Bath, a mysterious old lady in London whom nobody knows or ever sees, visiting alone, in hackney carriages and so forth. It's all tremendously intriguing. Everybody has a theory about you, my dear.'

I heard these words with some alarm. 'A theory, sir?'

He counted them off on his fingers. 'My wife thinks your late guardian must have gambled away your fortune, which would explain your familiarity with the playing cards. My mother says you must have suffered greatly, hence your understanding of the human heart. She claims an intuition when it comes to these things. Well, we've all suffered, I told her, not least when she starts talking about her wretched intuition.' He laughed delightedly. 'The boys think you are probably a pirate. Or perhaps a Jacobite princess. They have been listening to Archie, you see, who thinks you a perfect fraud.'

Damn Archie Montfort! He must have been sowing suspicion about me everywhere. But I affected levity and a boldness to match my uncle's words. 'You should see me climb the rigging with a sword between my teeth.'

He grinned. 'I like you. I'll take a fraud over a bore any day of the week.'

I smiled uneasily, but his gaze had already drifted away, following his mother's progress across the lawn, a great ship of state in a wide-skirted gown of scarlet brocade. 'There she is now,' he murmured. 'Come to cheer us all up, like Banquo's ghost.'

Mirabel joined Julius's party, and the thickset gentleman kissed her hand. I realized then where I had seen him before.

'Who is that gentleman in the Adonis wig?' I asked. 'I met him late last year in Bath, at an electricity show. He was with Mr Montfort.'

'Brinseley Radclyffe,' Septimus said. 'The Member of Parliament for West Devonshire. Speaks six languages, and has nothing of interest to say in any of them. He has lately returned from Spain, where he served as His Majesty's ambassador. I'm amazed the Spanish didn't start a war, just so they could give him back.'

Mr Antrobus had once told me that the Chinese ancients, when in battle, had burned great braziers of arsenic, using bellows to blow the smoke towards their enemies. So it was to be in the vicinity of my Uncle Septimus, whose malice seemed to poison the air we breathed.

'There was an older gentleman with him in Bath,' I said. 'He had long white hair.'

I remembered the old man's words about the elopement: *Such a monstrous thing. You poor girl.* Now that I knew so much more about those events, I wanted to talk to him again.

'His father, Piers Radclyffe,' Septimus said. 'I can't imagine you got much sense out of him. More conversation in a cabbage. Unless you get him started upon the De Lacys. He hates us with a perfect passion.'

'Why does he hate you?'

'Because he used to own Leighfindell, our Devonshire estate. When the Bubble burst, my father bought him out on very good terms. Only the Radclyffes didn't quite see it the same way. Oh, and Brinseley's older brother shot my brother, Virgil, dead. One might think the hate should be on our side, but the old lunatic seems to blame us for that too.'

'Is Mr Radclyffe's father in London?' I asked, surveying the assembled guests.

'Oh no, he hates to leave Leighfindell. You spotted him on a rare venture into the wild.'

'He still lives on the estate?'

Septimus grinned. 'If you're confused, then so are we. It's all my father's fault. When he bought the estate, he granted old Piers a life interest in the Dower House. And the wretched fellow won't die, so he's still there, stalking about, hating us all. Oh, look, Shrewsbury cake! Would you care for a slice?'

Wondering if his freedom in discourse might work to my advantage, I asked him if he'd like his fortune told.

'Heavens, no. The bishop would have my cassock.' Septimus laughed at my astonished expression. 'The Lord was ever optimistic in his choice of instrument. So Mother says anyway.' He shaded his eyes. 'Oh Lord, she's coming this way. I'm dreadfully sorry, Miss Antrobus, but it's every man for himself. No doubt I shall see you again ere too long.'

With these words, he scurried off to waylay a passing waiter with wine. I turned to greet his mother, and Mirabel took my hands in hers.

'Forgive me for not coming to find you sooner, my dear. I was ready to drown the Field-Marshal, he goes on so.'

'Our nation is only grateful for your forbearance,' I said. 'Would you like me to tell your fortune?'

She beamed, squeezing my hands. 'I have been thinking of little else since your last visit.'

My original intention had been to figure the elopement in her cards, but now I had more pressing matters on my mind. Everything I'd learned that day – the De Lacys' upcoming trip to their Devonshire estate; Piers Radclyffe, who hated the family, but seemed to know their secrets; most of all, the mysterious report concerning my parents' elopement – all pointed in one direction: to Leighfindell.

We seated ourselves in the Turkish tent, my fingertips dancing over the cards in my haste to despoil the Square. Outside, people applauded the archery.

'We begin with the four of clubs, influenced by a diamond,' I said. 'This card figures an imminent change. Often a journey.'

'For once there is no mystery,' Mirabel replied, with a smile. 'We are due to leave for Leighfindell in three days' time.'

'I shall be very sorry to see you go,' I said, pointing to the next card. 'The influence here is the ace of diamonds, which figures a prudent choice. If you are right, and the first card relates to your trip to Devon, then this card likely connects to that visit. Perhaps a choice you'll make while you are there – or before you leave.'

Without giving her time to mull this mystery, I tapped the master-card. 'The queen of clubs represents a female influence upon the querist. A person of authority, who might offer you good advice. This woman too may relate to your journey.'

It was not a time for subtlety. Nor would I dwell upon Tamson's warnings about the cards. I had one chance to change my destiny, and that moment was now.

CHAPTER SEVENTEEN

*Ace of clubs, influenced by a heart: a matter in which our
sentiments are specially enlisted, perhaps in contest
with judgement or tastes or duty.*

THE PLAYWRIGHT'S PEN moves jerkily across the page. There
is a whir of cogs somewhere beneath the machine. When the
automaton finishes writing, Morgan Trevithick picks up the paper
with a flourish, and hands it to a delighted member of his audience.

'I know this one, but I can't place it.' The man reads the lines aloud.

'Congreve,' someone says, and everyone applauds.

Lazarus studies the box below the machine, wondering if a man
could be concealed inside, moving the pen. It looks too small. A
dwarf? A child? He is distrustful by nature of such wonders. Life has
taught him that many things are not what they seem.

Lady Seabrooke is unenigmatic in her displeasure. This morning,
when he'd called on her, she'd had a letter in her hand.

'Have you heard from her? Miss Antrobus?'

'Not since my visit to the fair.'

'She has been to De Lacy House. I am told that she has paid three
visits there.'

Lazarus frowns. *'Your brother* is behind this business?'

'I don't think so. He appears to believe she's just some girl from
Bath with a gift for fortune telling. Mother is quite taken with her
apparently. She has talked Julius into inviting Miss Antrobus to
accompany them to Devon. They leave the day after tomorrow.'

Lazarus doesn't ask how she knows. He presumes that just as Julius has spies around her, so she has spies around him.

'I suppose the girl is looking for evidence to support her claim.' Her resourcefulness both troubles and impresses him. 'Can she really mean to go through with it? Assert her claim in court?'

'We must presume so.'

Lazarus thinks for a moment. 'She's clearly run away from home. I could write to Henry Antrobus, but he won't get here before they leave.'

Lady Seabrooke shakes her head. 'She cannot be allowed to set foot in Leighfindell. It is too dangerous. I want you to work her a mischief, Lazarus.'

He studies her uneasily. 'What manner of mischief?'

'You must know people.'

His voice is firm. 'No.'

'I only mean that we should scare her.'

'That is not the way I work.'

'You won't help me.'

He draws a breath. 'I didn't say that.'

'I need you, Lazarus. I can't have Leopold hearing those things in court.' She is very close to him now. A scent of Attar of Roses and desperation permeates her skin. She places a hand upon his arm, and her touch draws him away from moral certainty. 'This girl is a devious little meretrix and she needs to be stopped. By any means you can.'

Which has brought him here again, to the Bartholomew Fair. When the automaton show draws to a close, Lazarus remains seated. It is seventeen years since he purchased *The Square of Sevens* from Morgan Trevithick, on Nicholas De Lacy's behalf. Only a few months later, it was stolen along with the codicil. He wishes he knew what had happened to that document in the intervening years. Where did Antrobus really obtain it? Not from John Jory Jago. If he could only find out where, then the girl's case would fall apart.

Trevithick walks over to join him. 'This is about Red, isn't it?'

'Are you surprised? She claims to be the De Lacy heir. I doubt I'll be the last visitor you'll have.'

Trevithick shakes his head. 'She's naught to do with me. I told her to leave it alone.'

'You gave her a booth at the fair.'

'She tells a good fortune.'

'A good story too. Are you sure you haven't been helping her? Someone has.'

Trevithick regards him evenly. 'Are you so certain that she's lying?'

Lazarus laughs. 'You've grown soft-headed in your old age.'

The Cornishman shrugs. 'Not my problem, is it?'

'It will be if you're named as an accomplice. Has she given you any money? Because if you've profited from this enterprise, then that's collusion.'

'I just told her the truth. About me and John Jory. There's no harm in that.'

'That's for a judge to determine. Don't think my mistress won't pursue it. She's not the forgiving sort.' He waits a moment to let this prospect sink in. 'Tell me everything you told the girl, and I'll take it as a sign of good faith.'

Trevithick chews on his lip, then begins to talk. Lazarus listens carefully, putting himself in the girl's shoes. She's building a picture of John Jory, he thinks. Colour here, shading there – and I will cast light upon that shade.

'If you want me to throw her out, then it's going to cost you,' Trevithick says. 'That pitch cost me four quid.'

It's how he remembers Trevithick. A man who'll try to negotiate even when his neck is in a noose. Who'd invite his own sister up onto the gallows to take his place.

Lazarus's hesitation is imperceptible, he barely notices it himself. 'For the time being,' he says, 'I want her right where she is.'

Chapter Eighteen

Seven of hearts as master-card:
the card of trust and confidence approved of.

I LAY IN a dappled pool of sunlight, beneath the twisted branches of an ancient mulberry tree.

A dragonfly hovered into my field of vision, then out again. In that rare moment of contentment, the first I had known for what felt like an age, I turned my head to watch Tamson, her album in her lap, her box of watercolours open by her side.

I hadn't told her that I'd be leaving for Devon tomorrow. The truth was too dangerous, and I didn't want to lie. Nor did I want to face her disappointment. Or worse, her lack of it.

I had spent several hours the previous day making arrangements in advance of my departure. With great diligence, I'd forged a letter from Mrs Illingworth in a spidery hand, accepting the De Lacys' kind offer that I should accompany them to Leighfindell. Once it had been dispatched, I'd walked down to the shops on the Strand and used most of the money I'd earned at the *concert au jardin* to purchase several second-hand gowns, a new pair of slippers, a few other necessaries, and a trunk in which to transport them. I'd left the trunk in the care of Fernando, who'd promised to arrange a carrier to take it to De Lacy House. Finally, after taking advice from one of the escape-artists at the fair, I had visited a dark and rather insalubrious shop in Field Lane, where I had purchased a roll of lock picks, hoping I could still remember my lessons from Father on how to use them.

My plan was to rise early the following day and slip away whilst Tamson was still asleep. That morning, I'd written her a heartfelt note, which I intended to leave by the bed, saying that I'd had to depart London urgently, but would soon return.

We'd come to the garden to eat a leisurely breakfast of bread and sausage in anticipation of a hard day's work in the booth. It was the first day of the fair proper and we were expecting big crowds that night. When I'd expressed my bemusement, given that we had already been doing a brisk trade for nearly three weeks, Tamson had explained that under the terms of its charter, the fair was only supposed to last three days. From time to time, the authorities attempted to enforce this stipulation, but Sisyphus would have stood a better chance of success.

The garden was only a short walk from Smithfield, at the heart of the district known as Cloth Fair. Once the site of an Augustinian monastery, the neighbourhood was full of reminders of that earlier time. The old priory, St Bartholomew's, was now the parish church. An ornate archway of blackened stone led to an alehouse. Carved stone shields and fluted capitals adorned the walls of a print-shop. A tobacco factory was housed in a former chapel. The stubborn patch of green in which we were sitting had once been a part of the monks' infirmary garden. Somehow it had survived the speculations of the projectors. The grass was long and strewn with wildflowers; butterflies flitting between the fruit trees and the old vines that climbed the walls.

'Have you finished yet?' I asked, sitting up, rubbing my neck. 'You said I could see.'

Making a show of reluctance, Tamson tilted her book to show me the small pink flower she was painting. 'It's centaury,' she said. 'Used to treat a choleric temper.'

'You'd better give some to Gwen.' I caught her eye and she grinned. 'It's beautiful. I hope you know that.'

'I'm better at leaves and seeds,' she said. 'I'd like to try copper engraving one day. That's how you do real justice to flowers.'

'Have you ever thought about making money from your painting?'

She lowered her eyes. 'My dream is to publish a herbal. Like Elizabeth Blackwell's, only better, with knowledge about the stars and the best times to pick herbs or apply medicines. Maybe then I could buy a cottage with a garden of my own. Put down roots, watch things grow. No painting was ever as beautiful as the real thing.'

'I know a man in publishing. Perhaps I could talk to him?'

She shook her head. 'It's just a foolish idea.'

'You have to dream,' I said. 'That's how the impossible becomes possible. Show me a grand triumph that didn't start out as a dream.'

'So what's your dream, then?' Tamson said. 'No, wait, don't tell me. You want to be rich. I can see that glint in your eye, just like Morgan.'

'Not for its own sake,' I said, feeling unfairly judged. 'When you have money, men can't tell you what to do.'

When I claim my fortune, I thought, I'll pay to publish her book. Maybe then she'll forgive me for running away without saying goodbye. 'Who taught you all these things? Painting? Herbs? The stars?'

'My mother taught me to paint. The rest was our cook, Bessie.'

'You had a cook?' I'd always assumed she'd grown up on the road just like I had.

'For a time, when I was younger. We lived by the sea, near Sandwich in Kent. My father was a Frenchman in the wine trade. I don't really remember him. He left when I was four, taking most of my mother's money with him. He was living back in France the last I heard.' She gave me a sidelong look. 'Would it surprise you to learn that my mother's father was a gentleman?'

'I suppose it would. Was he rich?'

'Trust you to ask that.' But her tone was light – I was learning that friends were supposed to poke fun at one another. 'Yes, he was rich, but it's a complicated story. My mother was raised by a guardian, a former major in the East India Company's army. She looked like me, only more so, and she had memories of a white house on a lake, and a garden filled with sunlight and strange flowers. Sometimes she dreamed of a woman with black hair and brown skin, and bright blue beads she said were pieces of the sky. Given the major had served in India, it wasn't hard to make the connection.'

'Her guardian had served in the army with her father?'

She nodded. 'They were friends. My mother wanted for nothing, but her requests to meet her father were always denied. I imagine he'd left his family behind in England during his time in India, and took an Indian mistress while he was there. At least he owned his responsibilities. Up to a point.'

'What happened to your grandmother?'

'My mother never found out. I don't think she ever even knew her name.'

'That's cruel,' I said. 'Not knowing. All of it.'

'Many thought her fortunate. Major Gower told her that she would receive a settlement of five hundred pounds when she married. It made her the target of adventurers like my father. After he left, it was just me, my mother and Bessie. When Mother died, the house had to be sold to pay her debts. I started working the local fairs, which is where I met Morgan and the Players.'

Her story made me think of my own parents – all those years of not knowing. All those fictions I had written to fill the gaps. Yet those fictions had been more comforting than the truth.

'This is the part where you're supposed to tell me about yourself,' Tamson said.

Unwilling to lie, I wove her a story like a fine piece of Chantilly lace, embroidered with intricate detail to obscure the holes of omission. I made no mention of my father or Cornwall, but I told her about Bath and Trim Street, about Mr Antrobus and Mrs Fremantle. When I came to the part about Henry, Tamson squeezed my hand.

'That's why I came to London,' I said. 'It was intolerable.'

'You mustn't ever go back,' Tamson said, with feeling. 'Did you know the Cornish Players will be in London another six weeks? Until after the Southwark Fair? I'm sure Morgan would let you keep your place in the booth, if you ask him nicely. Maybe you could even come on the road with us? It's not so bad once you get used to it.'

Feeling like a wretch, I changed the subject. 'Do you never resent it? Giving Morgan half your money?'

She shrugged, plainly disappointed by my lack of enthusiasm. 'It pays for my food and lodging, pamphlets and protection. Morgan would look after me if I was sick, or got injured like Meg and Pierre. Not all companies would do that – and not all would take me on looking the way I do. Not Roland either. Did you know Morgan's training him up to take over when he retires?'

'He likes you,' I said.

Tamson blushed. 'Not like that.' She twisted a lock of her amber hair. 'Are you ever going to tell me about that gentleman who came to the booth? Was he the same man you told Gwen and Naomi about?'

It took me a moment to recall our conversation about Archie. 'No,' I said. 'He was just upset about a fortune I gave to a lady.'

She gazed at me sceptically. 'Does he have anything to do with this other business? The money? Your talks with Morgan?'

My face was a picture of innocence. 'What other business?'

Tamson sighed. 'Just make sure you call Roland if he ever comes back.'

I put my hand over hers. 'There's nothing to worry about. He won't come back.'

And if he does, I thought sadly, studying Tamson's concerned face, after tomorrow, I'll be long gone.

CHAPTER NINETEEN

Five of clubs, influenced by a spade:
an argument or dispute on a matter.

AT SEVEN O'CLOCK that evening, I excused myself from the booth, saying that I had an errand to run. I needed to call at Fernando's, as Julius De Lacy had said that he would write that evening, confirming the timings for our departure tomorrow.

'But we're so busy,' Tamson objected, breaking off from her customer's chart. 'Morgan was very clear that he wanted everyone at their posts tonight.'

'I won't be long, I promise.'

The streets were packed with excited revellers heading for the fair. My own excitement about Devon was mixed with trepidation and regret about leaving Tamson. At Fernando's, I waited in line, breathing the rich aromas of coffee and tobacco. But when I reached the front of the queue, Fernando said he had no letters for me. 'There is handsome gentleman waiting for you, though.' He winked.

Following his gaze, my heart sank as I spotted Archie Montfort. He'd risen from his seat in one of Fernando's mahogany boxes, and was trying to attract my attention by waving a letter in his hand. I made my way over to his table, ignoring the irritated glances of some of the gentlemen patrons, plainly appalled that a woman might overhear their tedious chatter.

Archie bowed rather stiffly and invited me to sit. I was very conscious of my appearance, having neglected to dress my hair and attend to my toilette with the same diligence I'd applied on my visits to De Lacy House. Pulling my cloak a little tighter around my shoulders to obscure my shabby day dress, I took the letter from Archie's outstretched hand.

'From my uncle,' he said. 'I was passing this way, and I offered to deliver it myself.'

'That was good of you,' I said cautiously.

'Goodness had nothing to do with it. I wanted to talk to you about this proposal that you accompany my family to Leighfindell.'

'Such a kind offer,' I said, not without a hint of triumph.

He regarded me sourly. 'I am here to advise you to reconsider that invitation.'

I met his gaze combatively. 'And why should I do that?'

'Because my grandmother was most distressed after your visit the other week. You had her speaking of her dead children, taking money to cause her pain.'

'That was not my intention,' I said, genuinely sorry to hear that she'd been upset. 'Nor did I ask her for money. She insisted, if you recall.'

'I don't remember you protesting so very hard. Look, it isn't the money. Lord knows we can afford it. But I will not stand idly by whilst my grandmother subjects herself to your cruel deceptions.'

His words inflamed me. 'Has it ever occurred to you that your grandmother needs to speak of her dead children? That it will benefit her to do so?'

'Benefit her? That's rich.'

I searched for the right words with which to convince him. 'When something in our past is difficult or disturbing to contemplate, it is natural to bury it deep inside ourselves, so that it cannot cause us pain. But like a splinter, those thoughts can fester. Sometimes it is better to prise them out into the air. Have you read *The Anatomy of Melancholy*?'

'By Robert Burton? No, though I have heard of it.'

'Burton writes about the causes and cures of human sadness and depressions of the spirit. He suffered from such maladies himself. His theories rest upon the assumption that melancholy is an ailment just like any other. One treatment he suggests, is that the melancholic patient should be persuaded to confess their sorrows to an empathetic friend.'

'That is hardly the same as a fortune teller charging money for fairground tricks.'

'If I was a doctor of the body, would you raise an eyebrow at my fee?'

He scoffed. 'A doctor is qualified, subject to the scrutiny of his peers.'

'Does the method matter if it convinces her to talk? Look on the cards, if you will, as a method of persuasion.'

'Manipulation, you mean. I heard how you tricked her into inviting you to Leighfindell.'

My guilt about that deception was tempered by my genuine belief that in Devon I could help Mirabel with her grief. 'Whatever you wish to call it, I tell you it works. There may be distress at first. The extraction of a splinter can be a painful business. But afterwards the wound will heal, and your grandmother will be the better for it.'

'Pretty words,' he said. 'And yet they rest upon a lie. My grandmother believes you can predict the future and divine secrets in her past.'

'Which I believe too. There is no lie.'

He breathed deeply. 'I have argued against this invitation, but my uncle, in his reckless indulgence of matters occult, refuses to listen. My stepfather believes you'll keep his mother occupied and out of his way. My mother adores your fortunes, and is all for this wretched enterprise. You also appear to have Emily in your thrall. But they will learn the truth eventually, I assure you of that.'

As one might imagine, I listened to these words in some alarm. 'The truth, sir?'

He sat back, regarding me with a crafty look. 'I wonder, Miss Antrobus, why you left Bath to come to London, at a time when everyone else travels the other way?'

'As I told your uncle, my new guardian has business in Ireland, and Mrs Illingworth kindly offered me sanctuary here.'

'Ah, yes,' he said, 'the famous Mrs Illingworth of Cheapside. I have asked around my friends in the City, and nobody seems to have heard of her.'

'That is hardly surprising,' I said. 'She rarely ventures out into society.'

He smiled scornfully. 'I wonder if your reason for leaving Bath so abruptly was rather different. Perhaps a complaint was made against you? Another unhappy widow, perhaps? One who'd parted with money she couldn't afford?'

I drew myself up. 'How dare you, sir. I was introduced to your uncle by the Countess of Arundel.'

'Who, I presume, had also fallen under your spell. As for this Mrs Illingworth, I'm starting to wonder if she even exists.'

It took every ounce of my self-possession to muster defiance in the face of his suspicious stare. 'Your allegations are as unwarranted as they are distressing,' I said, rising from my seat. 'I can only conclude that you are no gentleman, sir.'

He flushed, and I sensed I'd hit a nerve. Presumably he didn't much like the fact that his father had been the De Lacys' steward.

'If my candour offends you, Miss Antrobus, then so will my tenacity in just cause, should you insist upon accompanying my family to Devon. You still have time to change your mind, and I advise you to do so. Consider this fair warning of my intent.'

CHAPTER TWENTY

Eight of spades, influenced by a diamond:
a misfortune in an affair.

Lazarus is still thinking about Lady Seabrooke's hand upon his arm, still hearing his name upon her lips: *I need you, Lazarus.* He is sitting in the Cheshire Cheese, an old tavern just off Fleet Street, full of dark, unobtrusive nooks and hidden corners. As he awaits the arrival of the man he is meeting, his mind drifts inevitably to the past: Luna, the loose button, the soft kiss upon his cheek, all the kisses that follow . . .

Even then, in the arrogance of youth, he was never one of those men who courted danger. Each kiss fills him with foreboding – because how can it ever end well? – and it *must* end, he knows that, even as he craves more of this new way of being alive. He wonders if this is how his mother felt with her lover, and for the first time, he feels a stirring sympathy. Then he thinks about the wreckage of that affair, his father cold in a cheap, deal coffin, and he tells himself that he will end it, and do so today.

But instead, there are more discussions about Bacon, or Hobbes, or whichever moral philosopher is a pretext for that day's immorality. They talk about everything: science, politics, art, even magic. Everything, except the kisses and what they mean. He thinks they have been discreet, but he often feels the eyes of the world upon them: her father's cool, perceptive gaze; John Jory Jago's jealous stare. Do they know? How can they not? Lazarus's feelings shine out of him like the sun on a polished lens.

George Montfort catches him watching her from the window of the office they share at Leighfindell. Outside in the gardens, the sisters are arguing. Jemima is angry, as she often seems to be. Luna is giving as good as she gets, Virgil standing between them, playing peacemaker.

'Give me a sack and I'll drown the pair of them in the river,' Montfort says, his Viking-fair head hovering over Lazarus's shoulder. 'Pierrot too.'

Pierrot is Luna's black-and-white lapdog. 'What's he done now?' Lazarus used to know all the things that went on in this house, but now he is preoccupied with Luna, and he misses much.

'Destroyed a quill-work box,' Montfort replies. 'Jemima was making it for her father. She should save herself the effort. He won't change his mind.'

'Little Piers' Radclyffe has asked for Jemima's hand again – and been soundly rebuffed for the third time. The man cannot comprehend that such new wealth might find him wanting. His ancestors built Leighfindell and lived there for generations – until his father sold up to Nicholas De Lacy when the Bubble burst. The Radclyffes are as old as England, Catholic and proud; in their golden days they owned half of Devonshire. If his master will not entertain the suit of the Radclyffe heir, then how is he likely to respond should Lazarus Darke ever have the temerity to ask for Luna's hand? But Lazarus has always known the answer to that question. His master seeks a duke for Jemima – anything to best his brother, the earl – and a viscount at the very least for Luna.

'Little Piers should thank his guiding angels,' Montfort goes on, watching Jemima stamp around and shout. 'Imagine being married to that.'

'They are in love,' Lazarus says, a little more wistfully than he'd like.

Montfort snorts. 'You don't think her father's fortune has something to do with it?'

'I've seen the way he looks at her. She's a beauty, you can't deny that.'

'Dazzled by her money, dazzled by her cunny. There's a song there,' Montfort says.

Lazarus wonders why Montfort hates women so very much. His wife, Arabia, is young and extremely pretty – a trifle silly, perhaps, but perfectly pleasant. Their little son, Archie, is happy and healthy. They live in a sizeable house on the western edge of the estate. Yet Montfort seems eaten up with odd resentments.

'The old man should keep a tighter rein on them,' he says. 'Girls who flirt like that get themselves into trouble.'

He says it with relish. Is that what I am? Lazarus wonders. Trouble?

A few months later, trouble duly arrives – upon a scale unimagined, even by George Montfort. Little Piers abandons Jemima. Jemima goes out of her mind with grief. Virgil is shot dead by Little Piers during a duel. Like everyone else, Lazarus had liked Virgil, a smiling, uncomplicated boy. He chastises himself for not keeping a closer eye on things. His master is afraid that Jemima's madness might damage the marriage prospects of Luna and his younger sons. He has Lazarus pay off the newspapers to suppress the story of the duel, and Virgil is buried quietly in the local churchyard. Lazarus observes the family closely in their grief.

Nicholas De Lacy consoles himself with his investments. When he isn't absorbed by his financial papers, he has John Jory tell his fortune, or goes hunting with Julius. The middle De Lacy son possesses his father's calculating mind. He says and does all the things an heir should do if he has one eye on his inheritance. But Lazarus senses that Nicholas De Lacy, when gazing into this mirror, doesn't much like what he sees there. When Nicholas tires of his son's presence, he goes on long walks with Luna. Jemima used to be his favoured companion on these perambulations across the estate, but she is now confined to the attic infirmary under the care of the family physician, Doctor Crowhurst. Lazarus has advised his master to bring the very best mad-doctors down from London. But Nicholas is too afraid of her affliction becoming publicly known.

Mirabel wanders about the house, all in black, like one of the ghosts said to stalk the estate. Luna claims to have seen these apparitions, but she also claims lately to love him, and Lazarus isn't sure he believes that either. Mirabel believes that her family is cursed.

Fifteen-year-old Septimus is never invited to walk or hunt. For reasons Lazarus has never understood, Nicholas De Lacy detests his youngest son. Poor Septimus constantly tries to please him, which only earns him more contempt. The boy visits the church at the nearby village of Slaughterbridge, where he consults the parish priest, returning with a carefully transcribed biblical text upon grief. Lazarus is with his master, taking port after dinner, when the boy knocks and enters. His father listens to his stammered explanation, gives the paper a cursory glance, then tosses it into the fire. He dismisses his son with words of such tightly restrained fury, Septimus runs to his room and doesn't emerge for several days.

Lazarus doesn't fare much better with Luna. They meet in the woods, in the sort of glade where knights lose their honour to weeping maidens. There are many versions of this woman, different selves for different audiences. She has several versions for him, and he never knows which one he will get. The sparring partner, his intellectual equal; the tease who talks of her other suitors, men with money and land and titles; the cool Luna who keeps him at a distance when displeased; or the girl hot as an August moon, who brushes against him as she kisses his mouth, and is all he can think about at night when he tries to sleep.

Luna in grief is different, stripped of all pretence. Lazarus wonders if anyone else has ever seen her before. She cries for Virgil, and for Jemima too. He had thought that the girls did not much like one another – Luna was clearly jealous of Jemima's closeness to their father. But now she is angry with her father about the way Jemima is being treated, and she shows little appetite for her position as his new favourite. Sometimes she speaks about her sister's suffering with such bleak sorrow it touches his soul. For that girl, he thinks, he would do anything.

One day, in the woods, she pushes him away, gazing up at him with wet eyes. 'Run away with me,' she says. 'Somewhere far from here, where my father can never find us.'

He smiles uneasily. 'Where's that, then? The planet Mars?'

'At the moment of my birth,' she says, 'Venus, Mars and Jupiter were in conjunction with the Dragon's Head, which signifies destiny. John Jory told me once that he sees an unsuitable match in my future. A love that will anger my father, but won't be denied.'

Lazarus's mouth tightens. 'I rather suspect it isn't me your vagabond has in mind.'

'John Jory is harmless. Leave him alone. Give me your answer.'

He searches her face for confirmation that she is joking, but she only returns his probing stare. Just at the moment when he starts to wonder if she might be serious after all, she laughs. 'Your face. Remind me to never send a damsel in distress to Lazarus Darke.'

He'd laughed too, but for many years he has wondered about the truth of that moment. He imagines another world, one in which he'd said: *For you, I would go anywhere. Let's leave tonight.*

It is this stew of guilt and desire and regret, that has brought him, eighteen years later, to the Cheshire Cheese. Moral qualms assail him. He thinks about that strange, unhappy girl, Red, and all her lies. His actions might be in the service of truth, but that doesn't make them right. He suspects that they might be very wrong. But then he thinks about Lady Seabrooke. *I need you, Lazarus.*

Does she understand the effect of her words upon him? She cannot think he is really here for the money? Or is that now the only language she understands? He revisits that flicker of emotion he is convinced he saw on her face, wondering what memory inspired it. The day in the library? The day in the woods? The day he left Leighfindell? Of all the memories, this last is the one he can least endure – and he feels the weight of his sins like an anchor-stone.

A shadow falls across the table, a fat gentleman of about fifty. He has a brandy nose, his cheeks a web of broken veins. Propping his silver staff in a corner of the booth, he squeezes in to take the seat opposite Lazarus. Two sleek, silver greyhounds nestle at their feet.

'It's been a while, Darke,' he says. 'What do you want?'

CHAPTER TWENTY-ONE

Eight of diamonds as master-card: the unlucky red card,
meaning a personal event of importance going awry.

I WAS COLLECTING enemies at a quite alarming rate. Henry
Antrobus and his wretched pamphlets. Lady Seabrooke and Lazarus Darke. Archie Montfort, who was determined to prove me a
fraud. In going to Devon, I'd leave some of those dangers behind me,
though it seemed I would need a plan to deal with Mr Montfort. I
thought fleetingly of Mr Darke's theory that I had a fifth enemy too:
the person who had sent those villains to our house in Trim Street.
I doubted such a person really existed, but if he did, then I would
ensure that he would face justice. With the De Lacy fortune at my
disposal, all my enemies would suffer.

Occupied with this pleasing thought, I walked back to Smithfield,
the streets bottlenecked with people heading to and from the fair.
Thanks to Archie Montfort, I was late. I hoped Morgan hadn't given
Tamson any hard words on my account. The thought of parting from
her on bad terms made me quite breathless.

The lamps of the fair at dusk glowed with a dazzling intensity, the
taverns bright and inviting. Boys weaved in and out of the crowds
blowing penny-trumpets.

I heard the commotion before I saw it. Raised voices over the
music. Someone ran past me in a great hurry. When I turned the
next corner, I drew to a halt, spotting a crowd outside our booth,
some sort of argument in full sway. Morgan was in the middle of

it, a head taller than the rest, waving his arms around and shouting. Roland and one of the others were gripping Frank by the shoulders. He was struggling, and I wondered if he'd got into a fight. Then I saw two thickset men holding Meg, Tamson pleading with them to let her go. A portly man strode out of the crowd and I recognized the magistrate. He emptied Meg's basket onto the ground, poking at the contents with his silver staff.

'She's an astrologer,' I heard him say. 'There are books here, plates and charts.' His greyhounds sniffed around the basket.

'Where is the other girl?' he addressed Meg. 'Tell us and we'll let you go.'

Meg must have made one of her incoherent noises, because the magistrate hit her across the face. Frank made a lunge for him, but Lazarus Darke got there first. I stared at him in horror, everything falling into place. The magistrate was there to arrest me. Only they'd arrested Meg instead, because I was late.

Darke crouched down to talk to Meg.

'She can't tell you anything,' Tamson cried. 'Those charts aren't even hers, they're mine.'

Perhaps deciding that Tamson would be a better source of information than a woman who could barely talk, the magistrate barked an order. To my dismay, his constables released Meg and grabbed hold of Tamson.

Many thoughts flashed through my mind. Tamson. A year in prison. The pillory. Her beautiful face ruined. Her wits confused like Meg's. Because of me.

If I surrendered, they'd release her. Lazarus Darke's plan was plain enough. Put me in prison, facing the pillory, and he presumed I would sign anything he wanted. As I hesitated, my instincts at war, Gwen caught sight of me. She raised her arm and pointed. 'There she is.'

Self-preservation triumphed. I turned and ran. Shame clouded my vision, the stalls a blur on either side. The shouts behind me were drowned out by the shrieks of the customers seated on the Pleasure Windmill up ahead. Bernard, the strong man, was cranking the handle to turn the windmill. He called out to me as I ducked beneath one of the sails. I glanced back, spotting Darke and three constables in close pursuit.

Pushing past a startled ticket-taker, I ran into a large tent, where an Italian castrato named Antonio was dancing upon a rope with a duck on his head. I crept along the back of the tent, behind the audience, until I came to a gap where the tent met the grass. I rolled under it, just as the constables burst into the tent, finding myself on the fringes of the fair.

I walked swiftly, head down, trying to lose myself amongst the revellers coming and going from the taverns. At Smithfield Bar, I headed north towards Clerkenwell, where I could surely find an anonymous lodging-house to stay until morning. I tried not to think about Tamson. Perhaps they'd let her go, when they couldn't find me.

As I was passing the Porter's Block, where Tamson had told me they used to execute prisoners, I heard a shout. I turned, seeing that the crowd had parted behind me. Two of the Levantines were leading one of their bears along the street, and nobody wanted to get too close. Lazarus Darke was behind the bear, pointing at me.

'Stop that girl,' he shouted. 'The one with red hair. She's committed a crime.'

Turning back, I saw a pair of constables coming towards me from the other direction. Darke pointed and shouted again, but they had already spotted me. I was trapped.

I whipped out the snakestone from my pocket, determined not to let them take me without a fight. I wound the stocking around my wrist, gripping it tight. One of the constables made a grab for me, but I side-stepped him easily. His friend seized hold of my arm, pulling me back. I swung the snakestone awkwardly, and struck him reasonably hard on the side of his neck. He let out a shout, and stumbled backwards, falling into the path of one of the Levantines, who also fell.

Somebody screamed. The first constable grabbed hold of me by the shoulders. The crowd scattered around us like chaff on the wind.

I was still struggling in the constable's grip, when he released me abruptly. He backed away, a look of horror upon his face. Puzzled by my good fortune, I was poised to flee again, when a guttural roar echoed off the buildings around us. My flesh prickling, I turned.

The bear was up on its hind legs, staring right at me, the chain around his neck hanging loosely to the ground. The Levantines shouted at people to stay back. The bear roared again, and I smelled the meaty odour of his breath.

He looked from me to the constable, then back again. I glimpsed Lazarus Darke in the crowd, concern etched upon his face. 'Don't move,' he cried.

Instead, I backed away as the constable was doing, the bear following me with his yellow gaze. He dropped down on all fours, saliva drooling from his teeth, moving towards us with a slow, ambling gait.

Every possible outcome shuffled through my mind like a pack of cards. The bear dropped into a crouch, and the constable jabbed the air with his staff. If it was supposed to drive the creature in my direction, then it was a mistake. The bear tensed, then sprang. People screamed and turned away. I heard a clatter as the constable's stick hit the ground.

Then I was running, my feet flying over the cobbles. My chest hurt, my breathing was laboured, my brain foggy with fear. I heard shouts, more screams, another great roar from the bear. Then a gunshot, followed by a deathly silence.

BOOK THREE

Concerning a fortune told
of Mrs Mirabel De Lacy

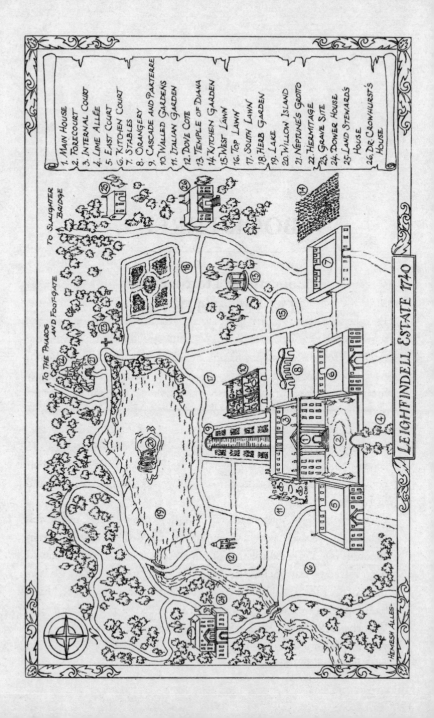

LEIGHFINDELL ESTATE 1740

1. MAIN HOUSE
2. FORECOURT
3. INTERNAL COURT
4. LIME ALLÉE
5. EAST COURT
6. KITCHEN COURT
7. STABLES
8. ORANGERY
9. CASCADE AND PARTERRE
10. WALLED GARDENS
11. ITALIAN GARDEN
12. DOVE COTE
13. TEMPLE OF DIANA
14. KITCHEN GARDEN
15. WEST LAWN
16. TOP LAWN
17. SOUTH LAWN
18. HERB GARDEN
19. LAKE
20. WILLOW ISLAND
21. NEPTUNE'S GROTTO
22. HERMITAGE
23. GRAVE SITE
24. DOWER HOUSE
25. LAND STEWARD'S HOUSE
26. DR CROWHURST'S HOUSE

TO THE PHAROS AND FOOT-GATE

TO SLAUGHTER BRIDGE

— HEWISH ALLES —

CHAPTER ONE

Four of clubs, influenced by a diamond:
it involves a change.

I T TOOK US over a week to reach Leighfindell. For the first part
of the journey, we followed the Bath Road, a reverse of the route
I'd taken to London. To my dismay, I had been allocated to the
second carriage, which carried Septimus and his family, including
Archie Montfort. The conditions in which we travelled could not
have been more different to my last journey, when I'd clung for my
life to the carriage roof. Our coach was large, the interior waxed
and polished and cushioned, our feet resting upon silver warmers
filled with embers. Archie barely looked up from his book, but Arabia
and Septimus chattered away, merrily slandering all their friends and
acquaintances. Sometimes they made an effort to include me in their
conversation, but all I could think about was the mess I'd left behind
in London.

The night of the magistrate's raid, I'd slept in a squalid Clerkenwell
lodging-house and taken a hackney carriage to De Lacy House in
the morning. I grieved the loss of my father's portmanteau, which I'd
been forced to leave behind at the Magpie – his copy of *Don Quixote*
most of all. I fretted about that poor constable, who I feared had been
badly mauled by the bear. Above all, I dwelled upon Tamson's fate.
Was she locked up? Would she be tried? Convicted? Sentenced to a
year in prison and the pillory? Did she blame me? How could she
not? It was all my fault.

I told myself that Tamson meant too much to Rowena for Morgan to abandon her. He would surely bribe the magistrate to secure her release. I told myself that once I had claimed my inheritance, I would fix everything. I'd buy her a cottage in the country. No, better than a cottage. I'd buy her a manor house with acres of garden where she could grow herbs and flowers. I'd visit and we'd talk fondly about our days at the fair. Such fantasies gave me cold comfort, when I pictured Tamson sitting in a prison cell silently hating me. Or chained in the pillory, facing a screaming mob armed with half-bricks.

We left the Bath Road at Hounslow, to take a more southerly course west, via Basingstoke and Salisbury. In every village and town, heads turned to witness the splendour of our procession. Armed manservants rode at the front, escorting the lead coach, which carried Julius and his family, including Mirabel and Ocho the parrot. Our carriage was followed by a vehicle belonging to Brinseley Radclyffe, who was travelling to Leighfindell to see his father. A fourth carried the twins, together with their tutor, Emily's governess, Julius's private secretary, and the man responsible for this grand enterprise, the household steward. Behind the principal carriages came half a dozen hired vehicles conveying the female travelling servants; a great many baggage wagons; and more armed manservants on horseback bringing up the rear. Sometimes our party would halt and fine stallions would be brought round for the gentlemen to ride out. Occasionally, a pair of gilded sedan chairs would be unloaded from one of the wagons, and footmen would carry Arabia and Lady Frances through the most picturesque stretches of countryside, such as when we passed the ancient stone trilithons near Salisbury.

At night, we lodged at inns in the market towns. When we were half a mile out, the head coachman would give a blast upon his horn: the signal for the footmen to run on ahead, calling out Mr De Lacy's name, so that the inn and everyone else would know that a great personage approached. These inns were nothing like the Magpie, or the places I'd stayed with Father in the old days. Small mansions in and of themselves, embellished with pediments and pilasters, they had room for dozens of guests to sleep at a time. The innkeepers were all known to Julius, the rooms booked well in advance by the household steward. This large, efficient gentleman had introduced himself to me in London with a bland, dimpling smile: 'Richard Whittington, at your service. Afraid there's no cat.'

As I was a last-minute addition to the party, Mr Whittington had decreed on our first night that Emily's governess, a Miss Webster, should share with Lady Frances's lady's maid, in order that I might have her room. The latter, a little, dark French girl, with large languid eyes and a small pinched mouth, gave me a look of daggers when she was told. Miss Webster was perfectly polite, but I sensed fury behind her smiles. Never let it be said that I didn't know how to make useful friends. Nonetheless, when I was settled in my spacious room with a four-poster bed, scented linens and mahogany furniture, I did not regret my situation so very much.

We ate our principal meal of the day in the evenings, in order to make swifter progress on the road. The conversation at table invariably centred upon the De Lacys' summer ball. This grand event, I'd learned, had been delayed due to the family's prolonged stay in London, but was to be held at Leighfindell in the last week of September. Lady Frances and Arabia could scarcely talk of anything else, and even Julius grew animated, boasting about all the important gentlemen due to attend. It seemed Mr Walpole might make the journey, and Mr Handel, the composer, and Mr Hogarth, the artist, as well as any number of dukes and earls and their ladies.

'Leighfindell will never before have witnessed such splendours,' Brinseley Radclyffe declared one night – I think we were in the market town of Blandford. 'Will Handel perform for us, do you think?'

'The amount I'm paying him to attend, he better had,' Julius replied.

'How good it will be to see him after so long. Did I tell you we were acquainted in Milan?'

As Mr Radclyffe is of some small significance to this tale, I wish here to pause to say a few words about him. We had been formally

introduced by Julius on the morning of our departure, amidst the
bustle of carriages in the courtyard of De Lacy House.

'The little redhead from Bath,' he said, peering down at me. 'I
remember. You gave my poor father quite a turn.'

'Miss Antrobus reads fortunes,' Julius said. 'Mother finds her a
delight.'

'So your daughter tells me.' Mr Radclyffe kissed my hand. *'Je suis
enchanté de rencontrer l'enchanteresse.'*

Why he was talking in French, I have no idea. Almost imme-
diately, he turned away to address Julius again: 'The Holy Roman
Empress once told my fortune with the cards of the *Tarocco Bolognese*.
Were you ever presented to her?'

Thus the conversation continued several inches above my head.
If I held little interest for Brinseley Radclyffe, he held some small
interest to me, given his father's hatred of the De Lacys, and his elder
brother's role in the death of Julius's brother, Virgil, which still caused
Mirabel so much pain.

Brinseley was about the same age as Julius, and I later learned that
the pair had been friends since their youth, thrown together, like their
elder brothers, by Nicholas De Lacy's purchase of Leighfindell. As
well as his Adonis wigs, Mr Radclyffe favoured striped fabrics, fur
trim, and coloured tassels in the *Turquerie* style. Arguably handsome,
in a robust, ruddy sense of the word, he liked to stand with his legs
very far apart. I knew how well the King's First Minister, Mr Walpole,
regarded his talents as a diplomat, because during the course of our
journey, Mr Radclyffe had seen fit to inform us several times. He was
certainly liberal with his compliments, finding warm words for every
innkeeper, speaking in French and Italian to the cooks, even praising
the wenches who poured his wine.

'It pays, you know,' he told Julius, after the latter had rolled his eyes
on one such occasion. 'The trading classes remember a kind word. It
makes them eager to please. I get the best service of anyone anywhere.
You can guarantee it.'

'I find my money fulfils that task just as well,' Julius said. 'Coddle
such people and it only demeans you both.'

Back to the night in Blandford and the Leighfindell ball.

'Handel introduced me to the great Anna Strada,' Mr Radclyffe went on. 'Did you know the Italians call her *La Scrofa*, the pig? Voice of an angel, plain as Lucifer, though I found her very charming in her manners.'

'I suppose one cannot have everything,' Julius said.

His wife smiled thinly. 'To hear him say it, one might almost think that he believes it.'

Julius grinned and Arabia laughed, though I wasn't altogether sure that Lady Frances had meant it as a joke. Perhaps it was just her manner. She had not warmed to me on our travels. Indeed, the curt words she had spoken to me at the *concert au jardin* numbered perhaps half of those she had spoken to me subsequently.

Mirabel let out a little sigh. 'Do you remember the ball we held in '22? How fine Virgil looked in his white dress suit. That was the last time I ever saw him dance.'

An awkward silence descended upon the table. Julius shot his mother a look of annoyance. Lady Frances glanced rather anxiously at Mr Radclyffe. Septimus watched in obvious amusement, whilst Emily, who had seemed somewhat subdued since we'd left London, stared down at her plate.

'It will be a turning of the page,' Julius declared.

Mr Radclyffe inclined his head in acknowledgement of the sentiment, but took out his watch and stared at it, looking rather displeased.

'Billiards, Mr Radclyffe?' Archie asked swiftly. 'I believe we owe the footmen a game.'

Thus any further awkwardness was avoided. Septimus went to watch, and Julius rose to attend to his papers, as he often did at this hour. Sensing Mirabel might be in a mood to talk, I asked her if she wanted me to tell her fortune, but she said that she was tired, and went up to bed. I withdrew with the other ladies to one of the parlours, where the conversation returned to the ball. I listened distractedly – *the ball, oh the ball!* – my thoughts occupied with Tamson. Perhaps an hour later, Mr Whittington appeared at the door. He bowed to his mistress. 'Mr De Lacy requests an audience with Miss Antrobus.'

Lady Frances eyed me rather balefully, then gave me a curt nod. I followed Mr Whittington upstairs to Julius's private parlour, where he left us, closing the door behind him.

Julius rose from his chair, gesturing me to an adjacent sofa. The parlour was large, with opulent brocade furniture, and paintings of the carnival in Venice. I sat hesitantly, fully aware of the impropriety of being alone with a gentleman like this. Yet given that I had repeatedly signalled my lack of concern for matters of etiquette during my visits to De Lacy House, I hardly felt in any position to object. Nor did I wish to displease my host. Reasoning that Julius might want his fortune told in private, I answered his queries about how I was finding the journey with polite reserve.

'Don't mind my wife, will you?' he said. 'She had some reservations about us inviting you upon this trip to Devon, but you mustn't take it personally. This wretched lawsuit of Lady Seabrooke's is very much upon her mind, and not everyone around us can be trusted. My sister has placed spies in my household before.'

I smiled to hide my concern. 'Should I have left my ciphers and invisible inks at home?'

He laughed. 'I told my wife that Lady Seabrooke would never send such an awkward spy. Your clothes, and so on. Your situation. It's so irregular, it would be bound to arouse suspicion. But please don't be offended if I don't ask to have my fortune told while we are at Leigh-findell. There is only one matter I would wish to ask you about, my current legal battles, and my lawyers insist upon discretion.'

'I understand,' I said, those polite words a mask for my disappointment.

Julius examined me with unabashed interest. 'Those clothes of yours won't do, you know,' he murmured. 'At Leighfindell, we will dress you up. Some lace, some stones, some sparkle.'

'Sir,' I began, 'I could not possibly—'

Julius frowned. 'It is my wish to see you transformed. Say no more about it.' He took a sip of wine and the candles flickered. 'In return, I ask only that you keep my mother occupied down in Devon. I'm sure you noticed her little performance at table tonight. I don't want her upsetting Mr Radclyffe by bringing up the past. Keep her distracted. Do you think you can do that?'

Of course, I said that I would, though I wondered why he cared so much about Mr Radclyffe's feelings. Hadn't the De Lacys supplanted the Radclyffe family and taken their estate? Hadn't Mr Radclyffe's brother killed his own?

'Good girl.' Julius reached out a hand, and fingered a lock of my hair. 'My mother is right, you know. The colour is lovely.'

For a moment, I sat rooted in shock. Then I sprang to my feet, upsetting his glass with my skirts. Dumbly, I watched the wine pool onto the floor.

'That was clumsy of you.' Julius picked up a sheaf of papers from a side table, and sat back in his chair to study them. After a moment, he looked up, as if surprised to find me still there. 'Send in one of the maids to clean up this mess on your way out.'

Chapter Two

Ace of diamonds, influenced by a club:
a prudent choice.

O N T H E E I G H T H day following our departure from London, we arrived at Leighfindell. We travelled across De Lacy land for at least twenty minutes, through beechwoods and purple moorland, past cattle farms and quarries, until finally we rattled between a pair of stone gateposts topped with praying angels that marked the boundary of the park. Soon we were descending into the valley at the heart of the estate. When the road levelled out, and we emerged from the trees, I glimpsed rolling lawns, more woodland, a herd of red deer, pavilions and temples ornamenting the grounds.

A deep sense of misgiving had settled upon me during the latter stages of the journey. Now that Leighfindell lay before me, my plan seemed to me a very grave mistake. How could I ever hope to find this report? Surely, I'd be discovered first? Especially with Archie Montfort watching my every move. I didn't even know for certain that the report would help me win my case. And even if it did, I hadn't the first idea how I'd ever pay for the lawyers I'd need to represent me. Yet it was too late to turn back now. I had made my choice.

Peering from the window, I saw that Brinseley Radclyffe's carriage had veered off to the left along a spur of drive, presumably destined for the Dower House. We entered an allée of majestic lime trees, and for the first time I could see the house ahead of us. Three storeys in height, built of worn yellow stone, two wings of seven bays each flanked a more ornamental building at their centre. Two further courts of buildings, one on each side of the forecourt, appeared to contain kitchens, laundries and the like.

'The first Piers Radclyffe was created Duke of Brecon and Clifton by Edward the Third,' Septimus said. 'For nearly two hundred years, the Radclyffes controlled three counties. This house was built by Piers the Ninth not long before the family's fall. He sided with pope over king in the matter of the King's divorce, and Henry took exception. Stripped them of most of their land, along with their title. Do stop me if Brinseley has bored you with all this already?'

'No, I'm interested in the history.' All being well, this house would soon belong to me.

'My sister, Jemima, was too,' Septimus said. 'Knights and their maidens. Old battles. Old legends. With the Radclyffe family, it's all simple enough. Show them a war and they will pick the wrong side every time. Pope over Elizabeth, king over Cromwell, Stuart over Orange. I'm sure old Piers is a perfect Jacobite even now.'

'Oh, he's no such thing,' Arabia cried. 'Don't listen to him, Miss Antrobus. Old Mr Radclyffe is a Catholic, to be certain, but I'm sure he's loyal as a Labrador. And don't hold it against poor Brinseley. He converted to the true English Church as soon as he came of age.'

'Of course he converted,' her husband said. 'He wants money and power and position. He'd be a Hindoo if it came with five thousand a year.'

'No one should be forced to choose between his religion and his family's interest,' Archie said. 'Reform of the laws against Catholics in public life is long overdue.'

Having grown up in the liberal environs of Trim Street, I heartily agreed. Yet I refused to give Archie Montfort the satisfaction of saying so.

'Brinseley's father is the fifteenth Radclyffe named Piers,' Arabia went on, trying to change this rather controversial subject. 'It is a charming family tradition, don't you think?'

'More like a lack of imagination,' Septimus said. 'You'll see traces of the Radclyffes everywhere at Leighfindell. Their dull books, their dismal paintings, their gloomy tapestries. My father bought their history lock and stock.'

'A house of ghosts,' I murmured to myself.

Septimus caught my remark. 'Ghosts?' he said, his smile fading. 'Oh yes, we can promise you plenty of those.'

As we approached the carriage circle, a pair of liveried footmen emerged from sentry boxes flanking the gate, and blew upon hunting horns. To my right, I saw the baggage wagons and servants' carriages heading off on another spur of drive, presumably destined for the stable yard. The moment we drew to a halt on the cobbled forecourt, a battalion of grooms swarmed around us, uncoupling the horses. The carriages were then hauled by hand beneath an arch that led through the very centre of the house into a vast central courtyard, enclosed on each of the other three sides by a mansion equally as large as the first. The carriage doors were flung open with great ceremony and the footmen handed us down, our journey finally at an end.

I gazed around myself in awe. Travelling beneath that arch, we might have been transported from Tudor England to Venice or Verona, surrounded by Doric pilasters and Roman statues, a chequerboard of pink and white marble beneath our feet. The courtyard lacked the weathered beauty of the older north front of the house, but one couldn't help but admire its magnificence.

Julius appeared gratified by my expression. 'My father's design. We greatly enlarged the house by building the east, west and south fronts. Wait until you see the south front from the garden side. It's really quite something.'

I smiled uneasily, the incident at the inn weighing heavily upon my mind. Julius had not mentioned it subsequently, and he had made no attempt to be alone with me since. Sometimes I wondered if I'd imagined the whole episode. Yet I knew I had not. I kept wondering if I'd somehow given him the wrong impression. I'd gone back and forth over my behaviour, castigating myself for imagined sins.

We proceeded up a flight of double steps, through vast bronze doors flanked by marble Romans, into an entrance hall dominated by a great oil painting of a red-haired Circe turning men into swine.

Immediately, my sense of unease deepened. My father had used to say that just as a gifted cartomancer can see the true soul of a person, so they can feel the true essence of a place. A battlefield, or the house of a murderer can afflict the senses most powerfully. So it was walking into Leighfindell now. My mind was consumed by an ominous energy that seemed to seep from the very stones. It all but paralysed me in the moment, before I was swept up by Mr Whittington's brusque efficiency.

He guided me along a line of manservants and housemaids waiting to welcome the family, headed by the land steward and a gaunt, stately housekeeper. It was bewildering to receive so many bows and curtseys as I progressed down this allée of servitude.

'My name is Mrs Vaughan.' The housekeeper gave me a wintry smile. 'Mr Whittington informs me that you have not brought your own maid here to Leighfindell. During your stay in this house, Rosie Denham will perform that task.' She beckoned forward a woman of about forty, dressed in a pretty floral gown and a white lace cap trimmed with a peach ribbon. She curtsied as elegantly as my dancing master had always wished I might.

'Rosie is my under-housekeeper,' Mrs Vaughan went on, 'but she was once a lady's maid herself, and is accomplished in all the usual duties you will require. If you have any trouble with her at all, then in the first instance you are to come to me, not Mr Whittington.'

Disliking the thought of someone else watching over me, I said that though I was grateful for the consideration, this would not be necessary.

'Oh, but it is,' Mrs Vaughan replied, her narrow nostrils flaring. 'No lady should be without her maid. Not at Leighfindell. Rosie, please show Miss Antrobus to the Chinese bedroom.'

From the expressions on the faces of the servants, I could see that I had already been judged a poor acquaintance unworthy of Leighfindell's splendour. I followed Rosie up a grand flight of stairs, while she explained that my room was located in the south wing of the house, where Mr Septimus and his family also slept. The rooms of Mr Julius and his family were in the north front, while more guest accommodation was to be found in the west wing, rooms currently being prepared for guests attending the ball. The east wing housed the senior servants, together with the various professional gentlemen who served the household.

Rosie was a little taller than me, with a brisk stride that had me hurrying along at her side. I admired the sway of her trim waist, and the glossiness of the mahogany curl that escaped her cap. At Leigh-findell, it seemed even the servants could make one feel wanting. We made a quarter-circuit of the house, along corridors hung with architectural drawings of the various fronts. Certain I'd never remember the way to my room, I counted the doors, and had reached the number fourteen, when Rosie halted before yet another door.

If I tell you that, in addition to the usual furnishings, my bedroom at Leighfindell contained a sofa, a japanned tea table, an escritoire, several cushioned chairs, and a *prie-dieu* for saying my prayers, then you will gain a good impression of the size. The bed's canopy was of apricot silk embroidered with hummingbirds, the spray of ostrich feathers at its zenith almost brushing the gilded ceiling. An adjoining dressing room was fitted out with cabinetry, a French-style fruitwood vanity table, and a marble-topped washstand. Yet even here, amidst all this splendour, my senses prickled at the dark, restless energy of the house.

Rosie unpacked my trunk, looking a little puzzled by its meagre contents. 'I'm at a loss to know what's happened,' she said, her speech a perfect emulation of the ladies of the house. 'I'll have Mr Whittington hunt down the rest of your luggage right away.'

'I'm afraid this is all I've brought,' I said. 'The footmen will be raising a toast to my restraint.'

Rosie's unsmiling nod made it plain what she thought about that. While she worked, I went to one of the windows, which overlooked a parterre, a cascade, and a quartet of walled gardens. Beyond the formal gardens, the full vista of the valley unfolded: a lake with an island, lawns dotted with specimen trees, and the steep slope of the wooded hills, a tall tower of yellow stone at the crest of the rise.

There soon came a knock at the door and Emily sailed into the room, followed by three maids. 'Father asked me to look these out for you. A few old gowns of mother's and Aunt Arabia's he thought you could use.'

The maids laid these 'old gowns' out on the bed for my inspection. Fine satins, brocades and silks, sable cuffs, embroidered velvet, spangles and seed pearls galore. Dressed like this, I would no longer resemble a poor companion, even if I still felt like one. Yet after the incident at the inn, I did not much relish the prospect of placing myself further in Julius's debt.

'Rosie, you are to give Miss Antrobus's measurements to the seamstresses,' Emily said. 'Make certain they understand that it is my father's command. He wants to see Miss Antrobus wearing these gowns as soon as possible.'

Emily dismissed the maids and then joined me at the window. 'That tower is called the Pharos,' she said. 'It's where Luna met John Jory on the night of their elopement. He had two horses waiting by the south gate. Nonny says he cast a spell upon the dogs and gamekeepers and the porters at the lodge, but Uncle Septimus says he fed the dogs poisoned meat, and bribed the gamekeepers and the porters to keep quiet.'

'Did nobody suspect them at all?' I asked.

'My father and uncle used to tease Luna that John Jory was in love with her, but nobody thought for a moment that his affections were returned. She must have hidden it well – and little wonder. My grandfather wouldn't even let her sister, Jemima, marry Little Piers Radclyffe, and he was of a good family – though a Catholic, of course.'

'I thought Little Piers rejected your Aunt Jemima? That's what your grandmother said.'

'Did she?' Emily raised an eyebrow. 'I suppose he did, in a manner of speaking, but my grandfather engineered it all. Everything that followed – the duel, the elopement – was all his fault.'

'How so?' I cried, eager to learn more about my family's history.

'At first my grandfather simply refused the match,' Emily said. 'He wanted Jemima to marry a man with a grand title to impress his friends. But Little Piers wasn't deterred. He was in love with Jemima and he asked for her hand many more times. And Jemima swore she would not marry at all, if she couldn't have him. That put my grandfather in a bind, and so he summoned Little Piers and offered him a choice. He could have Jemima for his wife with a dowry of just seven guineas. Or he could leave Leighfindell without her, with seven hundred. Well, the Radclyffes had lost most of their fortune in the Bubble – and so what do you think Little Piers did? He chose the money.'

'What a heartless thing to happen. Poor Jemima.'

'It was cruel,' Emily said fiercely. 'When Little Piers left for London, Jemima went out of her mind with grief. Archie said Nonny told you about the duel.'

'She did,' I said. 'What happened to Little Piers after he killed your Uncle Virgil?'

'He was filled with remorse. Ran off to Italy, where he died in squalor. Father says he drank himself to death.'

'And Jemima? Your grandmother said she died of a broken heart. But people don't die from broken hearts. Only in stories.'

'A broken heart? A broken neck, more like. After she went mad, my grandfather had her locked up in the attic infirmary. Only her maid and Doctor Crowhurst were permitted to see her. But one night, she somehow got out and wandered into the garden wearing only her nightshift. They think she was trying to find Little Piers at the Dower House. Only she fell down a flight of steps in the dark and they found her lying there the following morning.' Emily gave a heartfelt sigh. 'So you can see why Luna went so far. She must have felt like a prisoner, shut up here in this house of tragedy, waiting to marry some nobleman she could never love. She was determined to choose her own destiny, whatever the consequences. Her story is so romantic, don't you think?'

Emily reminded me of myself as a child, weaving foolish fantasies of my parents' great love. 'There's no romance in empty promises,' I said. 'Look at how it ended. They were only deceiving themselves. Or one another.'

Emily frowned. 'That's not true. I told you before, the deaths of

John Jory and the child must have been a dreadful accident.' She studied my face. 'Have you never fallen in love?'

'Not once,' I declared, cheerfully.

Nor would I. Men were nothing but a world of trouble, with their threats and their desires and their greed. If there was one promise I could make to myself that I was certain I would keep, then it was that.

♦

The family reconvened that evening for supper in the Stag Room, which Emily informed me was the smallest of Leighfindell's four dining rooms. Antlered heads gazed down at me, the candlelight giving a flicker of movement to their dead eyes. Famished after the journey, I devoured a plate of jellied calf's head, salad and potted lampreys, listening to talk of the morrow's hunting, which had supplanted the usual conversation about the ball.

'Perhaps tomorrow morning you might tell my fortune, Miss Antrobus?' Mirabel said, during a lull in this discussion.

Naturally, I said I would be delighted. Mirabel had only made this request twice during our journey, and on both occasions, Archie had made certain he was present. Her queries had concerned trivial matters, and she hadn't ventured any further confidences about her family. I suspected that she would not do so again until we were alone. I hoped tomorrow we might talk about my parents' elopement and the family's legal battles – and I might be able to help ease Mirabel's troubled mind at the same time.

'Come to my dressing room after ten,' she said. 'We will take breakfast together.' Catching Archie's eye, she laughed. 'Don't look like that, young man. You may judge, but you don't understand.'

'Oh, I think I do,' Archie said, with a stern look for me.

I smiled at him sweetly, determined to show him that I cared nothing for his censure. 'Our journey here made me think of our experiment in the park. Think how swiftly we could have covered the miles, travelling by Gusmão's passarola. Have you conducted any other experiments of late?'

'Regretfully not,' he said, rather stiffly. 'I've had little time to call my own. But if I can find a spare afternoon while we're here, I promised the twins that we would put Galileo's law of falling bodies to the test.'

'Not literally, I hope,' his stepfather said. 'Though they ate so much cake at the *concert au jardin*, they'd probably bounce.'

'I don't see why you always see fit to criticize,' Emily said, addressing Archie. 'How can you know that fortune telling is a nonsense, if you've never tried it? Don't you always say a man should make up his own mind based upon the evidence?'

'Why, yes, you do,' his mother cried, clapping her hands.

'I will happily tell your fortune, Mr Montfort,' I said.

'Thank you, Miss Antrobus,' he replied, with that condescending smile, 'but I prefer the contents of my mind to remain my own.'

Emily pushed away her plate of candied fruits and comfits. 'Perhaps he is afraid of what you might find there.'

The pair exchanged a hostile glance, and I resolved again to find out the cause of their discord.

After supper, Lady Frances declared that she was tired after the journey and was going to bed. Mirabel and Emily soon followed suit. I read a fortune for Arabia, and though I thought about manipulating the cards to prompt a discussion about the elopement, Archie was hovering, and I thought better of it. Once I had finished, I went up to bed myself. I was climbing the Oak Stairs, admiring the paintings, when I noticed Julius standing in the shadows of the hall below, watching me.

He bowed, raising his glass. 'Goodnight, Miss Antrobus.'

When I replied in kind, he did not move from his position, but simply watched me from behind as I continued up the stairs. Rather troubled, I hurried to my room and rang the bell for Rosie, who helped me to remove my dress and unlaced my stays. I asked myself again if I was overreacting to the situation, but the interest Julius was showing in me was definitely disturbing.

Once Rosie had gone, I pulled back the counterpane to climb into bed, frowning at the sight that awaited me there. Propped against the bolster was a playing card. The unlucky red card, the eight of diamonds. I picked it up to examine it. The card was from a De Lacy pack – of the same design as the one in the portmanteau and those I'd used at De Lacy House. Had it fallen out of my pack? Had Rosie found it and placed it here?

Taking the pack from my pocket, I riffled through the cards until I came to the eight of diamonds. Not mine, then. So where had it come from? Could it be a warning? A curse? Because of my manipulations of the cards? The ancient power of the Square of Sevens asserting itself? Or had someone placed it here as some sort of a silly prank?

Whatever the answer, it felt like an ill omen. I thrust the card into the drawer of the nightstand and slammed it shut. Climbing into bed, I told myself that I was a silly fool to let a playing card unsettle me. Yet my fears crawled around in my mind for an hour and more, as I lay there listening to the creak of that vast house.

CHAPTER THREE

*Queen of clubs as master-card: a marked female influence on the
querist, in the way of respect, judgement, advice, or authority.*

MIRABEL AND I stared down at the king of spades, smoke from
her silver pipe coiling between us. The card seemed to exert a
new power here in the oppressive airs of Leighfindell.

'Always, he is present in your parallelogram,' I said. 'The man who
hides his true malevolence. Can you think whom he might be?'

Mirabel smiled. 'My family has entertained every prince, bishop
and politician in the kingdom. If I had a sunflower seed for all the
malevolent characters I've met, I could fill Ocho's bowl.' She reached
out a hand to pet the parrot, who edged along his gilded perch to get
away from her.

Mirabel's dressing room was fitted out with duck-egg-blue
cabinetry, gilded mirrors and painted panels of lithesome nymphs
twirling ribbons. Her maid had brought us a breakfast of fruitcake
and carraway buns, preserves from the estate's orchards, butter from
their dairy, and honey from their hives. We were both in our dressing
gowns, our hair unpinned in loose coils. Mirabel took a sip of chocolate, and then drew on her pipe again.

'The recurring presence of the king of spades suggests someone
far closer than a passing acquaintance,' I said. 'He must be a man
of great significance in your life.' I pointed to the second and third
rows of cards. 'The queen, knave and king of hearts all appear in close
proximity. That is a most unusual combination. The queen figures a

woman beloved by a male relative, one who closely resembles you in appearance. This relative might be figured by the king of hearts, a man of good temperament. From everything you have told me, I'd say this sounds very much like Virgil and Jemima.'

Mirabel stared, her eyes very bright. 'They were reunited in heaven. The thought consoles me.'

I had let the cards fall naturally. Partly because I genuinely wanted to help Mirabel, and could only do so if the cards reflected what was truly in her soul. And partly because I was still unsettled by the eight of diamonds that I'd found on my bolster last night. I'd questioned Rosie that morning, and she'd told me she hadn't put it there, and neither had it been there when she'd made the bed. 'It might be the twins playing a prank,' she'd said. 'I wouldn't worry, miss.'

But I did worry. About my manipulations of the cards. About getting caught. About Tamson. What if I brought her more bad luck? What if . . . What if . . . What if . . . Catching my fears spiralling, I dragged my mind back to the present.

'It was Virgil who gave me Ocho,' Mirabel said, turning to smile at the bird. 'He bought him from a Spaniard at his club, some buccaneer who had spent time in the southern Americas. The Spaniard had named him for their silver coins, for luck. *Siete* would have been more apposite, but he answered to Ocho, and it would have been cruel to change it. Virgil said Ocho would watch over me, and so he—' She broke off, staring at the cards. 'But of course. Isn't it obvious who he is? My king of spades? That cowardly poltroon, Jemima's suitor: Little Piers Radclyffe. Didn't he break her heart? Didn't he shoot Virgil dead? What could be more malevolent than that?'

After everything Emily had told me, I believed there was another, more likely candidate. Yet it was a delicate topic to raise.

'See here, the knave of clubs,' I said. 'He figures a selfish man, one too easily influenced by others of greater art. Aren't those words that might describe Little Piers? Which means our king of spades probably refers to someone else connected to these events, perhaps that same person seen here exerting influence?'

Mirabel looked at me sharply. 'Have you been talking to Emily?'

'A little. She likes to talk about her family.'

'I suppose she told you about my husband's offer? How Little Piers made his choice?'

I saw no point in lying. 'Yes, she did.'

Mirabel sighed. 'Emily and Jemima are so much alike that it pains me. Romantic souls with romantic notions about the dead. Jemima's obsession was with the last Radclyffe duchess and she had been dead for nearly two hundred years. Whereas for Emily, it is Jemima and her sister who hold the fascination. Every romantic story needs a villain, and Emily has cast my late husband in that role. But Emily never knew her grandfather, and she is still very much a child, one rather innocent about the designs of men. My husband acted only to protect Jemima from an adventurer who was after her money. Whatever the tragedies that followed, his motivation cannot possibly be construed as malevolent.'

'Forgive me, madam. I did not mean to suggest that your husband—'

'Yes, you did.' Her eyes glittered, a little dangerously. 'My husband was a great man. Oh, I concede that he could be hard to love. Our match was arranged by our parents, and it took me several years to feel that great connection to which all young girls aspire. But I respected him from the first. His mind, his strength of character, his purpose. Nobody could measure up to him. Not in my eyes. That's why I never remarried, though I still possessed my looks, and I had several offers.' She preened a little, studying her rings.

'*The king of spades,*' Ocho squawked, with a great ruffle of his feathers – though it might have been 'the King of Spain'.

Although I wanted to help her and I felt that this card was key to her troubles, I also wanted to learn more about the court case and the report, my particular objective here at Leighfindell. Given her prickliness upon the subject of her husband, I took the opportunity to change the subject.

'Your estrangement from your younger daughter must grieve you greatly,' I said.

'More than you can ever know,' Mirabel replied. 'For years I have written to her, but my letters are returned unopened. I fear for her,

Miss Antrobus. In trying to destroy her family, she is only destroying herself.'

'I read in one of the newspapers that she might win her latest case?'

'I cannot think how. The courts will rule this codicil a forgery.'

'What makes you so certain?'

'Because the facts don't fit,' she said. 'There is no chance that the codicil survived. My husband destroyed it.'

'Why would he do that so soon after signing it?'

She shook her head. 'Forgive me, dear. Julius doesn't like the family discussing our legal matters with outsiders.'

'Everything we say is between these four walls,' I reassured her. 'No secrets are more sacrosanct than those between a fortune teller and her querist.'

She smiled rather sardonically. 'You are wrong, Miss Antrobus, at least in this house. My son's possession of the De Lacy fortune takes precedence over everything.'

Her tone was emphatic. I could see I'd get nowhere by persisting, yet I itched to breach the guarded citadel of her mind.

Later that day, I began my search for the report. Emily had shown me around the house on the day of our arrival. She'd informed me that Leighfindell had three hundred and thirty-seven rooms, a fact that filled me with trepidation. We had trooped through four dining rooms, a breakfast room, two morning rooms, any number of drawing rooms, five apartments of state, a library, a music room, a billiard room, and an enfilade of ante-rooms leading to a baroque Great Chamber, where the ball was to be held. Upstairs were countless bedrooms, dressing rooms, parlours and closets.

With so many rooms, it was easy to avoid company in that house unless one sought it. Julius and Archie were in the study attending to business. Septimus was out hunting. I could hear his gunshots echoing across the valley. Mirabel was still in her room; Emily was playing the harpsichord in the music room; Lady Frances was seeing to some piece of household management in the kitchen court; and Arabia was quilling in the morning room. The twins, I presumed, were upstairs with their tutor. I read for a time in the library, observing the patterns of the servants' movements in the hall, and then walked up the Oak Stairs to the first floor where the private rooms of Julius and his wife were located.

The door to their rooms was locked, but I had come prepared for such an eventuality. Over the past week, during the journey to Leigh-findell, I had been practising with my lock picks on the doors to my inn bedrooms, or on any lockable drawer or box I found within. The lock picks proved much easier to use than the hairpin with which I'd attempted to open the portmanteau. All my father's lessons came flooding back to me: how to apply the correct amount of tension, how to listen for each small click as the pins were sprung. Now I put those talents to good use.

My heart raced as I worked the pick, listening out for the sound of any approaching servant. It took me a few minutes, but eventually the lock gave with a satisfying snap. Opening the door, I walked into a private parlour. Like the exterior of the house, the interior had two distinct styles of decoration. The rooms in the north front retained the original Tudor fittings: rich oak panelling, coffered ceilings, and vast, blackened chimney pieces. The rooms in the modern wings were modelled after the Italian style of the courtyard, with intricate plasterwork, pedimented doors, and marble fireplaces. This parlour was positioned directly over the arched courtyard entrance in the north front, the dark walnut panelling and small, diamond-paned windows giving it a rather gloomy air.

My eye alighted immediately upon a walnut secretaire. A letter lay upon the desktop, though a quick glance was enough to ascertain that it contained only town gossip from one of Lady Frances's London friends. Swiftly, my heart pounding, I searched the shelves and drawers, finding only a few volumes on household management, a book of Lady Frances's plans for the ball, more dull correspondence, a box of watercolours, another of coloured silks, and a half-finished sampler. Also, five small bottles of diacodium, a concoction of the white poppy used to procure sleep. Our old cook, Mrs Grainger, had sometimes taken it for her gout, prompting Mr Antrobus to advise great caution. Perhaps this explained why Lady Frances went to bed so early, and slept so late.

Two doors led out of the room, in addition to the one by which I'd entered. The first opened onto a large chamber with patterned wallpaper and a bed surmounted by a cascading dome of golden silk. The faint scent of Lady Frances's perfume, *Royal Essence*, hung in the air. Reasoning that the document I sought was much more likely to be found in her husband's room, I returned to the parlour and tried the second door. Julius's bedroom was furnished with a carved four-poster bed hung with curtains of crimson damask, elbow chairs of red Morocco leather, and a collection of blue and white porcelain arranged on mahogany tables. As I took a few paces into the room, I was assailed by a powerful blast of the ominous energy I had felt everywhere in that house. Here it was more intense, and for a moment I was rooted to the spot by the shock of it – until I recalled the dangers facing me, and forced myself to move.

Two casement windows with richly carved wooden seats overlooked the carriage circle below. Between them was a marquetry desk, inlaid with the signs of the zodiac picked out in ebony, grenadillo and padouk. The astrological motifs reminded me sharply of Tamson, and I experienced a sudden surge of anxiety. Telling myself to remain calm, I tried a few drawers at random. Those which opened contained paper, packets of sealing wax, bottles of ink and other stationery supplies.

Three of the drawers were locked, and once again, I went to work with my pick. The first proved to contain bundles of letters relating to Julius's business interests. Eagerly, I went through them, running my eye over the contents, but to my disappointment, I did not find a single letter that concerned his legal battles with Lady Seabrooke, and no document that resembled the report I sought.

The second drawer contained a great many pamphlets, pictures and engravings, and it quickly became apparent that I'd find little to help me there. Every document in that drawer concerned the same particular act, depicted in all God's rich variety. I liked to think of myself as a woman of the world, and yet these images were beyond anything I'd ever imagined. Fascinated, I turned the pictures at different angles, trying to make sense of these strange activities: men and women, women and women, sometimes more than one woman, or more than one man. I'm not sure how long I sat there looking, but eventually I roused myself, and returned everything to the drawer in a great fluster.

The final drawer contained business contracts and other papers. I went through them all methodically, but I didn't find the report, and only one document held my interest. A letter from a London solicitor, a Mr Godolphin, together with the draft of a contract containing suggested amendments. Under the terms of this contract, Julius De Lacy was to provide Brinseley Radclyffe with the sum of ten thousand pounds. Furthermore, Mr Radclyffe was to be granted the use of a townhouse in Mayfair, a coach-and-six, and a manor house in the countryside at Hammersmith. The event that was to occasion all of this largesse was Mr Radclyffe's marriage to Julius's daughter, Emily De Lacy.

Chapter Four

Two of diamonds, influenced by a spade:
a service that one is glad of.

Lady Seabrooke's gaze is soft, gentle even. Her voice is calm, and yet it holds a note of strain. 'You must prepare yourself, my love. When our suit comes before the courts in the new term, our enemies may say unpleasant things about my past.'

Her son, Leopold, studies her face. He is fortunate to have his mother's looks: her creamy skin, her soft, red hair, her searching blue eyes. He sits proudly in his blue frockcoat, his gaze sometimes alighting upon Lazarus, no doubt curious as to his presence during this moment of family confidence.

'Can't we stop them, Mama?'

'We have tried, my love – alas, unsuccessfully.'

Somewhat to Lazarus's surprise, she had not castigated him for the failure of his plan to apprehend Red at the Bartholomew Fair.

'Of course,' she'd said, frowning, when he'd imparted the news. 'The eight of diamonds. It was there in my fortune. I should have known that your endeavour would end in disaster.'

Lazarus prefers to list more corporeal causes. Red absent from her post in the booth, when Trevithick had assured him she would be there. The magistrate's over-zealousness. The ineptitude of his constables. Lazarus's own mistakes, not least losing the girl in the crowd after the chaos with the bear.

Apprehending Red at De Lacy House the following morning

would have been out of the question. Lady Seabrooke is adamant that her brother mustn't learn of Red's scheme, and it wouldn't have taken much for Julius to discover their involvement. Lazarus prays Red will be careful at Leighfindell, and yet ultimately unsuccessful. Lady Seabrooke, mindful of her eight of diamonds, clings to no such hope. One way or another, she is convinced her past will be laid bare. It is with this outcome in mind, that she has taken the difficult decision to prepare young Leopold for the worst.

'Whatever they say about me,' she says, 'it is important that you remember that these stories come from a place of desperation on the part of our enemies. The truth will not serve them, and so they will resort to lies. They may even have evidence that appears to support their claims. I'm afraid their lies might be reported in the newspapers.'

Her son gazes at her steadily. 'What sort of lies?'

'The sort men always concoct about a woman they seek to destroy. They will try to attack my character, my virtue. Certain events in my youth—' Lady Seabrooke breaks off, looks at Lazarus helplessly. She is terrified of losing the love and respect of her son.

'They will seek to divide you,' Lazarus says. 'Not just the De Lacys. Perhaps another party too. Unity in the face of adversity. It is vital to your interests that you don't let them succeed.'

'Another party?' the boy says, looking from Lazarus to his mother.

'Lawsuits like ours, with much at stake, always attract such people,' she says. 'Vultures seeking to feast upon the spoils. But Mr Darke is right. As long as we let nothing come between us, we shall emerge victorious.'

'I understand.' The boy rises. 'Thank you for telling me, Mama. I will leave you now.'

His footsteps ring out on the parquet, and when the door closes, Lady Seabrooke clasps her hands to her breast. 'He will hate me.'

'How could he?' Lazarus says.

'Because my enemies will flay the flesh from my bones.'

'It may not be as bad as you think,' he says. 'The girl has no proof, or none that we know of. And as I told you, I think the De Lacys will hesitate to use the proof they have.'

'But the allegation will be made,' she says. 'The ghost of John Jory will stalk that courtroom. And my son will have to look him in the eye.'

'Would you like me to talk to him?' Lazarus says. He suspects this is the reason she was so insistent that he stay.

Her gratified expression fills his heart. 'I think if anyone could help him understand, then it would be you.'

Lazarus finds the boy in the card room, setting up his jade and ivory chess pieces. Together, they survey the problem on the board.

'Use your knight to take the bishop and protect the queen?' Lazarus suggests.

But the boy's mind is plainly not on chess. 'Those events in her youth. She means the elopement with the gypsy, doesn't she?'

So the gossip has reached his ears. Lazarus supposes he shouldn't be surprised. 'He wasn't a gypsy.'

'Then it's true?'

How to answer that? 'The important thing for you to remember, is that your mother was not at fault. People will put the worst construction upon it, but they will be wrong.'

'If it is in the newspapers, then everyone will know.' Leopold glares. 'I don't want people thinking of her like that.'

As an object of men's lust? As a victim of their desires? Or as the subject of society's condemnation?

'It would be strange if you did,' Lazarus says. 'But it is rather admirable, don't you think? The amount she is prepared to sacrifice in order to restore to you your birthright?'

His voice is sullen. 'This case is as much about her as it is about me. She wants to win, to hurt her family. I'm not sure I even know why.'

The boy has his mother's sharp mind too, and her ability to read people – which is fortunate, as his father made gammon look wise. 'Would you rather she walked away? She might, if you asked her to?'

Leopold thinks for a moment. 'That money is mine by right. My uncle stole it.'

'Then you owe it to her not to listen to anything they say about her character. You know the person she is. That should be enough.'

Leopold examines him. 'You knew her before she married my father, didn't you? What was she like back then?'

Lazarus might have written an essay upon this topic, but he chooses his words for the moment. 'Loyal to those who deserved it. Not everyone did.'

'I will not fail her,' Leopold announces, sitting up a little straighter. 'If anyone speaks unkindly about her in my presence, then I will fight them.'

His work done, Lazarus returns to the salon, praying that the boy's feelings will endure. He finds Lady Seabrooke pacing the floor.

'Your son is ready to take up a sword to defend your honour.'

She smiles uncertainly. 'Dear Lord, I ought to engage a better fencing master.'

Their eyes meet, and in that rare moment of intimacy, his feelings almost overwhelm him. Perhaps she senses it, for she moves away. 'We must be ready for them,' she says. 'My brother *and* the girl. My lawyers will deal with Julius. You remember the pond-man, Jemmy Woodford? It seems he was most forthcoming upon the subject of that poor maid. But I need someone to look into Red's past. To go to Bath, to Cornwall. Will you do it?'

There is more than one way to take up a sword. 'Of course I will.'

She studies his face, concerned. 'You must have the stomach for this fight, Lazarus. I want no quarter given to that girl. If you can't do it, then I'll send for someone else.'

'I said I'll go.'

She bites her lip. 'It all hangs by a thread. Too much and I will lose him. No son should ever know the whole truth about his mother.'

The whole truth. That elusive concept. There is so much he wants to say – and yet something still holds him back. John Jory's ghost again. The ghosts of his mother and father. The lies that bind, the truths that rend asunder.

After Bath, he tells himself. After Cornwall. To drink from the Grail, a knight must first prove his worth.

CHAPTER FIVE

Nine of spades, influenced by a high spade: a lie.

THOSE FIRST TWO days at Leighfindell set the pattern for the following two weeks. In the mornings, I would take breakfast in Mirabel's dressing room, where I'd tell her fortune. If I let the cards fall naturally, then either the duel, Jemima's madness, or the elopement would be figured there, along with the malevolent king of spades and either an error, or a lie, or both.

We talked in circles around these recurring cards, without ever really getting to the bottom of their significance. Mirabel had said that the lie must figure the one told by her husband to the newspapers to cover up the duel. Yet the lie was present even when the duel was not, and to me it seemed to possess some wider significance. Sometimes I felt as if Mirabel knew more than she was admitting about these cards, that she itched to ask me questions she couldn't bring herself to say out loud. Other times, she appeared just as perplexed as I was myself. Occasionally, her family's legal battles seemed to figure in her cards, but she refused to see it, growing irritated if I pressed the point. Once, out of frustration, I manipulated the cards to figure those battles so starkly she could scarcely deny it, but she only repeated her refusal to discuss them.

In the afternoons, I continued my search of the house. Julius's study proved a great disappointment, the drawers of his desk and cabinets containing only maps and plans and correspondence about the estate. I rifled through desks and escritoires in various parlours and bedrooms, and any number of cabinets, map chests and writing boxes. Yet I found no report. Nor did I find any of the usual private papers one would expect to find: deeds to the house, wills, stock certificates and so on. So where were they?

The servants proved a constant hazard during my search. Not least because there were so many of them: under-butlers and footmen, valets and ushers. Housemaids, lady's maids, kitchen maids, scullery maids. Cooks and undercooks, watchmen and lamplighters. A librarian, a gunsmith, an architect, a clerk of works. A fellow to wind the clocks, a man to sharpen the knives and swords, and a whole battalion of tiny sweeps to clean the chimneys. There were even servants to serve the higher-ranking servants. Fortunately, most of them went out of their way to ignore me, scarcely troubling to disguise their derision at my lack of wealth and status.

A far greater hazard was Archie Montfort. I often caught him watching me, listening in when I told his mother's fortune. Happily for me, his stepfather and Julius made many demands upon his time, and he was often called away to advise upon a matter of business or law, or to ride out in pursuit of game. Even then, I didn't relax my guard, not for a moment. Since our encounter in the coffeehouse, I'd given much thought to his threats to expose me, trying to imagine his next move. My best guess was that he would have written to Bath, making inquiries about me amongst his acquaintance there. I didn't know if it was common knowledge that I had run away from home, but if Archie discovered the truth, then he could call me out as a liar. If he learned of my connection to Henry Antrobus, I might even be forcibly returned to his care. I had to take every possible step to prevent this from happening.

Naturally, Leighfindell had its own postmaster. Every two days, at the crack of dawn, he set out upon the journey to Exeter to collect any letters for the household that had come in on the London stage, along with copies of all the London newspapers. He returned at around one the following day, when he handed the family and guest letters to the butler, who had the task of sorting them on a table in the Oak Hall. Under the guise of anxiety about the condition of Mrs Illingworth, I was always the first one there. I'd hunt for a letter I was supposedly expecting (which distressingly never came), and take a swift glance at Archie's mail, looking for any packet postmarked from Bath. It was terrible how many letters went astray down in the country.

Following this task, I would take the London newspapers to the library to search for news of Tamson in the lists of criminal trials. During all my time in Devon, she was never far from my mind.

Life at Leighfindell had its own rhythms, and in between my acts of subterfuge, I adapted to them. On clement days, the ladies of the house took walks around the lake, or sat in the rose garden beneath parasols, playing cribbage and piquet, or reading. When it rained, there was harpsichord and singing in the music room, or quill-work and painting in the library. I often found myself looking at Emily, thinking about that marriage contract in her father's desk drawer. It rather perplexed me. Brinseley Radclyffe, through his conversion to the Church of England and his seat in Parliament, was clearly attempting to rebuild his family's fortune. Yet he was not a rich or powerful man by De Lacy standards. I had discerned no marked affection between him and Emily, which made me doubt it was a love match. Nor did Julius strike me as the sort of man who'd willingly countenance an unequal husband for his only child. In sum, I could well understand why Brinseley Radclyffe should wish to marry Emily, but I struggled to see what was in it for the De Lacys.

Did Emily even know about the proposed marriage? This question was answered one day when we were strolling along the shore of the lake. It didn't take much effort on my part to turn the conversation to love and marriage, and soon Emily halted, turning her frank, appealing gaze upon mine.

'You might as well know,' she said, 'though it has been a secret up until now. My father is to announce my engagement to Mr Radclyffe at the ball.'

I affected amazement. 'Why, I had no suspicion at all! What a fine actress you must be to conceal your feelings so adeptly.'

She smiled a little uncertainly. 'Fourteen is not so very young to be engaged in great families like ours. Brinseley is to change his name to Radclyffe-De Lacy, which I think sounds very fine. When Parliament is not sitting, we are to live at the Dower House and raise our children here at Leighfindell.'

We turned instinctively to gaze back across the lake to the south front of the house: a vast Ionic facade of grey stone topped by a cupola. Fifteen bays wide, it dominated the valley: a stark message from Nicholas De Lacy to Leighfindell's former owners that the De Lacys had arrived.

'Father says it will be a long engagement,' Emily went on. 'We are not to marry whilst Brinseley's father is alive. He is still vigorous in body, for all that his wits are addled, so it could be ten years from now.' She pointed. 'Look. Speak of the devil and he will appear.'

Piers Radclyffe was striding along a path on the far side of the lake. I had seen him several times in the distance on our walks, marching to and from the Dower House on the other side of the valley. A spindly, dishevelled creature, not unlike a scarecrow, his long white hair blew rather wild in the wind. He carried a fowling piece over his shoulder, a lurcher dogging his heels, a brace of pheasants dangling from one hand. I still wanted to ask him about the elopement, and also about the night we'd met at the electricity show. He'd been the first person I had ever told that I was the child of John Jory Jago, and Mrs Fremantle had been murdered only a few weeks later. I still thought Lazarus Darke had probably been lying to unsettle me, but supposing he was right, and her murder was connected to the codicil, then perhaps it was my conversation with Mr Radclyffe that had precipitated it? I didn't think for a moment that Mr Radclyffe was responsible for the murder himself, but I wondered if he'd mentioned our conversation to somebody else.

What Piers Radclyffe's death had to do with Emily's marriage, I didn't fully understand, but I presumed it must concern a matter of inheritance.

'Don't think that I'm not eager,' Emily said. 'Brinseley is a learned man, known throughout the courts of Europe. And he has royal blood too. Not like ours; the proper kind. He took me through his lineage, right back to Edward the First.'

That must have been a long afternoon, I thought.

'Mother says she finds Brinseley very handsome. What do you think?'

As I listened to her trying to convince herself, my pity mingling with anger at her father, my eye was caught by Archie Montfort, riding out from the stable court upon a fine grey hunter. 'I suppose Mr Radclyffe is handsome,' I said cautiously, telling myself that this marriage was none of my business. 'Though isn't yours the only opinion that should count?'

'Brinseley wears his coat very well. And he does not look his age, I don't think.' Emily followed my gaze. 'Archie's off to Exeter, I suppose.'

'What's in Exeter?'

'My father's Devonshire solicitor, Mr Winterton. Archie is the only person Father trusts to carry his legal correspondence. He is too afraid of Lady Seabrooke's spies.'

'Is he still convinced he will win his case?'

'Oh yes, of course. Father's lawyers only need to disprove Lady Seabrooke's lies. Uncle Septimus is trying to find out where she claims to have found the codicil. Her affidavits are sealed until the court reconvenes, but she is not the only one with spies.'

Naturally, I heard all of this in some alarm. The moment the De Lacys learned that the codicil had been sold to Lady Seabrooke by one Henry Antrobus of Bath, every suspicion would fall upon me. I had to find that report before they did.

'The family are united against her,' Emily went on. 'Even Nonny plans to testify that she is lying.' She shaded her eyes to follow the path of the horse. 'All my friends think Archie is very handsome. Though he has no money of his own, and his father was barely a gentleman, so I don't suppose any of them will be allowed to marry him. Do you think he is handsome?'

'Not really.'

She smiled. 'Neither do I.'

'Why don't you like him?' I asked.

Her smile faded. 'I like him well enough.'

A lie is always intriguing. Several theories ran through my mind: a childish falling-out, an affection spurned – but I had too much else upon my mind to dwell on it for long. My failure to find the report, the threat of discovery, Mirabel's circumspection, the playing card in my bed, the scrutiny of Archie, the attentions of Julius. All seemed to me of far greater consequence than Emily's feelings.

I tried very hard to stay out of Julius's way. Yet at mealtimes, there was no way of avoiding him, and I was often subjected to his fulsome compliments and lingering glances. One afternoon, I came into dinner to find a yellow box tied with a red ribbon upon my plate. I looked up enquiringly, and Julius gave me a broad smile. 'Aren't you going to open it, Miss Antrobus?'

Everybody watched as I untied the ribbon. Inside was a tortoiseshell card box with silver clasps.

'I had it commissioned in London and sent after us,' Julius said.

'Oh, it's beautiful,' Emily cried.

'Thank you,' I said, feeling my skin grow warm under their scrutiny. I hated being the centre of attention like this, forced to smile politely at Julius. 'The generosity you have shown me is far more than I deserve.'

'It is precisely what you deserve,' Julius declared. 'We will play a game of cribbage tonight to christen your cards.'

That evening, after supper, not wanting to be cajoled into that game of cribbage, I pleaded a headache and went up to bed. After Rosie had unlaced my stays, I went to put the card box away in the drawer of the nightstand. Lying there in the bottom of the drawer was a playing card. The queen of spades, a female enemy.

I knew it hadn't been there that morning. My skin prickled as I picked it up, wondering again if it was a curse, or a threat of a more corporeal nature. One of the servants trying to frighten me? Archie Montfort playing games? The thought of being watched, schemed against, was deeply unsettling. Filled with a sudden revulsion, I held the card in the candle flame until it caught.

After I'd watched it burn, I went into the dressing room where my trunk was stored. On the day of my arrival, I'd stowed the snake-stone and stocking inside it, not seeing any reason to carry it here at Leighfindell. I revisited that decision now. The stone's weight in my hand was a comfort. From then on, I carried it everywhere I went.

CHAPTER SIX

Knave of spades as master-card: a man having no love
for you and inclined to wrong and hurt you; but
happily limited in opportunity.

ON SUNDAYS WE attended church at the nearby village of
Slaughterbridge. The first time I saw my Uncle Septimus in his
black cassock and white Geneva bands, it took some getting used to.
I'd met some unlikely churchmen at the Assembly Rooms in Bath,
but I'd never before met one who took such delight in human frailty
as him. Yet to see him up there in the pulpit, reading the prayers in
a sombre, forceful tone, one would think he'd been born to the part.

'It is sin and sin alone that makes the difference betwixt an angel
and a demon,' he declared, on the Sunday following my discovery
of the second playing card. 'Every sinner is a friend of the devil and
carrying on his work against God. And to be content to live in sin,
whether of sensuality or pride or falseness, is to wallow like a pig in
filth.'

Beside me, in the De Lacy pew, I felt Mirabel flinch.

Slaughterbridge, a cluster of forty thatched cottages on the banks
of a tributary of the River Dart, was surrounded by a brackish marsh
that gave a sulphurous aroma to the damp sandstone of the church.
The inhabitants, many of whom were employed on the estate or in the
De Lacy quarries, liked to knock on the church door to bring them
luck as they passed through it. I knew villages like this from the old
days. The sort of place where a sick cow could lead to an accusation

of witchcraft, and babies born of incest were said to be cursed and strangled at birth.

The villagers didn't like papists either – and from the looks they gave Brinseley Radclyffe, sitting ostentatiously alone in the new Radclyffe pew, once a papist always a papist. I wondered how Mr Radclyffe felt about his new religion, whether faith had played any part in his conversion at all? Did he secretly fear his father's God? Did a terror of everlasting fire creep into his bones at night? Or had he cast off his old religion as easily as he tossed aside his fur-trimmed cloaks?

Arabia smiled up at Septimus proudly, the twins fidgeting on either side of her. They made an odd couple: her willowy beauty, him bobbing along at her shoulder like a grinning ginger sprite. A passing observer might assume that she'd married him for his family's money. Perhaps she had, but I discerned much genuine affection between them. They were forever touching one another, or exchanging private smiles, or laughing at some wicked remark one or the other had made. Conversely, in all the time I was at Leighfindell, I don't think I ever once saw Julius touch his wife at all.

I studied the other De Lacys, thinking about the playing cards in my room. Lady Frances's lips moved silently along with the prayers, Emily's head was bent devoutly, while Archie listened with that same superiority of expression with which he greeted the subject of my fortune telling. Julius turned and caught my eye. Swiftly, I looked away.

Septimus was gazing directly at his mother. 'Lift up thy head, thou despairing and desperate sinner, whom thy unwillingness to leave thy sins hath brought to the dust of death. Thou are thy own hangman and executioner. The murderer knows David entered heaven, and hopes to follow him. But so saith St Paul "If you sin, fear". God's wrath like wind, shut up long in the caverns of the earth, shall break forth in a fiery tempest that will consume your soul.'

Mirabel's eyes were closed, her fingers knotted tightly, each word seeming to land like a scourge. When Septimus finished, she shuddered, as if from relief.

We filed out of the church, past white marble tombs of Radclyffe ancestors, laid to rest before the break with Rome. I dropped a coin into the collection plate carried by Septimus's young curate, who cared for his flock during the London season. A footman was waiting beside the lych-gate with a large basket of roses. Mirabel and I had picked them earlier that morning.

'These are De Lacy roses,' she'd told me on my first Sunday at Leighfindell. 'They are a cross between the *rosa damascena* and a new variety my husband had brought over from China. A botanist bred it especially to match my hair.'

Emily and I accompanied her to the very large mausoleum monument that dominated the churchyard. Three plaques of black marble engraved with golden lettering declared it to be the last resting place of Nicholas De Lacy; his much-loved son and heir, Virgil; and Jemima, his beloved daughter. Mirabel laid the roses beside the tomb and bent her head in prayer.

'The dead live on in our memories,' she'd said to me once. 'Sometimes they clamour so loudly their voices drown out the living.'

The following day at one o'clock, I took up my usual station in the library to await the postmaster's return. The moment the butler had laid out the letters, I was there to inspect them. Archie Montfort had received five letters that day, each annotated with the name of the post office where it had started out on its journey, together with the price of the postage. Three letters had originated in London, another was from Oxford, where Archie had once been a student, and the last was from Bath. The butler wasn't the most observant creature, but still I made a show of dropping a letter onto the floor, and as I bent to retrieve it, slipped the Bath letter into my pocket.

It was the third letter from my hometown that Archie had received since our arrival at Leighfindell. My instincts had been correct: Archie had indeed been making inquiries about me there. The first of his correspondents had never heard of me. The second had asked around, discovering that 'there is something of a mystery surrounding the whereabouts of Miss Antrobus'. Men being men, he had hinted at a pregnancy. I had tossed that letter into the fire, but it had occurred to me subsequently that Archie might grow suspicious if too many of his letters went astray. I therefore took great care removing the seal from this third letter, cutting around it with my quill knife in the privacy of my bedroom, so as not to damage it.

The letter proved to be from a gentleman named Captain David Black, a rather dissolute Guards officer known to me slightly from the Bath Assembly Rooms.

> *As to your enquiry about Miss Rachel Antrobus, the sobering rumour is that following the death of her guardian, a scholar of this city, she abruptly left the care of his cousin and is rumoured to be living in London. I have heard it said that the unfortunate runaway is suffering from a disorder of the mind, caused by her witnessing the terrible fire that occasioned her guardian's demise. Should you have knowledge of her whereabouts, I am certain that Henry Antrobus would be grateful for news, and might even be inclined to venture a reward.*

Not a letter I wanted Archie Montfort to read. Instead, I decided, he should receive another letter entirely, one that told rather a different tale about Rachel Antrobus.

Forgery is an art in and of itself. The task drew me back to my days on the road: those bad shillings we made in our crucible, Father painstakingly reproducing some official's signature on a permit for a country fair. I practised Captain Black's hand for over an hour before I was satisfied, and then set to work composing my new letter, using many of his original phrases, including his description of the fire and Mr Antrobus's death. According to this version of events, Henry was presently in Ireland, whilst I was staying in London with a dear and respectable family friend, Mrs Illingworth. I made certain to mention my honesty, and my bravery in the face of genteel poverty, when it was discovered that Mr Antrobus's estate was encumbered with debt. Finally, Captain Black paid tribute to my reputation for charitable works, in particular the funds I had raised to ameliorate the plight of Bath's distressed widows and orphans.

Satisfied with my creation, I turned my attention back to the seal. Carefully, I shaved the parchment from the reverse of the wax, and then heated my quill knife in a candle flame. I applied it to the seal, and painstakingly attached it to my letter. As I was returning to the Oak Hall to replace it on the table, I heard a woman crying in great distress.

Hurrying along the corridor towards the sound, I saw a maid-servant run into Mirabel's room, followed by Julius, who must have mounted the stairs in a great hurry. A footman stuck his head out of the bedroom door. 'Eloise,' he shouted. 'Salt of Hartshorn for Mrs Mirabel. Quickly now.' Lady Frances's French lady's maid ran out onto the landing and into Mirabel's room, clutching the bottle. I followed her inside, pushing my way through a throng of curious servants into Mirabel's dressing room. She sat weeping in a chair, her lady's maid fussing around her. Septimus and Archie were inspecting Ocho's gilded cage, which was empty. A path of destruction led from it: feathers, a smashed bowl, a broken mirror, the shredded petals of several De Lacy roses. Lady Frances was gazing out through the open window. 'We should tell Mr Whittington to speak to the gamekeep-ers,' she said. 'If they spot him out there in the woods, then they might catch him.'

'Oh, Ocho,' Mirabel sobbed. She turned upon her maid. 'I don't understand how you could have left his cage open.'

'I didn't,' the girl cried. 'I swear it, Mrs De Lacy.'

'I told you to put out his eyes,' Septimus remarked. 'A blind bird never flies away.'

Mirabel turned her distraught gaze upon mine. 'This is a sign, Miss Antrobus. A message from my son, Virgil. It is a warning about the plague that threatens this house.'

CHAPTER SEVEN

Six of hearts, influenced by a club:
a letter of more consequence than would appear.

DUE TO THE disruption of the parrot's escape, we dined much later than usual, at six o'clock, which Brinseley Radclyffe informed us was the Italian fashion. Dinner was always an elaborate affair at Leighfindell. The French Dining Room was a dazzle of mirror and crystal and green-and-gold panelling that Nicholas De Lacy had purchased from a former mistress of Louis the Fourteenth. The Meissen porcelain was painted with scenes from Leighfindell and bore the De Lacy crest. The silverware shone in the candlelight, reflections bouncing off our goblets of Venetian glass.

'The style of your hair is rather old-fashioned,' Lady Frances said, eyeing me indifferently. 'Make Rosie speak to Eloise. I always preferred a French lady's maid – they keep up with the latest styles – but Mirabel always insisted upon English girls for herself and her daughters.'

'Poor Rosie's only out of practice,' Arabia said. 'Luna's hair was always beautifully dressed, as I recall.'

I stared at her. 'Rosie was your sister-in-law's lady's maid?'

How remiss that I'd not asked her about her past. Hadn't Mrs Fremantle always said that no one was closer to a lady than her maid? I resolved to rectify this oversight at the first opportunity.

'Oh, Lord, don't speak of *her*,' Septimus exclaimed. 'It'll quite turn my stomach. And we're having swan.'

I was seated between Septimus and the family physician, Doctor Simon Crowhurst, who had been invited to dine with the family after attending to Mirabel. He'd given her a sleeping draught and she'd remained in her room. Her son had taken the opportunity of her absence to invite Brinseley Radclyffe and his father to dine. Emily had told me that her grandmother couldn't stand the sight of Piers Radclyffe, whom she blamed for encouraging the match between her dead daughter and his dead son.

It was the closest I'd been to Piers Radclyffe since the electricity show in Bath. Silently, I rehearsed all the questions I wanted to ask him about my parents, and our first encounter. Yet I could hardly talk to him about such matters here, surrounded by De Lacys.

'Maybe the parrot will mate with the pheasants,' Septimus was saying. 'Our woods might soon resemble the Amazon jungle.'

'Mother has agreed to have him blinded should we catch him,' Julius said. 'I only hope we do. She's entirely beside herself.'

'Someone should give that girl a whipping,' Lady Frances said.

'The maid? She denies it.' Julius swirled his wine thoughtfully. 'It might well have been Mother herself who left the cage open. She is getting a little forgetful, I regret to say.'

'Absalom thinks it was a ghost,' Arabia said. 'While Titus believes Miss Antrobus enchanted it open with her magical powers.'

'You should not let them say such things,' Lady Frances said.

'Which ghost does Absalom pick for the culprit?' Septimus asked. 'The Headless Horseman? Bloody Susan? The Weeping Drummer Boy? Have I forgotten anyone, Brinseley?'

Smiling, Brinseley counted them off on his fingers. 'There's the heir of the first Piers Radclyffe who was captured in battle and died in prison. He is said to walk around rattling a chain. There's a crying baby heard on full moon, a monk who seeks a lost crucifix, and the Scarlet Duchess who wanders the halls wearing a cloak stained red with her blood. She was the wife of my ancestor, Piers the Ninth, the man who built this house.'

'The Unlucky Piers,' his father interjected, his reddened eye interrogating the table.

'He was the last Duke of Brecon and Clifton,' Brinseley went on, ignoring the interruption. 'Do you know the story? It's really quite tragic.'

To my surprise, he was looking at me. I guessed that everyone else around the table had already heard the tale. Brinseley never passed up an opportunity to talk about his illustrious ancestors. I told him that I had not yet had the pleasure, and he beamed.

'The duke and duchess had a desperately unhappy marriage. Piers Nine was rather a brute, I am afraid. His wife sought solace in the arms of a neighbouring landowner, and they would tryst in the knot garden, which is where the Italian garden stands now. This was at the time of the Exeter Conspiracy against King Henry, and the King's agents suspected her husband of involvement. They searched this house several times, but the duke had spies upon the road and they never found anything incriminating. Until the duchess betrayed her husband by telling the King's men where to find his secret letters. The duke was arrested, tried and executed within a month.'

'Murdered. Betrayed,' old Piers cried, his searching eye coming to a rest upon me.

'Father,' Brinseley murmured, not without a hint of irritation. 'The duchess thought she'd be free to marry her lover, but as a fellow Catholic and a plotter, when he found out what she had done, he was appalled. They say he cut her throat, though her body was never found. It's probably bricked up somewhere in these walls even now.'

'My maid claims to have seen her,' Arabia said. 'She arrived in the forecourt riding upon a demonic horse.'

'You're getting her muddled up with the Headless Horseman,' Septimus said. 'He was a royalist cavalryman quartered here during the Great Rebellion. Until he was killed by a cannonball, which took his head clean off. Now he rides about the woods looking for it. Father said if I encountered him, he would chop off my head and substitute it for his own.'

'Please stop,' Emily said, with a shudder.

'I concur,' Archie replied. 'It is a foolish topic.'

How lofty, how superior. Yet science has never disproved the existence of ghosts. My father claimed to have seen them, and so did Mrs Fremantle, though Mr Antrobus had scoffed at the idea. If death causes the release of the soul, it does not seem to me to be so very far-fetched that in violent circumstances there might be a disruption to that process. The soul trapped in this realm, unable to pass beyond, in a state of being and unbeing, sometimes observable by man.

As I pondered the matter, I sipped my wine, discovering that it was thick with sediment. Given the riches of the De Lacy cellars, there was no doubt in my mind that this was a deliberate act. The footman who had poured my glass was a weasel-eyed bully named Patrick. Ever since my arrival, he'd addressed me with a slight smirk, delighting in pronouncing my name wrongly, bringing me tea when I'd asked for coffee, and countless other small humiliations designed to put me in my place. I'd ignored these slights, but my patience was wearing thin.

The swan was carried into the dining room by a quartet of foot-men. Stuffed and roasted, then redressed in its original feathers, the neck was supported by some piece of kitchen wizardry to make it resemble a living bird. We applauded and the French man-cook took a bow. I had never before eaten swan, and I cannot say I was enthused by the experience. It tasted as if I was dining upon the offspring of a chicken and a fish.

I took the opportunity of the lull in conversation to talk to Doctor Crowhurst. 'How long have you made your home at Leighfindell, sir?'

'I first came here in Mr De Lacy's father's day,' he said. 'Not long after old Nicholas bought the place. He'd read a treatise of mine on the structure of the heart, written when I was a student in Edinburgh.'

The doctor had an amiably ugly countenance: a large, fleshy nose struggling for dominance over a wide, rubbery mouth and bulging eyes. His pink ears were equally ungainly, protruding from beneath the rolls of his periwig – though his hands were long and delicate and seemed to belong to another man entirely. Life had seen fit to further diminish nature's design: a long scar running in a diagonal line from the lobe of one ear to the corner of his mouth.

'Mr De Lacy had long suffered from palpitations of the heart,' the doctor went on, 'and he had witnessed his father's early death from the same condition. He believed the best physicians were Scotchmen, and who was I to disabuse him? Especially when he made me an offer too handsome to refuse.'

'Then Mr De Lacy placed his faith in both science and magic?'

The doctor spread his hands. 'To my regret, his condition responded to neither.'

'I believe you also treated his daughter, Jemima?'

He nodded soberly. 'Another sad case. Jemima had always been a sensitive girl, and when she suffered a disappointment of the heart, it plunged her into a depressed state. I had high hopes for her recovery, but alas, the fates were cruel.'

'Emily told me about her accident,' I said.

'It should never have happened,' the doctor said, with evident feeling. 'In a case much like today's, her lady's maid left her room unlocked and she wandered off in the grip of a delusion. I should make it clear that this was after her condition had deteriorated. I would not normally countenance locking up a melancholic.' He smiled. 'But this is not a fitting subject for the dinner table, I think.'

'Emily said Jemima's illness greatly distressed her sister,' I said, hoping to lead the conversation around to the elopement.

But the doctor gave a rueful smile. 'Another unsuitable topic, I am afraid. Didn't you hear Mr Septimus?'

'Whereas Mrs De Lacy mentions her daughter often,' I said, still trying to understand Mirabel's recurring cards. 'I think she longs for a reconciliation.'

The doctor appeared distinctly uncomfortable at my refusal to let the matter drop, and attempted again to change the subject: 'So much tragedy in her life. Now this incident with the bird. It is regrettable.'

'She told me Ocho was a gift from her eldest son,' I said. 'Were you the doctor who attended to Virgil after the duel?'

Such talents I had – to turn even the smiling doctor into a frowning scold. 'Please, Miss Antrobus,' he said, lowering his voice, 'the Radclyffes are at table.'

'I only ask,' I persisted, 'because Mrs De Lacy's account of the whole affair left me rather puzzled. Jemima and Little Piers were never formally engaged. Her father had refused the match, and Little Piers persisted long after many other men would have been discouraged. He can hardly stand accused of treating her affections lightly. Most people would sympathize with his predicament. Granted, he took her father's money, but if he'd married Jemima without it, they'd have lived in poverty. Virgil can hardly have wanted such a life for his sister. Under the circumstances, it seems strange that he was so angry with his friend.'

The doctor was silent a moment. 'Miss Antrobus,' he said, at last, 'let me offer you a few words of advice. As you just heard from Mr Radclyffe, Leighfindell has long been a house of intrigue, one that hides its secrets rather well. I have lived here nearly twenty years, and still there is much that I can never know or understand. Yet, as a doctor, I have come to realize that knowledge can be a great burden as well as a blessing. There is a comfort in ignorance, I often find.'

His warning intrigued me, and I was left with the impression that Doctor Crowhurst understood a lot more about Leighfindell and its inhabitants than he claimed.

Once dinner was over, and the ladies withdrew to the drawing room, I took advantage of the exodus to return to the Oak Hall with my forged letter. The butler was in the dining room attending to the gentlemen and, thinking I was unobserved, I shuffled the letter into one of the piles of unclaimed mail on the table.

'I see you,' a voice cried out, and I wheeled around. Piers Radclyffe was peering at me from the doorway.

'What's that, sir?' I asked, my panic rising. Had he seen me interfering with the letters? I wasn't sure.

'I know you,' he said, his words thick and slurred. 'I remember.' He grinned toothily.

I walked swiftly to his side. 'I'd like to talk to you about all of this, sir,' I said, speaking as quietly as I could. The last thing I wanted was him shouting about me being a De Lacy again. 'Shall we meet tomorrow? When you're out walking in the woods?'

His mouth was slack on one side, as if pulled down by invisible hooks. A drool of turtle soup had run down his chin and dried to a crust. 'About your mother?' He grimaced. 'About your father?'

'About everything,' I said. 'Do you know the grotto? Below the Hermitage?' Emily and I had walked there the other day. Deep in the woods, hollowed into a rocky crag, it had looked like a good spot for a clandestine meeting. 'I'll wait for you there at noon.'

He reached out and stroked my face with his nails, as he had at the electricity show. 'Poor, dear girl. You should be dead.'

'You'll come?' I said, refusing to be unsettled by his macabre words. 'To the grotto at noon?'

To my alarm, he raised his voice, still resonant despite his frailty: 'The letter.'

I patted his shoulder, trying desperately to quieten him. 'No, sir. You didn't see what you thought you saw. Let's talk tomorrow.'

'Thank you.' He repeated the words rather angrily. '*Thank you.*'

I tried to move away, smiling uncertainly, but he grabbed hold of my arm and yanked me back. 'The letter,' he cried, louder still.

I heard footsteps behind us, then Brinseley Radclyffe's voice: 'Oh Lord, not again. Father, we've talked about this.'

Just as he had in Bath, he tried to prise the old man's hands free from my arm.

'Call Archie, will you?' he said, over his shoulder. 'Father always listens to him.'

Septimus had followed Brinseley into the hall. 'Archie,' he called. 'Come see to the old fellow, will you?'

'Just one meal,' Brinseley was saying, tugging away at his father's arm. 'Just one dinner without incident. That's all I asked.'

'He is unwell, sir,' I pointed out. 'Confused.'

Archie swiftly took charge of the situation. Taking a gentle hold of Mr Radclyffe's arm, he drew him away, speaking quiet words of reassurance. 'Why don't you come into the library, sir, where we can sit down?'

Would he tell Archie what he'd seen? Would Archie believe him if he did? Nobody else seemed to listen to a word he said.

Mr Radclyffe twisted around to look at me. '*The letter.*'

'What's he saying?' Brinseley said.

'I'm not sure,' I replied. 'Something about a letter.' Sometimes it is better to confront danger with a bold face.

Mr Radclyffe pointed at me, hostility burning in his wild, blue eyes. 'You're a liar.'

CHAPTER EIGHT

Five of clubs, influenced by a heart:
a wound or bruise.

R OSIE HELD THE curling tongs in the flame of the lamp to reheat them, a scent of burnt bergamot filling the air between us.

'I am told the seamstresses will finish work on the first of your gowns tomorrow,' she said.

'One cannot fault their efficiency,' I replied. 'I only wish the footmen were equally diligent in their duties. My wine was more sediment than grape last night.'

Rosie sniffed. 'It can sometimes take a little while to train the local boys up to London standards. If you have a complaint, then you should speak to the butler, miss.'

And doubtless make things worse. Rosie dipped her head, not meeting my eye, and I suspected Patrick's campaign against me was the talk of the servants' halls.

As she worked on my hair, I examined her in the mirror. Lines of strain around her mouth, lines of laughter around her eyes. Whomever she liked to laugh with, it certainly wasn't me. Her voice when she addressed me was polite and pleasant, but devoid of emotion. Her eyes, the colour of water, offered no clues to her at all. Seeking a subject to open her up, I asked her about the one topic guaranteed to animate anyone at Leighfindell. 'Are the servants looking forward to the ball?'

'They are servants. They look forward to seeing the famous faces. The Duchess of Portland and Mr Sterne and Mr Handel.'

She said this as though she wasn't a servant herself. Lady's maids tended to rest rather proudly upon their status.

'I am rather excited myself,' I said. 'I adore Mr Handel.' A few days ago, I had caught her humming 'Zadok the Priest' while she put away my nightclothes.

'Oh, so do I,' she replied, with something approaching enthusiasm. 'The first time I heard his music played, I felt quite breathless. All the girls were singing for days afterwards. This was at the academy where I trained.'

'When did you come here to Leighfindell?'

'Nearly twenty years ago,' she replied. 'Mr De Lacy's father was looking for two lady's maids for his daughters. He chose Etta and I out of all the girls at the academy. I was given the younger sister, Miss Patience – though everybody called her Luna. Etta got the elder, Miss Jemima.' She blushed, perhaps at the note of disappointment in her tone.

'What were they like?' I asked. 'The De Lacy sisters?'

She was starting to warm up, as people often do when you find a subject of mutual interest. 'Etta used to say they were like chalk and cheese, if the cheese came from the Japans and the chalk from the moon. Jemima was a sweet girl with a hot temper, who wore her heart upon her sleeve. She told Etta everything. Whereas Luna never told me a thing, and when she was displeased, she could be as cold as well-water. She liked to read about politics and philosophy, whereas with Miss Jemima it was romances and fairy tales. They were both beautiful girls by anyone's standard.' She wound a loose strand of my hair around the curling tongs. 'Etta used to say we had the easiest job in the kingdom. People judge a lady's maid by her mistress's looks.'

'I'm sure no one will hold your present commission against you,' I said. 'Does Etta still work here at Leighfindell?'

Her smile faded. 'She left not long after Miss Jemima died. It was a sad time.'

'So Mrs De Lacy tells me.' I tilted my head to look at Rosie in the mirror. 'She said another fortune teller spent time here at Leighfindell in those days. A man named John Jory Jago?'

'That's right, miss,' Rosie said, rather cautiously. 'Sometimes he would tell fortunes for the upper servants.'

'Did you never suspect him and Luna? Before the elopement, I mean.'

She frowned. 'Mrs Vaughan wouldn't like me talking about that, miss.'

'Come, Rosie,' I said. 'Is a little gossip so very bad?' Reaching for my purse, I pulled out a half-guinea, more money than she would earn in a week.

She made no move to take it. 'I'm not supposed to receive vails until the end of your stay.'

'I won't tell if you won't.'

She slid another pin into my hair and stepped away. 'That looks very fine, miss. I'll lay out your striped satin for dinner. Now if you'll excuse me, I'd better be getting along.'

A little later that morning, I set out across the lawn, past the cascade, in the direction of the woods. I did not know if Mr Radclyffe had properly understood my invitation to meet in the grotto, but on the assumption that he had, I didn't want to be late. Emily and her governess were strolling in the parterre, and I spied Septimus walking a pair of mastiffs by the lake. Faintly, I could hear the sound of hammers and saws coming from the direction of the workshops in the East Court. Leighfindell's carpenters and painters were busy with preparations for the ball. I'd heard rumours of lavish tents and grand spectacles that would astonish the guests. The noise unsettled the pigeons and doves, all a-flutter around their cotes and in the trees.

Out on the lake, swans glided unruffled through the reedbeds near to the island shore. I imagined Virgil and Little Piers Radclyffe meeting there at dawn. Paces marked, pistols chosen, the crack of a gunshot, lifeblood spilled. The precise nature of their quarrel still puzzled me, and Doctor Crowhurst's warning last night had done little to change my mind.

I had almost reached the woods, when I heard a voice calling my name. Turning, I saw Archie Montfort striding towards me.

'Miss Antrobus,' he called. 'Please wait. I wish to talk to you.'

I halted, eyeing him warily, wondering what Mr Radclyffe had said to him last night.

He bowed stiffly, taking a moment to catch his breath. 'One searches for the right words,' he said, 'and I am deuced if I know what they are. Wretch, there's a word. Vile toad, there are two more.'

'Mr Montfort?'

'I wish to apologize,' he said, looking suitably abashed. 'I know now that you told me the truth. About your guardian being abroad. About your reasons for being in London. About your poor friend, Mrs Illingworth. I have no right to ask for your forgiveness, but I do nonetheless.'

Then my letter had worked its magic, and Mr Radclyffe had held his tongue. 'You have been making inquiries about me, sir,' I said.

He blushed, highlighting the golden down on his cheek. 'Those words of censure you spoke in the coffeehouse are undeniable, I am afraid. I have not behaved as a gentleman should. I sought to wound you in word and deed, and it is much to my shame.'

I had hoped that my letter would assuage his concerns about me, and that he would curtail his investigations into my character. His contrition was something altogether more than I'd anticipated, and I wondered if there might be a way I could turn it to my advantage. 'Do you also regret the things you said about my fortunes?'

He frowned. 'I believe that you believe. That you are acting in good faith, if not in wise faith.'

'A fool, not a knave?'

His colour deepened. 'I have never thought you a fool, Miss Antrobus.'

Perhaps I might have tortured him a little longer, had I not needed to meet Mr Radclyffe. 'You are wrong about my fortunes,' I said. 'They contain great truths within them. But I do forgive you, Mr

Montfort. You were only acting out of concern for Mrs De Lacy. It might almost be described as admirable. Almost.'

He gave me a crooked smile. 'It is more than I deserve.'

Indeed it was. 'Tell me, how is your grandmother today?'

'A little better, I am told. Though she cannot accept that her bird simply flew away. She thinks it is some kind of an omen or curse. I thought I'd go and look for Ocho in the woods. Would you care to walk with me?'

How far we had come in such a short time. There were many questions I might have asked him about Leighfindell and its inhabitants, but they would have to wait. 'That is a kind offer,' I said. 'But I was intending to look at the grotto and then read there alone.'

He shifted rather awkwardly, and I could see he thought I had declined his offer because I was still sore at the way he had treated me. 'I shall leave you to stroll in peace,' he said. 'But if you are heading for the grotto, you should take the path on the western side of the lake. It is much quicker.'

I thanked him, he bowed, and I walked on, congratulating myself on the success of my forgery. I would continue to watch his mails and deal with his letters as I saw fit, but for the moment at least, I had countered any imminent threat from Archie Montfort.

The sun was blinding, dragonflies flashing scarlet and blue over the grass. I welcomed the shade of the woods, the greenery occasionally brightened by a glimpse of red deer, or a shimmer of bellflowers. I passed a group of gamekeepers armed with long nets, also out looking for Ocho. They lifted their caps to me, and I wished them luck in their endeavours.

Before too long, I came to a small clearing. Despite my eagerness to talk to Mr Radclyffe, I lingered there a moment, my eye drawn by a curious sight. To one side of the path, a crude wooden cross had been hammered into the earth. Many white rectangular stones surrounded it, about the size and shape of milestones. I counted fourteen in all. Several withered nosegays had been placed on the well-tended grass beneath the cross, as well as a few charms like the ones gypsies sold, and a straw doll that reminded me a little of Joan the Wad. Wondering who was buried here and why, I resolved to ask someone.

I walked on, occasionally glimpsing the conical roof of the Hermitage above the treetops. A round, flint building, like a witch's house in a children's story, it was perched atop a large outcropping of rock at the foot of the valley's steep, wooded rise. Emily had told me that it had originally housed a professional hermit, who had been promised seven hundred pounds by her grandfather to live there for seven years, on the condition that he never cut his hair nor beard, nor spoke to any of the De Lacys' guests who came to gawp at him. Unfortunately, after a month, they'd discovered he'd been frequenting the taverns in Slaughterbridge, and he'd been dismissed.

When I reached the grotto's entrance – a yawning maw at the foot of the crag – I could see no sign of Piers Radclyffe and I wondered if he was waiting for me inside. A shelf chiselled into the rock held a box of candles, a jar of tapers, and a flint upon a string. A metal plate was fixed to the wall for striking. I lit a candle, and walked along the short passage, which soon widened and heightened dramatically into a large, domed cave. The walls were studded with thousands of pieces of mineral and gemstone, winking and sparkling in the candlelight. Mr Radclyffe momentarily forgotten, I turned, entranced, picking out seashells and crystals, pieces of marble and alabaster, snakestones and spongestones and other petrified creatures.

Spotting the mosaic that Emily had told me about, I passed between stalactites and stalagmites to examine it. A muscular King Neptune flanked by a pair of mermaids, their red hair a blaze of garnets, spinels, and tourmalines. With his thin lips and hooded eyes, Neptune bore a slight resemblance to Nicholas De Lacy, whose portrait was hanging in Julius's study. I held my candle up to his eyes, and found the carving – *J & L* – that Emily had mentioned. As I ran my fingers over the grooves, I imagined my parents trysting here, wondering in that moment of weakness if they might have been in love after all. Maybe my mother had only become the person she was now because she'd believed us dead? Maybe there was still a chance of reconciliation? Then I remembered her cruel words and angry eyes, and I told myself I was being as foolish as Emily.

A very loud gunshot, very near at hand, startled me out of these thoughts. 'Mr Radclyffe?' I called, walking back down the passage. Blinded briefly by the sunlight as I emerged, it took me a moment to realize that somebody was lying on the grass outside. I ran towards the fallen figure, realizing from his long, white hair that it was Mr Radclyffe. The stock of his fowling piece protruded from beneath his body.

Dropping to my knees, I rolled him over. Acid flooded into my mouth, and I retched against my hand. Mr Radclyffe's face, or what was left of it, was a mess of blood and bone and teeth. Only his forehead was still intact, although badly bruised. I rose instinctively to get away, but my ankle turned over on a rock. I fell awkwardly, crying out as a sharp pain seared through my left wrist.

Grass against my cheek. Gunpowder in my nostrils. Blood on his shirt. Blood on my dress. Blood on my hands.

CHAPTER NINE

Four of hearts as master-card:
the existence of an obstinate sentiment towards one.

H is business in London concluded, Lazarus boards the Bath
Flying Machine. His employer, Mr Pardew, has refused his
request for a leave of absence, and nothing Lazarus could say would
change his mind. His future had forked before him, and yet such
mundane matters as jobs and money and common sense had counted
for little against Lady Seabrooke's gratified gaze. She is pleased with
the progress he has made since their discussion with Leopold, and he
revisits every compliment and kind word. Only one of his endeavours
does he judge less than satisfactory, and he cannot help but think on
it as he gazes out at the orchards and meadows racing past.

The bars over the window had cast shadows across his hands,
striping him as though he had been whipped. Many of the prisoners
awaiting trial at the Wood Street Compter faced such a punishment.
Or the pillory. Or a year or two in Newgate. Some, like the Anglo-
Indian girl he'd come to see, faced all three.

Her name is Tamson Adeline Lambert. Her father, it seems, was
French, though the pair are estranged, and the mother is dead. Lazarus has learned that not only did Tamson share a booth with Red
at the Bartholomew Fair, but they also shared a room at the Crown
and Magpie tavern. Morgan Trevithick, after getting nowhere with
the magistrate, has been to see Lazarus twice, arguing for Tamson's

release. Lazarus is not unsympathetic, but the girl has to help herself first.

Tamson's left eye is bruised, open a crack. The other, a striking blue, brims with hostility. Her hair is lank, and she smells as one would expect after a week in the Compter, a place of foul air and fouler villains. In a calm, measured voice, Lazarus lays out his proposal.

'The magistrate has two witnesses who will swear they saw you taking money to draw astrological charts.' He pauses to let this news sink in. 'He is angry because of what happened to his constable and has refused all Morgan Trevithick's attempts to purchase your freedom. But if you choose to help me, then I can help you. My patron is a woman of influence. She might intercede with the magistrate. But first, you need to tell me all about your friend Red.'

Tamson shrugs. 'We sold flowers together. Those witnesses are lying.'

'Morgan Trevithick will testify that he sold Red a pitch, and called the constables when he discovered she was selling fortunes.'

She looks stunned. 'Why would he do that? Did you threaten him?'

'Red's not a member of his troupe. He chose to save his own skin. I sincerely advise you to do the same. Now, did Red ever talk to you about a man named John Jory Jago?'

She glares at him, combative. 'I've never heard the name.'

'Are you sure? He was one of the Cornish Players once. Morgan's old partner.'

Her eyes narrow, trying to puzzle things out. 'Why would Red be interested in him?'

'Because she hopes to commit one of the most audacious frauds ever imagined.' He tells her all about Red's claims: the De Lacys, Lady Seabrooke, the suit in the Prerogative Court.

Tamson listens intently, and when she speaks, her voice is a whisper: 'Oh, Red.'

'She never talked to you about any of this?'

'No. She asked a lot of questions about the Cornish Players in the old days, but I thought it was the Square of Sevens she was interested in.'

Lazarus presses home his advantage. 'She lied to you, deceived you. She has made you an accessory to her crimes.'

'I don't know anything about her crimes,' Tamson cries. 'I'd never heard of these De Lacys before just now.'

'You never suspected anything was amiss? A canny fairground girl like you?'

Tamson is silent a moment. 'I thought she was hiding something. And I never did understand why she wanted to join the Cornish Players. But I never imagined anything like this.'

Lazarus suspects she's telling the truth. Red plays her cards close to her chest. 'Did she ever talk about her past? Where she came from?'

Tamson wipes her bad eye, suppressing a sigh. 'She said she was an orphan, raised as a lady in Bath by a guardian who died. Her guardianship passed to a cousin who stole all of her money, and so she came here.'

Lazarus suppresses a stab of anger at Henry Antrobus. He suspects they wouldn't be in this mess except for him.

'Did Red ever mention her mother?'

'She asked me to read her chart once. Her mother was a woman who lived for her passions. She had many secrets.'

'I'm not interested in your hocus pocus. Keep to the facts.'

Tamson blanches a little at his tone. 'All I know is what she told me. That her mother was dead and she never knew her. She woke me crying for her once.'

'When was this?'

'The night before you came to the fair.'

The same night Red had paid her call on Lady Seabrooke. Oh, she's good, Lazarus thinks. One of the best he's ever seen. 'She's a talented actress, don't you think?'

'This wasn't an act.'

'You're not saying you believe her lies?'

'I don't know. I don't care.' Tamson breathes. 'What are you going to do to her?'

'You should be more concerned about yourself.' He holds her gaze until she looks away. 'You said just now that you knew she was hiding something. That she struck you as devious, a liar.'

'I didn't say that. She struck me as kind and clever and sad. But she kept disappearing. She had too much money. And sometimes she looked scared.'

'Liars tend to be afraid of getting caught.'

'Or afraid of men like you who would put words into people's mouths.'

Lazarus studies her carefully, trying to understand her. 'Your friends haven't been so coy. Morgan, Pierre with one arm – they told me everything I wanted to know. Kerensa at the Crown and Magpie too. She was the one who first told Red about John Jory Jago. I have sworn affidavits and promises of testimony, should I need them.'

Tamson's expression is stony. 'If you have them, then why do you need me?'

'You were the one closest to her. The one who knew her best.' He glances down at the papers on the table in front of him. 'Your friends, Gwen and Naomi – they say Red didn't just use her wits to get close to people, she used her body too.'

'That's not true,' Tamson cries. 'It was just a silly misunderstanding.'

And yet one that might prove useful in a court of law, where a woman's reputation counts for everything and nothing. Lazarus hopes they will not have to use it, but he will if he must. 'Why are you still protecting her? Aren't you angry? You are only here because of her.'

'I think you and your friend with the greyhounds might have had something to do with it.'

Beneath the bravado, he can tell she is afraid. She feels the cut of the whip, hears the baying of the mob. 'Did you know she saw you that night and ran? Left you to your fate? What sort of friend does that?'

Her eyes flash. So she is angry with Red after all. Lazarus softens his tone. 'All you need do is sign a paper stating that you found her an untrustworthy person and a consummate actress. You will attest to the fortunes she told, and any other evidence of illegality on her part. If you can think of anything she said that undermines her story, so much the better. In return, you will have your freedom and maybe a little money for yourself on top of that.'

Her voice is sullen. 'I don't want your money.'

'You want your freedom.'

She is silent a moment. 'I won't do it.'

Lazarus almost bangs the table in frustration. He tells himself that this girl is not his responsibility. She was selling horoscopes at the fair, an illegal act, and rightly so. Yet he doesn't want to see her hurt, and so he tries again.

'You knew Red, what, three weeks? She made a fool of you and your friends. How can you owe her any loyalty after what she's done?'

Tamson smiles at him then. 'You wouldn't understand.' Her voice is rich with contempt.

Chapter Ten

Eight of spades, influenced by a club: an accident.

THE EDGE OF a stone was cutting into my cheek, the penny-taste of blood sharp in my mouth. My wrist pulsed with pain. *Don't look. Don't look.* And yet I did.

The bloodied pulp of Mr Radclyffe's face. Sitting up, I closed my eyes, letting out a moan.

'Miss Antrobus?' somebody cried. 'Are you hurt?'

Archie Montfort had run into the clearing. 'I heard a shot,' he said. 'Are you all right?'

Wordlessly, I pointed at the corpse.

'Oh, sir,' he said, taking in the horror of the scene. 'Oh no.'

He crouched down by Mr Radclyffe's side, but seeing that nothing could be done for him, his hands fell slack. I felt enormous pity for him in that moment. He'd been the only one who'd seemed to care about the old man.

'What has happened here?' Another male voice intruded upon my thoughts.

I looked up and saw Julius hurrying down the steps that led up the side of the rocky crag to the Hermitage. Even in that moment, I wondered what he had been doing up there.

'Mr Radclyffe is dead, sir,' Archie said. 'Miss Antrobus, do try not to look.'

It was like telling water not to be wet. My eyes kept returning to the corpse. I imagined it would be seared into my memory for ever.

'Poor devil,' Julius said, gazing down at the body with distaste. 'He must have fallen onto his gun and the damn thing went off in his face.'

Archie passed a hand across his brow. 'I told Brinseley that he'd do himself an injury, tramping about in these woods, but hunting was the only thing left that he enjoyed.'

'We should head back to the house,' Julius said. 'Send some men down here to deal with the body. Then I suppose I should go and tell Brinseley.'

'I'll come with you,' Archie said. He'd gone very pale.

'Good lad. He'll take it better coming from you.' Julius placed a hand upon his shoulder. 'Miss Antrobus, are you hurt? Can you walk?'

Rather shakily, I got to my feet. 'I fell on my wrist, but I don't think it is broken.'

'We'll have Crowhurst take a look at it, just to be sure.'

The full impact of Mr Radclyffe's death was only just now hitting home. Now I'd never find out what he knew about my parents. Never learn if he'd told anyone what I'd said at the electricity show. The thought prompted me to take another long look at the body. As I did so, a flicker of movement caught my eye. Up above, in one of the round windows of the Hermitage, just for a moment, I thought I'd seen a face. Yet when I looked again, it was gone. Had Julius been meeting someone up there? He certainly wasn't behaving as if he had. I wondered if it had been a trick of the light.

'Gad, there's flies already,' Julius said, swatting them away. 'We'd better have him taken to the icehouse. Come along, Miss Antrobus. Don't tarry.'

The three of us trooped back to Leighfindell in near silence. When we reached the house, Julius issued a string of commands to the footmen. Looking at Archie's careworn face, I wanted to tell him that I was sorry about Mr Radclyffe, but he hurried off to speak to Mr Whittington. Upon Julius's instruction, I was escorted by a footman to the music room and plied with brandy.

Word of the incident quickly spread throughout the house. Mirabel was still confined to her room, but the other ladies gathered in the music room to hear all about my ordeal. Even the twins came to listen.

'We should each send a note of condolence to Mr Radclyffe,' Lady Frances addressed her daughter. 'Make sure that yours includes a few words of tender regard.'

Emily nodded, her eyes wide, looking a little in shock herself.

'Did you kill him?' the bolder of the twins demanded of me, whether Titus or Absalom I was never quite sure. 'With a magic spell?'

'What a thing to say,' his mother said fondly, ruffling his hair. 'Didn't you hear what your uncle said? It was an accident.'

Was it though? I thought of the bruise upon the dead man's forehead. Could someone have killed him to stop him from talking to me? The same person who'd sent those villains to our house in Trim Street? Lazarus Darke had said that this third party must be someone who had an intimate knowledge of De Lacy affairs. Did Julius have a traitor living here at Leighfindell? The same person who had been leaving the playing cards in my room?

Almost as soon as I'd conceived this thought, I argued against it. Everyone in this household benefitted from Julius's wealth. They would only stand to lose from the sale of the codicil. The same went for Brinseley Radclyffe, who was due to marry Emily. A servant or one of the professional gentlemen connected to the household might have had more of a motive, but it seemed unlikely that they'd have had the resources to undertake the necessary inquiries in Bath and to recruit London villains to their cause. If such an enemy really existed, it was much more likely someone with a loose connection to the case, a lawyer, or a family friend.

Despite this chain of logic, the nagging suspicion would not leave me, and I was still dwelling upon the matter later that afternoon, when Doctor Crowhurst called. 'Forgive me for not coming sooner,' he said. 'I was in Slaughterbridge on calls this morning, and I only heard about the accident an hour ago. I encountered Mr De Lacy on his way back from the Dower House and he wanted me to take a look at the body. I've only just returned from the icehouse.'

He examined my wrist, turning it gently this way and that. 'Not a fracture,' he declared cheerfully. 'Just a mild sprain. Try not to use it for a day or two, apply a cold compress, and it should start to feel better before too long. Now, how are you feeling in your spirits? Lady Frances thought you might benefit from a little opium.'

'Brandy is proving more than sufficient,' I said. 'The shock is wearing off now. Yet I cannot stop thinking about poor Mr Radclyffe. Did you come to any conclusions about what had happened to him?'

'He was unsteady in foot,' the doctor said. 'I'd warned him, as had others, that he was doing too much for a man of his age. But like many older gentlemen who were once vigorous, he refused to be told. I presume he stumbled, and fell on his fowling piece, which regrettably discharged. He would have died instantly, for which we can be thankful.'

'Did you notice the bruise on his forehead?'

'Yes, he would have hit the ground rather hard.'

'Isn't it possible that somebody struck him? Knocked him to the ground and then turned his own gun upon him?'

The doctor's face contorted with surprise, rendering his features even more exaggerated than usual. 'Who on earth would want to do that to poor Mr Radclyffe?'

'I don't know,' I said. 'I'd just like to be certain.'

'Ah, certainty. That rare creature.' The doctor smiled. 'Rest assured, I am as confident as I can be, that there was nothing untoward about this tragic business.'

Was I turning windmills into giants, imagining enemies where there were none? I wished I shared the doctor's conviction.

As he was putting on his coat, I recalled the second macabre scene that I had discovered on my walk. 'Earlier, I passed by a grave in the woods. At least, I think it was a grave. A wooden cross surrounded by more than a dozen white stones.'

'Ah,' the doctor said, 'the lady in the lake. They found her body six or seven years ago, when they were dredging it. By all accounts, she'd lain there for two hundred years. Some people even say she might be the Scarlet Duchess herself. You recall Brinseley Radclyffe's story at dinner the other night?'

'Does the duchess have some sort of significance to people here at Leighfindell? I ask because flowers and what looked like offerings had been left on the grave.'

The doctor smiled again. 'You know servants and their superstitions. They probably think she will bring them luck.'

'And the white stones?'

The doctor's smile faded, and he glanced at the door, as if to check we were still alone. 'Those are the graves of Lady Frances's stillborn children.'

CHAPTER ELEVEN

Seven of clubs, influenced by a diamond:
beware of an indiscretion or error.

W E PASSED A sombre evening at supper and everyone retired
early to bed. That night my dreams were the children of my
fears. Black-Beard and Green-Coat, pressing their faces close to
mine, telling me all the vile things they were going to do to me. Mrs
Fremantle cowering. The glint of a blade, the stench of blood. Someone faceless stood in the shadows, directing them. The cold press of
metal against my skin, then hot as my blood spilled out. I awoke,
sheathed in sweat, my heart thumping.

I struggled to go back to sleep after that. All my suspicions and
unanswered questions revolved through my mind, until I wanted to
scream with the frustration of it all. Morning brought Mirabel's maid
to my door, bearing a note from her mistress, inviting me to breakfast. Eager to speak to her again, I went immediately to her room.

Mirabel looked as if she'd slept even worse than I had, her hands
fluttering as she took mine. She asked how I was after yesterday's
ordeal, but she barely listened to my replies, her own ordeal still
uppermost in her mind.

'Ocho has not returned,' she said. 'Virgil is sending me a message.
He is angry because Emily is to marry the brother of his murderer.
He thinks I haven't tried hard enough to prevent it – but what more
can I do? Julius won't listen to me. He's got himself a bargain. Doesn't
want his old mother souring the deal. Now that Brinseley's father is

dead, they will be married as soon as the court case is won. By Easter, if Julius gets his way.'

'So soon?' I cried, wondering about the meaning of Mirabel's cryptic words. *What deal? What bargain?* Why did Piers Radclyffe's death have such significance to Emily's marriage?

'Julius is concerned only for his legacy,' Mirabel brooded. 'Never mind what Emily wants. He tells her she will grow to love Brinseley in time – and perhaps she will. But if the blood in their children's veins is cursed, then it will bring ruin upon this house. We must ask the cards how I can prevent their match.'

'Mrs De Lacy,' I said carefully, 'if Ocho's escape was a message from Virgil, then I believe it concerns your own happiness, not Emily's marriage. Your son hates seeing you like this, tormented by the past. He grows frustrated by your refusal to confront the truth. Speak freely, unburden your soul, and he will be comforted.'

She gazed at me with red-rimmed eyes. 'Then Ocho will return?'

'It is possible,' I said, without much conviction. 'Perhaps the cards will reassure us upon that point? But there can be no more barriers between us, no forbidden topics.'

She nodded rather meekly. 'Only the truth.'

Was I taking advantage of the situation to serve myself? Of course. Yet I honestly believed that the truth was her path to salvation, the means of extracting that splinter from her soul. We would begin with the truth she had so far resisted: the legal battles between her children.

A death.

Money or an estate.

A quarrel.

A woman with a grievance.

An affair dealing with a lawyer.

And so on . . .

I hadn't intended to include the king of spades amongst her cards, but to my unease, he appeared there nonetheless. Mirabel gazed down at her parallelogram, looking bewildered. 'The lawsuit. I don't understand. What does any of this have to do with Virgil?'

'I told you, he wants to see you happy. This case is a cause of distress to you. Anyone can see it.'

'It is certainly that.' She blinked. 'Where to begin?'

I pointed to the queen of spades. 'With your daughter, Luna? She is the person most central to these events.'

Mirabel gave a heavy sigh. 'She hates me.'

'Emily tells me that you plan to testify against her.'

She stared at Ocho's empty cage. 'I plan only to tell the truth. My husband drafted that codicil in a moment of weakness, and then he changed his mind and destroyed it. Archie's father saw him do it. This document before the court is a crude forgery, an act of desperation on Luna's part.'

'Are you certain that Mr Montfort told the truth? Sometimes, when we harbour doubts, they can agitate the soul, upsetting the balance of the spirits.'

She frowned. 'Miss Antrobus, if my son—'

'We said no forbidden topics,' I reminded her. 'We go where the cards lead us. Look what they tell you.'

Mirabel's gaze returned to the table. 'I don't think that I harbour doubts.' She touched the ace of spades, the card of misfortune. 'The events that George Montfort described were entirely consistent with my husband's character. Nicholas fretted constantly about his will and he changed his mind several times, as you must know.'

'Why did he cut his sons out of his will in the first place?'

'Julius committed a youthful indiscretion with the daughter of a neighbouring landowner. I'm sure I don't need to tell you what boys can be like. Her father caught them together and demanded that they should be married, but Nicholas wouldn't countenance the match. The whole business was regrettable, and he was determined that Julius should learn a hard lesson.'

'Your husband was angry because Julius had ruined the girl?'

'He was angry because the girl's father was meant to sell him a parcel of land, but then he refused. It cost Nicholas a pretty penny to put everything right. The girl was married off in a hurry, and Nicholas paid for the dowry. That's when Julius was sent away to Oxford.'

'And your younger son?'

Mirabel sighed again. 'Nicholas never took to Septimus. I don't know why. His height, perhaps. I tried to foster an affection between them, but it was never any use. Nicholas said he'd rather leave his fortune to Seabrooke's brat. But that whim didn't last long. Seabrooke's boy was a pale imitation of his father: a pompous bore with a pudding for a mind. For my part, I am convinced it was always Nicholas's intention to restore Julius to favour. I certainly don't believe he intended to leave his estate to the child of a cunning-man who'd betrayed him – it makes no sense!'

'Will anyone testify in support of your daughter's claim?'

'Lazarus Darke, I suppose. Julius says that he is working for Luna now. I blame him for all of this. It was his theories that put these ideas into Luna's head in the first place. Darke never trusted George Montfort. He was jealous of anyone else who had my husband's ear.'

'He thought Montfort stole the codicil?'

She shook her head, a jingle of gemstones. 'Not him. Jemima's maid, a girl named Etta. She was a mere chit, but in Darke's mind, she was a master villain. So many shades of ridiculous. She'd never have known where to find the codicil, for a start.'

'It was well hidden?'

'In a place so secret, you wouldn't even know that it was there. Our carpenter discovered it during our initial renovations of the house. A lost piece of Radclyffe history, a hidden strongbox where they used to hide their papist books. Nicholas saw its attraction immediately. His greatest fear was that somebody would take steps to subvert his wishes after his death. Not even our children knew where his papers were kept. Only myself and Mr Winterton, my husband's lawyer.'

You can imagine the thought that leapt into my mind. Did Julius hide his own documents in that same secret place? Hadn't Emily said that the report was 'locked away at Leighfindell with my grandfather's papers'? A thousand questions sprang to my lips, but I was afraid of arousing Mirabel's suspicions by being too direct.

'Why did Mr Darke think Etta was responsible for the theft?'

'She left our employ rather suddenly around the time of my

husband's death. But servants come and go all the time. Just ask poor Mrs Vaughan. It signifies nothing.'

'Was she ever questioned about the disappearance of the codicil?'

'No, she was never found. Though I believe Mr Darke looked for her. These girls change their names like they change their ribbons. Common-law marriages, and worse.'

'How did Darke think she found the codicil?'

Mirabel smiled sardonically. 'He thought Jemima told her where to find it.'

'I thought you just said your children didn't know where it was kept?'

'They didn't,' she cried, rather triumphantly. 'But Darke supposed Jemima might have stumbled across it unwittingly. She could be rather obsessive about things, you see, just like her father. And one of her obsessions was the history of this house. It had belonged to Little Piers's family for generations, and he was all she ever thought about in those days. He was up at Oxford, and she closeted herself in the library, reading every book about his family she could get her hands on. She came across an old legend about a lost crucifix studded with jewels, and she thought if she could find it, it would help the Radclyffes restore their fortune. She believed her father might then look more favourably upon their match. Julius pointed out that if the crucifix was ever found, then by rights it would belong to the De Lacys. But Jemima wouldn't listen. She could be stubborn like her father too. That summer, she went hunting all over the house, tapping walls and floorboards, searching the attics and the cellars.' Mirabel sighed, a distant look in her eyes. 'Mr Darke believed she told Etta about the strongbox during her confinement in the attic. He thought it might have been an act of revenge against her father.'

'But why would Etta have taken it?' I asked. 'She'd have risked a hanging if she'd been caught.'

'Haven't you been listening? I told you, she didn't take it. Etta was an honest girl.' Mirabel studied my face. 'You appear to be the only one of us harbouring doubts, Miss Antrobus. Ask yourself this: if that codicil was stolen to benefit my son, as Darke supposed, then why wasn't it destroyed? Why would somebody steal it and then preserve it for all these years?'

Because my father had wanted me to one day claim my fortune. Surely he had known this maidservant, Etta? Rosie had said that he'd often told fortunes for the upper servants. He must have bribed or charmed Etta into stealing the documents for him, and erroneously, Darke's suspicions had fallen upon Julius. I still didn't quite understand my father's motive for stealing the codicil, but I presumed he must have believed that my inheritance was somehow under threat.

'I don't know why we are even talking about this,' Mirabel exclaimed crossly. 'The case distresses me, to be sure, but only because my children are at war. I don't countenance Luna's claims, not for a moment.'

'Then we will ask the cards again,' I said. 'We will grapple with all your doubts and all your fears. Until we have alleviated your unhappiness and soothed Virgil's concerns. I could lay another square now for you, if you wish?'

Mirabel put a hand to her head. 'Doctor Crowhurst is coming at eleven. But come again tomorrow, will you, please?' She gazed towards the window. 'Perhaps they will have found Ocho by then.'

Did I feel guilty about her distress? How could I not? I'd never expected her to treat the disappearance of her parrot as a message from her dead son, although I can't deny that I'd hoped to shock her out of her circumspection. I consoled myself with the thought that tomorrow I would guide her in the unburdening of her soul. She would help me and help herself at the same time. As for Ocho, he had never looked happy, and when I'd enticed him out of his cage, his eyes had burned with a new fire as he'd embraced his freedom. Judge me, if you will. I have heard it all before. If you'd wanted a saint, then you should have read a different book.

Chapter Twelve

Six of diamonds as master-card: the card of report.
Conversation about one, or action by another;
in a degree affecting one's outward affairs.

THUS JEMIMA DE LACY'S obsession with Leighfindell and its history became my obsession. I went directly to the library, where I scoured the shelves, selecting a number of volumes about the county during the Wars of Religion.

The room was a fitting setting for this voyage down the years, with its dark oak panelling and stone windows. A great fireplace was carved with pomegranates: symbol of Mary Tudor and her mother, the Spanish queen. The air held that scent peculiar to old books: grass and vanilla and leather. It reminded me sharply of Mr Antrobus, and I experienced a cruel pang of loss.

As I pored over these volumes, I discovered that Devonshire had not been fertile ground for the old religion, only a handful of the grandest families clinging to the Catholic faith. Under Queen Elizabeth, they were persecuted and imprisoned, their lands confiscated. Some were executed, just as King Henry had executed the unfortunate Piers the Ninth. One name that came up many times was that of John Culpeper, a carpenter, who was employed by many of these families to build secret places to hide priests and forbidden books. Leighfindell was mentioned several times within this context, the house raided on three occasions under Piers the Tenth without result. Yet these descriptions dealt in generalities, not particulars. How and where to start looking for this hidden strongbox? It must be in the north wing, the oldest part of the house, yet that would still involve a search of many dozens of rooms.

I'd been reading for two hours, when the door opened to admit Archie Montfort. It was the first time I'd seen him since our return to the house yesterday. Rosie had told me that he had stayed overnight at the Dower House, and I presumed he had just returned.

'How is Mr Radclyffe?' I asked.

'Shocked, but bearing up,' Archie said. 'And yourself? Yesterday must have been distressing.'

'Well enough,' I said. 'Though it is I who should be asking you. It was plain to see you cared for poor Mr Radclyffe.'

Archie sighed. 'He was a friend to me after my father died. His eldest son had died a few years earlier, and his wife had lately passed away. Brinseley was in London. My mother had a new husband and a new family. We were two lonely souls thrown together. His decline saddened me greatly, but I'd thought he would have a few years yet.' He peered at my book. 'What are you reading?'

'A volume about the history of Leighfindell during the Wars of Religion. I was intrigued by Mr Radclyffe's story at dinner the other night.'

'Ghosts?' Archie smiled. 'This place can have that effect. I read all about its history when I was a boy. I never understood why the De Lacys added all those modern buildings. I much prefer to surround myself with these old stones.'

'I suppose our lives will be a fraction of Leighfindell's,' I said. 'If I owned a place like this, I'd want to be remembered too. It's either build, or haunt the place, I suppose.'

'Aren't you going to ask me what I am reading?' Archie held up the volume he was carrying to show me.

'*An Anatomy of Melancholy*,' I said. 'Now there's a surprise.'

He ran a hand through his hair, giving me that bashful smile again. 'A closed mind is never an attractive thing, and so I have decided to open mine. I find Burton's arguments about the causes of melancholy rather persuasive. Even though, as an Englishman, I find the idea of discussing one's troubles with one's friends rather excruciating. Which isn't to say that it cannot work. Do you make any progress with my grandmother?'

'I'm not sure,' I said. 'It is my belief that she is shouldering a great emotional burden. I don't simply mean her grief at the loss of her children, but something else that she cannot bring herself to talk about. It is reflected in her cards, but I haven't yet been able to divine their true meaning.'

'If it will make her feel better to share this burden, then why doesn't she do it?'

'Because the truth must be painful to her,' I explained again, though this time he listened. 'She might have buried it so deeply within herself that she doesn't even believe that it exists. People do that sometimes – if they have witnessed a disturbing event in their childhood, or if they feel an emotion they don't believe they're supposed to feel. In your grandmother's case, I think it comes from a place of guilt.' I remembered her face in the church, her flinching stare. 'Whatever her sin, whether real or imagined, I believe it has something to do with her dead children. Perhaps she feels in some way responsible for their deaths?'

'And all she need do is confess the truth to you and she will be cured?'

'You say that as though it was easy. But if the cards show me the way, then I hope to extract it.'

Archie frowned. 'Forgive me if I remain sceptical about the power of the cards to show you anything. Yet I do see that you are adept at reading people. And my grandmother certainly believes in your powers. Sometimes belief is all that matters. Even if it flies in the face of scientific reason.'

'You were doing extremely well until the last sentence,' I said, and this time when he grinned, I grinned back.

'Is that why you're interested in Leighfindell's history?' he asked. 'The power of belief? It might be the perfect epitaph for the Radclyffe family.'

'I suppose so,' I said, not entirely untruthfully. 'The Radclyffes and families like theirs fought and died for their religion. Men told their priests their darkest secrets. They risked their lives to protect them. Have you ever heard of a man named John Culpeper?'

'The carpenter? He's rather a legend in these parts. Did you know he died on the rack? The pain must have been unbearable, but he never gave up his secrets.'

Sadly for me. 'I'm trying to find out more about his work, but these books only mention him in passing.'

Archie put down his book. 'Come with me. I want to show you something.'

I followed him to a heavy oak counter table that filled an alcove to one side of the fireplace. He removed a pair of candelabras and a few ornaments from the top of it, and then threw his weight behind it, moving it away from the wall. 'Pass me that quill knife on the table, will you?'

When I returned, knife in hand, he was knocking upon the panelling. 'It sounds quite normal, doesn't it? But these wooden pegs aren't fixed in place. They just slide out.' He went to work on them with the knife, and had soon removed them all. Then he lifted the entire section of panelling down from the wall, revealing plain red brickwork and a thick, upright oak beam.

'It still looks just like any other wall, does it not?' Archie said. 'You can see why Culpeper's work baffled the Queen's agents.'

He placed his hand flat upon the beam and pushed. A grinding sound came from somewhere deep within the wall, and a scattering of plaster-dust fell to the floor. Then, to my astonishment, the beam swung up and out into the room, rotating on some kind of central pivot. It left a gap about a foot wide, a dark void behind it.

Archie ducked beneath the beam. 'There's room enough for two,' he called.

I needed no more encouragement. Squeezing through the gap, I found myself in a dry, stone chamber, about eight feet long, three feet wide, and six feet high. In the gloom, I made out a wooden bench and a few shelves spattered with wax. No documents. Nor any place that looked likely to conceal a secret strongbox.

'Isn't it ingenious?' Archie said. 'There are holes in the floor to provide air from the cellars. And the heat of the fireplace keeps it warm.'

He looked down at me, smiling, and I was suddenly very aware of his proximity. I reached up to feel the warmth of the brickwork, and Archie placed his hand over mine to move it to the right spot. Startled by his touch, my mind lurched unbidden to that night at the electricity show. He was almost as close to me now as he'd been then. Unaccountably, I found myself thinking of those woodcuts and engravings in Julius's desk drawer. Alarmed by the direction of my thoughts, I pulled my hand sharply away, ducking under the beam to return to the safety of the library.

'Mr Landrake, the librarian, told me that Piers the Thirteenth sheltered an envoy of Charles the Second here during the Great Rebellion,' Archie said, as he followed me out. 'The poor fellow was in there for a week, while Cromwell's agents tore the place apart. That can't have been much fun. Not when you think about it.'

'Are there any other hiding places like this one here at Leighfindell?' I asked.

'Oh, dozens. The place is riddled with them. They find one every decade or so during a renovation. A few years ago, when they built the kitchen court, they knocked out the brick oven in the old kitchens. There was a hide in the back of it, big enough for two men. There's even rumoured to be a secret chapel somewhere.' He returned the beam to its original position, and then set about replacing the panelling. 'There are more books about the family's history in the Radclyffe archive over at the Dower House. If you like, I could see if there are any volumes about Culpeper and his work?'

'Oh, would you?' I cried, my gratitude entirely genuine.

'It is the least I can do after everything,' he said. 'I'm heading over there tomorrow morning. I'll have a look then. But there is one condition, I'm afraid.'

He answered my look of enquiry with another broad smile. 'After I've been to the Dower House, I'm meeting the twins up at the Pharos to conduct our experiment. Galileo's Law of Falling Bodies, if you remember? I'm in need of an assistant, so what do you say? There'll be a maid present, so it will all be perfectly proper.'

It seemed a small price to pay, and I readily agreed.

'Good. I shall see you there at eleven o'clock.'

He had just finished replacing the pegs in the panelling, when Arabia and Emily entered the room in the midst of a discussion.

'There you are, Archie,' his mother said. 'Lady Frances hopes you'll make a fourth for whist. Goodness, what have you both been doing?'

Looking at Archie and then down at my dress, I realized we both wore a powdering of plaster dust. 'I was just showing Miss Antrobus our priest's hole,' Archie explained.

'It was all I could do to keep him out of there when he was a boy.' Arabia glanced between us curiously. 'But what is this? A cessation of hostilities?'

'We have agreed to disagree,' Archie declared. 'Upon the existence of magic, in any event. Upon Miss Antrobus's motives, I have conceded that I was utterly in the wrong.'

'Wonders will never cease,' Arabia said. 'Normally it takes a miracle to make him change his mind about anything. It seems Miss Antrobus has the power to enchant us all.'

It was certainly much more agreeable having Archie for an ally than an enemy. Nevertheless, I was not complacent, and after he had gone to play whist, I went to see if the postmaster had returned from Exeter. There were no letters for Archie from Bath, and in rather upbeat spirits, I collected the London newspapers and returned to the library to read them. Their pages were full of speculation about the possibility of Walpole's fall from power amidst his various scandals, and conjecture about his likely successor. I was scanning the columns of criminal trials, when a name jumped out at me.

5 September 1740. Sir Tobias Smallwood committed to Newgate one TAMSON ADELINE LAMBERT, an astrologer, for defrauding two young men of money under false pretences and drawing up charts. Her imprisonment to last one year, accompanied by three floggings. Further to be committed to two sessions in the pillory, eight months

apart, the first to take place 10 October of this year. Of late this has become a very common practice; there are daily men and women plying such frauds at Bartholomew or Fleet-Ditch, about Chancery-Lane End and other places. It is the opinion of this newspaper and all educated men that more must be done!

My stomach heaved. My very worst fears realized. Tamson was going to be hurt and humiliated, perhaps much worse. Why hadn't Morgan Trevithick bribed the magistrate? Why hadn't he found her a good lawyer? I didn't know if it was still possible to save her from this barbarity, but I had to try. I'd earned about twenty guineas since I'd left London, telling fortunes for Mirabel and Arabia. But how could I take that money to the magistrate? He would arrest me.

Three weeks to find the report and get back to London. Three weeks to find a way to save Tamson from the mob. I prayed that with Archie's help, I'd find the answers I sought.

Chapter Thirteen

Three of clubs, influenced by a spade:
a matter to make one angry or heart-sick.

An odd expression, at once concerned and calculating, works its way across the features of Henry Antrobus. 'The welfare of my ward matters more to me than anything,' he says. 'I find your account of her exploits in London highly distressing. Should she return to this house, I'll have her placed under lock and key. But to involve the law as you suggest—' Henry sighs. 'The pillory, sir. Her lovely face.'

Lazarus had arrived in Bath earlier that morning aboard the Flying Machine. Trim Street is his first port of call. Henry appears very much at home in his late cousin's library. His tailoring has improved markedly, they are drinking a very fine claret, and a diamond ring twinkles on his little finger. He has just told Lazarus how Red destroyed his collection of eggs, and though he professed himself concerned only for her state of mind, he had quivered with rage as he described the destruction she'd wrought.

'I only mean to threaten her with the pillory,' Lazarus reminds him. 'All your ward need do is sign a paper renouncing her claim to the De Lacy fortune, and these charges will disappear in a heartbeat. Naturally, Lady Seabrooke will advance you a sum of money to compensate for your time and your distress.'

Henry is silent a moment. 'Your sad tale only adds to my conviction that poor Rachel is suffering from a derangement of the mind. She belongs in a hospital, not a prison cell. I have consulted a mad-doctor who believes that she would benefit from a stay in his institution. Alas, the cost is prohibitive, but with Lady Seabrooke's assistance, it might be arranged?'

Lazarus frowns, trying not to let his dislike of Henry colour their dealings. 'Your ward did not strike me as mad, sir. Merely devious.'

'Perhaps she's come to believe her lies herself? That is a sign of madness, don't you think? The treatment I propose would be very much to her benefit. And if I might say so, sir, to Lady Seabrooke's benefit too.'

Lazarus studies his face. 'Go on.'

'Have you considered what might happen if Rachel refuses to sign your paper?' Henry says. 'She can be very stubborn, you know, and rather persuasive. There is no law, after all, to prevent her from pursuing her claim from a prison cell. She might consider the pillory a price worth paying.'

Like her friend, Tamson, and their sisterhood of spells and stars and silence. 'No lawyer would take her case,' Lazarus objects. 'She has no money, for a start.'

Henry wags a finger. 'Don't be too complacent, sir. Rachel might sell her story to the newspapers. The public adore a long-lost heir. A Perkin Warbeck. A Lambert Simnel. Both were cheered by the mob. Did you know there was also a man who claimed to be Edward the Second? He said a servant had swapped him for a carter's baby. When he was exposed as a liar, he claimed his cat was the very devil. Apparently, it was all the creature's idea. They hanged the cat too, as I recall.'

'There's no cat whispering to your ward, sir. This story is all her own invention.'

'And if Lady Seabrooke wants to be certain that she won't tell it in a court of law, she should consider my plan. A lunatic, as you know, cannot testify before a judge.'

How far would he go for Lady Seabrooke? It is a question Lazarus sometimes asks himself, somewhat alarmed that he does not know the answer. Kill a man? Certainly. If her life was in danger. Kill an innocent? Certainly not – or at least, he thinks not. Incarcerate a fraudster in a mad-house to prevent her from testifying? It falls into that part of Lazarus's conscience where moral justifications teeter atop one another like a tower of cards. Henry's plan is not without merit. He knows what Lady Seabrooke would say if she was here. 'How much?'

Henry's smile widens. 'I shall go fetch the figures.'

Whilst he is gone, Lazarus rises to study the books upon the shelves. One is devoted entirely to British geography. His eye alights upon *Bradshaw's Handbook to Cornwall.* Taking it down, he leafs through it. The entry for Tretelly describes the town's principal land-marks: the Seven Stars inn, the cliffs above town, the ancient church. He imagines Red sitting here, harvesting facts to support her story.

Henry duly returns and names a very large sum that doubtless includes a fat commission for himself. 'I shall talk to Lady Seabrooke,' Lazarus says.

He gives Henry the fifty pounds they have agreed as a retainer, and Henry kisses his golden heart charm. 'All I desire is to see Rachel healthy and happy again,' he says. 'The doctor I speak of has many methods to restore obedience in his patients – and that is the precur-sor to happiness, as we know. Once Rachel's spirits find equanimity, she will return to live here under my protection, as she did before.'

'Your compassion does you credit,' Lazarus murmurs, the words sticky in his mouth. Red will see sense, he tells himself, as he walks out onto Trim Street. And if she doesn't, it is nobody's fault but her own.

Is Red mad? Lazarus doesn't think so. Or at least, it depends on what one means by madness. She is deluded, certainly, to think she could ever triumph over opponents as formidable as Lady Seabrooke and her brother, Julius. She is also angry, which can be a form of mad-ness, and somehow that rage has become fixated upon the De Lacy family. Is Henry right? Has she come to believe in her own lies? It is not so uncommon for an orphan to become convinced that they are a changeling in the cradle – the heir to a lost fortune, or a lost kingdom – though that is not the same as inventing a new past and believing it true.

The question makes Lazarus think of a favourite quote of John Jory Jago's that has stayed with him: 'Too much sanity may be madness – and maddest of all: to see life as it is, and not as it should be.' Perhaps that is what Red is doing, he thinks, as he dines at the White Hart Inn in Stall Street, Bath. Perhaps she is writing her life as she thinks it should be. Which, by Quixote's logic, would make her sane and the rest of us mad.

When he'd said it, John Jory Jago had been talking about Jemima De Lacy, who was certainly mad. Or at least, she'd behaved as mad people do in books. Refusing to speak, weeping uncontrollably, throwing plates, sometimes chairs. Once, she'd taken off all her clothes and come down to dinner that way. After that incident, her father had her confined to the attic infirmary, a room with bars over the window and a door enforced with iron. A person could scream themselves to death up there and never be heard.

Doctor Crowhurst bled Jemima daily with leeches, and prescribed belladonna. Later, he tried stronger treatments: blistering, cold baths, more bleeding. Lazarus's considered opinion was that the good doctor didn't have a clue what he was doing. He tried many times to convince his master to send for better doctors, but Nicholas always refused.

Lazarus's spy in the Crowhurst camp was Etta, Jemima's maid, the only other person permitted by Nicholas to see her. Etta had been anxious about her mistress too. Lazarus could see it in her eyes. A pretty, raven-haired girl with a forthright gaze and a sly good humour, Etta told him how Jemima talked at her for hours, barely pausing for breath. Her favourite subjects were her love for her brother, Virgil; her love for Little Piers Radclyffe; and her hatred of her father.

Lazarus had tried to persuade Mirabel to intercede with her husband. But Mirabel, an outspoken, modern-minded woman, had cited her submission to her husband as proof of her strength. 'I bow to my husband's judgement, because it is superior,' she said. 'I can say that of no other man. Not even you.'

His master's mind, when made up, could never be changed. Nonetheless, Lazarus had tried, because he'd promised Luna that he would.

'I told you, word will get out,' Nicholas says. 'Once people think madness runs through De Lacy veins, Luna's value will drop. I'll be paying through the nose for a husband, and no duke or earl will touch her. I must think of Julius too. I have the Earl of Macclesfield's eldest picked out for him. Her father has an aversion to madness of any kind.'

'Think of Jemima, sir,' Lazarus begs. 'She could die up there.'

Nicholas gives him the look: the one that has silenced generals and princes. 'Doctor Crowhurst has it in hand,' is all he will say.

Lazarus knows he will be punished for this conversation, his advice ignored for a month or more. But before he can retreat to lick his wounds, Etta runs into the room, red-faced and breathless. 'Please, sirs, you have to come. Quickly now.'

Lazarus mounts the stairs two at a time, leaving his master and Etta in his wake. The infirmary door is ajar, and Lazarus hears Jemima's screams long before he reaches the room.

'Liar!' she shouts. 'Liar, liar, liar!'

When he reaches the door, he freezes, shocked by Jemima's appearance. Her beautiful face is a skull, yellowed skin like vellum stretched tight over her bones. Her red hair is wild, her eyes wilder still. She is in her nightshift, and she has a knife in her hand. Lazarus guesses she has snatched it from Crowhurst's bag. The doctor reaches out to her. 'Put it down, Jemima,' he says, sternly. 'Come back to bed.'

'Don't touch me,' she screams. 'Don't look at me.'

The doctor makes a grab for the knife, but Jemima is quicker. The candles dance, shadows race across the walls. Then Crowhurst jerks away, clutching his face. Blood spills from between his fingers onto the floor.

The sight of the blood quietens Jemima. She stares at the knife, as if questioning why it is in her hand. Lazarus gently takes it from her and passes it to Etta. Then he takes Jemima in his arms, trying to soothe her.

Nicholas arrives and orders everyone out. He tells Jemima to go back to bed, where she huddles, weeping. The door closes upon her torment. And then there is silence.

Nicholas leans against the wall. He speaks sharply to Etta, telling her to take the doctor downstairs, and to send a footman for the village barber to stitch him up. Looking at his master's drawn face, Lazarus realizes he is afraid. His astonishment mingles with pity, until Nicholas addresses him curtly: 'You will not speak of this incident to anyone. You will not speak of my daughter in my presence ever again.'

Much later that night, Lazarus wearily climbs the Blue Stairs up to his room in the new east wing. Once again, he has failed Luna, as he seems destined to fail her in all things. Increasingly, she turns to John Jory for advice – as if his fortunes could ever help anyone with anything. Lazarus abhors the growing distance between them, even as he counsels himself that it is for the best. Yet when he reaches his door, and the light of his candle mutes the darkness within, he realizes she is lying in his bed.

Luna sits up. She is naked. Her hair is unpinned, grazing her breasts. Her eyes are dry, her gaze hot, but the skin beneath them is swollen like bruises.

'If you ask me to leave,' she says, 'I won't, so don't even try.'

Chapter Fourteen

King of spades, influenced by a club:
a cautious man unsuspected for his real malevolency.

WHEN I RETURNED to my room to dress for dinner, I discovered that the seamstresses had finished the alterations to the first of my new gowns. A very fashionable *robe à la Française* of blue silk, it gave me a silhouette that narrowed my waist, the flared skirts pinned back to reveal an underskirt of ruffled ivory satin. The silk was embellished with silver embroidery and as I admired my reflection in the mirror, the threads seemed to move like rippling water. Even Rosie summoned enthusiasm, dusting my face with pearl powder to give it an agreeable shimmer, weaving a chain of sapphires through my hair, a loan from Emily. When I entered the dining room, the gentlemen stared.

'Why, you look lovely,' Emily said, smiling proudly.

'Didn't I say you were in need of a little sparkle?' her father said, giving me a look that made my insides writhe.

After a few perfunctory exchanges about Mr Radclyffe's death, the conversation at dinner turned, as usual, to the ball, specifically the problem of finding enough additional servants to deal with the five hundred guests expected to attend.

'Lord Morval says he can spare three footmen,' Lady Frances said. 'Mr Fanshawe can only spare two, but we'll have the full complement from the Dower House. Even so, it won't be nearly enough.'

'We won't need footmen upstairs,' Arabia said. 'That's another eight for you, right there.'

'Six,' Julius said. 'I want two outside my door at all times.'

I had noticed earlier that day that two footmen were stationed at the top of the Oak Stairs, just yards from the door to the rooms of Julius and his wife. Emily had told me, when I'd enquired, that her father had a large sum of money on the premises.

'Surely you don't need them there all night,' Lady Frances said. 'Not once your business with Mr Walpole is concluded.'

'I'm afraid I do,' Julius said. 'Once it is done, Mr Walpole's door will need guarding.'

His wife sighed. 'Then we're still ten footmen short. I'll ask Mr Whittington to find some men from the village.'

Julius grunted. 'You'll have to compromise on height.'

'Not to mention feature,' Septimus said. 'Last time the carnival of grotesques came to Slaughterbridge, they paid to watch the villagers.'

I took little part in the conversation, lost in worries about Tamson – until, that is, my chief tormentor, the footman, Patrick, placed a dish of stewed red cabbage upon the table, setting it down rather hard, so that a great splash of the red liquor hit the front of my gown. Certain that he'd done it deliberately, I turned in outrage, swift enough to catch him hide a smile.

'Forgive me,' he said, in his Devonshire drawl. 'It slipped from my hand.'

Lady Frances suppressed a laugh, the first time I'd seen her amused. 'You look as if you have been hard at work in a slaughterhouse.'

Julius spoke a few words of mild reproach to the footman, while Septimus handed me a napkin. I dabbed ineffectually at the stains, my cheeks burning with humiliation. Somehow Archie's look of pity was the worst of all.

'I had better go upstairs and change,' I said.

Enjoy your moment, I thought, as I walked past Patrick on my way to the door. Because yours will come.

Upstairs in my bedroom, I rang the bell for Rosie, who helped me to remove my gown. She pursed her lips at the stains. 'Spirits of wine will remove the marks, though the rubbing may take the lustre from the silk.'

'You can only do your best, Rosie,' I said. 'Those seamstresses will be out for Patrick's blood after all their work.'

'That'll be no more than he deserves,' she said, with feeling – though I sensed her anger was at the prospect of the additional work for herself, rather than any heartfelt sympathy on my behalf.

'Rosie,' I said, when she was helping me back into one of my old gowns, 'can I ask you something else? I passed a wooden cross in the woods yesterday. Doctor Crowhurst told me that it was the grave of a woman whose body was found in the lake. Some people say she was the ninth duchess.'

I thought it unlikely that the grave had any significance to my goals, but given Jemima's obsession with the last duchess, I wanted to be certain.

'I've passed by it,' Rosie said, rather shortly.

'Do you know why people leave flowers and charms there? Does the duchess have some significance for the servants?'

'I cannot say,' she said. 'I rarely listen to the foolish notions of maids and porters.'

It was a dismissive response, bordering upon rude, and she was silent after that. When she'd finished lacing my dress, I thanked her for her help, but she didn't reply. Her gaze was fixed upon the window, her eyes glassy and distant, as if lost in thought.

Early that evening, I was summoned to Julius's study. Much to my relief, he was not alone. Septimus, Mr Whittington, Doctor Crowhurst and Brinseley Radclyffe were seated around the room in leather chairs. The decoration was fashionably modern: sage-green wallpaper, white marble busts of poets and philosophers, and fitted bookshelves of Doric design. Hanging over the fireplace was a large oil painting of Nicholas De Lacy.

The gentlemen rose and bowed, and I curtseyed. 'I am very sorry about your father, sir,' I said.

Brinseley inclined his head. 'Now that the shock has worn off, I feel it was, in part, a kindness. I mourned the last two years of his life, almost as much as I mourn his death. It was terrible to see what he'd become.'

Julius invited me to sit and Doctor Crowhurst enquired after my wrist. I told him it was much better, and he said he would examine it once we had finished here.

'I'm afraid I need to talk to you about your discovery of the late Mr Radclyffe's body,' Julius said. 'Mr Whittington travelled to Oke-hampton this morning and spoke to the coroner. As there were no witnesses to the death, the wretched fellow is minded to hold an inquest, and juries can be unpredictable creatures. A verdict of suicide would be a disaster. We'd have to call off the ball.'

'I believe the coroner might be persuaded to change his mind,' Mr Whittington said. 'But it would help to have testimony to support our contention that the death was a tragic accident. Doctor Crowhurst has kindly written a letter giving his opinion to that effect. All we need from you is an account of your discovery. You will state that you saw nothing untoward – excepting the body, of course – and your first impression was that Mr Radclyffe had tripped and fallen onto his gun. I have taken the liberty of drafting a statement for you to sign.'

I took the paper from his hand and read it through. 'Sir,' I said to Julius, 'it was not my first impression that the death was an accident. I didn't know. I'm still not sure.'

'Uncertainty only provides an opportunity for the scandalmongers to make mischief,' Mr Whittington said. 'We must leave no room for doubt.'

'But I do have doubt,' I said. 'There was a large bruise on Mr Rad-clyffe's forehead.'

'I don't understand your meaning,' Julius said.

They were all looking at me expectantly. 'Somebody could have struck him,' I said.

'You mean murder?' Julius exclaimed. 'Mr Radclyffe wasn't robbed. His purse was in his pocket.'

'I told Miss Antrobus that there was no medical reason at all to suspect foul play,' the doctor said.

'I only say that we should not discount the possibility.' I turned to Septimus. 'Did you see anyone suspicious at all, sir? While you were out walking with your dogs?'

'Not unless you count the twins. And even they would draw the line at murder.'

'Or you, sir?' I turned to Julius. 'When you were on your way to the Hermitage?'

'If I had, I'd have said so,' he said, in a tone designed to silence me.

'Have you talked to the person who was with you at the Hermitage?' I persisted.

'What person?' Julius said, no less unkindly.

'I thought I saw a face at the window as we were leaving yesterday. I wondered if you had been meeting someone there.'

Immediately, I knew that I had said the wrong thing. There was an intake of breath and an avoiding of gaze on the part of the other gentlemen. Julius's expression was a cold and forbidding thing. 'There was nobody else at the Hermitage, Miss Antrobus. I was reading my papers there alone, as I often do.'

'We cannot afford to have any suggestion of murder,' Brinseley said. 'I refuse to let my engagement become mired in a scandal. It would be the talk of the ball.'

'You mean to go ahead with the announcement, then?' Septimus asked. 'People will say it is rather too soon.'

'The word from Whitehall is that we cannot afford to wait,' Julius said. 'Mr Radclyffe and my daughter will not dance, but otherwise everything is to proceed as planned.'

Any curiosity I might have had about the significance of Whitehall to the wedding, was swept away on a tide of outrage at their indifference. I was glad Archie wasn't there to hear it. Piers Radclyffe was barely cold, and everyone, even his son, was simply thinking of their own convenience. 'Shouldn't we at least ask the local magistrate's opinion?' I dared to say.

'I am the local magistrate,' Julius replied. 'Now I'll ask you again to sign that paper.'

To my eternal shame, I signed it. My statement was not precisely a lie. I was far from certain that anyone had murdered Mr Radclyffe. Yet even as the ink was drying on my signature, I wondered.

Julius passed the paper to Mr Whittington with a flourish. 'Away to Okehampton with you, sir. Take my carriage. It will be a good reminder for the coroner about who he's dealing with. Emily is in the morning room, Brinseley. I am sure she'd like a stroll before supper. You go with them, Septimus. Not you, Miss Antrobus.'

My trepidation mounting once more, I waited as the gentlemen filed out. 'I'll be in the morning room when you're ready for me to take a look at your wrist,' the doctor said.

The door closed, and Julius studied my face for what felt like a very long time. 'My mother seems to have got it into her head that this business with the bird is some sort of message from my dead brother. She has tried to persuade me to call off Emily's marriage and when I refused, she said she was minded not to attend the ball. I asked her where all this had come from, and she talked a lot about you. Something about a king of spades and a great deal of foolishness about the past. I asked you to keep my mother distracted, not encourage her to dwell upon ancient resentments.'

'I told her it had nothing to do with Emily's marriage,' I protested.

He shook his head. 'I did not have you pegged as a troublemaker, Miss Antrobus. My wife thinks that I should send you home.'

Not now, I thought, my panic rising. Not when I was making progress at last. Sensing that any defence of my actions would only enrage him further, I answered with humility: 'I'm sorry, sir.'

My submission seemed to calm him. He rose from the desk and took the chair beside me. 'There now,' he said, in a softer tone, placing a finger under my chin, tipping it so he could look me in the eye. 'There's no need to be upset. But I think it better if you keep away from my mother for the time being. No more fortunes until after the ball. Is that understood?'

I nodded, regretting it bitterly. How could I make amends for the parrot now?

'Good girl.' Julius stroked a stray curl of hair away from my face, and it took every ounce of my will to remain in that chair.

'How alone you are in the world,' he murmured. 'Your guardian does not seem to be giving you the attention you deserve. Nor your friends. The butler tells me that you haven't had a single letter since you arrived. Your circumstances are not comfortable, that is plain enough to see. It pains me, Miss Antrobus. I should like to be a good friend to you, if you'll only let me.'

Hardly able to hear over the rush of blood in my ears, I mumbled a reply: 'You have already been more than generous, sir.'

'I can be more generous still,' he said. 'Let us take a walk together tomorrow and discuss all of your troubles then. I'll have a light repast laid out for us at the Hermitage. We can have that game of cribbage.'

There was little doubt in my mind what he would require in exchange for his generosity: a re-enactment of one of those scenes in his desk drawer. The nature of his invitation and the reaction of the other men made me wonder again who he had been meeting at the Hermitage. A maid, perhaps? Or Miss Webster, the twins' governess? Someone poor, or someone dependent upon his goodwill.

'Sir,' I said, grasping for an excuse that would not enrage him, 'I should like to very much. But I fear the weather will not be suitable for walking for a few days.'

'Not suitable?' he exclaimed, glancing at the window. 'The skies are clear, and I'm told they are likely to remain so all week. The— Ah,' he broke off and smiled. 'I understand,' he said. 'You come and find me just as soon as the weather improves.'

Rising, I bobbed a curtsey and fled the room. Yet all I had done was delay the inevitable. One week at most, before his attentions would become pressing again. Under no circumstances did I intend to set foot in the Hermitage with him. And yet I sensed that the promise of such an event was now the only thing keeping me here.

Chapter Fifteen

Two of clubs as master-card: a doubtful omen,
figuring a grave confidence, of interest to learn,
but burdensome rather than easily to be passed by.

EVEN BEFORE YESTERDAY'S incident, I had been keeping an
eye on my chief tormentor, Patrick the footman. The other day,
I had noticed him walk around a ladder, rather than go under it. This
morning, as I'd watched from the gallery window, I'd seen him spit
over his shoulder when he'd glimpsed a magpie on a windowsill, said
to be a harbinger of death.

I am not one to scorn a superstitious man. Gentlemen of reason,
like Archie Montfort, who sneer at such credulity, have so much less
to fear from the world than men like Patrick. If a poor harvest or a
sick child is all that lies between your family and destitution, you look
for luck in all sorts of unlikely places. Yet be in no doubt that superstition remains a weakness. There is no better route into a man's soul
than through his fears.

When I arrived downstairs in the hall, I asked Patrick for my
cloak. Giving me his usual insolent smirk, he sauntered off to get it.
When he returned and I went to take it from him, I slid out a pin I'd
concealed in my palm, and scratched his hand. He yelped, snatching
it away.

'What is it, Patrick?' said Lady Frances, coming into the hall.

He clutched his hand. 'She scratched me.'

Examining my sleeve, I drew out the pin to show them. 'An oversight by the seamstresses. I'm terribly sorry.'

Patrick had a chin shaped like a pair of buttocks, and long teeth to match his weasel eyes. He gazed at his hand, then back at me. 'She meant to do it.'

'Don't be foolish,' Lady Frances said. 'After yesterday, you of all people should know that accidents happen. Here, let me see. Why, it's barely drawn blood.'

'It's an enchantment, madam. A witch's curse. My grandad taught me as a boy. A scratch can kill.'

'Oh, what nonsense,' Lady Frances said. 'I don't want to hear any more of this talk. This is what I mean, Miss Antrobus, when I dispute that your fortunes are merely harmless fun. They put silly ideas into uneducated minds.'

She was right, of course. A scratch was just a scratch. I certainly had no power to curse or kill. But something bad would inevitably happen to Patrick over the next few days – a lost coin or a dropped plate, with a bit of luck, something worse – and I wanted him to remember my smile when it did.

In markedly better spirits, I walked across the lawn, past the lake, and through the woods, to the footpath that led up the side of the valley to the Pharos. Passing the spot where poor Mr Radclyffe had died occasioned me a shudder, but I kept my gaze upon a circling goshawk.

The walk to the top took longer than I'd anticipated. A soupy haze hung over the valley, and my lungs were tight with exertion. By the time I emerged from the trees, the sun was high in the sky. The ground up here was rocky, strewn with boulders and brambles, the shadow of the Pharos like a sundial pointing back towards the house.

The tower was round and very tall, with arrow slits for windows, and a crenelated top like a castle. An open chaise was pulled up nearby, the horses tethered to a tree, a maidservant conversing with the driver upon the box.

As I neared the base of the tower, something small and hard struck me smartly upon the cheek. I clutched a hand to my face, looking around to see where it had come from. Another small object struck me upon the back of the head. Reeling round, I saw it rolling across the path. An acorn. Another struck me on the back. I heard a giggle high above and, looking up, I glimpsed two small dark heads on the parapet of the tower.

'Hey, give me that,' someone cried, and the golden head of Archie Montfort appeared above them. 'I thought you weren't coming.' He grinned down at me.

'We were only defending the castle,' one of the twins cried.

'From the witch,' the other piped up.

'She's not a witch,' Archie said. 'For one thing, witches don't exist. Now apologize to Miss Antrobus at once.'

The twins obeyed in a half-hearted chorus. Archie disappeared and then reappeared a moment later, with a small ball in each hand. 'Now that Miss Antrobus is here, we can begin. One of these balls is made of lead, the other of wood. The first is five times as heavy as the second. Which ball do you think will strike the ground first?'

Of course, they both said lead. 'Let us put your theory to the test,' Archie said. 'Boys, you are to drop the balls upon my count of three. Miss Antrobus will bear witness, and tell us which strikes the ground first.'

He made the count, the twins dropped the balls, and they thudded to the earth a few feet from where I stood.

'They struck the ground at the same time,' I reported dutifully.

The twins chorused their disbelief.

'If you don't believe her, we'll do it again. Miss Antrobus, would you care to bring the balls up, so we can repeat the experiment? Boys, you take her place down below.'

I waited at the base of the tower for the twins to descend, and when they burst out of the door, I climbed the spiral staircase inside. The ground floor contained a cage that Emily had told me was where the gamekeepers imprisoned poachers. The five storeys above were used to hang deer. By the time I reached the top, I felt quite nauseous from the thick gamey stench, and I breathed in the fresh air gratefully. The view was inspiring: Leighfindell, its courts and gardens; the red-brick Dower House in the distance; Slaughterbridge and its church; a patchwork of purple moorland, green meadows and pastures.

I gave Archie one of the balls, and we repeated the experiment, much to the bafflement of the twins below.

'Aristotle said that heavier things fall to the ground first because they are more eager to reach the centre of the earth,' Archie called down to them. 'His thinking went unchallenged for nearly two thousand years. Then along came Galileo who proved it was balderdash. The lesson is not to believe everything that you are told, no matter how authoritative the source. Now didn't you promise your tutor that you would work out the height of this tower?'

Amidst a lot of grumbling, the twins set to work on this task, armed with a metre wheel and a protractor that they retrieved from the chaise. While Archie was giving them instructions, I turned my face to the sky. A flock of birds was flying overhead, and to my surprise, I spotted Ocho swooping among them. Archie hadn't noticed, and I stood there, torn, wanting to bring Mirabel some comfort by reuniting her with her parrot, but remembering what Julius had said at dinner about blinding the bird. Watching Ocho soar around joyously on the breeze, I joined Archie by the parapet to distract him until the birds were gone.

'Your brothers like you,' I said. 'Did you know your grandmother calls you the Pied Piper?'

'I am nowhere near so gifted. Marchpane is the only secret to my success.' Archie produced a paper bag from his pocket.

The heady taste of sugar reminded me of the fair, and I thought of Tamson.

'Did you see Nonny this morning?' Archie asked.

I had written Mirabel a hasty note, excusing myself from our breakfast. 'Your uncle didn't think she should be disturbed.' Unable to restrain myself any longer, I blurted it out: 'Did you find any books about Culpeper in the Radclyffe archive?'

'I did.' Archie burrowed around in his bag, retrieving a small, thick volume with a red-and-gold cover. 'It turns out the younger brother of the fourteenth Piers was even more obsessed with his ancestors than Brinseley is. There's a chapter in here all about Culpeper's time at Leighfindell. It's rather Romish in flavour, so don't let the curate see.'

I thanked him profusely. Not wanting to arouse his suspicion by appearing too eager, I resisted the urge to return to the house right away so that I could read it.

'In Culpeper's day, the Radclyffes posted a watchman up here,' Archie said. 'If he saw the Queen's men on the road, he'd light a fire on the parapet that could be seen from the house. Then they'd have time to hide the priests and their incriminating documents.'

'What's that house?' I asked, pointing to a large white villa to the west of the park.

'It's where Doctor Crowhurst lives. Do you see that house there?' He pointed to a red-brick house about a mile from Leighfindell. 'That's where I grew up. Until my mother married Septimus and we moved to the big house.'

'Quite a transformation,' I remarked.

'It certainly took some getting used to. I hope you weren't too upset by that footman yesterday. The servants here can be very proud and none too welcoming at times. The footmen treated my mother quite dreadfully when she first married my stepfather. They weren't the only ones.'

'Oh?'

He smiled wryly. 'Lady Frances is the daughter of an earl. My mother was the daughter of a taverner. It took five years before she could bring herself to speak to me. Everybody thought I should be grateful for my new situation, but I missed my father dreadfully. He died in a carriage accident when I was nine.'

'I'm sorry,' I said.

His eyes met mine. 'You understand the pain of loss, I know. My correspondent told me about your guardian, that you witnessed the fire in which he was hurt. I can't begin to comprehend the horror of it all.'

His sympathy caught me at a moment of weakness. I'd tried hard not to think about that terrible night. How strange to think that it was only five months ago. Noticing my distress, Archie kindly looked away, shouting a few instructions down to the twins.

'Can I ask you a question?' I said, once I had regained a hold on my feelings. 'Why will Emily be married so swiftly now that Brinseley's father is dead? It has something to do with Mr Walpole, doesn't it?'

His surprised expression told me that I was right. When he didn't answer right away, I pressed him. 'Does the wedding need to take place soon, because Walpole might fall from power? Is he to do something for Brinseley? Something that will save Julius money?' I was remembering Mirabel's words: *Deal. Bargain.*

Archie smiled. 'It seems there will soon be no secrets left at Leigh-findell. But yes, I will tell you in confidence that Mr Radclyffe's death removes the last obstacle from Julius's plans. Or rather, the plans of his wife, for I believe it was Lady Frances's idea. Mr Radclyffe was a Catholic, you see, which meant nothing could happen while he was alive. Now that he is dead, Walpole is to restore the Radclyffes to their dukedom. Or at least, the King is to do the restoring, but at Mr Walpole's behest. And so Julius will achieve what his father never could: outstrip the Seabrooke earldom. I'm told he made enquiries amongst the existing dukes with suitable heirs, and couldn't beat them down to less than thirty-five thousand pounds. Whereas Walpole will do it for fifteen.'

I remembered all Mrs Grainger's tirades about Walpolian corruption in our kitchen at Trim Street. It was a scheme suitably grandiose for a De Lacy. 'Does nobody think of poor Emily in all of this?'

Archie sighed. 'Don't think I am without sympathy. But it would be no use trying to change her father's mind, and I caution you not to try.'

'Can she not stand up to them? Surely they would not force her?'

'Her parents have convinced her it is her duty. Emily is a malleable creature. I learned that to my cost.' There was a bitter edge to his voice, and I looked at him enquiringly.

'Oh, don't mind me,' he said. 'I'm just feeling sorry for myself. You might have noticed that she thinks I'm the devil, but it wasn't always that way. For a long time, I was like an older brother to her. Until Lady Frances discovered that Septimus was trying to convince Julius to make Titus his heir. It was a silly plan that would never have succeeded. Julius wants that money to remain within his own bloodline and that means Emily. But that didn't stop my mother and stepfather from trying. Lady Frances convinced Emily that I was a part of it all, even though I'd tried to talk them out of it.'

'Have you explained all this to Emily?'

'More times than I can count. She only flings accusations back in my face.' He sighed again. 'But she is a sweet girl at heart. Or at least she would be without all of this.' He made a contemptuous gesture in the direction of Leighfindell. 'The De Lacy fortune would corrupt the soul of even the most honourable man.' He eyed me askance. 'If you think me a perfect hypocrite, then you'd be right. Julius gives me a generous allowance. Mother hopes he will make me a good marriage. But sometimes I dream of being free from it all. To be a man of science, which Julius thinks an ungentlemanly pursuit. To travel. To write. To marry a woman for herself and not her money.'

'Those are fine dreams,' I said.

'I'm afraid they don't survive a collision with reality. You must feel it yourself in your own situation. Yet I look at the De Lacys, my mother included, and I don't see any great joy, for all their riches. You and I are perfect paupers, and yet I think we are happier than the rest of them combined.'

What would he think of me, I wondered, when he learned that I'd been deceiving him all along? When he discovered that I'd only ever been interested in the De Lacy fortune? The thought was oddly unpleasant, and I tried to push it from my mind, as we stood up there on the Pharos, talking about science, literature and history, listening to the sound of the twins squabbling down below.

Later, when we'd descended the tower and the twins were scrambling into the chaise, Archie offered me his hand to help me up. 'Hold still a moment,' he said, and I felt his fingers in my hair. Something had been entangled in my curls, and he held it out to me: an acorn. Not quite knowing why, I slipped it into my pocket.

CHAPTER SIXTEEN

Ten of hearts, influenced by a club:
a marriage of reason, or of circumstances.

I HAD BEEN planning to read Archie's book the moment I returned to the house, but Arabia waylaid me in the drawing room. 'I need you to tell my fortune right away, Miss Antrobus.'

We joined Emily at the tea table, where she was working on her embroidery. 'I wish to ask you about a matter of the heart,' Arabia said.

After I had laid the Square and despoiled it, we studied her cards together. 'I see a handsome gentleman here,' I said.

'My Archie,' Arabia cried.

Emily met my gaze with a pointed smile, and I remembered our conversation by the lake, when we'd agreed that we did not find him handsome at all. I felt uncomfortable returning her smile, not least because I no longer clung to my old opinion with quite the same conviction.

'The queen of diamonds and the queen of spades,' Arabia said, pointing to the cards. 'What is their significance, Miss Antrobus? Tell me, please.'

I studied the surrounding cards. 'It looks to me as if they are rivals for the man's affections,' I said. 'I see a marriage with money in it. And this card here, the nine of diamonds influenced by like suit, is the card of material fortune.'

Arabia clapped her hands. 'Miss Raleigh and Lady Helena. I imagine they'll be all claws with one another at the ball.'

'The earl will never let Lady Helena marry Archie,' Emily said.

'Perhaps not.' Arabia sighed. 'But Miss Raleigh has five thousand a year and her grandfather was a grocer.'

'He owned a great many grocery shops,' Emily said. 'He became Lord Mayor of London.'

'I would never let Archie marry for less than five thousand,' Arabia declared. 'He is the stepson of a De Lacy, after all. Julius will undoubtedly turn his mind to a great match for him, once your own marriage is made.'

She chattered on in this vein for quite some time. All the young ladies who were in love with Archie. Names I'd heard, and names I had not. Their fortunes were tallied by his mother, and often found wanting.

'The worst part about having a handsome son, is all the unworthy girls who think to set their sights on him. Like that little baggage at Oxford. The less said about her the better.' Arabia glanced at the ormolu clock on the mantelpiece. 'Oh, I promised to remind Septimus to take his pills for his spleen.'

She hurried off, and Emily looked at me in some amusement. 'I do believe you have just been delivered a lesson.'

'I'm sorry?'

'Archie. It is Aunt Arabia's greatest fear that some girl without fortune will steal his heart and undo all of her plans.'

I almost choked on my wine. 'She thinks *I* want to marry Archie?'

'You do seem to have rather got over your squabble.' She gazed at me curiously.

'I want nothing of the kind,' I said indignantly. The last thing I wanted was to give people any more cause to suspect my motives in that house.

'Well, of course you don't.' Emily pulled a face. 'It's Archie. And you couldn't afford to marry him, could you? You're both adrift in the same boat, needing to marry well.'

'What did your aunt mean about Oxford?' I couldn't resist from asking.

'Oh, Archie had a girl there. They were going to be married, but it turned out that she didn't have the money everyone thought she had. My father put a stop to it, and in the end, she married somebody else. Archie moped about for weeks. I think he loves her even now. I'm sure we could find you someone much more suitable at the ball.'

'I don't want to marry anyone,' I cried.

Her smile faded. 'I wish I was in your shoes. Everybody wants to marry me, because of Father's money.' She fished in her pocket and placed a golden guinea upon the table. 'Rachel, would you tell my fortune?'

I gazed at her, surprised. She had never asked me that before. 'I thought you said your mother wouldn't like it.'

She smiled hesitantly. 'Mother's not here, is she?'

I should have refused. But my heart went out to this friendless girl in her gilded castle. Emily watched me solemnly as I laid and despoiled the Square. I hardly needed her to tell me the question in her heart. It screamed out of every line on her tense, troubled face: *Does he love me?*

I let the cards fall naturally. Why shouldn't Emily have the truth? And the truth could not have been figured there more starkly.

The ten of hearts influenced by a club, indicating a marriage of reason, or of circumstances.

The ace of clubs influenced by a diamond, figuring an affair connected to money or responsibility to others.

The eight of diamonds as master-card, the unlucky red card.

The knave of diamonds influenced by like suit, figuring a man who utilizes marriage or love for personal advantage.

I offered her no flowery interpretations, letting the cards speak for themselves. Emily bit her lip, looking increasingly distressed. When I turned over her wish cards, she choked back a sob, and fled from the room, scattering the cards.

Feeling desperately sorry for her, I picked them up. Emily had dropped her embroidery, a sampler depicting a vase of De Lacy roses. The silken blooms were wilting, three dead flies lying amidst the fallen petals, their bellies upturned.

CHAPTER SEVENTEEN

Nine of clubs, influenced by a spade: beware lest so is assumed
no greater responsibility than can be easily carried.

LAZARUS'S EYELIDS ARE gummed together. His teeth are dry
and sour. His skull is filled with a dull throb of pain. Yet the
sheets are soft and have an unfamiliar scent of lemon. Sunlight pools
upon boards thick with beeswax. He can hear soft voices near at hand.

A chink of crockery. The closing of a door. A sudden weight upon
the bed and he rolls over to find Araminta Davenport smiling down
at him. 'I was starting to think you might never wake up,' she says.
'Not that I begrudge a man his rest. Not if he's earned it.'

The sparkle in her eye alarms him. Memories of last night are
returning in disjointed flashes. The taste of wine mingles with the
scent of her perfume, making him feel rather sick.

It is unlike him to get so cup-shot. He racks his brain to remember
why. He had started drinking in earnest the moment Mrs Davenport
made it plain that her assistance to Lady Seabrooke was contingent upon those very labours upon which she has just commended
him. Guilt is not the right word to describe how he feels. If Lady
Seabrooke could see him now, she would probably congratulate him
on his fealty to her service. Yet every echo of his original sin – that
fleeting taste of paradise at Leighfindell – only serves as a reminder
of the cost of that moment.

'I should go,' he says, rising, uncomfortable in his own nakedness.
She pouts. 'Rather ungentlemanly of you, sir.'

No sense in undoing last night's work, however he feels about it now. 'Forgive me, madam,' he says. 'I should like nothing more than to while away the summer right here in your bed. Alas, my mistress's business will not wait. Yet last night . . .' he tries desperately to remember the right sort of words, 'was a draught of nectar to this beggarly palate.'

'A little much, Mr Darke.' But her smile is restored. 'You're quite certain that my affidavit won't upset Julius De Lacy?'

Lazarus's words come more easily now, some clarity of thought returning. 'Miss Antrobus's claim will only become the subject of scrutiny if and when the courts rule the codicil to be genuine. At that juncture, Julius De Lacy will have already lost. Did I give you the address of Lady Seabrooke's Bath solicitor? Be sure to tell him everything that you told me. Rachel's obsession with the De Lacys. How she questioned you and your friends. How you told her that Lady Seabrooke was Julius De Lacy's sister.'

She frowns. 'I'm sure I must have done. Why on earth wouldn't I? It's common knowledge.'

'It would seem very strange if you had not,' Lazarus agrees. 'That gossip you mentioned last night, about Antrobus being the girl's natural father. Did you give it any credence?'

'Oh, I never listen to gossip, sir,' she says. 'I wouldn't have repeated it to you, were it not for the seriousness of Lady Seabrooke's situation.'

'We may need you to repeat it in court.'

'Oh, Mr Darke, I never could. Mr Nash deplores a gossip. What would people think?'

'If asked about it by a judge, you can hardly deny that you heard it.' Lest she take this as a threat, he smiles. 'When you come to London, you must make sure to call upon Lady Seabrooke. She will be eager to tell you what a good friend you have been.'

'If I am asked about it on oath, then Mr Nash could hardly hold it against me.' Mrs Davenport pats her yellow curls, smiling at the thought of a London season under the patronage of Lady Seabrooke. 'And what of our own friendship, Mr Darke? Will I see you when I am in London?'

She had made it very clear to him last night that she only sought companionship of a transitory nature. *'A Handel concerto is enjoyed best only once a season.'* Lazarus supposes he should be flattered that she desires a repeat performance quite so soon.

'I should be very pleased to offer you my services as a guide.'

She reclines against the bolster, watching him dress with bold eyes. 'And what voyages of discovery we shall make.'

Lazarus walks back to his lodgings, the sun hot, his clothes sticky. Motes dance before his eyes like malevolent sprites. Wearily, he climbs the stairs, and packs his bags.

Before he departs for Cornwall, he pays a visit to a quiet street of small, but respectable houses near to the river. His knock is answered by Bartholomew Jennings, who is about twenty-five years of age. He has an athletic build surprising in one who spends his days hunched over a shop counter. Lazarus explains his business while Jennings listens, a thoughtful look upon his thin, intelligent face. A sum of money is exchanged and he invites Lazarus to step inside.

His wife, who is visibly with child, brews tea. They drink it sitting in the Jennings' dark, cramped parlour, which has framed sketches of Shakespeare and Milton upon the walls.

'How long were you a maidservant in the house of Robert Antrobus?' Lazarus asks.

Letitia Jennings brushes aside a lock of yellow hair that has escaped her cap. This conversation has cost Lazarus ten pounds, perhaps three months of her husband's salary as the manager of a Bath bookshop, but she doesn't look happy.

'About twelve years,' she says. 'I was just a girl when I started there.'

'Then you remember when Rachel first came to live with your master?'

She frowns. 'Why do you want to know about Rachel?'

Her husband gives her arm a gentle squeeze. 'Just answer his questions, love.'

She gives them both an uneasy glance, but she keeps talking. 'A scared little thing she was. Hadn't the first idea how to behave. Lord knows how her first guardian brought her up. She barely knew a knife from a fork. Bachelors!' She gives her husband a fonder glance.

'There is some speculation in Bath society that the story about her Cornish guardian and her dead parents was a fabrication,' Lazarus says. 'That she might have been your master's natural daughter.'

Letitia laughs. 'Who told you that? He loved her dear, but she wasn't his. They were unalike as a pea and a partridge.'

Lazarus persists. 'She might have got her looks from her mother?'

'He wasn't her father. Not a bit of it. Though I once heard him tell Mrs Fremantle that he wished he was.'

'That was the housekeeper? The one who was killed in the burglary?'

'That's right.' She looks away. 'Those villains were never caught.'

'Not many bachelors would take in a child, when they were under no obligation to do so. Is that really the sort of man your master was?'

She answers him tartly, as if the question has demeaned him. 'That is precisely the sort of man my master was.'

Lazarus rubs his temple. His headache still hasn't gone. 'Do you remember Rachel's portmanteau? She claims it contained various things that belonged to her father.'

She frowns. 'I remember an argument. Rachel must have been about twelve and Mrs Fremantle caught her looking inside a portmanteau stored under her bed. Though I think that Mrs F was less upset by the looking, and more that Rachel had lied to her.'

Then Red's narrative has been woven to fit verifiable facts. Lazarus admires her work, but he's not done picking holes. 'These fortunes she tells. Did she learn how to do it here in Bath? Or did she know how to do it already when she came here?'

Letitia thinks. 'I don't remember. I know the first time she read my cards, she was just a little girl. But I couldn't say where or how she learned it.'

Lazarus questions her about the old document, *The Square of Sevens*, but all she remembers is that it was kept in her master's cabinet. 'I've no idea where he obtained it. He was always buying old books and papers. Are you going to tell me why you're asking me all these questions? I'm not saying anything more until you do.'

When Lazarus tells her, she gapes like a carp. 'Rachel? A countess's daughter? How is that possible?'

'It's not,' Lazarus says. 'I need only to prove it.'

She bristles with indignation. 'That's why you're here? To trick me into calling her a liar?'

'I didn't trick you. You said yourself she was a liar, without any prompting from me.'

'That was different. All children lie. Especially if they think they're in trouble.'

But Lazarus isn't interested in all children, only in this one. 'Did you ever see Rachel with a little gold charm in the shape of a heart?'

'She took it everywhere,' Letitia says. 'Until she lost it last summer. There were tears about that, I can tell you.'

Lazarus wonders why Henry stole it – assuming it is the same golden heart charm, which he suspects it is. Perhaps Henry's feelings for the girl are more complicated than he first presumed?

'Did Rachel have it with her when she arrived? Or did she acquire it later?'

'She had it that first day when she came to Trim Street,' Letitia says. 'Clutching it in her hand, she was, and I had to prize it from her fingers when I bathed her. She looked set to fight me for it, said it had belonged to her father. So I put it on the side where she could see it, and I swear she'd rather have got soap in her eyes than take her gaze off it.'

However talented Red is, she can't have been planning all of this since she was seven years old. It's just a coincidence, Lazarus tells himself. You can buy charms like that at every fairground, and from every tinker in the kingdom. Red must have woven the charm into her story when she found out that John Jory sold them too. Yet Letitia's testimony is unhelpful, to say the least. He certainly doesn't want her saying her piece in court.

When he rises to leave, her husband shakes his hand, but Letitia just stares. 'How much are you paid to do this? I hope it's worth it.'

'Letitia,' her husband warns. 'I'm sorry, sir.'

'You're sorry, Bat Jennings? I'm sorry I ever let you talk me into this.'

Her question is one Lazarus is often asked in the course of his work. At least this time he has a decent answer. 'You won't believe it, but I'm trying to help her. If Rachel repeats these lies in court, she could be in serious trouble.'

Her lip curls. 'Has it ever occurred to you that she might be telling the truth?'

'I don't believe that. And I don't think you do either.'

'Are you a reader of minds now, Mr Darke?' Letitia shakes her husband's restraining hand free from her arm. 'Don't you think to quieten me. That little girl is dearer to me than my own sister. And he comes here like this, presuming I'll betray her because we're poor. Help her, indeed? Don't think you have me fooled. You might wear a fine suit and have charming manners, but you're no different to the bailiffs who came to question my ma, because they was convinced she had our Ben hiding in the attic. Just threats and cruelty dressed up as kindness. Slippery words for slippery ends. I don't know how it is you sleep at night.'

CHAPTER EIGHTEEN

Ten of spades as master-card:
an event or project to your disadvantage and regret.

T HE BOOK'S RED cover was richly worked in gold: circular patterns, quarter medallions, and filigreed borders. The title page
had a border of similar patterns: *A History of the Radclyffe Family by
Swithin Radclyffe, 1682.*

Seated at the tea table in my room, I turned the old vellum pages.
The book was hand-written, the script often hard to decipher, the
chapters cataloguing the lives of the various Piers Radclyffes in great
detail. I delved hastily through the volume until I came to the tenth
duke, and then turned the pages more slowly, searching the text for
the name of Culpeper. As Archie had promised, he had a chapter all
of his own.

John Culpeper was born in 1552 in Tiverton in the county of Devonshire in the reign of the Tudor pretender, Edward. His father was a
carpenter and he was apprenticed into that trade at the age of twelve.
The Culpepers, ever true servants of Rome, numbered three brothers
and two priests amongst their connexions, and Culpeper learned from
his father how his talents could be put to use in the service of the
Catholic faith. Under the reign of Elizabeth, Whore of Babylon, he
travelled the length and breadth of three counties – Devonshire, Dorset
and Somersetshire – offering his services to those great gentlemen loyal
to Rome. He worked by night, constructing hides and holes for men

and books, their ingenuity evading all detection by the Queen's agents. I verily think no man can be said to have done more good of all who laboured in the service of Rome. He saved the lives of many hundreds of persons, both ecclesiastical and secular.

As Culpeper's renown grew, his name became known to the Queen's serpent, Francis Walsingham, and he was forced to travel under several aliases. Though arrested twice, the Queen's agents did not realize they had in their custody a man of such fame, and he was released. On the occasion of his third arrest, his identity was betrayed and he was committed to the Tower. Here he was racked insufferably, but died without ever revealing his secrets.

Some of those secrets I commit to paper now.

Turning the page, I discovered three pressed flowers, a violet and two yellow pansies. I had no proof, of course, that Jemima had put them here, but eagerly I read on, looking for any mention of a strongbox.

In the year 1582, Culpeper came to Leighfindell at the behest of the tenth Piers. Here he constructed seven holes, several hides, and a private chapel.

In the chamber of the Twelve Martyrs, a discreet bedroom for a priest, Culpeper built a portal within the most innocent of cupboards. A hidden peg is removed and the back of the cupboard, shelves and all, is revealed to be a deceitful door into the chapel, one of the largest hides ever constructed in England. Over seventeen feet long and seven feet high at its highest point, religious rites were performed there in perfect secrecy. A trapdoor concealed in a tiny closet leads to a narrow flight of stairs communicating with the cellars below. From there a subterranean passage conducts to the gardens . . .

Frustrated, I turned the page. I was looking for a hiding place for books and papers, not for men.

In constructing a secret panel in the kitchens for the concealment of sacred books and relics, Culpeper was likely inspired by an earlier work of his own father at Leighfindell. Located behind a carved window seat in the principal bedroom of the house, the central petals of three Tudor roses, an outward display of conformity, comprise three fraudulent pegs. When removed, a panel opens by means of a spring, concealing a strongbox for the storage of documents and holy books. It was the whereabouts of this same store that was betrayed to the King's agents by the ninth duchess, leading to the martyrdom of her husband.

I read the paragraph again, my fingertip tracing each word. The old kitchens were long gone, knocked down in the renovation that Archie had told me about. But I remembered the window seats in Julius's bedroom. It made sense that he would keep his papers close. Hadn't I begun my search in the bedroom for that very reason? Hadn't Jemima been obsessed with the last duchess? Yet how to get into that room again? Two footmen were now stationed permanently outside, presumably guarding the money that would be used to purchase Brinseley Radclyffe's dukedom. I sat there, mulling the problem, until I remembered Julius's words at dinner. He'd said that once his business with Walpole was concluded, the footmen would be stationed outside the First Minister's bedroom, I guessed because the money was going to be moved there. Surely that was my chance to get into Julius's bedroom unobserved? The ball would provide plenty of distraction.

I didn't dwell on what would happen if I was wrong about the window seat. Or if I was right, but the report wasn't there. I went through my pack of cards to find the seven of diamonds, the card of good omen, and I placed it inside the book, next to Jemima's flowers.

Eager to put my plans into action right away, the next morning I rose early, and headed downstairs. Approaching one of the friendlier footmen, I asked him about travel from Slaughterbridge to Exeter, claiming the question was on behalf of a friend who had been invited to the ball. I ascertained that a coach departed the inn at

Slaughterbridge every day at eleven o'clock. On the day after the ball, at that hour, everyone would be in bed.

Assuming I managed to find the report, my plan was to leave a letter for the De Lacys explaining that I had been called back to London urgently as Mrs Illingworth's condition had worsened. They would think it highly irregular that I had departed in such a fashion, but I hoped my letter would be sufficient to allay any serious suspicion, at least until they discovered that the report was missing. From Exeter, I would take the stagecoach back to London, arriving there a week later, in time to help Tamson. My plan was to use an intermediary to bribe the magistrate to commute her sentence, perhaps Fernando from the coffeehouse on Fleet Street.

Determined to leave nothing to chance, I decided to walk up to Slaughterbridge to make further enquiries about the carriage. Yet as I made my way out of the courtyard, I encountered Lady Frances. 'Walk with me, Miss Antrobus, if you please.'

This was decidedly unusual. Normally, Lady Frances went out of her way to pretend that I did not exist. Not wanting to arouse her ire by refusing, I walked with her along the gravel path that led to the orangery. This handsome sandstone building had seven very tall arched windows in each wall, the interior filled with a dazzling light. Charcoal braziers warmed the air to a temperature sufficient for exotic fruits and flowers to flourish. Lady Frances's brisk step echoed on the marble floor as we strolled between the beds, breathing in the scents of oleander and hibiscus.

'I am told that you read Emily's fortune yesterday,' she said. 'Now she is crying in the music room, saying that she will not marry Mr Radclyffe. What did you tell her?'

I didn't know who her informant was – whether Emily herself, or the housemaid who had brought our tea.

'She asked the cards if Mr Radclyffe loved her. They told her that he did not.'

Lady Frances smiled, rather caustically. 'Of course he does not love her. They barely know one another. Love-matches are for milkmaids and servants. Brinseley is a decent fellow. He will not beat her or torment her. The worst he will do is look for love outside his marriage.' She paused to inspect a pineapple.

Perhaps I should have held my tongue, but now that the moment had arisen, I felt compelled to speak. 'That is the most that Emily can expect?'

'It is the price we pay for all of this.' Lady Frances swept a bejewelled hand around the hothouse. 'Did you know that I was originally supposed to marry my husband's brother, Virgil? The moment he was in the ground, my father told me that I was now to marry Julius. Nicholas De Lacy wanted an earldom to match his brother's title, and marrying his eldest son to the daughter of an earl was the next best thing. In return, he was to pay for a new west wing for my father's Norfolk estate. When Julius was disinherited, my father called off the match. But after the death of his father, Julius resurrected the original plan. My father explained his reasons to me quite succinctly: it was the only way Julius could get his hands upon his money. He was only nineteen when he inherited, you see, and would not come into his fortune for another eighteen months. But if he married a woman to whom the trustees could raise no objection, he would receive a marriage portion that would fund his life in London. My father was delighted. They called his new building the De Lacy wing. So you see, Miss Antrobus, I have no illusions about love.'

'You do not want more for your daughter?' I said, aware that I was venturing further into danger.

'More is precisely what I want for her. The De Lacys are a cadet branch of a family new to wealth and power. When you are as rich as my husband, people don't disparage you to your face. They do it behind your back, and make sure that you know it. My marriage demeaned my status, and I'll not have the same for Emily. I'll certainly not allow you to lay waste to my plans.'

This time I held my tongue, though I hoped that Emily would stay true to herself and stand up to her parents.

Perhaps reading my thoughts, Lady Frances fixed me with her jaundiced eye. 'What do you think my husband will do, when he learns that you have been meddling with this match? His mother's tantrums he could forgive, but this marriage matters more to him than anything. Perhaps you think your charms will win him round? I assure you they will not. The moment I tell him, he will send you packing without regret.'

Naturally, I heard this speech with some alarm. 'Lady Frances, all I did was read your daughter's cards. I offered no opinions of my own.'

'By all means try to convince him of that. It will afford me some amusement watching you try. Alternatively,' she dwelled upon the word, 'you and I could come to an arrangement.'

I studied her warily, confused by the suggestion of a reprieve. 'An arrangement?'

'I want you to go to Emily now and offer to tell her fortune again. You will inform her that the cards say Brinseley will grow to love her. Such contentment as he will bring her has rarely been known before. Children in abundance, fidelity until the end. Embellish as you see fit, but mend this problem.'

I halted. 'Lady Frances, I cannot lie about the cards.'

'Oh, yes you can,' she said. 'You are a cunning girl, Miss Antrobus. Don't think that I haven't noticed you at work. Perform this trick for me, and I shall turn a blind eye to all the other tricks you perform during your stay here. Those are between you and your God. And my husband, naturally. I hope your conscience is resilient. It will need to be.'

I had never presumed that I was the first girl who had been subjected to Julius's advances. The familiarity with which Lady Frances spoke of this situation, only confirmed me in that belief. I saw little point in denying her supposition that I'd set out to ensnare her husband. Her expression suggested she wouldn't believe me if I tried. My pity for her position was rather blunted by her proposal. I certainly had no doubt that she would see her threat through.

The thought of being complicit in their plans to marry Emily to a man she did not love and likely never could, filled me with shame. I'd feel responsible for her unhappiness for the rest of my days. And yet I could not be sent home now, not after all my hard work. Not when I was so close to getting my hands upon that report.

As I walked back into the south wing, I remembered Archie's words about the De Lacy fortune. *It would corrupt the soul of even the most honourable man.* Those words brought me a strange sense of comfort. After all, if even an honourable man would be corrupted, then what hope did I have?

Emily was seated on one of the sofas in the music room. She turned to look at me with tear-stained eyes. 'Dearest Emily,' I said. 'I have come to tell your fortune.'

CHAPTER NINETEEN

Ace of spades, influenced by a diamond:
in the eye of others.

SOMETIMES YOUR CONSCIENCE belongs in a box. The costs of my endeavour were steadily mounting. First Tamson, then Mirabel, now Emily.

After I'd told Emily's fortune that day in the music room, she had smiled tentatively.

'Then I should marry Mr Radclyffe after all? We will grow to love one another?'

'That is what the cards say,' I'd told her, with a thorn in my throat.

The following day, Lady Frances had given me a nod of satisfaction, and I presumed that Emily had capitulated to her mother's wishes. 'Don't look like that, Miss Antrobus,' she said. 'For all you know, the cards might be right, and they will find love.'

'And if they don't?' I said bleakly, my conscience drumming on the lid of that box.

'Then rank and respect will be my daughter's consolation. God willing, children too. Brinseley will have his money. The position of his family restored. And he will drink from the wellspring of her discontent.'

Over the course of the next few days, I set about putting my plans into action. I walked up to Slaughterbridge and booked passage on the Exeter coach for the morning after the ball. I'd take no trunk, only a small bundle of things that I would need on the journey. I forged a letter purporting to come from Mrs Illingworth's physician, that I planned to leave behind as proof of my story. And I committed the relevant passage about the strongbox in the Radclyffe history book to memory, reading it again and again.

At Leighfindell, preparations for the ball proceeded apace. A constant stream of wagons and carts brought haunches of beef and venison; salmon, carp and pike; crates of champagne and claret; and bolts of damask and velvet to dress the house. On the south lawn, the dining tents were being erected, the carpenters busy constructing a canal that would run along the centre of the tables, in which black and golden fish would swim about. In the west wing, the windows were opened to air the bedrooms, and the floor of the Great Chamber was waxed and polished until you could admire your face in it.

A few days before the ball, I returned to my room to find a magnificent gown laid out on my bed. The opalescent silk was hand-painted with coloured flowers, each embroidered, embossed with gold, and adorned with twists of coloured foil. There were matching slippers and a headdress of woven ribbons and silk flowers. A note upon my nightstand bore Julius's seal: a large red heart stamped into the wax. *For Rachel, who should have her heart's desire.*

'Mr De Lacy favours you,' Rosie said.

'I can't imagine I'll be able to carry it off,' I said dubiously, fingering the silk. It was going to be hard to be unobtrusive wearing this. The skirts were over four feet wide.

'I'll pile your hair,' Rosie said. 'Pearl powder, a patch on your cheek, and everyone will take you for a duchess.'

I turned, surprised by her enthusiasm.

'I heard what you did to Patrick, miss,' she said, her eyes sparkling with amusement. 'He dropped mustard on his best shirt today, right before the ball. And he tripped on the steps in the cellar and dropped a bottle of old Lisbon. He says it's because you cursed him. He's asking everyone if they know how to remove an evil enchantment.'

Poor Patrick. Every bit of bad luck he now laid at my door. His fear had probably made him clumsier as a result. I smiled at him at dinner that afternoon, and I swear he flinched.

Julius was in a buoyant mood that day. It seemed Mr Whittington had persuaded the coroner not to hold an inquest into the death of Mr Radclyffe. When I thanked him for the dress, he produced a flat shagreen box from his coat pocket and presented it to me. Inside, I discovered an emerald necklace and a pair of matching earrings.

'I had them sent down from London,' Julius said. 'Just a loan, I am afraid. They'll bring out the green in your eyes. Hold them up for us. There you go.'

Emily and Archie applauded, though Lady Frances and Arabia were hatchet-faced. As far as I knew, Lady Frances had stood by our arrangement, and made no further efforts to have me sent home. Yet her demeanour towards me had not improved, her sour moods a match for those of Arabia, who had been increasingly cool towards me ever since my excursion to the Pharos with Archie. I bore their slights patiently, with a martyr's smile.

Septimus grinned. I guessed, like Lady Frances, he believed me to be his brother's mistress, or on the verge of becoming so. Doctor Crowhurst, Mr Whittington and Brinseley Radclyffe probably believed it too. Then there were the servants. My face flamed at the thought of their gossip. At least Emily seemed oblivious, caught up in her own cares. And from the respectful way that Archie addressed me, I presumed he wasn't privy to the secret either.

I had tried to keep a careful distance from Archie, telling myself he was a distraction I did not need. Yet he often sought me out to engage me in conversation, and I experienced a little jolt of pleasure every time I made him laugh. I reminded myself what Emily had said about him still being in love with his girl from Oxford. He's only amusing himself, I thought, or he still feels guilty about suspecting me. Despite these words of caution, I sometimes found myself playing with the acorn in my pocket. Or thinking about his hand on my arm, as he'd helped me into the carriage.

Soon I'll be gone from this place, I thought, and the next time I'll see him we will be in court. And then we will be enemies once more.

That night, as I was going up to bed, Julius waylaid me in the Oak

Hall. 'I trust the weather has improved,' he said, with a sly smile. 'Shall we meet at the Hermitage tomorrow?'

'I regret that I already have an engagement,' I said. 'Emily is trying out different headdresses for the ball. I said I'd sit with her and give my opinion.'

He looked a little put out. 'You ladies and the ball! The day after, then.'

'I'm afraid Emily and I are to practise our steps for the dances.' I had deliberately filled my days with such tedious tasks in order to elude this very excursion.

Julius's frown deepened. 'Make an excuse.'

I searched for a reason that might convince him. 'Emily is feeling rather anxious about the announcement of her engagement. She says that my company helps to settle her nerves.'

'I see,' Julius said. 'Very well, our excursion can wait. But not too long. Let us meet the day after the ball. Shall we say three o'clock? There's a key beneath a stone next to the door of the Hermitage.'

By which time I would be in Exeter, and never have to simper at him again. 'Very well,' I said, smiling shyly.

'Wear those jewels when you come,' he said. 'Be a good girl for me, and I might let you keep them.'

I fled upstairs to my room, plotting all the various ways I would make Julius suffer when I took his money. As I approached my bedroom door, a figure emerged from the shadows, startling me, so that I almost dropped my candle. Patrick. He didn't look happy. My hand instinctively dropped to my pocket, finding the snakestone.

'Miss Antrobus,' he said. 'Please. I want to talk to you.' His face was a match for my own anxiety, his weasel eyes darting, his long teeth bared.

'You got my name right at last, I see.'

He clasped his hands together in a supplicant's pose. 'I want to say sorry.'

It is never a displeasure watching an enemy beg. 'I am all ears.'

'Everything is going wrong for me,' he said. 'I keep losing at cards, my mother is sick, and now I won't get to hear Mr Handel at the ball. Tell me what I can do to make amends. I want you to lift this enchantment.'

I studied him rather ambivalently, remembering my humiliation in front of Archie at dinner. 'Why should I?'

'None of it was my idea. I only did it for the money.'

Curious, I tilted my head. 'What money?'

'The maids took up a collection. They promised it to any footman who embarrassed you. I didn't realize you was a witch, or I'd never have done it.'

'What did the maids have against me?'

He hesitated, looking uncomfortable. 'It's just some of them. They see you as a rival.'

'For Mr De Lacy's attention?' And doubtless his money too.

Patrick nodded miserably.

'Do you know which of the maids was with your master at the Hermitage on the day that Mr Radclyffe died?'

He shook his head. 'It could be any one of a dozen. Mr De Lacy gives them a half-guinea a time, so they're mostly eager.'

Mostly. 'See if you can find out. Do you recall a body being found in the lake, about six or seven years ago?' Rosie's reaction had made me even more curious about that grave in the woods.

He shook his head. 'I've only been here five years.'

'Ask around,' I told him. 'I want to know why some of the servants leave flowers and charms on the dead woman's grave.'

'Very well,' he said, looking rather bewildered by my interest.

Fixing him with my sternest look, I asked the question that was uppermost in my mind. 'Have you been putting playing cards in my room?'

'Playing cards, miss?'

'That's what I said. They were designed to frighten me. Or perhaps it was one of those maids you mentioned?'

'I don't know,' he said. 'I never heard any talk about playing cards.' His voice caught. 'Please, miss. Help a sorry fellow. I don't want to live like this.'

'If you want me to help you, then you'll answer my questions first. Why did you say that you weren't going to hear Mr Handel?' I was eager for any intelligence about the servants' movements during the ball.

'I'm to be upstairs, guarding Mr De Lacy's door. We drew straws, and Rob and me lost out.'

'Do you know what time you are to go to Mr Walpole's room?'

He looked surprised by my knowledge, but he answered readily enough. 'Once the engagement is announced, Mr De Lacy and Mr Walpole are to come upstairs. Then Rob and I are to carry a chest from Mr De Lacy's room to Mr Walpole's.'

'And then you will remain there?'

'That's right, miss, though Rob is to return to guard Mr De Lacy's door. So I won't even have him to keep me company.'

I stared at him in dismay. 'Are you sure?'

'Yes, miss. Mr De Lacy was very particular in his instructions.'

Why the change? What did it matter? The result was the same. How long to carry a chest, heavy with gold, from the north wing to the west and then return? Fifteen minutes? A little more? A little less?

Not long enough.

'Can you get me a key to Mr De Lacy's room?'

He stared at me astonished. 'Miss Antrobus?'

At least that way I'd save the time it would take me to pick the lock. My mind was working swiftly to come up with an explanation that would satisfy him. 'I too have a rival,' I said. 'A girl in London. Mr De Lacy has made me certain promises, and I am not sure whether I should believe him. I'd like to take a look at her letters during the ball, to see if he is making the same promises to her.'

He seemed to accept my story, but he rubbed his temple in apprehension. 'I can't do that, miss. I might lose my place.'

'Then I can't help you.'

Patrick looked on the verge of tears. 'Please, miss. Wait. I can try.'

Three days before the ball, Mr Radclyffe was laid to rest alongside his ancestors at the church in Slaughterbridge. Only the gentlemen attended, as was the usual custom, though the ladies of the house sent a wreath of De Lacy roses to be placed on the grave.

Ocho had still not been found, and Mirabel remained confined to her room. I continued to make excuses to avoid our breakfasts together, and the following day, she came looking for me, catching me in the morning room.

'Why don't you come to tell my fortune any more?'

I smiled apologetically. 'Mr De Lacy told me that I should not do so again until after the ball.'

Her voice grew petulant, like a child's. 'But I want you to read for me now. Ocho will not return until Virgil is content. You said you could bring me peace of mind. My son need not know.'

I couldn't risk it. Not now, when I was so close. 'Please, Mrs De Lacy, I cannot go against your son's wishes.'

Her eyes glittered with tears, though they might have been tears of rage. 'I'm starting to wonder what is the point in having you here.'

On her way out, she pushed past Septimus in the doorway. He arched an eyebrow. 'Whatever you've done to upset her, I applaud it. Frankly, I'm amazed you've lasted this long, sitting up there all hours, listening to her self-justifying cant.'

He crossed to the decanter and poured himself a large measure of brandy. On days too inclement for hunting, he usually started drinking at eleven o'clock. From the look and smell of him, today was no exception.

'I shudder to think what you've had to endure,' he said, sitting down upon a sofa and crossing his legs. 'Let me guess. Dear Virgil, saintly Jemima. Her beloved Nicholas. Well, let me tell you a few home truths. Every time my father was in London, he had George Montfort take him on a tour of his favourite brothels. Had she been the one who had died, he wouldn't have mourned her a single second. My brother Virgil was a fool who believed every lie he was ever told. And nothing became my sister Jemima like her death. Sometimes I think that Luna is the wisest of us all. At least she is spared the grieving widow.'

He studied me appraisingly, with a sharpness of gaze that made me wonder if he was quite so drunk as he appeared. 'You intrigue me, Miss Antrobus. Peering into people's lives like a priest. It's good for the soul, you tell them, before they spill out their secrets. You must wonder about those of us who decline to receive your wisdom. What it is that we don't want you to know. Do you think that's why Brinseley really converted? Because he didn't want to confess? In the Church of England we let people keep their secrets close. Because too much truth is a dangerous thing.'

'What lies did Virgil believe?' I asked.

'What lies does my mother believe? That's the question you should be asking. Only she won't be able to tell you, because she wrote them all herself. And each lie is a perfect sonnet inscribed on her soul.'

Many children dislike their parents. To hate them is more unusual. It was one thing the De Lacy children had in common. Even Julius, I suspected, had no great love for his mother, though he hid it rather better than his brother.

That night, I returned to my room and took up the Radclyffe history book again. It fell open at the page I'd marked with Jemima's flowers and my playing card. Only someone had replaced the seven of diamonds with the ace of spades. I stared at it, my nerves a-jangle, my stomach a swill. Had somebody guessed my plans? But then why hadn't they exposed me? Who was putting these cards here and why? A dark feeling of foreboding settled upon me like a mourning veil.

♠

The day before the ball, Patrick caught up with me at the foot of the Grand Stairs. He looked furtively around, and then pressed a key into my palm.

'I filched the key to the butler's pantry,' he said. 'That's where he keeps the spare keys to all the rooms in the house. This one will open the master's door. Now tell me what to do to rid myself of this enchantment.'

'Walking by moonlight,' I said, having given this question a little thought. 'Seven miles a night for seven nights.'

He gaped at me. 'But I can't walk tomorrow night,' he said. 'It's the ball.'

'Begin the night after.'

'And then my luck will return?'

'If you are truly sorry in your heart.' It was a shame that I wouldn't be there to see it.

He bowed with true deference. 'Thank you, miss.'

'Did you find out which maid was at the Hermitage with Mr De Lacy?'

He shook his head. 'The girls called me names just for asking.'

I told myself it probably wasn't important. If the girl had seen anything suspicious, I imagined she'd have told Julius, and he didn't seem to be in any doubt that Mr Radclyffe's death had been an accident.

'I found out about the flowers on the grave, though, miss. Some of the older servants think the dead woman in the lake was a lady's maid who used to work here. Though the butler told me that it wasn't her.'

I frowned, rather disturbed by this intelligence. 'How does he know it wasn't her?'

'He said there was some anger about it amongst the servants when the body was found. So Lady Frances called the household together – the master was in London at the time – and she made the fellow who had pulled her out of the lake confess that he had found a bag of silver coins with the body. Doctor Crowhurst told them that the coins were over two hundred years old, and so it couldn't have been the girl they thought it was.'

Doctor Crowhurst, who'd told me that he didn't know why the servants had left flowers on the grave.

'But some of the servants still think it was her?'

He shrugged. 'I suppose they must.'

I didn't need him to tell me the maidservant's name. I remembered Rosie's strange response when I'd asked her about the grave. I remembered Mirabel saying that Etta had disappeared around the time of her husband's death and had never been found.

'Do you know his name? The man who found the body and the coins?'

'Jemmy Woodford – he used to be the pond-man here. I never met him myself, but some of the others still talk about him from time to time.'

'Does he live in Slaughterbridge?'

'No, miss. Butler said he moved away up north. Came into some money and bought a farm. Lucky fellow.'

Or perhaps luck had nothing to do with it, I thought grimly. Why would Lady Frances have paid a man to tell lies about the body? I could think of only one reason. Because she believed her husband had been a party to Etta's murder.

CHAPTER TWENTY

Nine of diamonds, influenced by a spade:
a valuable possession is endangered.

So much has already been written about the De Lacys' long-delayed summer ball in the year 1740, that my account will serve as a mere footnote. Suffice to say, the canal of fish in the supper tents caused a sensation, as did the allée of garlanded arches and dwarf fruit trees that connected the tents to the house. The trees were illuminated with crystal lamps, and covered walks had been constructed to enable the guests to promenade if the weather turned. Every table was laid with gold and silver plate, ready for the supper that would be served at one in the morning.

Julius and his wife received their guests in the Entrance Hall, seated beneath a canopy of crimson silk damask. Julius wore a diamond loop and button in his hat, while the skirts of Lady Frances's golden mantua were seven feet wide. Mr Handel came, together with his latest soprano. Art and literature were represented by Mr Hogarth and Mr Sterne, who wrote a satirical address to our hosts which was met with much laughter and applause. Over a dozen peers of the realm were in attendance, and many more knights and baronets. A few Bourbons, a Habsburg, even a Romanov. I regret to say that Mr Walpole proved a disappointment. Short and portly, with rather more chins than limbs, his plum velvet waistcoat was more fitting for a country squire than our nation's First Minister. (I overheard one guest say that his dowdiness in dress was a deliberate ploy to disguise the spoils of his corruption.) There was a minor incident when he was hooted by some of his fellow guests upon arrival, but politics soon surrendered to pleasure.

Rooms had been set aside for gaming and smoking and sitting, each decorated to a different theme: Chinese, Etruscan and Greek. The Great Chamber blazed with the light of two dozen chandeliers – one newspaper later likened it to Aladdin's Palace. Lady Frances preferred not to dance – the only subject upon which we were ever agreed – and so Julius made the first minuet with the Duchess of Portland. The serpentine lines of the dancers made a dazzling display, the light glinting upon their jewels and swords and buckles. Footmen weaved between the spectators bearing silver trays of iced champagne and punch. Everyone looked very proud to be a part of this glittering company.

And then there was me.

Between my gown and my borrowed emeralds and Rosie's efforts with her paint, patches and pomade, I did not stand out as a lady without favour or fortune. Yet inwardly, I stood apart, even as I smiled and curtseyed and conversed. Arabia was my chaperone, a task for which she displayed little enthusiasm, all but ignoring me. I declined all offers to partake in the dancing, pleading a residual pain in my injured wrist, though I watched Archie take to the floor with enthusiasm. He looked splendid in his white dress suit, his smile languid, his body lithe, his feet ambitious.

Amidst the crowd, I recognized a few faces from Bath, but Archie's letters had reassured me that it wasn't common knowledge there that I had run away from home. If anyone had heard the rumours, I reasoned they would assume from my presence here that the gossip had been mistaken. In any event, I would be back in London before Henry got to hear of it.

Under much persuasion from her son, Mirabel had consented to attend the early part of the ball, but said that she would retire early, before the engagement was announced. Knowing that I would not see her again after tonight – unless it was in court – I wanted to part on good terms, words she might remember once she discovered that I was her granddaughter. Yet when I approached her, she cut me deliberately, turning to the lady she was with, and announcing rather loudly: 'Let us adjourn to the Etruscan Room. I find the company much more pleasing there.'

Saddened by her anger towards me, I turned to find Septimus grinning, having witnessed the episode. He raised a glass of champagne in silent toast.

As I made my way back across the Great Chamber, Doctor Crowhurst caught my eye and bowed. Liar, I thought, as I bobbed him a curtsey, remembering his denial of knowledge about the body in the lake. It made me wonder what other family secrets he knew, and how many other lies he'd told to help the De Lacys conceal their sins. My belief that Etta had been murdered troubled me deeply, but I didn't have time to think properly about it now. I had a theft to undertake – from a man I now believed to be a cold-blooded killer.

At eleven o'clock, the music paused, and Julius made the announcement of Emily's engagement. Brinseley preened like a peacock when Mr Walpole shook his hand. Emily's face wore a sheen of sweat, her slight figure weighed down by heavy silks, pearls and other gemstones. I felt wretched for her, and ashamed of the part I'd played in bringing her here. Everybody applauded, though I overheard several unkind remarks about the surprising nature of the match, the youth of the bride, and the indelicacy of the announcement so soon after Piers Radclyffe's death.

'And so it is done,' Archie's voice intruded upon my thoughts.

I smiled at him, despite myself. 'I cannot think it is well done.'

He nodded. 'You and I will be in the minority, once the world finds out that she is to become a duchess. But let us speak of happier things.' He studied my face. 'Leighfindell becomes you, Miss Antrobus.'

Alarmed by the pleasure his words brought me, I sought refuge in self-deprecation. 'A few emeralds can work wonders. I scarcely recognize myself. It will be hard to return to my old life and my old things.'

'Not every woman needs gemstones to shine,' he said. 'Sometimes

I think of that night at the electricity show. The way we first met. Do you ever recall it?'

'How could I forget?'

'I thought I might try to experiment with electricity myself. I bought a book in London that has instructions upon how to do it. Perhaps you would help me?'

I longed to say I would. But there would be no more experiments. No more conversations about science or magic. No more smiles.

'I think your mother is looking for you,' I said.

'As it happens, I'm seeking sanctuary,' Archie said. 'She'll have me married off before dawn, if she gets her way. An auction, perhaps. A fatted calf sold off at market . . .'

My gaze had drifted. I had spotted Julius with Mr Walpole. They were walking together towards the door.

'Miss Antrobus?'

I turned back. 'I'm sorry?'

'I asked why you are not dancing?'

'My wrist,' I said. 'Or at least that is the lie that I prefer. The truth is, I find there are many less arduous ways to make a fool of myself.'

'That is a great pity,' he said. 'I had been hoping you would find room for me between your partners. We might have made perfect fools of ourselves together.'

I wanted to search his face for all the unspoken meanings I hoped that I'd find there. But Julius and Mr Walpole had almost reached the door. 'Forgive me,' I said. 'But there is someone I need to talk to.'

His smile faded and colour flooded into his cheeks. It was the height of rudeness for a woman to walk away from a man.

'I did not mean to monopolize your time.' He gave me a curt bow. 'Enjoy your night, Miss Antrobus, whatever it brings.'

As I hurried away from him across the Great Chamber, I reminded myself that I'd soon have lost his good opinion in any event. When he found out that I had lied to him, then made him ashamed of his suspicions, then manipulated that shame to serve myself, I didn't imagine he would ever want to speak to me again.

By the time I reached the Oak Hall, Julius and Mr Walpole were already at the top of the stairs. Over the strain of the orchestra, I heard them greeting the footmen outside his bedroom door. I idled in the hall below for a minute or so, until I heard the door upstairs close. There was another exchange of remarks, and then a period of silence.

Presuming that the four men had embarked with the chest on their journey to Mr Walpole's room, I climbed the stairs as swiftly as my gown would allow. Finding the corridor deserted, I took the key from my pocket and unlocked the door. In the parlour, I lit a candle, and then locked the door behind me. If anyone disturbed me, it would give me precious moments to hide. I walked into the bedroom and set my candle down on top of the window seat. Crouching, arranging my skirts, I went to work.

First, I set about prising out the central petals of the three Tudor roses with a quill knife I'd brought with me for that task. As I slid those old wooden pegs from their sockets, I thought of all those in whose footsteps I followed: Culpeper's father, the carpenter; Unlucky Piers, the ninth duke; his unhappy wife; Nicholas De Lacy; his daughter, Jemima; and the maidservant, Etta. When all three pegs were removed, I put my quill knife to the edge of the carved frontispiece, and worked it loose. Then I inserted my fingers into the gap and lifted the entire piece of wood away.

From all I had read in the Radclyffes' book, I'd thought the strongbox would fall open upon a spring. I could see the outlines of the box, fashioned from lead with a brass-fronted door – and a shiny brass keyhole. I stared at it, dismayed. There had been no mention of a lock in the book. The keyhole looked new, surely not of Tudor origin. I presumed Julius must have had it fitted since his father's day.

Thankfully, I had brought my lock picks with me as a contingency. Yet I would waste precious minutes getting the lock open, and I didn't have many to spare. Painfully aware of the tick of the mantle clock, I felt the pins move inside the lock as I worked my pick. I could barely hold the thing, I was trembling so much. At last the lock sprang, and the brass panel dropped down with a terrible clang that made my heart race. Inside was a dark cavity, and when I held my candle to it, I saw it was filled with documents. Title deeds, stock certificates, banknotes, correspondence. My heart sank. It would take me several hours to go through it all.

Then I glimpsed a number of old document tubes propped in a corner of the strongbox, identical to the one in which I'd found the codicil. I took one out and opened it at random. It was embroidered with the same initials as mine: NDL. Hadn't Emily said that the report was stored with her grandfather's papers?

I opened the tubes one by one, examining the contents of each. In the fourth, I struck gold. A sheaf of letters, each written in the jagged hand of Lazarus Darke. All dated from the latter half of 1723, which was when Darke had been searching the country for my father and mother. Hastily, I replaced them in the tube, and put it in my pocket. Then I returned everything else to the strongbox.

It took me at least a minute more to lock the box again, a task made harder as I had to hold the lead-and-brass panel in place as I worked. I'd just replaced the carving and the pegs, when I heard voices outside the door. Then a roar of Julius's laughter. They were back!

I froze, dizzy with dismay. How could I ever get out with the footman there? As I mulled this question, my terror was compounded when I heard the distinct turn of a key in the lock.

CHAPTER TWENTY-ONE

Six of spades as master-card:
a disappointment.

LAZARUS OFTEN ASKS himself when the end began. The night Luna came to his room? Or in the days that followed when he'd tried to live with his shame? Or the night he was shaken awake by George Montfort and informed that Jemima was missing? Surely that was the point of no return?

He can only bear to think of it here in the dark, listening to the grind of the wheels as the stagecoach rumbles on through the night towards Cornwall. Alarmed by Montfort's news, Lazarus had dressed hurriedly, and gone downstairs to join the search parties.

A clear black sky, bitter for March. Men and dogs, flaming torches. Nicholas in an uproar, upbraiding Doctor Crowhurst, who predictably blames the maid for not locking the door. Etta is weeping through her denials. Mirabel slaps her face. Luna cries out at them to stop, reminding them that they have to find Jemima.

Nicholas is convinced she'll have gone to the Dower House to find Little Piers. It is good logic, Lazarus thinks. Though she'll be disappointed if she has. From what he hears, Little Piers is presently consoling himself in London with his seven hundred pounds, spending days at a time in the brothels of St James's. The main search party sets off for the Dower House, and though Lazarus expects them to find her there, he decides to take a different route in case they are wrong.

'Where did they tryst?' he asks Luna. 'Where did she meet Little Piers?'

She stares at him, white-faced. 'Up at the Pharos.'

In her madness, it's possible that Jemima might think Little Piers is there. The quickest way is through the woods and up the footpath over the rise. He heads out.

In the woods, his swift stride disturbs resentful pheasants and foxes. Lazarus thinks about Luna, her skin by moonlight, her shuddering breath. Sometimes he cannot believe it happened. A living dream he inhabits. He despises himself, but he'd do it again in a heartbeat. He has tried to keep his distance, and yet he doesn't want to be a cad. Every night he opens his door, and he hopes she'll be there.

As he is passing the entrance to the grotto, something catches his eye: a twist of red cloth caught on a bramble about halfway up the steps that lead to the Hermitage. He retrieves it: a fine silk weave, perhaps a piece of cloak. Continuing up the stairs, he finds the door to the Hermitage ajar. It opens with a creak. 'Jemima?'

He spots her almost immediately. A cry of anguish rises from his throat. The roof of the Hermitage is made from the woven branches of silver birches. A knotted sheet is tied to one, Jemima hanging there. Her mouth is open and contorted, an expression of horror.

Lazarus rights the chair on the floor, clambers up, and unties her. He lays her upon the hermit's bed, chafing her hands, but her skin is cold. Taking her in his arms, he weeps for the waste of her life. Over Little Piers Radclyffe, an arrogant ass unworthy of her warmth or her beauty or her generous heart.

Upon her father's instruction, they tell people it was an accident. Nicholas says it is to protect Mirabel from the truth, but Lazarus knows he's still thinking of those marriages he hopes to make for Julius and Luna. Mirabel accepts what she is told like a blinking baby. Luna doesn't believe it. She demands to know the truth. He cannot tell her, but she reads it in his eyes.

The ground has shifted beneath his feet. All around him he can see wreckage. Lies and deceit. He hasn't felt like this since his father died. It unmoors him.

Luna wears the face of his sins. He cannot console her and he does not try. He sits in the grand salon with its painted sky ceiling and he wonders if this is what cast-out angels see as they are falling.

When business in London comes up, he volunteers to return to the city. Normally, he would have fought to remain at Leighfindell with Luna. George Montfort is happy enough to let him go. He'll have their master all to himself.

Lazarus needs time. He needs London's filthy air. He needs to think.

Luna comes to him in the office when he is packing up his papers. 'You are leaving.'

He cannot look at her. 'Business in London.'

'Let Montfort go.'

'Your father wants me.'

'Liar.' Her face is taut and distressed. The lie has hurt her. It is all he can do not to take her in his arms.

'I need to talk to you,' she says.

'Haven't we said it all already?' He is curt, because he's barely slept.

'This is important. Lazarus, I—'

He leaves the room, because she has always been able to talk him round. She calls after him, her voice cracking. 'Lazarus!'

In London, he finds new business to keep him in town. He sees a friend who talks about India. Would an ocean be far enough? He tries not to think about her, though he supposes she will endure. Luna is not the sort of girl who would take her own life over a disappointment.

He has been in London two weeks when a letter arrives. He recognizes her hand, though the letter doesn't bear her seal. He sits before the fire and stares at it. Then he tosses it unread into the flames.

A month later he receives the news that Luna has eloped with John Jory Jago.

BOOK FOUR

Concerning a fortune told
of Mr Lazarus Darke

CHAPTER ONE

Two of spades, influenced by a club:
a strong effort of no use.

I PINCHED OUT the candle, looking around myself wildly. The parlour door creaked open, and I heard footsteps, presumably belonging to Julius. As silently as my skirts would allow, I hurried into his dressing room, gazing about in the moonlight for a place to hide. I'd never fit into any of the wardrobes, not in these hoops. A Chinoiserie dressing-screen looked to be the only option. I stepped over a large wooden chest on the floor, wincing at the rustle of my skirts, and concealed myself behind the screen as best I could.

Peering between the cracks in the screen's panels, I saw a glow of light that gradually increased in intensity, as Julius walked into the bedroom, humming a minuet. For some moments, I heard him moving about in there, occasionally catching a glimpse of him as he walked in front of the door. Sweat prickled beneath my arms and ran down my back. Julius sneezed, once, twice, presumably having taken a pinch of snuff. Then, to my great alarm, he walked into the dressing room.

I tried not to breathe. Julius set his lamp down and took a key from his waistcoat pocket. He knelt on the floor, right in front of the screen, and unlocked the chest. I could see many cloth bags inside, and as Julius picked one up, I heard a chink of coins. Presumably Mr Walpole wasn't the only useful friend who was set to benefit from De Lacy largesse that night. Julius tucked the bag into the pocket of his coat, and rose from the floor.

As he walked back into the bedroom and paused by the looking-glass to smooth an eyebrow, I had a short moment of blessed relief. Then I noticed something lying on the bedroom floor by his feet, picked out in a puddle of moonlight. One of my lock picks. Julius turned and, to my horror, the toe of his slipper caught the lock pick, which slithered noisily across the floor. Julius halted and looked around – just as the room filled with brilliant flashes of red and green light. The fireworks. They were setting them off on the west lawn. I heard distant cries of wonder from outside. Julius turned, the thing he had kicked apparently forgotten. He retrieved his lamp and returned to the parlour, seeming in great haste to get outside.

The parlour door opened and closed, and the key turned in the lock again. I heard an exchange of voices between Julius and the footman. Only when the voices went quiet did I extricate myself from behind the screen. In the bedroom, I located and retrieved the lock pick, slipping it into my pocket with the document tube.

Yet my problems were hardly at an end. Returning to the parlour, I pressed my eye to the keyhole of the door. I could see the coat-tails and stockings of Rob the footman, just a few feet away. How to get out of the room without him seeing me? The windows were surely far too high from the ground to jump, and the carriage circle below was a bustle of vehicles and footmen.

I hesitated for some moments more, before coming to a decision. Then I walked back into the bedroom and stood before the looking-glass. Putting my hands to the beautiful silk of my neckline, I tore it open rather violently. Then I rubbed my eyes and pinched the skin to redden them, before tousling my hair. In this dishevelled state, I walked back into the parlour and unlocked the door.

The footman turned in astonishment. 'Miss Antrobus?'

I'd already turned back to lock the door, as if trying to hide my face. But as I turned again, I gave him a glimpse, and stifled a sob. A slow smirk spread over his features. I could all but read his thoughts. I had a key to the room, which meant someone must have given it to me. Considering that his master had just spent a few minutes inside and given my present state, the footman presumed that person to be

Julius. Doubtless it would soon be a fervent topic of gossip in the servants' halls, but I was gambling that Rob wouldn't dare mention the incident to his master.

With a final heave of my bosom and another sob, which only made the footman's smile grow wider, I ran off down the hall in the direction of my room.

♠

I didn't think anyone would miss me at the ball, and if they did, I would plead a headache. In my room, I lit candles, and removed my torn gown. My heart had slowed, and I breathed a little more easily. Settling myself upon the sofa, I took out the document tube.

Lazarus Darke's letters described his hunt for my father and mother. Many of the events he described, I already knew. Darke had questioned Kerensa and her husband, Pasco, at the Crown and Magpie tavern in Smithfield, who'd suggested that John Jory might be headed for Scotland. Darke had then ridden north-west to Worcester, where he'd discovered that my parents had stayed at an inn there two weeks earlier. Presuming Pasco was right, he had ridden as far as Gretna upon a false trail, wasting precious weeks upon the road.

Beyond their factual tone, I detected a note of desperation in these letters and I remembered how Darke had spoken of my mother that day at the fair. Next, he had journeyed to Cambridge, where he had caught up with Morgan Trevithick and the Cornish Players. Trevithick had given him much information about the people and places my father had known, and methodically Darke had criss-crossed the country, riding the ancient Roman roads and lesser-known highways from Warwickshire to Kent to Lincolnshire. He had presumed that John Jory would avoid Devon and Cornwall, but in early September in the South Downs he had picked up my parents' trail again, and concluded that they were heading west by back-country lanes. By then, Darke was only a week behind the couple, who seemed to be moving much more slowly on the road.

Darke wrote his next letter from a village on the Somerset–Dorset border named Melbury Bubb:

There is an inn here and a church, though a smaller backwater I have never visited before. I find no easy words to say this, sir, and so I will give it plain. On the morning of the eleventh of September, your daughter and John Jory Jago were married in that church. I spoke to the vicar, who relayed that he'd had concerns about the wedding, because of the strangeness of the groom, the youth of his bride – who from her speech and dress, he had concluded to be a lady – and her apparent absence of joy in this event. He consequently asked to speak to your daughter alone, to which request the consent of the groom was reluctantly given. The lady, though pale, declared that she desired nothing more than to marry John Jory, whom she described as her only happiness in this world. The vicar's concerns assuaged, he then performed the ceremony.

Sir, it is also my duty to acquaint you that your daughter was visibly with child. The vicar estimated that the baby would be born within the next few weeks, hence the couple's desire to sanctify their union.

I questioned several other individuals in Melbury, including a tapman at the inn, who had overheard a snatch of conversation between the couple. He believes that he heard mention of St Ives. Regrettably, I have been unavoidably delayed in Melbury, due to the lameness of my horse. Tomorrow, I will walk to Yeovil and purchase a new horse there, yet country fairs being what they are, I can only imagine the nature of the nag I will be riding. I therefore intend to call in at Leighfindell on my way through Devonshire to Cornwall. Please have ready the finest horse in your stables. Rest assured, sir, that as God is my witness, I will find your daughter and her child and bring them home.

My hands shook as I reread this letter. So many times I had told myself that my father had been a good man, that he had never forced or bewitched my mother into anything. Until that moment, I don't think I'd realized there had also been an insidious fear hiding inside me that I might have been wrong. To read of his innocence, in plain

English, written by the man who had hunted him on behalf of the De Lacys, occasioned me untold joy.

There were several more documents left to examine. One was a copy of a page from the parish register at Melbury Bubb. It provided a record of my parents' marriage, the copy witnessed by a notary. Accompanying it was a written declaration by the vicar, signed and witnessed by the same notary. I might have applauded Darke's thoroughness. As it was, I held those pages to my lips and kissed them. Here at last was the proof I'd need of my legitimacy.

Darke's next report had been written from St Ives. Between those letters, he must have called in at Leighfindell, where he'd witnessed the signing of the codicil and given Nicholas De Lacy *The Square of Sevens*. Darke's handwriting was increasingly erratic, and I deciphered it with some difficulty. It seemed Darke had encountered Morgan Trevithick again in St Ives, a meeting Trevithick had neglected to mention to me. Informed of the couple's plan to flee to Ireland, Darke had headed for the northern Cornish ports. According to the next letter, he had conducted a fruitless search of Padstow, before finally arriving in the town of Tretelly.

Sir, I can report that I have found your daughter and it is my joy to inform you that she is both safe and well. The same cannot be said for John Jory and the child she bore him. On the night of the 29th of October, your daughter was delivered of a baby girl. Not two hours later, the stable boy overheard a loud argument between the couple in their rooms. A short while after that, the inn's head ostler witnessed John Jory jump from the cliff outside the inn, with the child in his arms. I regret to say there is no possibility that either one of them could have survived.

Your daughter will say only that John Jory had a beast concealed inside him. She weeps for her murdered child and for her own situation. She is not yet sufficiently recovered from the birth to travel, but I hope that she will be well enough to do so in due course. Rest assured that I will make the appropriate arrangements

*in Tretelly to ensure that this sad tale does not gain a wider
currency.*

Had that been when my mother and Darke had concocted their
lies? Turning my father into a villain to spare my mother from the
condemnation of polite society? I swore that soon I would tell the
world the truth, and clear his name.

The next document was one of my father's star charts.

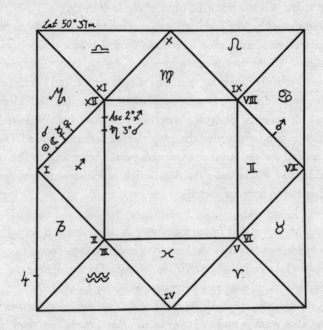

Regrettably, without Tamson's assistance, it could tell me little.
Putting it aside, I turned to Darke's final letter.

*Sir, I regret to tell you that your daughter refuses to return home.
I can only presume that the recent history of Leighfindell and the
malign influence of John Jory have combined to create an aversion
to the family home. She states that she will take her own life if
any attempt is made to force her. I have asked her where else she*

might go, and she has suggested her uncle's house in London. In the
interests of her well-being, I have therefore agreed to escort her to
Seabrooke House. It is my hope that Lord Seabrooke will provide
her with sanctuary, until such time as she consents to return to
Leighfindell. I regret beyond words that I have failed you in this
sad matter.

Two days after this letter had been written, Nicholas De Lacy had died. Around that same time, the codicil had been stolen. It was only about thirty miles from Tretelly to Leighfindell, where my father must have met with Etta the maid and induced her to undertake the theft of the codicil for him.

I had made great strides in my quest to prove my legitimacy. But how to prove that the ostler at the Seven Stars was lying or mistaken about my father's suicide? And how to prove that *I* was that child?

Those were questions for another day. I packed a bundle of things for the morning, and settled down to wait until dawn.

CHAPTER TWO

Three of clubs, influenced by like suit: a choice of two things,
both desired much, but one to be dismissed.

THE ORCHESTRA CARRIED on playing until long after the night
sky turned to pewter, and then pearl. At around six o'clock, it
started raining. At seven the breakfast was held, and the carriages
departed at eight. I listened to the clatter of vehicles in the courtyard
for over an hour. Finally, at nine o'clock, a hush descended upon the
house, as the family and overnight guests trooped off to bed.

This was the moment I had been waiting for. I hoisted my bundle
onto my shoulder, and went downstairs, pausing to drop the key to
Julius's bedroom into a vase on one of the hall tables, where I had
arranged that Patrick would collect it.

In the Entrance Hall, the sleepy butler eyed my bundle curiously,
but passed no comment, distracted by the columns of footmen passing
in and out carrying chairs, and the maids with piles of plates and pails
of rubbish. I walked out onto the south terrace, heading for the woods
and the path that led up to the foot-gate beyond the Pharos.

The rain was coming down harder now. Soon my petticoats were
spattered with mud, my cloak increasingly sodden. I'd be steaming
it off in the coach to Exeter. I picked up my pace, and had almost
reached the shelter of the woods, when I heard a voice behind me
calling my name. Turning, my heart sank, as I spotted Archie on the
terrace. I hurried on, into the woods, hoping he'd be discouraged by
the weather.

The paths between the trees were slippery underfoot, the drum of rain upon the leaves incessant. Passing the grave of the lady in the lake, with its sodden pile of flowers and charms, I resolved that I would make Julius De Lacy pay for all of his crimes.

By the time I reached the clearing by the grotto, the trees were bent under the force of the downpour. I was nervous about climbing the steep footpath in that weather and I didn't want to board the coach half-drowned. I debated waiting for a few minutes in the grotto, to see if the rain would abate. It was over an hour until the Exeter coach was due to depart, and only a quarter-hour's walk from here to Slaughter-bridge. Yet I was eager to leave Leighfindell behind me.

As I debated this decision, Archie ran into the clearing, holding his coat over his head. He was still wearing his white dress suit from the ball, and he looked as bedraggled as I imagined I did myself. 'Whatever are you doing out here in the rain?' he cried. 'Didn't you hear me shouting?'

'I'm just clearing my head after the ball,' I said, hoping he wouldn't ask me about my bundle. 'I don't mind a little rain.'

'A little? You are wet through. Come, we can take shelter in the Hermitage.'

I sensed that if I walked on, he'd be concerned for my sanity and come after me. Reluctantly, I followed him up the steps, resolving to wait there for a few minutes at most. If the rain didn't let up, I'd pro-voke some sort of a squabble and walk out. Archie retrieved the key to the Hermitage from under a stone beside the porch and unlocked the door.

Inside, it was cool and dry, a muted rattle of rain upon the roof. The furnishings were suitably sparse: a desk, a chair, two faded armchairs by the fire, and a bed made up with fresh linen. I had only taken a few steps into the room, when I became aware of another presence: a powerful, pulsing darkness that filled my mind. It was as if all that ominous energy that I'd felt at Leighfindell was concentrated here. The strength of it overwhelmed me, and I looked at Archie to see if he could feel it too.

He seemed blithely unconcerned, already down on his knees

before the fireplace, laying kindling. Soon he had a good fire blazing, and had lit candles against the gloom outside. I was starting to shiver in my wet clothes, and Archie insisted that I stand close to the grate to warm myself up.

'Miss Antrobus,' he said, abruptly, 'have I done something to offend you?'

I struggled to think over the pulsing in my head. 'Why would you think that?'

Just tell him no. Get rid of him.

'You seemed distant with me at the ball. And just now, when you were by the lake, and I called your name, I thought you had seen me and pretended that you had not. It made me wonder if Emily or somebody else had been telling you stories about me.'

'Stories, sir?' I could not help but say.

'About my time at Oxford. About a girl named Cloris whom I met there.'

'Your mother did say something in passing,' I said. 'Emily too. I didn't think it any of my business.'

'I can imagine why my mother would have told you that,' he said, rather bitterly. 'May I tell you what happened? I should like you to know.'

I gazed anxiously outside. The rain showed no sign of abating. 'Mr Montfort, truly there is no need.'

'I believe there is.'

The way he said it made me feel quite breathless. I needed to go, but I also wanted desperately to stay.

'Cloris was the sister of a fellow student,' Archie said. 'One summer I stayed with his family, and an attachment formed between us. She was due to inherit six thousand pounds from her uncle, and I knew my family would consider it a good match. Given my connection to the De Lacys, her father was agreeable to my suit, and it was settled that we would be married after my studies. Then Cloris's uncle died, and it transpired that her inheritance was only a fraction of what she'd anticipated. Given the change in her circumstances, Julius made it clear that if we married, he would cut me off. I begged her to marry me regardless. We wouldn't be poor, we just wouldn't be rich. But as it turned out, that wasn't enough, for her at least.'

He stared into the fire. 'We all have to make hard choices in this world. I don't blame her for that. Not any more. But her brother, in order to defend his sister's reputation, put it about that I was the one who'd rejected her. Because she didn't have the fortune that I'd anticipated. When I would have taken her to be my bride in a sackcloth. She knew this, and yet she didn't say a word in my defence. That was the part that I struggled to forgive.'

'I think anyone would,' I said.

'Not you.' He smiled. 'Did you not forgive me so very easily after all the dreadful things I said about you? You were kindness personified.'

The drumming of my conscience mingled with the drumming of the rain. 'Mr Montfort, I should resume my walk.'

'Please wait,' he said, as I made a move towards the door. 'There is more that I must say. May I speak freely?'

He took a few steps towards me, and I was unnerved by the intensity in his eyes. 'It is possible that you believe my feelings to be unchanged. That my heart, though wounded, still belongs to Cloris. Perhaps a month ago it did. But in that time, I find that another regard has grown to take the place of the first. I fear my family will think her an even less worthy match than Cloris, but to my eyes, she is quite the contrary.'

In that moment, I wanted to tell him everything. That my situation might be different. That I was the true De Lacy heir. Instead, I leaned forward and I kissed him.

Every sense that I possessed seemed alive in that moment. The ominous energy of the place, my haste to get to Slaughterbridge, my fear of discovery – all were forgotten, as I revelled in the softness of his lips. Then reality intruded, and I pulled sharply away.

'Forgive me,' he said, putting a hand to his lips. 'I did not mean—'

Taking advantage of his gentlemanly shame, I backed away towards the door. 'I am leaving now,' I said. 'Don't think to follow.'

I stumbled out into the rain, and was hastening down the steps when I heard a voice from below. 'There she is.'

Julius and a pair of footmen had entered the clearing. One of the footmen was pointing up at me.

I gazed down at them in confusion and dismay. It was too early for our assignation, so why was Julius here?

Archie had disregarded my words and followed me out. 'Sir,' he exclaimed, recovering his composure far swifter than I. 'Have you come to board our ark? I too got caught in the deluge, and decided to take shelter here, only to discover that Miss Antrobus had the same idea.'

Julius looked from him to me. Thunder rolled across the valley, a match for his forbidding glower. 'We need to return to the house,' he said. 'Something has happened.'

Chapter Three

Seven of clubs as master-card:
a troublesome situation dissolved.

THE DE LACY family were gathered in the Blue Drawing Room. Some were in their dressing-gowns, looking as if they'd just been pulled out of bed. Mr Whittington and a tall gentleman with a mole on his cheek stood by the fireplace, conversing in hushed tones. Everyone broke off their conversation as we entered, and I found myself gazing into a sea of hostile faces.

'This is Mr Godolphin, one of my London solicitors,' Julius informed me. 'We met after breakfast to discuss the upcoming case. Mr Godolphin has at last had sight of my sister's affidavit. It seems Lady Seabrooke claims to have purchased the codicil from a man named Henry Antrobus of Bath, who says he found it amongst the effects of his late cousin. I hope you won't insult our intelligence by denying a connection, and so I ask: what is your business in my house?'

I gazed at him in despair. To have come so close, only to be unmasked at the last moment. If only I hadn't let myself get waylaid by Archie Montfort. I might have been on my way to Exeter by now.

'Isn't it obvious?' Lady Frances said. 'Lady Seabrooke sent her here to spy on us. Didn't I warn you some weeks ago?'

'Indeed you did,' Septimus said. 'Archie too.'

'But I was wrong,' Archie said. 'Whatever has happened here, I am certain it is a mistake. Miss Antrobus cannot have known about the sale of the codicil.'

'Mr Whittington has spoken to the footmen,' Julius said. 'It seems Miss Antrobus somehow found her way into my bedroom last night. We found these letters in her room.' He tossed them onto the table. 'She must have been making good her escape when she got caught in the rain.'

'I did not wish to wake you with my troubles,' I said. 'What codicil, sir? I don't understand.'

Julius gave me a hard, contemptuous gaze. 'Turn out your pockets, girl, or I will force you to do it.'

Left with little choice, aware of Archie watching me, I took out the snakestone and stocking, my purse, and the document tube.

'That's one of my father's,' Julius exclaimed, snatching it up. Everyone watched as he opened the tube and went through the documents inside. 'It's Darke's reports on the elopement. After I threatened him in London, Lady Seabrooke must have tasked her with stealing them.'

I searched in vain for a friendly face to whom to appeal. Even Emily looked appalled. I couldn't bring myself to look at Archie at all.

'Well, Miss Antrobus?' Septimus said. 'Do you have anything to say for yourself before we place you under arrest?'

The room seemed to spiral around me. Bereft of lies, I reached for the truth. 'My real name isn't Antrobus,' I said.

The De Lacys listened to my story in silence – right up until the part when I declared myself the daughter of Lady Seabrooke, at which point, they all started shouting at once. Julius brought his fist down upon a side table, making the chocolate pot jump, and called for silence. 'Have this liar taken to the cage,' he said to Mr Whittington. 'Keep her locked up there until I can convene the bench. I want her charged with theft, fraud, and anything else Mr Godolphin can come up with.'

Mr Whittington grabbed hold of my arm, and began marching me towards the door.

'Treat her kindly, for pity's sake,' Archie exclaimed.

'Wait,' Septimus said. 'I want to hear the rest of her story.'

Everyone turned to him in surprise. 'Think about it,' he said. 'This girl is not a threat to us. Only to Lady Seabrooke.'

'Not a threat?' Julius exclaimed. 'She's trying to steal the bread from our table.'

Septimus studied me with interest. 'I presume you do intend to lay claim to the De Lacy estate?'

I thought about lying, but couldn't see the point. 'It's mine by right.'

'There you are,' Julius said. 'From the mouths of thieves.'

'She may be a thief,' Septimus said, 'but she's not trying to steal from us. If the codicil is found to be a forgery, you will keep your money, and her claim is worthless. If it is found to be genuine, then the only person whose money she can steal is Leopold De Lacy's.'

'They won't find it genuine,' Julius said. 'They can't.'

Septimus and the solicitor exchanged a glance. 'As I keep trying to tell you, our sister has a formidable array of witnesses on her side. Authorities on handwriting and parchment and all the rest. Mr Godolphin puts our chances at no higher than fifty per cent.'

'Fifty per cent?' Lady Frances and Arabia exclaimed in horror.

'What are you saying?' Julius said. 'Speak plainly, man.'

'If the ruling goes against us,' Septimus said, 'then we might decide, as a family, to assist Miss Antrobus with her claim.'

My own look of astonishment was a mirror for the rest of my family.

'Assist her?' Julius exclaimed. 'Have you lost your mind?'

'In exchange for her agreement, in the event of her victory, to provide generously for her family. Didn't Father always like to have a contingency plan?'

'But she's lying,' Lady Frances said. 'This is just another one of her tricks.'

'Does it matter?' Septimus said. 'The only question of relevance is whether she can convince the court of her claim. You must concede that she deceived all of us remarkably well.'

Mr Godolphin rubbed his chin. 'I don't see that you have anything to lose by hearing her out.'

Julius reached inside his coat for his snuffbox. 'Do as you please,' he said. 'But don't expect me to listen.'

And yet listen he did, his arms folded, as Septimus and Mr Godolphin questioned me for upwards of an hour. My gaze kept drifting to Archie, who sat looking down at his hands. When I told them how I'd made the decision to infiltrate my family, he shook his head. At one point in the telling – I think it was when I was describing my feelings when I was alone with Mirabel in De Lacy House that first time – my grandmother rose from her chair and came to clasp my hands.

'I believe her,' she said, looking around the room. 'Didn't I tell you how I felt a connection to her from the first? She has her father's gift, and a little of Luna's looks. Mr Radclyffe remarked upon it, even if the rest of us didn't see it.'

It was the first time anyone had said outright that they believed me. Tears sprang to my eyes, and for a moment, I couldn't speak.

'She's a shameless actress,' Lady Frances said. 'I'm not seduced by any of this.'

'I am who I say I am,' I said. 'I just can't prove it.'

'Julius,' she addressed her husband, 'lock this girl up as you first proposed.'

'Do you want to be in the poorhouse?' Arabia objected. 'That is the risk we face.'

'What do you think, Mr Godolphin?' Septimus said.

'I am all for dispassion,' the solicitor said. 'I would suggest a right of residence – at De Lacy House and at Leighfindell – for all members of the family. And an allowance for Mr De Lacy of, say, ten thousand a year? In exchange, we would provide Miss Antrobus with a full team of counsel. And the testimony of the De Lacy family in support of her claim.'

'I agree to nothing,' Julius said, rising from his chair. 'I need to think.'

He walked out into the hall, and Septimus hurried after him. Archie rose too, and went out onto the terrace. Emily turned to me, frowning. 'Are you really my cousin? It was unkind of you to mislead us all this time.'

'I can think of other words for it,' her mother said.

'What will Mr Radclyffe make of all this?' Emily said. 'I can't think he'll want to marry me if Miss Antrobus takes our money. Perhaps he will want to marry her?'

The Duchess of Brecon and Clifton. I won't deny it had a certain ring to it. But all the money in the world could not have induced me to marry Brinseley Radclyffe.

'Don't be foolish,' her mother snapped. 'He'll do no such thing.'

Poor Lady Frances. All her plans falling apart. I guessed Julius had been lying to them – and perhaps to himself – about the danger of defeat for many weeks.

'Excuse me,' I said, rising. 'I need some air.'

'Watch her,' Lady Frances ordered Mr Whittington. 'That girl would steal the coins from a dead man's eyes.'

The rain had slowed to a drizzle. Archie was standing on the terrace, leaning on the stone balustrade, gazing out over the parterre. Mr Whittington watched from the shelter of the doorway as I approached him.

'Archie,' I said, 'please, let me explain—'

'What a fool you must have thought me,' he said, without looking around. 'All that time I suspected you were a fraud, and yet I never began to comprehend your true design.'

'I wanted to say who I was in London, but I was afraid nobody would believe me.'

'Wasn't that your intention? To mislead us?'

'Only later – after I'd learned that the codicil had survived. I am entitled to that money, but I needed evidence to prove it. I couldn't think of any other way.'

'Spoken like a De Lacy,' he said heavily.

'I'm not like them,' I said. 'Truly, I'm not.'

Archie made no reply, and we stood there in silence, watching a bedraggled peacock strut across the lawn. He opened his beak and shrieked his outrage at the sky.

'Your interest in Leighfindell,' Archie said, at last. 'That book I got for you from the Dower House. Was that all a part of your plan? Did I help you to steal those documents?'

I couldn't bring myself to lie to him. 'I'm sorry.'

'How cleverly you orchestrated it all,' he said. 'I suppose that makes me your first violin? Maybe I should offer my services to Mr Handel.'

'I understand why you feel like that,' I said. 'But it wasn't all lies. The things we talked about up at the Pharos . . . Just now at the Hermitage . . .'

'How neatly you separate the two,' he said. 'I would find it a recipe for confusion.'

'But I *was* confused,' I said miserably.

He smiled rather sadly. 'At least you are relieved of that burden now.'

Less than an hour ago we had been kissing, and now the distance between us felt unbridgeable. I was still searching for better words, when Emily came out onto the terrace. 'Father is back.'

Whatever Septimus had said to his brother, it seemed to have worked. Julius studied me for a moment, an odd light in his steady gaze. 'I agree to my brother's proposal. Mr Godolphin will draw up the contract. I trust you are amenable to this plan?'

Did I trust the De Lacys? Of course I didn't. My uncles were venal, calculating creatures, and their wives were little better. I felt certain that they would find some means to cheat me. Yet nor did I wish to be put in prison. I needed to get back to London to help Tamson. And this proposal would at least solve the problem of how I'd pay for my lawyers. I told myself that I had outwitted the De Lacys for many weeks now, and that I was more than capable of outwitting them for a few weeks more.

'You are my family,' I said. 'I hated lying to you before. I would want to take care of you all no matter what.'

Septimus beamed around at our circle of solemn faces. 'What a convivial household we shall make.'

CHAPTER FOUR

Three of spades, influenced by a heart:
a sudden failure or fear.

L AZARUS OFTEN THINKS about the baby girl who died in John
Jory Jago's arms in the roiling waters of the Bristol Channel. She
is very much upon his mind as his hired chaise rattles into Tretelly,
and he catches his first glimpse of the crashing waves. He thinks of
another journey long ago, the silent desolation of the carriage back to
London. Luna huddled beneath a pile of furs, weak from childbirth.
He couldn't find the words then either. Because he was a coward.
Because it could change nothing. Because if a man has walked away
from a lady who has shared his bed, then he loses any right to speak
of the consequences.

Once they'd reached London, he had taken her to Seabrooke
House, where he'd explained the situation to her uncle. One of those
men whose moral code was all the more rigorous for his own failings,
Lord Seabrooke had reluctantly agreed to take her in to spite his half-
brother. Lazarus had returned to Leighfindell, where he'd discovered
that Nicholas De Lacy was dead. It gave him hope that Luna would
soon come home. We'll talk, he'd told himself, when she's ready. Only
the months had passed, and Luna never did return.

Lord Seabrooke had kept his niece shut up in a rented house
near Luton Hoo, out of her family's reach, in order to use her as a
pawn in his son's legal battles against his nephew. Lazarus had twice
ridden out to Bedfordshire to see her, and both times been turned

away – whether at her behest or at her uncle's, he was never quite sure. He'd written to her many times, coded words she'd understand, but, like Mirabel's, his letters were returned unopened.

When he'd given evidence before the Prerogative Court, he'd looked for her in vain in the public gallery. Even after his dismissal from Julius's service, he had stayed abreast of the family's affairs, scouring the newspapers for any intelligence of her. He had read of Julius's victory in court, and the untimely death of Lord Seabrooke, carried off by an apoplexy just like his half-brother. The second earl had kept his son well away from Luna, telling the boy that she was damaged goods. But the third earl had other ideas, and the moment his father was in the ground, he had ridden out to Bedfordshire to claim his bride. The same day that Lazarus had read of their engagement in the newspaper, he had sold everything he owned and booked passage to India.

He thinks of that voyage now, as he watches the boats in Tretelly harbour, the pull of the waves, the gulls crying overhead. The sailors on the Indiaman had seen Lazarus's like before: men running away from a debt, or a woman, or their own demons. They'd diagnosed him correctly, and taken turns to cheer him up, talking loudly about the wonders of the Cape Town brothels. Lazarus had hardly heard them, thinking of Luna's white face as he'd walked away from her at Leighfindell. Of the letter that he'd tossed into the flames without reading. Of John Jory's conviction when he'd seen Morgan Trevithick in St Ives that Luna still had two months of her pregnancy to go. Of the argument between the newlyweds at the Seven Stars inn after the child's birth a week or so later. Lazarus could count, and it seems John Jory could count too. As the ship had rounded the Quélern Peninsula, he had gazed north across the sea in the direction of Cornwall and mouthed a prayer for his dead daughter who had no name.

Red's claim should offend him, as it offends Lady Seabrooke. Instead, he feels only a lingering sadness that the girl's own tragedies have driven her to exploit the tragedies of others.

As he strides up the Tretelly headland, he feels a stabbing pain in his thigh. That's what four days in a stagecoach does to you at nearly forty. He'd left the coach in Bodmin, where Robert Antrobus's cousin on his mother's side, a gentleman named Christopher Williams, had once owned a substantial red-brick house and three neighbouring farms. The housekeeper of the current owner had remembered Williams fondly. She'd confirmed that he'd never had a ward living there, though that fact, of course, doesn't contradict Red's story. Nor did Antrobus have a little girl with him when he'd stayed at the house. Yet a month later, he had returned to Bath, together with a little girl. So where did he find her?

Not here in Tretelly, Lazarus is convinced of that. Before he'd left London, he'd written letters to all the principal medical schools, enquiring if they'd ever had a student named Kilderbee, the name of the doctor Red claims treated her father before his death. He has made similar inquiries about orphanages run by a woman named Sandbach and her assistant, Edward. On the journey between Bath and Bodmin, he'd questioned all the innkeepers along the route to see if anyone could remember Antrobus and the girl. 'Ten years ago?' one had cheerfully responded. 'I won't even remember *you* in a week's time.'

The Seven Stars inn looks just as it did in his memories: a grey weatherworn witness to six centuries of history. Old Chenoweth might be gone, but his niece welcomes Lazarus in her taproom. Amelia Fry has a pink, smiling face scarred by the smallpox, a pencil and two knitting needles stuck through her piled brown hair.

'I'd like to help you, handsome,' she says. 'But the registers from that time burned in a fire a few years back. My uncle was careless with his pipe. He was rather infirm towards the end, that's why my Jim and I moved here after the fire, to give a helping hand.'

'All the registers are gone?' Lazarus asks, with a sinking heart.

'Everything,' she says. 'All his books and papers. He'd have lost the entire place if it hadn't been for some swift thinking from one of the ostlers.'

Lazarus thinks. 'Did your uncle ever talk about a cunning-man who came here? One who died twice?' He gives Fry a brief summary of the story, leaving out any information that could compromise Lady Seabrooke. She'd told Lazarus that amidst her husband's financial woes, the annuity to secure Chenoweth's silence had not always been paid. Nor had Lazarus ever entirely trusted the landlord. Surely, if John Jory had returned, back from the dead, only to die again, he'd have talked about that?

Fry laughs. 'Sounds like a tall story. I certainly don't recall it. Though my uncle saved his best tales for his memoir.'

'His memoir?' Lazarus exclaims.

'*An Innkeeper's Life*,' she says, with a wry grin. 'He was convinced it would make his fortune. All the odd folks who had stayed here over the years, all the things he'd seen and heard. He wrote to the London publishers, but nobody wanted to read it. Everyone's writing a memoir now. They're ten a penny.'

Lazarus grips the counter in his urgency. 'Do you still have it?'

Fry shakes her head. 'Like I said, we lost all his books in the fire.'

Could Red have known about this fire? It's possible. 'There was a pot-boy here back in 1730. Does he still work here?' Red had said that her father had fought with the lad. Surely he would remember that?

'Sam Thwaite,' Fry says. 'God rest his soul. He saved his money for years, bought himself a fishing boat. It went down with all hands on his maiden voyage.'

Lazarus sighs. 'Does Edmund Bonny still work here?'

'Not for years,' Fry says. 'But he lives in the town and still comes in from time to time.'

At least that's something. Lazarus asks her for Bonny's address and drains his pot.

On his way back into town, Lazarus stops in at the parish church. The vicar is a young man named Longfellow, too young to have been here ten years ago. At Lazarus's request, he consults the records of his predecessor and tells Lazarus that no man named John Jory Jago or George the Tenth of Kernow was buried here in 1730. It fleetingly raises Lazarus's hopes, until he probes a little deeper.

'If it was a northside burial, then it wouldn't be listed here,' the vicar tells him. 'My predecessor was a stern man who preferred eternal fire to the cooling breeze of the gospel. He believed those poor souls buried upon the north side were best forgotten.'

Which, like so much else in this tale, is very convenient for Red.

An hour later, Lazarus is once more climbing the promontory that leads to the Seven Stars, this time in the company of Edmund Bonny, formerly the head ostler of the inn. Bonny has a weatherbeaten walnut of a face, a pipe clenched between his teeth, and fingernails blackened with dirt. He remembers Lazarus well, as one would remember a man who paid you a hundred pounds to keep your mouth shut.

Bonny points to one of the inn's buildings with his pipe. It has a door that opens directly onto the cliffside. 'That's where they stayed. Best room in the house.'

Lazarus remembers. Luna lying naked in the four-poster bed, the sheets soaked with the blood of childbirth, her glazed expression.

Together, they walk into the stable yard. 'I was out here working with young Tim Sullivan,' Bonny says. 'It was blowing a gale and all the horses was jumpy. I went inside to get something, and when I came back out, Tim said as how the couple had been arguing. Or rather, he said the man had been doing a lot of shouting.'

It's no use asking for the stable-lad, Tim Sullivan. Of all the people connected to these tragic events, his testimony was the one most damaging to Luna. Back in 1723, Lazarus had listened to his tale stony-faced, and then asked the lad about his hopes and dreams. America, came the answer. And so Lazarus had paid for his passage to the colonies and given the lad a tidy sum to make a new start there. On the condition that he change his name and never speak of that night, not to anyone, ever again.

'I knew the wife had just given birth,' Bonny goes on, 'because the doctor had just left. He told Mr Chenoweth that both mother and daughter would live. Everyone in the taproom raised a bumper to their good health.'

They walk back out to the cliffside. 'I was already leaking wet,' Bonny says, 'and the lightning was something proper that night. So after I finished up in the stables, I came out here to watch.'

They walk towards the edge. Lazarus, who has never liked heights, stops a few feet short. The wind whips his hair, tasting of salt.

'I was standing right about here,' Bonny says. 'The lightning lit up the whole sky, the rain like a wall of water. I'd been out here about ten minutes, when the wind dropped. That was when I heard the baby crying. I turned and there he was, the cunning-man.' Bonny points with his pipe to a spot about a dozen yards from the cliffside door.

'He was carrying something in his arms, huddled up in his cloak, and when I heard the baby crying again, I realized that's what it was. I called out to him, because he shouldn't have been carrying a newborn, not in that weather, but he either didn't hear me over the rain, or he ignored me. When he started crossing the grass towards the edge, I thought he had come out to watch the lightning too. Cooling off after their argument, that sort of thing. He stood there a few moments, and I was just thinking about going over and having a word, when he jumped.'

Lazarus peers gingerly over the edge. 'There's quite a slope here,' he says. A steep incline of about twenty foot, before the sheer drop to the rocks below. It's strewn with stunted shrubs and protruding rocks. 'Could he have lain here without you seeing him and then climbed back up?'

'Don't see how, not in that storm, not carrying a baby,' Bonny says. 'But in any event, where he was standing, over there, there was no slope. Just a straight drop down to the water.'

'And you saw the moment he jumped? Watched him go over?'

To his dismay, Bonny hesitates. 'Well,' he says, 'I didn't see the precise moment, not as such. But the lightning flashed and I saw him standing there on the edge. And when the lightning flashed again a few moments later, he was gone. I don't see what other explanation there could be.'

Had Bonny said this the first time, when Lazarus had questioned him back in '23? He isn't sure. But back then there was no question about what had happened.

Lazarus pays Bonny for his time and then walks over to the spot where John Jory had gone over. He inches forward to the edge on his hands and knees. It's at least a hundred foot down, and even today, when the wind is light, the waves are crashing against the rocks, gouging jagged maws in the side of the cliff. Yet as Lazarus gazes down, telling himself that no one could have survived that fall, an odd feeling comes over him. It takes him a moment to put a name to it.

Doubt.

CHAPTER FIVE

Queen of hearts, influenced by a spade: an amiable,
affectionate woman, rather one sentimental than of intellect.
She is not of wholly firm virtue.

IT WAS DECIDED that we would return to London immediately, in order that we could meet with the full cohort of De Lacy lawyers. Given my eagerness to get back to help Tamson, I certainly made no argument to this proposal. All the preparations were made in a great hurry, and the morning after the revelation of my identity, we boarded a procession of carriages in the courtyard. Only Brinseley Radclyffe remained behind at Leighfindell. I did not know what conversations had taken place between him and Julius regarding my true identity. Nor did I particularly care. I considered Mr Radclyffe an irrelevance to my plans.

I shall not bore you with all the details of our journey back to London. Suffice to say, I was now judged worthy of riding in the principal carriage, together with Julius and his family. I did not relish his company, but at least it spared me from Archie's disappointed gaze. I knew that I had hurt him, perhaps deeply. When he looked at me, I wondered if he saw another Cloris, the girl who had broken his heart in pursuit of money. I didn't know how to put things right between us, and my fear of making things worse made me reluctant to try.

At least the revelation that I was Julius's niece seemed to have cooled my uncle's ardour. He treated me with a curt politeness, that I suspected was underscored with resentment. Yet in our discussions with Mr Godolphin about the case, his questions were perceptive and his arguments sharp. However much he hated the prospect that I might take his money, it was clear that he wanted to deprive his sister of it more. I remained suspicious that the De Lacys would try to cheat me in some way, and I resolved to consult a lawyer of my own choosing about the contract of our agreement.

Where Lady Frances was concerned, at least I had the benefit of consistency. She hadn't liked me before, and she didn't like me now. Yet she was forced to exist on more equal terms with me and I addressed her as such, enquiring after her family and her friends and her interests as if we were the closest of acquaintances. She answered me politely, but I could tell each word was a torture, which only made me enjoy it all the more.

Among my leading supporters in the De Lacy family were Septimus and Arabia. When we stopped at night at the inns, they could not have been kinder or more solicitous: wanting my opinion on every small matter, giving me novels and ribbons and cake, and making great plans for all the delightful things we'd do together in London. Of course, all these kindnesses were entirely self-interested. It was possible that I might end up controlling the family purse-strings, and so they had determined to ingratiate themselves shamelessly with me.

I judged Mirabel's affection to be entirely genuine. All of her past resentments seemed forgotten. She asked me to call her 'Nonny' as her other grandchildren did. In the carriage, she sometimes liked to hold my hand. At night, after dinner, I often told her fortune, and we talked much more openly about my mother, Luna. She told me she hoped that my appearance in their lives might lead to a reconciliation, and I refrained from saying that I thought she'd lost her mind.

'It never made any sense to me,' she said fretfully. 'Luna's estrangement from her family. Oh, she was angry with her father over Jemima, and with me for taking his part, but the pair of them have been dead for sixteen years. Once she has got over the shock of your revelation, she will come round, I know she will. What mother could ever turn her back on her child?'

As others had said, Mirabel had a great gift for self-delusion. The recurring cards in her fortune were another instance of it. In our seven days upon the road, I did everything I could to tease out the meanings of her king of spades, the error, and the lie. Yet I felt a resistance in her, an unwillingness to let me probe too deeply, at odds with her expressed desire to understand.

Emily seemed to occupy a world of her own. Her spirits went up and down, as did her behaviour towards me, cool one minute and friendly the next. I suspected she was torn over everything that had happened. On the one hand, the prospect that she might be deprived of her inheritance, on the other, she was surely wondering what consequences that loss would have for her engagement to Mr Radclyffe.

Word of my revelation had quickly spread amongst the servants. The news that I might one day be their mistress prompted a revolution in their behaviour towards me. The footmen competed to help me down from the carriage, or to pour my wine – and these days there was never any trace of sediment! The maids were all shy smiles and respect.

Except for Rosie. I had asked to have her accompany me to London, yet I discerned no great enthusiasm upon her part for this mark of favour. During our time together at Leighfindell, the first green shoots of intimacy had flourished between us. Now she felt betrayed – and with some justification. She did not tell me this in so many words, but her former stiff politeness had returned.

One morning, when she was dressing my hair after a night in Basingstoke, I decided to confront it.

'I'm sorry I lied to you,' I said. 'You are entitled to be annoyed with me. I tried to induce you into betraying the trust of your employer to assist my scheme.'

She said nothing, pursing her lips around the pin in her mouth.

'You might have lost your place if they'd found out.'

She jabbed the pin into my hair rather hard. 'That's true.'

'Though I'd never have told them anything you said to me in confidence.'

My words seemed to anger her. 'You think they'd need proof to suspect wrongdoing? That's not how it works at Leighfindell, miss. They're always casting around for the nearest maidservant to blame.'

The bitterness in her tone gave me pause. 'Like Etta, do you mean?' I'd wanted to raise the topic with her ever since we'd left Leighfindell, but given the way things had stood between us, I hadn't judged it wise. Now I threw caution to the wind. 'She was blamed for Jemima's death. And for stealing the codicil. Why didn't you tell me that some of the servants believe the body in the lake was hers?'

Studying her face in the mirror, I could see she was startled by how much I knew. 'Why do you think?' she said. 'Lady Frances would have dismissed me on the spot if she'd found out.'

'I'd like to make things up to you,' I said. 'I'd like to help you understand what happened to Etta. Do you think it was her body in that lake?'

Rosie was silent for a long moment. I suspected Etta had meant a great deal to her, and she had wondered about her disappearance for all those years.

'I don't know,' she said at last. 'Sometimes I leave flowers upon the grave myself. Because if it *was* Etta in that lake, then I wouldn't want her to think that I had forgotten her.'

'Then you think it's possible?'

She set down the curling tongs, and moved round the table to address me more directly. 'She hadn't been happy at Leighfindell before she disappeared. It's possible she decided to leave of her own accord. But she left all of her clothes and other things behind. I don't understand why she would have done that. And she never wrote to me, not once in all those years. We were so close. We talked about everything. Then nothing.'

'I have a suggestion,' I said. 'We could ask the cards if the body was hers?'

I could imagine the debate taking place in Rosie's troubled mind. On the one hand, her fear of the De Lacys and, perhaps, of the truth. On the other, her fierce desire to know.

'Yes,' she said. 'But be quick, miss. Before I lose heart.'

We sat at the table, and I shuffled the cards. Rosie watched silently, as I laid the Square and despoiled it.

'The queen of hearts,' I said, pointing to the first card in her parallelogram. 'She figures an amiable, affectionate woman. I presume this to be Etta.'

Rosie smiled sadly. 'She had a quick wit, always making me laugh. Sometimes she'd mimic the De Lacys and have me in stitches. But she was never cruel. Always looking out for me and others.'

I touched the next card. 'The queen is influenced by a spade, meaning she is either not of firm health, or not of firm virtue.'

Rosie frowned. 'People always talk about a woman's virtue, don't they? Never a man's.'

'There is a man here on the second row,' I said, pointing. 'The king of hearts, also influenced by a spade. It figures a man with a defect of temperament. The spade in question is the three, meaning a folly and a warning from a friend.'

Rosie stared down at the cards, seemingly lost in thought.

'Was there a man in Etta's life?' I asked gently. Surely not my father. He'd only loved my mother. I recalled Lazarus Darke's certainty that Etta had taken the will to benefit Julius – and Mirabel's evasion of my question about why she would have done that.

'Rosie,' I said, 'was Etta in love with Julius De Lacy?'

Her eyes snapped up, and I knew I was right.

She let out her breath in a long sigh. 'Beneath all her sharp humour, Etta was a romantic at heart. Her and Miss Jemima both. Jemima liked Etta to read to her, novels about gentlemen in disguise who were secretly rich, and young girls from poor families finding great love. Julius was just sixteen, a little younger than her. But Etta wasn't his first, not a bit of it. I warned her about that. "I have no illusions," she'd say. "I know he can never marry me." But that didn't stop her falling in love. When he was sent away to Oxford, she wept for a week. She wrote him letters, and occasionally, he'd write back. This was when Jemima was sick and Etta was up in the attic all hours, thinking about him. Then Jemima died and Luna ran away and old Mr De Lacy had his first attack of apoplexy.'

'Mr Darke thought that Jemima knew where he kept his will,' I said. 'That she told Etta to get revenge upon her father. Presumably she thought that Etta would tell Julius.'

Rosie nodded. 'Mr Darke believed Julius asked her to destroy the codicil if his father ever looked like dying.'

Originally, he must have meant the Seabrooke Codicil, I thought. But the Grandchild Codicil would have been just as much a threat to Julius's interests.

Rosie bit her lip. 'I told Mr Darke she wouldn't have done it, because I didn't want her to get into trouble. But the truth is, I don't know. She said sometimes Julius talked about taking her to London. Setting her up in a fine set of rooms, where they could play at being husband and wife. A carriage, fine gowns and jewels. Children even. But he'd have needed money to do it.'

'You said she was unhappy before she disappeared? Was that because of Julius?'

'In part. She found out that something had happened between Julius and another girl – that's why his father disinherited him. So she doubted his constancy – and with good reason. But it was also because of what had happened to Miss Jemima. Her death, being blamed for it. Etta always denied leaving that door unlocked. She thought the doctor had done it, but he was a gentleman, and nobody would take her word over his. It enraged her. She said it was his fault that Virgil had died too. That Dr Crowhurst had made another mistake.'

'A mistake when he treated him after the duel?' I thought of Mirabel's recurring cards. They sometimes seemed to point to the duel. The error and the lie figured there time and again.

'I don't know. Maybe. Etta wasn't talking to me with her old frankness any more. I saw less of her too. After Miss Jemima died, she was sent to the Dower House to become maid to Mrs Radclyffe. People said Mrs Mirabel couldn't bear to look at her any more – because of Jemima. Whereas I was promoted to under-housekeeper. Sometimes Etta still came to the house on an errand, or to see me on her spare afternoons, but we didn't talk nearly as much as we had before. She was seen in the big house on the day before old Mr Nicholas died. Mr Darke said that she'd had no proper reason for being there.'

'And then she disappeared?'

'Not right away. Mr Nicholas died, the codicil was discovered to be missing, and the house was in an uproar. Then Mr Julius returned from Oxford – and later that same day, Etta vanished.'

'When was the last time anyone saw her?'

'One of the gamekeepers said he'd seen her with a man up at the Pharos. He was some distance away, and it was dusk, but he swore it was her. She was pretty, see, with glossy black hair and a bold eye. The sort of girl the gentlemen notice.'

'And the man?'

'The gamekeeper told Mr Darke he thought it was Julius. But Mr De Lacy said he was never there.'

Julius would have been hardly likely to admit to it, if that meeting had ended in murder. Our eyes met, and I could see that Rosie was thinking the same thing.

'Did Etta ever talk to anyone else about Julius?' I asked. 'John Jory Jago, for instance.'

'I don't know, miss. Perhaps. Etta liked to have her fortune told. And John Jory saw a lot. He guessed people's secrets.'

If my father had guessed Etta's secrets, it would explain why he'd thought that the codicil was at risk – and also how he'd known that Etta would be able to steal it. Perhaps he'd blackmailed her over her amour with Julius? I wondered if Father had ever had a proper plan of what to do with the codicil, or if it had been a simple act of desperation on his part?

As for poor Etta, I imagined she'd been frightened of telling Julius what she'd done. Perhaps she'd told him she'd destroyed the codicil just as he'd asked her to do – and Julius had killed her to keep her quiet.

'What else do you see?' Rosie was blinking back tears. 'Is Etta's death figured here? Was that her body in the lake?'

It was all there in her cards. A wound or bruise. A violent death at the hands of a man. But what good would it have done to tell Rosie that?

'I see a peaceful death at the end of a happy life,' I said. 'I see a man who loved her and brought her happiness. I see a child.'

Rosie's tears began to fall. 'Oh, how I have prayed for it.'

'I cannot say why she didn't write to you,' I said. 'But I do see a true friend here. I think she loved you and missed you until the end of her days.'

CHAPTER SIX

Five of spades as master-card: an expense.

IN LONDON, THE De Lacys' money and power swung into action on my behalf. My lawyers, sixteen of them, explained that the first task before them was an application to the Court of Chancery to request that Henry be stripped of my guardianship, in order that I might be made a ward of court. They would then apply to make me a party to the case due to be heard before the Prerogative Court concerning the codicil.

In order to assist them, I was asked to write an account of my life and I spent some days diligently working on that task. This version of my story differed in certain key respects from the book that you hold in your hands right now. I left out many things: my more troubling moments with Julius; the episode with Ocho the parrot; my manipulations of the cards; and everything that had happened with Archie at the Hermitage. When the lawyers read about the raid on the fair and the likelihood that there might be a warrant out for my arrest, three of them accompanied Julius and Septimus to the Guildhall, where the aldermen-magistrates had their court. They returned in very jovial spirits, smelling of beefsteak and brandy, and Julius informed me that all charges against me had been dropped. Of course, I also asked them to intervene to have Tamson released, but they wouldn't hear of it.

'Will this girl give testimony on your behalf?' one of the lawyers asked. 'Can she support your story?'

'No, I don't think so. She never knew who I really was.'

'Then all she can say is that you lied to her. And tell the court how you sold illicit fortunes, defrauding the public. Just as the other side will infer that you are defrauding the Earl of Seabrooke now.'

'The girl cannot be intending to testify,' Septimus said. 'Or she wouldn't be sitting in a prison cell right now. Best to leave her there.'

'You never know what inducements she might be offered to change her mind,' Julius said. 'Her freedom, for one. I'll make certain the magistrate understands that he is not to countenance an early release. No matter what bribes Lady Seabrooke might offer him.'

Of course, I begged and pleaded, but it was to no avail.

'You must be very careful, my dear,' Septimus said. 'So much rests upon your character now. The last thing you should be doing is consorting with a convicted fraudster.'

Not only had I failed to help Tamson, I had made everything worse. Now the magistrate would never accept my bribe to commute her sentence.

That evening, Rosie found me crying in my room. 'Why, miss, whatever's the matter?'

We had grown much closer since our conversation about Etta, and I told her everything.

'The poor child,' she said. 'I saw a man being pilloried once. His friends paid the constable to let him out after twenty minutes, instead of the full hour. Perhaps Tamson has friends who will do the same?'

Would Morgan and the Players be there for Tamson? Ordinarily, I'd have said yes. But who knew what Lazarus Darke had been up to while I'd been at Leighfindell? I could trust no one to help Tamson other than myself. And whatever the De Lacys said, I was determined to do it. Tamson had already paid far too high a price because of my endeavours.

The problem was, I was being watched. I was rarely left alone, even in the house, a De Lacy always sitting beside me, or a footman watching over me. If I tried to go for a walk alone, Arabia or Lady

Frances insisted upon coming with me, together with their attendant maids and footmen.

'We cannot risk anything happening to you,' Julius said. 'Your wellbeing is important to us all. Lady Seabrooke will surely know of our return to London by now – and if you think she would hesitate to harm you, then you'd be wrong.'

I'd already told the De Lacys that I wanted to consult my own lawyer about the contract they wished me to sign. Somewhat to my surprise, they had agreed that it was an excellent plan. I chose a solicitor at random, a name I saw in a newspaper, and arranged an appointment with him on the morning of the day that Tamson was due to be pilloried. Of course, Septimus and Arabia insisted upon coming with me in the carriage to his office in Chancery Lane. In turn, when we arrived at his door, I insisted upon going in alone.

'The whole reason for this endeavour is that I wish to seek independent counsel, and it will hardly be independent if you are present while it is given.'

'But Julius said we weren't to let you out of our sight,' Arabia said.

My gaze was steely. 'I won't go in, unless I'm alone. And I won't sign the contract without independent counsel.'

'Now then,' Septimus said soothingly, 'there's no need for cross words.' He turned to his wife. 'It is important that Miss Jago is reassured as to our fidelity in every respect. If our presence would undermine that trust, then we have no choice but to wait outside.'

'So suspicious!' Arabia cried. 'That's the De Lacy in you. Your grandfather would have demanded a receipt from St Peter for his soul.'

Number twenty-five Chancery Lane was a tall, narrow building of blackened brick, each floor containing two or three dark little chambers for a lawyer, each with a brass plaque affixed to the door. My solicitor, Mr Frederick Cowell, proved to be a neat, young, freckled man with thoughtful brown eyes and a trace of Essex in his accent. I explained my situation, his eyes widened at my story, but he restrained himself from passing comment upon my claims. He drew a lamp close, and spent several minutes studying the contract. His verdict rather took me by surprise.

'The risk here is not on your side, Miss Jago, but rather upon theirs. You are a minor, you see, and would not normally be considered competent to enter into a binding contract of this nature. Upon reaching your majority, you might choose to set this one aside, upon the grounds of your infancy when you signed it. Indeed, if Mr De Lacy were sitting here in your place right now, I would advise caution. It's entirely possible that a court would enforce this contract, because the terms undoubtedly benefit you. Should you inherit the fortune at stake, it would vastly outweigh the amount you are hereby contracted to give Mr De Lacy. That is surely what the De Lacy lawyers would argue in court, were you to breach its terms. But there is no certainty of it, which is where the question of risk arises. I wonder why Mr De Lacy doesn't simply wait until you are made a ward of court? The judge will appoint a trustee and a solicitor to act on your behalf, and they would be able to sign this contract in your name.'

'Perhaps he worries that the trustee might refuse to sign it? Or that I will change my mind about accepting his help, once I am free of Henry Antrobus?'

It certainly seemed unlike the De Lacys or their lawyers to miss a trick.

'In any event,' Cowell said, 'I am happy to tell you that this contract obligates you to do nothing to assist the De Lacys until such time as they have provided you with legal counsel and you have won your case. Should they renege on that agreement, or you lose the case, your obligation is entirely discharged.'

Perhaps I'd been wrong about the De Lacys. It seemed, under this contract, we both stood to gain. Unless I set it aside after I won.

The possibility gave me pause. I thought it reasonable to compensate the De Lacys for their assistance, and I actively wanted to take care of Mirabel, Archie and Emily. On the other hand, I believed that Julius was a murderer and I didn't want him profiting any further from that crime. In the end, I decided to worry about it if and when I won the case. I thanked Mr Cowell and paid him our agreed fee.

'It is a delight to have any connection at all to *Seabrooke v De Lacy*, however peripherally,' he said. 'I have followed your family's legal battles since I was an apprentice. Is there any other matter that I might help you with at this time?'

'Now you come to mention it, there is,' I said. 'Is there a rear entrance to your building?'

CHAPTER SEVEN

Six of clubs, influenced by a heart:
the call to assist another, near to one.

TAMSON HAD ONCE warned me about Seven Dials. A sprawling slum rookery notorious for its thieves and prostitutes, it was not a place for a lady, even by day. The buildings grew more and more dilapidated as I walked west of Drury Lane, the people more beggarly, the taverns more villainous. I'd read that the magistrate liked to pillory people here as an example, but that the locals were often sympathetic to the criminals. I'd hoped that would be the case for Tamson, but as I walked up Little Earl Street towards the hub of seven roads where the pillory was located, men started spilling out of the taverns, and I heard several of them mention with enthusiasm that an astrologer was about to be pelted. To my alarm, some were carrying cauliflower stalks, oyster shells and stones.

'I heard she was a witch,' one of them said. 'She goes around cursing people's children.'

'I heard she dabbles in herbs,' another said. 'That she has a poisoner's cabinet. I've heard it said she was the one who poisoned Queen Caroline.'

'No,' I said. 'That isn't true. She never poisoned anyone.'

They only laughed at me, and continued on down the street. Up ahead there seemed to be some sort of commotion: a crowd had gathered, and people were shouting. As I drew closer, I saw that a cart had been drawn up horizontally, blocking the road. Men swarmed around it, trying to get to the pillory site, shouting bloody murder at the driver, who was nowhere to be seen. A few of them attempted to climb over it, a task made harder by the fact that the cart was stacked high with bales and boxes. Just as one of them nearly reached the top, a man appeared from amongst the boxes with a stick, and jabbed it into the chest of the climber, knocking him off.

It was Frank from the Cornish Players! I spotted Roland up there too, also armed with a stick. One by one, they knocked the climbers off, ducking to avoid the missiles hurled their way. A few men tried to crawl beneath the cart, but soon retreated, clutching their eyes or bleeding from their mouths. I surmised that more of the Players must be on the other side of the cart at the level of the street.

'Let's try Great White Lion Street,' one of the men called out to his friends, and the rest of the crowd followed their lead, racing off down the street.

'Roland,' I cried. 'It's me, Red.'

He gazed down at me with hostile eyes. 'What do you want?'

'To help Tamson. Let me through. I've got money to bribe the constables.'

'Morgan's already tried,' he said. 'Sheriff won't take it. Morgan thinks the magistrate threatened him.'

'At least let me try. I've got twenty guineas. That has to tempt him.'

Roland hesitated a moment, then he turned. 'Stand back. A friend is coming through.'

I crawled beneath the cart, and when I emerged on the other side, I found myself looking up into the very unfriendly faces of Gwen and Naomi.

'You little fuckstress,' Gwen cried, gripping her stick.

'I thought you said it was a friend,' Naomi cried.

'She's got money,' Roland said. 'More than Morgan. It's worth a try.'

Scrambling to my feet, I looked around me. 'Where are the others?'

'Blocking the other streets,' Roland said. 'But the trouble with this spot is that there's seven roads in and out. We're spread too thin. They'll break through before too long.'

'Why are the crowd so angry?' I asked.

'That constable who got mauled by the bear. His friends spread stories around the taverns. Most of it is lies, but they've got the neighbourhood all riled up.'

'Your fault,' Gwen said.

'I know,' I said. 'At least give me the chance to put things right.'

Gwen and Naomi looked at one another, and then stood back. Distantly, I heard a shrill blast upon a whistle, and the sounds of another commotion on a nearby street.

'That's the start of her hour,' Roland said. 'What are you waiting for? Go.'

Lifting my skirts, I ran down the street, eventually emerging into a round cobbled space where the seven roads converged. A wooden platform had been erected here, and my heart surged as I saw Tamson. Her head and arms were locked in the pillory's wooden block, her hair wild and loose, her eyes wide with fear. A few constables stood around the pillory, waiting for the crowd. I span round, seeing that each of the roads was blocked, as Roland had said. The mob seemed to have concentrated their efforts upon one street in particular, where they were locked in a pitched battle with the Cornish Players. I saw Morgan striding about, directing the action. It didn't look as if they'd be able to hold the crowd back for very much longer.

Tamson looked up and our eyes met. How to convey everything I felt in a glance? I tried nonetheless. She didn't smile, but she didn't look away.

I gazed wildly around for the sheriff, my eyes coming to a rest upon a gentleman dressed in black, sitting in a chair outside one of the taverns, enjoying a tankard of ale. The ceremonial chain around his neck left little room for doubt.

I hurried up to him. 'I have a fine gift for you, sir, if you'll only blow that whistle now.'

'Popular lass, isn't she?' he said. 'I've already told her other friends that I can't help them. See that there?' He pointed to a large clock hanging outside the premises of a watchmaker. 'I'm under strict orders not to let her out even a minute before her time.'

'I have twenty guineas,' I said, opening my purse to show him the gold.

I could see the desire in his eyes, but he tore them reluctantly away. 'That magistrate's a vindictive fellow. If I cross him, he'll take my job.'

Hearing shouts behind me, I turned. Three men had succeeded in getting past the Players, and were sprinting towards us. Another man came out of one of the nearby houses, stooping to pick up a loose cobblestone.

I ran to block their path to Tamson, using my arms to shield my head.

'Silly bitch,' one of the men cried. 'Get out the way.'

He threw a cauliflower stalk which struck me on the ear. One of the constables ordered me to move out of the way, or I'd be hurt. The man with the cobblestone hurled it, and it smacked into the wood of the pillory by Tamson's head. An oyster shell whizzed past my ear, and caught her on the cheek, drawing blood. She cried out in pain and fear.

Two more men ran in to join the others. One hurled a brown paper parcel, which struck the wood above Tamson's head. It burst, covering her in excrement. The men hooted, pointing and laughing. Another threw a stone, which struck her on the hand.

I glanced up at the clock. Tamson couldn't take forty-five minutes more of this. Yet the clock gave me an idea. Protecting my head with my arms, I ran for the watchmaker's door, getting hit by a rancid potato on the way. I burst through the door, and an old man looked up from his counter. I could see a flight of stairs behind him.

'This is an emergency,' I cried, ducking beneath the counter. His howls of protest followed me up the stairs. I found myself on a landing with several doors, and I headed for the room at the front, which appeared to be the watchmaker's parlour. A heavy armchair faced the fire, and I heaved it across the floor to barricade the door. Then I ran to the window and threw it open.

More men were hurling missiles at Tamson, a large group of them now. Blood was dripping from her mouth. I leaned from the window, and found I could just reach the hands of the clock. The watchmaker was rattling the door, trying to get in. I moved the hands forward to two o'clock. Then I ducked back inside, and moved the chair. The door burst open, and the watchmaker stumbled into the room. I dodged past him, and he made a grab for me – there was a tearing of silk, but then I was free. I ran back down the stairs, onto the street.

As I crossed the road, a huge crash echoed around the buildings. Glancing in the direction of the sound, I saw that the mob had overturned the cart. Men were scrambling over it, dozens of them, shouting to their friends, running down the street.

I tugged on the sheriff's arm. 'Look at the time.'

He frowned. 'That can't be right.' He took out his pocket watch to show me. 'She's not half-done yet.'

'Those weren't your orders,' I reminded him, taking out my purse, and giving him another flash of my gold.

Again, I saw that avaricious glint in his eye. He hesitated a moment longer, then snatched the purse from my hand. Then he gave a long blast on his whistle. A couple of the constables started to protest, and I wondered if they were friends of the man who'd been attacked by the bear, those same men who had been spreading stories in the taverns. The sheriff barked an order, and two of the constables mounted the platform, just as a huge tide of men swept into the space where we stood. Realizing that the constables were unchaining Tamson, they gave a great howl of outrage. The sight of her blood seemed to inflame them all the more, and they made a charge for the pillory. The other constables beat them back with sticks.

The constables on the pillory were having difficulty unlocking the block. Stones and half-bricks rained down on them. The sheriff was looking alarmed, backing towards the door of the tavern. His blasts upon his whistle went ignored.

At last the constables had Tamson free, and they half carried her from the platform, while the mob yelled their fury. I followed them into the tavern, where the sheriff gave curt orders to a pair of men drinking in the taproom, whom I presumed to be his drivers. We hurried through a series of back rooms and out into a yard. A pair of battered black coaches were waiting there, one with bars over the windows. As one driver opened the gate, the other opened the door of the prison-carriage. Two of the constables lifted Tamson inside and before anyone could stop me, I hopped in too. One of the constables started to object, but the mob were hard upon our heels, and nobody wanted to waste any time getting me out.

The door slammed shut, and moments later, the coach lurched off. Through the window behind us, I saw a group of red-faced men burst into the yard. We headed down a narrow alley, and out onto Tower Street, stones and other projectiles bouncing off the carriage roof.

Tamson wiped the blood and excrement from her face, and then pressed along one of her cheekbones, as if checking for a fracture. Seemingly reassured, she spat a rose of blood into the straw that covered the floor of the carriage.

'Are you all right?' I asked.

One of her eyes was swollen. She fixed me with the other. 'I'll live.'

'I'm sorry,' I said hopelessly. 'I'll get you out of here. I promise.'

'And how exactly do you propose to do that?'

'I'll have money soon. A lot of it. More than you ever dreamed of.'

'I never dreamed about money. That was you. Now we're all paying the price for it.'

'I didn't mean for this to happen.' Tears came to my eyes and I blinked them away. 'I know that doesn't count for much. But I will get you out.'

'You really think this scheme of yours is going to work? That they're going to believe you're this countess's daughter?'

I stared at her in surprise.

'That man came to see me. Lazarus Darke. He wanted me to test-ify against you. Said it would get you out of prison.'

'Why didn't you?'

She only closed her eyes and leaned her head against the side of the carriage, moving with the sway.

'It's not a scheme,' I said. 'It's the truth.'

She didn't reply at first. 'Darke has Morgan in his pocket. The others too. They'll say bad things about you, Red.'

It shouldn't have come as any surprise. 'I can't help that.'

'Yes, you can,' she said, suddenly impassioned. 'Stop all this. It's madness. You're going to wind up in prison and believe me, you don't want that.'

I tried not to dwell upon these dangers. It was what Lazarus Darke wanted. 'I have my family behind me now. I think I can win.'

She shook her head. 'I fear for you, Red.'

Emboldened by this evidence that she still cared, I edged closer and took her hand. She applied no pressure of her own, but nor did she pull away. 'I missed you in Devon,' I said.

She gave me that look again. 'What do you want? A parade?'

I shrugged. 'I just wanted you to know.'

'Now I do.'

'Can I show you something?' I asked, reaching into my pocket to take out the star chart that I'd found with the reports at Leighfindell. The lawyers had taken the reports, but nobody had seemed interested in this. 'I think my father drew it. It looks like his hand.'

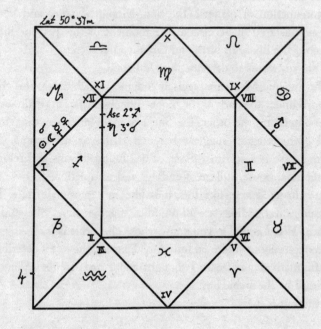

Tamson studied it, frowning in the gloom of the carriage. 'Is it another birth chart?'

'I think so. Can you tell me when and where this person was born?'

'Not without an ephemeris,' she said.

'Is there anything you can tell me?'

She studied it again. 'It is another unusual chart. Sagittarius is in the ascendant, which is a bold, optimistic sign. But Saturn is squatting like a toad in the first house, conjunct to this birth, which is an ill omen. The arrow of Sagittarius represents the future. But here it is impeded by Saturn from the moment of birth. Saturn is often associated with fathers.'

I frowned. 'In the myths, he devoured his own children.'

Tamson pointed at the chart. 'There is another ill omen here. Jupiter is in Capricorn, where he is never happy. Jupiter is the planet of luck, and here it is lacking. Mars, the planet of war, is in Cancer, which is the sign of the mother. It suggests parental discord. That is mirrored here in the twelfth house.' She pointed again. 'Do you see this conjunction of planets? The Sun, Moon, Mercury and Venus were all clustered in Scorpio at the moment of this person's birth. Scorpio is the house of birth and carnality and secrets.'

More apt words to describe the De Lacys.

'The Sun and Moon are precisely conjunct, which means this child was born under the dark of the moon. This life began in shadow, one light obliterating the other. The Sun is a male influence, the Moon female, which again suggests parental strife, or misfortune. The twelfth house is a spiritual place, of death and dreams and rebirth. It is the final house, a place of endings and completion. To have the planets clustered here like this, it is like an explosion of fate. The beginnings and endings are all muddled together here.' She studied my face. 'What is it? Do you know whose chart this is?'

I thought about where I'd found it, alongside the letter describing the aftermath of my birth. I thought about my parents' argument, overheard by the stable boy.

'I think it is mine.'

CHAPTER EIGHT

Eight of hearts, influenced by a diamond:
a lost article recovered.

I T IS A cold and bitter January, the London air thick with sulphur which leaves an unpleasant taste in the mouth. Much like relations between the De Lacys and their Seabrooke cousins, say the wags. Three months have passed since Lazarus returned from Cornwall, carrying his doubts. He crosses a little courtyard, the flagstones slippery with frost, and passes through a green baize door in one of the surrounding red-brick houses. Beyond is a draughty lobby, and beyond that, a large, high-ceilinged chamber with crests and shields on the wall above the tall black wainscotting. The courtroom is divided into two by a stone triumvirate of arches, like a rood-screen in a church. On one side are the public, who are steadily filing through the door to fill the benches. On the other is a raised semi-circular dais, where sit a dozen gentlemen in scarlet gowns and plump grey wigs. The judge is settled upon an elevated throne behind them, from where he can catch the eye of the proctors seated in the pit below. The registrar, a grinning, impish fellow, occupies an armchair at the end of the proctors' table, facing the judge. On the public side of the arches, seated at two green baize tables, are the barristers representing De Lacy and Seabrooke. Behind them, occupying the first two rows of the public benches, sit the parties themselves, surrounded by their teams of solicitors and clerks.

The Officer of the Court, a burly fellow in a black gown and gloves, recognizes Lazarus, who has attended every sitting of the court since the Michaelmas term began. The Hilary term is upon them now, and the Officer is in a buoyant mood. He ushers Lazarus through the door with a swing of his silver staff.

'You're in for a treat,' he tells the couple coming in behind Lazarus. 'This one is a lively case indeed.'

So it has proved. Since the middle of October, the Prerogative Court of Canterbury has been considering the validity of the document known to the newspapers as the Grandchild Codicil. Lazarus and Henry Antrobus have given evidence about how the codicil was found. The publisher, John Gowne, and various learned gentlemen of Robert Antrobus's acquaintance have given testimony about the document known as *The Square of Sevens*. And the court has also heard from several gentlemen considered experts in the study of handwriting and the provenance of parchment, who all share an opinion that the codicil is genuine.

Naturally, Julius De Lacy has his own authorities on such matters, who have testified that it is a crude forgery. His counsel, a rangy, slope-headed gentleman named Figg, pointed the judge to George Montfort's testimony from seventeen years earlier, that he witnessed his master destroy the document in question. In turn, the Seabrooke counsel pointed to the large sum of money in George Montfort's possession at his death – of which there is a record in probate – an amount unaccounted for by any satisfactory explanation.

Lazarus edges along the benches. The De Lacys do not look at him, but stare fixedly ahead. Julius has been in court most days, and when he is not, Septimus is there in his place. Today, they are all there: Julius, Septimus, Mirabel, Lady Frances, Arabia, Emily, and Montfort's lad, Archie, who has the height and Viking good looks of his father.

Lazarus takes the vacant seat next to Lady Seabrooke, who gives him a nod. He can read the tension in her taut gaze, in her tight, curled fingers. Leopold gives Lazarus a tentative smile. The journalists scribble away in their books, taking it as a sign. Today the judge is expected to rule upon the validity of the codicil, and the newspapers think he will find in the young Earl of Seabrooke's favour.

The registrar gives a long and tedious preamble and when he sits, the judge rises. Sir George Lee, a desiccated septuagenarian with a cracked voice and a steely eye, uses obscure words of many syllables to make his ruling. Yet between all the *deponents* and *revocations*, the *testamentaries* and *executrixes*, it becomes apparent that there will be no surprises today. When Sir George declares that in his opinion, the codicil is genuine, that it is the same document lost at the time of Nicholas De Lacy's death, a great murmur goes up from the public benches. Figg, for Julius De Lacy, leaps to his feet immediately, begging leave to appeal to the High Court of Delegates, but the judge tells him to sit down, adding that there will be no ruling upon the distribution of the estate today. This prompts another great murmur, and the Seabrooke counsel, a rotund gentleman named William Rich, whose name has been the subject of much satire in the newspapers concerning the avarice of lawyers, objects at once.

Lady Seabrooke's face is impassive, the journalists puzzled by her lack of elation. She knows what is coming, has known it ever since Red returned to London and took up residence at De Lacy House. First, the girl's lawyers had applied to the Court of Chancery to strip Henry Antrobus of his guardianship. With Lady Seabrooke's financial assistance, Henry had contested the application vigorously. He had testified in person to the Lord Chancellor in chambers, weeping as he spoke of her insanity. His mad-doctor had given a long affidavit, speaking of his history of treating patients delusional in the mind, and his conviction that Red is suffering from such a malady. But the De Lacys had their own mad-doctors, who had examined Red in person, and who testified by affidavit that she was perfectly sane. The De Lacys had also produced an accountant, who had looked into the disappearance of Robert Antrobus's fortune. He was not able to conclusively prove that Henry and the lawyer, Mr Edwards, conspired to steal her money, but the whole business appeared murky to say the least.

Finally, there was Red herself. The Lord Chancellor had questioned her *in camera* in his chambers, and whatever she said to him there, it seemed to have settled the question. He'd ruled that she was of sound mind and granted the application that she be made a ward of court. He'd also approved her stated desire that she remain in the care of the De Lacys.

This combining of forces was always the worst fear of Lady Seabrooke. Lazarus shares her concerns. It has occasioned him sleepless nights. He has tried several times to get a warning to Red, but she is always surrounded by De Lacy women and footmen. Her letters are undoubtedly being intercepted before they reach her, and Lady Seabrooke refuses to risk the exposure of her spies in the household to pass her a note. She says Red wouldn't listen anyway, that she'd mistrust their motives. She's probably right.

'Before making a distribution of the estate,' Sir George declares now, 'I must first consider an application for another bill, a third party who wishes to join the suit.'

This news delights the public gallery and the journalists, who had feared the curtailment of their sport. They crane their necks, hoping to catch sight of this third party, speculating feverishly about who it might be. A young, neat, freckled gentleman rises from his seat and approaches the bench.

'You are Mr Cowell?' the judge says, looking down at his papers.

'I am, Your Honour. The Court of Chancery has appointed me to oversee the financial and legal affairs of Miss Red Jago, a minor. I stand here as her *prochein ami.*'

Her litigation friend. This had been the only real surprise in the Chancery hearings. It seems Red told the Lord Chancellor that she wished to entrust her affairs to Mr Cowell, rather than the solicitor the De Lacys had intended for that task. She doesn't entirely trust them, Lazarus thinks, and it gives him hope. As a minor, Red cannot bring suit on her own behalf, but Cowell will act in her stead. When he retakes his seat, another gentleman rises. He is wearing a peacock-blue waistcoat and an astonishing pair of blue-glass spectacles through which he squints at his notes.

'Mr Bagshott,' the judge says, 'I believe you are counsel to this deponent?'

'I do indeed have that honour. Miss Jago was, until recently, a resident of the city of Bath, where she went by the name of Rachel Antrobus. She is the daughter of Lady Seabrooke by her first husband, a fortune teller called John Jory Jago. Her age at this present time is seventeen years and three months, making her the eldest grandchild of the late Nicholas De Lacy.'

This announcement provokes an uproar, the registrar forced to call for order several times. Not a muscle moves on Lady Seabrooke's face and, as ever, Lazarus admires her fortitude.

'My client made an approach to her mother some months ago, when her assertion of kinship was denied. Yet other members of the De Lacy family accept my client's claim of consanguinity.'

Sir George peers around the chamber. 'Is Miss Jago here in court today?'

'She is, Your Honour.'

Lazarus cranes his neck with the rest of the court. A door opens at the rear of the chamber, and Red enters, followed by more solicitors. She looks very different to how she did when Lazarus last saw her at the fair. She is wearing a day dress of Indian cotton in a muted shade of blue that makes her look both younger and more innocent. Her red hair is unpowdered, in order to heighten the resemblance to Lady Seabrooke and her siblings. Lazarus studies her face. Could it be true? His doubt is like the flame of a lamp, sometimes bright, sometimes dim, but never extinguished. Red curtseys elegantly to the judge, and then takes a seat amidst the De Lacys. Mirabel places a hand upon her shoulder.

The registrar calls for silence. Sir George clears his throat. 'Let us begin.'

♥

Even Lady Seabrooke is forced to admit that Red makes a compelling witness. For three days she gives testimony and the court hangs on her every word. Jemima's locket is produced as evidence, along with the pack of De Lacy playing cards. Red talks movingly about her quest to find her mother's family. When Mr Rich calls her a liar and a fraud to her face, she trembles with emotion. Some of the crowd start wearing badges: *I believe Red*. Lazarus's own doubts multiply, but he voices them to nobody, least of all to Lady Seabrooke.

Red's barrister, Henry Bagshott – or Hotshot Harry, as he is now known in the newspapers – issues a subpoena compelling Lazarus to testify. Now that the De Lacys have nothing to lose by using Lazarus's reports against Lady Seabrooke, it comes as no surprise that they have given those reports to Red. Lazarus is forced to stand and read them aloud, every word a blow to Lady Seabrooke's reputation. The journalists revel in it, and the next day the newspapers talk of little except the elopement. *A fortune teller! A gypsy! She was already carrying his child!* It is a worse purgatory for Lazarus even than their years of separation. Yet endure it he must, as she endures it too, greeting each insinuation and insult that flow so politely from the lips of Mr Bagshott with that same impassive stare.

When called to give evidence, Lady Seabrooke tells the court that she was raped by John Jory and, in her shame, could not bring herself to tell her parents. She duly discovered that she was with child. (Here she breaks off to weep, but, having heard Lazarus's report, the judge and the proctors are stony-faced.) It was in this state of distress, heightened by grief, Lady Seabrooke says, that John Jory tricked her into meeting him at the Pharos. There he assaulted her and kidnapped her from her home, subjecting her to months of abuse on the road, which turned her into a creature under his control. As for the ceremony of marriage, she says that she believes she was bewitched, prompting a ripple of laughter from the rational London crowd.

The newspapers the next day make for dismal reading. Censoriously, they report Lady Seabrooke's derisory excuses, her lack of contrition or shame. She cares nothing for their disapproval, even when crowds hoot at her in the street. Only once does Lazarus see her unnerved. During one of the arguments of Mr Bagshott, when he is speaking about Lady Seabrooke's loose morals, her lack of every good womanly virtue, her hand creeps over her son's – who pulls away.

Lazarus talks to the boy, settles him down, reminds him that this is precisely how his enemies would want him to react. He says victims of crime often behave in unlikely ways. He says fault lies with John Jory, with the neglect of his grandparents and their servants, but not with his mother. The boy seems to listen, and the next day in court, he takes his mother's hand in full view of the journalists and the judge. Yet Lazarus now shares Lady Seabrooke's fear that in staking everything upon victory, she runs the risk of losing something more precious to her still.

Mr Bagshott produces various witnesses who give evidence in support of Red's claim. Letitia Jennings testifies that she remembers the portmanteau and the argument about it, as well as the golden heart. Nobody can deny that *The Square of Sevens* and the codicil were in the possession of Robert Antrobus, even if the Seabrooke counsel very much disputes how he came by them. Mirabel gives moving testimony that she believes Red to be her long-lost granddaughter. She is followed by all the other members of the family, with the exception of Archie Montfort, who doesn't count.

When Edmund Bonny, the ostler from the Seven Stars, is called to give evidence, he sticks stubbornly to his story.

'Let us be quite certain on this point,' Mr Bagshott says. 'You never saw Mr Jago jump from that cliff?'

'Not the moment itself,' Bonny says. 'But he was there one minute and gone the next. There's nowhere else he could have gone except over that cliff.'

'Couldn't he have walked away without you seeing him? It was dark and you have testified that it was raining heavily.'

'I'd have seen him. When the lightning flashed, you could see everything.'

'Might he have landed upon a ledge, and climbed back up after you had returned to the inn?'

'With a baby in his arms? In a storm?'

'Difficult, perhaps, but not impossible.'

'He was a cunning-man,' Bonny says. 'Perhaps he flew.'

The laughter doesn't put Mr Bagshott off his stride. 'How much did you have to drink that night?'

Bonny looks discomforted. 'I'm not sure, but I wasn't lathered.'

'You were in an inebriated condition, in the middle of a terrible storm – isn't it possible that you simply made a mistake?'

'No, sir,' he says. 'I know what I saw.'

Arguments rage in the letters pages of the newspapers. Questions are asked in Parliament. A fight breaks out in one of the theatres between supporters of the two sides, and there is nearly a riot.

And so, in the second week of February, the court comes to the subject of the maid.

As Jemmy Woodford's name is announced, Lazarus notices Red looking confused, and presumes this part of the plan is not of her design. She passes a note to Mr Bagshott, by way of Mr Cowell, who appears to ignore it.

A shuffling fellow with a cadaverous skull and hollow eyes, Woodford tells the court that he was formerly the pond-man at Leighfindell. His evidence was supposed to be Lady Seabrooke's principal attack on her brother's character, but it seems the De Lacys have found a way to turn it to their advantage.

The court listens, enraptured – *another murder!* – as Woodford describes finding the body in the lake. How some of the servants believed it might have been the maidservant, Etta. How Lady Frances gave him a bag of old coins and offered him a large sum of money to say that he'd found them on the body.

The court erupts. Lady Seabrooke's counsel looks to her for guidance, but she shakes her head. 'John Jory,' she murmurs to Lazarus. 'They are absolving him of one murder, only to implicate him in another.'

So it proves. Lady Frances is next to testify.

'Let us be very clear, My Lady,' Mr Bagshott says, with all due deference. 'Did you believe that the body in the lake was that of the maid, Etta Morgan, when you gave this money to Mr Woodford?'

'Of course not,' Lady Frances says. 'Or I would have involved the law. I only wanted to put an end to the agitation of my servants.'

Liar, Lazarus thinks. You thought your husband was as guilty as the rest of us did.

'I submit to the court, Your Honour,' Mr Bagshott says, 'that the body in the lake was indeed that of Etta Morgan. That she was not murdered by Julius De Lacy, nor anybody affiliated to him, but by John Jory Jago, who bribed or blackmailed Etta into stealing *The Square of Sevens* and the codicil, and then killed her to conceal that crime.'

Red rises, starts to object, but Julius pulls her back down. The indignant reaction of a daughter, who refuses to believe in her father's guilt? Or a consummate actress? Lazarus's doubt flares again.

'Who can say why Jago took the codicil,' Bagshott goes on, 'a document that would have enriched his own daughter? We have heard testimony that John Jory was a dark and brooding man. It is possible that he nurtured unfounded suspicions that somebody might tamper with that codicil and so he sought to preserve it. Whatever his reasons, he secreted it away for many years, in the hope that one day his daughter would be reunited with her fortune.'

With that, Mr Bagshott is done. He has acquitted himself admirably, and yet he has not produced a single witness who can testify that he met John Jory in the seven years after 1723 when it is claimed he was alive. It is now the turn of Mr Rich, for the Earl of Seabrooke, who takes enormous pleasure in pointing this out.

Henry Antrobus, still smarting from the Chancery hearing, testifies that he never saw or heard a single thing that would corroborate Red's claim. He repeats his conviction that she is mad, and is reminded sharply by the judge that the Court of Chancery has already found her sane. 'I say it, Your Honour,' Henry says, 'because the alternative to me is so unthinkable. That she is lying for personal gain, to enrich herself.'

Throughout Henry's evidence, Red stares at him steadily, as if she is measuring him for his funeral suit.

Mrs Davenport tells the court how Red was constantly asking questions about the De Lacy family, and that she lied about not knowing that Lady Seabrooke was Patience De Lacy. Mr Rich asserts that this trail of gossip, along with Red's discovery of the codicil, put the idea of this fraud into her mind. He says the De Lacys don't really think she is telling the truth, but that a nefarious arrangement has been concocted to deprive Leopold De Lacy of his rightful fortune.

Morgan Trevithick and several of the Cornish Players provide the court with much evidence of Red's dishonesty. She is a thief, a fraud, a liar, by their account – and, indeed, her own, in her affidavit. The two fairground women, Gwen and Naomi, attest that she is also a whore, an assertion that is fiercely contested by Mr Bagshott, and yet one which might well lodge in the mind of the judge. There is something of Lady Seabrooke in the way Red holds her head high as her character is traduced. Lazarus feels a creeping sense of shame, and yet it is nothing to the worry in the pit of his stomach, that little nugget of fear that she might not be lying.

'So many parts of this story are conveniently opaque,' Mr Rich says. 'Impossible to prove or disprove. Mired in uncertainty. The northside burial of Mr Jago. The deaths of Robert Antrobus and Mr Chenoweth. Miss Antrobus's convenient lapses of memory about her early life, when her recollection of her father's death is clear as ice. So many witnesses at the inn – the drivers, the fellow guests, the doctor who treated her father, the woman from the orphanage and her assistant. And yet not one of them appears before you today. All the records from the inn, burned in a fire, along with the innkeeper's memoir that might have settled this question beyond doubt.'

As he says this, a gentleman rises from the public gallery, and approaches the Officer of the Court. It is the young vicar from Tretelly, who had given testimony earlier that day about the northside burial and his predecessor's lack of records.

The pair exchange a few words, and then the Officer approaches the registrar, who, a few moments later, approaches the judge. The judge calls the three barristers to his throne, including Mr Figg for the De Lacys, who has sat silently all this time. A conversation is had, and then the judge asks the vicar to come forward.

'Mr Longfellow,' he says, 'do I understand it correctly, when I say it seems as though this memoir was not lost in the fire after all?'

Lazarus draws a sharp breath. The vicar has a slight stammer which he puts down to nerves. 'That's right, Your Honour. The volume in question is in my possession.'

Every person in court turns to his neighbour, talking excitedly. Red and the De Lacys look astonished. At least Lazarus wasn't alone in his dereliction – if he missed a trick, then they did too.

'After the publishers declined his memoir,' Longfellow goes on, 'Mr Chenoweth was in a brown study about it all. He intended to burn his book, but I convinced him not to do it. I have an interest in the history of our town and I felt it was an artefact that should be preserved. I purchased the volume from him to place in my own library.'

Lady Seabrooke clutches Lazarus's arm. 'Proof of her lies.'

'It seems likely that these incidents would have been mentioned in the memoir,' the judge says. 'The first visit to the inn, when John Jory was believed to have jumped from the cliff with his baby daughter. And the second visit, when it is claimed that he died again, this time quite genuinely. If Chenoweth made mention of both incidents, then it would settle this matter once and for all. Conversely, if the first visit is in this memoir, but not the second, I would think it highly likely that Miss Jago is lying about her identity. I therefore propose an adjournment, in order that this memoir can be brought to London. I suggest we reconvene in a month's time.'

'I am staying with my sister in Northampton for the next two months,' the vicar objects. 'I won't be able to return home to Tretelly to collect the volume until after that.'

'Three months, then?' the judge asks, with infinite patience.

Mr Longfellow agrees, and the court is adjourned until that time.

Lady Seabrooke turns to Lazarus. 'By the time he returns to Tretelly, there won't be a memoir in his library. Not if my brother has anything to do with it. You must go to Cornwall, and secure it.'

But Lazarus isn't listening. This is the moment of maximum danger. The court rises, and he worms his way through the crowd, trying to attract Red's attention. But the De Lacy footmen spot him and hold him back. 'Oh no, you don't, sir.'

In desperation, he calls out to her, and she turns. But Septimus takes her arm, and she is soon swallowed by the crowd who are swarming towards the door. By the time Lazarus fights his way outside, through the courtyard, onto the street, the De Lacy carriage is already clattering away.

Lady Seabrooke appears by his side. 'Didn't you hear me? The De Lacys will be sending a man to Cornwall. When they find this memoir conflicts with her story, they'll destroy it. You have to get to it first.'

'What about the girl?'

Lady Seabrooke gazes in the direction of the dwindling carriage. 'She has served her purpose in court. Now they kill her.'

Chapter Nine

Three of diamonds as master-card:
a sudden surprise in an event.

GIVEN THE RELENTLESS interest of the newspapers in the twists and turns of our court case, I will not bore my reader by rehashing it all here. It is enough to say that everything had gone precisely as my uncles had predicted – with one major exception. The revelation that old Chenoweth, the innkeeper, had written a memoir of his life was news to both myself and my uncles. We hurried away from court following the adjournment, piling into our carriage, my uncles already intent upon their plans to secure that volume.

Septimus sat scribbling away with his quill on a portable desk, a task made harder by the swaying of the carriage. Julius tapped his fingers impatiently upon his knee. I tried not to look at Archie, who had caught me looking at him rather too many times of late. We'd been a smaller party in court that week. Lady Frances, Mirabel and Emily had gone to stay with Lady Frances's sister near Taunton in Somerset. Arabia had remained in London, though today she had pleaded a headache.

'Archie, I need you to go to Cornwall and find this memoir,' Julius said. 'You'll ride faster than Whittington and you'll need less rest upon the road. It's essential that we get to it before Lady Seabrooke. She'll be sending Lazarus Darke, I imagine. If the memoir supports Red's story, he'll have orders to destroy it.'

'What if it doesn't?' Archie said. 'What should I do with the memoir then?'

'It will support my story,' I said. 'I know it will.'

'Just bring the book back to Leighfindell, and we can discuss it there,' Julius said.

'To Leighfindell?' I said. 'Why are we returning to Devon?'

'For your own protection,' Septimus said. 'You are now the only thing that stands between Lady Seabrooke's son and Father's fortune.'

'But I've been perfectly well protected in London up until now,' I objected.

'You forget your little escapade to help that friend of yours,' Julius said.

Tamson. Those moments in the prison carriage had only served to underscore how much she meant to me. Our time together had been all too brief. At Charing Cross, the carriage had halted, and the constable had ordered me out. Tamson had smiled rather bleakly. 'Remember what I said. Stay away from these De Lacys.'

And yet how could I?

When I'd returned to De Lacy House, tattered and stained with the residue of rotten vegetables, stern words had been exchanged. Search parties had been out combing the streets for me. Archie had looked for many hours.

His relief when he returned to the house to find me unharmed was plain to see. It had given me reason to hope that we might be reconciled, though since that day, I'd been watched ever more closely, and I hadn't found an opportunity to be alone with him.

I had clashed with Julius again over my decision to make Mr Cowell my legal protector, and then again over Mr Bagshott's assertion in court that my father was responsible for Etta's murder.

'Mr Bagshott needed to give the judge a theory about how the codicil ended up in your father's hands,' Septimus had said. 'It doesn't mean that we believe your father was guilty of that crime.'

I had gazed at Julius, still convinced he was the guilty party. My belief that he was capable of murder unsettled me at times – and now it made me even more anxious about returning to Leighfindell. Yet

I told myself that he needed me alive, a reasoning Septimus under-scored for me.

'With the court adjourned, it seems sensible not to subject you to any unnecessary risk. We're thinking of Archie too. He'll be vul-nerable alone on the road with that memoir in his possession. Once he's safely back at Leighfindell, we can make the return journey to London more safely, with guards around us.'

I certainly didn't like the idea of Archie being in danger. Septimus passed one of the letters he had written to Julius, who signed it upon his knee, and then passed it to Archie. 'A letter of credit,' he said. 'Take the fastest horse at every inn. Spare no expense. We'll travel through the night, so we'll only be a couple of days behind you.'

Septimus held a lit taper to a stick of sealing wax, and red drops fell upon the fold of his second letter. He drove his signet ring into the wax, and passed it to Archie.

'Give this to Mr Lightfoot at the White Hart in Okehampton. There's a little business that I need him to take care of.'

We had reached the Golden Cross Inn at Charing Cross. Archie opened the door, and jumped down from the carriage. 'I hope to bring back what you need, Miss Jago.'

What I needed in that moment was a hard question to answer. For a second we gazed at one another, and my hope kindled again. Then the door slammed, and our carriage pulled away.

◆

Brinseley Radclyffe called at De Lacy House later that afternoon, as we were making preparations for our departure. He'd presumably been back in London since the start of the parliamentary session, but this was the first time I'd seen him since we'd left Leighfindell. Given everything that had happened in the court case, when I passed him in the hall, I wondered if he'd come to break off his engagement to Emily. Yet when he departed, he and Julius appeared to be on good terms, shaking hands and clasping shoulders.

It occasioned me another flicker of suspicion, until I recalled that the bribe to Walpole had already been paid. I suspected that the

Radclyffe dukedom meant more to Brinseley than anything, even the De Lacy fortune – and he had no wish to make an enemy of Julius whilst he still had the power to call a halt to the restoration. It was even possible Brinseley still meant to go through with the marriage. I resolved to have a conversation with Emily about her future at the first opportunity. I would promise her an income even if her parents cut her off, so that she wouldn't feel compelled to marry Mr Radclyffe or anyone else of their choosing.

We left London an hour later, just three carriages – one for the baggage and one for the servants – and a party of armed retainers riding front and rear. Arabia had decided to remain behind in London, not liking the idea of travelling through the night, leaving me to make the journey alone with my uncles.

Throughout the course of that journey, I grew increasingly uneasy. The scrutiny that I had been under at De Lacy House seemed to have tightened even further. Every evening when we stopped at an inn to eat, Julius and Septimus barely let me out of their sight. Even when I went to make water, I was followed by Rosie or one of the other maids. I told myself that the De Lacys were only concerned for my safety, protecting their investment, even if it made me feel more like a prisoner at times.

In Dorchester, we stopped at the King's Arms, a large hostelry with a curved window projecting out into the street above the main portico. The innkeeper, a Mr Hedges, came out into the yard to shake Julius's hand, ushering us inside with great ceremony. Many of the innkeepers along the Exeter Road had previously served as butlers in the great houses, a role that gave them the necessary connections to entice the aristocracy into their establishments. Mr Hedges was one such example, having once served as the butler at Leighfindell.

Soon we were ensconced in the inn's oak-panelled dining room, a repast of roast meats, pickled salmon, Cheshire cheese, and gooseberry pie laid out before us. I thought it rather odd that we were sitting here under the curious gaze of so many fellow travellers, when I knew from my previous journeys to and from Leighfindell that the inn had a private dining room. I presumed it was already occupied or under renovation. The food was delicious, though the wine tasted a little bitter.

'I wonder how Archie is,' I said. 'Do you think he'll have reached Cornwall by now?'

'He'll arrive sometime tomorrow, I should think,' Septimus said. 'He'll probably beat us back to Leighfindell.'

'Unless Darke gets there first,' I said, rather fretfully. Would Darke hurt Archie? He certainly had a ruthless streak. Hadn't he conspired with Henry to have me put in a mad-house?

'Oh, don't worry about Darke,' Julius said. 'We've taken care of him.'

I turned. 'What do you mean?'

Septimus stared at me. 'Miss Jago?'

The innkeeper was staring at me too, and one of the serving maids. 'What is it?' I said, alarmed.

'Your words,' Julius said. 'They sound slurred. Are you drunk?'

As he said this, I became aware of an odd taste in my mouth. My tongue felt too large, and a curious tingling sensation had broken out over my body. Frightened, I rose from my chair. The room span around me. I gripped hold of the table to steady myself, but the world seemed to tilt on its axis. My knees went from under me, and I fell.

'Somebody fetch a doctor,' Septimus cried.

CHAPTER TEN

Ten of spades, influenced by a club: a hindrance.

LAZARUS RIDES THROUGH the night, feeling the sting of rain and hail against his chapped cheeks. It is his third night on the road. Every fall of the horse's hooves jars his bones, and he feels every one of his thirty-eight years. He stops to change horses every fifteen miles or so, and each time, he discovers that the same rider has been there ahead of him. From the description, he sounds very much like the Montfort boy. Archie has fifteen years on Lazarus and the first pick of the horses. At every stop, he finds he has lost a little more ground.

The De Lacys will be about a day and a half behind him – if they're riding through the night, swapping horses and coachmen, as he imagines they will be. He is convinced they'll kill Red at Leighfindell, out of the gaze of the court and the newspapers. An accident? A drowning? Questions will doubtless be asked. But Julius has scant regard for appearances now; he only cares about the money.

'The girl is responsible for her own fate,' Lady Seabrooke had said. 'What's she to you?'

How can Lazarus tell her that he no longer knows? That the question has come to mean almost as much to him as she does herself? To Julius De Lacy, of course, the question is moot. He doesn't care if Red's a fraud or not, as long as the judge believes her story.

Julius's plan is obvious. Lady Seabrooke, desiring to keep her first marriage a secret from the world, had never taken legal steps to have John Jory declared dead. If the court accepts that Red is her mother's child and that John Jory survived for seven years after he was believed to have died, then Lady Seabrooke's marriage to the third earl was bigamous. *My eldest grandchild lawfully begotten*, says the codicil. Which means if Red should meet with some tragic accident at Leighfindell, then the next grandchild in the line of inheritance is Emily De Lacy.

Unless Lazarus can prove that Red is lying. Unless he can get his hands on the memoir before the Montfort boy. If it proves she is a fraud, then Leopold De Lacy will inherit just as Lady Seabrooke had always planned. Which might be enough to save Red's life.

And if the memoir proves her story? What then? Lazarus will have to make a trade. Offer the De Lacys the memoir and his testimony that he is Red's real father – paving the way for Emily to inherit – in return for his daughter's life. Lady Seabrooke will never forgive him, but he cannot stand by and let Red die.

He has slept only a few snatched hours since he has been on the road. Sometimes the world starts slipping away, and he has to grab hold of the saddle to steady himself. He has come to welcome the needles of rain, which at least keep him sharp. He alternates between a fast trot and a canter. A gallop would tire the horse too quickly. Yet when he glimpses the lights of Okehampton up ahead, he spurs her on.

By the entrance to the White Hart Inn, in the light of the lantern over the door, a stable boy is playing nine pins with some bottles. Lazarus ties up his horse next to the trough, and pays the lad a penny to watch him. He steps into a blast of warm air, a fiddler playing, travellers' laughter. In the old days, Lazarus knew all the innkeepers along this route, but this man is a stranger. Lazarus introduces himself and tells the fellow he wants to change horses. 'The best you've got. This one to go back to Exeter.'

'Another fellow took my best horse not two hours ago,' the innkeeper says.

'A fair-haired lad, about twenty?'

'That's right.'

Every part of Lazarus wants to stop and rest, but Montfort will be only about twenty miles from Tretelly by now, and he suspects the boy will keep going. It'll take him time to find the memoir – if the vicar's housekeeper even lets him in at this time of night. 'I'll take the best you have to spare. And a pot of ale.'

'That'll be a half-guinea,' the innkeeper says, running his eye doubtfully over Lazarus's bedraggled clothes.

Lazarus counts out the money, and the man bites each coin before he pockets it. Then he steps out to talk to his ostler. Eager to get back on the road, Lazarus drains his pot.

When the innkeeper returns, he smiles. 'Go see my ostler out in the stables. I've told him you'll take your pick.'

Lazarus heads back out into the yard. The boy is gone, but his horse is still there. Muttering a curse about the unreliability of youth, Lazarus unties the reins and leads the horse towards the stables. He is halfway across the yard, when the big lantern over the door gutters and goes out. The yard is plunged into darkness, but the door to a tack room or a feed store creaks open and a large figure fills the frame.

'Where do you want me to put her?' Lazarus asks.

The man walks towards him. He has something in his hand the size and shape of a club or brickbat. Lazarus reaches for his pistol, but his assailant swings the bat, connecting with his right hand. The pistol clatters across the cobbles, and the pain in his hand is so intense, Lazarus almost surrenders to a wave of blackness.

He turns to run for the taproom, but a second man has followed him out of the inn. From the size and shape of him, Lazarus surmises that he is not unacquainted with the man who has just broken his hand. He backs away from the pair, and they circle him, not speaking. He shouts for help, but no one can hear him over the music. He spots a broom, and grabs it, but even the act of grabbing causes his hand another surge of pain so fierce he thinks he might vomit.

The first man makes another swing with his brickbat. Lazarus parries it, and the broom breaks. He steps forward, the broken shaft gripped in his good hand, and drives it into the first man's thigh. His assailant gives a high-pitched squeal – and yet Lazarus's rear flank is undefended. The second man grabs him from behind. His friend limps forward, and Lazarus can see the whites of his angry eyes. He jabs his brickbat into Lazarus's stomach, slamming the wind out of him. The second man lets him fall to the floor.

His face strikes the cobbles and they fall upon him, kicking him – in the ribs, in the groin, in the head.

'Beshittened arsehole,' the first man says, bringing his bat down hard. There is a distant crack, and then Lazarus knows nothing at all.

CHAPTER ELEVEN

King of clubs, influenced by a low heart: it is secret or remote;
or it may be that it is religious, in part.

S LOWLY MY SENSES returned. I could taste that troubling bitterness, and smell something sour, like sickness. My vision was
blurred, everything spinning. I gazed up at a beamed ceiling. Voices
were talking, but they sounded oddly muted. I heard my name. Julius's
voice – and another man's I did not recognize.

'She was complaining of a fever on the journey,' Julius said.

The man he was addressing possessed an implausibly large head.
Or at least, he might have done. Everything was distorted. Familiar,
and yet wrong.

The man with the large head was backing away from the bed. 'I
don't wish to alarm you,' he said. 'But my presumption is the typhoid.'

I heard this with detachment, as if they were talking about somebody else.

'Oh, dearest Red,' Septimus exclaimed.

'We should get her back to Leighfindell at once,' Julius said. 'Place
her under the care of Dr Crowhurst.'

I tried to say that I just wanted to lie here, but the words wouldn't
come. My vision clouded, and I was sucked away on a river-tide of
darkness.

♣

When I next awoke, everything was swaying. It took me a while to realize that it was the movement of the carriage. It made me want to vomit. My head ached and I was gripped by a terrible thirst. I was lying on the carriage seat, a fur draped over me. We jolted over a hole in the road and I let out a moan.

'She's awake,' I heard Julius say.

A bottle was held to my lips and I drank eagerly, despite the bitter taste. 'There you go,' Julius said. 'Take your medicine.'

I don't know how many hours passed, but when I next awoke, it was dark outside. The men were talking and, instinctively, I kept my eyes closed.

'This wasn't my idea, if you'll recall,' Septimus said. 'My way was better.'

'It was too risky,' Julius said. 'The judge might have found against us.'

'You think what you're doing is without risk?'

'Hence the witnesses. Everyone in that tavern saw my concern for my niece and can testify to it.'

I recalled Julius's peculiar resilience in the face of losing his fortune. The bitterness of my wine. Had he poisoned me?

'That doctor in Dorchester will testify that we did everything we could – so will Dr Crowhurst.'

'That won't stop people speculating that you killed her,' Septimus said. '*Cui bono*, they'll say.'

'Better a wealthy murderer than a poor saint.'

'Have you thought about Emily in any of this? What will she make of it all?'

'She'll do as she's told,' Julius said. 'So will Brinseley, if he wants this marriage to go ahead – which I assure you, he very much does.'

Slowly it was all making sense in my sluggish brain. The oddities about that contract, one they'd never intended to be honoured – because I would be dead. But they'd needed me in court, because it was essential that the world saw me stand up and speak the truth. Their lawyers would do the rest. Then Leopold could be declared illegitimate. And if I was dead . . .

'You're sure Darke won't be a problem?' Julius said.

'Lightfoot is dependable,' Septimus said. 'Poor fellow. I always rather liked him.'

I struggled upright, reaching for the carriage door – but I was too weak, too slow, too giddy. Strong hands gripped me, and returned me to the carriage seat.

'This tincture of yours had better do the job,' Septimus said.

'I'm assured it will,' I heard Julius say, as I was sucked away into nothingness once more.

I dreamed I was lying in my bed at Trim Street, suffering from a fever. Mr Antrobus was gazing down at me with concern. Mrs Fremantle was holding a compress to my brow. I tried to tell them that I wasn't sick, that I was being poisoned by the De Lacys. But Mrs Fremantle's face dissolved into a terrifying visage: a pair of bulging eyes, a terrible scar, and a wide rubbery mouth, contorted into a smile.

'It's all right, Red,' Dr Crowhurst said. 'You're at Leighfindell now.'

It all came back to me in a rush. The inn. The carriage. Julius.

'They poisoned me,' I told the doctor. 'They want to steal my inheritance.'

'You can see how delirious she is,' Julius said. I tried to lift my head to look at him, but it was all too much. I made out a bright light, a window with bars across it. My head fell back heavily onto the pillow.

'I fear the doctor you consulted on the road is correct,' I heard Crowhurst murmur. 'This looks like the typhoid.'

'No,' I tried to say. 'He's trying to kill me.'

'You'll come tomorrow?' Julius said to the doctor.

'Of course. Keep her isolated,' the doctor said. 'And make sure to burn those clothes.'

'Ask Travers to send up Mrs Vaughan,' Julius said.

The door closed and Julius's face swam into my vision. He gripped one of my wrists rather painfully, and dragged it above my head. I felt something rough against my skin, and realized he was strapping me to the bedstead. I tried to resist, thrashing feebly, but it was no use.

'You're thirsty,' Julius said. His eyes were perfectly cold, no pretence at charm at all. 'Here, drink.' He held the bottle to my lips again, but I turned my face away. He gripped my chin, wrenching me back. With his other hand, he pinched my nose, until I was forced to open my mouth to be able to breathe. He tipped the liquid inside my mouth, filling my throat. Then he clamped my jaw shut, still holding my nose. 'I'll only let you breathe, once you swallow,' he said.

To die quickly or slowly? It wasn't much of a choice. I swallowed, feeling the liquid flow down my throat. A few moments later, came a knock at the door. Then I heard the crisp, unfeeling voice of Mrs Vaughan.

'How is she?'

'The doctor says it is the typhoid. I want you to take those clothes away and burn them.'

I watched between heavy eyelids as Mrs Vaughan went to the chair where my gown and stays and other clothes were piled.

'Help me,' I said. 'They're trying to kill me.'

She tutted and shook her head. 'The De Lacys were kinder to you than you ever deserved.'

'It's just her illness,' Julius said. 'She is delirious. It's why we've had to strap her down. She keeps refusing to take her medicine.'

Mrs Vaughan was going through my pockets, putting everything she found into a drawer in the dresser. Then she bundled the clothes in her arms and they both left the room. I heard the sound of bolts being slid across the door. I tried desperately to stay awake, to come up with some sort of plan, but my thoughts puddled together and soon I knew nothing.

My dreams were full of bloody scenes: men decapitated upon the block, men burning in fires. I felt as if I was burning in hellfire myself. I heard the words of Septimus's sermon, Mirabel's flinching gaze. *God's wrath like wind, shut up long in the caverns of the earth, shall break forth in a fiery tempest that will consume your soul.*

When I next awoke, it was dark outside. My thoughts were a little less muddled, though my skin burned and the sheets were wet. My heart raced unnaturally, as if I had been running. I pulled against the straps, but they were tight, and I felt so weak. Whatever was in that draught seemed to be having a cumulative effect. Each time I had one of these periods of lucidity between doses, I felt weaker and more confused. Presumably, they were trying to mimic the progression of the typhoid. Dr Crowhurst wouldn't look too closely or ask too many questions. He'd spent years hiding from the truth.

I wondered if they'd sent the ladies of the house away to Somerset in anticipation of this devilish plan. Perhaps it was also why they'd dispatched Archie to Cornwall, rather than sending Mr Whittington. Rosie was somewhere in this house, but she had presumably been ordered to stay away because I had the typhoid.

If I was going to escape, then it had to be now. Another day or two of this, and I'd be too weak to do anything. I tugged again at the straps, twisting my head to look at them. They looked old, the leather mottled, and I twisted my wrists, trying to loosen them. Nothing seemed to do any good. I tugged harder, my despair mounting, until I was startled out of it by a sharp stab of pain. Something warm crawled down my wrist. A drop of blood.

I moved my wrists more slowly, trying to locate the source of my pain. My skin caught again, on the rough head of a nail, protruding from the oak panelling. Hope mounting, I moved my wrist back and forth, sawing the leather against the head of the nail.

I don't know how long I lay there, working at the strap like that. Sometimes I drifted off, awaking with a start. My wrists ached, my strength ebbing away, but slowly, surely, the nail wore away at the leather strap, and eventually, when I gave my bond a hard tug, it snapped. Twisting around, I undid the other strap with my free hand. Then I climbed from the bed, shivering, my legs trembling uncontrollably, taking stock.

Of course, I tried the door, but I'd heard those bolts slide across it and it was shut fast. I went to the window, peering out at the darkened estate. In the moonlight, I made out the allée of lime trees, and the lawn very far below. I guessed I must be at the eastern end of the north wing, up on the attic floor. The straps made me wonder if it was the same room where Jemima had been confined. It was far too high to climb down, even if I could somehow get past the iron bars.

Refusing to give up yet, I went to the drawer where Mrs Vaughan had put my things. My lock picks had been in my trunk, and there was no sign of my luggage here. But the snakestone was there, loosely wrapped up in the stocking. The whereabouts of my purse was a mystery, but my slippers were in the drawer. I put the slippers on, and slipped the snakestone into the stocking, tying it tight.

Could I ambush Julius when he next came to give me his poison draught? Even if I managed to incapacitate him, I doubted I'd get past the footmen on the Oak Stairs in my nightshift. On top of the dresser was a candlestick, tapers and a tinderbox. I lit a candle, and looked around for anything else that might help me.

Only then did I take in the carvings upon the wall. Each section of oak panelling was richly carved with an image of human suffering. Men with swords thrust through their chests, or being broken upon a wheel, or consumed by fire. Little wonder my dreams had been so fevered. In one corner of the room was a large oak cupboard, and I opened it to see if there were clothes inside. I found only a few folded blankets and a chamber pot. I tried the other drawers of the dresser, but they were all empty.

In frustration, I paced, the snakestone swinging from my hand. A blow to the groin, another to the head. Get him on the ground and crack his skull. As I imagined this scenario, it felt desperately improbable. Yet as I imagined Julius lying in a pool of blood, a memory stirred. I studied the carvings again. Martyrs.

What had the Radclyffe history book said? *In the chamber of the Twelve Martyrs, a discreet bedroom for a priest, Culpeper built a portal within the most innocent of cupboards . . .*

I turned, counting the carvings. Twelve in total. And hadn't Etta sworn that she hadn't left the door unbolted when Jemima escaped? Jemima – who, I believed, had also read that book of Radclyffe history.

I opened the cupboard again, pulling out all the blankets in great haste. Trying desperately to remember the instructions in the book, I felt around inside for the hidden peg. Eventually, I found a small, protruding knob of wood at the very bottom of the cupboard, near to the back. I tried to pull it out, but it was stuck fast. I tugged again, and it gave a fraction. Little by little, I worked at it, until I could get a better purchase upon the head. Then I tugged it all the way out, discovering that the peg was attached to a long, very old piece of rope. I pulled the rope all the way through the hole, until it went taut. I tugged harder, fearing that the rope might snap, until I heard a faint grinding sound, like the one I'd heard when Archie had shown me the priest's hole. Then the entire back of the cupboard swung out and upwards upon a hinge, leaving a black void where it had been.

Uttering my silent thanks to the ingenuity of Mr Culpeper, I stepped into that void. As the light of my candle filled the chamber beyond, I heard a scurrying of mice or rats. I picked out the illuminated face of a woman on the wall: Mary holding up an infant Jesus. I turned in wonder, making out other objects in the gloom: a wooden crucifix, an iron chalice upon a shelf, a basin. On the floor were what looked like the remnants of cushions for kneeling, the fabric rotten, made into nests for mice. At the far end of the room a marble altarpiece shone in the darkness. As I approached, I saw the top of it was thick with dust, three ancient books lying there. I imagined some frightened priest turning the pages.

What had the Radclyffe book said? Something about another cupboard and stairs to the cellars. There was a cupboard behind the altar. I crossed to it, my feet freezing, imagining how cold it was going to be outside. A piece of paper was secured to the cupboard door with a jewelled pin, a message written upon it in a brown ink that might have been blood.

My name is Jemima De Lacy. I am an angel now. Don't trust Dr Crowhurst. He called me a liar.

Chapter Twelve

Six of hearts as master-card: an inclination,
a desire, or action, is well-rewarded.

I OPENED THE cupboard door and a plague of moths flew out. In my hair, in my face, in my mouth! I swiped at them frantically. My brain seemed to pulsate with these exertions, and I put out a hand to steady myself.

When I felt calmer, I examined the base of the cupboard. There were two knotholes at the base of it, and when I inserted my fingers into these holes, I found that I could lift the piece of wood out altogether. In the flickering candlelight, I made out a narrow flight of steps, descending deep into the darkness below. Afraid that the years might have rotted the wood, I stepped gingerly onto the first stair. It creaked ominously, but it held my weight, and I descended slowly into the void.

The narrow space was only about three feet wide, and I guessed it must be concealed by a false wall. I was painfully aware of every creak upon the stairs, my candle guttering in drafts through the brickwork. Once, I froze, hearing voices. Through a chink in one of the walls, I made out a glimmer of light. When I put my eye up to it, I found I could see right into one of the corridors at Leighfindell. Mr Whittington was holding a candle, talking to Julius's secretary, who was yawning in a doorway in his shirtsleeves. I was looking directly into the east wing, where the bedrooms of the senior servants were located. The pair looked as if they had just woken up, which meant it must be about six in the morning. The maids would already have been up for an hour. The threat of discovery was very real.

As I descended the stairs, Tudor brick gave way to much older stones. The temperature had dropped and I presumed I must be inside the old cellars. Finally, I reached the bottom of the stairs, a stone passage stretching away into the darkness. I followed it until I came to an open doorway. It led into a long earthen passage propped up by timbers. The tunnel under the gardens described in the Radclyffe book!

Stifling my fear that the passage might collapse and bury me alive, I walked down it, breathing in mulchy scents of mushroom and earth. Before too long, I came to a vast pile of earth that almost blocked the tunnel. It looked as if one of the timbers had given way. I could not climb over it holding my candlestick, and so I was forced to leave it behind. I tied the snakestone to my wrist, and then scrambled up the mound, worming my way through a narrow gap between the earth and the splintered timber above.

I slid down the other side, into pitch-blackness. The ground was damp, and I walked on, shivering, feeling my way along the passage in the dark. Eventually, I felt a faint breeze against my face and heard a sound of running water. The noise grew steadily louder, the darkness somewhat muted up ahead. I picked up my pace, in my eagerness to be free of this terrible house and all its tragic history. Until I walked into something heavy and metallic in the dark, and fell awkwardly against it.

A metal gate. I rattled the iron bars, but it didn't open. On the other side of the gate, I could see a night sky thick with cloud, clumps of reeds, and what looked like a stream in the moonlight. As my eyes adjusted to the light, I saw that the gate had a handle but no padlock or keyhole. I tried the handle, but it wouldn't turn, and I guessed it might be rusted up inside. Gripping my snakestone tightly, I drove it hard into the handle again and again, the effort causing me a great wave of dizziness. I tried the handle again, and this time it turned. When I eased the gate open, it gave a terrible screech.

I stepped directly into the ice-cold waters of a running stream, and almost cried out at the shock of it. My thirst was powerful, and I eyed the water longingly, but the stench of lye filled my nostrils. I guessed this was the stream where the laundrymaids did their scrubbing. Scrambling up the muddy bank, I peered over the top. I was about fifty yards away from the eastern front of the house. Directly ahead of me was the East Court, where the laundry, brewhouse, bakehouse and other outbuildings were located. An odour of smoke and baking bread hung in the air.

I anticipated that nobody would discover I was missing until Julius came to give me another dose of his poison draught. He usually didn't rise until eleven, which gave me several hours. But where to go? I couldn't turn to the law. Not here in Devon, where the De Lacys were the law. And I hadn't any money to get to London.

Archie, I thought. He was surely back at Leighfindell with the memoir by now. I didn't believe for one moment that he was a party to the conspiracy to kill me. Like Emily and Mirabel, they'd wanted him out of the way while the deed was done. He'd have been told that I was in isolation with the typhoid, but surely, if he learned what his family had done, he would help me? Could I get a message to him? I pondered the question. All the servants would presumably have been told that I was sick, and if I was spotted in the house, or asked a servant to take a message, I ran a high risk that someone would raise the alarm.

Perhaps if I walked to Slaughterbridge, I could get someone to take him a message? I could ask him to come and meet me in one of the taverns. Or maybe Greater Domstowe would be safer. It was a little further to walk, but my face would not be recognized there.

Yet I could hardly walk into a tavern in my shift. Then there was the problem of the cold. If I didn't find something warmer to wear, and soon, I was going to freeze to death out here. The bone-aching chill warred with thirst, warred with hunger, warred with weariness. I gazed across the grass to the East Court. Surely I'd find something suitable in the laundry yards? I ran towards it, praying that no one would happen to be looking out of the window of the big house. Reaching the shelter of the gateway, I peered into the court, and then ran across to the laundry-yards, where sheets and clothes were pegged out on the ground to dry. I could hear the chatter of the laundry-maids inside the boiler-house and, fearful of discovery, I grabbed the first few items of women's clothing I could find. Then I ran back to the shelter of the gateway.

Examining my booty – a dark blue linen petticoat and a plain gown of striped white cotton – I found they were several sizes too large. Beggars couldn't be choosers. I dressed quickly, putting them on over my damp and muddied shift. I was still wearing my white lace cap, and I untied it. Winding my hair into a tight knot, I pulled the cap on again and tied it fast, trying to conceal every distinctive red curl beneath it. The clothes hung shapelessly upon me, and I was still shivering violently, but at least they offered me a little more protection against the elements.

My stomach growled at the smell of baking bread. I gazed longingly at the bakehouse, yet the bakers would be hard at work inside, and there was surely no chance of me getting my hands upon a loaf without being spotted. The sky was starting to lighten, the heavy banks of cloud tinged with an edge of sapphire-blue. I had no time to think about breakfast. I needed to get going, before the rest of the household came to life. I decided my best plan was to follow my original plan of escape from Leighfindell, and leave by the foot-gate beyond the Pharos, thus avoiding the lodge-keepers.

I made my way out of the East Court, onto the East Lawn, heading for the cover of the woods. From this distance, in these clothes, anyone seeing me from the house would presume I was a maid embarked upon an errand. I therefore walked briskly, with purpose, but I did not run, nor do anything else likely to arouse suspicion. It took every ounce of will I possessed, my legs trembling with every step, and when I reached the woods, I almost cried with relief.

Now I ran, through the trees, all the way to the Hermitage. Thinking I might find some food there, I ran up the steps, found the key beneath the stone, and unlocked the door. Again, I was assailed by that powerful, ominous energy inside. Trying my best to ignore it, I quickly searched the place. I found no food, but I did find a gentleman's cloak hanging on a peg, and an old sixpence in one of the desk drawers. A washstand held a bowl of soapy water, and I eyed it with revulsion. Then I held the bowl to my lips and drank it down. I retched and almost vomited, but at least it soothed my scratched, dry throat. Bundling myself up in the cloak, I resumed my walk.

My ascent up the side of the valley was hard won. Stones cut into my slippers. Several times I was forced to stop and rest. Yet I found a stick to lean upon and, armed with a fierce determination to escape Leighfindell, I eventually reached the crest of the rise. By now, the sky was cygnet-grey. Soon the sun would be up. I headed towards the Pharos and the path that led to the foot-gate.

As I rounded the side of the tower, I almost walked straight into a gamekeeper, enjoying a pipe of tobacco.

'Where you off to, then?' he said in a Devonshire drawl, studying me with interest.

'Slaughterbridge,' I said, keeping my face low and mimicking his dialect. 'An errand for Mrs Vaughan.'

'Too lazy to go herself, is she?' The man peered at me. 'Are you new?'

'That's right, sir,' I said.

He smiled. 'What's your name?'

'Sukey, sir,' I said.

'You're not from Slaughterbridge, Sukey,' he observed.

'No, sir, but my ma, she has a cousin who lives nearby. It was her who got me my place.'

He nodded. 'You know that gate is locked at night? Head game-keeper opens it up in the morning.'

I hadn't known. As I gazed at him in dismay, he grinned.

'Luckily for you, I'm the head gamekeeper. Dan Halloran, that's my name. I'm not supposed to unlock it for another hour, but I can't think it will hurt.'

I smiled at him, keeping a tight grip on my snakestone in case he got any ideas. But it seemed Mr Halloran was a benevolent sort. He strolled with me along the path, produced a key from his greatcoat and unlocked the gate. He even held it open for me with a flourish.

'Mr Halloran,' I said, 'Mrs Vaughan asked me to take a message to Mr Montfort's room before I left. Only I forgot. I don't suppose there's any way you might help a girl out?'

He frowned. 'Funny that she'd ask you and not his valet.'

'I believe she looked for his valet, sir, but she couldn't find him.'

'Sleeping it off, I suspect.' He chuckled. 'I'd like to help you out, Sukey Sue, but Mr Montfort isn't here. I heard Mr De Lacy and his brother having words about it in the stable yard last night. A right agitation they had. It seems they expected him back by now.'

I frowned. It was only about thirty miles from Tretelly to Leigh-findell. Had Darke caught up with Archie and waylaid him on the road? Or had he been ambushed by thieves? Or thrown from his horse?

As my thoughts spiralled deeper into despair, I caught myself. More likely he'd been delayed by inclement weather, and decided to spend a night or two in Tretelly because of the roads. If I headed towards Cornwall, I'd probably meet him coming back the other way. And then I wouldn't have to fear my message being intercepted.

'Never mind, Mr Halloran,' I said.

He raised his hat. 'Mind yourself, Sukey Sue.'

I walked in the direction of Slaughterbridge. Yet as soon as I was out of sight, I turned off along a footpath into the fields, doubling back round until I was clear of the gate, when I rejoined the road. I felt a powerful sense of freedom, and yet I was hardly out of danger. I was cold, hungry and alone, with only sixpence to my name. The minute the De Lacys discovered me missing, I had no doubt they would come after me with men and dogs. I kept close to the verge, ready to duck out of sight if I heard horses, walking as fast as I could, heading west.

CHAPTER THIRTEEN

*Queen of diamonds, influenced by a spade: a woman not
devoted to benefiting others; and threatened by misfortune;
or with a hidden grievance.*

I HOPED THE De Lacys would assume that I'd head for Exeter and
London, but I couldn't guarantee it. Which meant I needed to
put some distance between myself and Leighfindell. I hoped that in
Greater Domstowe, a taverner would let me tell fortunes for an hour
or so, and I could earn enough to pay for passage to Launceston and
Tretelly beyond. I would keep an eye out for Archie on the road, and
likely intercept him soon. Once I explained everything to him, he
could use Julius's letter of credit to get us both safely back to London.

The sky had lightened a little, but the clouds were ominous in
colour. Somewhere in the distance, I heard a rumble of thunder. The
cold gnawed at my limbs, the world still swaying upon its moorings.
I walked as briskly as my unsteady legs allowed, keeping my eyes
and ears open for any riders upon the road. If they were coming
from behind me, I would hide. Ahead of me, and I would stand my
ground, in case it was Archie. Soon I came to a stream, where I knelt
and drank, scooping the water into my mouth like a man in a desert.
Even as it soothed my parched throat, I battled the urge to vomit. But
I managed to hold the water down, and kept walking.

I passed only a few country folk on the road. By the time I made
out the spire of Greater Domstowe on the horizon, I was already
exhausted. My vision was playing tricks: things moved that shouldn't

move and vice versa. There were more vehicles on the road now, carts laden with cloth, or heading to and from the breweries and iron foundries on the outskirts of town. When I reached the High Street, the clock over the corn exchange was striking ten. Spotting a busy-looking inn, I walked into the yard, which was a jumble of carts and carriages and talkative drivers.

The taproom was full of drovers talking about a cattle fair. I wanted to ask the tapwoman if she had a pack of cards so I could tell fortunes, but my stomach was an aching void, and I imagined I'd get a better reception from the woman if I spent some money there first. All I had was the sixpence that I'd found in the drawer in the Hermitage.

'Bread and sausage do you?' the tapwoman said.

It most certainly would. I took a seat in an unobtrusive nook away from the door. The food tasted better than any of the dinners I'd eaten at Leighfindell. I washed it down with a pot of small beer, delighting in every mouthful. When I'd finished, I returned to the bar to ask the woman about telling fortunes. She was serving another customer, and I waited there a moment, until a familiar voice carried to me from the yard.

'She's about so high. Long red hair. Not a beauty, but pretty enough.'

Ever so slowly, I turned. Julius De Lacy was just outside the door, talking to some of the carters. My panic was matched only by my despair. He must have risen earlier than usual and discovered me missing not long after I'd left.

'She stole a sum of money from my mother. Fraud is her game. She tells fortunes, so she'll likely be frequenting the taverns.'

One of the drivers said something I didn't catch, and Julius shook his head. 'Our best guess is London, but it's possible she's heading west. Can you put the word around between here and Truro? I'll pay fifty pounds if she's caught.'

I was already creeping away from the door, grateful for the cap covering my hair. Ducking into a busy smoking room, I made my way out of the rear of the tavern into a garden. A gate led down to the river, and I walked swiftly along the towpath, trying to put distance between myself and the town. Those carters would overtake me on the road, and if they spread the word about me in the taverns they passed, it would be too risky to try telling fortunes anywhere. Which meant I'd have to walk. The thought filled me with dread, but I told myself that I'd surely meet Archie soon. On the western side of town, I rejoined the main road, continuing my trek west.

On I walked, stopping occasionally to drink from a stream or to rest for a few minutes. I passed through Lewtrenchard with its great manor house, and Lifton with its tall church tower. My legs ached and sometimes seized up with cramp. Beyond Lifton it started to rain, a persistent drizzle that turned into a steady downpour. My cloak was soon soaked through, my breath coming in icy clouds. I had no more money with which to buy food, and I'd have been too nervous to stop at the taverns in any event. As the day lengthened, I grew increasingly anxious about Archie. Surely he should have passed me by now?

Gradually, the landscape changed from rolling green countryside to a bleaker brown. The road followed the edge of Bodmin Moor, past swathes of purple heather and giant granite boulders. Once I passed a stone circle, haunting against the sky. I thought of my father's old stories about the ancient power in these Cornish lands. Would Joan the Wad guide my journey, or would she only lead me further into danger?

Before too long, it started getting dark again. I had a blister on one foot, and all I wanted to do was sleep. I heard hoofbeats and glimpsed a rider in the distance. Thinking it might be Archie, when he drew close, I called out to him. He wheeled his horse around, but when he lifted his hat to peer at me, I saw that he was a much older man. I apologized and he muttered an oath, cantering on.

The road took me past slate quarries and tiny hamlets of run-down cottages. Lightning lit up the night sky and thunder rolled across the hills. I was wet through, shivering, but somehow I kept moving, steadily putting one foot in front of the other. Sometimes I heard the call of a seabird, and a little later, I tasted salt on the wind. I could see lights ahead of me, and when the wind dropped, I heard the roar of the waves. I passed a few old timber houses on the outskirts of town, and then I was walking through the cobbled streets of Tretelly.

So many memories crowded in on me. It had been raining that night too. I passed the inn where the owner had called father a gypsy, and the woman had told me that I should be in bed. Up ahead, I could see the church where the cruel vicar had buried father on the north side of the graveyard. Truly afraid for Archie now, I knocked at the vicarage door. It was after eleven, and the house was in darkness. I knocked again, louder this time, and soon I heard feet descending a staircase. The door opened a crack, and I glimpsed a woman of about fifty, presumably a housekeeper, bundled up in a dressing-gown, clutching a candle.

'I'll give you sixpence,' she said, 'but the master's away, so you can't come inside.'

'I'm not a beggar,' I said, though I presumed I must look like one. 'I'm looking for a gentleman. He was on his way here to collect a book that belongs to your master.'

Reassured by both my words and the manner of my speech, she opened the door a little wider. 'You must mean Mr Montfort?'

'Yes,' I cried. 'Then he has been here?'

'Two days ago,' she said. 'He explained all about the court case, how the judge sent him here. It took us a time to find the right volume, but we did eventually.'

My delight that Archie had secured the volume before Mr Darke mingled with my fear for him. 'Do you know if he left town right away?'

'He said he intended to take a room for the night up at the Seven Stars. The weather.' She made a gesture at the rain. 'He looked half-drowned.'

I worried he'd been taken ill. If so, then perhaps he had stayed a second night at the Seven Stars? It would explain why I hadn't passed him on the road.

I thanked the woman, and resumed my walk through the town. Willing my weary legs on, I strode up the headland to the inn, battling the rain. The wind howled around me, lightning flashing over the sea. I remembered holding father's hand, the hollow rattle of his breathing as we'd climbed towards the lights at the top of the cliff.

So many memories . . . When I staggered through the arch into the inn's stable yard, it was all I could do not to break down and weep. I remembered clutching Father's cold body, willing him to wake. That villain Edward casting Joan the Wad into the flames. Mr Antrobus plucking me from Mrs Sandbach's carriage right here in this spot.

Collecting myself, I walked into the taproom. Everyone stared at me in surprise – just as they had when father and I had walked in here ten years ago. The welcome I received now was much more friendly than that given to us by Mr Chenoweth. A lady with knitting needles in her piled hair gave me a sympathetic smile. 'You're leaking wet, child. Come warm yourself by my fire.'

'I'm looking for a man named Montfort,' I said.

Her face broke into a smile. 'Such a charming gentleman.'

'My brother,' I said, seeking an explanation that would satisfy her. 'I was supposed to meet him here, but my carriage had an accident on the road.'

'He just put his head in here for some wine,' the landlady said, 'so I know he's still awake. Would you like me to take a message to his room?'

Archie was still here! And if her words about wine were to be believed, not at death's door! 'Just show me, please,' I said.

My claim of kinship with Archie clearly assuaged any concerns she might have had about propriety. We walked down a corridor, and the landlady knocked at a door. With a great stab of recognition, I realized it was the same room where my father had died, perhaps the same room where my mother had given birth to me. I heard footsteps, the door opened, and Archie stared at me. 'Miss Jago! Good Lord. What has happened?'

On the verge of tears after everything, I simply walked inside. Archie murmured a few solicitous words to the landlady and closed the door.

'They tried to kill me,' I said, turning to gaze upon his concerned face. 'Julius and Septimus. They poisoned me. So that Emily would inherit my fortune. But I managed to escape and I came here to see if I could find you.'

To my enormous relief, he didn't scoff at my claims. 'That is appalling. Thank heaven you are safe.'

His words made me want to throw myself into his arms. Perhaps I might have done so, had I not caught sight of a large leather book on the desk.

'Is that the memoir?' I said.

'Yes, it is,' Archie said.

'Have you read it?' I asked. 'Does Mr Chenoweth talk about my father?'

Before Archie could reply, the door to the bedroom opened. To my astonishment, Emily came into the room. 'Were you intending to let me sleep—' She broke off when she noticed me, and gave me a glare of surprising hostility. 'What's she doing here?'

'Emily!' I exclaimed. 'I thought you were in Taunton with your aunt?' I turned to Archie, frowning. 'What are you still doing here? Why haven't you returned to Leighfindell?'

'He was waiting for me,' Emily said. 'Archie sent a man from Exeter who made it all happen. I cannot tell you how hard it was getting away from under Mother's nose.' She gave me a little smile, hard and triumphant. 'Oh, and you need to address me properly from now on.' She crossed the room to take Archie's arm. 'My name is Mrs Montfort now.'

CHAPTER FOURTEEN

Ace of spades, influenced by a heart:
ill-fortune in the affection.

I STARED AT Archie, so many things falling into place. Outside the wind howled, the rain hurled against the window like fistfuls of gravel.

'Emily,' I said, 'it isn't you he wants. It's your money.'

She smiled at me scornfully. 'What money? You're going to steal it all. Or my aunt is.'

'No,' I said. 'Your father tried to kill me. Because if your lawyers can prove I am who I say I am, then it means Leopold is illegitimate and you will inherit. Archie must have known or guessed what your father intended to do.'

'Ridiculous,' she said. 'For one thing, Archie doesn't even care about money.'

'Yes,' I said, giving him a hard look. 'He told me that too.'

His gaze was measured, his eyes perfectly calm. I could almost hear his brain working, like one of Morgan Trevithick's automata, as he turned this new problem over in his mind.

'He was just pretending to like you,' Emily said. 'To put my family off the scent. We fooled everybody into thinking we hated one another. When nothing could have been further from the truth. I'm sorry you were caught up in it. I did try to warn you. It was plain as day how much you liked him.'

'It was you who left those playing cards in my room,' I said.

She shrugged, unabashed. 'I didn't like watching you make a fool of yourself. I wish you had heeded my warnings. But here we are.'

'Did he tell you that we kissed?' I asked.

'She kissed me,' Archie said. 'It meant nothing, Emily.'

'Oh, I don't doubt that,' I said. 'But he wanted me to think it did. It was always about the money with him. I think Archie must have learned at Leighfindell who I really was. Old Mr Radclyffe must have told him what I'd said at the electricity show. He was hedging his bets, waiting to see if the court would find the codicil genuine. If I had been set to inherit, it would have been me he'd tried to marry. As it was, your family got involved, and he had to rethink his plans.' I broke off, as a new realization struck me. 'It was you, wasn't it? Who sent those men to our house in Trim Street? You are responsible for the murder of Mrs Fremantle.'

Archie gazed steadily at Emily. 'I don't know what she's talking about.'

But I knew I was right. Rage consumed me – at him but also with myself. How could I have let my head be turned by this manipulator?

'I can see why you wanted the codicil,' I said. 'It would have been useful to have something to hold over Julius, to guarantee he'd accept you as a son-in-law and not do anything foolish like leaving his fortune to Titus or Absalom. But you don't need to force his hand now, because she'll get everything.'

I could see we were both thinking the same thing. *Only if I am dead.* Archie had committed himself now. Which meant I was in as much danger from him as I had been from the De Lacys. Perhaps I should have run the moment I realized, and sought safety in the taproom. But my eyes kept returning to Chenoweth's memoir lying on the table. I couldn't leave without that book.

'Where's Darke?' I said. 'Weren't you worried about him catching up with you?'

Archie smiled. 'Darke is dead.'

The matter-of-fact way he said it chilled my soul. Yet he could do nothing without Emily. If he tried to hurt me, then she would be a witness to that crime. And she was the one person he couldn't silence. Not without losing the De Lacy fortune.

'Archie's been manipulating us both,' I said. 'Do you remember how he tried to get rid of me at first? He did everything he could to turn your family against me.'

'He was worried you'd guess our plan to elope. That I'd give it away. It's why I didn't let you tell my fortune for so long.'

'No, he was worried that I might work out that he was the one behind the murder of my guardian's housekeeper. Then when he learned that the courts would likely find the codicil genuine and he realized I intended to claim your father's fortune, he had another idea. He could pretend to fall in love with me. Just as he pretended to fall in love with you. Did he tell you the story about the girl in Oxford? Her brother who slandered him, saying he'd abandoned her after she lost her fortune? I'll bet that is precisely what happened.'

'She's just jealous of you, my love.' I could see from Archie's face that he was utterly confident in his ability to talk her round. 'She's trying to hurt you.'

'He's a liar,' I cried. 'I think you know it deep down inside, Emily. It wasn't all an act, was it? Your rancour with one another. That's why you wanted me to tell your fortune. I thought you were asking me about Brinseley, but you were asking me about him. You were worried he didn't really love you.'

'I was just upset because everything was taking too much time,' Emily said. 'To make the arrangements for our elopement. To sort out the money.'

'When did he start dragging his feet? Around the time that Lady Seabrooke produced the codicil and brought her new legal suit?'

I could see from Emily's face that I was right again. 'The cards gave you your answer,' I said. 'He doesn't love you.'

But Emily didn't want to hear the truth. 'Stop it,' she said. 'You are making a fool of yourself again.' She opened the door to the hall. 'Go. Leave now. Before you embarrass yourself further.'

Archie leaned over and closed the door. 'It's not quite so simple as that,' he said. Reaching into his pocket, he produced a pearl-handled pistol, which he pointed at me. 'We'll say she came here looking for me, but when she discovered we were married, it broke her heart.'

Emily looked at him. 'Archie?'

'He's going to kill me,' I said. 'But he can't do it unless you stand with him.'

She frowned. 'You can't really mean to kill her?'

'We have no choice,' Archie said. 'Love and money. We can have it all. Who wouldn't take both, given half a chance?'

I could already see in her eyes that she wouldn't have the strength to stand up to him. They were standing in front of the door. The second door, the one that led out onto the cliffside, was closed, yet I could see a key in the lock. Lightning flashed and the wind gave a long, low moan.

'Trust me,' Archie said, gazing into Emily's eyes. 'I know what's best for both of us, remember?'

The wind howled again, and one of the windows burst open. The curtains danced, a violent spray of rain guttering half the candles. Seizing my chance, I grabbed the book and made for the door. I turned the key, yanked it open, and ran out onto the cliffside. Behind me, I heard a shout, but I didn't look back. Cursing my ill-fitting skirts, clutching the memoir to my chest, I ran alongside the inn, trying to get to the stable yard and the safety of the taproom.

I was running against the wind, the ground a quagmire that sucked at my feet. Skidding, I went down on one knee. I heard more shouts behind me. I got back up and ran again, but something hit me with great force, knocking me down.

I lay there, dazed and coughing in the mud. Archie stood over me. He grabbed the book and passed it to Emily, who had run after us.

Archie hauled me up. He still had the gun in his hand. 'A broken heart,' he said. 'Leading to a tragic suicide. A jump from the cliff in the midst of a storm. It will be a fitting ending to your tale, don't you think?'

CHAPTER FIFTEEN

*Nine of hearts as master-card: a card of good augury
for what we wish for another.*

LUNA IS LYING in his bed. Lazarus kisses her eyes, her lips, her breasts. A blinding light fills his vision, and he sighs. Other truths become known. He moves to kiss her again, but his bed is empty. A pain tears through him, and it isn't just his heart. His head aches. And, oh sweet Jesus, his hand. He stares at it in the half-light. It resembles a blown-up bladder.

Everything comes back to him in flashes. The road. The inn. The man with the brickbat. How long has he been out? He isn't sure.

Light is stealing through the window. He sits up with great difficulty, and takes stock of all his pains. The sharper ones worry him most. He is certain his ribs are broken too.

His clothes are lying on the floor. He is wearing only his undershirt. Sliding his legs out of the bed, he catches his hand on the sheet and almost screams. The effort it costs him to reach for his clothes is almost too much to bear. He dresses awkwardly, with one hand, and once his boots are on, he opens the door, finding himself in a hall with stairs. From somewhere, he can hear a chink of crockery. He descends the stairs gingerly, emerging into the same taproom he'd been in the night before. The innkeeper is behind the counter, wiping tankards.

'You're awake, then,' he says, when he sees Lazarus.

'Those men who attacked me last night,' Lazarus says. 'Have they been caught?'

'Last night?' The innkeeper raises his eyebrows. 'You've been out over two days.'

Lazarus sags against the counter. Red is surely dead. Montfort will have the memoir, and if it supports Red's claim, it will be carried to London under armed guard. And it will support her claim. He knows it for certain now. As if something in him has shifted while he has been under.

'You were lucky,' the innkeeper says, sounding entirely indifferent. 'My stable boy found you in the yard and raised a clamour. If you'd lain out there overnight, you would have died for sure.'

Lazarus eyes him sceptically. He is certain the attack on him wasn't a coincidence, but he has no time to pursue those suspicions now. Surely there is still a chance. The Montfort boy might have had an accident on the road. Or a lame horse? Lazarus clings to each unlikely possibility. He might have failed his daughter, but he might still serve Lady Seabrooke.

'The horse I paid for. Is it still in your stable?'

The man shrugs. 'Take a look in the mirror. You can't ride.'

'Just answer the question.'

He shrugs again. 'Go see my ostler.'

Once again, Lazarus heads out to the stables. The ostler is a big man, walking with a slight limp. Lazarus glances down at his fists as the ostler silently saddles the horse. When he tries to mount the horse, the pain is too much.

'Have you got a mounting block?' he asks.

The ostler gives him a scornful look, and shouts to his boy to fetch it. Unsteadily, unable to grip with his broken hand, Lazarus climbs astride the horse. Reaching into his pocket, he is surprised to find his purse is still there. He tosses the boy a silver crown for saving his life.

Every fall of every hoof is like crawling on glass. It is forty miles to Tretelly, but he can't ride at his old pace. Not with only one hand to hold the reins. By the time he reaches Launceston, it is dark and raining. He changes horses, and the endeavour is an agony he can barely describe. But he rides on, skirting the moor, soaked to the bones. The pain in his side worsens, until he fears it is more than broken ribs.

Near Camelford, he is gripped by a terrible shivering that unsettles his horse. Memories flash though his fevered mind. The kiss in the library, that day in the woods at Leighfindell. *Run away with me. Somewhere far from here, where my father can never find us.* He catches Luna listening at the door, only she has the face of Red. The pain intensifies, as does the ache in his heart. For seventeen years he believed her dead, and now she is dead again. Before he had a chance to tell her: *I believe you.*

His horse is slowing, but he must be nearing Tretelly now. Lazarus spares the whip as much as he can, willing her on. Forks of lightning cleave the sky, and the pain searing through him feels like the continuation of that fire. He has been riding for eight hours, when he spots the lights of the town, and soon the horse's hooves are clattering over cobbles.

It is nearly midnight, and the woman who comes to the door of the vicarage looks mightily displeased, especially when she takes stock of Lazarus's bruises. 'Madam,' he says, in his most refined tones, 'do you remember me? Mr Darke. I called here a few weeks ago and was received by your master. I saw him again more recently in London, where he asked me to collect a book for him from his library.'

'That book again!' She explains to him that Montfort has already taken it, and Lazarus's heart sinks. Yet she adds that Montfort had intended to take a room at the Seven Stars, and Lazarus thinks he might as well try there. He knows in his heart how unlikely it is, and so he gives little thought to the question of how, in his current condition, he expects to wrest the book away from a man almost half his age.

As he gallops along the cobbled streets, bedraggled patrons leaving the taverns shout out at him to slow down. Lazarus hardly hears them. The town is soon behind him, and he turns off the main road, onto the track that leads up the headland to the Seven Stars. Flecks of lather spray from the horse's muzzle. Thunder rolls across the ocean. He is about to turn into the yard of the inn, when he hears a cry.

Heaving on the reins, he turns. Three figures are out on the clifftop.

Two of them are grappling, one big, one small. The wind snatches away the cap of the smaller figure, and there is a flash of red hair.

Lazarus stares. How can Red be here? But it's not a product of his fevered mind. She is alive. Wheeling his horse around, he charges across the grass towards them, shouting. The figures turn and he recognizes Archie Montfort and Emily De Lacy. Montfort has Red by the arm, dragging her to the edge of the cliff. She is fighting him all the way. Lightning flashes blindingly. Montfort gives Red a hard push. Lazarus lets out a cry of anguish, as she tumbles over the edge.

Chapter Sixteen

Six of spades, influenced by a diamond: a fall.

I PLUNGED DOWN the steep incline amidst a rattle of loose stones, picking up speed, hurtling towards the sheer drop to the water below. I tried to grab at rocks, at anything, gripped the slim trunk of a stunted tree. It arrested my slide, and my legs swung around. Then the trunk ripped out of the earth and I was sliding again. My foot struck a large rock, and I made a grab for another tree. This time it held, and I hung there, pinned to the face of that cliff like a butterfly on a board. The wind howled, threatening to tear me off and send me tumbling down to the rocks and the roiling sea.

Up above, I heard a gunshot and a woman's cry. Another rock was digging into my thighs, and I edged one leg up towards it, finding purchase. I hauled myself a little way up the slope, terrified the tree would snap. I rested my foot upon the rock. Then I pulled myself up again, grabbing hold of another rock with my free hand. In this fashion, I wormed my way up the slope, buffeted by the wind and the rain. My hands were numb, my feet slippery, fear coursing through me. Occasionally, when the wind dropped, I heard the sounds of a violent struggle up above.

About four feet from the top, the cliff steepened dramatically. From my position on my belly, there was no plausible way I could reach the top. I scrabbled for a handhold to pull myself up, but I only succeeded in dislodging a few stones and a shower of earth that bounced off my back on a long descent to the rocks below. As I clung there, impotent, the wind billowing my skirts, I knew I wouldn't be able to hold on very much longer.

'Emily,' I cried. 'Emily!'

A moment later, her white face appeared over the edge of the clifftop.

'Help me,' I said. 'Don't let me die here.'

She glanced over her shoulder and then back to me, her eyes wide.

'I won't tell anyone what Archie did,' I cried. The wind snatched away my words. 'I won't take him from you. I'll make sure you get everything you want. You can have your money.'

She only stared at me, looking lost in indecision.

'You're a good person. Not a killer. But that's what you'll be, if you don't help me. Please, Emily. I never tried to hurt you.'

My fingers were cramping, my voice growing hoarse. Emily leaned out over the edge, extending her arm towards me. Could I trust her? I had to, or I'd die. I reached up, trying to grab her hand, our fingers inches away from one another. She edged out a little further, and I pushed with my feet against the rock, making a clumsy sort of leap. She clasped my wrist as I clasped hers, more stones and earth rattling past me. My arm wrenched, and I feared I was going to carry Emily over the cliff with me. But she hauled, pulling me up, and I found new purchase with my feet. Then I was vertical against the cliff, looking straight into Emily's eyes.

'Hold on to the edge,' she gasped.

When I did, she let go. If she pushed me now, I'd surely die. But she put her hands beneath my arms and hauled again, while I pulled myself up, and in this awkward fashion, I climbed back over the edge.

Panting, catching my breath, I heard Emily cry out. Turning, to my astonishment, I spotted Lazarus Darke. He and Archie were circling one another, dangerously close to the edge. Darke made a jab with his fist, hitting Archie in the face. He seemed to be holding his other hand rather awkwardly. Archie was bleeding from the mouth, but he looked lighter upon his feet. He came forward at Darke suddenly, striking him hard in the ribs, then aimed another punch at his injured hand. Darke cried out and staggered. Archie cannoned into him, and the pair of them went down.

Archie climbed on top of Darke, and hit him once, twice in the face. Then he got to his feet. Darke groaned, turned his head, and vomited. Archie walked a few paces away, and bent to pick something up. The moonlight glinted upon the pistol in his hand.

I was on my feet by now, and I'd taken the snakestone and stocking from my pocket. I ran towards them, knowing I'd never get there in time. Archie stood over Darke, the pistol pointed at his head. In a last desperate endeavour, I swung the snakestone in an under-arm arc, and let it go. It sailed through the air, and struck Archie square in the forehead. He took a step backwards, then another to steady himself. Confusion washed over his face, as he realized he'd stepped into space. He teetered there for what seemed like a very long moment. Then his weight carried him backwards over the cliff.

'Archie!' Emily ran to the edge. Afraid she would be carried over it by the wind, I ran to her, holding her back. Together we peered down the slope, but Archie was gone.

Emily was shaking violently, and I held her as she screamed and sobbed. I looked around for Darke, and saw he had crawled to the place where Emily had dropped Chenoweth's memoir. He climbed unsteadily to his feet, holding the book in his hand.

'Read it,' I said to him. 'That book contains proof of my story. I know it does.'

He gazed at me, emotion working across his face. 'I'll escort you back to London,' he said. 'I won't let anyone hurt you.' He walked back towards the edge of the cliff, and I guessed his intent.

'Please,' I said. 'Don't do it.'

Darke stopped at the edge, gazing out at the forks of lightning over the sea, the wind whipping at his dark curls.

'Please,' I said again. 'I thought you cared about the truth.'

He gazed at me once more with an intensity I didn't understand.

Then he drew back his arm, his expression set hard, and he hurled that book into the air, out to sea.

I will not dwell upon our journey back to London. The three of us sitting silently in a hired carriage, me hating Darke; Emily, inconsolable, hating us both; Darke looking as if he hated himself. We took Emily to Okehampton, where the innkeeper was known to Julius De Lacy. He gave Emily a private room, and said he would send word to Leighfindell in order that her family could collect her. Then Darke and I, having no wish to encounter the De Lacys, continued our journey.

In London, I threw myself upon the mercy of my solicitor, Mr Cowell. He and his wife kindly took me into their home, pending the conclusion of the case in the Prerogative Court. He advises me that I would have no prospect of success if I brought a private prosecution for murder against Julius De Lacy. My family would say that I was confused by a sickness of the body, and I have no evidence to prove otherwise. Yet I know what I know and what I saw.

In order to pay for the lawyers I will need to fight my case, I have decided to publish this account of my life, with the assistance of Mr Gowne of the Mask bookshop. To lay myself bare to the judgement of the public, warts and all, is a daunting thing. And yet, I believe it is necessary for you to know the truth. How Julius De Lacy tried to kill me. How my own mother has traduced and slandered me. Most of all, how she and Lazarus Darke conspired to destroy the only evidence that could prove my story.

Without that evidence, I can only tell the truth, and have faith in the law and in justice. Win or lose, I speak with integrity, which is more than my enemies can say. I know that my father, John Jory Jago, looks down upon me with pride. I carry him in my heart, along with all those who have loved and believed in me. *The truth may be stretched thin, but it never breaks, and it always surfaces above lies, as oil floats on water.*

Let the truth prevail. Let justice be done.
Here, by my hand, it is written:

***Red Jago of Kernow, also known as
Miss Rachel Antrobus of Bath
27 April 1741***

CHAPTER SEVENTEEN

Seven of diamonds, influenced by a club:
a communication of importance.

L AZARUS SIGHS AS he closes the book, and turns it over to contemplate the cover:

THE TRUE *and*
ASTONISHING LIFE
of RED JAGO

Rightful Heir to the Fortune of
Her Grandfather, Nicholas De Lacy.

Memoirs are ten a penny, Amelia Fry had said to him at the Seven
Stars. Not this one. The title is worked in gold upon ivory calfskin
inlaid with red hearts and diamonds, black clubs and spades. This is
the collector's edition and it costs a guinea. For that price, the reader
gets diagrams of the various fortunes Red has told, the red playing
cards picked out in vermillion ink. The popular edition can be bought
for twelve shillings from the Mask bookshop and a few other selected
purveyors. It went on sale five days ago, and is said to have sold two
thousand copies in that time.

'She paints us as villains,' Lady Seabrooke says, looking up from
her own edition. 'Me a liar and a cruel mother. You a mercenary who
will stop at nothing to conceal the truth. The mob threw dung at

my carriage yesterday. One of my footmen was almost blinded by an oyster shell.'

'You should have heard the names I was called coming in here today,' Lazarus remarks with a wry grin. 'There is quite a crowd outside your door, I'm sorry to say.'

'The judge won't be swayed by chapbook lies,' Lady Seabrooke says. 'When I have won, I will sue her for slander. She'll end her days in a debtor's prison.'

'Except that we did all the things that she says we did,' Lazarus points out. He places the book upon the table, wincing a little. The pain in his ribs is getting better – except when he makes sudden movements like this – and the doctors tell him his hand will mend, even if it won't ever be quite the same. Yet his guilt about everything that happened in Tretelly is a wound that festers. In the weeks since his return to London, he has tried to justify his actions to himself countless times. If he is a servant to the truth, then it has to be to the whole truth. *Lawfully begotten*, says the codicil – and however else he chooses to describe the night Luna came to his bed, the position of the law is entirely clear.

And yet the truth is, the truth had nothing to do with it. It is fitting, he thinks, that his last service to Lady Seabrooke should have wreaked such havoc upon his conscience, because when was penance ever an exercise in frivolity? His two selves have warred within him ever since his return. Is he the man he was on that clifftop, or the man he always thought himself to be? It is the latter who finds his voice in that moment: 'What if the rest of it is true too? What if she is –' he still can't bring himself to say the word 'our' – 'your child?'

Her look is contemptuous. 'Don't say she has got to you too?'

'I saw her face,' Lazarus says. 'When I threw that memoir into the sea. I think she believes her story, and she thought the proof of it was there in that book.'

Lady Seabrooke considers. 'I suppose it's possible the Montfort boy forged the evidence before his death. He had time to do so in Tretelly, don't you think?'

He is silent. She'll never accept it. He remembers her pale and shivering, lying beneath furs, frail from childbirth, silent in shock. It has taken her seventeen years to mend herself after what she believed John Jory had done that night, and perhaps she is not entirely mended even now. To let other truths uproot all of her certainties would come at too great a cost to herself. In those circumstances, he thinks, I'd do the same.

'Lazarus,' she says, 'don't be weak. Not now. Not you.'

Ultimately, he has already made his choice, and if the destruction of the memoir was a reckoning for his past, then it has also opened a new account in his future. His daughter hates him now. She says it plainly in her book, but he already knew.

There are things he might have told Red, during their long carriage ride back to London. That he'd have given the memoir to the De Lacys in a heartbeat if he'd needed to save her life. That he almost certainly *did* save her life on that clifftop. That she doesn't understand the past, how this was the only way he could make it right. That he is her father.

But none of it would have made a difference. Red is like her mother; she nurses her wrongs like grit in an oyster. The truth might even make her hate him more.

Leopold comes to the door. 'The carriage is here.'

◆

The De Lacys have come to court in force. All of them, even Emily. Dr Crowhurst is sitting in the public gallery too. Red turns to stare at Julius. Is she wondering why the De Lacys haven't given up? Lazarus turns to Lady Seabrooke, feeling afraid for her.

Red's solicitor, Mr Cowell, explains to the judge that his client has parted company with Mr Bagshott, the De Lacys having withdrawn their funding of her legal costs. Her new barrister, a Mr Crispin St Claire, is a Lincoln's Inn man who looks barely old enough to buckle his own shoes. Red might have made enough money from her memoir to pay for a lawyer, but Mr St Claire is a long way from the best. When he informs the court, in outraged tones, about the destruction of Chenoweth's book, he swiftly gets himself into trouble.

'You will know, Your Honour, from Mr Darke's affidavit, that he claims to have dropped the book by accident in the aftermath of an attempt on my client's life. I submit that this is laughable. Mr Darke cannot expect this court to believe that the very piece of evidence that would establish my client's claim was lost by his own hand – except by a deliberate act of perfidy.'

The judge, Sir George Lee, grunts. 'It is not for you to tell this court what it believes, sir.'

The lad flushes, an ugly colour that makes its way down his long white neck. 'You cannot let this piece of wickedness go unpunished.'

The judge looks down at the proctors, one or two of whom nod. He writes something on the parchment in front of him, and then gives Mr St Claire a hard stare. 'Even supposing you are correct, and the volume was deliberately destroyed, we have no way of knowing what it contained. Isn't it right that neither your client, nor Mr Darke, nor Miss De Lacy, had occasion to examine it? The only person who did so was Mr Montfort, and he is dead. So you cannot assert that it would have helped your client's case. And that is, after all, the principal question before this court today.'

'Mr Darke wouldn't have destroyed it had he not believed that it would help my client's case.'

'But we cannot be certain,' the judge says. 'That is the point. It is regrettable that the book was lost, but I am minded to disregard Chenoweth's memoir entirely from my consideration of this matter.'

'Then Your Honour is rewarding the Seabrooke interest for a criminal act.'

'Be careful, Mr St Claire. No wrongdoing has been established. And I assure you, in my courtroom, I can do as I please.'

To the surprise of everyone, except Lazarus Darke and Lady Seabrooke, Julius De Lacy's counsel, Mr Figg, steps into the breach.

'Your Honour, the argument of m'learned friend, Mr St Claire, is not without merit. As you will know from our bill, my clients also have an interest in this matter. We support Mr St Claire's contention that the memoir was destroyed deliberately by Mr Darke, because it provided proof of his client's claim that she is the daughter of Lady

Seabrooke. You will see from the affidavit of Miss Emily De Lacy, who was also a witness to these events, that she supports Miss Jago's version of events entirely.'

The court murmurs. *What bill? What standing do the De Lacys now have in this matter?*

Lazarus steels himself for what is to come. Julius might have failed in his attempt to kill Red, but there is more than one way to take her out of the line of inheritance. From what Red says in her memoir, Lazarus suspects this was Septimus's plan all along – but then he was always a far subtler creature than his brother.

'I have the privilege of drawing Your Honour's attention to *Armory v Delamirie*,' Mr Figg says. 'This was a case heard by the King's Bench nearly twenty years ago. Armory was a chimney-sweep's boy who found a jewelled ring in the course of cleaning a chimney. He took this ring to the shop of Delamirie, a silversmith. An apprentice acting for Delamirie removed the jewel from the setting and returned the ring to Armory, stating that it was worth three halfpence. Armory asked for the jewel back, and was refused. The court found for Armory, and when the jewel in question could not be produced in court, the Chief Justice ruled that the jewel should be presumed to have the maximum value that a jewel of that form could possibly have – under the principle that a wrongdoer should not derive gain from the effects of his wrongdoing.'

Everyone in court strains to catch a glimpse of the wrongdoer in question. Lazarus keeps his face perfectly still.

'I submit that this precedent means that the court should apply a maximum value to this memoir, and presume that it would indeed have provided proof of Miss Jago's claim.'

Mr Rich, acting for the Earl of Seabrooke, immediately jumps to his feet, raising a number of strenuous objections to the point of law. The argument rages for three more days. Yet by the end of it, Lazarus can see that the judge has been swayed. Sir George retires to confer with the proctors for half an hour.

'Mr Figg makes a powerful argument,' he says, when he returns. 'I will give it due consideration.' He nods to the recorder, who scribbles in his book.

'Returning to the question of Miss Jago's deposition,' the judge says. 'There being no further witnesses listed in my papers either in support or refutation of her claim, I propose that we move on to your bill, Mr Figg. I believe, in this matter, you act on behalf of Miss Emily De Lacy, her father standing as her *prochein ami*?'

'That's right, Your Honour.'

The judge makes a note. Here it comes, Lazarus thinks.

'Sir,' Figg says, 'although my client is content to accept without dispute that Miss Jago is the daughter of Lady Seabrooke, born shortly after her marriage to John Jory Jago, we do not accept that he was the father of that child.'

The court erupts, and the judge has to call for order several times. Red stares at Lady Seabrooke. Julius smiles.

'I submit that Miss Jago is the child of Lazarus Darke.'

CHAPTER EIGHTEEN

*Nine of clubs as master-card: the need of much decision in
our own judgements in an affair of importance;
a need of disregarding counsels of others.*

RED TELLS HERSELF that it's just another De Lacy trick. She
sits there, listening in appalled silence, as Mr Figg declares the
De Lacys' intention to have her declared illegitimate by the court,
and by Act of Parliament, leaving the way clear for Emily to inherit.

While he is talking, Red remembers how Darke had spoken with
feeling of Lady Seabrooke at the fair. She remembers the star chart
and the argument overheard by the stable boy at the Seven Stars.
Most of all, she remembers the way Darke had looked at her on the
clifftop. Is it possible that Figg is telling the truth?

The journalists are scribbling frantically. Lady Seabrooke leans in
to murmur something to her son, Leopold, who stares at his shoes.

The judge calls for order again. 'I will allow it, Mr Figg. But I
remind you that Lady Seabrooke is a dowager countess. I will take a
dim view of any questions that overstep the mark.'

Mr St Claire leans back from his table. 'Do you know anything
about this?' he asks.

Red shakes her head, adopting a tone of conviction. 'They're lying.
They have to be. Why would my father have raised me for all those
years if he'd thought I was another man's child?'

Mr Figg's first witness is sworn in. Arabia is wearing black, her face more pinched than when Red had seen her last. For all her faults, and they are legion, Arabia had adored her son.

The judge offers his condolences on her loss, and Arabia tells him how grateful she is for his kindness. Red swears he blushes.

'Mrs De Lacy,' Figg says, 'during the time Lazarus Darke was employed by Nicholas De Lacy as his secretary, you lived on the Leighfindell estate, is that right?'

'Yes, sir. At that time I was married to my first husband, Mr George Montfort. He was Mr De Lacy's land steward.'

'Did you have much to do with Mr Darke?'

'He and my husband worked together. Sometimes he would dine at our house on the estate.'

'And did you have much to do with Lady Seabrooke – Patience De Lacy, as she was then?'

'I saw the daughters often around the estate. Sometimes they would stop and talk to me on their walks. But in the autumn of 1721, I saw rather more of them.'

'Why was that?'

'Their governess had to leave rather abruptly, and it took their father some weeks to find a new one to his satisfaction. During that period, he asked me if I would spend time with the girls, so they were not lacking in older female company.'

'Did you witness any sort of attachment between Lady Seabrooke and Mr Darke during that autumn?'

'They were certainly close. Patience was a great reader, and Mr Darke is a learned man. They would talk about their books or some political matter in the newspapers. Patience admired him, I think, and anyone could see that he was in love with her. I told my husband no good would come of it, but he only said that I should watch them and say nothing.'

'Why was that?'

'He and Darke were rivals for Mr De Lacy's favour. Nicholas knew of their mutual distrust – indeed, I think he rather encouraged it – and my husband didn't want to denounce Mr Darke without firm evidence of impropriety.'

'Did you ever see Mr Darke behave improperly towards Miss De Lacy?'

'Not as such. But one day, when I was out walking in the woods, Mr Darke and Miss De Lacy came out of the trees ahead of me, laughing. They stopped when they noticed me, and Patience said that she'd been out looking for her lapdog. Mr Darke added that he had encountered her by chance in the woods and offered her assistance.'

Lady Seabrooke is murmuring to her lawyer and when Mr Figg sits down, Mr Rich rises to cross-examine.

'Did Lady Seabrooke have her lapdog with her when you met her in the woods?'

'Yes,' Arabia says, 'I believe she did.'

'Then I submit that she told you the truth. That Lady Seabrooke encountered Mr Darke quite by chance.'

'All I can tell you, is that there was an air about them,' Arabia says. 'It made me think that they were up to something in those woods.'

'An air.' Mr Rich gives her the full penetrative weight of his stare. 'It seems very convenient that this story should arise now, at this crucial juncture. You and your husband depend upon his brother for most of your income, is that right? The loss of his estate would cause you much personal detriment.'

'I am motivated only by a desire to see justice done,' Arabia says primly. 'As are we all, I would hope.'

'Quite so, Mrs De Lacy,' the judge says.

Mr St Claire has no questions for Arabia. Red has no evidence to counter any of this. To her dismay, Rosie is the next witness to be sworn in.

The judge explains the proceedings to her as if she is a halfwit. Rosie answers him rather crisply. 'I understand, sir.'

'Miss Denham,' the De Lacy counsel says, 'you were lady's maid to Patience De Lacy during the years she spent at Leighfindell, is that right?'

Rosie glances at Lady Seabrooke and gives her a tentative smile. Lady Seabrooke stares back, stony-faced. 'Yes, sir.'

'Did you ever witness her in the company of Lazarus Darke?'

'Yes, sir, I did. I often sat with them while she asked him about her books and other matters.'

'Did you think that an attachment existed between them?'

Rosie pauses. 'I suppose I did. They had a way of looking at one another. But I always thought it was harmless. I felt Mr Darke was an honourable man. He always behaved perfectly properly towards her. And it wasn't as if it could ever come to anything. Her father had grand plans for her marriage.'

'Did anyone else ever talk to you about them?'

Again she pauses. 'My friend Etta, Jemima's maid. She said Jemima had told her that Patience had said that if she was free to marry anyone, she'd choose Mr Darke.'

Red looks over at Lazarus, sees a muscle working in his face. The space between him and Lady Seabrooke seems both minuscule and vast.

Her barrister rises. 'This is hearsay, Your Honour, and m'learned friend knows it.'

Sir George nods. 'I will certainly disregard the tattle of maids. Stick to what you witnessed with your own eyes, girl, if you please. Mr Figg, you should know better than that.'

Mr Figg inclines his head. 'Forgive me, Your Honour. Can you tell me what happened at Leighfindell after the death of Jemima De Lacy?'

'Mr Darke left for London not long after. Patience was distraught. About her sister, of course, but I also thought she was upset about Mr Darke leaving. It was my impression that he had left Leighfindell in order to stay away from her. I believe it broke her heart. Etta and I talked about it and we decided it was for the best. But we felt sorry for her, and she was not someone who easily inspired pity.'

'What did you think when you discovered that she'd eloped with John Jory Jago so soon afterwards?'

'I was shocked,' Rosie says.

'And why was that?'

'I'd never witnessed any affection between them, though the servants used to say he had a great fancy for her. I presumed that she'd done it to get back at Mr Darke – and her parents too. She blamed them for Jemima's death, and I think she couldn't bear to be at Leigh-findell any longer. Sometimes young girls do unpredictable things with a broken heart. Perhaps she looked to John Jory as someone who could put her back together?'

'Did you know that Patience De Lacy, or Patience Jago, as I suppose we must refer to her then, gave birth to a baby daughter in the October of 1723?'

Rosie swallows. 'I didn't know it then, sir, but I do know it now.'

'When did Lazarus Darke leave Leighfindell?'

'It must have been around the beginning of March.'

'The beginning of March,' Figg repeats, placing great emphasis on these words.

'You're implying something I didn't say,' Rosie cries. 'I never saw anything of that nature between Patience and Mr Darke. He treated her with great respect and courtesy.'

'Be quiet,' the judge says. 'Answer only the questions that are put to you. Mr Figg, do you have any more questions for this witness?'

'No, sir, I do not.'

In his cross-examination, Mr Rich merely has Rosie repeat her belief in Mr Darke's propriety and Patience De Lacy's virtue. When he sits back down, the judge looks at Mr St Claire, who shakes his head again.

'Finally,' Figg says, once Rosie has been dismissed, 'I call Dr Simon Crowhurst to testify.'

Red watches the doctor walk towards the bench, her eyes narrowed. The light catches the scar on his cheek. Mr Figg begins with a long preamble about the doctor's qualifications and his respectability.

'I believe you were also resident on the Leighfindell estate during the time that Mr Darke was employed there?'

'That's right,' the doctor says.

'Did you witness Mr Darke in the company of Patience De Lacy?'

'On many occasions.'

'Would you say that they were close?'

'Yes, she would flirt with him. That was not so very unusual.

Patience liked to flirt with men to gauge their reactions – even with me.'

Around Red, people murmur. The journalists scribble.

'With Mr Darke, I sensed it was different,' the doctor says. 'Once I came across them in the library, talking to one another, and I felt that they were too close for propriety. When they noticed me, they immediately sprang apart.'

'Did you mention this incident to your employer?'

'I did not. I liked Darke. He was intelligent company, which was often lacking at Leighfindell. Nor did I wish to see him punished or dismissed. But I did have a word with him. I don't remember what I said. Something awkward about forbidden fruit, I expect.'

'And did Mr Darke listen?'

The doctor hesitates a moment. 'I fear he did not.'

'What makes you say that?'

'Something that occurred shortly before Miss Jemima died. I was treating her for a depression of the spirits, a malady that overcame her after a disappointment of the heart. Jemima had grown rather violent in protestation at her treatment, and an incident had occurred a few nights before.' The doctor traces the length of his scar with his finger-tip. 'She asked for her maid, Etta, but because of what had happened, Nicholas De Lacy had ordered that only I should attend to her. For the safety of the maid, you understand. I told Jemima this, and that's when she asked me to take a message to her sister.'

For the first time, Lady Seabrooke turns to study the doctor.

'What did this message say?' Mr Figg asks.

'She wanted me to tell Patience that she should run away with Mr Darke and never come back. Of course, I intended to do nothing of the kind. But I did ask Jemima about her sister and Mr Darke – because of my own concerns in that regard. Jemima said that her father must not be permitted to destroy their love, as he'd destroyed her own with Little Piers Radclyffe. I asked how she knew that they were in love, and she said that she had seen her sister leaving Mr Darke's room early one morning.'

Amidst the murmuring, Mr Rich rises to his feet. 'Hearsay again, Your Honour.'

'I will allow it,' the judge said. 'The doctor is a gentleman of standing, and we can safely presume that Jemima De Lacy did say those words to him. Whether or not she was telling the truth is another matter.'

Red leans over and grabs Mr St Claire's notebook and quill from his hand, gesturing for the inkwell. At last, she has an answer to this. She scribbles furiously, trying not to think about that chink of light upon the secret staircase at Leighfindell. It looks directly onto the corridor where the upper servants have their bedrooms, and she knows Jemima was familiar with that staircase too. Instead, she thinks about that note pinned to the closet door in the private chapel: *Don't trust Dr Crowhurst. He called me a liar.*

'Did you give any credence to this story?' Figg asks.

'I had no reason to doubt it,' the doctor says. 'Jemima's emotions were often overwrought. She fluctuated between mania and periods of sullen silence. Sometimes she behaved inappropriately, which was entirely out of her previous character. But she was never delusional. Nor was she malicious. She seemed to be acting out of concern for her sister, however misplaced.'

'Did you say anything to Nicholas De Lacy about what she told you?'

'No, I did not.'

'Why not, given you've just said that you believed it to be true?'

The doctor sighs. 'Only a few months previously, I had shared a piece of information obtained in not dissimilar circumstances, with tragic results. I blamed myself for what had happened, and I was determined not to repeat the mistake. Perhaps I was wrong to hold my tongue. I will never know.'

'Thank you, Doctor. I have no more questions.'

The judge seems impressed by the doctor's testimony and sits for a long time making notes. When he looks up, he nods at Lady Seabrooke's counsel.

Mr Rich rises with a flourish of his silk robe. 'Your Honour, we do have questions for this witness, but we have had no time to consult our own medical authorities about the state of Jemima De Lacy's mind. That being so, we beg for an adjournment.'

'I see no harm in that,' the judge says. 'If all are content?'

Red leans over to put her paper into Mr St Claire's hands. He reads it through, and then gazes at her with a look of puzzlement.

'Just ask him these questions,' Red says.

'Mr St Claire? I don't have all day,' the judge says.

'Your Honour,' St Claire says, squinting at the paper. 'I beg the court's leave to cross-examine this witness before we adjourn.'

The judge pulls out his watch and sighs. 'Very well.'

St Claire turns to the doctor. 'You've said Jemima De Lacy was not delusional, which I accept without dispute. But did you ever accuse your patient of lying?'

He frowns. 'Not to my recall. She was a sweet girl, quite without guile.'

St Claire looks down at Red's paper again. 'You spoke of another incident just now, one where you had told the truth and it ended in tragedy. What was that?'

Dr Crowhurst looks at the judge. 'I don't see the relevance, Your Honour.'

Mr St Claire responds: 'I ask Your Honour's indulgence. We believe there may be a connection between that event and the incident this witness has just described.'

'I will allow it,' Sir George says. 'But my patience is not infinite, Mr St Claire.'

The barrister inclines his head. 'Please answer the question, sir.'

The doctor frowns. 'Very well, though I wish it to be noted that I do not speak of my own volition. I have no wish to cause undue distress to the De Lacy family.'

'Your position is noted,' the judge replies.

'You are correct in thinking that the incident bears a connection to Jemima De Lacy,' the doctor says. 'She had been in my care for some months with her mental affliction, but I was also growing increasingly concerned for her physical health. She was often running a fever, and

I therefore undertook to give her a physical examination.' He clears his throat. 'In the course of that examination, I discovered that she was suffering from gonorrhoea, more commonly known as the clap.'

Lady Seabrooke emits an audible gasp, and puts a hand to her face.

'Her condition may have exacerbated her malady of the mind,' the doctor goes on. 'I treated her with mercury, also with arsenic, and I debated long and hard about what to say to her father. The De Lacys had taken their daughter's illness very hard, and I had no desire to compound their distress. On the other hand, I felt a responsibility to act. In the end, I shared my concerns with Virgil De Lacy, Jemima's twin brother. He shared my belief that the guilty party was the man she had wished to marry, Little Piers Radclyffe.'

'And Virgil challenged Mr Radclyffe to a duel?' Mr St Claire says.

'To my enduring regret. I knew nothing of it, until a footman banged on my door early one morning. He told me the news, and I grabbed my bag and hurried down to the lake. We crossed by boat to the island, where I found Virgil dying of a gunshot wound. You can understand why I felt the responsibility was mine. Which was why I held my tongue when Jemima told me about her sister and Mr Darke.'

Red has always known that there was more to the duel than she'd been told. And it seems, to Jemima's tragic tale too. The truth was ever a slippery thing at Leighfindell. Now she has a terrible feeling she knows what it is.

She scribbles more questions, while Mr St Claire plays for time. When she leans over to give him the paper, she earns herself a reprimand from the judge.

'Did Mr Radclyffe say anything to you at the scene of the duel?' her barrister asks the doctor.

'Yes. He said he had never touched Jemima.'

'Did you believe him?'

'No, I thought he was lying.'

Mr St Claire looks down at the paper again, and then looks at Red doubtfully. She gives him a hard stare. *Ask the question.*

'Did you ever treat Mr Radclyffe for gonorrhoea?'

'No, I did not. But he'd spent much time in London and Oxford, and could have easily sought treatment there.'

'Did you ever treat anyone else at Leighfindell for that disease?'

'Yes, naturally. There are many young men on the estate. They visit the brothels in Okehampton and doubtless women nearer to home. Sometimes the clap can be successfully treated, sometimes not. Sometimes it appears to have been treated, only to return some years later. Such are the vagaries of Venus, I am afraid.'

'Did you ever treat any gentlemen at the house for that disease?'

Over on the De Lacy benches, Red observes a ripple of unease. The doctor looks to the judge. 'Sir, it would not be proper—'

'I'm asking in the most general terms,' Mr St Claire says.

The judge nods, and the doctor clears his throat again, looking increasingly uncomfortable. 'Yes, from time to time I have treated gentlemen on the estate for that condition.'

Mirabel is wearing the same flinching expression she'd worn in church. Red remembers her cards: the error and the lie. The error, she now feels sure, was Doctor Crowhurst's. But the lie was Mirabel's own, one that had governed her existence ever since. *Nonny only believes what she wants to believe.*

'Did you ever ask Jemima De Lacy who had given her that loathsome disease?' Mr St Claire asks.

The doctor pauses for a long time. 'Yes, I did.'

'Did she tell you that it was Mr Radclyffe?'

'No,' the doctor says. 'She named another man.'

The courtroom is perfectly silent, as if the crowd senses that they are about to hear something of great significance.

'Why, then, if she named another man, did you tell Virgil that you thought the guilty party was Mr Radclyffe?'

The doctor seems to be having difficulty breathing, and adjusts his cravat. 'It would have been natural for Jemima to want to protect Mr Radclyffe. She was in love with him.'

St Claire's tone is sharp. 'You thought she was lying?'

'No.' The doctor sighs. 'I believe she must have been confused. She blamed the person in question for many of her problems. I believe that's what she must have meant. That this man was at fault in a general sense. Not the particular sense. She couldn't have meant that he had given her the disease.'

Mr St Claire smiles. 'Then couldn't she have been equally confused when she told you about her sister and Lazarus Darke?'

The doctor seizes upon the change in subject eagerly. 'Yes, I suppose so. I didn't think so at the time, but you could be right.'

Red studies the doctor. This shabby, compromised man. Lady Seabrooke stares at him too, her hand over her mouth, looking as if she might vomit. Lazarus Darke looks from her to the doctor. Leopold frowns, looking confused.

Mr St Claire draws a breath. 'Will you tell the court who it was that Jemima said was responsible for her condition?'

'No,' Mirabel cries, rising to her feet. 'My daughter was mad. A liar. No credence whatsoever should be given to any of her claims.'

Mr St Claire turns back to the judge, raising his eyebrows. 'We should like to add Mrs Mirabel De Lacy to our list of witnesses, Your Honour.'

'I daresay you would.' The judge studies Dr Crowhurst with interest. 'Well? Answer the question, sir.'

But another voice rings out in the courtroom, clear, cold and precise. 'I ask the court's leave that I be heard.'

The judge glances at Lady Seabrooke, looking irritated by the interruption. 'You will have an opportunity to rebut these allegations in due course, My Lady,' he says.

'No,' she says. 'I wish to withdraw my suit.'

Everyone stares at one another in astonishment. Red is as confused as everyone else – until she meets the gaze of Lazarus and reads the agony in his eyes. As realization crashes in, an acid spike of sickness rises in her throat.

Lady Seabrooke presses on. 'Miss Jago is my daughter. I have been fighting the knowledge, but I find I can do so no longer. These desperate claims from my family about Mr Darke are preposterous. There was only one man I ever loved: my late husband, the Earl of Seabrooke. Yet for a time, I believed that I was in love with John Jory

Jago, and our marriage, however unwise, was legally made. Which makes Miss Jago the heir of my body, lawfully begotten, and the rightful heir to my father's fortune.'

Red can think of only one reason why she would be doing this now. Only one reason why she'd be prepared to give up everything, rather than have that question answered in court, in front of her son. She thinks of old Mr Radclyffe's words when she'd told him she was the child of Patience De Lacy and John Jory Jago. *Such a monstrous thing. I didn't know.* Then on their second meeting at Leighfindell: *You should be dead.*

Lady Seabrooke meets Red's gaze, and the message written on her face is stark. *You have what you want. My words are the price of your silence.*

Blood throbbing at her temples, Red catches Mr St Claire's eye and shakes her head.

'I withdraw the question, Your Honour.' The barrister sits back down.

Red recalls Lazarus Darke's testimony in court. How the first thing Nicholas De Lacy had done when he'd learned his daughter was with child, was to change his will. How he'd called that child 'a new beginning'. Not John Jory's child. Not Lazarus Darke's. But the child he'd believed to be his own, begotten upon his own daughter.

'You're going to win,' St Claire whispers to her excitedly.

Yet in that moment, all Red can do is stare at Lady Seabrooke, consumed by a deep abiding horror at what she's just learned.

Chapter Nineteen

Five of hearts, influenced by a spade:
an ache, pain, or breaking.

I T ALL SEEMS so clear to Lazarus now. That piece of Luna that he never quite understood. Her changing selves. Her hatred of her father, of her mother. *Run away with me, somewhere far from here where my father can never find us.*

How had he been so blind? Or had he just not wanted to see? Like Mirabel, had he averted his eyes from the horror? Or was this lie so big and so monstrous, it had consumed them all?

He thinks of that day in the library. *When powerful men die, their lies still endure.* As they endure now.

It is three days since Lady Seabrooke withdrew her suit. She had risen from her seat and walked from the courtroom, followed by her footmen and her confused son. Lazarus had caught up with her by her carriage.

'Luna, wait.'

She turns, but he has no words. Only the knowledge of quite how much he has failed her.

'Why did you come back?' she says.

'To put things right.' He is aware of how foolish and inadequate those words sound now.

'Impossible dreams,' she says. 'They were always my curse. Not yours.'

Then she climbs into the carriage, and the footman ushers him away as he closes the door.

Like a fool, wanting to give her time alone with her son, he had waited a day before calling at Seabrooke House. He had found it all locked up. 'Fled in the night,' a passing coalman tells him. 'To escape her creditors.'

Over the next few months, Lazarus follows the case in the Prerogative Court in the newspapers. Having failed in their attempt to have Red ruled illegitimate, the De Lacys have few enough options left. The judge is satisfied by a new affidavit from Lady Seabrooke, dispatched before she left town, and he rules that Red is the rightful heir to her grandfather's fortune. The newspapers report that you wouldn't know from the young heir's pensive expression when the judge made this ruling, that she was now the richest woman in the kingdom.

The De Lacys appeal to the High Court, claiming that Sir George erred in his original ruling that the codicil was genuine. When they lose that appeal, Julius sues in the Court of the King's Bench for breach of the contract he signed with Red, arguing that he is owed ten thousand pounds. Red's barristers argue, quite reasonably, that Julius broke the terms of that contract when he withdrew his funding of her legal costs, and once again, the court rules against him.

On the sixteenth of September 1742, the newspapers report that a body pulled from the River Thames is that of the impoverished financier, Julius De Lacy. Nobody saw him jump, but the coroner rules his death a suicide. Under the terms of her husband's original will, Mirabel was left an annuity of two thousand pounds a year, a provision unaffected by the codicil. The De Lacys retreat to a small manor in the countryside, but when Mirabel dies of the smallpox that winter – her annuity dying with her – the family are evicted. Lady Frances throws herself upon the mercy of her brother, the Earl of Macclesfield, who gives her and her daughter use of the Dower House on his estate. Having lost his rectorship at Slaughterbridge – a position in the gift of the owner of Leighfindell – Septimus is forced to take up an ill-paid living in Gloucestershire, where his brimstone sermons achieve some local renown.

The scandal caused by Red's memoir prompts many awkward questions in Parliament about Julius's plan to buy Brinseley Radclyffe back his dukedom, and both Mr Walpole and the palace refute that any such arrangement was ever made. It seems Brinseley will go to his grave as plain Mr Radclyffe. Nobody is surprised when he breaks his engagement with Emily, and for a time the name 'Radclyffe' becomes synonymous with a cad.

As for Red, she simply disappears. The newspapers become obsessed with her whereabouts, but the trustees of her estate are tight-lipped, saying only that she prefers to live quietly in the countryside until her majority. Leighfindell is sold, together with De Lacy House and the property in St James's once occupied by Septimus and his family. Sometimes there is a story about Red in the newspapers: that she has appeared at a ball in Hertfordshire, or become engaged to a gentleman of Exeter, but other reports dismiss these stories as unfounded rumours.

Still Lazarus wonders. Just because Nicholas De Lacy believed her to be his child, it doesn't mean she was. He wants to offer Red that comfort – he thinks constantly about her anguished face in court. He tries to arrange a private audience, but the trustees refuse his request. He writes her letters, but receives no reply.

Yet over the course of the next year, he catches little glimpses of her work. Not long after Julius's death, Morgan Trevithick calls upon Lazarus at his lodgings. 'Have you seen her? Red? I need someone to tell her to stop.'

Slowly, Lazarus gets the story out of him. Trevithick's biggest rival amongst the companies of players has a new and significant investor. Bolstered by these funds, his rival has been stealing his best players. Roland has been poached, along with Frank and many others, the Cornish Players reduced to a rump, playing village fairs.

'I'm sorry,' Lazarus tells Trevithick. 'I haven't seen her.'

In January, he happens to read an article in the newspaper, and makes his way down to the deadhouse in Thames Street. The beadle on duty shows him the bodies. A large man with a black beard, and a smaller fellow with a white face, pitted with the smallpox. They'd been found together, their throats cut, near Cotton House Quays.

'Who are they?' Lazarus asks.

'Local villains,' the man says. 'The big one with the beard is named Benjamin Kind. The little cur is Simpson. I suppose they must have picked a fight with somebody better.'

Lazarus supposes they did, and it sets him wondering about the supposed suicide of Julius De Lacy.

By now, he is working again in the insurance trade – for a different company, no less exacting in their demands. In the May of 1743, he has cause to visit Bath upon business. It is a dull matter: a claimant in town for the season had a carriage accident upon the road. His masters suspect the damage is not quite so great as has been alleged.

Whilst he is there, chivalry demands that he call upon Araminta Davenport. To his surprise, given her eminent position in Bath society, he finds her house rented out for the season. His inquiries at the Baths soon provide him with the tale. It seems that certain letters of Mrs Davenport's, gossiping about the great and the good, had somehow found their way into the hands of Mr Nash. Indeed, Lazarus is told, Mr Nash himself featured in her letters, and is said to be furious. Banished to Tonbridge, Mrs Davenport is said to be licking her wounds, and nobody can say when she might return.

In the course of his work in Bath, Lazarus visits a solicitor in the High Street, making inquiries about the company who undertook the carriage repairs. Mr Alexander Bigham, attorney-at-law, has lately acquired the practice after the respective death and bankruptcy of the two senior partners. A local man, eager to make connections in London, he happily provides Lazarus with all the answers he seeks.

It is whilst he is there, that Lazarus notices an advertisement for an auction upon Bigham's desk: the sale of a property on Trim Street. 'I knew the former owner,' he tells Bigham. 'Robert Antrobus. Henry is selling up?'

Bigham sighs. 'A sad matter. That family truly is beset by tragedy.'

It transpires that Henry too has lately been declared bankrupt.

'It is doubly unfortunate,' Bigham says, 'because he believed he was on to a sure thing. A colony established in the southern Americas. The returns were extraordinary at first. So much so, he mortgaged the house and borrowed more to purchase new stock. Then it turned out that the colony didn't even exist. He wasn't the only one to lose everything. Mr Edwards, who was once the senior partner here, lost all his money investing in the same stock.'

Like grit in an oyster. Lazarus imagines these incidents linked like a string of pearls, each one polished to a glorious shine.

'Is it possible to see the house?' he asks. 'I have a client who might be interested.'

He's not even sure why he wants to. Perhaps because nothing else connects him to Lady Seabrooke except this affair. He thinks of her every day. She is a void in his soul, an ache in his heart.

Mr Bigham gives him the key, and Lazarus walks down to Trim Street. He wanders through the empty rooms, each one bathed in a golden glow. To Red, he imagines, this house was a symbol of everything she had lost.

In the room that had once been Antrobus's study, a brighter glint of gold catches his eye. He bends down, and tries to extract something stuck between two floorboards, but he can't get it out. Eventually, with the aid of his quill knife, he succeeds. A golden heart. He slips it into his pocket.

Despondent in mood, he returns the key to Mr Bigham, and walks along the High Street. He passes a haberdashery named Illingworth's, the name of Red's mythical friend in London, and he hopes her money has made her happy, for all it has cost. As he passes Mr Moss's cakeshop, his stomach growls noisily. He goes inside and buys a local specialty, a saffron-and-brandy cake. As he is leaving, another customer greets the serving-woman with a friendly smile. 'Good morning, Mrs Kilderbee,' he says.

Lazarus turns, remembering all those letters he wrote to the medical schools, inquiring about Dr Kilderbee, whom Red had claimed had treated her father in Tretelly.

He leaves the shop, still thinking, and then turns, and strides back down the High Street. When he reaches Mr Bigham's legal practice, he almost runs up the stairs.

'What is it?' Bigham says, looking slightly alarmed by Lazarus's flustered appearance. 'Did you forget something?'

'The partner here,' Lazarus says. 'Not Mr Edwards, the one who died. What was his name?'

'Solomon Sandbach,' Bigham says. 'Why do you ask?'

Mrs Sandbach from the orphanage and her assistant, Edward. Dear God, he thinks. She was lying all along.

CHAPTER TWENTY

Nine of spades, influenced by a club: a secret told.

LAZARUS REVISES HIS plans and remains in Bath for three more days. He attends the auction for the sale of the property on Trim Street. It is a fine house, and competition is fierce, but a small, dark man in a purple suit is determined to see off all bidders. Lazarus is told he is an agent down from London. When he approaches the man, inquiring about the identity of his client, he is unforthcoming – and when Lazarus presses, grows decidedly rude.

Lazarus refuses to be discouraged, and talks to a connection in one of the Bath insurance companies. He discovers that ownership of the property in Trim Street has been transferred to an obscure legal entity named the Marcella Company. The address given for this company is in Duke Street, London, a set of rooms owned by a gentleman named Abraham Smollett. Lazarus calls on Mr Smollett, but finds nobody at the address. The neighbours seem surprised to learn that someone has been living there. He leaves Mr Smollett a letter, but receives no reply.

Guessing that the Marcella Company is underpinned by a common-law trust, Lazarus visits the Court of Chancery and, by liberal use of his coin, obtains the relevant declaration. He discovers that the Marcella Company is owned by an equally obscure entity named the Sancho Company. He digs through records, burrows in archives, and bribes a great many clerks, following a long chain of companies through solicitors' offices and the courts. He compiles lists of trustees, none of whom are known to him, and when he calls on them, all refuse to talk to him. Eventually, after several months of dogged work, he strikes lucky. He is at the Court of Chancery, looking into the declaration of yet another trust, the Mancha Company. The overworked clerk lets him look through the record, and Lazarus finds a misplaced document: a copy of a land deed filed with the Middlesex Registry.

When he calls at the relevant office, he discovers that the land in question is a hundred and fifty acres of woodland and pastureland in the Elthorne Hundred, not far from Harrow-on-the-Hill. Lazarus hires a carriage and a driver, and travels out there. When they reach the spot, he jumps down from the carriage, and climbs a stile in the fence to look out over the woods and fields. In the distance, he can see a red-brick manor house of Queen Anne's time. He waylays a passing labourer with a rake over his shoulder, and asks him if he knows the owner of this land.

'You looking for old Gerrity?' the fellow asks. 'He up and died six month ago. Everything's been bought by the folk up at Holly House.' He points at the red-brick manor.

Lazarus has his driver take him there. They find the gate locked and the porter says the family are not receiving visitors, but when Lazarus gives his name, insisting that it be conveyed, the man strangely lets him in without further argument. His carriage proceeds down a gravel drive, lined with well-tended topiary trees, to a carriage circle in front of the house.

The front door is opened by a young woman in a floral-patterned gown. It takes him a moment to recognize her.

'Mrs Jennings,' he exclaims in surprise, and now he knows he is in the right place.

Letitia Jennings gives him a cool, assessing glance. 'My husband is land steward here now. I am the under-housekeeper. She said I was to let you in when you came.'

Leaving him in no doubt that she is acting under orders, rather than her own pleasure, she shows him into a large drawing room with paintings of flowers and herbs on the walls. He has been sitting there, sipping tea, for about five minutes, when Red walks into the room.

'Mr Darke,' she says. 'It has been some time.'

He bows, studying her curiously. She is elegantly attired in a gown sewn with sparkling crystals, the only trace of Leighfindell he has noticed here.

'I am glad to find you looking so well.' He reaches into his pocket to retrieve the golden heart. 'I came to bring you this. I found it when I visited your old house at Trim Street.'

As she takes it from him, he sees her struggle to hide her emotion. 'Thank you. I am truly glad to have it back.'

They sit in a pair of comfortable chairs before the fireplace. A breeze from an open window riffles the pages of a newspaper and disturbs an arrangement of playing cards on the table.

'I heard about Henry's misfortunes,' Lazarus says.

A smile plays around her lips. 'It seems his luck abandoned him.'

'And Mr Edwards too. Did you hear that his senior partner had died, and the practice had to be sold? Old Mr Sandbach?'

To drink from the Grail, a knight must first prove his worth. And it seems he has, because after a long moment, she meets his gaze. 'I wasn't quite ready for you that day at the fair. Or I might have come up with better answers.'

'Chenoweth's memoir must have come as quite a shock,' he says. 'All your other plans were so carefully laid.'

'I had a lot of time,' she says, 'when Mr Antrobus was dying. I needed a design for my future and this was it.'

'That memoir contained no proof,' Lazarus says. 'Only an absence. Of any visit made by John Jory Jago and his daughter to the Seven Stars in 1730.'

Red's smile cleaves her face. 'And you destroyed it.'

'I'm not here to cause you trouble,' he says. 'I just need to know. About what happened at Leighfindell. Not while you were there. I mean before.'

She nods soberly. 'I don't know when it started with Jemima. My fear is that it began when she was very young. Her father used to take her to the Hermitage. I imagine that's why she chose to kill herself there.'

'It was after she lost her mind, that he started going walking with

Luna,' Lazarus says. 'She changed after that. I thought it was because of Jemima.'

Red nods. 'She never knew whose child it was. It might have been yours. It is important that you know that. She wasn't trying to trick you when she came to your bed, like she did with John Jory.'

Lazarus closes his eyes. 'She wanted to run away with me. I thought she'd be ruining her life. Why didn't she tell me?'

Red gives him the sort of look that a woman gives a man when he's asked a stupid question. 'She felt disgust at herself, ashamed. The last person in the world she wanted to know was you. Then you left her, and she only had one other place to turn.'

Lazarus's voice is thick. 'Jago was more of a man than I ever was.'

'Let's not canonize him,' Red says. 'Luna was half his age. He desired her and he didn't think twice to take what was offered. Luna thought that when her father discovered that she was with child, he would lock her up, like he did with Jemima. She'd be disgraced, not allowed to marry, imprisoned there with him until the end of his days. She didn't love John Jory, but a life on the road with him was better than the alternative. Unfortunately, John Jory was a man with dark impulses beneath his smiles. And he didn't take it kindly when he discovered he'd been played for a fool.'

Lazarus wants to ask how she knows all this, but Red keeps talking. 'She told him the child had come early, that it was a miracle, but John Jory wasn't taken in a second time. When he confronted her, she was caught between two truths. The truth concerning you, and the truth concerning her father. She decided that the latter would be more palatable to him, but as it turned out, she was wrong. Men like John Jory believe that infants born of incest are cursed. In the villages, they are often drowned or strangled at birth. He wanted to punish her, I suppose. He was bitter, enraged, drunk. So he jumped to his death with that baby girl in his arms.'

'Mirabel knew?' Lazarus remembers her intervention in the courtroom. 'I can't comprehend it.'

'About Jemima? I think she knew and didn't know. I think all of them did. Dr Crowhurst certainly did, and I think that Septimus guessed. Maybe Julius too. We cannot be too hard on Mirabel. What could she have done if she had admitted the truth to herself? Her husband would have denied it and at Leighfindell he was the law. When a man is powerful and evil, other people surround themselves with lies, until they're not sure if they're protecting him or protecting themselves.'

'Still, she should have done something,' Lazarus says.

Red nods. 'Yes, she should.'

To his surprise, he sees guilt on her own face too. 'I didn't know all this at the start,' she says. 'Later, I had suspicions about Jemima, but I didn't put it all together until Dr Crowhurst testified in court.'

'Are you saying you wouldn't have gone through with it, if you had known? About Lady Seabrooke, I mean.'

She thinks. 'I would have done it differently.'

Lazarus is silent a moment, his feelings overwhelming. 'How did you conceive all of this?' he asks eventually, unable to keep the wonder from his tone. There are so many things that don't quite make sense to him even now. 'Who even are you, if not a De Lacy?'

'Not a De Lacy?' she says. 'Oh, I'm afraid you're quite wrong there. A De Lacy is the one thing I always was.'

CHAPTER TWENTY-ONE

Ten of clubs as master-card:
success in a matter long pursued.

RED TELLS HER story simply, in the same clear voice she'd used in court.

'I grew up in an orphanage in the city of Exeter,' she says. 'It was not a benevolent place. The owner was a woman of temper, not unlike Mrs Sandbach in my story. The children were a rough breed, many of them raised on the streets. There I learned how to pick a pocket and a lock, how to open and forge a letter, how to fight and how to survive. For the first seven years of my life, I was perfectly wicked.

'I never knew who my parents were. I was left at the orphanage with that golden heart charm, and a note from my mother saying that it had belonged to my father. Not long after my seventh birthday, I was called to the office of the owner. That was the first time I laid eyes on Robert Antrobus. I was told that he was taking me to live in Bath, and just like that, my existence was transformed. In that house in Trim Street, I found love and kindness, and yet I never stopped wondering who my parents really were. I always suspected that Mr Antrobus knew the truth. I believed he had come to the orphanage specifically for me, that I had some special significance to him. I listened at doors, and I became convinced that the answers might lie in a portmanteau stored under Mrs Fremantle's bed.'

She smiles. 'The next part of my memoir was mostly true. I looked in the portmanteau, and I divined that I had a connection with the

De Lacys. I heard about Lady Seabrooke's elopement with John Jory Jago, and the rumours of a child, and I came to believe that *I* was that child. It was only when I found the codicil that I was disabused of that belief. Because in the lining of that document tube, alongside the codicil, was a letter from my mother.'

The truth is dancing just out of Lazarus's reach. 'Who was she?'

'Her name was Loretta Morgan,' Red says. 'I believe you knew her once – at Leighfindell.'

Lazarus stares at her. 'Etta was your mother.'

'The things in that portmanteau were all she had left from the old days. A few gifts from Jemima, like that old shawl and the pack of cards. The locket given to her by Nicholas after Jemima's death. And a birth chart drawn by John Jory Jago, mapping the destiny of the man she loved, the same man who had given her that golden heart charm. My father, Julius De Lacy.'

Lazarus shakes his head slowly, thinking about the carving in the grotto, the piquet score Red had found. *J* and *L*.

'In my mother's letter, she confessed that she had stolen the codicil for him, and unwittingly taken *The Square of Sevens* at the same time. Nicholas De Lacy must have put them away in the same document tube, the day you had brought him *The Square of Sevens*, when you witnessed the codicil. My mother met Julius up at the Pharos, and she told him she had destroyed it as he'd asked. Julius had promised to set her up as his mistress in London, you see, and she loved him very much. He said she had to leave Leighfindell that same night – I imagine he was afraid that she might talk under questioning. She left only with what she could carry in that portmanteau. Julius paid for her transport to London, but when she arrived, she discovered that the accommodation he'd arranged for her was in an insalubrious part of town, nothing like the splendour she'd been promised. She waited there, weeks passed, and he didn't come. Until eventually, George Montfort came to see her. He told her that if she ever breathed a word of what had happened, Julius would deny everything, and she'd be hanged. Montfort offered her a sum of money, saying that Julius wanted nothing more to do with her.' Red toys with the golden heart, holding it up to catch the light. 'I don't treasure this because of him, but because it reminds me of all that we endured, my mother and I.'

'Why hadn't she destroyed the codicil?' Lazarus asks.

'I imagine some part of her suspected that Julius might do something like this. My mother had a romantic heart, but she was never a fool. Thoughts of revenge occurred to her. She might have sold the codicil to Lady Seabrooke, but she was too afraid of the consequences for herself. So she simply kept it, sewing it into the lining of that document tube to keep it safe.'

Lazarus frowns. 'Whose was the body in the lake, if not hers?'

'I don't know. Some poor woman from history. Perhaps it even was the last Radclyffe duchess. You thought Etta had been murdered, because you couldn't find her, but it never occurred to you that she was simply resourceful and knew how to hide. The servants, already suspicious because of your line of questioning, presumed the body was hers. Even Lady Frances believed in her husband's guilt, but in this matter, at least, Julius was quite blameless. He had no need to kill her. He had power enough over her already.'

'My theory about the murder served you well,' Lazarus says. 'You needed a convincing explanation for how that codicil could have ended up in John Jory's possession. So you implied that Etta had stolen it for him and he had killed her.'

'The De Lacys did that,' she reminds him. 'Poor John Jory. Slandered in death, as well as in life. But after what he did on that clifftop, I shall not dwell on it unduly.'

Lazarus shakes his head again. 'I still don't understand how Mr Antrobus fits into all of this.'

'Have patience,' she says, with a smile. 'I haven't finished telling you my mother's story. Etta was forced to leave London, and by then she knew she was carrying Julius's child. She returned to Exeter, her hometown, and there she gave birth. She hated to give me up, but she was determined not to let Julius be the end of her. In her past, she'd had a sweetheart, a milliner from Bristol. He'd loved her honestly, she'd broken his heart, and now she regretted it.

'They were married later that year, and lived quite happily for a time, though regrettably, their marriage was never blessed by children. A few years later, when her husband died, she was threatened by penury once again. Which was when she made a decision to apply for a post as a housekeeper in the nearby city of Bath, in the service of a scholar named Robert Antrobus.'

Not for the first time that day, Lazarus stares. He'd never asked in Bath for a description of Mrs Fremantle, the housekeeper. But then why would he have done? He recalls a line from Red's memoir and speaks it aloud: '*The truth is, she was a mother to me, the only one I ever knew. My only regret is that I did not know it, until it was too late.*'

'I couldn't bring myself to disavow her,' Red says. 'It was a risk, I suppose. But isn't that true of everything worth having?'

'Etta persuaded Mr Antrobus to take you into his care?'

She smiles sadly. 'They fell in love, and she told him almost everything. And because Robert Antrobus was a very good man, he went to collect me from that orphanage, and constructed stories to ensure I could be raised as a lady. But I was never a lady, not at heart. I would never take no for an answer. When I found *The Square of Sevens* in the portmanteau, I kept it secretly and studied it, teaching myself to read fortunes. It was Mr Antrobus who caught me with it – and his anger was tempered by his fascination for that old document. I was allowed to continue telling fortunes, but that was when they put a lock on the portmanteau.'

'Why did your mother keep the codicil and *The Square of Sevens* for all those years? When they were such a threat to her?'

'Because they were a part of her plan for me. She could do nothing with those documents in her own lifetime, not without risking a hanging, but she believed rightly that we were owed by the De Lacys. She knew how inquisitive I was, and how determined – and she knew I'd find those documents after her death. In her letter, she said I was to go to Lady Seabrooke. I should sell her those documents, and I shouldn't take less than a thousand pounds. I thought about it, naturally, in those days after the fire. But then a different plan occurred to me. Why should I content myself with a thousand pounds, when I might have it all?'

'Old Mr Radclyffe,' Lazarus says. 'It was Etta he recognized in Bath, not you. Mrs Fremantle. That's why he took you for a De Lacy, because in his confusion, he thought she was your maid.'

Red nods. 'My one consolation is that nothing I did brought about my mother's death. It was simple chance that Mr Radclyffe was there and recognized her, and ill fortune that he told Archie. Archie must have known enough about our family's history to wonder if Etta might still possess that codicil. Especially once he discovered that I knew the secret of the Square of Sevens.'

'*The letter*,' Lazarus says. 'That's what you said he shouted that night at Leighfindell. Only he didn't say that, did he? He said: '*Tell Etta.*''

'Very good, Mr Darke. Mr Radclyffe wanted me to thank her. I'm not entirely sure why. It has occurred to me that when she departed for Leighfindell, she might have left him a note. I think Jemima told her, you see, about the things her father had done to her. And my mother might have wanted Mr Radclyffe to know that his son hadn't been at fault.'

Red's memoir was an astonishing creation, Lazarus reflects, written more to obscure the errors and weaknesses in her story than to promulgate it.

He has to ask the obvious question. 'Did you kill him? Mr Radclyffe?'

She stares at him, astonished. 'Of course not. I had no quarrel with him. Archie killed him, I think, to protect me. Marrying me was his contingency, if you recall. Though it's possible Mr Radclyffe simply fell. We'll never know.'

'Then Archie always knew that you were lying about who you were?'

'At the beginning, I think he simply thought that I was the ward of Robert Antrobus. When I first came to De Lacy House, he wanted me gone, if you recall. I imagine he thought I was there to divine who was responsible for the burglary, and I think for all his professed belief in rationality, he was afraid of my fortunes. He changed towards me after that night at Leighfindell. I thought originally it was my forged letter that had caused that change, but now I think it was his conversation with Mr Radclyffe. He must have told Archie that I'd said I was the daughter of John Jory Jago, which was when he guessed my true purpose at Leighfindell.'

'Why did you accept the De Lacys' help in London? Didn't you guess Julius would try to kill you?'

'For one thing, unlike you, I knew he hadn't killed Etta. I did wonder if he had it in him, faced with the loss of his fortune, but I'd thought if he was going to strike, he'd do it at Leighfindell. I needed to get to Cornwall quickly, remember, to head Archie off on the way back home and secure the memoir. My plan had been to go most of the way in the carriage, and then make my escape when we stopped at one of the Devonshire inns. I'd intended to make my own way to Tretelly from there. That was my biggest mistake. That and Archie. I'd thought he had feelings for me, or that he might be corruptible. I never realized that he was making a play of his own.'

'Then you never loved him?'

She thinks for a moment. 'He could be very charming company, and I can't deny he was a fine place to rest the eye. There were times when I found him quite distracting. Otherwise, I like to think that I'd have seen through him earlier.'

Lazarus grunts. 'I should have known that Red would never be drawn away from her goals for a trifle like love.'

She only gives him one of her smiles, the sort that suggests she knows a great deal more than he does. Then she rises, and he presumes their audience is at an end.

'Walk with me,' she says, rather to his surprise. 'I want to show you something.'

He follows her into the hall, along a corridor, and out through a door, onto a stone terrace overlooking the gardens. And such gardens they are! Neat borders of box line the paths, leading to groves of foxgloves in purple and white. Bright splashes of scarlet peonies and hedges of hydrangeas. In the distance are specimen trees, fountains, and a maze. Peacocks strut across the neat, clipped lawns.

There are several people out here, and to his surprise, Lazarus sees faces he knows. At a table sits Tamson, the Anglo-Indian girl from the fair. She glances over at them, neither welcoming, nor hostile. On one of the lawns, a tiny boy with a mop of yellow hair is being walked around by a tall, slender woman of about forty. Rosie Denham, Luna's lady's maid from Leighfindell. He wonders if the boy is Letitia Jennings's child. A few paces away, the disfigured girl from the fair, the one who was nearly arrested on the night of the raid, is grinning lopsidedly at them both.

To one side of the terrace, a young redheaded man is hunched over a chessboard. As he reaches to move his knight, he gives Lazarus a nod of recognition. With a start, he recognizes Leopold De Lacy.

Lazarus stares wildly around, not quite believing she could be here. Then Luna emerges from a planting of trees with a ball in her hands. She throws it to the little boy, and then stops as she catches sight of him, her hand halfway to her face.

'And so we have washed up here,' Red says. 'Survivors amidst the wreckage.'

Lazarus wants to run to her, but he is afraid. 'How is this possible?' he hears himself say.

'Mr Cowell found her in France,' Red says. 'She was hiding there from her creditors. It took some persuading to get her to come, but in the end pragmatism conquered pride. I tell her fortune every day. She talks about you often now. We cannot change the past, Mr Darke, but we can write the future.'

Darke isn't listening to her any more. His lips move, and Red catches Luna's name on his breath. He takes a step towards her and then another, down the steps, onto the grass. Red crosses the lawn. Tamson lays her brush aside, and smiles.

'You said he would come.'

'I saw it in the cards,' Red says. 'They never lie.'

Tamson gives her a look. 'Sometimes they do.'

'Hush,' Red says. 'Just look at them.'

They turn to watch Darke's progress across the lawn, and Tamson's hand creeps over her own. Lady Seabrooke hasn't moved, but her lips are parted, her cheeks flushed. The boy throws the ball. It catches the sun as it spins. Lazarus clasps her hands, everything bathed in a golden light.

Historical Note

The Square of Sevens was my lockdown book. At a time of fear and isolation in the modern world, I wanted to write something mythical and magical, a sweeping Dickensian story with a twist. My first ideas were sketchy: a large family and a disputed inheritance, plus fortune telling in the age of the Enlightenment. I also wanted the book to have a structural element connected to the fortune telling.

Whilst finishing my second novel, I did some initial research into eighteenth-century fortune telling, which was when I came across *The Square of Sevens* by the American author and journalist E. Irenaeus Stevenson (Harper and Brothers, 1897). The book purported to contain an eighteenth-century method of cartomancy which is described in great detail, together with diagrams and lists of the various meanings of the cards. A fortune told by this method consists of twenty-one cards, and I soon hit upon the idea that my novel would have four parts, each consisting of twenty-one chapters headed by a playing card – the meaning of the card mirroring the events of that chapter. The four parts would correspond to four different fortunes that my main character, Red, would tell during the course of the story. (*The Square of Sevens* is a short read and can be found online at Project Gutenberg.)

The preface of *The Square of Sevens* also intrigued me. Stevenson claimed to have discovered the method in an eighteenth-century book also titled *The Square of Sevens*, written by a Bath scholar, Robert Antrobus, and published by John Gowne of the Mask bookshop in London. Stevenson states that most of the original editions were destroyed in a printing-house fire and that the few surviving copies were much sought after by collectors. He adds that the book has a

foreword, which explains how Antrobus first acquired the secret of
the Square of Sevens.

According to this foreword, Antrobus spent a few weeks in Cornwall in the year 1730, and whilst staying at an inn in the town of
Tretelly, made the acquaintance of a dying gypsy named George X – a
name Antrobus suspected to be a pseudonym. George had a daughter
of six or seven years, but was estranged from his family and friends
for reasons relating to his marriage. In exchange for agreeing to take
the child into his care, George X gave Robert Antrobus the secret of
the Square of Sevens. Ten years later, after the printing-house fire,
Antrobus returned to Bath and died there. He left his ward half his
estate – the other half presumably inherited by his cousin, Henry
Antrobus, who is also mentioned in the text.

I had already decided that my main character would be a young
female fortune teller, and it wasn't a great leap from there to the
idea that she should be the little girl in that foreword. The events
in Tretelly, I decided, would comprise the first three chapters of the
book, and I also decided to incorporate the publication of *The Square
of Sevens* and the printing-house fire into my story. Even the dedication of Stevenson's book, 'this new forth-setting of an old mystery is
cordially offered' felt like a sign that I should write this novel.

Upon closer study of the text, I was amused to realize that Stevenson's *Square of Sevens* was an elaborate hoax, a nineteenth-century
invention of an eighteenth-century story and method of fortune
telling. The book is prefaced with a quote from Hamlet: 'Tis easy as
lying,' and ends with another quote from an entirely made-up play:

BRADAMANTE: But is this authentic? Is it an original? Is
    it a true, original thing, sir?
GRADASSO: Madam, 'tis as authentic as very authenticity
    itself – 'tis truth's kernel, originality's core – provided you
    are but willing to believe it such.

The town of Tretelly was also invented by Stevenson, as were
Robert Antrobus, John Gowne, and the Mask bookshop. Other

inconsistencies, such as a reference to Robert Antrobus's study of the Cock Lane Ghost, a famous eighteenth-century hoax that took place over twenty years after Antrobus's supposed death, are further tongue-in-cheek clues that point to a gentle literary fraud (at least one contemporary reviewer clearly recognized it as such, and was greatly entertained by the project's eccentricity).

It was then that the idea came to me of writing a hoax within a hoax, my main character laying claim to a vast fortune, having invented a backstory for herself that mirrors the invented backstory in Stevenson's account. Thus the seeds of *The Square of Sevens* were sown. The Quixote epigraph seemed perfect to sum up the book's theme of truth and lies, and linked nicely to a second theme of knights and quests. The next part of the plot to fall into place was the interweaving of a love story (that incorporated the backstory of the De Lacy family) around Red's investigation into her family's past. I greatly enjoyed writing the character of Lazarus Darke and his quest to serve both the truth and the woman he loves – and for once I decided my characters deserved a happy ending.

The year of 1740 was an interesting time in 'enlightened' and 'rational' England. Only a few years earlier, the 1735 Witchcraft Act had been passed by Parliament, the first time it was acknowledged in English law that witchcraft did not exist. Those who practised magic (including astrology and fortune telling) would no longer be executed or otherwise punished as witches, but as fraudsters intent upon the exploitation of the credulous. Fortune tellers were usually imprisoned and pilloried (blocking the streets and changing the hands of the clock were real tricks sometimes employed by friends of the pilloried miscreant).

Yet despite the efforts of the authorities, many people from all classes of society still believed in magic, and arguments about the subject raged in pamphlets and newspapers – a clash of ideas that seemed fertile ground to explore in my novel. Two excellent books on the role of magic and superstition in Georgian society are *Witchcraft, Magic and Culture 1736–1951* by Owen Davies (Manchester University

Press, 1999) and *The Decline of Magic: Britain in the Enlightenment* by Michael Hunter (Yale University Press, 2020).

What did eighteenth-century people even mean by magic? I found this an intriguing question, particularly in the context of science and discovery. Electricity shows were extremely popular from the 1740s onwards and both 'The Flying Boy' and 'The Electrifying Venus' were real experiments performed for the paying public. *Sparks in the Dark: The Attraction of Electricity in the Eighteenth Century* by Paola Bertucci (*Endeavour*, Vol. 31 No. 3) is a delightful account of this theatrical and scientific craze. The overlap between science, religion, popular culture and magic in early modern England is a fascinating subject I could only touch upon lightly in this novel, but I was especially intrigued by the human desire to write stories to explain phenomena we don't fully understand, whether it be The Clockwork Universe or the origin of snakestones (ammonites).

The use of fortune telling as therapy was entirely my own invention, but seemed to me entirely plausible. Robert Burton's *The Anatomy of Melancholy* (1621), a medical study of what we would now call clinical depression, contains some suggestions for treatments that sound surprisingly modern, including confessing one's sorrows to an empathetic friend. It goes without saying that many of his other suggestions, such as boring a hole in one's skull, should not be tried at home.

My bright idea of using the four fortunes to structure the book proved a more arduous and frustrating task than I had at first appreciated. Every time I changed the order of a chapter, the whole thing fell apart and I'd spend days at a time fiddling with layouts of playing cards and Post-it notes. This was further complicated by my determination not to use any influenced card more than once, and my desire that each card in the fortune should have relevance not only to the character whose fortune was being told, but also to the point-of-view character in the chapter itself (whether Red or Lazarus Darke). Red says in the novel that just as the querist influences the cards in their fortune, so the fortune influences the querist. Similarly, whilst the plot clearly influenced the cards I chose for the chapters, so those cards often came to influence the plot. There are clues in the cards that my more perceptive reader may have spotted, though I am reconciled to the likelihood that some readers will ignore them entirely!

I had a wonderful time exploring eighteenth-century Bath, both in books and in person. *Bath Under Beau Nash* by Lewis Melville (Eveleigh Nash & Grayson, 1907) is a particularly useful guide to the architecture and society of the Georgian spa. General Wolfe's house in Trim Street was my inspiration for the house of Robert Antrobus, and Mrs Davenport could live nowhere other than Queen Square. Other useful books I read when researching Red's upbringing were *The Gentleman's Daughter* (Yale University Press, 1998) and *Behind Closed Doors: At Home in Georgian England* (Yale University Press, 2009) both by Amanda Vickery. Tamson's backstory is loosely inspired by Mary Wilson, the Anglo-Indian daughter of an East India nabob, who was raised by a friend of her father's in some comfort, but was never acknowledged publicly by him.

Amidst many great books on eighteenth-century London, the one I come back to time and again is the magnificent *London in the Eighteenth Century: A Great and Monstrous Thing* by Jerry White (The Bodley Head, 2012). In writing about the world of the De Lacys, I returned to another of my favourite books about the period: *The Beau Monde* by Hannah Grieg (Oxford University Press, 2013). De Lacy House was inspired by both Burlington House, and the now demolished Devonshire House, two of the finest mansions on Piccadilly. The Cheshire Cheese is still standing, though its neighbour, the coffeehouse Fernando's (more commonly known simply as 'Nando's'), is sadly no more. Hanover Square, home of Lady Seabrooke, has lost most of its eighteenth-century buildings, but two of the original houses survive and are an evocative glimpse into the history of one of Mayfair's oldest squares.

The Bartholomew Fair, then one of the largest fairs in Europe, occupied the site of the Smithfield meat market every August for over seven hundred years. *The Theatre of the London Fairs in the Eighteenth Century* by Sybil Rosenfeld (Cambridge University Press, 1960) provides an excellent history of the fair, as well as a wonderful flavour of the stalls, shows, plays and other spectacles that brought Londoners flocking in their thousands.

Leighfindell was inspired by the estate of Lyme Park, which I transported with my pen from Cheshire to Devonshire. I wanted a house that retained its Tudor core, but that also had a stamp of Georgian grandiosity, and Lyme Park perfectly fitted the bill. The Legh family, who owned Lyme Park before it was given to the National Trust, have a long history of naming their eldest son Peter or Piers. I appropriated this tradition for my fictional Radclyffe family, though in all other respects they bear no resemblance to the Leghs.

In bringing Leighfindell to life, I found the following books extremely useful: *The British Country House in the Eighteenth Century* by Christopher Christie (Manchester University Press, 2000); *The Georgian Country House: Architecture, Landscape and Society* by Dana Arnold (Sutton Publishing, 1998); and *A Country House at Work: Three Centuries of Dunham Massey* by Pamela Sambrook (The National Trust, 2003).

John Culpeper, my Tudor carpenter, is loosely inspired by Nicholas Owen, a renowned maker of priests' holes and other hiding places in the houses of the Catholic gentry. For examples of Owen's work, I recommend Harvington Hall in Worcestershire which has at least seven priests' holes and possibly more that remain undiscovered to this day.

After reading about ornamental hermits, I was determined that Leighfindell should have a hermitage. I stole the background to my hermitage from the estate of Painshill in Surrey, whose ornamental hermit was employed for seven years under very strict terms of isolation, but was sacked after three weeks when he was found in the local pub.

Armory v Delamirie (1722), the case involving a jeweller and a chimney-sweep's boy cited in court by the De Lacys' barrister, was a real case that established a precedent in English law. It was recently cited in the High Court of Justice, in the libel case *Rebekah Vardy v Coleen Rooney (2022)*, in reference to the dropping of a mobile phone into the sea and the loss of computer data.

Finally, given my previous career, I could not resist a light sprinkling of Walpolian corruption into my plot. Robert Walpole, England's first Prime Minister, occupied an unparalleled position of power and influence for over twenty years, until his fall from office in 1742 mired in scandal. Walpole first came to power in the aftermath of the South Sea Bubble, and was alleged to have protected many politicians and friends implicated in the Company's collapse. *Money for Nothing: The South Sea Bubble and the Invention of Modern Capitalism* by Thomas Levenson (Head of Zeus, 2020) is a fascinating account of the financial disaster and its repercussions for Georgian England. It felt very fitting to me that the De Lacys should have made their fortune from the Bubble, a tale, like my novel, of fraud, excess, illusion, and the vagaries of fortune.

Acknowledgements

As ever, my heartfelt thanks are owed to my agent, Antony Topping, who is the most wonderful champion to have in my corner. He is always there for everything I need, whether it be advice on my early drafts, strategic wisdom, therapy, or very enjoyable lunches that turn into long afternoons in the pub. I'd also like to thank everyone else at Greene and Heaton, especially the wonderful Kate Rizzo, who has put my books into the hands of readers in many different countries.

I am doubly fortunate to have a truly amazing editor, Maria Rejt, who has such great instincts and experience, and such commitment to her authors and their work. I will never forget how Maria and her team came into the office the day before lockdown to make certain that advance copies of my last book got into the world before the shutters came down. Which says everything about Mantle and Pan Macmillan and their dedication to their authors and their readers. This time round, Maria let me write the book of my heart and gave me the time to do it justice. Her enthusiasm for *The Square of Sevens* has made all the hard work seem worth it.

I'd also like to particularly thank Alice Gray at Mantle, not least for speaking Latin and helping me come up with the De Lacys' motto: *Fortuna Favente* – let us hope it proves auspicious for this book! And huge thanks are due to Ami Smithson, who designed such a beautiful cover, capturing all the elements of history, magic, mystery and wonder. Also to Lucy Hale, Stuart Dwyer, Claire Evans, Becky Lushey, Rosie Friis, Laura Sherlock, Kate Tolley, Laura Carr, Lindsay Nash, Jonathan Atkins, Leanne Williams, Becky Lloyd, Rory O'Brien, Richard Green, Kate Bullows and everyone else at Pan Macmillan who has worked so hard to bring my books to readers at home and abroad.

I am thrilled that *The Square of Sevens* is going to be published in the US, and I would like to thank Jennifer Weltz at the Jean V Naggar Literary Agency; my American editor, Kaitlin Olson; and everyone at Atria and Simon and Schuster. And to the translators who have worked on my books, and the editors and publishing teams behind my foreign language editions.

Many people helped me with their time and expertise, and to them I owe a particular debt of gratitude (needless to say, any errors are mine alone). Kate Griffin saved me weeks of research by telling me all about eighteenth-century astrology and consulting her ephemeris on my behalf. She also drew the natal charts and gave me great spiels for Tamson's readings. Amanda Bevan from the National Archives (big thanks to Jessamy Carlson for the introduction) helped me navigate the very complicated world of eighteenth-century wills and the legal system. I'm sure she will wince at a few of my simplifications, but the balancing act between strict historical accuracy and readability was at times a delicate endeavour! Georgina Clarke gave me some much-needed help on eighteenth-century sermons and dissolute clergymen. Hallie Rubenhold had many suggestions to help Red plausibly circumnavigate the terrifying rules of eighteenth-century etiquette. And Hannah Grieg very generously gave me some wonderful research on eighteenth-century balls.

I always like to seek inspiration from history for the people and places that appear in my books, and I was searching for the right inspiration for the De Lacys' country house in Devon when my old friend, Lee Findell, suggested Lyme Park. It was absolutely perfect and, by way of thanks, I named my fictional house, Leighfindell, after him. Another friend, Katie Myler, introduced me to Hugo Legh, whose ancestors owned Lyme Park for generations. Hugo very generously gave me some wonderful anecdotes about his family and the house, including the rumours of a secret tunnel under the gardens. The name Leighfindell seemed doubly fitting, given my shameless plundering of the Legh family's history and traditions.

Big thanks are due to my friend and former neighbour, Paul Heneker, who designed the layouts of the playing cards for the four title pages of this book. Paul and his wife, Helen, have championed my writing career from the first, and I can only pity their poor family and friends who have received countless copies of my books as gifts.

So many people in book-land have provided love, support and practical help along the way that I cannot possibly list them all here. But a few deserve a special mention: to the Ladykillers, the History Girls, and Colin Scott, I missed you so much over lockdown and it is so lovely seeing you all again now. To David Headley and the brilliant booksellers at Goldsboro Books, thank you, sincerely, for everything. To my dear friend and wonderful writer, Anna Mazzola, who read an early draft of this book and gave me many helpful comments. To her daughter, Iris, for Joan the Wad. And finally, to Abir Mukherjee for all the pictures of Pavarotti.

My family have been as wonderful as ever, and their Zooms and distanced visits during lockdown made everything seem less bleak. Thanks in particular to my dad and Lou who read a very early plan of this book and made many interesting and useful suggestions.

This book is dedicated to my eldest niece, Holly. I never wanted to have children myself, but being an aunt is the best job I have. To be a part of Holly's life over the last thirteen years has been a joy, not least because she is clever, funny, kind, talented, and an absolute delight to be around. I felt that this book's dedication should mirror the dedication in the original *Square of Sevens* (see my historical note), but what I really wanted to say was: *This book is for you, because you're amazing.*

Lastly, and most of all, thank you to Adrian . . . Like everyone else, lockdown held its share of challenges for us, but never once did those challenges include one another. On our walks, we talked through my plot wrangles and Ade had many excellent suggestions. The South Sea Bubble and the Clockwork Universe were both down to him, and he was great at acting out action scenes at two in the morning. He also insisted on making me a spreadsheet to organize the four fortunes that structure the book, having tired of finding Post-it Notes all over our flat. This book would have been so much harder to write without his support. I wake up every day and love him more.

Discover Laura Shepherd-Robinson's
first novel *Blood & Sugar*

'A brilliant book . . . Absolutely superb'
James O'Brien

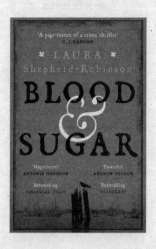

Waterstones Thriller of the Month

Winner of the Historical Writers' Association Debut Crown

June, 1781. An unidentified body hangs upon a hook at Deptford Dock – horribly tortured and branded with a slaver's mark.

Some days later, Captain Harry Corsham – a war hero embarking upon a promising parliamentary career – is visited by the sister of an old friend. Her brother, passionate abolitionist Tad Archer, had been about to expose a secret that could cause irreparable damage to the British slaving industry. He'd said people were trying to kill him, and now he is missing.

To discover what happened to Tad, Harry is forced to pick up the threads of his investigation, delving into the heart of the conspiracy Tad had unearthed. But by doing so he risks threatening his political prospects and his family's happiness, and exposing secrets from his own past that have the power to destroy him. And that is only if he can survive the mortal dangers awaiting him in Deptford . . .

'A page-turner of a thriller . . . This is a world conveyed
with convincing, terrible clarity'
C. J. Sansom

Discover Laura Shepherd-Robinson's
second novel *Daughters of Night*

'Spectacularly brilliant. Once-in-a-blue-moon levels of fantastic.
One of the most enjoyable and enduring stories I have ever read'
James O'Brien

London, 1782. Caroline 'Caro' Corsham discovers a well-dressed
woman in the bowers of the Vauxhall Pleasure Gardens – mortally
wounded and alone.

When the Bow Street constables unearth the identity of the dead woman,
they cease to care entirely. However, Caro has motives of her own for
wanting justice done, so sets out to solve the crime herself, enlisting the
help of thief-taker Peregrine Child.

Their inquiries will throw them headlong into the deepest hidden corners
of Georgian society, a world of artifice, deception and secret lives. And
with many gentlemen refusing to speak about their dealings with the dead
woman, and Caro's own reputation under threat, finding the killer will be
harder and more treacherous than she can know . . .

'The best historical crime novel I will read this year'
Antonia Senior, *The Times*

'A stunning tour de force . . . Breathtaking stuff'
Chris Whitaker